Al-Qata'i
Ibn Tulun's City Without Walls

A NOVEL

Reem Bassiouney

Translated from Arabic by Roger Allen

Georgetown University Press / Washington, DC

Library of Congress Cataloging-in-Publication Data

Names: Bassiouney, Reem, 1973– author. | Allen, Roger, 1942– translator.
Title: Al-Qata'i : Ibn Tulun's city without walls / Reem Bassiouney ; translated from the Arabic by Roger Allen.
Other titles: Qaṭā'i. English
Description: Washington, DC : Georgetown University Press, 2023.
Identifiers: LCCN 2022002028 (print) | LCCN 2022002029 (ebook) | ISBN 9781647122874 (hardcover) | ISBN 9781647122881 (ebook)
Subjects: LCSH: Egypt—History—640–1250—Fiction. | Aḥmad ibn Ṭūlūn, 835–884—Fiction. | LCGFT: Historical fiction. | Novels.
Classification: LCC PJ7816.A768 Q2813 2023 (print) | LCC PJ7816.A768 (ebook) | DDC 892.7/37—dc23/eng/20220510
LC record available at https://lccn.loc.gov/2022002028
LC ebook record available at https://lccn.loc.gov/2022002029

∞ This paper meets the requirements of ANSI/NISO Z39.48-1992 (Permanence of Paper).

24 23   9 8 7 6 5 4 3 2 First printing

Printed in the United States of America

Cover design by Trudi Gershenov
Interior design by Paul Hotvedt

"These pages can keep us busy for a lifetime or more . . . Pick them up carefully . . . When they're read, they'll take us back to former times without the slightest difficulty."

To someone who read these pages and was not satisfied merely to understand them. He has eagerly prepared an excellent translation of them into a different language. I dedicate these pages and this novel to Roger Allen.

REEM BASSIOUNEY

I want Al-Qata'i to remain a city with no trace. I want every stone to be pulverized into grains of sand, neither covered nor heated, but rather scattered to the winds with no goal or purpose. This city is intended to be forgotten, to be nothing. Should any part of it remain, then we have lost. Should the smallest stone be restored to its former self, then there is no hope of eradicating sedition or acknowledging fate.
—*Muhammad ibn Sulaiman al-Katib, 905 CE*

This world loves not my brother.
It views the world-lover only through toils of misery.
Sweet mingled with bitter,
Ease mingled with hardship.
Tread not for a single day in the garb of conceit;
From clay and water were you created.
—*Abu al-Atahiya, Abbasid-era poet (d. 828 CE)*

Contents

The Third Story: The Pledge

List of Characters

Listed in order of appearance.

Sultan Fuad (1868–1936), later King Fuad I after Egypt obtained independence in 1922: Ruler of Egypt from 1917 until 1922

Adil: worker at the Ibn Tulun mosque site, preparing for Sultan Fuad's visit to the mosque in 1918

Hamza al-Skandari: father of Anas and Ali, head fisherman of Alexandria; he commits suicide by drowning after being tortured by Ibn al-Mudabbir's men

Zayid: Hamza al-Skandari's servant

Anas: son of Hamza al-Skandari and husband of Maisoon; bookseller and copyist, he becomes a friend and supporter of Ahmad ibn Tulun; appointed Deputy Police Chief, he is twice sent by Ibn Tulun to negotiate with the Abbasid Caliph in Baghdad, Iraq

Ali: son of Hamza al-Skandari, brother of Anas, tortured and killed by Ibn al-Mudabbir's men

Abd ar-Rahman ibn Abdallah ibn Abd al-Hakam: Anas's teacher

Shaikh Bakkar ibn Qutaiba: the chief judge (*qadi*) of Egypt

Saeed ibn Katib al-Farghani: architect in Ibn Tulun's era and builder of the house of Anas, son of Hamza al-Skandari

Ahmad ibn Tulun (835–84): initially appointed Deputy Governor of Egypt by the Abbasid Caliph in Baghdad, he took over control of the country and built the new city of Al-Qata'i, including the famous mosque that bears his name

Asma: daughter of Mahmud the tailor, Ibn Tulun's Egyptian wife and Maisoon's mother

Saneeya: daughter of Mahmud the tailor and Asma's younger sister

Ja'far ibn Abd al-Ghaffar: secretary of Ahmad ibn Tulun

Muhammad ibn Sulaiman al-Katib: secretary to Lu'lu', a general in Ibn Tulun's army, who joined his master in defecting to the Abbasid administration; later, army commander in charge of the campaign to end the rule of Ahmad ibn Tulun's successors

Maisoon: daughter of Judge Yahya ibn Isa and wife of Anas, son of Hamza al-Skandari

Ahmad ibn al-Mudabbir: appointed Tax Administrator of Egypt by the Abbasid Caliph, he used the office to exert a tyrannical hold over every aspect of Egyptian life; opponent of Ibn Tulun (868–71), and rival for Maisoon's affections

Judge Yahya ibn Isa: Maisoon's father

Abla: hairdresser and facilitator of Ibn al-Mudabbir's encounter with Maisoon

Ruqayya: Judge Yahya's daughter, Maisoon's sister

Gameela: Ali's servant-girl who also served Maisoon in hiding

Bahnas: the Pyramid Witch, resident in the Great Pyramid at Giza, consulted by many of the characters in the novel

Abu Sha'ara: confidant of Ibn al-Mudabbir

Shuqair: Postmaster-General of Egypt and colleague of Ibn al-Mudabbir

Yarjukh: a Turkish commander, appointed by the Abbasid Caliph as Governor of Egypt; he appointed Ibn Tulun Deputy Governor, then Governor of Egypt

Mughith: Anas's servant (along with his wife)

Al-Wasiti: Anas's travel companion to the Caliphal capital, Baghdad, in Iraq; he later defects to the Abbasid commander, Al-Muwaffaq

Tulun: a Turkish soldier who rose to become the commander of the Abbasid Caliph's private guard; married to Qasim, their son was Ahmad ibn Tulun

Qasim: Ahmad ibn Tulun's mother

Bayakbak: a Turkish commander who was married to Qasim, Tulun's widow and Ahmad ibn Tulun's mother

Khatun: daughter of Turkish commander Yarjukh and wife of Ahmad ibn Tulun

Al-Abbas Ahmad ibn Tulun: Ahmad ibn Tulun's son

Mayyas: a slave-girl given to Ahmad ibn Tulun by the Caliph, mother of Ahmad's son, Khumarawayh

Khumarawayh: son of Ahmad ibn Tulun and Mayyas, and Ahmad ibn Tulun's successor

Anduna: an Egyptian monk

Lu'lu': a general in Ahmad ibn Tulun's army and governor of northern Syria who defected to the Abbasid Caliph's army

Aisha: initially portrayed as an orphan girl, adopted by Ibn Tulun's secretary, Ja'far ibn Abd al-Ghaffar, and cared for by Saeed al-Farghani; married to Abd ar-Rahman; later identified as a daughter of Ahmad ibn Tulun by his wife, Asma

Abd ar-Rahman: son of an Arab tribal chief, Musa ibn Uthman, husband of Aisha

Qatr an-Nada: Khumarawayh's daughter and Ahmad ibn Tulun's granddaughter; wife of the Abbasid Caliph, Al-Mu'tadid

Azza: Abd ar-Rahman's cousin and fiancée, who becomes a friend of Aisha in Abd ar-Rahman's absence

Musa ibn Uthman: Abd ar-Rahman's father, chief of his tribe

Atika: the youngest wife of Musa ibn Uthman and opponent of Abd ar-Rahman within the family structure

Saleema: Azza's elder sister who later becomes the chief tormentor of Aisha in the absence of Abd ar-Rahman

Khalisa: Shaikh Musa's first wife, now living in a separate wing from the family

Abu l-Asakir Jaish: Khumarawayh's son and successor; ruled for one year (896 CE), was deposed, and subsequently killed

Harun: Khumarawayh's younger son, Jaish's successor, killed in an army mutiny (904 CE)

Shaiban ibn Ahmad ibn Tulun: Harun ibn Khumarawayh's uncle and successor, the last Tulunid ruler (904–5 CE)

Rabi'a: Musa ibn Uthman's brother and Azza's father, who, in the absence of Abd ar-Rahman, takes over the leadership of the tribe

Salih: a member of a poor branch of Shaikh Musa's tribe who argues with Abd ar-Rahman; he doggedly defends the tribe's traditional values and seems to be concerned about Aisha's safety; he is eventually killed by Abd ar-Rahman

Qasim al-Khurasani: leader of a troop of soldiers sent by the Caliph to support Muhammad ibn Sulaiman; vicious implementer of Ibn Sulaiman's destructive commands, he is the primary advocate of the need to destroy the Ibn Tulun mosque

Isa an-Nushari: appointed Governor of Egypt by the Caliph following the dismissal of Ibn Sulaiman

Muhammad al-Khalanji: former general in the Tulunid armed forces and part of the group of former soldiers being sent to Baghdad to be punished by the Caliph, he joins Abd ar-Rahman and Khafif an-Nubi in returning to Egypt and taking over the government of the country

Khafif an-Nubi: a member of the Tulunid army being sent to Baghdad who joins Abd ar-Rahman and Muhammad al-Khalanji in returning to Egypt; he pursues the armed forces of Isa an-Nushari, the Abbasid-appointed governor, and initially defeats his forces, but is eventually defeated in battle

1918 Cairo

Sorrow still lurks deep down, though everyone has been extolling his achievements for some time. An apparently successful marriage, a job in a government department, and a parcel of land that gives in plenty. Yet here he is, with women all around him yelling non-stop. He is shocked to be cursed as a tyrant, maybe evoking a cruel streak he had never known before. He feels insecure; understanding has become an impossibility. Ever since he has been working in the Arab Monuments Department, he has been counting the days, as though he were in a brutal prison. He neither understands nor cares about what is going on. Every day, he spends an hour or two sitting in his office, then goes home. But today, the situation is different. A surface calm has been replaced by resistance; when water stagnates, vision becomes clearer. The new Sultan is different. He is very ambitious, and yet he does not follow custom. People say that he is challenging the Caliphate and wants to understand the past. Understand? What does that mean? What history is it that the Sultan wants to uncover?

The yelling women compelled Adil to shout back at them.

"If I hear any more noise from you today," he yelled loudly, "I'm going to give orders for you to be imprisoned. These are commands from His Majesty Sultan Fuad. He wants to pray in the Ibn Tulun Mosque."

"Listen, my son," one of the women pleaded, "this isn't a mosque. It's a house for the indigent and sick. It won't work to pray there. No one's ever done that."

"His Majesty the Sultan's commands must be carried out," he insisted.

"So why does the Sultan ignore all the other mosques in Cairo and knock down our houses?" She slapped her face in consternation.

"The Ibn Tulun Mosque isn't meant for prayer," she muttered. "That's forbidden. Don't people say that stolen money was used to build it, and the architect was a Copt? How can a Muslim pray in a mosque built with stolen money?"

"Don't argue with me," Adil told them firmly. "The space will be cleared in an hour. His Majesty the Sultan is showing you his mercy; he's going to build new houses for you."

When the police arrived, the argument subsided. Men started bringing in equipment.

"The houses attached to the mosque will have to be destroyed," the policeman whispered to Adil. "His Majesty Sultan Fuad can't possibly see such poverty and filth."

"You'll have to stay with me while they're knocking the houses down," Adil replied angrily. "I don't know how I'm supposed to answer the women's questions and put up with their yelling."

"Questions?" the policeman asked in amazement. "Women? Since when have women asked questions? Since when have inhabitants of poor quarters needed to know anything? Why haven't they asked before? These are strange times. His Majesty Sultan Fuad has decided to give forty thousand pounds as compensation to all those who have suffered damage. No ruler has ever done that before."

Adil moved closer to the policeman and asked him the question that his wife had been nagging him about. "I've heard, brother, that when the Friday prayer is over, the Sultan is going to be photographed with the other worshippers, and the picture will be published in the newspapers."

"Yes," the policeman replied, "he's going to allow all the people who've helped get the mosque ready to pray with him."

"As soon as the prayer's over, I'll come to be photographed with him. The photograph will be taken outside the mosque, won't it? I won't hide this from you: my wife has told all her friends that I'm having my photograph taken with His Majesty Sultan Fuad. I can't make her angry."

"Just make sure you're not late. Sultan Ahmad Fuad won't wait for you."

Adil closed his eyes, then opened them again to witness the debris and rocks scattered all around him. In the mosque courtyard, there were piles of ancient debris that no one had thought of removing for a thousand years or more. All around the mosque were the ruins of houses that their owners had built inside and around the mosque. They had made use of a thick wall of unknown history in order to fashion themselves a seat or light a fire.

A British scholar had appeared, someone with a superior knowledge of history and was particularly interested in what could be discovered. What exactly was there to discover among the ruins?

Right next to the ruins of a house that was attached to the mosque wall, there appeared a new entry, a magical gate, and a staircase, its whiteness as fresh as if it had been built the day before. The concealment of the past made the discovery that much more trenchant and disturbing; the beast's burial beneath rubble made it even more provocative.

The scholar focused his attention on the chips flying up as the axes hit the houses. Every time a roof caved in, some new reality appeared; every crack in a wall revealed another gate beneath it or around it.

"Don't go near the rubble," he shouted. "It's all treasures. Leave it to us."

The policeman stared at him in astonishment. Meanwhile Adil's inner self was preoccupied, collapsing with each wall. The unease in his soul felt no less incomprehensible than the language of birds and the chunks of stone strewed in front of him.

The workers carried on knocking down all the houses that impinged on the mosque. They made a pathway for Sultan Fuad to enter the mosque, he being per-haps the first person to perform the Friday prayers in the Ibn Tulun Mosque since the Mamluk era.

The British scholar appeared calm. He was continually soaking up the atmo-sphere of the place.

"Do you see all the stones?" he asked, looking at Adil.

"Stones are all I can see," he replied.

"You sound angry, and I don't understand why. Are you angry with me or yourself?"

"With the stones, Professor."

The British scholar looked over at a collapsing house a hundred meters from the mosque staircase that they had just uncovered.

"Al-Qata'i!" he yelled for the very first time, his voice trembling.

He rushed over to the house. By the wall that had collapsed was another wall, decorated with gypsum in the style of the city of Samarra in Iraq.

"Adil," he said, running his fingers over the wall, "this house that we've just un-covered must be the home of Saeed ibn Katib al-Farghani. What do you think?"

"All I see is old stones. I can't understand, Professor, why Sultan Fuad is so con-cerned about this particular mosque at this point in time. Fire's consuming the country, and the whole world is engaged in vicious warfare."

The British scholar did not respond. He was busy looking at the decoration. Then he looked over at the piles of stone again and the workmen carrying them out of the mosque.

"Make sure you take them to the Arab Monuments building," he insisted again.

The men put the stones down angrily. The policeman kept telling them to get rid of the stones, while the British kept saying to keep them. They all wanted to go home before the sunset prayer. When some stones came crashing down to the floor of the mosque, the earth shook and revealed some papers from its interior. They were scattered all over the house in which the British scholar and Adil were standing.

"Pick them up, one by one," the scholar said in a quavering tone. "The Sultan will want to read them, all of them . . ."

Adil started picking up the ancient papers.

"I've no idea what His Majesty the Sultan wants, Professor," he said.

"He wants a lot . . ."

"Why pray here? People won't be happy for him to conduct prayers here."

The scholar smiled, then turned away.

"These pages can keep us busy for a lifetime or more," he said. "Pick them up carefully."

"They're all eaten away and old."

"When they're read, they'll take us back to former times without the slightest difficulty."

At the outset, Adil came across these words on a separate sheet:

This house in Al-Qata'i belonged to Anas ibn Hamza al-Skandari, then it became the house of Saeed ibn Katib al-Farghani. It is all that is left of Al-Qata'i. These papers have been collected by Saeed ibn Katib al-Farghani from Ja'far ibn Abd al-Ghaffar, secretary to Ahmad ibn Tulun, from Asma, Ahmad ibn Tulun's wife, and from Muhammad ibn Sulaiman al-Katib, Ahmad ibn Tulun's enemy. Then Saeed recorded everything he knew and had witnessed. God is all-knowing.

In erasing the city there is the stench of fear and the taste of risk.

In erasing the city there is war on the memory, with swords and lances.

In erasing the city there is revenge and blessing. Cities long past lurk in memory.

Cities past are always in bright sunlight and have lofty buildings.

In the quest for the city, the heart draws its final breaths.

Far from the city, the traveler awakes.

Close to the city, its dweller is heedless.

This is the story of a city unlike all others, its construction a meeting of foe and beloved.

In its alleyways, an approach to a chasm loaded with treasures, with no mercy for the hesitant, and connection solely to those who would vanish into them.

They said that it was neither here nor there. They said rather that it was by a mountain that would fend off death. They said that its inhabitants were scattered all over the globe, with neither memory nor knowledge.

They said that ancestors collected the stones and put them in a ditch as deep as the seabed itself.

Then they obliterated all its features, so as to protect the papers from destruction.

They said that time will ravage the heart, weaken the body, and destroy all cities.

But on this land, monuments do not disappear, nor is history lost.

Here they can perfect the preservation of all documents, even if they have not read them.

Come now, and I will tell you about the city—lovers, dreaming, arrival, and more than forty years of wandering.

—Saeed ibn Katib al-Farghani

The First Story: Maisoon
Part One

Chapter 1

I shall keen until the bird realizes
That I am sad, the cooing dove pities me,
And I may kiss a land wherein you dwell.
Perhaps my burning flame may be cooled
  by the earth's soil.
—*Antara ibn Shaddad, pre-Islamic poet*

When she reached the market square in Fustat, the guards abruptly told her to stop. People clustered all around Maisoon. For just a few seconds, she thought they were struck by her beauty and wanted to find out who was the judge's daughter whose beauty was being talked about by everyone in Fustat. But the people were clustered for another reason. She looked over at the center of the square and noticed a young man in iron fetters, his head lowered as though he were unconscious. She looked at the black stake that the guard was about to insert into the young man's body. She could not look away. She watched as the stake's tip penetrated the young man's rectum. The screams were different, tasting of blood and reeking of death. The guard continued his job, carefully thrusting the stake till the vision became clear and the stake's tip emerged from the young man's torso. Blood poured from his eyes (or that's what she thought), from his lips, and from his sides. Now the screams quieted down, followed by a groan that stayed with her for the rest of her life. Maisoon's mother moaned, then seemed to lose consciousness. Maisoon's thoughts meanwhile had plunged inside the young man's body and envisioned his exposed guts in all their detail and the flesh stripped away on both sides of the stake. All around the young man, the silence of death prevailed, and his death groan continued to spread feelings of impotence and humiliation among men and women alike. That day, no one dared raise their head. The guard grabbed the young man's hair and showed everyone his head.

"People of Egypt," he yelled, "anyone who defies the tax authorities defies the caliph's instructions and deserves the fires of hell! Taxes are the caliph's right, and the caliph is Commander of the Faithful. Ahmad ibn Mudabbir is the Tax Administrator and must be obeyed by all, good and bad alike."

Loud prayers for the caliph arose, as though each one was a blend of hope and desire to stay alive for another day, a month, or even a year, if possible. Maisoon did not faint the way her mother had. She stared at the young man's eyes. Why was the blood mixed with black bile? Was there a general gloom today, one wondered, or were the stars angry?

"My lady Maisoon," she heard a quiet voice say.

Looking up, she lifted her veil. Their eyes met—no excuse and no warning. Her heart leaped. She could not be sure whether it was from looking at the young man who was not about to die today, tomorrow, or the next day, or from seeing the bookseller, carrying the books: Anas, who had called her name and was looking at her gently with his big eyes and thick, black eyebrows. Could she be in love with those eyes and grow to like them more forever, or was it just that the blood was obliterating all her common sense?

"Your mother needs some help," he said with a smile.

Maisoon did not say anything. She had come to the market with her mother in the hope of meeting her beloved Anas, the bookseller. She loved listening to him recite his poetry and seeing the gleam in his eye whenever he was close to her. Today everything had changed. Their eyes met, spoke to each other, and overflowed with stories. For a year, love had been inundating their minds. Their meetings had been brief, like a sword drawn swiftly from its scabbard to sever the necks of wrongdoers.

The maidservants gathered around Maisoon's mother and asked the bookseller to leave them, but he insisted on helping. He threw some water on her mother's face, then looked at Maisoon.

"My lady," he said, "your mother's not used to seeing objectors punished. It's happening every day. I'm on my way to your house to give the judge the books he ordered. If you'll allow me, I'll go with you."

Maisoon lowered her head. "What about the Tax Administrator?" she asked, her mind distracted.

"He's carrying out orders," he replied firmly. "He's very good at his job."

He walked beside her and spoke to her in a muted tone that no one else could hear. "Were you to display the contents of my chest and scatter my limbs so that my heart could just once capture your beaming glance, and then were my body to be carved up just like that young man today, were that to happen, I wouldn't mind. With your eyes on my heart, I could suffer and be obliterated, your very breaths pursuing me like the air of paradise itself."

Maisoon pretended not to have heard what he had said and did her best to hide the pleasurable smile that showed itself without permission.

Anas continued, "'And may I kiss a land wherein you dwell. Perhaps my burning flame may be cooled.'"

"Those aren't your own words!" she countered flirtatiously in Coptic.

"I'm quoting Arabic," he replied, also in Coptic. "They've perfected love-talk, just as the stars have mastered self-immolation. Love that cleaves the spirit," he continued, "only emerges in the tongue of the ancients. I love you, Maisoon, and someday I will marry you."

Happy to hear his words, she batted her eyelids.

Ever since he had fallen in love with Maisoon, the bookseller had known only the scent of light and the flavor of freedom. Before, his life had been empty and sad, his days monotonous and routine; when they were nerve-racking, it was painful. Then Maisoon had appeared. The first time he had seen her was totally by chance, when he brought her father the books he had ordered from the bookstore in Fustat. Ever since setting eyes on her, her image had filled his days. It was not her radiant beauty that captivated him, nor her arrogant expression, but rather the wildness in her restless pupils and the stubborn streak evident in her mouth, so perfectly crafted by the Supreme Creator. She had entered to quickly hand her father a letter from her mother, with her face veil removed. She had not seen him or even bothered about his being there. But from then on, she had never left his heart. Day after day, his eyes would follow her, brimming with a mixture of passion and despair. He had transferred to Cairo two years earlier, when his life had changed, and his fate had become tied forevermore to the Tax Administrator.

The day that Bahnas, the Pyramid Witch, had whispered her words to him was riveted in his memory. He had told her what had happened.

"Anas," she had responded in her quiet voice, "sometimes spirits are united because the love between them can never fade. Others are united through a hatred that never fades. Life often comes to an end with us finally realizing that we have lived as prisoners of those who have done us wrong, not those who have treated us well. Your steps are following the track of the wrongdoer. Your vision is clouded by dirt. Think about who you really are."

"A fisherman's son," Anas the bookseller had responded at the time.

"Are you a bookseller, a fisherman, a warrior, or a lover?"

"I'm Anas, all those people."

At the time, she had laughed, then faded into her own darkness.

For two years now, his life and earnings had been transformed. Hamza, Anas's father, had settled in Alexandria, although the sea there was anything but settled. He would spend his days hovering around his two sons and counting his profits. He had wanted his business to succeed and was eager for his two sons to inherit so many ships that anyone standing on the shore could not see the end of the line. He had two sons: Anas was the elder, and Ali the younger. Anas baffled him and kept him awake at night. He had no patience when it came to gathering in the fishing-nets and waiting for profit; he showed no inclination toward commerce.

Ever since he had gone to Quran school, reading had been his main interest. He was fascinated by paper and its manufacture, and ink and inkwells. Anas was not yet twenty when he traveled to Fustat to meet a scholar named Abd ar-Rahman ibn Abdallah ibn Abd al-Hakam, who was famous at the time for writing about Egypt and the Islamic conquest. His writings were different, enough to blow the mind. When he spoke, it was like no one else, discussing ancient civilization and great ancestors, and incorporating geography, astronomy, and a new science called algebra. Anas plunged into a totally different world. In the process, he forgot about love or consorting with slave-girls as his brother and father did. He was economical with his father's gifts so that he could purchase the books he wanted. He had no friends or companions. When his father insisted that he return to Alexandria and learn his father's trade, he reluctantly agreed because he had no funds of his own. He returned, but his heart was still in books and the magical craft that could make of one and the same book, ten, twenty, or a hundred copies. People started making snide comments, suggesting that the fisherman's son was crazy or weird, saying nothing for hours and not caring about women or money. Ali, on the other hand, learned how to fish and kept company with male friends. Sometimes he would have some fun of his own, at others he would come home drunk, and at still others he would perform the prayers precisely and beg for forgiveness.

When Ibn al-Mudabbir demanded that taxes be paid, the head fisherman resisted at first, then brought the merchants together to submit a complaint to the caliph. But no complaint was going to stop Ibn al-Mudabbir or any other administrator. When the caliph paid no attention to the complaint, head fisherman Hamza al-Skandari objected to the taxes, and there was a confrontation between him and Ahmad ibn al-Mudabbir.

The day came when the merchant was whipped, and his entire property and fleet were sequestered, changing life for everyone in Alexandria. It was unheard of for a merchant to dare submit a complaint or raise an objection. The two sons watched as their father was whipped by a fisherman who worked for him. The man cursed their father and accused him of dreadful things. Ibn al-Mudabbir's men had the place surrounded and stopped anyone from interfering. With every stroke of the whip on Anas's father's back, the links of his previous life broke apart.

If only Anas had been able to forget about the sight of rope in his father's mouth, his father's blood being spilled, and a sword penetrating without reaching his father's depths. How he had wanted it to penetrate that far. There were a hundred men or more, while they were just two, Anas and Ali. Later they were able to understand that Ahmad ibn al-Mudabbir had wanted to teach the people of Alexandria a lesson and to make their father an example to anyone who dared defy him. He had come in person, Ahmad ibn al-Mudabbir, the Tax Administrator, but he had not come close. He maintained a distance, like a rugged mountain. Anas had seen his face and turban and noticed his silk gallabiyya that fluttered in the Alexandria breeze as the whip fell on his father's back. Over a hundred men had come. The men began by shackling Hamza over the objections of Anas and Ali.

Yes indeed, Anas protested, but a man punched him in the face, and blood started dripping from his mouth.

"Leave my father alone!" he yelled, wiping the blood from his mouth. "Zayid, you wretch, that's your master! Remember this. I'll cut your limbs off."

Every time Anas yelled, the man only hit him, his brother, and his father all the harder. He could not fight back for more than an hour. After they had kicked him, pounded him, and hit him on the head, his strength gave out. They bound his limbs with a thick rope and moved away from his line of vision so that he could watch his father being humiliated. However, his eyes were focused on Ibn al-Mudabbir and the folds of his silken garment flapping in the winds that accompanied his father's screams. He noticed the expression in Ibn al-Mudabbir's eyes: he looked steady, smiling, and content. Then he looked at Zayid's expression. His eyes were a tissue of rapture and revenge.

"I want to hear you beg, you tyrant," Zayid yelled as he flayed Hamza. "Come on, I want to hear you beg."

Anas closed his eyes. "Don't do it, Father," he muttered. "I beg you, don't do it. You've always been generous to Zayid; he's a servant. Don't give him this triumph."

This time the whip stroke hit his father on the face. He screamed at the top of his voice. Zayid was determined to hear him beg. The blows kept coming, increasingly cruel, until his father finally did beg Zayid, and then asked Ibn al-Mudabbir to forgive him, once, then twice. The whipping continued.

Ibn al-Mudabbir smiled. When Zayid had administered a hundred lashes, he stopped and let the father fall, half-dead, to the ground. Zayid turned to Ibn al-Mudabbir and bowed his head.

"My lord," he said, bowing in front of the Tax Administrator.

"The Tax Administrator is being lenient with the Egyptian people," Ibn al-Mudabbir now proclaimed. "Otherwise, he'd be slaughtering everyone who resisted the tax obligation. From today onwards, I don't want to hear any whisperings or raised voices. I want fishermen to breathe calmly. The sea-fish will come to me first, and I'll then distribute the catch to those who are deserving and obedient. Obedient people will be the winners. Anyone who refuses will die right here. I'm here, and I've no plans to leave. Your only hope is to comply."

He then looked at Anas, and their eyes met. Anas did not recognize the expression in his eyes. Ibn al-Mudabbir spoke to his men.

"I don't want the fisherman's sons to stay here," he said. "They must leave today."

"My lord," Zayid said delightedly, "I'll make sure of that myself."

Ibn al-Mudabbir's men left. The fishermen all lowered their heads in despair. Night had fallen by the time Hamza returned home, his head bowed, not uttering a single word. While Ali bound his wounds, his father remained silent. Anas held his hand, then kissed his head.

"What can brave people do, Father, when they're confronted with desert beasts? Let's just forget what's happened."

His father did not respond.

"They're just ignorant, Father," Anas went on gently. "Tyranny inevitably comes to an end."

"There's no end to tyranny," his father responded firmly.

"Even in this era," Anas insisted, "there's still justice to be found. We must raise a complaint with the governor."

"Don't you dare do that!" his father insisted. "Nothing ever reaches the governor. Ibn al-Mudabbir's men have seized control of the very air Egyptians breathe."

"But the world is just," Anas responded angrily. "Tyranny will get its due recompense!"

"We no longer have anything," the father commented.

"We'll get it all back," Ali retorted with a scowl. His father said nothing.

At midnight, Anas heard waves crashing against the door of the house and wind whistling through the windows. He decided to check on his father and went to his room, but he was not there. He roused his brother in total panic, and they both rushed out of the house. No waves were crashing against the house, nor were the winds whistling through the windows. It was their father. He had taken his small boat and everything he still owned and set out to sea at night. The two brothers looked all around the place, then seized a boat belonging to one of the fishermen and tried to catch up with their father. While Ali kept talking nonstop, Anas was rowing as hard as he could, sweat pouring off him.

"What does he want?" Ali kept asking. "To go fishing at night? The sea's not safe now. Why's he out here now? Anas . . ."

"Father," Anas yelled when they finally caught up with their father's boat, "wait!"

His father turned around and gave him a look that he could not interpret in the dark. His eyes were gleaming, or that was how it looked to Anas. Then his father threw himself into the sea and disappeared in seconds. Ali let out a yell, and Anas jumped into the sea and searched all around the boat in total despair. All he could see was seafoam. He grabbed the edge of the boat, and his brother pulled him back on board. They both returned to the shore without saying a single word. The father had taken refuge in the sea and now dwelled within it. Zayid spread the good news among all the fishermen.

"Hamza's killed himself," he told them. "He's not a man. He's nothing. He's an infidel."

Ali collected their belongings from the house and kept talking nonstop. "Don't listen to Zayid," he told Anas. "We're leaving here."

Anas left the house slowly, his gaze following Zayid, who was leaping around like a monkey over a fire, hysterical in his delight. Anas went up to him, put his hands around his neck, and throttled him. Zayid tried to call for help and opened his mouth to get a breath. No one interfered. Anas must have broken his neck. All his hatred and bitterness were mustered in his actions, and he ignored Ali's pleas to stop. He left Zayid a lifeless corpse.

"Hamza al-Skandari is the head fisherman," he proclaimed, surrounded by the other men. "Zayid is one of his servants. Just remember that."

They then started running as fast as they could and escaped. For a while, Anas's heart felt a sense of calm, but it did not last.

How often had Anas told himself that murder was impossible? Anyone who could trace letters with his pen could only be proficient at acquiring knowledge. Such a person should not seek slaughter. The fire in the soul would die down the moment breathing stopped. Throughout his life, he had believed in reprisal, even when, as a child, he took revenge on his own self or refused to confront it. Now he no longer knew who he was. When he plunged into his self, all he found was dust. It was ignorance that really scared him; ignorance of the self was incurable.

The two brothers escaped from Alexandria and went to Fustat. Anas resorted to his teacher, Abd ar-Rahman ibn Abdallah ibn Abd al-Hakam, who found him a job in a tavern in the Booksellers' Market in Fustat. Anas started making copies of books, selling them, and occasionally talking to people about them. Ali tried working as a fisherman, but had no experience at freshwater fishing. Thus far, he had not managed to find a job. It was then that Anas met Judge Yahya, Maisoon's father, who read a lot and admired Anas's script and conversation.

Every night Anas would see his father, his eyes gleaming with impotence and disappointment. Every day, he swore to take revenge. His anger was not directed solely at Ibn al-Mudabbir. He was just as angry with himself, and his father who had surrendered. Even though Anas was secure in his job, and no one had any doubts about him, Ali was a worry for him. Anas was older, but he was devoted to making and selling books. Such a person regards himself as a giant and a magician. Even as a child, he was the most spoiled boy in the whole of Alexandria. His father Hamza used to give him anything he wanted. When it came to food, he would only choose the very choicest meat and fruit. At that time, Hamza had regarded himself as the most powerful and important man in the world. Then Ibn al-Mudabbir had arrived and cut him down to size, until he became tinier than a mustard seed. Ali realized the extent of the humiliation; even if his father was the head fisherman, he would never be able to defeat the Tax Administrator. Anas told himself that his father had been mighty enough to reach the stars and probe the earth's very depths. Ali felt sorry for him. He dragged Anas to see the judge and Shaikh Bakkar ibn Qutaiba, who was famous both for his loathing of tyranny and his ability to keep people's secrets. Ali came in, leading his brother by his shoulders, and they all performed two prostrations of salat. Ali was hoping that the shaikh could persuade Anas to give up on his plan for revenge. Anger is more likely to kill than poison; wrath invades the liver like a sword and lance combined.

"Shaikh," Anas told Shaikh Bakkar at the time, "I've come here with a heart full of fire. Tyranny is the most ruthless of fighters, the most poisonous of snakes. Do you have an antidote for it?"

The shaikh smiled. "It's as though you're asking a human being to clasp a star that's fallen from the heavens," he replied. "The only cure is in God's hands. He's the One to repel tyranny. Make sure you don't assume that your own efforts are enough. It is God who knows both wisdom and time."

"I've realized," Anas retorted, "that there's no justice in this world. I'm not content to get my rights from the people who have wronged me in the next world. It's in this world that I want them first, then in the next world. Does not God say: 'In retaliation there is life for you, you of sound minds'?" [Quran, Sura 2 [The Cow], v. 179]

The shaikh smiled, but did not respond.

"You understand, don't you, Shaikh?" Anas insisted.

"Faith has yet to enter the heart of anyone who claims to know everything," the shaikh replied. "I'm learning and trying to understand. I fail, I succeed, but I'm still trying. Perhaps you need to think afresh and try to understand."

"On the contrary, I used to be indifferent, but then the light flashed in front of me and blinded my sight. I don't want to understand any more than that. Anger is consuming my entire spirit."

"Understand your anger first, then appreciate the meaning of justice. You need to realize that you cannot know His purpose. He is the One who knows that best. I know you, Anas. Shaikh Abd ar-Rahman has told me about you. You're a reader and scholar. After a while, if angry people hand over the reins to their heart, they will come to a realization; those who resolve to question themselves will always find the answer. Whenever you're angry, turn to God and repeat His words. You're praying to Him today because you're scared of Him or crave His gifts, not because you love Him. Those who love will receive His judgment; those who love will never be angry with human beings. How can you be angry with an ephemeral human being when you have with you the One who knows the inner workings of everything? He envelops you in His love, so how can you think of any other? Did not Rabia al-Adawiyya state that:

My beloved is forever with me. For His love I can find no substitute. His love is my ordeal among mortals. O beloved of my heart, O my every hope . . . grant me a union with You to cure my ordeal.

"I told you I'm angry," Anas responded in confusion, "and you're quoting poetry at me?"

"I told you that anger is closely tied to fear. When you can love, you'll have a better understanding. But you need to realize that, as part of your love-relationship with Him, there can be no way to understand everything because He is the One who knows, and you are ignorant. You must learn to trust Him; then use your love to overcome anger. Anas, given your love for your father or mother, would you lose your trust in them, even if they were to try to kill you? Did Ishmael lose his trust in the Prophet Abraham, even when he tried to kill him?"

"I'd never lose my trust in either of them."

"God is even closer to you than your jugular vein. His mercy is all-encompassing, but it is also the love-relationship between the strong and the weak . . . the One whose knowledge is all-encompassing and the one who seeks yet more knowledge, even though he has already learned."

"And what about justice? Doesn't He call Himself 'the Just'?"

"My son, the issue of justice has exhausted shaikhs. Every time they've reached a decision, they've been worried that an innocent person will be wrongly treated. It's faulty justice because we don't see everything. Only He sees and knows all. My son, love involves surrendering yourself to Him and dwelling within the realms of His light and words. You realize that sometimes you're weak, and, more often than not, you're deficient."

"And yet, powerful people take everything," Anas insisted.

"You have not made your way inside His heart or recognized His efforts. A wise man once said that we're all fighting a battle of which other people are unaware."

"Those are Plato's words."

"I know. Didn't I say that you were a reader? I too read in order to understand. How hard it is for you, as a flawed human being, to accept opinions. You're not convinced by what I'm saying. Perhaps you aren't ready to listen to them. Do you realize why? Anger is also a sign of loss of mind, as intoxicating as wine or even worse. Before you stop drinking wine, try to stop getting angry so you can let it salve your wounds. My son, your father is with God and His all-encompassing mercy, as I've told you. Don't worry about your father. Submit and rest assured that he would not do wrong or be cruel even if shaikhs do so."

Anas did not respond.

"You're eager to take revenge," the shaikh continued. "Revenge is a mirage where thirsty people imagine there's water, but it neither waters the thirsty nor feeds the starving. In the long run, weakness is a companion to the human body. That same deficient body is Adam's tribulation and punishment, a weak, puny body in a world that is long gone before your eye can even blink."

Anas had not expected to hear what the shaikh was saying. His words did nothing to assuage his heart, disturbing him instead. At the time, he did not realize that some worshippers were listening silently to the conversation. Anas approached the shaikh and looked into his eyes.

"You know who I am," Anas said. "Aren't you going to ask the police to arrest me? The Tax Administrator is searching for me."

"You know I won't do that," Shaikh Bakkar answered quietly. "Otherwise, why did you come to see me?"

Anas stared at him for a moment, then stood and left without a word.

✦

He never wanted to forget the past, but then Maisoon arrived and opened gates of light all around him. Whenever she was close, his heart would leap. When he set eyes on her face, it appeared illuminated by a light as pure as the rivers of paradise. For two whole years, he had imagined that joy would never return. His heart would never again pound, but simply linger. But then her glances and her forever bold and modest eyes changed everything.

Anas was a bookseller, and his relationship with books was unlike that of anyone else. Pain had tugged at his heartstrings. Having lost everything, he had become the strongest and most courageous of men. There are times when wisdom accompanies loss. Loss erects a formidable, protective wall for the heart, as stolid and resistant as the stones of the pyramids themselves. What did he have to lose? His eyes envied the impaled young man as he had groaned in agony. Anas realized that the young man's end had been very near, whereas Anas had neither certainty nor an end in sight. He wrote skillfully in his notebook. When vengeance resembles arithmetic, the anticipated result arrives quickly.

Ever since he was a boy, he had been fascinated by the works of Al-Khwarizmi. He had cracked the riddles of his symbols and understood algebra. He realized that difficult equations could be solved, but you needed to divide them up, solving each example on its own. The entire world was made up of squares, roots, and numbers; it consisted of an equation with six examples. It was easy to understand if we divided things up and looked for the result and the root. Every problem had a solution. He had one column for love, and another for slaughter. People being tortured should never plead with their torturer. That is an unforgiveable sin. Was he responsible for his father's death? Had his father noticed the blame in Anas's eyes without saying anything about it? Did his father not always notice everything? When their eyes had met, had his father seen some sorrow and frustration in Anas's expression? A third column was for punishment, and a fourth for victims. Who belonged there? Maisoon? He stopped writing for a moment, then wrote her name in a beautiful script. He had never felt weak when faced with a woman before. After some study and reading, he had formulated his strategy. She was successful, with a clear result, root, and number . . . Was he exposing Maisoon to danger, he wondered, with the squares he was writing down now? In his equation, she would not be in danger. He smiled to himself as he contemplated the moment of union between the two of them. Love was a different sensation, but it too was subject to the same equations—that much was certain.

In a fifth column, he wrote Ibn al-Mudabbir's name. How would he act? When was he going to die? Death would bring rest, but there had to be torture of some kind: humiliation, begging, severing limbs—cutting off a limb every day and giving him no water. He needed to read more and memorize things by heart. He needed to add another column for surprises. The first of them was that he was more in love than he had ever expected and his hopes were too high. He had thought that, with the heart dead, the body would calm down. But he desired the judge's daughter. He was passionately in love with her.

His brother yelled in his face that he must be crazy. He promised to bring him a

Greek slave-girl that very day; she would be more beautiful than the judge's daughter. Women were all the same: pretty face and nice body, that's it.

"I only desire Maisoon," Anas insisted. "I won't marry anyone else."

"You're a fugitive killer," Ali scoffed, "and she's the judge's daughter. Be sensible, Anas. Every day I see these pages with their weird equations, numbers, and letters. I don't know, are they devil's magic or a touch of madness? Even if you drew in the language of birds and kept company with the Pyramid Witch, you wouldn't be able to take revenge on the Tax Administrator, or reach the judge's daughter."

"I'm the head fisherman's son," Anas replied proudly, "and she's the judge's daughter. There's no difference between us."

"Open your eyes, brother," Ali reacted in shock, "and stop living in delusion. You're the son of a man who killed himself. You've no hope."

Love, it seemed, does not conform to the rules of algebra or astronomy. Faced with his energy and efficacy, even the stars were at a loss. That day, he prayed, made a vow, and spoke to God. He said that he was willing to forget everything in the past. He would leave the tyrant to face his reckoning with God. He would tear up his notebook or bury it in the columns of the ancients, on one condition: that Maisoon would be his. She had taken over his emotions; the very image of her removed all self-hatred, and the unforgettable look in her eyes toyed with his memory and made him forget his goal. He no longer wished to forfeit a single moment of his life without thinking about her and imagining her in his arms and enveloping his soul. But the Pyramid Witch had talked about the union of enemy souls. If only she had never known. For the Tax Administrator and Anas, that time now drew close when the Administrator found out about Maisoon's beauty.

Chapter 2

The day the stars fell from the sky, the Egyptians anticipated the misery to come. One governor followed another, but Ahmad ibn al-Mudabbir did not leave the country or show any intention of doing so. Anger intensified, and tyranny took hold. All lamentation was suppressed; groans were stultifying and useless. On the day the stars fell, a near-miracle occurred, or almost. The news spread in Fustat, and passersby carried it as far as Giza, crossing boundaries all the way to the sea. Some people laughed, others were confused, and still others expected the Day of Resurrection. The news that confused the Egyptians was not about stars falling or the new governor of Egypt who was not going to come himself, but was sending a deputy instead. No, the news that baffled the mind and flew faster than crows after a fight was even weirder and more significant. Ahmad ibn al-Mudabbir, the Tax Administrator for Egypt, whose term in office had coincided with one governor and caliph after another, someone who had established his position in Baghdad, Samarra, and at the Abbasid caliphal court, who had made Egyptians taste the humiliation of need after plenty and poverty after wealth, who had claimed to own the salt of the earth in Egypt and the fish in the sea, that same Ahmad ibn al-Mudabbir was in love with the daughter of Judge Yahya ibn Isa and had written poetry about her. Women laughed, and the story of how the tyrant, Ibn al-Mudabbir, had encountered the judge's gorgeous daughter outdid the news about the new governor and stars falling. Not only that, but several ladies had suggested maliciously that stars had fallen because of the power of love. Ibn al-Mudabbir had a fragile sparrow's heart; it had been shattered by the hips of the judge's daughter. Men listening to the story were eager to know how it would end. Would Ibn al-Mudabbir be married to an Egyptian woman with whom he had fallen in love? Would he simply snatch her from her father? Once he was married, would his heart soften toward the people of Egypt? Or once he had obtained what he was after, would he become more and more brutal? They said that the judge would never allow his daughter to be married to that Satan. Others said that she loved him like a slave-girl, and he showered her with poems and jewelry. Now she was seeing nobody else. People were saying that he was ignoring his wives and no longer spending any time with his slave-girls. News of his infatuation with the judge's daughter had by now reached the caliph's court. The old poetry that he had written about his famous slave-girl, Uraib, was nothing when compared with the poetry he was writing now about Maisoon, the judge's daughter, describing her hips and breasts. He would melt into her eyes, plunge headlong into her lips, and bury his head into her long tresses. He described passion and pleasure in her arms, savoring the warmth of her arms and kissing her lips. Surely he composed from experience, in order to include such detail and passion. Women slapped their faces, simultaneously titillated and shocked, covering their mouths as they shared the story with each other. It was trickier and more dangerous than men imagined. Abla the hairdresser had told the whole story; she could enter every house, and knew every woman. In fact, she knew Ibn al-Mudabbir as well. He had given her a pure gold necklace in order to arrange the meeting that was now the talk of every segment of Egyptian society—indeed the news had now reached Syria and Iraq.

Abla the hairdresser told the whole story. She said that it had started when she had gone to the judge's house to prepare his daughter Ruqayya for her wedding. She had made up Ruqayya's face, decorated her feet and hands with henna, combed her hair, and wrapped her head in a turban. Ruqayya had looked even more beautiful than the caliph's own wives. When it came to decorating the daughters of amirs and judges, no one in the whole of Egypt was finer and more costly than Abla the hairdresser. She was also the only woman in the country who could help girls get married and had a handle on the secrets of houses and palaces.

When Abla the hairdresser had entered the house of Judge Yahya to prepare Ruqayya, her eyes had fallen on his other daughter, Maisoon; her mouth had gaped in sheer astonishment. Never in her life had she seen such a lovely face, long hair, and profound, pure eyes, all part of a peerless body that was bound to arouse enough lust to make men lose their minds. When she left the judge's house, she rushed over to Ibn al-Mudabbir's palace and told his wives and slave-girls about her, with entirely pure intentions and not intending to arouse his curiosity or passion. It just so happened that, on that very same day, one of Ibn al-Mudabbir's senior wives decided to annoy one of his junior wives, so she told Ibn al-Mudabbir what she had just heard as a way of distracting him from his beautiful, younger wife. Ibn al-Mudabbir summoned Abla the hairdresser and listened to her detailed description of Maisoon the judge's daughter. He did not believe her, so she arranged a secret encounter with Maisoon. She invited her, along with her sister Ruqayya and their mother, to her house to view some gowns made of pure decorated silk that she had specially imported for the bride from Syria. When they entered the house and took off their face veils, Abla the hairdresser started taking the gowns out of her wardrobes. Ibn al-Mudabbir was hiding behind a curtain, his eyes riveted on Maisoon, his mouth gaping in amazement. Swallowing hard, he uttered some curses to fate and Abla the hairdresser who had managed to make him lose his mind. Never in his forty years had he ever seen a woman's face of such purity. When the women left Abla's house, he sat in front of her like a little boy.

"That girl's mine!" he said in a commanding tone.

"She's a virgin," she replied with a smile. "She's only ever left the house once or twice."

"I must marry her."

"Will her father, the judge, agree, Sir?" she asked.

He gave her an angry look. "Listen, woman," he replied, "who would dare oppose the Tax Administrator? Even the governor himself has no hold over me, nor even the caliph."

She interrupted him. "Love often impairs the mind, Sir," she said cunningly. "I beg you not to talk about the Muslim caliph that way. Walls have ears that can hear even more than spies. In matters of marriage, dreams fare better than brutality."

"I'll be married to her before this month is out," he responded swiftly.

She moved closer and held out her hands. "If the judge's daughter falls in love with the Tax Administrator," she said with a smile, "then nobody will be able to interfere in their marriage plans. The girl has her own way of getting what she wants."

"What does she want?"

"How much is the love of Maisoon, the judge's daughter, worth to you, Sir?"

"All the gold in Egypt."

"All the fish in the sea," she replied with a sigh, "all the salt on land, all the gold in the tombs of the ancients, all belonging to Abla the hairdresser . . . a dream, Sir. Let me arrange a meeting. You aren't the only arranger [*mudabbir*], Sir. Then we can discuss how much I deserve and what you'll pay me."

"If you'll arrange a meeting, you'll get more than you could ever want."

She gave a malicious smile. "Remember, Sir, that she's just a young girl," she said. "Don't scare her with a passion she won't understand and a devotion even more powerful than her young heart. Take your love slowly. Girls are often won over more by shiny jewelry and sweet talk than by burning kisses and the kind of fiery passion that they have never experienced before."

Abla the hairdresser then invited the judge's wife, Ruqayya the bride, and Maisoon to visit her house again. The judge's wife declined the invitation at first, but Abla stuck to her guns and insisted until the judge's wife agreed. The meeting that all Egypt was talking about took place in Abla the hairdresser's house. People say that Ibn al-Mudabbir surprised them by coming into the room. The mother was shocked, and the two daughters screamed. The Tax Administrator ordered them to go out and leave the room to himself and Maisoon. The mother was terrified, but refused. He insisted, stating that he intended to be married to Maisoon. The girl stayed where she was, not saying a single word, neither objecting nor fleeing. The mother yelled at Abla and threatened her, and Abla replied that she knew nothing about it and was as surprised as they were. They all left the room, but Maisoon's mother was determined to listen to the conversation from behind the door. Abla joined her at the crack in the door and watched them both carefully. Ruqayya was in shock. She could not believe what had just happened, and had no idea what her husband would do when he found out about it. The mother listened to the words of love and the ghazal poems. The Tax Administrator kept his voice low and soft; she could not hear what her daughter was saying. For a moment, there was silence.

"What's he doing to her, Abla?" the mother asked in total shock.

"Calm down, my lady," Abla replied. "I swear that he's asking her to marry him."

After a while, Ibn al-Mudabbir opened the door.

"I'm going to visit the judge's house," he said gruffly, "in order to ask permission to be married to his daughter. Inform your husband, the judge, that the Tax Administrator will be paying him a visit today."

With that, he opened the door and left.

Maisoon's mother now went crazy. She called for Abla, and then turned to her daughter. Ruqayya was in tears. "My husband's going to divorce me today," she mumbled. "That's for sure." She squeezed Maisoon's shoulder. "What on earth have you done, you cunning little devil?" she screamed. "Your father's going to kill you."

What had happened between the Tax Administrator and Maisoon floated through the dusty air like fragments from stars that had fallen that night. Some faces were lit up with feelings of hatred and vengeance, others with despair and dejection. Abla the hairdresser described what had happened to the women of Egypt. Ibn al-Mudabbir, with his henna-dyed beard, trimmed hair, silk cloak decorated with pure gold, silver-embossed shoes, and gallabiyya long enough to reach all the way to Fustat, had managed to catch Maisoon's attention. Abla herself could hear the passionate kisses and, from her place by the crack in the door, saw Maisoon's robe fall off her shoulder to reveal a flawless shoulder underneath and breasts that would drive anyone to insurrection. Kissing her shoulder and breasts, this maximally powerful man now whispered despairingly in her ear. Never in his entire life, he told her, had he seen anyone so stunningly beautiful. Everything he owned was at her disposal; the entire land of Egypt was not enough for a single kiss from her lips. He would withdraw his sword from its scabbard and slay anyone who so much as looked at her from then on. His life had begun today. Shuddering modestly, she gave him a flirtatious smile. She told him that she was just some unknown girl and did not deserve a man like him. Abla the hairdresser swore that he had then prostrated himself in front of her and put his head on her feet.

"No," he insisted, "I've only started living since I've seen you."

Maisoon now lifted her hand and put it on his hair. "This star in the heavens that's fallen into my hands today!" she responded gently, "How wretched I feel today, Sir, since I do not deserve you."

Kissing her, he assured her that she was his, and they would be wed that very day if not earlier.

This is the story that Abla told. She was shocked at Maisoon's guile, as she was not yet nineteen, at her expertise in dealing with men, and at the way she had been able to take control of such a wild beast and lion as the Tax Administrator. For some time, she had been hearing about the way slave-girls were able to hold sway at the Abbasid caliph's court, but those women were Persian or Byzantine. Never had she heard of an Egyptian girl being so masterful at flirtation and deceit.

Judge Yahya listened to his wife in complete shock. Judge Yahya ibn Isa was acquainted with Ibn al-Mudabbir, the way a prisoner knows his jailer and camels know their trainers. Two years earlier, they had both been involved in an incident, one that the whole of Egypt knew about—the so-called fisherman's son incident.

The judge could recall how Ibn al-Mudabbir's time in Egypt began, when the caliph appointed him Tax Administrator in 248 AH [861 CE]. The Abbasids had their own way of governing, especially when it came to Egypt. They divided authority between several men so that none of them would have sole authority and try to declare independence. The governor was only in charge of war and prayers. People would pray for him in mosques after praying for the caliph, and, on orders from the caliph, he would declare war, but that was the limit of his authority. The Tax Administrator was the controller of money and influence. He always came from the caliphal court itself; he would be the one to collect and distribute the money. He had to be someone they could trust and rely on. The caliph would also appoint the chief of police. Each man had his own specialty and prestige. However, the one with the least prestige was the governor; he had no power to dismiss either the police chief or the Tax Administrator. In fact, the governor of Fustat and Egypt did not even have control over the border regions, and thus over Alexandria. Ibn al-Mudabbir was the only one with control over the whole of Egypt. One governor after another arrived in Egypt. Occasionally, a governor might try to dismiss Ibn al-Mudabbir, when complaints about his actions had multiplied. But the governor would fail and leave. One year, four governors arrived successively; one might govern for seven days, another for a whole month, and someone in luck might govern for a year or a year and a half. Ibn al-Mudabbir's regime was firmly fixed like a tent-peg in fertile ground. He started laying down his regulations without consulting shaikhs or judges. He decreed that taxes would be imposed on all Egyptians, on mineral salt, crops, and animals, and later on fish as well. People came out to object, prime among them Judge Yahya. He had addressed Ibn al-Mudabbir in no uncertain terms.

"In God's noble book," he said, "He has spoken to humanity: 'Permitted for you is the fish of the sea and its food as a pleasure for you and travelers.' [Sura 5 (Table) v. 96] How can the Tax Administrator claim that the fish of the sea are his property or the caliph's?"

However, Ibn al-Mudabbir insisted and dispatched spies to Alexandria, Al-Farma, and Dimyat. He produced the accounts of every fish merchant and told them all that the fish were the property of the caliph and Tax Administrator. Merchants would be required to pay taxes for everything extracted from the sea. People in Alexandria rose up, but the Tax Administrator's men put a swift and brutal end to their protests. The previous year, Hamza the head fisherman, Anas's father, had protested, and what had happened had happened. Hamza himself had recounted what Ibn al-Mudabbir had said: "I want you to announce to everyone that the merchant died an infidel." He asked Hamza to recount the story as an object lesson for any wrongdoers who chose to resist the Tax Administrator's orders.

At the time, Judge Yahya had refused, pointing out that he controlled neither heaven nor hell in order to pass judgment on human beings. Hamza al-Skandari was now with his Lord. He would be passing judgment on him and certainly knew him far better than either the Tax Administrator or the judge. He was a judge who would pass judgment on the affairs of this world, not on what was to happen when God welcomes His servants. Ibn al-Mudabbir was furious and punished him by preventing him from delivering sermons and confining him to his house for three months. Eventually, Shaikh Bakkar ibn Qutaiba himself intervened. He had some influence with the caliph, and Ibn al-Mudabbir was forced to pardon the judge.

The judge remembered everything from the past as he looked at Ahmad ibn al-Mudabbir, who had come to ask for his daughter's hand in marriage.

"What does the judge think?" Ibn al-Mudabbir asked after he had made his speech.

"You have three other wives, Sir," the judge replied hesitantly. "My daughter's very young. I'm worried about how she'll fare among your other women."

"She'll be the primary wife over all of them," Ibn al-Mudabbir said firmly.

"This is all very serious," said the judge, in despair. "We need time to think. Give me some time to consult with the rest of her family and ask her for her opinion."

"What family can be more important than the Tax Administrator?" Ibn al-Mudabbir retorted. "Who's going to object to such a family connection? Just ask her. If she says 'no,' then I won't be married to her. If she agrees, then she's mine."

The judge gasped in astonishment and was furious.

"Have you met my daughter, Sir?" he asked, controlling his nerves.

"Just do what you're told, Judge," he roared. "From today, your daughter's my wife."

"Don't women merit any respect these days?"

Ibn al-Mudabbir gave him an angry stare. "I've come to ask for your daughter's hand."

The judge stood up. "We're duly honored, Sir," he said, keeping his anger in check.

"The marriage will take place before the week's out."

"We'll need some time to arrange things."

"The marriage will take place before the week's out."

The judge remained silent.

"Yahya, I know you," Ibn al-Mudabbir said with a smile. "I realize that you're full of hatred and anger. You're angry with me because I do my job and you're an Egyptian. If you weren't, you'd understand more. I'm here on behalf of the caliph for whom you pray every single day. I'm here to carry out his orders. I do my job very well because I'm loyal to him. When people protest and fishermen refuse to pay their taxes, I must teach them a lesson. Stand on the side of what's right, and don't follow your fancies. In this case, right is that the money belongs to the caliph."

The judge remained silent.

"Egyptians haven't perfected Arabic yet," Ibn al-Mudabbir went on. "They keep making mistakes. As long as their language supersedes Arabic, they'll need someone to teach them. You're a model for that, Judge. Your language is just like that of people in Basra, no irregularities and no mistakes. Does Maisoon speak Coptic? Have you taught your daughters Coptic?"

"What's language got to do with marriage?"

"If Egyptians learned Arabic, they'd understand that they have to obey people in authority and not protest against the caliph's decrees."

The judge paused for a moment. "When an animal's in milk," he said, "it needs an experienced person who's familiar with it and can help it produce a lot of milk. Your orders regarding cow's milk are one thing, but for me to teach you how to do the milking without scaring it, that's something else."

"I get the impression I'm talking to a peasant, not a man of faith and learning."

"What I'm saying, my lord," the judge replied firmly, "is that the caliph's orders are clear to us all, but their implementation requires a certain level of wisdom and a good deal of patience. Cruelty only produces drought. You don't get milk-tasting water from inside rocks, Sir. But no matter. Let me think things over."

Ibn al-Mudabbir was emphatic. "Yahya, shaikh and judge, is fully aware, of course, that his own daughter's opinion is important."

"No, Sir, it's her guardian's opinion that matters, my lord. We've been honored by your visit."

Once Ibn al-Mudabbir had left, Judge Yahya remained in the room, neither speaking nor moving. His wife had given him a summary of what had happened in Abla's house. She had told him that Ibn al-Mudabbir had come in behind them, then left. She had not told him about Ibn al-Mudabbir being left alone with Maisoon or about the scary silence that had prevailed inside the room. For just a moment, the judge stared at the floor, then he stood up calmly and went into his daughter's room. Their eyes met.

"Father," she pleaded.

He raised his hand and slapped her on the face. She fell to the floor. Silence ensued.

"You, Maisoon," her father said in a suppressed tone, "you studied religion, you memorized God's book, and now you're causing me this humiliation? What is it you're after? Treasure and money? Power? You want to be married to a tyrant, someone who is cursed in every Egyptian household day and night? Do you want to shame and humiliate your own father? You . . . , if I'd buried you alive, it would have been better for me than having Ibn al-Mudabbir come to me with all his brute power and tell me that you want to be married to him, the very same Ibn al-Mudabbir who imprisoned and discredited me because I refused to kowtow to his oppressive regulations. Do you remember?"

She stayed silent, staring at the floor and not looking at her father.

"My girl," her father went on forcefully, "Judge Yahya will die before marrying his daughter to that despotic tyrant. If I killed you with my own hands today and buried you, it would be better for both me and you. You're a stain on your own family. I used to think you were more intelligent than your sister and more devout. I never expected this kind of perversion."

Tears turned to stone in her eyes and failed to fall.

"Look at me!" her father said brutally.

She turned and looked at him. He could see anger and blame in her expression, and that made him even more annoyed. He started having some doubts, but angry moments can set stars ablaze.

"Have you something to say?" he asked defiantly.

She wanted to sound calm, but her reply came out in a quiver.

"You know everything, Father," she said. "You know me better than my own self."

"Are you going to defend yourself? Of course, you won't do that. Today I can recall how stubborn you were as a child, defiant and foolish. If only you'd died!"

She opened her mouth to speak, but he interrupted her.

"I don't want to hear any more," he said. "What the Tax Administrator has just told me is enough. Do you want a husband, daughter of Judge Yahya? Yes indeed, I do know you, and today you've allowed yourself to be perverted by power and glory. I promise that you will never be married to Ibn al-Mudabbir."

With that, he left the room and closed the door.

A general gloom pervaded the judge's household. Whom could he ask for help? What could he do? His wife did not dare talk to him or let him know about the widespread rumors and comments. He had one or two meetings with Ibn al-Mudabbir and managed to delay the marriage for a month or more so that the girl could prepare her trousseau. He avoided looking at his daughter so he would not feel compelled to strike her again, something he hated doing. But she had raised no objections to Ibn al-Mudabbir, had met him on her own, and did not ask for help. Maisoon, the girl who had memorized God's book and studied jurisprudence and hadith with him. Maisoon, who had turned down marriage proposals from several men so she could keep herself to be cared for by a man of religion and faith. She had now agreed to be married to Ibn al-Mudabbir. And why not?! Was he not the most powerful man in Egypt, all the way from Alexandria to Albuja? Why not? Could anyone take care of her and drown her in gold the way Ibn al-Mudabbir could? She was just young, that's all. He was well aware of what awaited her. What was that? The Tax Administrator was showering her with love while he waited patiently for the day when she would be his and he would willingly fulfill the judge's conditions to the letter. Maybe some kind of triumph would be awaiting her in Ibn al-Mudabbir's household. Who knows? Maybe the judge himself would also attain a rank he had never even dreamed of achieving. So why fight fate and close off the doors opening in front of him? That is what his friends kept saying. That is what his wife kept trying to tell him. And yet, Judge Yahya hated nothing in life so much as tyranny. He realized that fairness was the key to paradise and a quiet life in this world, and that people who consorted with tyranny would be consumed by an insatiable and unquenchable fire in their bellies.

By nature, Maisoon was tough. With her father present, she was as self-controlled as a bride on her wedding day, only to explode later like a shower of poison, baffling her mother. Maisoon picked up the water jug and threw it as hard as she could. Her mother leaped to her feet and gave her daughter a look that was a blend of sympathy and blame. But she refrained from commenting. Without scolding her daughter, she asked the servant-girl to pick up the pieces. As Maisoon watched the girl carefully picking up the fragments, her mind was swinging wildly between the bookseller and Ibn al-Mudabbir. Her father had accused her of flirting with men, that she had fired up and encouraged Ibn al-Mudabbir, and she wanted him as a husband. Her father had accused her of deceit, lying, and maybe even immorality. But it was other people who had pounced on her. She had stayed all alone in her own room amid doubtful and censorious glances, memories of love poetry that enveloped her, and Abla the hairdresser's tongue that never stopped wagging. She was the victim, not the killer. She was the one whose world that man had invaded and set on fire. She had been the prey in Ibn al-Mudabbir's trickery. Her father had been furious . . .

She recalled that day.

She had totally panicked, recited some verses from the Quran, and looked at the Tax Administrator. He had sat down in front of her and stared at her hair and face.

"You're Maisoon, the judge's daughter," he had said. "I've never set eyes on a woman as beautiful as you."

She shuddered.

"Do you realize," he went on, "how people in love can be struck by swords they've never encountered before, struck by glances like yours?"

She remained silent.

"If I asked to be married to you, would you agree?"

"You've shocked me, Sir," she replied.

"I didn't mean to shock you," he said gently. "It was just the sight of your lovely face, thou desire of my heart!"

She did not say anything. She had no idea how to respond. She was afraid of her father, of Ibn al-Mudabbir, of her mother, of everything.

"Your silence suggests both confusion and promises. Can you reassure me?"

She must have said something after a pause. Maybe it was:

"How can the Tax Administrator possibly need any reassurance from someone like me, when he holds all the reins of power in Egypt?"

"On the contrary, I've never felt so restless and worried as I do today. Just give me one word of reassurance, and I'll leave."

"You always have such reassurance, my lord," she replied quickly.

She did not say that because she wanted him as a husband. What else was she supposed to say to the Tax Administrator when she was in the room alone with him? He neither harassed nor even touched her. She was shocked. Ibn al-Mudabbir scared her but, when she looked into his eyes, what she saw was a lover's gentleness, not an aggressor's lust. Only she knew his heart and true feelings. Perhaps those rays of power and conceit might follow her.

The man who had confessed his love in front of her, who had fought for her, was the most powerful man in all of Egypt. That fact was somewhat satisfying. Ever since she was a girl, she had known that she was the most beautiful and richest, the judge's daughter, desired by every mother for their sons. She had always turned them down. She wanted a man with power and influence, whether in money or learning, a merchant perhaps or a judge, but she had never even dreamed of the Tax Administrator. His wives were from Iraq, and he had slave-girls from Byzantium and Persia. She was not going to kid herself. After he had spoken to her, she had returned to her house feeling scared. But once that feeling had died down, she had imagined herself as his wife, with complete ownership and control over him. There would be no room for any other women inside his house. He would have to abandon his wives and get rid of his slave-girls. Then he would be completely under her sway, and hers alone. She would ask him to treat the Egyptian people more kindly, and he would do it. She would become the country's savior. Ibn al-Mudabbir would build a huge mausoleum in her name and invite all Egyptians to visit it in her memory. People would say that his young attractive wife had managed to change him; he had become more sympathetic and less aggressive. She certainly entertained such hopes; she would not deny it. Yet she also hurriedly recited Quranic verses, seeking aid against the devil. She told herself that, even if she did manage to gain his exclusive affection at the expense of his other wives, that would still be a sin. Every time she pictured herself in the Tax Administrator's arms, her whole body rebelled and screamed in pain. Her well-established love for Anas was disquieting, with no room for negotiation or accepting spoils. Her father kept talking about the Tax Administrator's actions. Love would not be able to cope with every kind of infamy or atone for every sin. In fact, love only served to intensify sins and induce pain.

When she was just fifteen, she had formed an attachment to a relative but, when he had come to offer her his hand, she had rejected him. She had not liked the intensity of his affection and the abundance of love-talk he had used. She had received him twice at her sister's house. He had not touched her, but had started panting every time he looked at her. He had sent her one letter after another. She had ignored him and sworn to herself that no man would ever gain control of her heart. She was Maisoon, the most beautiful and most powerful girl on earth. Maybe Ibn al-Mudabbir was not the most powerful man . . . Who knows? Perhaps fate was keeping another man hidden from her, someone who was even more powerful and wealthy. Her ambition knew no bounds, stretching all the way from Fustat to the outskirts of Giza.

Sometimes her mother used to scold her. "You've no heart, Maisoon," she would say. "You were born with a beautiful face and a hole where your heart should be. I've no idea what it is you want."

All she wanted was someone who deserved her, but it seemed as though such a man had not yet been born. She had no feelings for Ibn al-Mudabbir, but his passion watered the headstrong soul and sated the eye's cravings. What if Ibn al-Mudabbir divorced all his other women and swore to change and treat Egyptians more generously? In that case, perhaps she would marry him. Why not? But he had no heart.

What about the bookseller? He had pierced the heavens and spread enchantment. Every time he drew close, her heart beat faster. Her eyes used to pause and long to gaze at him for the rest of her life. She put her hand over her heart in case it would yield and submit. If it did not, then the stake would do it, just as it had done with the rebellious young man. What kind of madness was besetting her? What was she expecting from a man she did not know and who possessed neither gold nor power?

She read from a book of poetry, then put it on her chest and fell into a deep sleep.

"Maisoon will be married to the Tax Administrator," she muttered to herself, half-awake, "even though she's really in love with the bookseller. She'll travel to Iraq. The caliph will set eyes on her and kill Ibn al-Mudabbir so that he can have her for himself, and she can be queen of Baghdad and the whole earth. The caliph will die, and then she can marry Anas. Yes indeed, that ending is fine."

She sighed in her sleep, sometimes seeing the caliph in the bookseller's face, then seeing the Tax Administrator in his face. But she was well aware of where power lies and how gold shines much brighter than all the gleaming of lovers. It would be fine to be married to the Tax Administrator; the heart could be mastered, but power had yet to be overcome. Were she to be married to Ibn al-Mudabbir, her name would be repeated throughout the ages, ahead even of Uraib, the caliph's concubine, about whom court poets, including Ibn al-Mudabbir, had composed verses. Indeed, she would become like Khuzairan, Haroon ar-Rasheed's mother, who ruled alongside her son and signed state documents along with him. She was more beautiful and powerful than even Khuzairan.

Maisoon took a slave-girl and went to the market, looking for Anas. Did he believe, she wondered, that she had managed to seduce the Tax Administrator? Would he slap her the way her father had?

She strolled through the trees and asked her slave-girl to buy some vegetables. Anas arrived.

"Maisoon," he told her firmly, "you're not going to be married to the Tax Administrator."

She stared at him.

"Anas . . . ," she said without even thinking.

He walked away and disappeared from view. She went looking for him, and eventually found him again.

"You desire only me," he told her.

"Be polite," she said, "or I'll tell my father."

"So tell me now!" he insisted. "Am I supposed to fight, or disappear into the foliage and live in the desert?"

She wanted to see him, but was puffing because he was walking so fast, disappearing amid the trees. "Do you believe what people are saying about me?" she asked him.

"No, I don't," he replied, "but I do believe that you know your own worth. I own an ancient Greek necklace that my father found in the sea and gave to me. The Tax Administrator will give you gold and silver, and I can give you a necklace that the ancients offered as oblation to the gods, something even more beautiful than anything to be found in either Persia or Byzantium. I can give you something, my beloved, that no other man can."

For a moment, she said nothing.

"Can I see it?" she asked.

He took it out of his pocket and put it in front of her.

"Did you but know," he whispered, "love has its own prestige and cost."

She was stunned by its sheer beauty and grabbed it.

"If you owned this necklace," he said as he took it back from her, "you'd be even richer than the Tax Administrator. It's your dowry, Maisoon."

She shuddered and was about to move off.

"Wait a minute," he told her. "You're generous of heart. Camels can survive with little water, but if you leave me permanently thirsty, I shall die even sooner than the young man killed by the Tax Administrator."

She put her hand over her heart.

"Did he die quickly?" she asked.

"He lasted the rest of the day and the next morning," he told her gently, his eyes fixed on hers. "He kept groaning and longing for death. I went back to him after a while. Every dying person needs water, perhaps as a way of tying him to a desert existence he has finally realized, or out of a desire for the rivers of paradise. I gave him a drink of water while the guard was asleep, but he just spat up blood and died."

She closed her eyes in pain.

"Lovers suffer twice," he whispered, running his hand over her fingers. "First, realizing that life isn't fair; second, knowing that we're not Noah who can face the flood in a boat. I'm suffering twice as well: first, recognizing I'm just a bookseller, while you're the judge's daughter, desired by Ibn al-Mudabbir; second, knowing for certain that there's no water to quench my thirst and no rivers of paradise waiting for me on this earth."

She looked at his fingers covering her hand and could not pull away. Sweet talk had never moved her; she had heard such words from lots of men. But the bookseller's eyes were unlike anyone else's, and so was his voice. She clung to his pupils as though they were the sweetest milk, and found consolation in his voice that sounded like angelic melodies.

"I'm afraid of seeing you on the stake," she said. "It pains me."

"It happens dozens of times a day; it's just part of the world we're living in. Don't let it grieve you. Even were you to see me dying for your sake, you should know that my heart would be at peace."

"You're lying."

"If I were lying, I wouldn't be fighting. If I were fighting, I wouldn't be lying."

"You're crazy, that's for sure. But the man who fights for Maisoon's sake is the one who'll win her, that's for sure too."

"You're right," he declared.

So much was happening these days. She had grown used to her own beauty, even as a young girl. She realized that she was not like other girls. Whenever any man looked at her face, he would utter words of praise to God. How often had her mother told her that whoever was to be married to her would come from the elite, a governor or amir? The man would never find another with a face like the full moon, a cascade of hair, and eyes that shone bright without candle or fire. But from the outset, Maisoon's beauty had been a trial for her father. He was afraid for her and sometimes even wanted to bury her alive. Ever since he had set eyes on her face for the first time, he had had a sense of foreboding. Being a girl's father was a problem, as far as he was concerned. Even if he tried to find a suitable husband for her while she was still young, beauty always provoked intrigue and stirred up rebellion. Ever since she was just ten years old, he had had his doubts about her. He used to yell in her face and lock her up if she did something wrong. He would make the punishment more severe for fear of a recalcitrance with no good outcomes. His wife did not dare stop him from being so severe. He was much more severe with Maisoon than with Ruqayya, who was not as beautiful as Maisoon. Ruqayya was not a threat, nor did she open the gate to an assault from some unknown location. Now the assault had finally come from Ibn al-Mudabbir. Even though Judge Yahya always did his best to be fair, his cruel streak had now managed, without him even realizing it, to sneak its way in and affect those closest to him. He neither listened to her nor spoke to her. When she occasionally rebelled, he used to lock her in her room or slap her; she would neither cry nor complain. That only increased his worries and sense of foreboding. She would often stare at the ceiling without saying a word. Then, everything that her father had feared now happened. Ibn al-Mudabbir wanted Maisoon for himself. Maisoon had accepted that, or even more. But the bookseller had arrived and scrambled the entire past.

He brought with him an affection that she had never encountered in a man, speaking as though he knew everything. And he was very good-looking. Did she want a man who owned the world, or one who treated her like the entire world? How was a man supposed to be affectionate with a woman, she wondered? If the bookseller really loved her, how would he treat her? He had no wife or children. If he loved her, she would be his entire life. Had she lost her mind? Was she giving up the Tax Administrator in favor of a bookseller? Or was it that the necklace had dissolved all her doubts? Her imagination wandered off to life after marriage. Closing her eyes, she imagined the Tax Administrator rubbing his mouth all over her body. She frowned a little and felt irritated. Standing up, she went out to the water fountain in the garden and looked at her reflection, shimmering, then stable, in the water.

"The one who fights for Maisoon's sake is the one who'll win her," she said.

Not a week passed before the poems were on every woman's tongue, the Tax Administrator's verses about Maisoon.

> O Maisoon, never have I seen such beauty in a human,
> If only you would moisten a heart only watered by counsels!
> She has a body that flees before sparks can ignite,
> And a breast that burns the lover without embers and intoxicates without wine.
> By God, never have I seen such beauty in a human

Anas recited the poem in a muted tone, his eyes on the judge's face.

"Forgive me, Sir," he said modestly, "I've wanted to place before you a reality so that you won't have to confront it during some surprise confrontation or when you're faced with a group of the damned. You are both shaikh and judge, and I hold you in the very highest respect. It is totally out of the question for the Tax Administrator to publicize the judge's daughter and write ghazal poetry like these verses about her, even if he plans to be married to her. These aren't the actions of a man who controls Egypt's finances."

The judge remained silent, his eyes afire with anger.

"I've brought you the book you asked for," Anas the bookseller went on. "And I have a request to make."

The judge looked at him, his expression one of total sorrow and humiliation.

"Judge Yahya is not like other judges," the young man continued. "He learned at the hand of a pupil of Sayyida Nafeesa. His house is one of purity and righteousness."

"Leave, my son," the judge mumbled. "Thank you for the book."

Anas did not leave, and for just a moment there was silence.

"Forgive me, Shaikh," the young man said, "I'm talking to you as if you were my father. Ever since you came to my shop in the Booksellers' Market, I've looked on you as my father. Will you give me the opportunity to speak?"

"Go ahead, Anas," the judge replied, looking at nothing in particular.

"You don't approve of this marriage," Anas said gently. "I realize that. People who aren't unnerved by fear won't be unnerved by greed either."

"I don't agree, my son."

"What about your daughter?" the young man asked.

The judge did not respond. Anas was well aware of what was going through his mind.

"Infatuation," he said calmly, "is something that can affect both men and women. It has the power to kill, Shaikh, at the speed of lightning. What do you expect from a girl when she's faced with the Tax Administrator, someone every girl in Egypt dreams about?"

"But not the judge's daughter."

"Even her," Anas asserted.

Suddenly the judge looked at him, as though he had not noticed him there before.

"You've brought me the book," he said. "Thank you. You can go now."

Anas had no intention of leaving.

"My lord judge is preoccupied," he said. "I have a solution for all his concerns."

The judge gave him a suspicious look.

"Ibn al-Mudabbir has lots of enemies," Anas went on. "How many houses has he destroyed, how many people has he imprisoned for failure to pay, how many men have lost their property and business because of him? He has lots of enemies. You can hear stories from Christians and Muslims alike. The judge must surely be aware of all that."

"Yes, I am," the judge replied.

Anas changed his position and looked around him. "Is it safe here?" he asked. "Can I speak freely?"

"Yes, you can. Go ahead."

"I'm an orphan, Sir," Anas continued. "As you know, I work in the Booksellers' Market. Were it not for the shop owner who taught me how to copy and do calligraphy, I would have ended up as a vagrant. But I listen, learn, and read; I spend my entire life reading. Ever since the year when Ibn al-Mudabbir jailed the priests, and the Coptic Pope fled for fear of an uncertain fate, Ibn al-Mudabbir has been bent on seizing the church's property. Why do monks need gold and silver, he asks. As you know, the Pope has not conducted mass for a year because he fled to escape Ibn al-Mudabbir's brutality. I wonder, when will a shaikh be forced to flee the Friday prayers because he's scared of Ibn al-Mudabbir? This isn't just the first phase of this trial, nor is it the mere beginning of greed."

"I know."

"You realize that Ibn al-Mudabbir raises taxes so he can guarantee his status in Egypt. Every time he does that, he can build palaces for himself here and for his family in Baghdad. Every time taxes are raised, his roots here are fixed and his branches reach the heavens. For some time now, no one has bothered about the Egyptian people."

The judge stared at him. "What do you mean?" he asked.

"Last year, the people in Alexandria rebelled against the Tax Administrator. They came out with weapons and attacked his servants and soldiers. That never happens in Egypt; Egyptians don't fight, they're farmers. What tips the balance and makes women come out with men to fight and grab tax money? Needless to say, Ibn al-Mudabbir snuffed out their rebellion and made them pay for it. But tyranny has a foul stench that wafts through the air, even if you plant a jasmine garden all around it. Don't marry your daughter to the Tax Administrator. The day you do that, one of Ibn al-Mudabbir's enemies will kidnap her, and she'll disappear from the earth's surface. Even Ibn al-Mudabbir's servants will never find her."

The judge gave him a confused stare, without saying a single word.

"The judge needs to contact the Police Chief," Anas went on, "and meekly complain that, now that the Tax Administrator has written poems about his daughter, she's become a target for his enemies. Who'll kidnap her, one wonders? Someone from the South? Or from Alexandria or Fustat?"

"What are you saying?"

"Your daughter needs to disappear."

"The Tax Administrator will find her. Nothing stands in Ibn al-Mudabbir's way."

"I'm standing in his way."

"Are you out of your mind, boy?"

"Solomon enlisted the jinn for years. They're much more powerful than Ibn al-Mudabbir. Then the Beast of the Earth came [Quran, Sura 34 (Sheba), v. 14] to purge their ignorance and expunge their pointless actions. Consider me the Beast of the Earth."

"This is an age of insanity."

"Insanity thrives whenever greed is widespread. We all realize that."

"Why do you want to help me?"

For a moment silence prevailed.

"My lord," Anas continued, "I've watched you stand up to evil with all the resolve of believing soldiers confronted by infidel swords. I've wanted to learn from you. You were going to face the Tax Administrator and place yourself in peril. I can't accept that."

"Will you help me in God's cause?"

"I'll help you because you've always stood up to wrongdoing."

The judge moved closer to Anas.

"And perhaps you'd like my daughter for yourself," he said slowly.

Anas smiled.

"My lord Judge," he replied, "I've never set eyes on your daughter. But the Tax Administrator has described her breasts and hips for anyone who speaks Arabic. She must be beautiful."

The judge stood up and was about to slap him.

"I did not mean to say anything bad about her," Anas said.

"I'm going to flay you now for what you just said."

"I remind you, my lord, those words are not mine. They're from the Tax Administrator's poems. The person who deserves to be flayed is the Tax Administrator. I've a sister in Giza who lives there with her husband. I can hide your daughter safely with her and ask her husband to leave the house. I've no need of women, Shaikh. I just want to help you."

"What kind of madness is this? You expect me to hand over my daughter, when I don't know anything about your sister."

"You can hand her to me, to the Blue Genie, or to the Tax Administrator."

"I'll give her to the Blue Genie," he replied without thinking.

"She'll stay in my sister's house."

"Till when?"

"Maybe till the Tax Administrator forgets about her."

"And if he doesn't?"

"It's your decision, Shaikh."

Once again, there was silence. Then the judge looked at the young man as though noticing his presence for the first time. Anas had had a firm place in the judge's heart ever since they had first met. Anas devoured books the way lions devour lambs. Readers of books are to be trusted; no evil lurks on the pages of books, and no envy resides with the possessor of learning. Whenever the judge asked for a book, he discovered that Anas knew of it and had memorized its contents. Maybe he wanted Anas to be one of his own children. How he longed for someone who really valued book-paper and excellent copying. He trusted Anas as much as someone who has fallen into a burning well trusts a hand extended to him.

"Maybe you're deceiving me," the judge said. "Perhaps you're one of Ibn al-Mudabbir's men."

"Perhaps," Anas replied, "but you're a judge with eagle eyes. You can see and understand things that we can't. Have you ever detected any evil in me?"

"What do you want in recompense?"

Anas smiled.

"Marry me to her," he said.

The judge looked at him and his shabby clothes.

"The judge's daughter married to you?" he asked. "Is that what you want?"

"Do you want to marry her to me or the Tax Administrator?"

"To someone who deserves her."

"The one who really deserves her will not balk from asking for her, or from confronting the Tax Administrator."

"Let me think about it," the judge declared firmly.

"Ibn al-Mudabbir is not going to exert his power over your daughter, even though he could. Instead, he has been knocking on a much riskier door, the lovers' door. When powerful people come knocking on the doors of the weak, defeat is inevitable. Listen to me, my lord. Your daughter is young, while Ibn al-Mudabbir has the kind of experience and power that no one in Egypt even realizes. Who's ruling Egypt today? The caliph appointed a new Turkish governor, but he has refused to leave the court in Iraq and has sent a deputy here instead. Fustat today is being governed by a deputy governor who has no control over Alexandria or finances. All he has is the authority to declare war. Do you even know the new deputy governor's name, my lord? Are you even interested? People say that he's from Bukhara, was born in Iraq, and his name is Ahmad ibn Tulun. He's arrived in shabby clothes and a fighter's garb. He has neither men nor money. I've heard that Ibn al-Mudabbir makes fun of him at every meeting, imitating his gait and dress. He doesn't wear sackcloth because he's an ascetic, but because he doesn't own anything else. By contrast, Ibn al-Mudabbir's clothing is made of jewel-embossed silk. His cloak is the envy of every woman on earth, and he sports a trimmed, black beard. His sweet talk enhances the effect of his gold. Who's going to protect your daughter? The deputy governor whom men scoff at whenever he leaves the house? The caliph? The only way to save her is to marry her to me. If you do that today, it'll be hard for Ibn al-Mudabbir to get her divorced. Even the Tax Administrator will hesitate to get her forcibly divorced. Thus marriage is both shelter and protection."

The judge listened to him, broken-hearted and increasingly fearful.

"Are you looking to take revenge on Ibn al-Mudabbir?" the judge asked.

"All Egypt wants to do that."

"I'm scared of throwing my daughter into a fire she's never encountered before," the judge said. "Ibn al-Mudabbir might well take revenge on her as well. If he killed her . . ."

"She'll be under my protection," Anas insisted.

"And who are you? A bookseller, that's all."

"If I fail to protect her, you may slay me with your own hands."

That night, the judge got no sleep. Anas's words never left him, and the boy's ideas overwhelmed his mind. He imagined his daughter far away, with Ibn al-Mudabbir unable to reach her. Anas in front of him was not leaving the Booksellers' Market. He would check on his daughter every single day and, if Anas had betrayed or tricked him, he would be able to ask Ibn al-Mudabbir for help and rescue his daughter. He would rather throw his daughter into tongues of flame or waves of the sea than throw her into Ibn al-Mudabbir's arms. He had only known Anas for a short time, but he was a reader; and readers never betray. The bookseller's shop now relied on Anas's copying knowledge. The shop owner praised Anas and told the judge that he had never employed anyone who knew the ancients as well as Anas did. He had read Greek and Byzantine sources. The judge had discovered the way out; he was always an advocate of truth and justice. However, the project would be difficult if his daughter did not go along with the idea. The judge kept things to himself and listened as his wife talked about Ibn al-Mudabbir's gifts, his gold, and his desire to see their daughter. His wife did not object to the marriage, but she did not express her agreement openly, in order to avoid making him angry. At sunrise, the judge went to his daughter's room. No sooner did he enter than she leaped to her feet, her gaze fixed on the floor.

"Sit down, Maisoon," he told her gently and with a slight frown.

She sat down slowly, still remembering the way he had slapped her. It had been the first time he had hit her since puberty. It had not been the slap that had humiliated her so much as his expression and the words he had used.

"You've always been the most precious of my daughters," he told her after a while, "the one closest to me. I've taught you everything I've learned, even though I've always been worried about the way your beauty might conspire against your own critical self."

She remained silent.

"What do you think of Ibn al-Mudabbir?" he continued.

She did not answer, and that annoyed him.

"He keeps reciting love poetry about you all over the place. Does that make you happy? Does the Tax Administrator's passion for you please you? Do you realize how evil he is? Did you notice that when you met him?"

"No, I didn't, Father," she replied quietly after a pause.

He nodded, as though he was expecting that reply.

"Being married to him is totally impossible," the judge went on. "I'll die before marrying my daughter to a tyrant, even if he controlled the entire earth and everything on it, and even if you wanted to be married to him. Were you to be married to him, it would be the end for me. Is that what you want?"

"I'd sacrifice my very soul for you, Father," she responded in a pained tone.

He gave a sarcastic smile.

"I'm not so sure of that," he said, "but I'm totally sure that I'm going to fight to the death. I'll never marry you to Ibn al-Mudabbir. But I have a plan. I want you to listen and carry it through. If you don't, I'm going to resist Ibn al-Mudabbir to the death."

"I'd sacrifice my very soul for you, Father," she repeated.

"Don't lie to me. I know you, and I'm well aware that power and wealth can tempt you. The way he fawns over you satisfies your vanity. You've constructed an eternal wall between us, Maisoon. I'll forgive you if you do everything I ask of you. We're going to claim that you've been kidnapped."

She frowned.

"Do you long to be married to him?" he asked her. "Do you want me to die?"

"I'm scared for you, Father," she replied deliberately. "I don't believe that the Tax Administrator will believe such a story."

"You know him better than I do, of course. He'll believe it because you're going to vanish from the whole area of Fustat. All he'll be able to do is to search for you for years till he forgets about you. Every single man in Egypt is better than Ibn al-Mudabbir. Don't you dare argue with me. You're going to carry out the instructions without a word. Otherwise, I'm going to kill you with my own hands before you can get married. Do you hear me?"

"Yes, Father, I hear you."

"I'm going to marry you to the bookseller," he said.

Lowering her eyelids, she managed to suppress her pulsating heart and conceal her happiness at her father's decision.

The judge gave his daughter in marriage between evening and the following day. It was done in secret, and he brought in close friends as witnesses. Once the ceremony was over, the bride's father looked at her.

"He is now your husband; you have no other husband but him. I want you to be kind in your dealings with him. Anas will carry out the plan we've agreed to. Don't utter a single word to anyone. I'll leave you with your husband for a while. He's made that request of me."

Her father left. Anas took her hand and kissed it slowly. He sat down beside her.

"I promised that you'd be mine," he said.

"You're crazy," she replied. "You're standing up to the Tax Administrator? You're going to kidnap and hide me? Even if my father can't stand up to him, nor even the governor himself? Aren't you scared, bookseller?"

"We're all scared, my lady. Plato says that courage involves knowing what should not make you scared and what should. Ibn al-Mudabbir doesn't scare me. The only thing that does is your fickle heart after I've fought on your behalf. What is it that scares you?"

"My father's temper," she replied without even thinking.

"What if I promised you that, after today, he'll never be angry with you again?" he told her with a laugh.

"So what special powers do you have, Anas? All of Egypt fears the Tax Administrator. Even the governor."

"Anas is not scared of him."

"Do you have some extraordinary power, or are you some kind of genie, monk, or prophet?"

"What's so scary about the Tax Administrator?" he asked with a smile. "Life's a destiny deferred, and we're all doomed to suffer. What can he do?"

"Maybe he won't kill or torture you. Who knows, perhaps he'll kill someone you love."

For a while, no one spoke. He put his finger on her lips.

"There's no way he can get to you," he said.

"Am I everything you love, bookseller?" she asked flirtatiously. "Do you want me for my beauty or because of my father's position?"

He took out the necklace and put it in her hands.

"Here's your dowry, Maisoon," he said.

She was totally dazzled as she ran her hand over it.

"Before you're my wife," he went on, "you need to know who I am."

Her eyes widened as he told her.

He took her arm and laid her head against his chest. She remained silent, doing her best to take in the madness all around her and the fact that her husband was the son of the head fisherman and a killer as well.

"Your father's going to come in at any moment," he told her as he kissed her hair. "You can tell him the truth about me, and he can give you a divorce from me."

She tried to pull away, but he clasped her shoulder and kissed her cheek.

"Stay here," he said, "beside the person you've just heard about. Are you feeling guilty?"

She raised her head and looked at his face.

"What is it I've just noticed?" she asked.

"Don't ask me that," he replied, breathing hard as he moved closer to kiss her mouth. "My breaths are all astray in longing for you. Give me just one kiss, then I'll leave for today. Tell me you love me and long for me."

She opened her mouth to speak, and he gave her a passionate kiss. She tried to push him away, but then she surrendered to his lips, and all resistance crumbled. His caresses made Ibn al-Mudabbir's face disappear. She had no idea that love could feel like this, and his lips could erase both past and present. She pulled away gently.

"Have you forgiven me?" he asked, kissing her ear. "I don't want there to be any lies between us."

"Stop, Anas," she sighed. "I forgive you, but you have to stop."

"I know," he replied firmly, staring at her lips. "How can you be so alluring and beautiful? What are you doing to me, judge's daughter?"

She pushed him playfully in the chest.

"I'm not doing anything," she replied. "You're the one with the plans."

He heard her father opening the door, and she moved quietly away. He stood up and, still looking at her, bid her father farewell. With that, he left.

Chapter 3

The judge sat in front of Ibn al-Mudabbir. Their eyes met. Ibn al-Mudabbir exhibited all the enthusiasm of victory, while the judge seemed to be waiting like a panther before pouncing. Maisoon's mother's screams echoed inside the house; her daughter bride had been kidnapped. She rushed to her husband, who scowled as he made for his daughters' room with Ibn al-Mudabbir and his men behind him. The judge asked his wife what she had seen, and she replied that she had not seen anything. She had heard her daughter calling for help, but when she went to her room, she could not find her. The judge looked at Ibn al-Mudabbir, his expression a mixture of blame and resentment.

"My lord," he said, "you're responsible for my daughter's life. Whoever's kidnapped her was bent on revenge."

Ibn al-Mudabbir's piercing eyes were riveted on the judge.

"Whoever's kidnapped her is going to die for sure," he made abundantly clear, "but not before he confesses who his helpers were. No one's ever dared defy the Tax Administrator, and it's not going to happen now."

Ibn al-Mudabbir departed furious, his entire being devoured by sheer evil. He did not trust the judge; he found him intolerable. He was not so naive as to believe his story. The judge had hidden his daughter in order to crush and humiliate him. Now he was not just at war with fishermen and peasants; now it involved Judge Yahya. His plan was to find Maisoon, marry her, and then kill her father—but not before parading him around Fustat, naked on a donkey, with children pelting him with stones and proclaiming him a measly liar. As Ibn al-Mudabbir plotted, his love and passion for Maisoon never ceased.

For the first time in a month, the judge had a peaceful sleep. He had put his daughter into an excruciating situation so that she could be picked up by travelers. He did not know the bookseller at all well and did not trust anyone. But a little pain was certainly preferable to her being married to Ibn al-Mudabbir, at least as far as he was concerned. If the bookseller killed her so he could steal her hair, even that would be better than her being married to Ibn al-Mudabbir. He had shown Anas all the house's secrets and exits. His wife had started keening and bemoaning her lot. She swore that she would go to the witch in the Great Pyramid to ask her where her daughter was and who had kidnapped her. He had not responded or bothered to calm her down. He had slept peacefully.

The first night that Maisoon spent in the mud-built house on the riverbank in Giza, she commenced waiting for Anas to arrive. He had promised to return in two weeks. The servant-girl of Ali, Anas's brother, had welcomed her and given her some food. Maisoon had not slept. Her entire life had changed, thanks to the book-seller with his ruggedly determined eyes. In two weeks, she would be his; he would hug her again and maybe kiss her. If his touch could shatter the feeling of loneliness and estrangement, then she would be content. She may have sacrificed all the Tax Administrator's power, but her beloved's courage was worth the power of a thou-sand administrators and his determination brought with it all the treasures of the ancients. She was not aware that she had ever followed her heart before, but her father was happy and so was she. What would Anas do, she wondered, when he returned? Would he take her in his arms again? Let her melt into his chest? Would he keep kissing her till she forgot who and where she was? Would his kisses be enough to compensate for tolerating life here? For how long?

At dawn she went out and washed her face in the Nile water. She looked at her reflection in the water. It moved, then was washed away by a wave, but came back even clearer and more profound. She focused on the way her pupils were reflected in the water. They looked shiny, as though they had been cleansed of every sin. Perhaps she smiled or repeated some words to herself, but then someone threw a big rock into the water. The face broke up into two parts and the features were scattered all over the place. She gasped in shock at the way the rock had hit the water and smashed the image of her face before her very eyes.

The judge waited for a week before visiting the Booksellers' Market to ask Anas the bookseller how his daughter was faring. He still had his doubts about his decision and his trust in Anas. Every time he hesitated and rued his decision, he thought about Ibn al-Mudabbir and was overwhelmed by fear and despair. He wished that he had buried her alive to protect her from marriage to that man.

While heading for the bookseller's shop, he looked around. Once he was sure that Ibn al-Mudabbir's men were following him as usual, he went slowly into the shop and took a seat as he opened one of the books.

"Abd al-Azeem," he said as he looked for Anas, "has Anas the bookseller come today? I asked him to look for a book two weeks ago."

Abd al-Azeem gave him a sad look.

"I'm so sorry about your daughter's kidnapping," he said.

"The Police Chief has told us," the judge replied, "that he's searching for her now. He'll find her."

Abd al-Azeem, the shop owner, called Anas from the other end of the quarter, and he came running.

"Forgive me, my lord," he said as he sat in front of the judge. "I've been looking for the book I promised you. It's all fine."

Anas reassured him, but he was not reassured.

♛♛

For Maisoon, the first week passed like a dream. The house had just two rooms, a tiny hut almost drowning in the water. She went out to the river, spending hours thinking about her situation and sometimes about the people around her. The servant-girl of Ali, Anas's brother, was Gameela, but, as far as Maisoon was concerned, she was not pretty [Gameela]. She always wore a smile, and had big teeth and thick lips, along with the enthusiasm of lovers and the politeness of gracious hosts. From the very first moment she had treated Maisoon like a queen, preparing her food and calling her "my lady." Every day she would lay out her bedding and wash her clothes. She talked nonstop. After three days, she asked Maisoon for permission to let her master visit her at night. Maisoon agreed. She did not see him arrive at first, but she could hear passionate sounds coming from Gameela's room. Ali visited Gameela regularly at night in the tiny house.

♛♛

One night, she gazed at the stars, watching for one to fall, as they had on the day when Ibn al-Mudabbir set eyes on her. Anas would be coming, whether today or tomorrow. How could he possibly stay away from her for two weeks? Her mind understood why, but her heart longed for her beloved.

He sneaked up behind her and hugged her from behind.

"I've missed you," he told her. "Things weren't in my hands, I swear to you. I wanted to stick to my plan. The Tax Administrator's spies are following every Egyptian now."

She did not reply, but moved away flirtatiously.

"We were married in a way you don't deserve, judge's daughter," he told her, "but I want our life together to make you happy. I don't have any money, but I promise you . . ."

She had planned to frown, but could not stop her lips from bursting into a smile.

"Don't make promises you can't keep," she said.

He carried her inside the house. No sooner were they in their room than he kissed her with all the passion of many long years. She pushed against his chest, but his lips were glued to hers. She tried to speak, but could not say a word. She saw twilight's hues; grains of sand scattered, and her mind was totally confused. Her hand was still trying to push him away, but now she was accepting his kisses and allowing him to enter her. The kisses seemed never to end and penetrated to the very depths. Now that time had come to a stop, its premonitions came back. What was coming would be even worse. Suddenly she moved away.

"Ibn al-Mudabbir," she said, "stands between us. I want you to promise me first that you'll forget about taking revenge on him."

Their eyes met.

"You're right to be scared of him," Anas replied resignedly. "But you need to realize that this kiss was created by falling stars, blended with the scent of light."

"Light doesn't have any scent."

"Yes, it does. You need to smell it, if only just once."

He drowned her with his kisses as she grumbled and asked him to slow down and talk. She was shocked by the audible pounding of her heart and the way her mind was getting baffled. She put her arms around his neck.

"Listen to me first," she said, panting.

"I agree to everything you ask," he replied, kissing her neck.

"Forget about Ibn al-Mudabbir," she told him sharply, fearing for herself in his arms. "Forget about revenge. Start with me again."

He stopped suddenly and looked straight at her without saying a word.

"Promise me you'll forget about revenge," she insisted, worried about his reaction.

He sat up.

"But he's not going to forget about us," he replied.

"We can live here in peace," she said gently.

"As fugitives."

He moved closer and gave her mouth some short kisses.

"I'll forget the man," he said. "I want you. Do you even realize how much I want you?"

She moved her face away.

"Promise me first," she said.

Closing his yes, he took her hand and kissed it.

"I promise," he said.

She sighed in relief and rubbed her cheek against his.

"You've just promised me," she said, desire now firmly fixed inside her.

"I have," he replied, losing all sense of reason in her arms.

"I want gold as well," she went on. "You haven't brought me any gold or given me any money. That necklace is not enough for Maisoon's dowry."

"That's easy, if you only realized. It's your first demand that's more challenging."

After quite a while, she buried her head bashfully in the pillow, while he put his arms around her waist. She grabbed his head and cradled it, feeling that that was its proper place. The previous days without him had been dreary, lacking water and the scent of light. He swore that he would sacrifice everything for her sake. His love for her was overflowing and impetuous, as though his life was either ending or beginning. With her he searched for the scent of light, the taste of color, and the glow of flowers. He treated her body gently and with a good deal of determination, inscribing the rest of his life on its surface.

The next morning, she grabbed his hand to move it away.

"Where are you going?" he asked her, as he sat up and hugged her.

"What happened yesterday . . . ," she started somewhat shyly.

"The best day in my life," he said, still hugging her. "It was like I'd been waiting for it all my life."

She was still searching for the right words.

"What happened," she repeated, "what you promised me . . ."

"I love you," he told her firmly.

She shuddered suddenly.

"What awaits us, Anas?" she asked, moving closer.

He brushed her hair off her face.

"We'll take things one day at a time," he said. "Today, tomorrow, and every day to come, I want you in my arms."

She ran her hand over her sleeping-place.

"Maisoon deserves to sleep on silk," she told him passionately. "You promised me that as well."

"Maisoon deserves to sleep between silk and brocade," he replied, drowning her in his love.

She blushed shyly at Gameela's glances and did her best not to talk to her. Her husband had not been lying. He did spend most of the day with her, sometimes taking her in his arms, at others walking by the river, and often going for a swim with her at dawn. He took good care of her, as though she were some rare plant or a piece of pure gold. Every day, when she was left on her own, she would put her hand over her heart, happy and very proud. Her sense of closeness to a man of Anas's sort was completely different from what she had been expecting. Sometimes she thought about the future, and at others, she would become worried.

"What are we going to do, Anas," she would ask him, "if Ibn al-Mudabbir finds us? I'm scared."

He used to calm her down and reassure her that only death would be able to part them.

This type of pleasure was new to him; the plunge into the glories of passion could erase all loneliness and bitter feelings. Tomorrow he would think about what he was going to do. Perhaps they could flee to Syria, the Hejaz, or even Baghdad. Maybe he could settle in the North or South. But the entire repertoire of astronomy could not shift the heart's direction or deflect the soul's impetuous instincts.

When she laughed, all lights were fused together. He realized at that moment that paradise would exist on earth, if only Ibn al-Mudabbir disappeared; that would bring assurance and happiness. He had thought that bookselling had no need of women's embrace. At first, he had imagined that he would have sex with her, then go back to his books and manuscripts, but she had not given him the chance. Her very existence was a temptation, and her continuing need for someone to worship her body and face and to openly acknowledge their stunning superiority had made him forget all about his books and even his desire for revenge.

Anas's arms, his love, and his words, they were what she had been living for. He had become the light radiating into every nook and cranny. She forgot all about Ibn al-Mudabbir, her father, and her former home. If there was a man to honor her and kiss her, as though she were an angel that had appeared all of a sudden, she would not need gold or silver, would she? If the river was there right in front of them, somewhere they could drown themselves in passion, she would not need to exert authority, would she? Farewell to all those silly dreams and modest hopes! Maisoon was in love, waiting for his gazing eye, smiling lips, and powerful kiss. She would wait for his words of reassurance amid the earth's alarm and countries' confusion. For a moment, when she would laugh and he would stare at her lips, he looked like he owned the world and was asking her to laugh one more time, or even twice.

By the dawn light, he would take her hand and throw her in the river. She would scream because she could not swim and was scared of river water and wind currents. He promised to rescue her before she drowned. She would cling to his neck and scream again, as she swallowed the sweet water and cursed and swore, only to repeat herself again the next day.

She had never met a man who was so good at talking as Anas was. He told her about the Greeks and ancient Egyptians, and she listened with all the enthusiasm of a child eager to learn. He would listen to her carefully, as though she were the caliph himself. Until Anas, no one had ever listened to her, neither her father nor her mother. Her father was worried about her beauty and the problems that it would bring. Her mother was proud of her beautiful daughter and wanted her to be married to a governor. Her only sister was jealous and avoided her most of the time. Anas was friend and companion. How handsome he was! Every time she spoke to him, he seemed to fully understand and know what she was saying. She complained a lot about the harsh way her father had treated her, how he had locked her in a room on her own till she apologized; but she never did. Sometimes, he would hug her and tell her about his own father and how he had devoted his entire life to Anas's and Ali's education. Even though he was head fisherman and every woman had desired him, he had never married or bothered about slave-girls. She would comment bitterly that she wished she could have had a father as affectionate as Hamza al-Skandari, but even so, she loved her father. When she and Anas spoke to each other, it was in Coptic sometimes and Arabic at others. When she was talking about her family, it would be in Coptic. She complained to Anas that her father banned Coptic inside the house and pretended that he did not know it, even though he was perfectly fluent; it was as though he were ashamed of his own language. Her mother did not know Arabic as well as Coptic, so she only spoke to her daughters in Coptic. That led to frequent arguments with her father. Yes, Judge Yahya was a fair man, but with his daughters he was rigid to the point of being cruel. That was in spite of the fact that he gave them both a fine education and concerned himself with what they wore and what they ate. She told Anas that they had never traveled to Alexandria. He promised to take her out to sea in a boat for a whole night, just like the nights of paradise.

She spent two whole months like this, in his arms and listening to his words, enjoying his company, his caresses, and his existence all around her. Beginning to forget about gold and power, she began to blend with the beauty that meshed with the stars. It was as though she were the only thing he could see in the world. They never spoke about Ibn al-Mudabbir, and Anas seemed to have forgotten about him. Every day, she would feel proud of herself; she had managed to use her beauty to make him forget about tyranny. When Anas had been preoccupied with Ibn al-Mudabbir, Maisoon had been preoccupied with herself; now they were preoccupied with each other. The whole world revolved around the two of them, and stars only fell to illuminate their path.

Chapter 4

The witch dwelled at the base of the Great Pyramid, feared more by men than women. No one had yet solved the mystery of the pyramid; the caliph Ma'moon had managed to enter it just several years ago. When the caliph had visited Egypt to quell the Coptic revolt against the Abbasids, he had decided to open the Great Pyramid. He felt sure that it contained enough treasure to last for the rest of his days. This was a country where earth could be changed into black musk, then gold would shine from the depths of the earth. There were no limits to its bounty, and no avoiding a plunge into its interior. The caliph spent money opening up the pyramid, waiting to go inside with a mixture of awe and anticipation. After some effort, Al-Ma'moon did go inside the pyramid and discovered treasure and statues within. The treasure was worth as much as he had spent digging a hole into the pyramid, no more and no less. He could not understand what the purpose of the statues was. The ancients seemed to have buried their dead and their bounty together, as though the bounty were for death, not life. No one knew the meaning of this. However, the hole remained open, worrying Egyptians about people going inside. They heard about the jinn living there and beautiful naked women emerging at night to attack and devour men.

Nevertheless, Maisoon's mother decided that she was going to visit the witch living with the jinn. She would not fear the darkness of the ancient tombs and the awesome sight of the lofty structures. She had heard from her relatives and neighbors about Bahnas, the witch. Bahnas could read people's hearts, but could not predict the future. She could trace lost people, but would not be able to restore what love and war had corrupted. She never accepted money, and only ate cake made of wheat, sugar, and dates. For her visit, Maisoon's mother made a perfect cake. She kept it hidden from her husband, who regarded astrologers as liars even in their truth-telling. She took her daughter, Ruqayya, with her, saying that she was going to pay a family visit. Then she set out for the pyramid, in search of the witch.

She shuddered as she entered the pyramid through the dark hole and grabbed Ruqayya's hand.

"If it weren't for Maisoon," she said in despair, "I would never have entered this place. But she's my daughter. I've no idea what's happened to her."

"Be strong, Mother," Ruqayya said, shuddering like her mother.

Maisoon's mother heard a noise inside the dark cavity and screamed, then clasped her daughter's hand even harder.

"My lady," she begged in Arabic, "we've come to ask for your help."

The witch's face loomed out of the pitch dark. She was sitting at ease amid colorful statues, drinking some water. Her long hair almost touched the ground. Her features were awesome, and she looked in the prime of life. She possessed all the luster of a jinn and the beauty of houris of paradise. She was dressed in a white gown and had applied a lot of kohl to her eyes. She resembled the statues of the ancients and seemed to have assembled in her ideal body all the sins and splendor of the past.

"I don't understand you, woman," the witch said in Coptic.

Maisoon's mother praised her God because the woman spoke Coptic. Her husband had never learned it and often stopped her talking to her two daughters in it, but she always used it to talk to them both in secret.

"I need your help, my lady," she said in Coptic.

Bahnas the witch smiled in pleasure.

"I know," she replied. "Come and sit here beside me."

Maisoon's mother sat down, shocked. The witch lit a candle, and her huge eyes gleamed in the dark. Maisoon's mother had never been sure whether the witch was human or jinn. She swallowed hard.

"My daughter," she pleaded, "I've lost my daughter. Plotters kidnapped her on her wedding day."

The witch gave a nod.

"Give your greetings to the ancients," she said.

Maisoon's mother stared at her, not understanding.

"Give them your greeting," the witch insisted.

"I don't know what to say. They're not Muslims or Christians."

"Ask them for peace of mind," she told her firmly. "Thank them for preserving the earth and gold."

"I thank you for preserving the earth and gold," she repeated. "My greetings to you."

"Ye ancestors . . ."

"My lady," Maisoon's mother said, "they're idolaters. I'm afraid of offending God with my words."

"Ye ancestors," the witch insisted. "They're your forebears, whether you like it or not."

"Ye ancestors," Maisoon's mother eventually recited in resignation.

"Bahnas knows everything," the witch said confidently.

"So reassure me. Is my daughter safe or in danger?"

"She's both safe and in danger."

The witch ran her hand respectfully over one of the statues.

"Our ancestors are keeping a careful eye on us," she said. "Something's about to happen in the country, and our ancestors are concerned."

"My daughter, my lady? How is she doing?"

"She's awash in the delights of passion and love-death. There's no point in res-cuing her; that never works with lovers."

"Is she in love with the Tax Administrator? If that's the case, maybe we can find her and marry her to him."

"The ancients are expecting a moon or star to shine. The day the stars fell, all wild trees were burned so that the past could emerge from the bowels of the earth."

"What has my daughter to do with the ancients?"

"As I've told you, we're all from them and belong to them. Your daughter is en-veloped by the stench of hatred, the aversion of loathing, the passion of ascetics, and the despair of the possessed. You will come to see me again, perhaps with her, who knows? And he will come too."

"Who is he?"

"The gleaming star."

"Reassure me about my daughter."

"She's not doing well. I've told you."

"Is there no hope of finding her? Will her kidnapper kill her?"

The witch was silent for a while.

"There's no hope of finding people you know," she said. "Her kidnapper will kill her, but there are different ways of doing that. The easiest is death, which is linked to life. The nastiest is despair, for which there's no cure. Leave now, after greeting the ancestors. Remember. Something's about to happen in Egypt. The star's draw-ing close."

The witch's words left her feeling even more confused and desperate.

👪

Tossing in her sleep, Maisoon moved closer to Anas, laid her hand on his shoulder, and fell into a deep sleep. A few hours later and before dawn, he woke up with a start and a sense of what was going to happen. He woke her up.

"What's the matter?" she asked, half-asleep.

He got out of bed without responding, put his clothes on, and rushed out of the room. Grabbing the sword that he had kept ever since his father gave it to him as a boy, he opened the door. Seeing men surrounding the house with swords drawn, he froze in place. One of them approached him.

"You're Anas, aren't you?" the man asked him sternly.

He put his hands on the door. She was standing behind it, her hand over her heart.

"We want you alive," the man said. "That's what Ibn al-Mudabbir has ordered. If you don't resist and come with us now, you'll save yourself."

Maisoon grabbed his hand from behind the door.

"Don't go with them," she insisted. "They'll kill you."

He looked around at the men surrounding the place.

"Do you just want me?" he asked the man.

"Just you," the man replied.

"And what about the other people in the house?"

"We're going to kill the judge's daughter."

"Kill me first," he replied defiantly, raising his sword.

"Maybe if you come with us," the man responded in the same calm voice, "we'll let her live."

"But maybe not?" Anas said.

She grabbed his shoulder and closed her eyes.

"Are you going to fight fifty men on your own?" the man asked. "The judge's daughter defied the Tax Administrator. The punishment is death."

Another man interrupted.

"Listen to us," he said. "If you come with us, the judge's daughter can stay here safe and sound for a week."

"You can't trust the word of Ibn al-Mudabbir's men."

While Anas kept trying to resist, a sword reached his neck and another his wife's. The men tied him up and carried him out of the house.

"I'll never desert you," he muttered to himself, staring at the distant horizon, "even if the mountains crumble and the waters of the sea cover the dry land."

Part Two

Never shall you blame me for my departure,
The day I left without meeting you.
I feared stopping places;
With separation spills the absence of your eye.
I realized that our weeping
Equaled my passion and yours.
I recalled what the leaver discovers
In your hug and embrace.
So I left it all on purpose,
As I departed, avoiding bidding you farewell.
—*Al-Buhturi, Abbasid poet*

Chapter 5

Looking around, Anas saw a large house in a wide area surrounded by men. As time passed, his courage increased like the pounding rain during thunderstorms. He was convinced that death was inevitable and victory had been short-term. But no death could erase victory, and no life could erase defeat. He had defeated Ibn al-Mudabbir, even though it was only a minor victory. An oily patch can foul water, even an entire river. How, one wonders, would he inform Ibn al-Mudabbir that his beloved Maisoon was still his beloved. Now time had changed things, and he was no longer the sole master of his fate. Now someone else had that control and could use it. Anas had not composed any poems. Instead, he had condemned them and torn them to pieces, so that they were now pieces of paper in his innards. He was the victor for sure; she was his today and tomorrow. He was on his own and without support, just as he had been before, when he was with his father's fishermen in Alexandria. No one had helped him or treated him nicely. He had left, fearful and cautious; everyone would now be scoffing at him and rejoicing at his defeat. Could he forget Maisoon in such a flood of fear and aspiration? She had yielded and settled into his arms, but there was no way of downplaying Ibn al-Mudabbir's methods of torturing the rebellious and breaking the spirit of the powerful.

After some time, a man came in. Anas noticed that the hem of his cloak was worn through a good deal of use. He was surrounded by soldiers and guards, but he was not Ibn al-Mudabbir. Anas looked carefully at the man's face and general appearance. He looked like a fighter, so he had to be the Police Chief. He did not look that much older than himself, five years perhaps, no more.

The man sat down in front of Anas.

"Head fisherman's son," the man began confidently, "scholar-reader, someone who kills on purpose and kidnaps the judge's daughter."

Anas did not respond.

"I wonder," the man went on, "what did you want to achieve with those actions?"

"Are you the Police Chief?" Anas asked.

"I'm not Ibn al-Mudabbir, that's for sure," the man replied. "You above all know what he looks like; you have his features memorized by heart. They haunt your dreams every night to remind you of what was. I know. This is a strange country. The deputy governor has arrived. Have you heard his name? Maybe not. What's the point of having a deputy governor who has authority in Fustat and Giza, but not in Alexandria? What's the point of a deputy governor when all the funds are in the Tax Administrator's hands?"

"Ahmad ibn Tulun?" Anas asked slowly.

Ahmad took a seat.

"I thought that Egyptian men didn't know my name," he said. "Ibn al-Mudabbir's is the only one they bother about."

"I heard that the governor had refused to leave Iraq," Anas replied, "and sent a deputy in his place, a young man from the army. I must know who he is. This country hasn't been governed by a young man for some time."

"I've been looking for you," Ahmad said, "and you've been looking for me."

"So let's complete the equation," Anas replied.

Ahmad smiled.

"Was it the root or number you were lacking?" he asked.

"Have you read Al-Khwarizmi, my lord?" Anas asked.

"I've tried, but your knowledge is better than mine. Why don't you ask me how I found you?"

"Instead, I'll ask you what you plan to do with me."

"I'll answer both questions, even though you've only asked about one of them. I was looking for you, then heard about your conversations with the judge and Shaikh Bakkar ibn Qutaiba. That's how I found out who you were."

Anas looked at him without saying anything.

"I'm going to hand you over to Ibn al-Mudabbir, of course," he went on. "Perhaps he will come to trust me and realize that I'm better able than him to learn the intentions of men, Anas, son of the head fisherman."

"Why haven't you already done that, my lord, Ahmad ibn Tulun?"

Ahmad smiled. "You can aspire to get rid of Ibn al-Mudabbir as a way of taking revenge for your father, or else you can aspire to get rid of tyranny to take revenge for Egypt. The choice is yours."

Anas did not understand and was speechless. "Getting rid of tyranny," he replied, "that's loftier than humanity, something that's baffled prophets, my lord. You're asking me to do something beyond my means. The haven of justice is not one of perdition."

"If every governor thought like you, he would never try to exercise justice. All of us strive in accordance with what we know. What you have done so far is admirable. You alone have challenged the Tax Administrator and persuaded the judge to marry you to his daughter. You've used love to convince her and keep her prisoner. All that you've done while a fugitive from crime and sin. You're crazy, young man!"

Anas looked at him, but said nothing.

"But it's the kind of madness I like," Ahmad continued. "There are a lot of things I want to talk to you about. You'll stay with me for a day or more."

"You won't be handing me over to Ibn al-Mudabbir?"

"Maybe later. I don't know."

Ahmad dismissed the men, then offered Anas some water. "I came to Egypt," he said, "knowing full well that the governor would only stay here for a month or so.

I understood Egypt was Ibn al-Mudabbir's territory, and that the Egyptians were suffering under his brutal tyranny. But the governor has no purpose where Ibn al-Mudabbir is concerned. Do you know why? Because the governor must hold out his hand each month to receive his share of funding from Ibn al-Mudabbir. I'm not even governor, just deputy governor. I have no authority to make any decision. Ever since I've arrived, it's been clear to me that my enemy is firmly established, while I'm floating through the air like leaves on trees. He's offered me money to break my will, but I've refused. I haven't come here for money."

"Speaking that way, my lord, you're putting a good deal of trust in a killer you don't even know."

Ahmad smiled.

"Your lord is talking to someone who's already one of the dead. Nothing beats pouring out your heart to a dead man. When you know that all your secrets are buried underground, you can empty your heart of its troubles."

"So has my lord Ahmad ibn Tulun decided to kill me?"

Their eyes met, and Ahmad did not respond.

"I've heard, Anas," he went on, changing the subject, "that fishermen in Alexandria used to make fun of you because you were different. You used to read and busy yourself with pens and books. You weren't interested in fun, fishing, and slave-girls."

"That's true."

"How hard it is to be alone among other people! How miserable it is to lose in your own country and amid your loved ones! Do you realize, fisherman's son, that the caliph's own men in Egypt make fun of me, my modest appearance, and my lack of taste when it comes to dress? Needless to say, I wasn't born to enjoy a life of luxury; I was born to fight. Fighters aren't like people who wallow in pleasure."

Anas smiled in despair.

"My lord," he said, "allow me to speak frankly before you kill me. Pack up your things and leave here. This is a country that's inured to tyranny and tyrants. You can't change anything or introduce justice here."

"Your love of this country seems to drive you to anger, and your anger at your loved ones leads you to despair. People who are angry are showing love; people who are sad are also passionate. What you're saying is encouraging, not discouraging. Call me Ahmad or Abu al-Abbas. I'm not leaving, and tyranny will not find a haven in this country. Tyranny is like a plant with large, flowering branches that can deceive the eye, but has no roots. If you only knew, it's easy. Before I arrived, two things happened."

"What happened?"

"I had a dream. I'll tell you about it in a while."

"What's the other thing?"

"I read about the ancient Egyptians. You're Egyptian, and you can speak Coptic and Greek and read them both. I realize that."

"My lord, I'm just a poor servant. I'm Anas, son of a fisherman."

"You're the head fisherman's son. You realize that the sword is important; that much is certain. But you also realize that the pen is even more dangerous and profound."

"Pardon?"

"You'll learn how to hold a sword."

"Egyptians aren't fighters," Anas said.

"Since when?"

"A thousand years or more. The last time Egypt had an army made up of Egyptians was in the time of Pharaoh and Moses. It was destroyed at sea. Ever since then, Egypt has been without an army. It was ruled by Greeks first, then Romans, and then the Arabs arrived."

"The army was made up of Arabs," Ahmad continued, "and its task was to defend the caliphate. Then the caliph decided that the army would be made up of non-Arabs."

Anas gave the deputy governor a dubious look.

"My father's from Bukhara," Ahmad went on, "and I was born in Samarra. But today, I'm an Egyptian."

"How do you choose who you are?"

"The same way you choose who'll be your wife, whom you're going to kidnap, whom you're going to cajole, and how you're going to win."

"People say that Egyptians are only good at farming," Anas asserted. "They can't go to war and don't like it either. The army protects the caliph, residing in Baghdad, the seat of the caliphate. What is it you want, my lord? What have you read about the ancients that has so impaired your vision? Forgive me for speaking so frankly to you."

"I have a dream."

"Right," Anas replied. "You said you'd had a dream."

"I dream, or I hope . . ."

"Hopes never work to their owners' benefit . . ."

"I dream of an army for Egypt, as was the case before the Pharaoh and Moses."

Anas gave a contented smile.

"Are you thinking of yourself, my lord, as one of the ancient Egyptian monarchs? Even the Arabs have never done that, nor the Byzantines before them. That's an era that's over and done with. We don't remember the ancients and don't even understand their language."

"If you knew about my dream, you'd change your mind."

"Forgive me, my lord, but . . ."

"I'm a bit crazy, and so are you. The Greek philosopher Aristotle declared that greatness involves a little madness. No great man is ever rational. They're all crazy. You're talking to me today as a friend, but tomorrow I'll be governor and amir. Listen to me."

"My lord Ahmad knows Aristotle?" Anas asked bashfully.

"I actually prefer Plato. He's one of the greatest philosophers. Do you imagine, Anas, that you're the only one to delve into the secrets of the Greeks?"

"Forgive me, my lord. We've never expected the governor to know about the Greeks and study their writings."

"Ahmad is not just any governor."

"Ahmad isn't modest either," Anas muttered to himself.

Even so, Ahmad understood his intent and smiled.

"The way you win," he said, "is proportional to your belief in your own strength."

"Ibn al-Mudabbir is not going to form an army in Egypt, nor will the caliph. That's impossible. As I've told you, it hasn't happened for over a thousand years."

"I know Ibn al-Mudabbir won't give me the money needed and the caliph won't permit it. I'm deputy governor here, with no authority, no friends, and no ancestry. Ibn al-Mudabbir wants to get rid of me today, not tomorrow. He and the Police Chief have already tried, and he'll try again. He'll be sending letters to the caliph, employing spies, and making my life here hell until I leave."

"My lord," Anas said hesitantly, "will you let me say a word?"

Ahmad nodded.

"When you're working for Egypt," Anas declared forcefully, "you're building and creating an army. You're not working for the caliph. As the Abbasids put it, Egypt is the Sultan's treasury. Ibn al-Mudabbir will claim that you're challenging the caliphate."

"On the contrary, I'm working for the caliph."

Anas did not pursue the topic.

"How can I help you?" he asked.

"How did you know that I need your help?"

"You're not intending to hand me over to Ibn al-Mudabbir."

"I want a soldier in my army . . ."

"You don't have an army, my lord."

"I'm going to have one. Patience is the true model for achievement; strife doesn't involve only swords. You'll work with me and be trained how to fight. But more important, you'll train in the arts of government. You're keen to take revenge on Ibn al-Mudabbir and restore your father's rights, but you'll need to be cautious."

"Why have you chosen a man like me who's running from certain death?"

"Anas, you're not like other men. You read and understand; you're good at languages and intrigue as well. Beyond all that, your hatred of Ibn al-Mudabbir makes you an ideal friend. No one realizes that the bookseller is the head fisherman's son. I admire you, Anas. I can see a fighter in you. Despair means courage. The person wronged possesses power greater than the armies of Caesar and Chosroes combined."

Anas gave him a bashful look.

"My lord," he said, scarcely able to believe what he was hearing, "I'm just an auxiliary, an Egyptian. Are you planning to induct Egyptians into your army?"

"People in the country always know secrets that others don't. I'm going to co-opt them in every sphere, not just the army."

"No one's done that," Anas said, "ever since Amr ibn al-As invaded Egypt."[1]

"Your teacher, Shaikh Abd ar-Rahman, writes about history," Ahmad replied slowly. "He has something different to say. It's as though this is a country that conquers you before you can conquer it, enters you before you can do the same to it, and swallows your treasures before you can swallow its."

"Those aren't Shaikh Abd ar-Rahman's words, my lord."

"No, they're mine. But that's what the shaikh intended in his writings. But let's go back to Ibn al-Mudabbir. Have you heard his sarcastic comments about my gait, my clothing, and my general demeanor?"

"Yes, I have."

Ahmad smiled. "If you're going to work with me," he said, "then all kinds of wrongdoing must be your primary focus; you must fight it and crush it. Egypt needs an army made up of Egyptians and other peoples."

"I know."

"You'll have to leave the judge's daughter."

"That's not going to happen."

"Do you love her?"

"My lord . . ."

"Anas, I've left my own wife and son in Iraq. Do you know why? Because they'd be pawns here. Ibn al-Mudabbir might get angry with me, and then with the caliph. He would demand that I go back. If I didn't, my wife and son would be pawns in his hands."

"My lord, my wife has to be protected."

"Not only that," Ahmad continued, "but I'm planning to build an army. When the time's right, I'll bring my wife and son here. Leave the judge's daughter till the time is right. Understand what I'm saying and take it to heart. If Ibn al-Mudabbir finds out that you're her husband, Anas, he'll kill her. He won't just kill you. Do you understand? Do you want her to die?"

Anas remained silent.

"I want you to spy on the caliph's men in Egypt," Ahmad continued. "You know everything. You'll be working with me and in my army. If you send the judge's daughter back to her father and promise her that, when the time is right, you'll come back for her, you'll have rescued her before yourself."

"He'll marry her to Ibn al-Mudabbir against her will."

"That he can't do, I promise you and swear to you. We'll say that she's married,

---

1. Translator's note: Amr ibn al-As led the Muslim invasion of Egypt in 639 CE and served as its governor.

but we won't say that the head fisherman's son is her husband. She'll go back to her father's house and stay there till we've managed to defeat Ibn al-Mudabbir. Then you can go back to her, and I can go back to my own wife."

"I can't do it."

"Fighters have to use their brains and work for the public good, not their own. You can either put an end to Ibn al-Mudabbir's tyrannical hold over the Egyptian people, or you can go back to the judge's daughter and spend the rest of your life with her fleeing from one country to another while Ibn al-Mudabbir continues with his brutal tyranny. Think about it and don't respond today. Just think that, by staying with her now, you may actually end up killing her. You realize that equations need time and analysis in order to reach a conclusion. If you run away with her, Anas, he may find you both, and when he does, he'll show no mercy, and especially not to her."

Anas stayed silent.

"If it's difficult for you," Ahmad continued, "I'll let you go to her as you wish, as though I've never met you and you've never heard of me. But when Ibn al-Mudabbir slaughters her before your very eyes, you'll only have yourself to blame."

Silence prevailed. Anas was in a quandary, but hope managed to find a path to his heart. That made him even more confused, and his heart kept racing.

Ever since he was a child, he had realized that he was different. Ever since he had taught himself Greek and had started translating books for himself so that he could give them to people who deserved them; ever since he had devoted himself to learning and avoided frivolous activities, had learned how to fish but did not intend to become a fish merchant; ever since then, his father had realized that his son was different. For the business, he had relied on Ali and asked him to take it over. The father had sacrificed a lot for his two sons and devoted no attention to anyone else. He had spared no expense in order to buy books for Anas, up until the confrontation with Ibn al-Mudabbir.

And then there was Maisoon. With her, Anas unleashed his tongue, and the words came pouring out, so much so that he did not dare reveal them to anyone else. His brother had accused him of being shy with women, and he often thought that he would never be able to admit his love for a woman. He could not find the right words, till he saw her. No, he did not love her for her beauty, even though it was enough to stymie poets from the pre-Islamic era till today. He loved her for her gentleness, and maybe also for her eyes, sparkling with life that reached down to the very depths, and her intelligence that could pierce the very soul. His entire being was disrupted, and he no longer desired anything other than her arms. Even when she was around him, the hunger was insatiable and the thirst unquenchable.

Today, the deputy governor was telling him to leave her for a while. Yes, he had also said that Anas could go back to her once Ibn al-Mudabbir was gone. But what if Ibn al-Mudabbir didn't go? How could he give her up now she was his? He would be leaving the only prize he had taken away from ibn al-Mudabbir. Amid the frenzy of his passion, he had forgotten all about revenge and, for a while, had incinerated his hatred for everyone on earth. But then Ahmad had arrived like the Angel of Death to remind him.

How could he convince her to wait? Was the deputy governor confident that the judge's daughter would never talk? If she said that the bookseller was the man to whom she was married, then all the deputy governor's plans would fail. But he was sure that she would never reveal who her husband was. Why was he so certain? Was he not sure himself that she would not be angry and assume that Anas had deserted her? Would she wait for him? Could she ask for a divorce and then be married to Ibn al-Mudabbir? Would he be able to leave her? The deputy governor assured him that he would make sure she would never be married to Ibn al-Mudabbir.

Ahmad ibn Tulun, the deputy governor, seemed different. He was from Bukhara, and yet his Arabic was better than Anas's. His eyes knew where to look and how to get what they wanted. He seemed obsessed with a particular idea that Anas did not fully understand. He did not know what Ahmad's eventual goals were, but he had confidence in him. He spoke about Egypt, justice, and a frequent dream he had had. Sometimes, Anas did not understand everything he was saying, but he trusted him. A firm bond developed between them, two men who loathed Ibn al-Mudabbir.

He was beset with anxiety when he opened the door to find her standing there in front of him, her eyes huge. For just a moment, she stared at him in amazement, but then she rushed forward and threw herself into his arms.

"Anas," she said, "I thought you were dead."

He put his arms around her waist. "My darling Maisoon," he said, doing his best to sound firm, "you have to go back to your father's house."

"I know you agreed to do that," she replied quickly. "Ibn al-Mudabbir threatened you and told you to leave me. Thank God he didn't kill you. Did he intend to? Answer me, Anas."

He avoided looking at her. "If I asked you to wait," he said slowly, "would you do it? If I promised to come back and to get rid of Ibn al-Mudabbir and come back to you, would you wait?"

"Of course I'll wait for you," she replied without even thinking. "But you can't get rid of him. Why did he let you go?"

"He's not the one who arrested me. It was the Police Chief."

"He's forced you to give me up, right? But we can flee today. If he let you leave with me to take me back to my father, we can escape instead."

He looked into her eyes and put his hands around her face. "I love you," he said.

"Did he threaten you?" she asked again.

"Will you wait for me?"

"I don't understand anything."

"The Police Chief has promised me that Ibn al-Mudabbir will never be married to you. You'll be going home as though you've escaped from your kidnappers. Don't mention his name or anything about him. Ibn al-Mudabbir is not going to be married to you. That's a promise. When you go back, I shall always be around you. I won't be able to contact you or send you messages, but I'll still be all around you. I shall come back to you, I swear that I will. I will never betray you, and I desire no one else. Do you believe me?"

She stared hard at him, then firmly removed his hand from her waist.

"You haven't been forced to give me up," she said. "You've decided to do it."

"I shall never give you up. You're my wife."

She stamped her foot on the floor like a child that has lost all patience. "You must choose now between me and Ibn al-Mudabbir," she said. "If your love for me was greater than your hatred for Ibn al-Mudabbir, then we could escape together."

"Maisoon, we have no future if we run away. Just think about it. Are we going to spend the rest of our lives on the run? If he found us and killed us, would that make you happy?"

"Choose between me and Ibn al-Mudabbir," she insisted.

"You need to use your brain," he told her angrily.

"You want me to use my brain now?" she yelled. "Now? Why weren't you using your own brain when you convinced my father that we could escape here? Why didn't you use your brain when you were married to me and made love to me? Today you want me to use my brain?"

"Maisoon," he told her firmly, "like it or not, you're going back to your father and waiting for me. You're going to wait for me, and I shall come back. Have no doubts about that."

All the way there, he did not say a word to her. The dagger thrust had settled deep in his soul and hers. When he was close to her father's house, he covered his face.

"I don't want to leave you here with so much anger between us," he said.

"I don't know what's going to happen to me."

He stretched out his hand and grabbed hold of hers. "Let your conviction overcome your pride," he told her. "I want to live with you forever. I shall return."

She pulled her hand away. "Don't worry," she said. "I won't tell anyone who you are. Go back to the Booksellers' Market and take revenge on Ibn al-Mudabbir."

"No, I shall come back to my wife. I have no one else."

"You've got Ibn al-Mudabbir."

"Maisoon . . ."

"Take me home," she said.

"Like it or not, you're going to wait for me," he told her forcefully. "Ibn al-Mudabbir will only set eyes on you when I'm dead."

She walked away a few steps, then turned around hesitantly.

"Anas . . ." she pleaded.

"My darling," he replied passionately.

"You have to choose between me and Ibn al-Mudabbir," she said. "Who's more important to you, Maisoon or the Tax Administrator?"

"Try to understand," he said gently. "How can we live as runaways?"

"Answer my question."

"How can you compare love and hate?"

"On the contrary, love can only be compared with hate. Answer my question."

"I shall return to you," he replied firmly. "I'll send you letters. Wait for me."

"Who knows?" she replied angrily. "Maybe you set the whole thing up. Perhaps you were happy that the Tax Administrator had fallen in love with someone you loved as well. Your fates were joined. Did you arrange for him to see me, Anas?"

He opened his eyes in fury and grabbed her waist. "What nonsense are you saying?" he asked. "Make sure—do you hear me?—make sure you don't imagine for a single second that I'm not coming back."

She walked steadily with the guards, and her image moved away, faded, and disappeared. Her every step snatched at his heart. He had not expected his heartbeat to be affected, his liver to bleed, and all his senses to shudder. He closed his eyes and let out a sigh. This was the kind of pain his father had felt before dying, or maybe even worse—who knows. Why had he not chased after her, held her in his arms, and forgotten about everything that had been and would be? He would be putting ten men around her father's house to watch over her the entire day. He would send money to her father and use the first payment he received from his work with Ibn Tulun to buy her gold. She would forget and forgive. Lovers could not be angry; they had soft hearts. Anyone who had lived in his arms would never leave such a haven because of a certain degree of distance. Separation happens all the time, but it does not last. He was as full of worries as a field is with water. He found himself on his way to visit the Pyramid Witch. He wanted to ask her to help him and tell him whether what he was doing was right. Loss and passion both have a potion to protect against extinction.

"Welcome to the competent scholar," she said, "possessor of impossible missions and distraught heart."

"I've come to ask for advice."

"They all come asking for advice. Then arrogance gets the better of them, and they forget all the moments of hesitation and degradation. Anas the Egyptian is being crushed by humiliation. Hatred has taken over and thrown you to the ground. You had everything, but then Ibn al-Mudabbir reminded you that you're weaker than a frog in a snake's mouth. It's a reader's disease, Anas. Every time you delve into your books, you forget who you are. It kids you that you've acquired the entire world. When you return to this world of ours, you realize your real worth, and weakness gnaws at your soul. You're fighting the Tax Administrator and the caliph who appointed him. You're trying to collect all the air particles in your two hands till the tyrant is throttled to death. What kind of fool are you, what sort of madman? Sheer delusion has eaten your heart, Egyptian!"

"I vowed to avenge my father. Moses managed to defeat a pharaoh."

"You're not Moses, and you don't have a magic wand."

"I've come because I'm exhausted."

"Your exhaustion hasn't even started yet."

"Do you want me to give in to humiliation?"

"Take your revenge slowly. War is destructive, and the stench of weakness seeps from killing. Slaughter dries up the slaughterer's blood before that of the victim."

"I'm going to take revenge."

"You read about the ancient Egyptians. You're the only one who knows about them. They would speak about tyranny, justice, and revenge. They were perpetually at war, which never ends. But the tyrant is not a tyrant all the time, nor is the just person always impeccable. Time spins us around like the Nile before it floods. Ibn al-Mudabbir has taught you that you're weak. Weakness is the very first lesson for humans to learn. You should be thanking him."

"You're speaking in riddles and making me lament your infatuated mind."

"You're weak, Ibn al-Mudabbir is weak, and so is Ahmad ibn Tulun. Everybody has a particular moment when they realize their real worth, their ignorance, and their helplessness. That time comes, whether you like it or not. It's come to you early, so you can be aware of it. Weakness is accompanied by knowledge, and ability is linked with ignorance."

"Do you want me to forget about Ibn al-Mudabbir?"

"Even if I asked you, you wouldn't do that. He's wounded your pride and reminded you that you're a lone fox in the desert till the wolves catch up with that wound of yours. But why have you assumed that they'll never get there? Sooner or later, wolves always manage to get everywhere. Where's the knowledge to go with the weakness?"

"Where's the knowledge to go with the weakness?" he repeated in confusion.

"Just remember, Anas. You're all weak; in fact, we're all equally weak. In the Islamic religion, the individual thinks that no one will have power over him. Then what? He falls from the loftiest peak. In the face of powerful waves today, there's no protection or stratagem. Wisdom goes along with a long life, and awareness of weakness brings power. Self-deception is a worm burrowing its way into the spirit, so it's destroyed."

"Your words alarm me. I came here to ask for advice."

"Ancestors are no help. Their messages are contradictory, and their stories are all magic and fables." She smiled. "Even so, I wanted you to talk to them. Come back after a while when you've opened your heart to know."

"Bahnas," he said sadly, "love has crushed me."

"Love has often crushed people. It's destroyed entire armies. Love is like wine. It deceives you into thinking that you're all-powerful. Then you wake up to the agony of your own weakness and lack of discretion. That's the way it always is, with no peace. But it's as sweet as honey and as smooth as pure milk. There's no way to avoid a plunge into the honeyed sweetness and a drink from that milk. Anas, where's the cake I asked you to bring?"

Chapter 6

Entertainments had a double advantage, a precision and an offer. Deals would often be made there, and whole states could be created and disappear. A fascinating face would appear for men to fight over, or a soft voice would numb the ear so it would submit to every command. Governors and amirs knew such venues well; they had brought them from Baghdad, along with their pageboys and slave-girls. The Egyptian people had learned from them, and sometimes senior businessmen had imitated them, seeking that sense of absolute drunken bliss that did not finish with the end of night.

Today, the assembly was different. Ibn al-Mudabbir had invited the deputy governor to his entertainment. He had invited him because he was not sure about him. The deputy governor had rejected his offer of money as a gift; that was a declaration of war. He had invited him so that he could make fun of his gait and dress and assess what his plans were and how much of a risk he presented. If the deputy governor persisted in his frowning gaze and conceit, he would have to be deposed today. Ibn al-Mudabbir could do that.

The singing-girl started with words from the poetry of Ulayya bint al-Mahdi, accompanying herself on the oud. She batted her eyelids in a coquettish gesture:

Passion pulsates in my heart, and my tears flow freely, then dwindle.
I long, then I raise my hopes, but despair draws me to it, and I subside.

Ibn al-Mudabbir looked at Ahmad ibn Tulun, who was listening carefully, and smiled. The singing-girl finished her performance.

"Did you like her, Abu al-Abbas?" Ibn al-Mudabbir asked.

Ahmad looked straight at him. "More important," he replied, "did you like her?"

"I'll give her to you today," Ibn al-Mudabbir continued, "since you turned down my first gift. Do you prefer boys?"

"No," Ahmad replied, "I prefer the young men with whom you surround yourself, a hundred or more."

"They're not for pleasure. They're trained soldiers."

"I'm aware of that, brother."

"Why would the deputy governor need guards?"

"You did ask me to choose my gift."

Ibn al-Mudabbir looked angry.

"I've come to see you today," Ahmad continued, "to talk about the judge's daughter."

"Maisoon," Ibn al-Mudabbir replied, his passion floating on the surface.

"Forgive me, brother. I don't remember her name. My soldiers found her today and freed her from her kidnappers."

Ibn al-Mudabbir looked at him, shocked.

"Where are the kidnappers? We need to cut them in two in front of the whole of Egypt."

"It looks as though they escaped. That's not the important reason why I've come to see you. Judge Yahya does not agree to his daughter being married to the Tax Administrator."

Ibn al-Mudabbir blanched. "I didn't realize," he said, claiming to be surprised, "that the deputy governor had come to Egypt specially to adjudicate matters of love and marriage."

"No, brother. He's come here to adjudicate matters of justice. The man does not want his daughter to be married to you."

"So he's the one who hid her, just as I thought."

"The matter's in my hands now. I'm afraid the news may reach the caliph that governors are now compelling Egyptian women to be married to them, thus exposing themselves to matters of honor."

"Are you threatening me, Abu al-Abbas Ahmad?"

"No, I'm just making things clear. The girl is now under my protection. I've promised her father that you won't be importuning her. She'll be staying inside her house and not leaving it."

Silence prevailed.

"The girl wants to be married to me," Ibn al-Mudabbir said. "You're not introducing matters of honor about that."

"Since when, brother, does any girl make decisions with which her father doesn't agree? But let's discuss state affairs and forget about matters involving women. There's no point in that."

"You came with two requests, although I don't know which of the two is more significant. You want men and the girl."

"Let's put her aside for now. Perhaps the judge will change his mind after a while, without insistence or threats."

"The deputy governor seems to have come here to ingratiate himself with the Egyptians and to despise the caliph's people."

"On the contrary, I've come here for the caliph's sake and in order to elevate his words. But, brother, how I've been stunned by the conditions of the people in this country! Ever since Amr ibn al-As first conquered Egypt, it's been a mountain of pure gold, its bounty pouring from its sides to inundate Muslim lands and flood non-Arab territories. Yet the mountain has crumbled into non-existence. People are poor, food is scarce, and money is violently snatched from between their very teeth. What has happened to Egypt, brother?"

"Your words are a grave insult to the Abbasid caliphate and a criticism of the caliph himself. They were about to appoint you Governor of Wasit in Iraq."

"Then the governorship of Egypt came up," Ahmad replied. "It was all predestined fate, brother. I want the caliphate to receive the entire mountain of gold, and not just bits of it."

"Are you criticizing me, Deputy Governor?"

"I've been shocked by the fact that Egyptians are going hungry when there is enough gold to inundate their homes. You're sending a lot of tax revenue to the caliph, but if the Egyptian people had enough to eat, you'd be able to send a lot more tax. Hand over some of the money to me. I have an idea."

"We'll talk about your ideas in a while," Ibn al-Mudabbir told him. "If you stay with us, Ahmad, we can exchange a whole lot of ideas."

"'If,' you say. That 'if' in language is a useful way of saying 'no.'"

"You're very knowledgeable about Arabic, even though you're a non-Arab."

"Linguistic knowledge and loyalty have nothing to do with origins. It's the place where you're born that matters. I was born in Iraq, brother."

Ahmad stood up and headed for the door. Once he had said farewell, Ibn al-Mudabbir exploded in anger. "Ahmad has to leave today, not tomorrow," he repeated.

His friend, Abu Sha'ara imitated Ahmad's gait. "He walks like wild toads," he said. "He needs a lion to slaughter him. Have you looked at his clothes and his beard? What was the caliph thinking? Maybe you should give him some money so he can change his appearance."

"The caliph didn't appoint him. It was his mother's husband." Ibn al-Mudabbir smiled as he looked at Abu Sha'ara. "If your mother's husband was an intimate acquaintance of the caliph and took over the governorship of Egypt, he could make you deputy too. These non-Arabs have ways of doing things that are different from ours."

"Qasim, Ahmad ibn Tulun's mother . . . They say that she married General Bayakbak for her son's sake."

"Maisoon," Ibn al-Mudabbir said sadly.

Abu Sha'ara gave him a sad look. "I know," he said.

"No, you don't know," Ibn al-Mudabbir replied. "Until I saw her, my life had no meaning. She enslaved me with a single glance, like some genie."

"Behold, Ibn al-Mudabbir," his friend Abu Sha'ara teased, "someone before whom court officials quake in fear. Now he's passionately in love like a teenager!"

"Be polite!"

"It's the wine, my friend. What is it about her that you don't find in that slave-girl?"

"Don't question the lover about his heart, or else you'll do wrong to both mind and heart. We'll wait for a while till we can get rid of Ahmad ibn Tulun."

Abu Sha'ara laughed. "Maybe Bayakbak will get rid of his mother, Qasim, and then exile him from all the caliph's lands. Who knows? It all depends on Qasim and her skill in the arts of passion."

"No," Ibn al-Mudabbir replied. "Passion can't be taught or perfected. It's a God-given blessing and gift."

"Your words distress me."

"I've purified my soul of all evil. She is my only desire now."

"What about your slave-girl?"

"After Maisoon, I've no desire for anyone else."

Anas now moved to a house in the military complex called "Authority Town" because of its size and many gates. Ahmad ibn Tulun lived there with his own men and retinue and the police. Each category of men had their own gate. Ahmad ibn Tulun entered through a gate that overlooked the Abu Qadeera reservoir. Anas's way in was through the police gate, now that Ahmad had appointed him a deputy in the Superior Police, charged with supervision of Fustat and the army.

Every single night, he remembered hugging her and the scent of paradise from having her so close; her laughter, and the loving looks in her eyes. Every night, he had the same dream. She would be looking at him cautiously, clutching his neck, and begging him not to throw her in the river.

"I can't swim, Anas," she would whisper.

"I'll pull you out before you drown," he would reply firmly.

"But what if you can't find me in the dark?" she asked like a forlorn child.

"Even were the water to swallow you," he reassured her, "I could still locate you within the folds of my limbs and the depths of my ribs."

He was giving her father money and handing over generous amounts for her personally. With his earnings, he had bought her a pure gold necklace and handed it to the guards to give to her.

Anas spent two whole months in hard training. In the morning, he would train in combat with the slave-soldiers that Ahmad ibn Tulun had taken from Ibn al-Mudabbir in place of his gift. In the evening, he sat with Ahmad ibn Tulun, reading to him and translating works of Greek philosophy. In Plato, Ahmad had discovered wisdom and purpose. He could not forget his words of wisdom or stop listening to them every day. After two months, Ahmad asked Anas to take on the task of spying on Ibn al-Mudabbir. Ahmad explained that Anas was someone Ibn al-Mudabbir would never be able to buy, not that day or any other day. He also asked Anas to investigate all the letters from the Postmaster to the caliph. Shuqair, the Postmaster, was a close confidant of Ibn al-Mudabbir, and was also loyal to the caliph's mother. For that reason, it would not be possible to get rid of him. But what Ahmad could do was to keep an eye on things and intercept the Postmaster's letters to the caliph. Ahmad gave Anas a lot of tasks. Every night he sat down with him, and the two of them laid out their plans for everything.

Ibn Tulun kept his eye on Anas and learned a lot about him. He knew that he was a fox, not a wolf. He loved the life of an individual and did not follow communal rules. Whenever possible, he would dive into his books and his private world. He had no desire either to lead a community or follow a leader. Yes, he had learned how to use a sword and spear very quickly, but Ahmad could not see in him a soldier who would follow orders and work with the army. He was good at digging holes and excelled at precise planning fueled by knowledge and reading.

"Do you realize, Anas," Ahmad told him one day quite spontaneously, "that you're my friend today, but you won't be forever because you won't follow orders?"

"My lord," Anas replied, "you know that people who follow every order cannot be trusted. People who won't object in public will do it in private."

"A man like you is a fine friend, but not an army commander. He's a teacher and planner for the future."

"The future's in Alexandria, my lord," he replied forcefully. "I said we're friends. Alexandria must come under Ahmad ibn Tulun's control. Till that happens, its taxes won't be going to the caliph."

Ahmad opened his mouth, scared. "What you're proposing may end up finishing me off before anything else."

"You asked me how to get rid of Ibn al-Mudabbir and his tyranny. I'm helping you."

"I never asked you to avenge your father and steal the taxes."

"The Alexandria taxes belong to Ahmad ibn Tulun. They're going to be stolen at night by thieves without the Police Chief's knowledge. Ibn Tulun will then be able to carry out everything he's dreamed of doing in Egypt. He'll be able to build if he wants or give money to the peasants. He'll set up a center for manufacture, and another for agriculture."

"And there's the police," Ahmad said slowly.

"The Police Deputy is going to be furious," Anas said. "He'll be searching for the culprit."

"You're a cunning devil, Anas. Sometimes I'm scared of you. I used to think that all you could see were Al-Khwarizmi's books."

"Yes, they're his books on algebra, as I know. Let me help you. When Ibn al-Mudabbir's aura fades and the caliph realizes that Ibn al-Mudabbir has no power over the Egyptian people, that'll be the end for him. There can be no authority without prestige and no permanence without a treasury and cash. I have another request too, my lord."

"Go ahead."

"The Deputy Police Chief will release the Coptic Pope of Alexandria. Throughout its history, Egypt has never known days like these. Christians are afraid of celebrating their masses. Churches are worried about bringing out their censers and vessels for fear of the Tax Administrator's greed."

"Are you planning to challenge the Tax Administrator's decision?"

"The Deputy Police Chief has some discretion in the matter."

"But you aren't the Deputy Police Chief, Anas."

"Free religious authorities, and Egyptians may put up with poverty for a while, but they won't tolerate insult for long."

"Do what seems right to you," Ahmad said. "But bear the consequences in mind."

As Anas put his plan into action, his dream drew ever closer to fulfillment. He would get rid of Ibn al-Mudabbir and go back to his beloved. He could picture the day and the hour. He remembered her scent and her arms as she embraced him. He would sneak along her balcony, burst in on her all of a sudden, and give her a big kiss. She would welcome him with the same passion and ardor. When he had asked about her after a month, the messenger had neither reassured nor alarmed him. She had just taken the letter. He tried writing to her again and dearly wished that he could see her. But that was impossible as long as Ibn al-Mudabbir was keeping watch on her house. Anything that would rouse suspicion about Anas would make it impossible to get rid of Ibn al-Mudabbir. He had to be patient, and so did she. When he left her, they had been at odds, but his heart had already made peace with her even before the argument. He could understand her sorrow and frustration. He would ask her to forgive him and explain things to her. She would love him for the rest of her days. He knew no comfort in her absence. He hurried to see Ahmad, hoping to find a way of going back to her; he could no longer stay away. But Ahmad asked him to be patient for at least a year. He would find a way even if Ibn al-Mudabbir did not leave.

From the very first day, he managed to sever the route by which Shuqair, the Postmaster, sent letters to the caliph. That same day, he learned that the letters were demanding that Ahmad be removed from office. He was not fit to be Governor of Egypt; his appearance was scruffy, and he had no prestige. Shuqair and Ibn al-Mudabbir both accused him of disrespect for the caliph; his eyes were full of a desire for independence and rebellion. Ahmad ibn Tulun was a danger to Egypt. Once he gained control, no one would be able to stop him. He had to be dismissed before it was too late. These letters all fell into the hands of Ahmad and his men. He changed them as far as he could. Since he could write and make copies quickly, he was able to do it rapidly without Shuqair or his men noticing.

Once Ahmad had appointed Anas Deputy Police Chief, he was able to infiltrate Shuqair's men as he had been asked, and then to do the same with Ibn al-Mudabbir's men as well. He learned about lying, trickery, cunning, and deceit; in the space of a few months, he learned a lot. But then, sorrow is the best teacher of all, and an inability to reject tyranny solidifies the heart's resolve and gives it yet more strength and courage. He mastered everything and worked night and day, engaging in political conflicts and realizing that justice was not easy, tyranny had to be fought using every means available, and that, while unity was power, isolation was weakness personified. Every time he managed to put a stop to Ibn al-Mudabbir's evil ways, some of that sense of weakness was cured. When his men had managed to steal the Alexandria taxes and hand them over, part of his heart felt better, or almost so. Victory was near, even nearer than he expected.

✦

Anas was doing his best to apply justice, and now he had the weapon with which to do it. But he never wore a police uniform. Even with his hold on power and swords, his heart was still that of a bookseller. Every time he looked into a particular matter, he discovered the Tax Administrator behind it. Whenever he arrested a thief to put him in the dungeon, he longed for it to be the Tax Administrator. Ibn al-Mudabbir was dominating his every day, and he kept thinking about him as a way of diverting his heart from what he had lost and left behind.

His heart rejoiced as he made his way to the dungeon to release the Pope and everyone who had supported his cause. He opened the gates and removed the covers from the walls. He gave the Pope his respects and apologized on behalf of Ahmad ibn Tulun. He then ordered the release of everyone who had been imprisoned with the Pope. He stood there, watching the joy in people's eyes and the hopeful expressions on their faces. Then a man came up behind him.

"We didn't realize that the governor was appointing Egyptians to these positions. I wonder, are you an Egyptian or a spy?"

Anas turned round in a fury. "Curse you! What did you say?"

The man looked around him in confusion. "I didn't say anything, my lord," he said.

"Yes, you did. I heard you. Repeat what you just said in front of these men so I can throw you back in the dungeon."

"When prison is subject to the whims of the Deputy Police Chief," the man muttered, "then you know you're in Egypt."

Anas grabbed his collar. "I get the impression that the Tax Administrator put you in jail because you haven't learned your manners."

"Or maybe he put me in jail because I took the same kind of risks as you have, head fisherman's son."

Their eyes met. The man looked about the same age as him. Anas dismissed his men and sat down on a bench. He asked the young man to sit in front of him.

"Who are you?" he asked.

"Saeed."

"Saeed who?"

"Saeed, son of Katib al-Farghani."

"I've just set you free, but I haven't heard a word of thanks."

"We were extolling your heroic deeds, Deputy Police Chief. All of us in prison know you, but we weren't sure exactly who you were."

"What do you know about me?" Anas asked in Coptic.

"I told you, all Egypt knows who you are. News about rebels reaches prison before it gets to the caliph's court. When Ahmad ibn Tulun appointed Anas ibn Hamza al-Skandari as Deputy Police Chief, we realized that every rebel has his price."

"Ahmad isn't Ibn al-Mudabbir. He's released the Pope from prison."

"We've no business with rulers."

"On the contrary, you need to understand before getting angry. Don't strike without any knowledge. Know your enemy before your friend. Once you find out who your enemy is, then go looking for your friend."

"I don't know Ibn Tulun, but I do know Ibn al-Mudabbir. Traces of him still decorate my heart and back."

"So, Saeed, son of Katib al-Farghani, be on your way."

"I have no way," Saeed replied suddenly. "Nothing pleases me."

"What do you want, man?"

"Does Ibn Tulun only appoint Muslim Egyptians?"

"Do you want to work with Ahmad?"

"No, I want to work with you."

"You're not right for the police."

"Why, because I don't lie?"

"No, you're too thin. You're not healthy or strong."

"I've just spent a whole year with no sun and no food."

"Be on your way, or I'll put you back in the dungeon."

"I want to work with you. I've no job and no family."

Anas said nothing for a while.

"Let me think about it," he said.

"While you think about it, I'll stay with you. I have no home."

"Have you lost your mind?"

"I won't leave this spot."

Anas took out his sword and put it on Saeed's stomach. "If I kill you now," he said, "you won't be leaving this spot."

"I've nothing to lose," Saeed replied, "and nothing I expect to happen. Do what you like."

Anas was shocked as he looked at him. Leaving him by the gate of Authority Town, he spent the whole day finding out about him, so much so that, for a while, he forgot about Ibn al-Mudabbir.

Anas learned Saeed's entire story. Saeed grew up in Farghan in the Nile Delta with a father, mother, and four brothers. His father went to Iraq to look for a job and returned after a few years a rich man. He purchased a large house in which to raise his sons. The family remained Christian, even when some relatives converted to Islam. His mother continued to pray and attend mass. The people of the quarter knew all about Saeed's story with the orphan girl. People say that an orphan girl aged five appeared in the quarter. Saeed's father took pity on her and asked his mother to bring her up as one of their children. The mother complained, but still took the burden on her shoulders. In fact, she paid no attention to her and treated her like a household servant, no more. But the orphan girl was strange. When she was ten, she took to sitting beneath one of the Pharaonic statues for hours and talking to it. When Saeed's mother told her not to do it and said that it was just a statue, the girl stated firmly that it was her father. Before the entire quarter, she claimed that she was the statue's daughter and proceeded to weave an elaborate tale about her mother and father. Saeed's mother now started to complain about her; she blamed her, chided her, and sometimes even struck her.

But somehow a love developed between Saeed and her, the like of which the people of Babylon had never encountered over the ages. He was the same age as her and had always accompanied her as a child, never leaving her for a second, believing her story and listening to her patiently. He had taught her how to draw and read. When they were both fifteen, they exchanged a passionate kiss that Saeed never forgot for his entire life. Saeed asked his parents for permission to marry the orphan girl, but they refused outright, not because she was an orphan, but rather because she was peculiar. She used to sit in front of statues and stay with them. For Saeed to be married to her would be a scandal for the entire family. He was sad, and so was she. The girl stuck with him. People say that she used to slink into his room and sleep in his arms. God knows, she waited for his love to triumph, but he did not dare. A row broke out between her and the people of the quarter. She claimed that Saeed was her family, and she would be married to him. Amid the shocked looks of neighbors and people in the quarter, Saeed said nothing for a moment, neither denying nor supporting her. Two years later, he opened his eyes, and she was no longer there. It was dark all around, and the stars in the sky faded away. He stayed in his room for months, and his mother asked the priests for help. She was afraid that the orphan girl had bewitched him. She spat three times by the door of the house and declared that the orphan girl had gone to hell, and Saeed would find himself a suitable wife. But he never married. The darkness dwelled deep inside him and dug out spaces for loneliness and longing, leaving no space for anything else. His family perished in the plague, and he was left on his own in Egypt.

Saeed adopted the gate to Anas's residence as a home, pitching a tent and putting some clothes and food in it. He would greet Anas every morning, but Anas would never respond. Every night, he would ask him what he had done, but again Anas would not respond. Saeed's presence there began to aggravate and scare him, but he could not remove him or expel him from Fustat entirely.

Anas contacted his brother, Ali, and asked him to join him in the police force. But all Ali wanted to do was to go back to Alexandria and work as a fisherman like his father. He knew no other life. He had traveled to Al-Farma because, for him, the sea was closer there than the Egyptian Nile. He took Gameela with him, settled there, and worked as a fisherman. One day, he hoped to be able to go back to Alexandria, head held high, with no fear of the Tax Administrator. Anas promised him that once he was rid of Ibn al-Mudabbir that would happen. But getting rid of him did not seem all that easy.

There were revolts in Egypt; the Alawis rebelled, and so did others. Poverty and corruption were widespread. Ahmad ibn Tulun wrote to the caliph asking that Ibn al-Mudabbir leave him some funds so that he could purchase men and have enough power to put down those revolts. The caliph immediately rejected his request. When Ibn al-Mudabbir heard about it, he immediately wrote to the caliph, telling him that he had been expecting that Ahmad ibn Tulun would make such a request. Ahmad ibn Tulun needed to collect men in order to make Egypt independent. If the caliph gave him money for power and an army, then it would mark the end of Egypt as part of the Abbasid caliphate. The caliph began to have his doubts, and looked forward to the day when he would be rid of Ahmad, or maybe the real governor. That real governor, the husband of Ahmad's mother, was killed, and Ahmad's presence in Egypt seemed almost at an end. What would be awaiting him in Iraq? Death or prison?

Four months later, Ahmad ibn Tulun asked Anas to go to Iraq and start spying on the men at the caliph's court so he could find out who was fomenting conspiracies against him and who had killed Egypt's governor, his mother's husband. He gave him a letter to take to the caliph and asked him to stay in Iraq for several months to listen to what the palace personnel were saying and report any dangers or slander back to him. Anas did not like the idea of traveling; he was just a client person from Egypt, working with his father as a fisherman and reading books. He was afraid that the caliph's men would not receive him or trust him. Since when did Egyptians carry important letters? The caliph was bound to have his doubts about him; he was from a client people, not a real Arab.

But Ahmad insisted and told him that, at that point, he did not trust anyone else. Anas was still sending Maisoon a letter every day, but she never replied. He had no idea why. Was it because she was afraid her letter might fall into the wrong hands, or that she was still annoyed with him? How he missed her and how he longed for the day when they would be together again! But his trip to Iraq would delay that for half a year or more. He walked past her house. If only he could hug her once before he left! He hesitated. If he allowed the heart to make the decisions, there would be no success and no escape. Patience would reunite them; that was certain.

That day, when he returned to his house, he found Saeed gathering his things, as though he was planning to leave.

"So," he said, "you've finally come to your senses!"

"No," Saeed told him, "I'm going to Iraq with you. I'd like to see Samarra and its wonderful buildings. Didn't I tell you I have no family?"

"What are you talking about, my brother?" Anas asked.

"I was searching for water to put out the fire of regret, but I didn't find any. People say that when you collect all your belongings and travel on God's path, your heart is cleansed of desire and passion."

"Do you know where your beloved is? Why don't you go back to her?"

Saeed gave a scary laugh.

"Be careful not to annoy women, brother," he said, "especially the passionate ones!"

"I don't know what you're talking about."

"I no longer have a home. She went away and left me a vagrant."

Anas's heart was in knots; he did not know why.

"Perhaps she's died," he said.

"Don't say that," Saeed replied. "I have to find her. Please, Deputy Police Chief, help me. You can help me. Make me your travel companion. I don't need any money. But, when we come back, I shall ask you for something."

Anas stared at him, shocked. "What's that?" he asked.

"I want to meet Ahmad ibn Tulun," Saeed replied, "and tell him what I can do. Like my father and my entire family, I'm an excellent builder. Mention my name to Ahmad ibn Tulun, and I'll never forget it. Construction brings some kind of solace. I'll be loyal to you for the rest of my life and do whatever you ask me."

Their eyes met.

"In your eyes," Anas said slowly, "I detect both pride and suffering. I'll pray to God for you and me."

Saeed started to tail him like a shadow, even all the way to Iraq. His only goal seemed to be to reach his beloved who had died some time earlier. Without Anas even realizing it, Saeed had now made his way to his heart, and he had become a friend and companion. Anas sympathized with Saeed's predestined fate. While searching for her, he had lost his mind; Anas could empathize with his despair and confusion. But Saeed was patient and listened to Anas all the way to Iraq as he read to him the letter in Arabic that was addressed to the minister and caliph. Anas kept trying to pronounce the Arabic sounds "qaaf" and "zaa" and spent a lot of time pronouncing the "j" sound the way people do in Iraq. Sometimes Saeed would laugh.

"You've studied jurisprudence," he said, "but you don't know how to pronounce Arabic consonants!"

That annoyed Anas. "Look who's talking!" he retorted. "You speak Arabic like the Greeks."

At nighttime, Saeed sat warming himself by the fire. "You think I've lost my mind," he said. "You don't realize that you're crazy. When wind and fire are mixed, then every face is revealed. Look at me, Anas. What you see in my pupils is yourself."

"Here you are going back to fear again, man!" Anas replied. "Wake up from your stupor!"

"Do you realize that regret is worse than loss and harder to bear than tyranny? If time moved backward, I would yell at them all and say that she was my beloved and my wife. Cowardice is compliance and shame. Do you hear me?"

Anas was not listening; he was thinking about Ibn al-Mudabbir.

"The Tax Administrator follows you like your own shadow," Saeed continued. "Isn't that true?"

Anas did not respond, but he was listening. The whole story fascinated him, or at least aroused his curiosity. He found his eyes following in the footsteps of the orphan girl Saeed had talked about, and then tracing Saeed's tears falling without any embarrassment as he told the story. As he talked, he held nothing back and was not in the least shy. For some time, he told Anas, the orphan girl had got used to sleeping in his arms. When his mother scolded her and promised her that the devil would be following her footsteps, the girl shuddered in silence. At night, she went to Saeed and buried her head in his chest. From that very day, she had a place in his heart and never left it. Every morning she would sneak back to her own room from his. No one noticed, and she never had the slightest doubt that he would be married to her. One day, she told him that he was much closer than any husband, since she had grown up in his arms and all around him. She had a lot to say. She told him that he was her entire soul and world; security lay in his arms and affection in his breaths. How much he had promised and vowed! He would protect and help her. At the moment of confrontation, he had hesitated; just hesitated without deserting her. Perhaps he had hesitated for fear of the disapproval of people in the quarter and did not realize his own sense of shame and the way his soul would die when she was not with him. When people in the quarter yelled at her that she was a prostitute and devil, when his own mother talked about the sin and offense that her own son had committed—and that it was the orphan girl's fault, he had said nothing. At that moment, their eyes had met. Her eyes had a lot to say, while his begged for help. She asked for a delay, some time, but she erected a barrier without waiting to hear his defense. "Courage," she said, "neither follows nor counts the hours. Courage is a moment, a spear that knows its course."

Anas paused, then stroked Saeed's shoulder without saying a word. But the tears did not stop and blended with light from the fires, giving them the hues of dawn and its transformation.

"Dry your tears, brother," Anas said softly. "She's a woman, that's all."

"I've never told anyone before. I wonder, why have I told you now?"

"Maybe because we're alone in the desert," Anas replied. "My advice to you is to forget about your beloved and get married to someone else."

"No, I'm going to find her. There's no one like her."

"Madness, Saeed, involves hanging on to the impossible. You realize how impossible it is."

Saeed laughed as he cried.

"Madness, Anas," he replied, "involves hanging on to the impossible. You realize how impossible it is."

"Why are you just repeating what I said?"

"Because you're my friend."

"I'm not your friend."

"You've no time for friends. Even so, you're my friend. As long as you've listened to me, you're my friend."

"Friendship has no benefit and no purpose. What you want from me is a job. That's not friendship."

"If you could raise yourself far enough to see other people, you would realize that we're friends. There's no discretion when it comes to our friends and the people we love. It's all predestined. When you listened to me, you inevitably became a friend. We don't choose our friends, just as we don't choose our livelihood or the day we die."

"There's no friendship to unite us, Saeed. I don't have time for friends. Today, you're a travel companion; tomorrow you're a stranger."

Saeed laughed till his eyes teared up. Suddenly he frowned.

"You've promised," he said, "to mention my name to Ahmad ibn Tulun. Construction is my only job. I won't be building for the intelligentsia; I'll only be building for madmen."

Chapter 7

She missed him. She was convinced that a month would not go by with her on her own before he was back with her again. No man could possibly give up the embrace of Maisoon, the world's most beautiful woman. Now that he had sampled the sweet taste of honey, how could he possibly live on rotting fish? There was Maisoon's love for Anas, and then there was Maisoon's love for Maisoon. The twin loves were intertwined and could not be separated. Maisoon understood victory was her constant ally. If the Tax Administrator had savored a glance from her eyes, how could the bookseller possibly resist the idea of staying with her? It was a moment of sheer delusion to imagine that he could overcome the Tax Administrator. That moment would end, and he would come back to his senses. He would plead with her; yes, he would plead with her, construct a shrine around her body, and beg for forgiveness every day. She would never forgive him; his crime was unforgiveable. She would not talk to her mother and father about him. Maisoon's only friend was Maisoon. She had an intimate relationship with her own self. That self always obeyed her, raised her self-esteem, and assuaged any occasional doubts she might have.

Every day hope came closer. Two weeks went by, then another two, then another month. He had made no attempt to see her or get in touch with her. When the new moon appeared, she wished that all the stars would fall from the heavens and burn Fustat and everything in it. Without any warning, she screamed, buried her head in the pillow, and started to weep. She shuddered and sobbed for hours. Her mother came in and asked her what was the matter, but she did not reply. A few days later, she stopped eating and talking. A servant-girl approached her and said that a stranger had told her that he was with her, and she needed to wait for him. A letter came, but it was delayed. The fisherman's son was always late. She did not respond. When her mother asked her how she was, she did not reply. In the dark night, she went out on to her balcony, looked up at the stars, and asked God to bring them down. She wanted every Fustat star to leave the skies and settle on his chest. After two months, she heard her sister whisper to her mother that Maisoon may have gone crazy. She was not eating or talking to anyone. Indeed, sometimes her mother heard her screaming at night or crying like someone possessed. They read her verses from the Quran, but she did not improve. As month after month went by, she lost even more weight and was even more miserable. She heard the whispers growing and words spreading: it was love; she loved him, and he had gone away. Ibn al-Mudabbir. He had bewitched her. The only cure for bewitchment was the Pyramid Witch. She was in touch with the jinn. Some people had spotted the witch wandering naked around the pyramids at night. She had predicted this sorrow and realized that ruin was on the way.

They had to carry Maisoon because her own legs would no longer hold her. She did not resist. Her father saw the sorrow in her eyes. Anas was still sending him money every month since he had brought her back to the house. He was keeping it for Maisoon. In fact, when one of Ibn Tulun's guards brought him a gold necklace as a present from Anas for Maisoon, she threw it out of the window and did not tell her father. But he found out, recovered it, and kept it for her along with the money.

Her mother cursed fate that had driven her daughter to this state. Her sister, Ruqayya, grabbed her under one arm, and her mother did the same with the other. They took her to see the Pyramid Witch.

Maisoon's eyes kept looking all around the place, but she could not see anything. Her mother called to her, but it seemed as though she did not even recognize her. She kept looking all around her as though danger was bound to come. Then she screamed as though she had seen a ghost and closed her eyes. Her mother stared sorrowfully at her. Maisoon sat down, her eyes glued to the pyramid ceiling.

"Do whatever it takes," her mother pleaded with the Pyramid Witch, "to bring my daughter back to the way she was before the criminals kidnapped her."

The witch stared knowingly at Maisoon and shook her head.

"I warned you," she told her mother

"I beg you, my lady."

The witch looked first at her, then checked Maisoon.

"The sorrow never leaves you, beautiful lady," she said. "Tell me, is the sorrow overwhelming?"

Maisoon avoided looking at her.

"Yes, it is," she replied.

"Are you waiting for the stars to fall?"

"Yes, every day and night. But they don't fall."

"Do you think your salvation lies with falling stars?"

"I know it does," she replied swiftly.

"Maisoon," the witch said hopefully, "our ancestors perfected magic and astronomy. They buried their secrets with them inside the pyramids. Every day, I try to crack the codes. Some of them I can understand, but others are impossible for me. However, there is advice to be had in astronomy. I've known it for some time."

She went over and held Maisoon's hand, while her mother watched fearfully.

"Your hand's like ice," she said, "as though you were born before the clouds. The ancients said that when you want a star to fall, you're not prepared for it. Wait till it brings itself close to you. Your current quest brings with it danger and fire. Only when it's close is there light and salvation."

Her mother shuddered and swallowed hard.

"My lady," she said, "I don't understand what you're saying."

The witch rubbed her hands over Maisoon's face.

"Maisoon understands," she said. "Maisoon only listens to herself. Remember that it's the heart that stimulates evil; in the searing heat of passionate love, many fiery specks come straight from hell itself. Maisoon must be patient so as not to set herself on fire. Loveliest of all women, with fire, your soul will never sigh. Do you know why? Because that soul of yours has inured itself to obedience and acquiescence. Ask it to show some defiance."

Maisoon's lips started moving, as though she were speaking fast. Her mother stared at her in alarm. The witch reached into her jar and gave her some herbs.

"Put them in hot water every day before she goes to sleep," she told her mother. "Make her drink it. She'll calm down."

"Will she go back to the way she was?" the mother asked pleadingly.

"That's impossible," the witch replied, "but she'll be calmer."

"Will she recognize us and stop screaming?" the mother again pleaded.

The witch focused her attention on Maisoon.

"Maisoon needs to recognize herself first," she replied with a smile. "Then she'll recognize you."

"My lady . . ." the mother tried to continue.

"The visit's over," the witch said, standing up. "Take your daughter and say farewell to the ancestors."

The herbs helped Maisoon. She started sleeping at night, not observing the stars and wanting to burn them with her own hands. She no longer opened her arms to the moon and prayed to fire to consume all hearts. She no longer traced a land with her fingers on the sun's surface, a land that was all light and had no scent to shock the eye and shake the heart like earthquakes. She no longer whispered things that no one else could understand. No longer did she pick up discarded bits of heart amid the wars of the powerful. She could no longer remember his arms and kisses, but she had never forgotten his despicable behavior and betrayal. She erased the entire past and convinced herself that she would not remember the future or the present either. Various hands had taken hold of her as though she were a wooden doll in children's hands. A father who loathed Ibn al-Mudabbir and prevented her being married to him, a man who wanted revenge and was married to her, while, among men, she was a piece of red meat dripping blood with no purpose or end. After a few days, she calmed down and gradually started eating. She acknowledged her mother and sister, and even spoke to her father. Her mother told her excitedly that she had been cured thanks to the Pyramid Witch who had learned from the magic of the ancients.

After several months, Maisoon resumed her usual world, although with no smile, a hollow heart, and lame soul. With her return, sorrow was inevitable, but she managed to bury it in a deep pit. Now it was anger and contempt that dominated her; Anas deserved to die. He had humiliated and belittled her. When his end would come in front of her, her soul could calm down and her heart could hope once more.

"When you're going to die," she had told him once when they were together beside the river, " they'll cut off your limbs and discard your guts."

At the time, she had been scared for him, but now the fulfillment of that prediction was the desired goal.

When several months had passed, her father allowed her to go out, surrounded by guards. Her husband kept sending her letters, but she never answered them. Instead of reading them, she often tore them into pieces.

Every night, she could not go to sleep without thinking and reminding herself. Ibn al-Mudabbir had made his choice, and it had not been her. Every night, she remembered the way her father had locked her up when she was just ten.

"You're disobedient," he told her firmly. "You have a touch of the devil in you. You don't do what you are told. Perhaps if you spend some time on your own, you'll come to realize your mistake."

When she was left on her own for a day, then two, then three, she did not realize it at the time, but she only became more annoyed. In the room's shadows she started seeing her own beautiful face, the beauty that would save her from everything. She saw her eyes gleaming in the dark, telling her that tomorrow would be better. She was more powerful than the Pyramid Witch. With a smile she started following her shadow and trusting it. She was alone, and so was Anas. They were both peculiar. Ibn al-Mudabbir had made his choice. After tempting and deceiving her, his hatred had defeated his love. She would not be forgiving. In the past, her father had slapped her if she and Ruqayya had done something wrong. Ruqayya would apologize or start crying, and her father's heart would soften, but Maisoon never apologized or burst into tears. Instead, she could remember the slap daily, angrily cursing the day she was born into that household and amid those people. She loved her father, and yet fear prevailed over love, just as her hatred of Anas prevailed over his love for her. Her father had forgiven him, but Anas would have to pay the price for his actions.

She would drink the witch's potion before going to sleep, then close her eyes. She could see her shadow around her, keeping her company in her loneliness. The day the stars fell was all for Maisoon's sake. In her dreams, Anas was burning, falling into a fiery pit. She watched him turn to dust, then eagerly gathered up the dust in her hand, blew on it, and scattered it all around till it covered her. She gave a happy smile. Not a day went by without her seeing Anas on fire in her dreams.

Ibn al-Mudabbir missed no opportunity in his attempts to see her. He sent his guards with letters, but she ignored them. When she went to visit her sister, escorted by both the governor's guards and those of Ibn al-Mudabbir, she discovered him inside the house. Her sister told her that he had insisted on seeing her and that neither she nor her husband could stand in the Tax Administrator's way.

She was still surrounded by guards when she entered the room. Ibn al-Mudabbir did not ask them to leave the two of them alone. As far as he was concerned, guards did not matter that much, or maybe it was that Ahmad's guards would not allow it.

"Maisoon, my heart's desire, more precious than my own eyes," Ibn al-Mudabbir said as soon as he set eyes on her, "if only you knew how much I suffer being far away from you. In former times, you had some sympathy for my feelings. Tell me, how are you?"

She looked all around her as she opened her eyes in a pleading look.

"I'm not well," she replied. "They've made me suffer, my lord."

"Who has?"

"The people who kidnapped me. They had no respect for women or the innocence of the judge's daughter."

He frowned. "I myself will tear them limb from limb," he said.

"I want to be there," she said sincerely. "I want to see them suffer."

He looked at her pale face and her languid eyes that seemed to recede into the bones of her face.

"What is it that makes you so sad?" he asked.

"That sinner," she replied forcefully. "He was married to me, my lord. I'm his wife now."

"No marriage can work that way. Don't worry yourself."

"No, only his death will give me any peace of mind."

"Judge's daughter, it seems that your hatred is more powerful than your love for Ibn al-Mudabbir. It looks as though Ibn al-Mudabbir's love no longer means anything to you, is that right?"

"I can't discuss love, my lord. I'm another man's wife. If it's possible, let's allow time to cure me."

"How can your cure resist time itself, judge's daughter?"

"Because, when confronted with my illness, time is weak. Sin is not forgiven and cannot be ignored. Did you but know, it still gnaws at the soul."

"I'll talk to your father."

"I beg you not to do that. Leave things as they are for now."

"You're mine, Maisoon."

"Maybe dust is my lot, not normal life."

"Don't say that."

"The world never gives us what we want. It's as though its primary purpose is to crush and manipulate the heart. My own heart has learned and accustomed itself to sorrow."

"What do you want from me?"

"Have you come here to ask for me, my lord?"

"I've come because I've longed for you for an entire year. Tell me that you still long for me."

She did not respond.

"Surely you're not toying with my heart," he told her firmly. "No woman would ever dare do such a thing."

"I have no heart, my lord. When sorrow's in charge, it makes seeing light difficult and enjoying life impossible. Forgive me if I've been waiting to be cured."

"I can help you be cured."

"There's no treatment for me. Leave me to fade with the seasons and wait for the stars to fall."

"Maisoon, I don't understand you. But I still want you to know that my love for you has not diminished. Seeing you like this has only increased my grief and does nothing to lessen my longing for you. Even if the judge, the governor, and the caliph were standing in front of me, I would still want to marry you."

She started to leave the room. "One man's just like a palmtree in his determination," she said slowly, "while another is like air in his flight."

"What are you talking about?"

"About you, my lord. I appreciate your feelings and respect. I wish you victory against all the traitors who surround you. But as long as I'm someone else's wife, it's not right for me to meet you and talk to you. I beg you to respect my situation."

With that, she left the room, followed by the guard.

What happened to Maisoon that year would need hundreds of pages and pens to write it all down. Every night, she would see him in her dreams. He would come full of passion and ask her to forgive him. He would tell her that his only wish was to be with her. When she lost all hope of having her dreams fulfilled, she sank into her own shadow and self, convinced by fancies and removed from reality. She roamed in empty circles, her entire soul rent by anger. She no longer heard or saw anything. For a while, she had been cut off from the world, and when she came back, she was still angrier, oppressed, and disquieted. His letters meant nothing. What he had done was a betrayal, something unforgiveable and irretrievable. Maybe he was having fun in Iraq; perhaps he had gotten married or purchased a slave-girl. No matter. But how could someone who had savored the wonder of Maisoon desire another woman? Was she not the most beautiful woman on earth? How could he abandon her like some scabby dog, when she was so incredibly dazzling? How could she let him enjoy his life after the crime he had committed against her?

She went to sleep, but then screamed during the night. Her mother rushed to her room and started stroking her chest.

"Wake up, my darling," she said. "It's a dream."

She opened her eyes and stared at the candle in her mother's hand.

"I can't see anything," she said.

"Maisoon," her mother said gently, "it's dark everywhere. Look at the candle."

"I can't see anything," Maisoon insisted. "Where's the candle?"

Her mother started reciting some Quranic verses.

"My daughter," she said gently, "you were getting better. What's happened to you?"

"Don't leave me in the dark," Maisoon replied in despair.

"Look at the candle in my hand," her mother said again.

"He has to die," she said again.

"My daughter . . ."

"He's sucked all the light out of my eyes. He promised me that I'd be smelling the scent of light. But then, mother, he sucked all the light from my eyes. Wrongdoers must be punished. People who run away have to pay the price . . ."

"Go to sleep, my daughter."

"But I can't see the light," she cried.

"Go to sleep, my daughter."

She closed her eyes. The next morning, she seemed calmer. She had decided to pay Ahmad ibn Tulun a visit.

She left on her own, walking with all the determination of a fighter and the resolve of someone sure of victory. If her father found out, he might well kill her. These days, how wonderful that would be—body flayed, and all hope incinerated! She waited by the gate of Authority Town until the chamberlain would allow her to meet Ahmad ibn Tulun. She was certain that he would permit it and that Ahmad ibn Tulun knew who she was.

She removed her face veil slowly and then fixed her gaze on the floor.

"My lord governor," she said, "forgive me for resorting to you when I'm aware of the extent of your responsibilities and tasks."

He looked at her for a while.

"Maisoon, daughter of Judge Yahya," he said, "what is it that you want? Why have you come here without your guardian?"

"Because what I want is personal," she pleaded. "I've never revealed it to anyone before, my lord."

He sat down in front of her. "Speak," he said.

She looked all around her. "One of your close confidants," she told him in a low voice, "has done me great wrong. I've come here to ask for revenge."

He looked at the guards, and they left the room. "What has this man done to you?" he asked.

"If I tell you," she asked hopefully, "I'd like you to listen to what I say. Every man has a heart containing both profligacy and piety. Everyone who seems loyal on the inside is a steadfast traitor. Those who appear powerful have the odor of weakness in them. This man kidnapped me, then forced me to have sex with him, even though he may say otherwise. He persuaded my father to marry me to him. Then he treated me badly and went away."

"All I know is that the Tax Administrator is eager to marry the judge's daughter. I know nothing about some other man harming her."

"Open wrongdoing is always less apparent than the kind that lurks behind a gloss of gentleness and mercy. Let me tell you what has happened to me. I hope that you'll be fair with me, even if my father is not. I seek justice. Anyone who's forced me needs to be punished."

"How am I supposed to know that he forced you? Why don't you take your complaint to the judge?"

"Because the judge is my father. If the Tax Administrator finds out the man's name, he'll kill him."

"So then you don't want him to be killed. You just want him to be punished."

"He's not fit for work under the orders of Amir Ahmad ibn Tulun."

"Listen, girl," he said. "Since when is the amir supposed to take women's opinions into account concerning his men? Go home! This conversation's a waste of time."

"I just wanted . . ."

"Go home!"

"My lord, I've heard that robbers got hold of Alexandria's taxes. I know who they are. In fact, I'm certain that this wrongdoer is one of them."

"The malice and insolence with you are unbecoming for a judge's daughter. The fact that you're not married to the Tax Administrator is a piece of salvation. Do you know the penalty for someone who makes false accusations? It's a very serious matter."

"Just listen to my complaint. That man did me wrong."

"Do you want him to come back to you?"

"No, I want him to divorce me and let me live in peace. Then, if you find that the way he's treated me is wrong, you can punish him. You're the scholar, my lord, not me."

"What punishment do you want for him, woman?"

"Whipping, or maybe prison. Most importantly, he shouldn't be working under your leadership. That's an honor for any man, and he doesn't deserve it."

"What about killing him?"

"Killing brings peace and serenity," she said after a pause.

"Do you think he was behind the theft of the taxes?"

"It's an idea, although some ideas are wrong. All I want you to do, my lord, is to look into the matter."

"I will look into it. Now go home."

"My lord, forgive me for speaking to you. I'm fully aware of how just and wise you are . . ."

"My duty is to protect the Egyptian people," he interrupted her.

"Egyptians pray for you every single day."

He was not sure whether she was as simple as a lamb or more cunning than he had imagined. Why had she come now, rather than at the outset when she knew her demand could not be met? Maybe she would be annoying the governor. She certainly realized that the governor would not carry out her wishes; her complaint was trivial and without evidence. But her complaint had revealed a lot. Maisoon had acted rashly and would do so again. She had mentioned Alexandria and her desire for a divorce. She had not mentioned his past or the story of his flight. He was well aware that she knew. Maisoon was saying that the heart always shakes on the point of making revelations and that Anas's closeness to the governor might well lead to serious problems. Maisoon was as mysterious as the stars in the dark of night. In a few days, Anas would come back, and everything would be clear. He would not think any more about the judge's daughter, but now he realized why Ibn al-Mudabbir had lost his mind.

Chapter 8

Anas returned to Egypt from his visit to Iraq, having learned a lot. He had thought that he had mastered the arts of war with sword and spear, and knew how to crack the codes of Greeks, Copts, and algebra. But what he did not appreciate was that the current wars were more vicious and difficult; the caliphal court was full of conspiracies. Some of the information that he brought back to Ahmad ibn Tulun was good, and some was worrying. All the way back he was thinking about his own future and that of Ahmad ibn Tulun. Now that future was one and the same. After the caliph had expressed his pleasure that Ahmad ibn Tulun had sent Anas to him with some letters, the caliph had been suspicious as to his intentions, as he was with everybody's, Arabs in particular, more so than non-Arabs. The best news that Anas brought was that Shuqair, the Postmaster, had lost the taxes; that was because of his major support for the caliph's mother. Once the caliph al-Mu'tamid had died, his mother no longer had either evil intent or authority; she was condemned and put in prison. That meant that Shuqair, the servant, had now lost all his authority. Now Ahmad ibn Tulun could get rid of him. Ibn al-Mudabbir was now more powerful, and his brother, Ibrahim, still had influence at the caliphal court. The worrying information was that news of the Alexandria taxes had now reached the caliph, and he had his doubts about Ahmad ibn Tulun. Anas did not know the best way to tell Ahmad ibn Tulun. He had made up his mind to go back to Maisoon, either the next day or the day after; he could not stand being away from her any longer. He stood in front of Ahmad and told him about Shuqair first. Ahmad listened.

"What do you think, Anas?" he asked.

"We have to get rid of Shuqair," he replied without thinking, "and then Ibn al-Mudabbir. You've read for yourself what he's written about you to the caliph. If we hadn't been watching the post, that would have been our fate."

"Death or prison," Ahmad interrupted him. "That was to be our fate."

"Yes, my lord."

"Do you believe, Anas, that, if I killed, imprisoned, or exiled Shuqair, the Postmaster, the caliph would defend him? I wonder, do you think the caliph will let me hit his men and stand there with arms folded? I'd do it if I could."

"Now he's lost his support with the deposition of Al-Mu'tazz Billah, the evil woman's son. Today the caliph . . ."

"You haven't learned caliphal ways yet. I was born in Iraq. I know and understand things. If I could kill him, I would have done it ages ago."

"Let me get rid of him," Anas said, looking at the ground, "without any bloodshed."

Ahmad stared at him for a while.

"Anas, son of the fisherman, is talking like Ibn al-Mudabbir. I didn't realize before that you were so crafty."

"Traitors always deserve to be punished. Only trickery can repel tyrants. I'll get rid of Shuqair for you."

"What about Ibn al-Mudabbir?"

Anas remained silent.

"The caliph has his doubts about me, doesn't he?" Ahmad went on. "He thinks I stole the Alexandria taxes."

"My lord," Anas replied in a muted tone, "the caliph's heard what you're doing in Egypt. He knows you're building a center for manufacture and have already constructed canals and bridges for farmers. He keeps wondering where the money has come from. Every dinar gets counted, and Ibn al-Mudabbir sends all the numbers to the caliph. One of the caliph's men confronted me and asked me the question straight to my face!"

"I wonder, who sowed such doubts in the caliph's mind?"

"I don't follow you, my lord."

"Continue with your report. When the man asked you straight about the money I had used, what did you say?"

"You'd sent me to Iraq even though I was only from a client people," Anas replied. "Maybe your vision was more acute than that of many other people. I managed to convince him that you and your men had nothing to do with the Alexandria taxes."

"How did you manage that, Egyptian?"

"I told him that you'd found treasure in the desert."

"Did he believe you?"

"Yes, but he requested that, from now on, you inform the caliph about any treasure that you find."

Ahmad smiled. "You've done well, just as I expected," he said. "The idea of doubt creeping into the caliph's mind may be connected to a visit that your wife paid to me."

Anas stared at him in shock.

"Before we talk about her," Ahmad continued, "tell me about Ibn ash-Shaikh, the Governor of Syria. What do the caliph's men in Iraq have to say about him?"

"They're worried about his treachery and expect him to declare independent rule. They anticipate that he's going to hold back this year's tax revenue."

Ahmad smiled again. "God is opening a door for every independent thinker," he said. "With pure intentions come suns that we can only see through sacrifice."

"My lord . . ."

"An army for Egypt, that's what's needed."

"My lord Abu al-Abbas Ahmad ibn Tulun, what's my wife done?"

"Anas, when a woman is deceitful, she has to be sent away, or else her deceit flies all over the place. That woman's deceit is more relentless and dangerous than the combined armies of the caliph. You'll have to control your wife, or else I'll have to accuse her as a traitor. This time, I'll leave her to you, but giving her any kind of discretion is a danger to both you and me. If the caliph splits my head open and stamps on my corpse, you won't get any mercy for her from me. You can deal with her as long as she keeps her tongue inside her mouth. If she shows the slightest inclination in Ibn al-Mudabbir's direction, I'll kill her. I won't stand for traitorous conduct. I want you to divorce her, Anas."

"I'm not going to do that," Anas replied without thinking.

"She'll open fire on Egypt, but not on me. Ibn al-Mudabbir will know everything. If you go back to her, he'll know who you are, even if she almost . . ."

"That fire has to happen. I'll keep her under control."

When he left Ahmad's place, he wandered around in confusion, as though he were somebody else he did not know. Maisoon had loved him and had asked him to take her far away. She had wanted him to stay. She had not replied to any of his letters. He had thought she was scared, but still remaining true. It was impossible for a woman's heart to turn in a month or year. He had gone to Iraq, dearly hoping to spend his life with her once he had returned. He had been planning how to win her back. They had been apart for a long time, and Ibn al-Mudabbir had never left Egypt. Now what? Had he returned to Egypt only to hear what Ahmad had just told him?! He hurried to see his men who were working with Shuqair, the Postmaster, and asked them to search for any letter sent to the caliph by a woman. He told them to ask questions, remember things, and do some spying. Then the guard who never left his wife's side came to see him, the one who used to deliver letters to her, Ahmad's guard who brought him information about her all the time. When he came that day, he seemed hesitant.

"My lord," the guard told him, "I have kept from you the fact that she was ill; she never left the palace, and then she recovered. Forgive me. I only found out about her illness a month ago. It didn't last long, and I knew nothing about it because, needless to say, I didn't go into her room. But I gathered from the household staff that it wasn't serious."

"She recovered?"

"Yes, she recovered. Then she went to visit her sister, and the Tax Administrator was there."

The guard gave him full details about what had happened, and Anas listened with a stony glare and eyes aflame.

"How was she?" Anas asked once the guard had finished his account.

"I've told you everything."

Her words echoed in the depths of his soul. She had told Ibn al-Mudabbir that she was being oppressed and suffering cruel treatment at the hands of her husband.

"Why didn't you stop him?" Anas asked. "Did she know he was coming? Did she arrange the meeting? Did she want to see him?"

The guard looked confused.

"I've no idea, my lord," he replied. "God alone knows the workings of hearts. She was neither dismissive nor welcoming; somewhere between the two."

"Somewhere between the two," he repeated.

He sat where he was, picturing his own father. It was a gloomy day. Where had all the stars gone? When they disappeared, the waves would pick up, gather strength, reach all the way to the edge of the house, and crash against the balcony. Did that wave actually crash against the balcony or did it just seem like it? Did he hear his father battling the waves or was he riding peacefully with them? Why are realities mingled at night, and why does memory follow fugitive stars?

"Father!" he screamed.

What father doesn't hear his son's screams? What father is ever treacherous and deceitful? What father longs for the hangman and submits to him?

Anas feared the constant flow of breaking waves. Whenever he saw them curving over on themselves and burying a chunk of darkness in their folds, he was frightened as though they marked the end of life. At the end of life, the surprise happens. Perhaps his father never intended to kill himself by drowning; maybe he just wanted to plunge into the breaking waves and discover the secret of darkness. Darkness comes to an end at the porches of eternity, and pain comes to an end when darkness does. If the stars themselves have fled from the darkness of this night, then how could he be blaming his father? Was he more powerful, loftier, brighter than the stars? Anas took the plunge, remembering, plunging in despair as he searched for his father's body in the pitch-black waves. But each spray tossed him higher, as though refusing to acknowledge his desperate and dangerous search. All someone like him could do was to float on the surface, never plunging or escaping.

As he covered his ears, his father's scream reached all the way to the depths.

He had read and transcribed; he had spoken like Arabs and non-Arabs, and yet he had been deceived regarding his own wife. He had observed her with all the passion of lovers and the naivete of tiny fish close to the shore, exploring, darting, and waiting for light. In her he had detected a certain amount of stubbornness and arrogance, maybe some vanity as well; in fact, a lot of it. She might have been so bound up with herself that she did not notice anyone else. He was aware of all that, and yet he had admired her blazing feelings, her loyalty to him—like a fisherman's net, and her heart whose apertures were as wide as the very heavens. When he had left, perhaps love had seeped out of her heart. Perhaps she had thought about Ibn al-Mudabbir's wealth and power. She thought that she had given herself to the fisherman's son who had now fled, and now she had to wait a year or two while the Tax Administrator was there, ready and waiting for her arms. What a traitor! If it was the Tax Administrator she wanted, why had she gone to see Ahmad ibn Tulun? Why such enmity and malice, as though she was out to kill and humiliate him? Did she regret melting in his arms and whispering words of love? Was she sorry to have given her feelings free rein and not protected herself from his kisses? Did she regret the fact that he had been the first man in her life, and not Ibn al-Mudabbir? Was it revenge she wanted, because he had been bold enough to marry her, because he had had to leave her unwillingly, or because he had not listened to her, left his entire life behind, and gone into exile with her? His mind could not cope with it.

As a boy, he had thought he knew more than his peers. He could read and copy; he would discover new words and pieces of wisdom. Did not Plato state that all men were poets when it came to love? Did he not say as well that love was a kind of madness, but it was also a gift from the heavens? He had said many things. Every time Anas had read something, he had imagined the day when he would fall in love. While his friends were playing and kissing slave-girls and pretty maids, he was dreaming, realizing that what he wanted was not a body in his arms on which to expend his energy, but rather a soul that would swim in the waves around him, someone who knew how to embrace the waves, how to follow them sometimes, and how to withdraw when needed. He was asking for a lot. His brother Ali had scolded him.

"You're just like a monk, brother," he said. "I've had sex with five girls, but you haven't even with one."

He had not bothered about his brother's words. He had no wish to be satisfied with just half of paradise, half-pleasure, half-rapture, half-ease, and half-life. When Maisoon had come to him, she had smothered him with her affection out of a desire to protect him. She had shuddered in his arms, and together they had discovered a life fulfilled. They had learned together, achieved happiness together, and used exceptional power to swim together in the tempestuous sea. There had been neither hesitation nor fear. But now what?

The police arrived at the judge's house to demand that Maisoon appear before the Police Chief.

"Maisoon, the judge's daughter?" the judge asked, incredulous. "How dare you force her to go to the prison?"

"Orders from the Police Chief, my lord. Excuse us. No one will touch her."

"Then I'm coming with her."

"Impossible, my lord."

"You're not going to tell the judge what's possible and what's not."

"I'm worried about the Police Chief's anger, my lord."

"He's not going to do you any harm."

"I'm afraid that he'll do it to you."

When they reached the Authority Town precinct, the gate to the Police Chief's house was wide open. It had two sections: one for men, the other for women. Senior police officers gathered there, the Deputy Police Chief among them.

The judge went in with his daughter, and they waited for an hour or more. The judge was getting nervous, but his daughter was calm until Anas came in.

"Anas . . ."

"Welcome, Judge Yahya ibn Isa," he said curtly.

She stared at him as though she were not seeing him, but he did not look at her.

"What are you doing here?" the judge asked.

"I'm arresting your daughter so she can be put in prison. That's her natural place."

"What's this drivel you're spouting?"

"It's not drivel. Your daughter's interfered in things that don't concern her. She's leveled false accusations against her husband. Your daughter's been meeting the Tax Administrator, Judge."

The judge opened his eyes wide in shock.

"Ahmad ibn Tulun might prefer to kill her immediately. Is that what you want?"

"Yes," the judge replied decisively.

Anas asked him to sit down. He then looked at his wife for the first time in a year. Their eyes met. In his was a mixture of sorrow and anger; in hers, frigidity and indifference.

"Come with me," he told her as he headed for the door.

She followed him with a slight smile on her lips. He went into another room. She followed him, and he shut the door. He had vowed to himself that she was not going to win and he was not going to lose his authority. If it was her idea to defeat him, he still knew a few things about Maisoon. He calmly read back to her everything she had told Ibn al-Mudabbir.

"This husband of yours who's forced you and made you suffer. How is he? Has the Tax Administrator managed to rescue you from him?"

She was out to annoy him. "If only he had," she said.

"But he didn't. I agree with your father that you need to die. That'll be a mercy for all of us, but for you as well."

"If I'd realized that visiting the governor would make you so angry, I'd have done it ages ago."

"Aren't you afraid of the consequences?"

"Consequences don't scare me. When the final pain evaporates, all that's left is apathy. My heart's a barren desert."

"Killing brings relief, Maisoon," he said as though he had not heard her. "I've sworn to make sure that, as long as I'm alive, your heart's going to roam through hell with no peace."

"What if you die?"

"Did you ask Ibn al-Mudabbir to kill me when you met him secretly, my wife?" He suddenly grabbed her hand. "How sad it makes me to part two hearts that loved each other. But mine's not going to see you ever again."

Now she wanted to crush him, to see him suffer, just as he had once robbed her of her mind. "Does Ahmad ibn Tulun appoint a murderer as Deputy Police Chief?" she asked. "I wonder who's better, him or Ibn al-Mudabbir?"

"Any woman who meets a man when she's married to someone else is unfaithful."

"I told you I knew everything. Don't accuse me of dishonorable behavior when you know full well that I'm free. I'm not a slave-girl like the ones your brother and you have sex with."

He drew his sword. "Be warned. Every word out of your mouth from now on will get you a hundred lashes."

"You've become powerful now. What is it you want? Put me in prison or divorce me. Do what you like. I'm not afraid."

"Divorce you? That's impossible. Prison, whipping, and beating are all still possible. But all that's not enough."

"So kill me, then."

Suddenly he put his hands around her face. "Maisoon," he told her, "you're going to remain an unreachable hope for Ibn al-Mudabbir until he dies. If your tongue spouts evil things, then it'll have to be cut out as well. Prison's always there, and so is my own house. I'm going to put you in a room there, and then, as year follows year, forget about you. Eventually, the day will come when you'll emerge with your beauty long since gone and find my wife and children waiting to welcome you. Your heart will crack and break into two pieces or more. I shall witness it all myself. There was a time when I thought I hated Ibn al-Mudabbir, but when the unfaithfulness comes from someone you love, it pierces your heart and takes away your sanity. Don't ask me for mercy, not today or tomorrow."

"Assuming that my hatred for you is as great as the number of drops of water in the river, fisherman's son," she asked quietly, "why do you think that the sight of your wife and children is going to upset me?!"

"Then perhaps being far removed from Ibn al-Mudabbir will upset you." he said, "That, and seeing him defeated before your very eyes. Will that upset you, Maisoon?"

"Yes, it will," she replied, her eyes fixed on his.

He raised his hand to hit her, but then he stopped. "You're trying to provoke me, aren't you?" he said. "You want to annoy me so I'll hit you and yell and scream. Do you know why?"

She looked at him, but said nothing.

"I know why, most beautiful girl in all Egypt," he said. "It's because you can't accept the idea of a man being able to stay away from you for any reason. You can't imagine a man leaving you for a month or two. You've crushed your arrogant self for no purpose. You weren't interested in my letters or my words. I swear to you, judge's daughter, that, for the rest of my life, my sole purpose will be to crush your arrogant self. As far as I'm concerned, you're nothing. Ever since you met the Tax Administrator, you're nothing. You're just like a fruit fly, annoying, but not piercing or destroying the fruit."

He grabbed her by the shoulder till she looked at him.

"I neither love you nor hate you," he said. "I don't want you. You need to be re-trained. And you'll be the first witness to the Tax Administrator's downfall."

He headed for the door. "Infidelity has to be punished," he said. "Eighty lashes over four days. That's not a lot. The police will supervise the whipping."

"I know that you stole the taxes," she said suddenly. "I thought of sending a message to the caliph, but I was afraid he'd kill you, not because I was worried about you, but because I wanted you to stay alive so you could suffer. You deserve that."

He stared at her for a moment, then left.

He thought that the sight of her might stir some old worries and maybe even some affection, but she was like the sight of a piece of solid rock, neither splitting nor tumbling in storm flood. When their eyes met, there was no trace of love, only fury and loathing. How could a single year change two hearts so much? How could the heart have any confidence when it turned over as fast as the governors of Egypt? Now things were much better: he had shown no pity and no mercy in dealing with her. He had not made up his mind yet as to whether he would whip her. He had read a lot and learned things. In spite of his limited experience with women, he had learned that she had been out to stir him up and make him angry and aggressive. He realized that she had wanted him to treat her as a powerful adversary. That was not going to happen. She was just a woman, one with no sense, who had been destroyed by sheer vanity. She had not kept the pact.

"It's not right to whip your wife, the judge's daughter," the judge said in alarm. "Anas, you remember what our relationship was, don't you?"

"She's been disloyal," Anas replied languidly. "If I don't whip her, the deputy governor is going to kill her. She has to be punished."

"There are still principles and rules, Anas," the judge said.

"She can ask me for forgiveness," Anas responded without looking at him. "She can promise not to leave my house and not talk to anyone. I'll think about it."

"She'll do it," the judge said firmly.

He then went to see his daughter and scolded her, turning his hands up to show that he had no idea why she had behaved the way she had and not understanding what curse had been afflicted on him by her being born.

"I want you to stay here," he made clear to her. "Don't go out, or else you'll die. Maisoon, ask him to forgive you in front of me. It's not right to whip the judge's daughter. The pain you've already caused me is enough."

Her stony eyes looked far away at nothing. "That's not going to happen," she replied. "He can whip me a thousand times or kill me. I'm never going to ask that bookseller to forgive me."

"And what if your father asked you? Would you obey me?"

"Father . . ."

"I want you to realize how much I've suffered ever since you had that meeting with Ibn al-Mudabbir, or actually, ever since your mother gave me the good news of your birth."

For a moment, she said nothing.

"I'll do whatever you order me to do," she said.

He took her by the hand and went back with her to appear in front of Anas. Anas leaned his back against the wall, waiting for her to ask for forgiveness.

"I've done wrong," she said, not looking at him. "Forgive me. I swear that there was no advanced planning to my conversation with Ibn al-Mudabbir. Actually, he surprised me."

"Anas," the judge said gently, "she's your wife."

"Kiss his hand in front of me," the judge told her, pinching her shoulder. "Say you were wrong. Come on . . ."

She stayed silent, and her father pushed her forward. Anas was standing there, looking at her without saying a word. She moved closer, bent down, grabbed his hand, pursing her lips in anger, and kissed it.

"I did wrong," she said.

She was about to stand up.

"Keep his hand on your forehead," her father told her, "till he allows you to stand up again. What grief you bring me! You haven't learned anything."

Swallowing hard, she kept his hand on her forehead.

"That's enough," she muttered. "Tell me that you forgive me."

"No," he replied, withdrawing his hand.

He told her to stand up.

"I returned from Iraq two days ago," he told her father. "My plan was to visit you and take back my wife."

"Nothing's happened," the judge told him. "She's here now, compliant with your wishes. If she annoys you, just let me know."

"She's not going to annoy me," he replied forcefully. "We're going to start all over again, now that she's regretted her actions. Don't worry yourself."

The judge paused for a moment.

"I'm worried about you, Anas," he went on hesitantly. "My son, you're starting a fire. Once Ibn al-Mudabbir finds out . . ."

"Don't worry about me or her. Ibn al-Mudabbir's end is in my hands. Just remember that, whether today or tomorrow."

The judge was somewhat relieved as he left because he had managed to get rid of Maisoon. Whatever she did from then on was not his responsibility.

She lifted her head toward Anas, and they both stared at each other.

"I have no regrets in my heart," she told him in a muted tone. "Everything I said was for my father's sake."

"I know," he replied tersely.

"Do whatever you like with me. It doesn't matter."

"I'm not going to do what you expect. Punishment can take a variety of forms and types. Each one has a different smell to it. There's a whole lot of life left . . ."

"Whenever I come into your room," he told her forcibly, "you're to get up, come over to me, and kiss my hand, the way you've done today. I want you to work with the servant-girls in the kitchen and learn the things that you didn't learn in your father's house. I'll be the one to decide on your working hours."

Before she could say anything, he told one of the servant-girls to take her to her room.

Today Anas did not send back his friend's gift, something he usually did every day. His friend kept sending him beautiful slave-girls, and he would send them back. But today, he did not do that. When the girl knocked on his door, he opened it and looked at her. She was of Maisoon's age, maybe even prettier. Why not? She had a svelte figure, her large eyes were decorated with kohl, which showed off their whiteness, and her eyelids were soft and attractive. When she gave him a smile, he seized her hand and took her into his room. She was finely dressed and well perfumed. She was an accomplished lover and knew it all by heart. She gave him more than she took and did not forget to extol him and his gentle sweetness. He looked at her, lying by his side, and closed his eyes. What had just happened? He had had sex with a woman, and she had given of herself with passion and skill, maybe even more than Maisoon. She was certainly prettier than Maisoon. All those years past, he had not understood the world; he had not been satisfied with just one woman. Once he had uncovered her unfaithfulness, he had been angry and sad. If only he had realized that the body was just body, and not the soul, and that fish go on their way without mingling with other fish and only befriend the enemy. Had he realized that, he could have saved himself. Maisoon could go to hell.

As day followed day, he found himself getting bored with the slave-girl and sending her back to his friend with thanks. He would give the girl the money she wanted.

"I understand you, Anas," his friend said with a smile. "You don't want to pay for her. You want someone who wants you for yourself. Come with me."

The next day, Anas discovered a different side of the city. The two men visited a woman, probably in her thirties. She was a widow who had been married to a merchant in Fustat who had died. She had been married to him when she was thirteen and he was in his fifties. She was in her twenties when he had died. She had found herself alone and did not want to be married again. She had seen Anas once or twice and had liked him; in him, she found what she was looking for. At first, she did not satisfy him, and he did not try to have sex with her. He preferred relationships in which he had no need to explain himself or to waste any effort on words or satisfying the heart. He just wanted to satisfy the body to the point of satiation. Then he could forget about Maisoon. That is what he needed to do. One, two, three, four women, trying a different one every day. If one pleased him, he might keep her perhaps for a week, but no more than that. He would leave her with no promise of return. One of them once asked him, while clasping his back, if she could stay with him.

"I don't want anything," she told him. "I just want to stay with you."

"No," he had told her firmly.

With that, she left. The body was sated and irrigated. Heart and soul no longer felt any inclination to ask or impose conditions.

After a while, he would be married to a daughter of one of the generals. The father would need to choose, not the daughter. When the heart's owner cannot be trusted, it needs to be plucked from its roots, even though that may result in death. Now his manuscripts became his real friends once again, and it was with them that he spent his hours of sorrow and weakness.

Maisoon's life in the house of the Deputy Police Chief, her husband, in Fustat was not what she was expecting. She expected him to whip her, beat her, or have sex with her against her will. But he did not do any of that. In the Deputy Police Chief's house within Authority Town there was one wing for women and another for men. Between the two, there was a garden with date palms and grapevines. Four senior police officials lived there, Anas being one of them. They each lived with their wives, children, and slave-girls. Maisoon's own room was modest, but she was allowed to stroll around the garden and to get to know the other wives. From the very first day, she attracted the attention of all the other women. They all said that they had never seen anyone so beautiful, and they all knew the story of her encounter with Ibn al-Mudabbir. Such was their curiosity that they used to line up in front of her room out of a desire to talk to her and hear what had happened. Never in her life had she had so much attention. All that separated her from her husband was a garden, no more. Even so, he made no attempt to see her even once in two months. She did not bother about him or expect him to come. If he was having sex with slave-girls, that was to be expected; it did not upset or shock her. For some reason, she was not miserable, either because she had made her way into his heart and crushed it, or else because she was in his house and he was all around her even if she did not see him. She did not know for sure. It was her hope that the primary reason was to soothe her troubled heart and to make sure she did not lose her mind again. She convinced herself that sorrow was capable of changing all feelings; that much was certain. Her presence in this house made her happy because all the women acknowledged her beauty and were jealous of her for it.

"How come your hair is so shiny?" one of them asked her.

"Why is your skin so soft?" another one asked.

"Where did you get such a figure, Maisoon? How long did you have to wait patiently till your hair reached your thighs? What happens to men when they set eyes on you? Do they lose their minds? Maisoon . . ."

As the questions spread all around her and their interest increased, she was able to bathe in the sweet waters of illusion and certainty. Sometimes at night, she would remember moments between the two of them that she had thought would last: when he would throw her shivering into the river, then pick her up with her almost throttling him. He would be on the point of throwing her in again, and she would beg him not to do it. She would remember moments of gentle discord, of tenderness accompanied by provocation. When she went into the garden at night and looked up at the stars, she would have the troubling sense that her current satisfaction might result from her being there with him. She had not lied to Ibn al-Mudabbir. Anas had forced her. Maybe he had not forced her to have sex with him, but he had forced her to love him. He might not have tortured her with lashes, but he had gnawed her guts and sunk his teeth in her liver.

She started hoping to bump into him in the garden, but that did not happen. She was afraid of losing her mind. She had been tailed by her shadow and darkness before; these days, the darkness accompanied her at night, even when the lamps were lit. There were other times when she did not want to see him. She would pray to God not to see him, walking quickly to avoid stopping if she happened to see him, as though the very sight of him were a heavy burden.

From the very first day in the house inside Authority Town, she conspired against him. She did not do any work in the kitchen. Instead, she stayed there all day, talking about her own beauty and ordering those around her to do the cooking. They would obey without any argument. She would tell everyone that she was cooking; sometimes she would ask Mughith's wife to taste her delicious food, and the woman would thank her. After a while, Maisoon's husband asked her to come to his room. Now fear blended with a passion that had previously overwhelmed him and mingled with the knowledge that she had deceived him once or twice.

When she went in, he was seated. He looked at her for a moment, then told her to sit down. With a defiant look she sat down. This time, she stared at his face for some time. What was his heart concealing, she wondered, and how would he be surprising her this time?

"You're to look at the floor, Maisoon," he told her, "not at my eyes. Don't you dare look at me."

She opened her mouth.

"What lies are you telling?" he asked her forcefully. "You can deceive servant-girls, but not forever. I told you to work, not to boss them around."

"They know who I am," she replied firmly. "They don't let me do any work."

He looked at the papers in front of him. "Do you know how to write?" he asked.

"What kind of question is that?" she replied angrily. "I'm the judge's daughter."

He stood up, grabbed her hand, and looked at her. She had no idea what had happened. Her eyes teared up without any warning.

"You're going to write and copy books," he told her, holding her hand hard. "Maybe then, you'll see and understand. In my room. You'll come here in the morning and stay till evening. I myself will look at what you've been doing every day."

She suppressed a smile and said nothing. He ordered her to leave. When she left and went back to her room, her body was pulsating with life, as though she had just fought a wild beast and scored a victory.

She would come to the room every day, early in the morning, and begin copying slowly. At first, he scolded her and told her to produce more so he would not have to whip her. He seemed impatient, and never even looked at her. She started working seriously, reading and writing for her own sake to cope with her loneliness. Sometimes he would come back to the room, not even look at her, and tell her to leave. Then he would look at what she had done. At other times, he would come back late, and she would know; she could smell a woman's scent on him. A week went by without him paying her any attention, as though she were a folded piece of paper or a dry inkwell. She was even more furious than she had been the previous year. What was odd was that he gave her gold and silk and left everything she dreamed of in her room. Then, it seemed, he went away. When she went back to her room, she would scream sometimes, bury her head in the pillow, and rip up some cloth. She had no idea what was causing the pain: was it the soul or the heart, the spirit or the mind? She decided to stop going to his room and copying books. What would he do? Beat her? That would be better than simply obeying his every instruction. When she was late in the morning, he sent two servant-girls. She told them that she was not going to come. The two girls told her bashfully that the Deputy Police Chief had told them to drag her there if she refused to come willingly. She fully understood his game and his plan. She went to his room and entered without saying a word.

"I shall want to see what you've copied today," he told her as he left the room.

That day, she did not copy a single word.

Chapter 9

ihihihihihihihihihihihihihih

Ahmad ibn Tulun had never told anyone the dream he had had as a boy, but he asked for a meeting with the Pyramid Witch. Men told him that she did not speak Arabic, so he took Anas with him. When they reached the Great Pyramid, Ahmad stood there fearfully for a few moments.

"I want you to translate for me," he told Anas. "I need to know everything."

"No one here knows everything, my lord," Anas replied with a smile. "Even us. Knowledge is stingy, like justice and treasure."

Ahmad lowered his head as he went inside the pyramid, with Anas behind him. He sat down to wait for the witch to look at him. She was busy sorting a whole pile of papers, then cleaning a wooden coffin. It took half an hour for her to notice him.

"You're late," she said clearly as soon as she saw him.

Ahmad looked at Anas, and he translated.

"Did we have an appointment, woman?" he asked in confusion.

"I was expecting you the day the stars fell," she replied. "You've come to ask about the magic of the ancients and the treasure."

He opened his mouth.

"Arabs say that the magic of the ancients is buried inside their tombs," she went on. "We've no idea what they made with the stars, and we don't understand bird language. I'm telling you that we do wrong to magic. We extol it when it's the work of human beings. But inadequate knowledge demands justification."

"Do you mean that the ancients didn't practice magic? Doesn't the Quran refer to Pharaoh's magic?"

"I don't explain my words, Ahmad."

"How do you know my name?"

"I've been expecting you."

"Why?"

"As I've told you, I was expecting you the day the stars fell. You've come here to ask because the dream disturbs you. You don't know if it's true or a kind of madness."

"How did you know about the dream? You're a witch, that's for sure."

"Or maybe I know things that you don't and have read things that you haven't. So certain symbols that you don't understand are clear to me. The difference between a witch and a governor, my lord, is that the witch understands symbols and is good at interpreting words, while the governor can only read what he knows. If you've come to ask about magic, then wait for the dream to be interpreted and the past to be understood. But if you've come here to ask about the treasure, then you've been lying to the caliph. What the caliphs regard as treasure is actually the resources of this country. Amid the grains of sand, there are many stories and thousands of treasures. You will find lost cities, long-dead kings, dreams like yours, and more. This is the king's coffin. Do you know what he said?"

"Tell me," Ahmad replied quickly, "what did he say?"

"He said: 'Ahmad, I am Surid the King. I built the pyramids and completed the project in six years. Anyone who comes after me and claims to be like me, let him destroy them in six hundred years, even if he's learned that destruction is easier than construction.'"

Ahmad was apprehensive and said nothing.

"Epochs disappear," the witch went on, "but the pyramids don't. What is it that distinguishes those kings from others? Why has their heritage been cut off for a thousand years or more? Explain it to me. You need to understand, Ahmad. Don't give up. Do you love Egypt? It's a dream and prize, a reward from God."

She bent down and picked up some sand. "Have you dug in this earth before?" she asked him. "Every time you dig, you find a city, and each one has its story to tell. In every city, there's a fighter, a lover, a hermit, and a lunatic. You're all those things. Don't despair. Cities don't vanish. On the contrary, they remain as stories in the folds of life, reminding us of what was. With knowledge, the magic becomes clear. The stars shine with an uninterrupted brightness. Whenever you dig deeper into the earth, you find what you need. Make your passion pure and your purpose unwavering."

Ahmad shuddered, maybe for the very first time.

"And you," he said, "who are you?"

"Ahmad, make your passion pure and your purpose unwavering. Remember . . ."

"What do you want me to remember?"

"Sorrow is for the powerful. Only those with stolid hearts can tolerate heavy burdens. When your heart has been weighed down by distress, I know that you've risen above it as though you were one of the ancient kings."

"My lady . . ."

"They're with you."

"They're all helping me."

"Because you're a passionate soul who's come after a thousand years or more. This soil, O king, gives to those who search; it gives to people who aren't satisfied with the glint of gold. Gold disappears. If you don't recognize its true essence, it has no value. Ponder, O king, and try to understand."

"What burden and what concern is this? I'm not a king."

"The concern is bound to come. When it does, seek help from a monk or shaikh. Don't come to see me again. I've told you everything I have to say. Farewell!"

"I wish you safety and good health!"

"There can be no safety with greatness and no evanescence with stories and legends."

Ahmad read what the Arabs had written about the ancient Egyptians. It was Surid who had constructed the Great Pyramid. Ahmad would be the one who would try to understand the bird language. The witch had to know it, or else she would not have known about his dream. Her words were saddening and predicted a heavy burden yet to come, but it was inevitable. Whom would he kill, and who would be defeated? The Arabs had conquered Egypt some two hundred years ago. Then what? Islam arrived, and the Arabs and Fustat . . . Sometimes there would be an Ibn al-Mudabbir, and at others, an Ahmad ibn Tulun. The Abbasid Empire's limbs stretched far and wide, and power had become more difficult. Then the fisherman's son had arrived, seeking vengeance for his father. He wanted to shake a planet, extinguish a star, and light another one. He had arrived as though he owned Moses's rod and Solomon's power, as though he would drown the tyrant and treat all humans as equals. His dream was like Ahmad's, but it was even more implausible and painful.

The first spoils of war belonged to Ibn al-Mudabbir, as did the first victory. He had killed Bayakbak, Governor of Egypt and husband of Ahmad ibn Tulun's mother, the man who had appointed Ahmad as his deputy in Egypt. It seemed a new governor would be taking over Egypt; and he would not be retaining Ibn Tulun as deputy governor. Ibn Tulun did not lose his composure. He sent Anas with some men to Baghdad with letters to his friends and one to the caliph in which he explained everything. More important still, he sent Anas with another important letter informing him of Ibn ash-Shaikh's maneuvers in Syria. He provided the caliph with all the early phases in the revolt that would involve the whole of Syria. Ibn ash-Shaikh was moving closer to Damascus and would take it over for himself. If he did that and then refused to pay taxes, he would be in revolt against the caliph. That was far more important than all the trivial things Ibn al-Mudabbir was speaking about, and also more important than Maisoon, the judge's daughter, and the utterly infatuated Ibn al-Mudabbir.

Ahmad's guess proved right. Ibn ash-Shaikh refused to pay taxes. When Al-Mu'tamid succeeded to the caliphate, Ibn ash-Shaikh refused to pray for him in mosques. Indeed, he went so far as to cut off the route by which all Egyptian taxes made their way to Baghdad and commandeered the entire Egyptian tax revenue. Ahmad gave a satisfied smile. He now sent another letter, this time to the caliph Al-Mu'tamid, asking for something else. In the letter he stated that his first and last duty was to protect the caliph and the tax revenue. He would be able to deal with

Ibn ash-Shaikh in Syria; he had been trained as a soldier since childhood and had fought for the caliphate many times in Baghdad and Samarra. However, he did not have an army with which to fight. If the caliph allowed him to purchase men and create a force to oppose Ibn ash-Shaikh in Syria, that force would be in the service of the caliph and the caliphate. Moreover, if the caliph wanted to help Ahmad, then Ibn al-Mudabbir would have to release the funds so that he could purchase the men and create his army.

It was by far the most significant letter in Ahmad's life. He exaggerated the extent of the danger that Ibn ash-Shaikh posed to the caliphate and the way he set out to convince the caliph that such a precedent as this would have a lasting negative impact on the caliphate's prestige. He waited for a response.

After several weeks, the caliph assigned the governorship of Egypt and its ports to Yarjukh, a decision that Ibn al-Mudabbir resented. Yarjukh was the father of Ahmad's wife, Lady Khatun, whom he had left in Iraq along with his son as hostages to the caliph. No sooner had Yarjukh taken charge of Egypt than he sent Ahmad a letter. Shuqair read it in a clipped tone before handing it to Ahmad.

"From you to you," he said.

Yarjukh made Ahmad Governor of Egypt and added Alexandria to the appointment. Fate seemed to be backing Ahmad, and Ibn al-Mudabbir's intrigues could not dislodge him. In fact, Ahmad was to marry Maisoon to one of his own men instead of Ibn al-Mudabbir. Now the conflict was out in the open. Anas kept track of the letters between the caliph and his spies in Egypt and between the caliph and Ibn al-Mudabbir. Ibn al-Mudabbir talked about Anas and Maisoon; in a letter, Anas told the caliph what had happened. The caliph showed no sympathy for either Anas or Ibn al-Mudabbir. His primary concern was Ibn ash-Shaikh, who had taken control of Damascus and had refused to pray for the caliph.

After several days, a sealed letter arrived from the caliph and was delivered to both Ahmad and Ibn al-Mudabbir on the same day. Ahmad was as thrilled as he had ever been; he forgot all about losing his wife and son, everything except for his dream and his visit to the Pyramid Witch. Ibn al-Mudabbir, on the other hand, was very disappointed, painfully acknowledging that fate was with Ahmad today, but certainly would not be tomorrow. The letter arrived some three months after Anas's trip to Baghdad. The caliph instructed Ibn al-Mudabbir to release the funds to Ahmad so he could purchase men and create an army as quickly as possible to stand up to Ibn ash-Shaikh in Syria.

Ibn al-Mudabbir's enmity—he being the most important man in Egypt—had to be directed at the fisherman's son, who was both worthless and powerless. The new governor had arrived, bent on change and on establishing his presence. He had resorted to the Egyptian people, but why? He scoffed as he asked the question. What did Egyptians have? They did not even know their own ancient history. They moved from one savagery to another, from one treacherous ruler to another who only erased and destroyed. They had lived through eras of martyrs and lunatics. They no longer had the will to resist or rebel. They would walk over treasures with a patient insouciance, neither wanting the treasure nor appreciating its value. All they wanted was a loaf of bread, albeit dipped in broth; that would last them for an age or more. Ibn al-Mudabbir knew and understood them, and today he knew about the fisherman's son as well. Why had he kidnapped Maisoon? What was he planning to do? He understood it all, and now the enmity was out in the open. Anas had defied the Tax Administrator, so he would have to be punished. But Ahmad was still a roadblock, erecting a wall to keep him away from the fisherman's son. He would have to get rid of both Ahmad and the fisherman's son.

Anas tossed in his sleep and leaped out of bed. He had not punished her yet, neither whipping nor crushing her. But in her eyes, he could see that she wanted it; she was out to prick his authority and composure, to get to his liver and eat it. But he was not humiliating her or teaching her a lesson. What had he done except threaten her? What kind of man was he? His feelings were a mixture of a desire to burn her now as he pictured her meeting with Ibn al-Mudabbir, and his longing for her as his wife. He was having sex with one woman after another, and yet she was still his wife and subject to his will. She certainly needed to stay subject to his will. He looked toward her room; he did not keep it locked, but she did. She avoided looking at him, which was much preferable. Even though the room was close, it seemed far away. Between the two of them were rivers full of muddy water and rapacious fish. Why did he want to go to her room? Was not every kind of woman enough?

He went out into the garden and sat on the wet grass. She held the same level of control over his heart as numbers did on the pages of Al-Khwarizmi's book. Maisoon giggling in his arms, true laughter from the depths of the soul; Maisoon, batting her eyelids in moments of rapture; Maisoon who deserved what was left of his life.

He noticed her shadow in the dark night; it was no dream. She was sitting on the grass, talking to the stars like the Pyramid Witch. Then, in a gesture of weakness, she put her head between her hands and bent over as though life had crushed all her strength. She lifted her head again and looked in his direction.

He leaped to his feet and went over to her. "What are you doing here at this time of night?" he asked her forcefully.

She looked at him, but said nothing. She did not tell him that she had no idea as to why she had come out, why she was looking for him, why she was missing him, and why her fire went out whenever he was around her.

"Go," he said without looking at her. "Go back to your room."

Without saying a word, she went back to her room. The next day, he came back again at night. She was seated, writing slowly. She felt him coming close, but did not move. She tightened her grasp on the pen and pursed her lips, pretending that she had not noticed him. He raised his hand, put it on her hair, and started stroking it gently. She opened her eyes wide in shock and stopped writing. He looked bewitched.

"Have you finished writing?" he asked as he stroked her hair.

She said nothing. Their eyes met. She looked baffled. Her heart sank at first, but then rose high in the sky. The moon was eclipsed, and the sun shone bright. She stared at him without saying a word.

"When I'm standing," he told her firmly, "you need to stand in front of me and await my instructions."

She closed her lips, got to her feet, and stood in front of him. He did his best to avoid looking at her, all his senses in revolt.

"Have you learned anything from your copying?" he asked. "Tell me what you've learned."

"Did you want to punish me or teach me?" she asked with malicious glee.

"Teaching you was punishment enough. Once you realize that the world is not interested only in Maisoon, perhaps you can be more modest and know your place."

As she looked at him, she could see the alienation in his eyes.

"I've learned from Aristotle," she responded dryly, "that love of self marks the beginning of love for all humanity."

He sighed in despair and grabbed her wrist. "Is that all you've learned?" He pulled her to his chest and hugged her hard. For just a moment, she pushed him away.

"Stop resisting," he told her forcefully, as he rubbed his cheek against hers. "You wanted silk and gold, and I've brought you silk and gold. Your room's filled with them, isn't it?"

There was his smell, the light that he had extinguished before, unreliable, tickling the ribs and boggling the mind. How she had missed it!

"Hug me round the neck," he whispered. "If you do, you won't do any work all tomorrow. What do you think?"

She hugged his neck, then frowned and lowered her eyelids. Her soul was screaming how much she had missed him, for a year or more. Tears clustered in her throat, then stopped. If she killed him now, she could still keep the memory of past passions. Could she strangle him with her bare hands? Did she have the strength?

"You realize that I want to kill you, don't you?" she muttered. "I want to do it with my own hands."

"Yes, I know," he replied firmly, her heartbeats pounding again his chest.

She pushed him away with her two hands.

"If you stay away from me," she said, "I'll never kill you."

He moved away a bit, then put his hand on her cheek and came close again. He gave her cheek a slow kiss deeper than well water. She closed her eyes.

"Can I go back to my room?" she asked.

His kiss moved to her ears. "I want to remind you of who I am," he told her.

She remained silent.

He put his hands around her face and kissed her ear, then her neck. Her entire body shuddered.

"Who am I, Maisoon?" he whispered.

"The Deputy Police Chief," she replied, grabbing her hand angrily.

"Your husband."

He could feel her body pulsating to his touch. Her breaths came out short; confusion and passion blended together, he realized.

"Do you remember?" he whispered, bringing his lips close to hers.

"No," she replied at once.

"Oh no, you can't forget. Your breathing tells me that you remember. Did you have some hope, I wonder, or did some devil whisper in your ear that one day you would be married to him? Did you think that would ever happen, that I'd let you be married to him? I gave you a gold necklace. I sent it to you with the guard. Where is it?"

"I threw it into the street," she replied, recovering her self-control. "I used all my strength to hurl it as far away as I could."

"What strength are you talking about?" he asked with a droll smile. "Women are so fickle."

"Tonight, you're going to sleep in my bed," he told her casually.

She opened her mouth, but he interrupted her.

"I want to find out whether or not your passionate love for me has faded."

"What do you want?" she asked, giving him a dubious look.

"I want you," he said, coming close.

She scoffed and, at the same time, there were tears in her eyes.

"Listen, man," she said. "If you could leave me for a whole year, think of me as unfaithful, and have doubts about my fidelity, then what is it you want from me? Aren't you afraid I'm going to kill you while you're indulging in passion?"

"I'm not even thinking about all those details," he replied firmly. "Okay, take your clothes off and come to me as a wife."

Her hand shook, and it was not clear whether it was fear or anger.

"Then what?" she asked.

"You'll await my instructions," he replied forcefully. "Don't imagine that I'm ever going to forgive you for what you've done."

"How many women have you had sex with this year, Anas?"

"Before I learned about your attempts to kill and slander me, I'd never had sex with any woman but you. In the past two months, I've had sex with ten."

Now she wanted to crush him all over again. "You still want me, even after that! Why? Couldn't you find someone more beautiful than me in all of Egypt and Iraq? Or is it that you always want whatever Ibn al-Mudabbir wants?"

She almost crushed him, and he had to grab his hand to stop himself from slapping her. He took her hand and put it over his heart.

"There's no love in my heart for you," he said, pretending to be calm. "It's all over. But when I want you the way a man wants a piece of fruit he's kept in the cupboard, you'll still be mine whenever and wherever I choose. Come on, take your clothes off."

She stayed where she was, hiding her shaking hand and not responding. She was not sure what to do or how she should feel. Could anger blend with melancholy? Could fury be the equal of hope? Or was it rather that relationships depend on fidelity? What relationship can there be that deprives a man of his mind, so he cannot distinguish his mother from his sister, or life's bitterness from the sweet savor of memories?

He pushed her against the wall and put his hand over her heart.

"You'll never mention the Tax Administrator's name in front of me again," he said. "If I hear it from you, I'll cut your tongue out. Then I'll cut open your heart with my sword and take out all the deceit and infidelity."

"Do you still want me, fisherman's son?" she asked shivering. "What kind of defeat is that?"

Before she could decide what to do, he went over, picked her up in his arms, and threw her on his bed. The shock made her scream. He kissed her, and she remembered. He did not kiss her like a tender lover, but with an angry passion. She pushed him away and almost fell out of his arms. Her heart started racing, and the days all blended together. If he hit her, it would not matter; her father had done as much. If he kept her in prison, it would not matter either; her father had done that too. If he whipped her, she would never submit. When the kissing was over, their eyes met. Her eyes gleamed with a new light, as though it were a star that had ignited.

"You still want me," she said, putting her hand over his heart, "and you don't want anyone else. Even after you've gone to Ahmad ibn Tulun. What do you plan to do with your heart, Anas?"

He covered her body with his, and the shock made her scream.

"I'm going to cut it up into little pieces," he said, "and throw it from high up as hard as I can, just as you did with the necklace."

He moved close to her, and she kissed the edge of his lips slowly.

"I don't like the feel of silk," she muttered. "It slides and slips through your fingers."

He did not hear her disconnected words. No sooner did her lips touch his than he kissed her with a vicious perfection, passion eliminating all discretion. When she moved away, he clutched her hand.

"Don't toy with me," he said. "Don't ever kid yourself that you're in charge."

He kept her close to his body.

"Who's in charge, Maisoon?" he asked.

She closed her eyes and clamped her arms behind her back so she would not touch him. She heard screams inside her, and maybe outside as well. Loneliness can cover more than ice and soil. She opened her eyes again as though she were looking at a genie.

"Don't touch me, Anas," she yelled, pushing him away as hard as she could.

He stood up and moved away, staring at her as though he were about to kill her.

"What's this game you're playing?" he asked her.

"If I don't want you," she replied forcefully, as she stood up, "you're not going to force me. How come you need to force me when you're Deputy Police Chief and have all those women around you?"

"But you want me," he said, pulling her by the arm.

She looked at him and pulled his hand away from her arm.

"No, Anas," she said, "I don't want you."

With that, she rushed over to the door and left, with a sense of victory and pleasure that she had not felt for a year.

She went into her room, headed for her bed, and closed her eyes. Traces of his kisses still hovered over her ribs, and his touches plunged their way into her bloodstream. Passion was still gnawing at her soul; the rest of her life would only be safe if she stayed with him and killed him. Her shadow emerged and toyed with her vision and foresight. Passion blended with anger, and the flames of separation died down. New realities emerged: she was out to crush him. She wanted to make him suffer; indeed, she longed to do it. She could only be satisfied by being by his side. He wanted to treat her like some receptacle. How different was Anas then, the one who used to melt away in love and awe at her beauty, and Anas now! She pictured him today, with all the longing of a vagrant, crushing her between his hands and lusting after her. Now that he had deprived her of life, he could not do without her. Even though he had not done those things yet and was behaving like a piece of solid rock with her, why was he still toying with her mind like this? It was the devil's own doing. Why was she suddenly feeling so content? She dearly hoped that staying by him was not the only thing she wanted. She hoped that her own shadow would not chase after her on those dark nights and make her lose her mind. Today she had seen the candle, and her shadow had disappeared. What could be worse for a mind than following the spirit of an untrustworthy man, a man who followed his angry feelings, not his affection?

Intense attachment leads to collapse. Attachment is a feeling that causes confusion, that plunges the heart into a deep well from which there is no escape. What if he were to disappear again? If he died? If he kept on humiliating her? Would she keep on living just because he was by her side? What had Anas done to her? Why just Anas? Was not the Tax Administrator deeply in love and desiring her? What had she found in Anas? Had his shadow stayed with her throughout her life? Or was it that her own heart hated her so much as to forge the attachment with Anas?

When she woke up, she felt herself enveloped by ardor, energy, and triumph. She had no idea what form victory would take today, nor did she know how she would react if Anas desired her again with such passion and a touch of madness. Did she not loathe him so much as to make her long to see him die slowly right in front of her? Was she not out to defeat him? Did she not long to level the ground bit by bit till all trace of his existence was erased from her memory? What was happening today? When he had wanted her, she had refused. She had taught him that she was not like other women. She picked up the sheet she had been sleeping on and used it to bang on the wooden window ledge. Today he would choose the most beautiful slave-girl he had had sex with once or twice, and all because his own wife had refused to have sex with him. Today he would be making a child with one of them and would forget all about her. She clasped the window's delicate woodwork in her fingers and squeezed it hard so it could splinter. But it did not, and she had a raging fit, the like of which no one had ever experienced. She screamed as loudly as she could, and Mughith's wife rushed in to find out what had happened. Maisoon told her that she wanted to smash the window. For a moment, Mughith's wife looked at her, then asked her again what was the matter, muttering some Quranic verses.

"This window needs to be smashed," Maisoon said with determination. "I want to smash it today. I want to break this wood into little pieces. The very sight of it is disturbing me."

Mughith's wife gave her a look showing that she fully understood what Maisoon was going through. She gave her some food that she had cooked.

"Maisoon," she said craftily, "don't let him get away from you again. Take control and get to his heart."

She concentrated on the wood. "He has lots of women," she said.

"All men have slave-girls, but a wife has a different status. If you let him rely on slave-girls, he'll have children by them and . . ."

She used all her strength to pull out the delicate piece of wood, and it moved from its place. "See, it's moving," she told Mughith's wife. "Leave me alone for a while till I've destroyed the rest of the window."

Mughith's wife pursed her lips, then left the room.

She closed her eyes in the middle of the day and dreamed about him. He had shown his love for her as in the past, and she had hugged his neck and squeezed as hard as she could. She could feel the touch of his taut arteries. She let out a pained sigh that cures all wounds. The shadow appeared, then disappeared. The shadow inhaled his breaths, then wafted into the air. Anas remained in front of her, her alone, neither running away, nor lying, nor leaving. She realized that she was not like other women; not because she was the most beautiful, but because she was crazy. What was it that she did not understand? She screamed, then felt regret. Despair prevailed even before daylight covered her.

She went back to her work. Every night he would come in and look at what she had written so perfectly. He would ask her what she had understood and learned, and she would explain to him without looking at him. He did not ask her to stay. He was having sex with other women, that was certain. She kept hearing whispers from slave-girls and the chatter among the womenfolk.

He could not understand his wife. Did she crave Ibn al-Mudabbir's power and so had decided to be rid of him? Or had she been humiliated by his departure for Iraq, something over which he had had no control? Why had she not resisted his kisses? Why had she turned him down? She would copy all day without getting tired; she would do what he asked, but without any forgiveness or opposition. But she refused to submit. He could break every bone in her body and whip her for what she had done, but he realized that she would not care. He noticed that today Maisoon was different. Along with her supercilious looks, there was also a hidden weakness and sense of humiliation. Within the folds of her bitter talk there lay a quaking heart that he could not bear. He closed his eyes against his own doubts. Maisoon was Maisoon, someone who could only see herself and only loved power and wealth. But sometimes her words came out with no meaning. Her eyes would roam as though they were looking at the clouds and talking to them. She pretended that her eyes were just playing a game. Maisoon was his mistake, but he would have to be cruel in order to win. Soft hearts never won, and the sword was the only path to revenge.

He raged against her. Summoning her once or twice, he accused her of sloppy work. He sat her down in front of him to copy for hours. He stared at her without saying anything while she made perfect copies. She had inured herself to the fact that he would not be touching her again. His pride would not allow him to force her. Every time she detected a sad look in his eyes, she felt reassured and content. Every time he noticed sorrow buried in her pupils, he hoped patiently. His only comfort lay in humiliating her, and hers involved making him suffer. As long as they were so far apart, neither of them felt at ease. At night, she could see her shadow pounce on her and throttle her slowly. She let out a groan that only she could hear. She was thinking about the glint of swords, but only daggers fascinated her. She liked their shape and grip, suggesting a power over the rebellious heart. They had blades that brooked no compromise and could pierce rock without hesitation. Sometimes she hoped he would plunge one into her chest or that the blade would flirt with the veins in her neck, shedding compliant blood. She had not found the appropriate dagger yet, but darkness promoted rebellion. Sometimes she would hear a whisper, and at other times a sob. There were other times when her heart would blame her for not winning and not learning.

She had a small dagger with her that she used to tear up the pillowcase amid suppressed screams. All humanity was in agreement, and loneliness was always fixed and silent.

⛪

He went to visit his brother in Fuwwah. He had missed being with him. Even though their temperaments were different, they were united by a strong bond, going back to the time in childhood when they had played together in the sea and battled the sands with wooden swords. How many victories together and how many defeats! When Ali greeted him, he was happy and content. Ali was always that way, as though everything that happened on earth had no effect on him. When their father died, Ali had said it was God's will. When they lost all their money, Ali said that days are a rotation among people. When tyranny worsened, he said that the world was never stable. When Anas had killed Zayid, both brothers had become fugitives, and Ali said that the world was a succession of tribulations. How Anas wanted to be like Ali, to find some pleasure in a slave-girl's arms, and to expect to catch a fish or two with all the enthusiasm of innocence and the joy of lovers. Ali knew how to live and what to expect from life.

"Live your life," Ali told him as he fried the fish, "as though evil can never reach your heart, and die content with what has happened. Ever since you became aware of the world, Anas, you've been bearing burdens like shaikhs. I give thanks to God that I didn't learn to read and never learned the things that you know. Here I am with the fish, king and amir!"

"Hiding in the hole is not the solution, Ali," Anas told him. "The day will come when the fisherman will destroy it and find you."

"You've become a warrior, brother," Ali replied. "You've mastered the act of killing. I'd rather live in peace."

"There can be no peace with tyranny," Anas said. "The only way out of war is defeat. We're doomed to fight even though we find it hateful."

"You're the eldest and wisest. You've read and learned. Eat the fish and enjoy the sea breeze. Tell me how things are going for you."

He enjoyed being with his brother; he had no one else in the world. Even when they disagreed, he felt a sense of serenity and devotion in his brother. If there was a day or two left in his life, he would not want to go back. If only he could forget the world all around him.

When he returned to his house, he paused for a moment. He thought he would summon her to his room now and force himself on her or even argue with her. He closed his eyes and put his hand on his heart. Words kept sneaking their way into his soul, and for the first time he was afraid. He did not try to recall the Tax Administrator's words and made an effort to forget the killer instinct that had hit him and the evil lurking in his eyes: "You don't rip out the soul by killing the body. You won't have any love left alive." The words echoed all around him, filling his room like smoke from old lamps. He had a terrible fit of anger, leaped to his feet, and rushed over to the women's quarters to look for his wife. Then he came back without waking her up.

He promised Ibn Tulun that this year's Alexandria taxes would be his as well. Ibn Tulun did his best to dissuade him, but Anas insisted that Alexandria had never submitted before, even in caliphal periods, and was not about to submit to Ibn al-Mudabbir now. Alexandria would use its waves to blow away the avaricious and invoke its courage to contrive against time. This year was not like others: Ibn ash-Shaikh in Syria was preventing taxes from reaching the caliph, and Alexandria's taxes had to pass through Syria. The taxes would have to be retrieved before they reached Ibn ash-Shaikh. Anas laid his plans carefully. He realized that this time he would have to kill people; in particular, he would need to kill Abdallah As-Sa'adi, who was transporting the taxes. As-Sa'adi had flayed several Egyptians, and four people had died under torture right in front of their relatives. He had to die, Anas told himself, without any ambiguity. He would be implementing justice, no more. If there was to be justice in Egypt and if Ibn Tulun was able, he would impose the penalty on As-Sa'adi. Since all power today lay in Ibn al-Mudabbir's hands, it was inevitable that he, Anas, would implement that justice, being someone who recognized and kept watch on tyranny. He asked the men to bring him As-Sa'adi's head. They would be disguised as Bedouin and would attack the caravan on the Syrian border. At first, only three highly trained men would emerge; they would pretend to be defeated by As-Sa'adi's men and would run away. A day later, the tables would be turned, but with a hundred men, each of whom would keep part of the tax revenue. The rest of the money would be for Ibn Tulun to construct an army and city and to restore the money to its rightful owners. Shaikh Bakkar might be of the opinion that the Abbasid caliph deserved obeisance, but Anas was not inclined to give it. He would never stop until Ibn al-Mudabbir died at his hands. If the caliph was unable to stave off tyranny, then he, the fisherman's son, would have to do it.

What Ahmad ibn Tulun was planning to do seemed like a fit of madness. He was a strange personality, neither a good angel nor incapable of understanding. He had none of the ambition and viciousness of the Iraqi Turks, none of the cunning of the caliphs' pageboys, and none of the serenity of Sufi shaikhs. By now, Ibn al-Mudabbir had concluded that Ahmad ibn Tulun had streaks of madness in him: he had no taste when it came to dress and never wore silk decorated with rubies and silver. He did not enjoy beautiful slave-girls or singing. What was even more peculiar was that Ahmad did not belong to any of the cliques who surrounded the caliph. It was as though he walked down the street on his own. Yet he was both vicious and merciless, dealing with his foes with both violence and cunning. If there was one thing that Ibn al-Mudabbir could not stand, it was bluntness. Ahmad was blunt in his behavior and his tastes; he never listened to poets or attended their sessions. He had brought in the fisherman's son as Deputy Police Chief; that was an outrage and a secret declaration of war. He had claimed that the fisherman's son had paid the ransom for Zayid and had committed no crime.

Ibn al-Mudabbir expected Ahmad to gather all the Bukhara men around him and purchase young men from there to add to his army. He reluctantly released the funds, certain that his own end was nigh. Ibn al-Mudabbir had a plan in place to get rid of him. Ever since he had released the funds, he had been looking on in confusion.

Ibn al-Mudabbir realized that the way that Ahmad had used the funds was frightening, reflecting the ideas of a mind that had to be taken seriously. He had hired men from every quarter and location. He had purchased them from Sudan, Nubia, and the Turks. Then he had asked the Arabs to form separate groups and had promised them rewards. He had also bought men from Byzantium. Then he did something amazing that no one had ever done before, even before Amr ibn al-As's conquest of Egypt. Ahmad ibn Tulun created an army of soldiers from among the client peoples in Egypt—Egyptians. Since when did Egyptians fight? This had never happened before, and Ibn al-Mudabbir knew nothing about it. People said that the last Egyptian soldiers had drowned along with the Moses's Pharaoh. Ever since then, Egypt had never had an army or soldiers. People said that the Greeks had ruled the country with their soldiers, then the Byzantines, and then the Arabs. How was it that Ahmad was losing his mind and drawing the lightning sword on a quiet night? What did he want, and what would the Egyptian people think in the wake of such brazen behavior and chaos? Ibn al-Mudabbir watched as Ahmad selected six thousand soldiers from the young men of Egypt. He neither bought nor forced them; instead, he tempted them with the offer of gifts and power. They duly emerged from every deep valley, six thousand Egyptian men who would be trained to use weapons and be loyal to Ahmad. News of this madness had to reach the caliph. Making use of Arabs in the army would reignite the flames of divided loyalties and blood. Why had Ahmad not assembled an army of Turks? From the outset, Ibn al-Mudabbir understood that Ahmad trusted no one; his only concern was for his wife and son who were both being held hostage in Iraq. As long as Ahmad's son, Al-Abbas, remained a hostage in Iraq, the sword was still in Ibn al-Mudabbir's hand, even if Ahmad controlled all the armies on earth.

Ibn Tulun continued to assemble men, counting them till they overflowed like the Nile. There was no room for all of them in Fustat or the army camp, so he went out to the northeast and instructed his men to divide the land and build their homes in the new location. They said that he was going to build a new city even larger than Fustat and the camp. A hundred thousand soldiers would live there, and the gates would not be closed to Egyptians. On the contrary, the entire Egyptian population would be making its way there, intent on building so it would last for a thousand years or more. If Ahmad was constructing a new city, then he was planning to stay for a thousand years or more. That was alarming enough, but it was his first mistake, the first thing the caliph was going to hear about. Ahmad's status was an even greater threat to the entire caliphate than it was to Ibn al-Mudabbir. The stars would soon be falling from the sky, so let him gather his men and engage in battle with Ibn ash-Shaikh. Let him build his city. Ibn al-Mudabbir would demolish it once he had put Ahmad ibn Tulun in prison.

The fisherman's son could defy Ibn al-Mudabbir, but after he had been demeaned and humiliated, he would soon disappear. Maisoon could lose her way and be confused and belittled. Then she would wake up and realize Ibn al-Mudabbir's true love, for which there was no parallel. The whole world was in his hands. Ahmad could play around for a while, but then he would pay the price for his innocence and naivete.

Part Three

Verily shall I leave the world and their love.
None shall sense it in my heart.
Twixt myself and sorrow have I proposed an acquaintance
That never ends, else eternity does.
—*Bashshar ibn Burd, 8th century*

Chapter 10

The land that Ahmad ibn Tulun set aside for Anas was both broad and fertile. Every time Anas pictured his wide, welcoming house, he could only see Maisoon inside it, an unconscious fetter on his heart. After she had been so unfaithful, he had intended to be married to the daughter of some Turkish general, to have lots of slave-girls, and produce many sons. He would forget all about Maisoon. Longing and passion do not make walls or kindle fires to warm houses. Women who give birth to sons and bring them up cannot be disloyal and change with time's vicissitudes. His mind would be in charge, but that did not prevent Maisoon's being his wife. His thirst for her was still not quenched. If he could rip her out of his arteries today rather than tomorrow, he would certainly do it, but he still could not picture the walls of his home without also imagining her around him.

He heard a voice and turned round abruptly to look at the man who had called out to him. It was Saeed, who had disappeared after they reached Iraq.

"Anas, son of Hamza al-Skandari!" Saeed said enthusiastically. "Do you remember me?"

"Saeed, son of Katib al-Farghani," Anas replied with a smile, "the one who traverses the earth's corners searching for the orphan girl! I assumed you'd drowned yourself with love of the Samarra slave-girls! I forgot that you were my companion on the journey."

"Yes," Saeed replied, "I fell in love, but it was with the buildings in Samarra. My heart only has room for my beloved."

Saeed pointed at the ground.

"I'll build the house for you in less than a year," he said enthusiastically.

He bent down and started drawing on the ground with his finger, talking nonstop.

"Here there'll be a fountain to dazzle the heart," he said. "Here windows to delight the very stars, and here we'll plant some trees to please the eye. What's your wife like and what kind of temperament does she have?"

Anas stared at him in amazement.

"If I knew what she's like," Saeed went on, "I'd know what she wants the house to look like. Don't tell me; let me guess. But why guess when the whole of Egypt knows who your wife is? When it comes to architecture, I have no rival in Egypt."

"You're not very modest, are you?" Anas said with a smile. "You're just like Ahmad ibn Tulun."

"Modesty's for important people. I'm just a vagabond! I've no job and no income. I studied architecture, but I'm not working in that sphere. These days, people don't like building. Just look at the houses and mosques in Samarra. Where are we amid such glory?"

"Ahmad ibn Tulun's going to build something like it, and even better."

"That's why I've come to see you."

Anas looked at him, but said nothing.

"I'll build you a house," Saeed told him. "You provide the building materials, and I'll design a house like the homes of amirs and caliphs. It'll be right here in the middle of the new city so that you can enjoy it with your wife. The judge's daughter will want a spacious mansion full of light and life."

"I don't care what she wants."

"Women always cause trouble," Saeed replied in Coptic with a smile. "But you, fisherman's son, wear a perpetual frown, as though you've never solved Al-Khwarizmi's equation! I'll build you a house," he continued, "provided that you mention my name to Ahmad ibn Tulun. You promised me. Tell him that a Coptic Christian has built your house; he's a skilled architect and wants to be of service to the governor. Has he become the governor yet, or is he still deputy governor?"

"He's governor now," Anas replied. "But I'm not going to mention your name because I don't know you. How can I be sure that you're a good architect?"

"You'll be sure when I build you a house of incredible beauty. You're one of his closest confidants. As I've told you, the whole of Egypt knows the story of the fisherman's son. All Egypt loves you."

"When I was weak, brother, the whole of Egypt banished me to the wilderness in disgrace."

"There's nothing they can do about Ibn al-Mudabbir. People never admire the weak; they're bewitched by the powerful. In our religion and yours, only God loves the weak. Most people prefer power and glory. Tell the governor that the poor servant is Egyptian. People say that the governor likes Egyptians. Why?"

"Because he's in charge in Egypt. What kind of question is that?"

"How many governors has Egypt had who loathed and despised Egyptians? There are Egyptians, but there's one Egypt consisting of land and gold, and another one made up of people and ancient palaces. Which one are you talking about?"

"Both."

"No one will ever have seen a house as beautiful as yours," Saeed told him enthusiastically. "It won't be inlaid with gold, but every wall will be covered with works of art and glories of the ancestral past. Mention my name to Ahmad ibn Tulun. I'm your friend."

"I'll try. But I'm not your friend. I don't have any friends."

Killing had seemed like a major sin, but now it had become like a grain of sand in an inflamed eyelid. Was he upset? Yes, for a few moments perhaps. He did not know how he had become so inured to death. Ever since his father had died, death held no terrors for him; now that he had witnessed humiliation and death, it brought a sense of peace. If he were responsible for the death of one of Ibn al-Mudabbir's men, he would be happy and would celebrate.

Today he had planned the death of Shuqair, the Postmaster, one that would be part of Ibn al-Mudabbir's downfall. He knew that Shuqair had a pale complexion and was portly. He sent some men to arrest him, then agreed with them to tie him to a plank of wood, leave him in the sun, and threaten him all day that Ahmad was planning to cut open his body and take out his guts. Ahmad was well aware of all Shuqair's intrigues and how he had intended to drive a wedge between him and successive caliphs until Al-Mu'tamid arrived. When night came, they untied his restraints and took him back to his house. They told him that Ahmad was going to kill him before dawn. When Shuqair came home, broken and terrified, he died in his own bed before dawn. When Ibn al-Mudabbir heard what had happened, he went crazy. He sent word to the caliph that Ahmad ibn Tulun's Deputy Police Chief, Anas, the fisherman's son, had murdered the postal worker. The caliph dispatched investigators and police to look at Shuqair's body and establish whether he had been murdered. The body showed no signs of beating or sword wounds. Ahmad claimed that he had had an argument with Shuqair, and he had died of fright; he had not been killed. The caliph's men could not pin anything on Ahmad ibn Tulun, and left Egypt loaded with gifts and food.

Ibn al-Mudabbir abstained from women. Even Abu Sha'ara's sarcastic remarks about Ahmad no longer made him laugh. He wanted Maisoon as a contented lover and was eager to crush the fisherman's son. If Anas's father's death had not managed to crush him, then something else was needed. Let him lose every lover. But before crushing Anas, he needed to come up with a plan to kidnap Maisoon, who was suffering inside the house in Authority Town.

Stones lay scattered about, waiting to be installed on the roof. Morning and night, pillars and structures were being erected. Anas stared at the horizon, deep in thought. All cities are doomed to disappear; it is said that we are swimming over the cities of our ancestors, sometimes floating, and at others, plunging deep inside them. Pharaoh chased after Moses with his entire army and drowned. Arabs read some words and discovered that, with the disappearance of Moses's army, Egypt never again had one. They read about a city called Menouf. No one knows if it was destroyed by an enemy or simply disappeared with the vicissitudes of time. Then Ahmad ibn Tulun constructed Al-Qata'i. Had he forgotten that cities are doomed to disappear? What would remain of his city? A few fables perhaps, and some tales repeated by women.

Al-Qata'i, a city with an army unlike any other, one with Egyptian soldiers and others of every color and country. Maybe one of them would want to erase what

Ahmad had brazenly built. Human beings will always alternate the days and forget about the Egyptian army. The sands will blow to cover over the entire past; the sword will eliminate all traces; the years will erase memory. People will ask themselves what was and what remains. With no traces, there is no tale to tell; without walls, hope has nowhere to reside. The vestiges of stones will be scattered and blend with those who departed and went away. Would the city survive? A thousand houses or more, each one with light and dark, absence and presence, contempt and prestige. Ahmad's name and dream would be repeated in every house. Egyptians have perfected the reading of scripts from the past; they love living in the folds of past triumphs and collapsed buildings with lofty structures and minarets reaching to the skies. If only every Egyptian city could witness this day. Anas looked at his sword. If only every Egyptian could recall a time when they held a sword in their hand, when memory enfolded the city. Perhaps a different era, a different day was coming. Some might claim that Egypt had no army, that they were not proficient fighters. Others might say that the pharaohs vanished just like their cities. But people investigating cities discover a shadow as they wait, shadows, a shining light, and another that is dim. Here lived Ahmad and Ibn al-Mudabbir, Anas the fisherman's son, Shaikh Bakkar ibn Qutaiba, and Saeed, son of Katib al-Farghani.

Anas could also remember the young man's groan as blood oozed from every orifice in his body; screams from the body's belly, groans from the depths of the soul. Maisoon was far away and fixed inside the liver. She herself had become close, while her heart had traveled to a land beyond the twin rivers. If only the screams of love would emerge thick and fast like the pouring rain during thunderstorms. If only the gremlin would shove the desert wastes of loneliness toward oblivion, the way camels are driven back to their abodes. But groans are mingled with pride as the lonely soul cringes before its tormentor. When her eyes searched for him inside his room, did she see him? When she walked amid the women, her heart overwhelmed with longing, did she see him? Was the hope of being married to Ibn al-Mudabbir still playing within her? Had hatred and spite won her over? He was searching for her, but not finding her. He had often searched for his own self, but no longer recognized it. He had started reciting every kind of poem, but was not understanding them; he kept shouting every name, but not remembering them. He no longer wanted anything. Who can sate the sick person's hunger when the disease intensifies and becomes chronic? Can the satisfaction of hunger sometimes be a cure? Is the person who provides water for the thirsty hoping for fulfillment? Does drinking water in times of absence slake the thirst?

"Forgive me, Father," he muttered again. "What you've seen in my eyes today is not blame. I promise you that I won't disappoint your hopes in me."

Every day, Maisoon asked for a pillow that she could attack and rip apart, taking out her craziness. None of them dared speak of it in front of the Deputy Police Chief. Then one day, Abla the hairdresser paid her a secret, unexpected visit. Even the guards did not recognize her. Her complexion was pale as she sat down in front of Maisoon.

"You poor woman," she said, "the fisherman's son treats you badly. I know. The Tax Administrator wants to rescue you. He can do it. Hear me out till I've finished. Don't say a single word, or I'll die and you'll die with me. The Tax Administrator trusts you and wants you to run away from here. His men will be waiting for you outside the house after dinner. Thieves will pounce on your husband at the same time. They may not manage to kill him, but thieves have a special way of breaking bones. Do you understand what I want, Maisoon? Do what I say without a word. Your husband's a thief, and thieves have their hands cut off. That's what Ibn al-Mudabbir says."

"What's he stolen?" Maisoon asked in a choked voice.

Abla rubbed Maisoon's thigh. "Don't bother yourself about that," she said.

Maisoon swallowed hard, but said nothing. Abla stood up to leave.

"I'm going now," she said, "before anyone recognizes me. We'll meet after dinner, as agreed."

Abla left. Maisoon stared at the pillow and scoffed at herself, not at the Tax Administrator. She put the knife by her side to feel safe and took deep breaths as though they were weeping hot tears. Closing her eyes, she walked slowly to Raihan, her husband's slave-girl. Closing her eyes, she tried to recover a sense of decency that she did not possess at that point. They would be cutting off his hands, then torturing him, and then killing him. He would be paying the price for all the wrongs he had committed against her. Anas . . . if any harm touched him, she would die that day. The impact of the love she felt for him could only be assessed by a madman, someone who has lost his mind because of the intensity of his passion and whose entire memory has been wiped clean by the fiery flames. Oh Anas, my torturer yesterday and tomorrow! You, the one whose absence has put an end to my breathing, even though you're all around me!

She went into Raihan's room and grabbed her hand. She handed her pen and ink, then grabbed her fingers and started writing these words: "Danger is coming from Alexandria tomorrow."

"Before you have sex with him," she told Raihan in no uncertain terms, "give him this piece of paper. If you don't, I'm going to slaughter you tomorrow. If you mention my name, I'll do it today."

The slave-girl looked at her in confusion.

"Don't think that he knows you, my beauty," Maisoon went on. "Anas only knows his goals."

With that, she left her and went out.

These days, having sex with beautiful women was no longer enjoyable. Greed has no place in paradise. Drinking water without being thirsty does not satisfy the ardent or moisten a lover's belly. At nighttime he would approach Maisoon's room and think about going in, hugging her hard, and penetrating her the same way he had transfixed and humiliated Ibn al-Mudabbir's men. Men's courage was more important than their discernment and pride. Such pride was always brutal. He realized that if he were to take her by force, she would know how far his ribs would yield when faced with her love and how firm the soul was with the memory of a past now gone. He would never grant her that victory, even if he would feel sorrow a thousand times each day, a feeling that would be renewed every morning and change with the color of the sky.

When the lovely slave-girl came into his room that day, she was speaking rapidly. She told him that she loved him and wanted to stay with him. She said a lot of things that he did not hear and did not even reach the air around him. Maisoon's smile was shining bright and spreading; moments spent with her reminded him of heaven's delights. Those moments would never return. When the body was sated, he would remember his papers and books. He had left her to look for Ibn al-Mudabbir. How he wished he could be the fisherman's son again, teaching algebra to slave-girls. When he had finished, he turned his face away and told her to leave. She held onto his shoulder.

"Is my lord angry with me?" she asked coquettishly.

She lay back on his bed and took off her dress. The blue tattoo with Arabic letters was now visible on her shoulder. He had noticed it many times before, but was only paying attention to it today. He read the words loud enough for his heart to hear:

Majnun was only truly present when I was as he,
But he revealed love's secret, and I dissolved in concealment.

She gave him a flirtatious glance.

"Those are Laila al-Amiriyya's words," she said, "which could well apply to me too. If only you realized how much I love you! People say that free women don't have tattoos. But how can slave-girls express their love if not with tattoos?"

She moved close and gave him a kiss.

"Tell me," she whispered, "what do you need to love me?"

He told her again to leave, as though he had not heard what she had been saying. She put on her dress again and went over to him.

"I love you, my lord," she said, handing him the piece of paper. "I want to save you. One day, you'll realize how loyal I've been. Maybe you'll pay me some attention."

When she left, he opened his eyes and looked at the piece of paper that the slave-girl had written. He read it and sat up.

Of course, Ibn al-Mudabbir was out to get rid of him. He realized that it was now open warfare. Everyone involved now had their weapons drawn; in love, there could now be swords drawn, even if spies were clustered around fighters' corpses in so many rows. Maybe his wife had been conspiring against him. Did she not want to kill him, had she not tried? But Raihan could not read or write.

He summoned Raihan and all the womenfolk. He learned about the unknown woman's visit to his wife, told them all to leave, but kept Raihan with him. He told her to tell him the truth. She insisted that she loved him and had learned to write for his sake. She cried and pleaded. He started to lose patience and insisted that she tell him the truth. With that, she confessed what had happened.

"My lord," she said by way of blame, "I've done this because I love you. But your wife . . ."

He looked at her.

"Give me your assurance," she went on, "and I'll tell you."

He nodded.

"All the women in the household are talking about . . . how crazy she is," she continued. "She rips up cloth, talks about fires, and speaks to the devil. Send her away, my lord, and you'll be safe."

His heart kept reminding him of what his anger had tried to bury.

"Who talks about her?" he asked.

"Everyone who knows her. She prefers to be alone with her demon. She claims to be sick, my lord, so she can talk to her jinn. She's visited the Pyramid Witch, so she's been touched by madness. Everyone who visits the Pyramid Witch loses his mind."

"Raihan," he told her firmly, "I want you to tell all the slave-girls and womenfolk that, if I hear a single whisper about my wife, I shall cut out their tongues without any excuse and whatever their status."

"But, my lord . . ."

"Go and save your friends, go on!"

"I thought that we . . ."

"Our relationship has stopped me killing you today. But it won't stop me tomorrow."

He left with all the enthusiasm of a little boy and all the doggedness of a fish in the sea, eager to catch even a tiny fish in the river, and with the heart of a lover. A hundred years ago, he had lost his beloved, but now, at the point of death, he had suddenly found her in his arms. All his pains had disappeared, a life of despair had faded to nothing, and he found himself collapsing into the sweet savor of pleasure and the soul's self-quenching of thirst. He tried to look natural, but his heart was pounding loudly, and his eyes were shining with a cryptic gleam.

He told Mughith to get his men ready and to arrest anyone who approached the Authority Town complex the next day; their presence would be a danger for Ahmad ibn Tulun. He gathered his own men and counted them.

Then he opened the door to her room without asking permission. She leaped to her feet and shrieked, clasping her heart. Their eyes met. His eyes were gleaming in a way that she had never seen before. She closed her eyes, then opened them again to see if the gleam in his eyes had disappeared. But he was still looking at her, the glint of pleasure and triumph still visible in his expression.

"Don't you dare come any closer," she yelled at him, "or I'll tell everyone in the house that the Deputy Police Chief's wife doesn't want him!"

He went over to her, seized her wrist, and pulled her toward him.

"You endured a year of suffering while I was far away," he said, "but my heart was with you. And another year, with me far away, but my heart has been all around you."

She looked in embarrassment at the feathers scattered all over the room. Who knows, maybe he would confine her to the house once he discovered that she had lost her mind. Could there be any greater revenge?

"I've often wanted to kill you," she told him.

As he looked around the room, both of them were dominated by a mad streak. He sat down on her bed.

"Okay," he told her steadily, "kill me, then. I'm waiting."

She went over to him but avoided looking at him.

"Don't defy me," she said in a muted tone. "Didn't your slave-girl tell you that I'm mad?"

He grabbed her hands and held them tight, then put them on his neck.

"I don't need a slave-girl for me to know you're mad," he said.

Her fingers were quivering as she raised her head and looked at him. She squeezed his neck as hard as she could. After a while, she let her hands drop. She moved closer and rubbed her cheek against his neck.

"Did I kill you, Anas?" she asked in despair. "Answer me."

"Maisoon," he replied, "you've killed me time and time again."

"You're responsible for the misery that every Egyptian is suffering; in fact, everyone living from Africa to India. Now you've come to see me after your slave-girl told you. That slave-girl of yours can't be trusted with secrets."

He removed her hands gruffly.

"No," he told her in a tone that scared her, "you don't know anything. That's because you were everything. I was waiting for the day when I'd wake up and see your face again."

She said nothing, but clasped her hands.

"There's caution in your eyes," he went on, "conceit in your smile, and defiance in your nose. I've loved everything that's evil, not just your beauty. Do you realize that? Can your heart be in love? Why didn't you let Ibn al-Mudabbir kill me?"

"Because I wanted to do it myself."

"You're exposing yourself to his vengeance."

"I've nothing left that he can destroy."

He wrapped his hands around hers.

"Do you love me, Maisoon?" he asked.

"No," she replied without thinking. "That was in the past, and it's over."

He pushed her away slowly and then covered her body with his. She did her best to resist, but he lifted her arms and looked into her eyes.

"Such intense anger, Maisoon, betrays a passion for Anas."

Her heart was racing.

"That's true," she replied. "There's no anger like yours."

He drew close to her cheek and gave her a long kiss. It was not gentle, and with it came a fresh bout of violence from inside him.

"There's no anger like it," he repeated. "If you loved me . . ."

He stopped talking, closed his eyes, and took a deep breath.

"If you loved me," he went on, "I'd spend my days in agony like so many grains of sand."

"Grains of sand are better than seeing darkness and one's own shadow," she muttered.

He did not understand what she had said, but did not bother about it.

He drowned her in painful kisses that exorcised the killer who had melted inside her.

"If only you realized what you've done to me," he said.

Tears were pouring down her face, but she did not know whether they were the result of his painful kisses or because she was still in love with him. Her heart was keeping pace with the heavy breathing.

"Leave me alone, Anas," she said. "Don't force me. Your pride won't allow you to force me."

He stopped the kissing, looked at her, and ran his hands over her arms.

"Even if Ibn al-Mudabbir arrived here now with his army and cut off my head, if every star in the heavens fell, if the soil enveloped our ancestors, I would never leave you."

She opened her mouth to reply. He pressed his body against hers, his chest impeding her breathing.

"I don't love you, Anas," she told him breathlessly, "and I don't want you."

As though he had not heard her, he took off her dress, then ran his hands over her entire body.

"I used to tell myself," he said, "that moments spent in your arms were glimpses of days in paradise, heart's fulfillment and censorious heart's delight. I told myself that our separation was inevitable, and those moments would never last. Tonight I want you in my arms. I need to confirm whether they are to last."

She tried to remove his hand, but without success.

"They won't last," she replied immediately.

He grabbed her arm and hugged it to him till she could feel her ribs cracking. She sighed and tried to push him away as hard as she could, but failed. She put her arms around his neck.

"Do you think I can't kill you?" she muttered.

He was gnawing and devouring her with every limb in his body.

"You kill me every single day," he told her between breaths. "With you, death's nothing. It's ongoing, and there's no single end to it. Anyone who kills you, Maisoon, is going to need an entire age to bring it off."

She shuddered as she clasped his shoulder with her arms in order to hide her face. She wanted to hurt him the way he had hurt her. Heart-pain is not like any other. He did not seem to care. She dug her fingernails into his shoulder. She had no idea whether she was hurting him so he would go away, or because he should be paying the price for what he had done.

He did not care; maybe he did not even feel it. The kiss he gave her went straight to the soul, a kiss that reminded her of a past that she had almost forgotten, not like all his precise and vicious kisses, but instead a kiss that involved innocence, hesitation, weakness, and power. It was as though they had never separated; she had never deceived, and he had never left.

Her tears were shivering before her limbs. Her insides knew him better than her mind. Her body was longing for him, even though her heart was still mired in bitter darkness. She was still wandering in the depths of the sea and had yet to surface.

Time seemed to pass with both of them semi-conscious and semi-drowned. All the stars in the sky shone, but they did not ignite the fires of passion in her. If only it had died down after a while, a period, a year, or an age. He was in despair that the passion had gone, while she bit her lips till they bled. He awoke from his stupor, with fires all around him.

She saw him; she had not been dreaming. She saw him, his mouth on her breast, searching for her heartbeats so he could live. She could feel the impulsive wave of passion that was overwhelming him.

"How I love you!" he whispered.

That day, she was his, once, many times. Every time he was about to come round, delirium took over. All around her, the shadow spread, and bone fragments were scattered. The body no longer had any power, and only tenderness filled the soul.

She clasped her body with her hands and moved away. He pulled her back and put her head on his chest. He brought her hand up to his mouth, then kissed it.

"I longed for you," he told her, "as the stars have longed for the heavens, then fallen. What can I do? I love you. We'll start afresh with no blame. Everything in the past was hurt and error. We'll have to maintain control over what lies ahead. If this experiment didn't lead to love before, then nothing will end it from now on. You're not the one I left two or more years ago, and I'm not the one who left you two or more years ago. But the soul's cohesion doesn't change over time."

Maisoon stared at the traces of the savage war on both their bodies, and let out an exhausted sigh.

"What did we just do, Anas?" she asked.

"You loved me with your whole heart," he replied with a smile, eyes closed. "Your heart's a ferocious desert beast."

She must have gone to sleep out of a sheer exhaustion that she had never felt in her entire life. They both lost consciousness and fell into a deep sleep that lasted for an hour or more. When she woke up, she put her arms around his neck.

"Yes," she said angrily, "I love you. Do you want to know? I love you so much that, when you left me, I lost my mind. I could not tell my mother and sister apart. I love you so much that I let darkness shroud what was left of my judgment and erase everything I'd learned. I love you, even though the shadow no longer leaves me ever since you went away. Can you forgive me for wanting to torture and defeat you? But how can I forgive you when you made me lose my mind and reason?"

For a while, he just looked at her without saying anything.

"If I did that," he said, "then I ask you to forgive me."

She let out a sob, but no tears fell.

"Here's Anas asking for forgiveness," she exclaimed. "That's even harder than getting Ibn al-Mudabbir out of Egypt!"

He kissed her hand. "Ibn al-Mudabbir is going to leave Egypt," he said. "I'm asking you to forgive me, and I'm promising never to leave you again."

"Don't make promises you can't keep," she replied bitterly.

"Even though I've bedded hundreds of women," he said, "I promise you that I've never seen anyone but you. No other woman can make her way into the heart's recesses and plunge inside the soul. In our house in the new city, you and I will be there alone."

She said nothing.

"There'll be no slave-girls around, Maisoon," he went on, "and no other wives either."

She looked at the feathers scattered all around the room. "Haven't you noticed, Anas?" she asked him.

"Let's pick them up together," he replied, almost without thinking. "I swear to you," he went on seriously, "that I've only ever felt happy in your arms. My heart has only quenched its thirst from your mouth."

"Using poetic talk, you're toying with what's left of my mind. Do you want a crazy wife, Anas? Sometimes I'm aware of the extent of my madness, but then there are other times when I'm not. The scandal involved will be worse than Nile floods; it'll flood whatever's left of your world. I no longer recognize my own self."

"I want you along with all your craziness," he replied.

He said nothing for a while. The fragments of his mind that remained were eager to assess the precise amount of what he had lost and what he had gained, but it was impossible.

"What's our house like in Al-Qata'i?" she asked, caressing his shoulder.

"It's a house that'll suit you, judge's daughter," he whispered, as though he was forgetting the entire past. "It has a fountain and wooden window frames. It's wide, with lofty ceilings. Light comes in from every side."

The words seemed to satisfy her vanity. "Were you thinking of me, Anas," she asked, "when you were building it?"

"We'll have lots of children," he told her, as though he had not heard what she had said. "I wanted it to be big, and I've always hoped for a big family. You know I used to live with my father, brother, and . . ."

He spoke for an hour or more, and she did not hear everything he said. The river appeared and flooded the night with eyes. Moments of union and affection can erase all memories. When destiny opens its arms, life starts to moderate.

Saeed ibn al-Farghani finished building the house in a month, just as he had promised. It was more splendid than anything Anas had ever seen, well-lit and full of warmth. Maisoon moved there, taking her mother and sister and bringing clothes and jewelry. Her eyes shown with delight.

Chapter II

Two weeks later, Anas received a letter from Ali in Al-Farma city, saying that he needed some money; fishing was not what it used to be. Ali did not usually complain about anything. Anas's brother seemed to be facing a problem, but he had no idea what it was.

He prepared some clothes and informed his wife that he was going to pay his brother a brief visit. There would be a couple of guards at the house, and he did not want her to go out until he returned. She tried questioning him, but he did not respond.

He rushed to Al-Farma with a troubled heart. No sooner did he get there than he heard Gameela screaming. He found his brother splayed out on a wooden plank, his entire body ripped apart by whips that caused blood, flesh, and bone to mix together. Anas grabbed hold of the plank and started untying Ali's bonds while he lay there, eyes shut.

"Quick," Anas told Gameela. "Get some water."

"Brother," she said in despair, "he died an hour ago. Don't tire yourself."

He stared at his brother's eyes, then shook him hard, begging him to move, but he did not.

"Ibn al-Mudabbir's men demanded money from him," Gameela told him breathlessly. "He didn't own anything. He gave them all the money you sent, but they weren't satisfied. They said he was secretly trading in fish and accused him of this and that. They tied him up and flayed him to death. It all happened on the same day. There was no time to let you know."

He kept trying to wake up his brother and talked to him incessantly. He finally stopped four hours later.

"Ibn al-Mudabbir," he told himself and her.

"Brother," Gameela said fearfully, "manumit me, and I'll go back to my family. I have nothing to do with these disasters."

He did not respond, but picked up his brother in his arms.

"I'm going to bury him in Al-Qata'i," he said. "You can go your own way."

She gathered her things and was gone in minutes. He put his brother's body on his horse. Before he could move, he found himself surrounded by Ibn al-Mudabbir's men.

"The Tax Administrator has not ordered the rebel's burial," one of them said. "He refused to pay what he owed."

"Get out of my way," Anas said forcefully, "or I'll kill you here."

The man drew his sword, and so did Anas.

"If it's blood you want," Anas said, "then let's fight it out!"

"It's the Tax Administrator's orders!"

"If you don't get out of my way, I'm going to kill you, and your companion too. Then I'll bury my brother."

The man wielded his sword, so Anas chopped off his arm and pierced the other man's heart. He felt possessed by all the power of jinns and demons. Screams arose, but his soul did not calm down. Clutching his brother's body, he looked at the man who was screaming as his arm lay on the ground. He buried his sword in the man's neck.

"I need to relieve you of a life that's all tyranny," he said.

With that, Anas shook his horse's reins and took off as fast as possible. His brother's body kept pulsing to the horse's movements, so that it seemed as though he were talking to Anas, blaming him for being angry and despairing for what was past and what was to come.

"Speak, Ali," Anas yelled. "What is it you want to say? Haven't I told you that the mouse in its hole isn't safe?! Which of us was right, brother?"

He took him back to Al-Qata'i, but shed no tears. He seemed to have lost all senses. Father first, now brother. He had no one left. When he reached Al-Qata'i, he buried his brother and prayed for him on his own. Ibn al-Mudabbir was not simply going to die. Death would bring peace and happiness.

Anas headed for the mosque. For a year or more, he had been going there in a bad mood. When he went there that day, his anger had abated, the situation was different, and his mood was one of anxiety.

When he went into the alcove, the shaikh greeted him, but he did not respond. He raised his hands in praise to God and started praying slowly and deliberately. After the final prostration, he delayed raising his head and standing up. Instead, he stayed quietly where he was for a while.

The shaikh stared at him and smiled with pleasure.

"Did you talk to Him?" the shaikh asked Anas once he had finished. "Did you complain?"

"Today the complaints were lengthy," Anas replied.

"Submission is a confession of weakness before Him," the shaikh said, "and confession of weakness before Him is the path to strength. He's the One closest to you, even with all your blame and anger. Perhaps you were not aware or sensitive to it. But He was always there inside you, holding you and dwelling in your depths. Maybe He was too close for you to see. Such closeness can often make people alarmed. The bright light burns the eyes. We have no idea where we're going or what's the end."

"Maybe you can offer me guidance. My suffering's now double, and so is my sorrow and anger."

"Today it's not anger at Him, but at yourself. Only the self can offer guidance to the self. If you inure yourself to the bright light, then you will see things more clearly. If you acknowledge your own ignorance, you could achieve the acme of your knowledge; if you admit your weakness, you could attain ultimate power. He is generous when the believer is miserly; He is perfect when the believer is in error; He is merciful when the believer sins. He is forgiving, that is certain. Remember that so you do not go astray."

"What do you want me to remember?"

"Bear in mind that humans are always seeking vengeance; with that, the will always dominates every single endeavor. That's always the case. However, if sometimes you forgive or forget, you can recover your power and self-control."

"That I can't do."

"Don't let your passion set fire to your own soul and the souls of your loved ones."

Anas paused for a moment. "I no longer know," he said.

"The only refuge from God is with Him," the shaikh replied firmly. "When intrigues wear you down, seek refuge with Him. He can bear with your anger and tolerate your doubts and lack of vision. He is the One who created the heart and understands that it faces trials. If you allow your heart to be crushed by anger and hatred, you do it wrong when it deserves better. Your Lord can bear with you because He loves you, a love that disowns anger. Allow some mercy and gentleness into your heart and remember His qualities and perfection so you don't meander through the halls of despair. Despair is always the enemy of faith. Allow your certainty about God to overcome your despair about His servants. For all of us, my son, He is the goal. Whenever you let rancor delve its way into your heart, every time you see Ibn al-Mudabbir in your own features, you'll never be able to get rid of him or fight him. He'll take up residence inside your heart."

"There can be no victory without power, Shaikh, and no justice without weapons."

The shaikh interrupted him. "Power resides in the heart's abandonment of hatred and malice, not in burning eyes and carving up bodies."

As Maisoon kept company with her husband, she felt a sense of alarm that baffled her. It was as though she were walking alone in the fields, aimless and miserable. She had never felt so listless. Anas had gone into his room and not allowed her to come in. She started tossing and turning on her pillow. Ali had died or been killed. Ibn al-Mudabbir had killed him. Was she the cause of all his problems, she wondered, or was she rather his means for vengeance? She could recall Ali's smiling face, his modest ambitions, his innocent laughter, his spontaneity, and his pure heart. He had none of Anas's bitterness and hatred. Death was always for the innocent above all else.

She heard Anas's door open. Maybe he wanted some water. She stood up without thinking and opened the door to her room where she had not been sleeping. She saw him there, walking as though he were somewhere outside this world, neither hearing nor seeing anything. He grabbed the jug and drank some water. Then suddenly he looked at her, and the two of them stared at each other without saying a word.

"Ali was the very best of men," she said softly. "But death always comes."

"Yes," he replied without thinking, "death always comes to the weak."

"I don't think the powerful can live forever," she replied.

He gave her a dubious look as though he did not recognize her. For a moment, she hesitated and looked at the water. Her eyes grew unfocused, and she could no longer see her face in the clear water. The water was ruffled and roiled by multiple faces. Then Anas's face emerged, the eyes full of affection. She went over to him and hugged him from behind without saying anything. A different kind of affection now poured forth, devoid of selfishness and blame. She laid her head against his back.

"Your grief is enough to split blood and carve up the guts," she whispered. "It's fanning the flames of a body that's already burning. Come to me, my darling."

She let go of him slowly, clasped his hand, and sat him down on their bed. Then she pulled him to her and buried her head in his chest.

"Do you realize," she whispered, "that I'll never get angry with you again as long as I live? My heart's run out of anger."

He gave her a bitter smile. "That anger lasted a long time, Maisoon," he replied.

"I swear to you," she told him, "that, whatever you do, I'll never lose my temper with you again. But don't be sad. Your sorrow penetrates to the very depths, and I can hardly breathe."

He put his arm around her shoulders. She thought he let out a sigh, but shed no tears. But he did let out a groan which echoed through every house in Al-Qata'i. She did not know whether to say something or remain silent.

"You're possessed by hatred of Ibn al-Mudabbir," she said after a while. "Such hatred is as tempting as love itself."

"If he killed me," he told her, "it would be better. I used to want to die. I envied my father his courage, and he wanted to live. I was just like my father, and he was like my mother. They both died too soon. My father stayed alive long enough to suffer, but now he's left me alone with only memories, most of which have gone, leaving behind only defeat and delusion."

She pronounced his name in a voice he did not understand. Then she kissed his hand and ran her own hand over his face and hair.

"Don't be sad," she said. "There has to be a way out. God will make one for us."

When he went out, he had made up his mind to punish Ibn al-Mudabbir's men. With his men sufficiently scared of the consequences of their actions, they refrained from broadcasting the news of Ali's death to other people. He ordered his men to bring all those involved in the plot to murder his brother at night. He tied them up and flogged them to death. There were three of them, and he witnessed their deaths, their screams, and their pleas. He thought he might feel some pity, but he did not; he thought too that he might be forgiving, but he was not. When the three men were dead, he took their corpses and dumped them in front of the Tax Administrator's house and in full sight of his men so that they had to take notice. There were no words, no message.

Ibn al-Mudabbir was furious, knowing full well who had done it. Time had caught up with his men, and he, the Tax Administrator, would get hold of Anas. He would torture him first and then rip his body apart slowly. He had just killed Anas's brother, and before that his father. Once Maisoon was his and he saw how much they loved each other, Anas would be torn apart like the victims of wild dogs without dying, and then stripped of his flesh piece by piece. But as long as Ahmad ibn Tulun was in Egypt, there was no hope of getting rid of Anas.

Maisoon sneaked into his room at night and hugged him from behind without saying a word. He was not asleep, nor was she. He was thinking about the corpses of his father and brother, the loss of life, and the heavy tread of tyranny. He put his hand on hers and squeezed. He had felt no pity for her, nor had he felt that, without him, she had been lost and with nowhere to seek refuge.

At midnight, he heard a knocking on the door. A slave-girl asked him to come quickly. He left his wife asleep and dressed himself. Ahmad ibn Tulun was waiting for him in the main square. He was expecting this and understood. Ahmad ibn Tulun scolded him angrily for killing Ibn al-Mudabbir's men. He said that they had died from the whipping, but Ahmad counted out for him the number of men killed since Anas had become Deputy Police Chief, many of them Ibn al-Mudabbir's men and associates. The caliph would not overlook the way his Tax Administrator had been humiliated or the threat that was facing him. When Anas returned to his house, Ahmad's words caused a pain that ate at his entire body. If he had disturbed

Ibn al-Mudabbir's sleep, he was happy; if he had humiliated him, he was satisfied. When sorrow spreads, it eats away at flesh like leprosy. The only cure for leprosy is God's mercy. Those who kill are killed, even if it happens later. God's mercy is for the weak before the strong, but he did not know whether he deserved to be forgiven. If only he felt some regret, but he did not. Even if he killed all Ibn al-Mudabbir's men, he would never regret it.

When he reached his house, he found her asleep. He went to sleep beside her without waking her. Half-asleep, she put her head on his chest.

"Do you think," she asked fearfully after a while, "that, whenever I'm the only one to see the shadow or don't see anything else, it's a touch of madness? I mean, when my loneliness afflicts me, life becomes impossible, and my heart collapses when faced with the very first darkness and doubt. I find myself helpless inside the prison of the heart and the confines of the soul. But when you're around me, even if you are far away, my soul expands and feels secure. I'm afraid that this condition of mine may be a touch of the jinn. People will say that your wife, Maisoon, is crazy. If you left me, I'd plunge into the pit of helplessness."

He put his hand on her hair.

"Before I'll ever leave you," he told her forcefully, "I'll die first. In fact, I'll cut up my body like so much wild fish. It'll never happen."

Anas sent letters to Ibn ash-Shaikh, but received no replies. Ibn ash-Shaikh had made up his mind to declare independence. His men had infiltrated the caliph's court, so he had no fear of reprisals for his rebellion. Ahmad was forced to take his army to Syria. He took all the different sections, hoping that he would not have to confront Ibn ash-Shaikh. He was well aware that, even if he defeated him, he would lose some of his men and the caliph would not be able to punish Ibn ash-Shaikh. Ahmad had lived with Abbasid caliphs and the machinations of power, and realized that once territory expands, it is impossible to maintain control. One caliph is killed, another is deposed, and a third loses his authority. In Samarra he had learned and observed. Anyone who does not wrap the picture in words has no hope of governing.

However, it looked as though the ancestors were following in Ahmad's footsteps, or he convinced himself that they were. When his mother's husband had been killed, his father-in-law had taken over as Governor of Egypt, and now Ibn al-Mudabbir had been conspiring against him. He had managed to save his army. A letter from Ibn al-Mudabbir had reached the caliph in which he warned the caliph about Ahmad ibn Tulun. If he managed to defeat Ibn ash-Shaikh, he might take over Syria and claim Egypt as his as well. He might well become so powerful that it would be impossible to depose him. Military victories always impair the mind. After Ahmad had already left with his army to confront Ibn ash-Shaikh, the caliph sent him a letter demanding that he stop and ordering him to return to Egypt. Then Amajur al-Turki took the caliph's army to face Ibn ash-Shaikh and defeated him. He did not kill Ibn ash-Shaikh, who fled to Armenia.

Ahmad brought his army back complete and focused his attention on Egypt.

At this point, Ahmad took the initiative and decided that he would be the one to depose Ibn al-Mudabbir. If the caliph had not been concerned about Shuqair's death and Ahmad had an army of a hundred thousand men, then maybe the caliph now realized how powerful he was. He ordered Anas to take some soldiers to Ibn al-Mudabbir's house and inform him that the Governor of Egypt, Abu al-Abbas Ahmad ibn Tulun, had decided to remove him from office, and he needed to leave Egypt within two days. Ahmad appointed Ibn Hilal Tax Administrator in his place.

Every steed can stumble, and boldness is the greatest of faults, inspiring death and expelling fear from tranquil souls. Ahmad ibn Tulun removed the Tax Administrator from office without asking the caliph's permission. Not only that, but he appointed his replacement. This was an initiative to traverse time and establish principles, an initiative to fulfill the dream. He was wrong to assume that the city built without walls would protect him; he was wrong to think that a hundred thousand men could alter the course of the stars and the sun's orbit; he was wrong to assume that ancestors were standing with him and watching him from on high and that the fallen star was foretelling the days to come and the gleaming sun. Hurry up and stop! That was the destiny of everyone who kidded themselves about independence for this country. The caliph Al-Mu'tamid ordered him to immediately restore Ibn al-Mudabbir to his position. The caliph had started to have doubts in the Governor of Egypt. Ibn al-Mudabbir promptly prepared a lengthy letter in which he discussed Ahmad ibn Tulun.

Ibn al-Mudabbir could not send such an important letter to the caliph with a normal messenger. Following Shuqair's death, he needed someone he could trust, someone with enough cunning to converse and convince. In his letter, Ibn al-Mudabbir described Ahmad ibn Tulun's actions over the two years he had been Governor of Egypt. He described in detail the city that Ibn Tulun had built, with each of his soldiers receiving a plot of land. It was less than a year old. Anyone who builds a city for his soldiers has no intention of leaving the country. When Amr ibn al-As had built Fustat, he had meant it to be a new capital for Egypt, far away from Alexandria. He had been working for the caliph, not for himself, and his army had consisted of Arabs. When the Abbasids had constructed the fortress city, it was for their soldiers, not for a governor or his soldiers. Ahmad's building Al-Qata'i, with a splendid palace on its outskirts, suggested disloyalty and conspiracy. He stressed that Ahmad had no intention of leaving Egypt, either that day or the next.

Ibn al-Mudabbir wrote that people who build things are not going to leave; people erecting pillars ascend to the throne of the ancients. Ahmad was not just and knew nothing about fairness. Ever since he had arrived, he had been oppressing the Tax Administrator. Not only that, but the Tax Administrator had managed to confirm that Ahmad and his aides were the ones who had stolen the Alexandria tax revenues. Moreover, Ahmad had appointed a murderous spy named Anas, who had avoided paying taxes. If the governor appointed as a deputy police chief someone who was a fugitive from an accusation of murder and who stole and plundered, then he could no longer be considered reliable. He had started acting without asking the caliph's opinion and dealing with the caliph just like Ibn ash-Shaikh, or actually worse. Even Ibn ash-Shaikh had not mustered an army around him like the one Ahmad ibn Tulun had. When he had dismissed the Tax Administrator without the caliph's permission, he had brazenly breached his allegiance to the caliph. Ahmad had to go. The caliph could possibly let his wife and son stay in Iraq. He would not object or betray anyone, even though Ahmad had wanted to do so.

After receiving the Tax Administrator's letter, the caliph did not spend much time thinking before deciding. Ever since Ahmad had built his city and formed his army, the caliph had sensed Ahmad's independent intentions in Egypt. But he also realized that soldiers make rules and calculations. Ahmad's behavior and reactions were not what the caliph was expecting.

If the caliph ordered Ahmad to return to Baghdad at once and hand over the governorship of Egypt to someone else, he might well refuse and declare war. If the caliph threatened Ahmad's wife and son, he might well decide to sacrifice them. He needed a subtle plan to get rid of Ahmad ibn Tulun. The caliph thought of making use of Ibn al-Mudabbir to help in formulating a quick plan. The caliph would instruct him to go to Egypt with a large army to take over the government. At the same time, the caliph would send Ahmad ibn Tulun a warm, friendly letter, informing him that an even better position was awaiting him; indeed, he needed to be in Baghdad alongside the caliph. The caliph would invite him to come back as soon as possible, and Ahmad would have to go back; Ibn al-Mudabbir was sure that Ahmad would never sacrifice his own son. His son would be all he had left, even if he decided to sacrifice his wife.

The caliph's letter to Ahmad ibn Tulun read:

> We have seen fit to restore to you the conduct of our caliphal court and the administration of our kingdom. Hand over to anyone you choose your Egypt and the city that is yours and in your name. Come back to us to take

up the position that we have chosen for you and for which we have deemed you well qualified. Farewell.

Ahmad fully understood the import of the letter and the covert threat it contained. He realized that his time in Egypt was at an end.

Ibn Tulun's era ended before it even began. He had only been in Egypt for two years, noted the Egyptians sarcastically. But they had to admit that those two years in which he had been Governor of Egypt had seen unprecedented developments. The day he had arrived in Egypt, a star had fallen from the sky. That was certainly a bad omen, even though the senile Pyramid Witch had declared that ancestors were hailing his advent and the way he lit up the earth and temples. Astrologers only lead you astray. Ibn al-Mudabbir would never leave Egypt. Egyptians had become inured to the Tax Administrator for an age or more. Over a thousand years past, they had learned that reformers disappear and those who collect money and brandish the sword stay around. They all realized that the last era of prosperity was at an end, that time is tossed back and forth among us all, that humans are not equal, and that Noah's flood and Moses's sea were their last link to their ancestors.

Regarding their ancestors, they did not know very much about them. They always had gold in their guts and maybe they worshipped idols; yet their buildings were full of magic and pride. People said that they had invented astronomy, burying along with their monarchs all the secrets of magic and learning. They said that their ancestors had worshipped knowledge and kept it hidden from every conqueror and adventurer. People went even further and suggested that their ancestors hoarded knowledge in their tombs, along with wooden sarcophagi and pottery bowls to challenge all ages. No one had known Ahmad's dream; there was no point in knowing it. Even if Ahmad were to come out on top in today's struggle, he would still have to face thousands of others. Egypt was a land ablaze with conflicts. All who passed by were driven; those who remained were acolytes. Quests were the keys to the secret. The quest was the buried treasure, but entering tombs was an impossibility. Poor Ahmad! He had nearly realized his city; Egyptians had moved there with their ovens, their stores, their markets, and their grills. Then came the caliph's order.

People were saying that the caliph was keeping Ahmad's wife and son as hostages. If Ahmad thought about an independent Egypt, he would never see his son again; and his son was his entire life. Every man has a particular love and a soft spot that can crush and destroy him. Ahmad loved his wife and son, but his son in particular. Who does not love his son and want to keep him for his entire life?

Alas for Ahmad and his army; they would be scattered over the earth like so many swarming locusts. Perhaps the caliph would summon them and send them into losing conflicts that would do away with them within a year. All Egypt knew what was going to happen to the fisherman's son. He would be cut down by the swords of Ibn al-Mudabbir's men, and would see his wife in Ibn al-Mudabbir's arms. He would be burned alive in the ovens of Al-Qata'i, along with hunks of old bread. Ibn al-Mudabbir would cut out his tongue so he could not scream and stick a pole in his rectum, but he would not die. Alas for the fisherman's son; but he had been brash and seemed bent on revenge. Secure escape was preferable to stupid courage. Ahmad had been bold and dreamed. The fisherman's son had been bold and loved. Ibn al-Mudabbir did not need to be bold. He had known and observed what they had not. Yes, indeed, time is tossed back and forth among us all. A thousand years ago, time drew near, then it moved away again. Such separation was part of inevitable destiny. Defeat was always at hand. When Ibn al-Mudabbir died, he would be replaced by hundreds or more just like him. What did Ahmad want? Did people not understand? Had he built a city and established an army? What for? What was his goal? They said that Maisoon was spectacularly beautiful. Would Ibn al-Mudabbir kill her or show her some understanding? She was his only soft spot. What if the entire population of Egypt went to Maisoon and asked for mercy? Courage might work, or it might not.

News of Ahmad ibn Tulun's dismissal as Governor of Egypt struck Anas like the powerful waves in which his father had drowned many years earlier. Hope had been a constant, and stability had grown some green shoots. But then the end had come so quickly, so unexpectedly. Once Ahmad left, Ibn al-Mudabbir would exact his vicious punishments. Anyone who had acknowledged the dream and tried to learn would be punished. That was standard operating procedure for the caliph's men and holders of governorships. Anyone who had learned and hoped would have to be punished. Both knowledge and hope were a government monopoly and a crime for anyone else. Everyone should remain in his place: no need to change location, dig the soil, or extract worms and precious stones. Everyone should remain in his place: no need to build walls, houses, or silos. Construction calls for planning and hope, and hope requires knowledge. As just noted, knowledge is both a monopoly and a crime.

"This time, brother," Ahmad told Anas knowingly and calmly, "Ibn al-Mudabbir's won."

"My lord," Anas replied, "if we sent a letter to the caliph or you let me go to Baghdad again and talk to the vizier, we might be able to get the decision changed. I've succeeded before, and I'll do it again this time."

"You need to learn when to stop resisting," Ahmad told him forcefully, "and when to raise the flag of peace!"

"I won't raise any flag to Ibn al-Mudabbir."

"Anas, separate your personal anger from this problem. You have to keep heart and mind separate in making decisions."

"Ibn al-Mudabbir's never going to win."

Their eyes met. "He's already won," Ahmad said. "It's all over. But I'll be back, that's for sure."

There was silence. "My son, Al-Abbas," Ahmad went on, "is all I have. How often have I dreamed of him drowning in blood! You don't have any children, Anas. When you do, you'll understand."

"Give me a chance to try."

"I'll think about it. I'm worried about Egypt. In fact, it's overwhelming me and controlling my pulse. Maybe we need to visit the Pyramid Witch so she can tell us again why the stars fall."

Ibn al-Mudabbir's triumph was not yet complete. He rested his head on the back of his chair. After so much worry and exhaustion, it was time for some quiet. Things had almost reached a crisis point, but now everything was stable and calm again. He still could not believe that Ahmad had removed him from office in such a cunning and deceptive way, but now he had paid the price for such outrageous conduct. Now that the caliph had restored Ibn al-Mudabbir to his position, it marked Ahmad's first defeat in the eyes of Egyptians, the army, and the Abbasids. Then the caliph had deposed Ahmad from his position.

"Now you can kill her husband," Abu Sha'ara told him, "and have her for yourself. This time, no one can stop you."

"You fool!" Ibn al-Mudabbir replied. "I tell you I love her, but you talk to me as though I've no heart."

"You mean you're going to let her husband live for her sake?"

Ibn al-Mudabbir was silent for a while.

"Maybe she loves him," he went on. "I don't want her to be miserable. If I killed him, I'd be digging a spot for him inside her heart forever."

"I don't understand, my lord."

"I want her to know the truth about him and to realize who loves her the way Qais loved Laila, the love of the treasure thief."

"These profound thoughts confuse me, my lord."

"That's because you don't understand poetry and love. Once I give her the choice, she'll come to me willingly."

"Do you intend to deceive her?"

"Why deceive her? Who deserves her love more, me or the fisherman's son?"

"You, of course, my lord. There's no comparison."

"She'll realize that. All I want is to make sure that she realizes it before my heart wilts for love of her. She'll realize it very soon."

The summons that the fisherman's son received to visit Ibn al-Mudabbir's house did not alarm Anas. He pictured himself stabbing Ibn al-Mudabbir in front of his men. Whenever he smelled blood or tasted it in his mouth, he would remain calm and hopeful. He had no idea why Ibn al-Mudabbir wanted to see him, but realized that he had been wanting such a meeting so that he could chop his head off slowly, even though that would never happen.

The two men looked at each other.

"I haven't had the chance," Ibn al-Mudabbir said calmly, "to offer you my condolences on your brother's death."

Anas did not respond.

"You don't know me, fisherman's son," Ibn al-Mudabbir went on. "If you did, you'd realize that I prefer fun to violence, and poetry to whipping. I have no choice; it's my job. I have to be tough, just like your father, who used to kill the fish that came trustingly into his nets to feed. What kind of cruelty was that? What crime had those fish committed? You'd love to kill me right now; I realize that. Maybe you want to torture me first."

Anas still said nothing, lips pursed.

"I could keep Ahmad ibn Tulun in the Egyptian government," Ibn al-Mudabbir went on, "but if I did, it would be the end of me. That's certain. He hates me the way fish hate deceitful fishermen. Or Ahmad can leave, and I'll kill you and be married to Maisoon. It's your choice."

Anas still did not respond. He realized that anything he said in anger would end his life.

"You'll be saving Egypt," Ibn al-Mudabbir continued, "and leaving Maisoon. I promise you, I won't force her to do anything. Think about it."

"It won't happen, my lord," Anas replied forcefully.

"You won't need to leave her until the caliph agrees to let Ahmad stay," Ibn al-Mudabbir continued. "I'm going to cancel the taxes on sea-fishing, natron, cattle, and agriculture. I'll write a decree to that effect. You won't need to leave her until after I've sent it to the caliph. The men will witness our words, as will Ahmad himself."

Anas opened his eyes wide and swallowed hard. He had left his sword outside. Could he pierce the Tax Administrator's heart with his own hands?

"If Maisoon refuses to be married to me," Ibn al-Mudabbir said, drawing closer to Anas, "I won't send that decree. Egypt's fate is in your hands, and so is Ahmad's. The fisherman's son has the power to decide whether the governor stays, and whether the necks of farmers, fishermen, and all Egyptians are to be spared. She's just a woman. Do you want to save thousands and sacrifice yourself, or do you want all Egyptians to suffer the same fate as your brother?"

"The people of Egypt are already suffering," Anas replied firmly.

"Maybe Maisoon has a different opinion?"

"She doesn't have an opinion," Anas replied, "because she already knows."

"What does she know, Anas?"

"She knows that I've vowed to kill anyone who takes her from me and kill her as well."

Ibn al-Mudabbir raised his sword and put it on Anas's neck.

"You can't fight the caliph and his men," Ibn al-Mudabbir said. "The sword will go through your neck, and you'll be dead in an instant."

Perhaps that is what Anas wanted. He did not flinch or close his eyes.

"I'll take that threat as coming from a lunatic," Ibn al-Mudabbir said, his sword still on Anas's neck. "Love is madness. Abla the hairdresser now tells us everything. If you left Maisoon and she refused to be married to me and went back to you, I wouldn't stop her. I'll say that in front of my men and Ahmad. I realize that you're going to ask me how I'll keep Ahmad in Egypt. I know how to keep him in office, the same way I know how to depose him."

"You're just like the king who claims to be able to bestow life or death. Can you move the sun West to East, my lord?"

"I'm not fond of Egyptian sarcasm. I don't know if it springs from knowledge or ignorance."

Anas did not respond.

"I promised you, do you remember?" Ibn al-Mudabbir went on triumphantly. "I'm going to kill your spirit before your body. You'll have no lover in this world. The judge's daughter can be with me or with her Lord. The Deputy Police Chief can leave now."

Anas's heart shuddered as he left without saying a word.

He rushed home, his heartbeats clearly audible, and called for Maisoon as he opened the door. She was sitting and staring at the floor, her hands clasped around her legs in despair and frustration. No sooner did he set eyes on her than he realized she knew everything.

"That lunatic!" he said angrily as he sat down. "I'll die before I leave you."

She looked at him.

"No," she said. "This time I won't blame you if you do it."

He held her hands.

"What do you read in my heart?" he asked her.

Her tears started flowing, but she said nothing. He sat down beside her and clasped her shoulders.

"Don't worry," he said.

"Our separation might save everyone around us," she whispered. "If Ahmad stayed and Ibn al-Mudabbir canceled the taxes, the people of Egypt could breathe again, and maybe even thrive."

"Ibn al-Mudabbir's death will solve everything," Anas said emphatically.

"Do you trust his word, Anas? I do. He won't break it. If he said that in front of his men and Ahmad as well, he won't break it."

"He wants to create a barrier between Ahmad and me. Ahmad has a soft spot too, his son, Al-Abbas. Ibn al-Mudabbir knows how to get to that soft spot, then eradicate everyone standing in his way."

"He doesn't lie," she replied firmly.

He said nothing. Suddenly she shuddered and rested her head on his chest.

"Hold me," she said.

He held her tightly. "Why are you so worried?" he asked. "I've promised you that, even if the entire world collapsed, I would never leave you."

"If you stay with me here, Ahmad will go. Then Ibn al-Mudabbir will take over. After a while, he might kill you. Who knows? Tyranny will be back and firmly implanted in Egypt. If Ahmad stays, Ibn al-Mudabbir will run amok. But why would he bother doing that? What for?"

"I know what for."

"You think he wants me."

"I think he's in love with you."

"Don't say that!" she said, hugging his neck.

"You know it, and so do I."

"If you knew that you could save hundreds of people and sacrifice yourself," she asked, wiping away her tears nervously, "or you could live while hundreds of people died, what would you do? If we separate, I'll die."

"So will I," he replied without even thinking.

"But you'll make that sacrifice and fly high," she said firmly. "You'll hover in the sky like eagles and falcons, unbothered by mundane issues down on earth. From your lofty position, you'll see the heads of black snakes firmly fixed in a bottomless sea; you'll view the central rust on street squares as rubies gleaming from above. You're different from me and Ibn al-Mudabbir."

"Why are you crying?"

She buried her head in his neck and kissed it. "I know the choice you've made before you even say it," she said. "You've made up your mind."

"Yes," he replied firmly.

"You're not going to fly high."

"No, I'm not."

"You'll never leave me, Anas. I've known that from the very beginning. It's not because you love me or related to all the qualities you don't like; it's not because you can't bear to separate us, even though you might be killing the entire Egyptian people. No, it's because you're bent on revenge. The biggest revenge of all is to deprive Ibn al-Mudabbir of me. I know you. Didn't I say that I know you?"

For just a moment he stared at her. "That's strange talk," he said, giving her an angry look.

"It would be better," she said, wiping away her tears, "if you just killed me and sent my corpse to Ibn al-Mudabbir. You'd break his heart the way he did yours over your father and brother. That'll make you very happy."

"Have you finished?" he asked her calmly.

She let out a loud scream and shuddered. "Kill me," she muttered, "or else I'm going to kill myself. But don't leave me again. My love is like a grain of mustard seed in comparison with your hatred for Ibn al-Mudabbir. Your heart is incapable of making the adjustment between love and hate. Hatred has ravished your heart and smothered its every corner, enfolding love inside it. It can't move any more. But don't leave me. This time I'll kill myself. I'll kill myself if you don't leave me, or if you leave me, or if . . ."

"Stop!" he told her, grabbing her arms. "Don't say any more. Listen to me, and don't interrupt. Maisoon, Ibn al-Mudabbir will break into pieces, burn, and die one thousand times before he ever sees you again. I'll never leave you. I'll go with you to every spot in earth and sky. I'll attach your heart to mine so that there's no escape and no hesitation. You're mine for evermore. Time may bring some unknown misfortune, but if you remember these words of mine, you'll be safe. Do you understand?"

She kept shivering as she strummed her fingers on the wall and muttered some rapid words to herself.

"Maisoon," he said firmly, putting his hand over her heart.

"Maisoon's crazy, Anas," she replied in despair. "She's not right for you. I asked you to hold me, but you didn't. Why not?"

"After what I've just promised you," he whispered in her ear, "no shadow will follow you and no darkness will cloud your mind. Calm down. If you do that, I'll hold you."

He pressed on her heart till it hurt and pushed his fingers against her bones. She closed her eyes.

"I can have no happiness," she said, "as long as my mind keeps leaving me and running away. Death puts an end to all pain."

He used his fingers to wipe away her tears. "Do you want to put an end to your tears and kill my spirit?" he asked. "You'll never do that. Remember that you have an inner strength, perhaps even more than you know. Maisoon, it's patience we need."

He put his arms around her. "We're all fighting the shadow and the heart demons that envelop us," he told her. "You're not alone, Maisoon. Very few people manage to avoid this war. Either you work with your heart demons or else you have a violent confrontation with them. Any separation between us will be temporary. If I tell you that you're more important to me than anything else, do you believe me?"

She nodded her head vigorously. He hugged her even harder.

"Perhaps if they realized how crazy I am," she said in despair, "they'd ask you to leave me and put me in the clinic that Ibn Tulun is building."

He turned her toward him and held her again.

"If they realized how crazy they, I, and all humanity are," he said, "they'd stay silent for shame. I want you to say farewell to your father and to tell him that you're going away with me. Ask him to keep it all a secret; no one should know."

"We're running away together?" she stammered.

"Yes, we're leaving for Iraq."

He picked her up in his arms and carried her like a child that has just lost both parents. He kept on rocking her as he told her repeatedly how much he loved her. His heart was heavy with thoughts about an unknown future, one that might lead to separation or destruction. He did not know as yet. She closed her eyes and fell asleep sobbing.

Every crop has its season, and every heart its appointed time. He had to have been thinking about killing Ibn al-Mudabbir for some time. Why had he not done it? If his destiny was also to die, then people would at least regard his evil deed with sympathy. Was it her arms he wanted? Had that diverted him from revenge? Was it a new house in Al-Qata'i that he wanted, along with a sword and prized horses? If he killed Ibn al-Mudabbir now, Ahmad would leave and a new Ibn al-Mudabbir would arrive.

Words accumulated around Anas, from lots of people. It was as if he were both the cause and the solution; he had destroyed and built, he had been cruel and forgiving. The earth might quake all around him, and yet he would still be convinced that death would be easier than surrender. Saeed, son of Katib al-Farghani, rushed over to remind him to mention his name to Ahmad ibn Tulun. He then asked him to give up Maisoon for the sake of the Egyptian people. As long as Ibn al-Mudabbir remained, everyone had to adjust to tyranny and placate it. Love was neither the end nor the guide. Saeed himself was still wandering in despair because of a love over which he had no control.

There was another meeting in Ibn al-Mudabbir's house, between Ahmad ibn Tulun and Ibn al-Mudabbir, and Maisoon's name was a constant in the conversation.

"I'm really sorry to see you leave, Abu al-Abbas," Ibn al-Mudabbir said, "but I understand that the caliph needs you for something bigger and more important than Egypt."

Ahmad gave him a fixed stare. "What's bigger and more important than Egypt?" he asked, repeating Ibn al-Mudabbir's words.

Ibn al-Mudabbir looked at Ibn Tulun. "I swear to you, Abu al-Abbas, that I'm prepared to make sacrifices for your sake—only after the caliph agrees, of course. I'll lower taxes and give you due consideration."

"People say that you're in love with the judge's daughter," Ahmad said with a smile. "You're of a certain age . . . Who's this girl for whose sake Ibn al-Mudabbir is willing to keep his hands off Ahmad?"

"You seem to have some doubts about my loyalty, Abu al-Abbas. I'm your brother and friend. Maisoon is a victim of her father; she was married against her will to a man she did not even know. There must be agreement in marriage. I merely wanted them to let her choose."

"Would she choose you, brother?"

"The Tax Administrator does have a heart, Abu al-Abbas. Turkish soldiers may not know anything about love, but we love and have passions. There's nothing wrong with that. As you point out, I've now reached a certain age, and the world is no longer my primary concern."

"Your primary concern now is the judge's daughter!"

"Have you come to make fun of me, Abu al-Abbas?"

"No, I've come to let you know that you're a friend. I've never wanted to do you any harm. Even when I dismissed you from office, it was because of my appreciation for you. I wanted you to have the Syrian taxes because I realized the significance of your presence in Egypt and what Egyptians were expecting from you. You're loyal to the caliph, and so am I."

"The fisherman's son will divorce the judge's daughter. He was married to her against her will."

"I can't order that," Ahmad replied with a smile. "I don't know how you can intercede on my behalf with the caliph, as if you had a magic ball that controlled people's destinies. It's all in God's hands, brother."

"Those who show modesty toward God, Ahmad, are raised up by Him. And you're not modest."

"Can there be any modesty greater than my coming to your house to tell you that you're the winner for today? I feel pity for your heart, dealing with a love that can transform and adjust a person's very being."

When Ahmad left Ibn al-Mudabbir's house, he had made up his mind. He wanted to confirm how confident of certain victory Ibn al-Mudabbir was and to reassure himself about the story of the judge's daughter.

He went back to the square and found Anas waiting for him. Anas insisted on going to Iraq and having a meeting with the caliph's vizier. Anas's suggestion to Ahmad ibn Tulun was his final attempt at victory.

Ahmad ibn Tulun agreed to Anas, son of Hamza al-Skandari, traveling to Iraq, along with Al-Wasiti, to have a meeting with the caliph's vizier, Hasan ibn Makhlad, and explain the situation to him. He started putting together gifts, precious jewels, and rare food. He collected money, fine Dimyat cotton, mules, and horses, along with treasured ornaments, silk, and brocade. This would be the final effort, but it had to be tried. He was not going to defy the caliph; that would lead to his son's death. If he defied the caliph, he might win, because he had a powerful army that was much larger that Ibn ash-Shaikh's, but his son would die; that was certain. He could not gamble with his son's life; he was all he had left. He could not leave Egypt; it was everything he had dreamed. This was the final effort. He had sent a letter in which he explained what had happened. He said that he had not been involved in the murder of Shuqair, as the evidence had made clear. Shuqair had died alone, and he, Ahmad, was prepared to cooperate with Ibn al-Mudabbir to give the caliph's message more prominence. The question of the fisherman's son was a trifling matter that need not concern the caliphate. In fact, the fisherman's son had come to the caliph in Baghdad in person so that he could decide on the matter.

He realized that Anas's journey to Iraq was a risk. The caliph might put him in prison or even kill him. Ahmad did not usually sacrifice his own men, but this was a last resort. What he was hoping for was greater than any one man, revenge, or the judge's lovely daughter. Ibn al-Mudabbir had won this conflict. He, Ahmad, needed to lower his flag, admit defeat, and start all over again. Egypt was not big enough for both Ahmad ibn Tulun and Ibn al-Mudabbir. But as long as Al-Abbas was in the caliph's hands, there was no hope of an independent Egypt. The dream was still haunting him. He would ask the caliph to restore his wife and son to him in exchange for these gifts. They had to be very expensive and flashy.

This was exactly what Anas wanted: to travel to Iraq. He knew it could well be his final trip there, and he might never see Egypt again.

Anas returned to his house, surrounded by guards, in order to prepare for the journey and join the caravan to Iraq.

Maisoon looked into his eyes to read her fate.

"This time," he told her, "I don't know if I'm going to make it out alive. It all depends on the caliph and his whims."

"He won't pardon you," she said quietly. "He's afraid of Ibn Tulun and wants to teach him a lesson."

"You're coming with me," he told her firmly. "That's an order."

She lowered her head, and he pulled her toward him.

"Did you tell your father and say goodbye?" he asked her. "Did you ask him not to tell anyone that we were traveling, no matter who it was?"

"Yes."

He hugged her and kissed her cheek slowly. As he whispered in her ear, her eyes were closed, and her mouth shut tight.

"Your father has connections with shaikhs and judges in Iraq," he said. "You'll be staying in the house of one of them. I'm hoping that the judge will help us."

"When do we start the journey?"

"Today. The guards are waiting outside. We're leaving for Iraq today. Get your things and put your veil on."

Maisoon left the house after night had obscured all features and eyes. She followed her husband, walking hand in hand through Al-Qata'i for an hour or more. The quarters seemed deserted, except for bits of meat and bread, and the calls of crows. Wild dogs emerged from their lairs to scavenge. The lanes twisted and turned like snakes. Buildings blended into each other. She kept feeling her way and searching for his hand. Al-Qata'i fell away, its buildings and inhabitants disappearing gradually. Or was the darkness removing each inhabitant, inducing forgetfulness and departure?

A lot happened that night. The caravan awaited Anas and Maisoon on the outskirts of the city, free of fences or walls. The people who lived there were soldiers. It was protected by crowds of inhabitants by day, and was safe at night within the city. But there was no security on its outskirts. Ibn al-Mudabbir did not like Al-Qata'i and did not live there. Egypt was his personal treasury, or so he said.

She screamed and put up a fight. Lighted candles appeared in the houses as people tried to see what was happening. Who had been killed and who had survived? Men covered his mouth, and a sword was put to his neck. Fifty men or more, and he was alone. Some of them fled amid all the screams.

"You were on your way to Iraq," one of them said. "We'll make sure you get there. Carry on with the journey. Your wife has gone back to her father."

He continued to put up a fight, but twenty men threw him to the ground and knocked him out.

When Anas opened his eyes again, he was in the desert. He had been tied with a thick rope before he could move. One of the men stuck the point of his sword into Anas's hand.

"The Tax Administrator's always merciful," he said. "He wants you alive and will ensure that you complete your journey."

The sword hit some stubborn bones, but it managed to make it all the way through. Anas suppressed his screams.

"This is to make sure you'll never write again," he heard the man say. "The bookseller's been aggravating the Tax Administrator. Everything he writes is harmful."

The man left the sword in his hand for a moment, then withdrew it slowly.

"We don't want to kill one of Ahmad's men," the man said. "That wouldn't be right."

Anas did not scream, but he knew that now life had no value. Taking the sword out would destroy all the sinews. Leaving it in place would be a guarantee of continuing pain. Sometimes leaving a dagger in place is an act of mercy only known to people who have had a dagger inside them for years.

The man looked at Anas and noticed blood oozing from his mouth where he had bitten his lips because of the pain.

"People say the Deputy Police Chief killed Shuqair, the Postmaster," the man said. "He also killed a lot of Ibn al-Mudabbir's men."

The man grabbed a hammer and slowly moved closer to Anas. "Deputy Police Chief," he said, "your hand's going to be no good for writing or killing."

He brought the hammer down on Anas's fingers as hard as he could. Anas heard his fingers splinter like so many mountain rocks. He shut his eyes, hoping that the pain might take pity on him, but it did not. He bit his tongue, and more blood spilled onto his lips and chin—cold drops. Were they, he wondered, thick, black drops like the ones that dripped from the young man before he died of impaling? Their coldness turned into teeth that gnashed at his entire face.

"The Tax Administrator considered severing all your limbs," the man said, "but he changed his mind. Instead, he wants you to hope, to long, to grieve, to feel pain, and to regret what you've done. Spending twenty years in prison without a woman is much worse for a man than having both legs cut off, especially when he realizes that there's a woman who used to be his wife now enjoying the embrace of a man like no other, namely the Tax Administrator. We're going to leave your legs in a tight clamp. You won't know what to do with them. At that point, you'll want to amputate them with your own hands, but you won't find a hand with which to do it."

His vision blurred; he could no longer see the man clearly. The man came close and raised his sword.

"But you're a thief as well," he said. "You stole the Alexandria taxes and the judge's daughter. Thieves have their hands cut off, fisherman's son."

He brought the sword down as hard as he could on Anas's wrist and severed the uninjured hand.

"It wasn't any use, brother," the man said, holding the severed hand. "Why bother keeping it? Your right hand now knows how feeble it is. You can probably use it to fight flies, but not Ibn al-Mudabbir. I showed you some mercy and used a drawn sword."

Anas could not speak. He remembered the man with the pole impaling his innards. Bright light dazzled his eyes, but he had no idea where it came from. He could almost swear that he could see the fingers moving on his amputated hand. He saw his father's face as he pleaded with the servant. He shook his head, then heard a voice somewhere near him.

"That's enough. Bind his hand, or he'll bleed to death."

The man put him on his horse.

"Ibn al-Mudabbir wanted to teach you just one lesson," the man said. "He orders you never to return to Egypt. This horse is going to take you to the caravan in Syria, whether you like it or not. Continue your journey to Iraq."

All he could remember were the drops of blood that kept falling slowly. That sword had opened the dam, and now the contents were spilling out. In his imagination he kept seeing images and shapes of his own father, chiding him for being angry and resentful.

"Anas," his father kept saying, "you're responsible for my death. I saw your eyes. I saw your contempt as I pleaded with the servant during the whipping. Do you remember? You chided me for feeling pain, and now you're feeling it too. When there's pain, there's no difference between courage and cowardice. With loss, Anas, all destinies are the same, and life has no purpose."

His father's voice blended with his brother's. Ali would always laugh, but that day he was crying and begging. Those who love the world are the first to depart; those who can tolerate its treachery are the first to get rid of it. The journey is a long one, and the path is filled with the dead and blood. Many people laugh, among them now his father. They were laughing at him: the fisherman's son wants to fight the Tax Administrator?! He's completely crazy, imagining that he's a blue jinni emerging from beneath the earth and the depths of the sea. As if he could fight a caliph in Iraq on his own. When ants stand in front of a herd of cows, they deserve to be trampled underfoot.

"You kept blaming me," his father was shouting angrily. "Why?"

Chapter 12

He put his hand on his head, hoping that the pain would diminish. His eye understood and learned. He tried to move his hand; his fingers were hurting, but there was just a stump at the end of his wrist.

"Anas," his companion Al-Wasiti said.

"Where are we?"

"On the Syrian border. You can go back if you want, or go ahead if you plan to see the caliph. The men who kidnapped your wife handed you over to us to join the caravan. You have a deep wound. I've cleaned it and bound it up. They cut your hand off. If you go back now . . ."

"We're going to see the caliph," Anas said without even thinking. "Then I'll go back. And when I do, I'm going to be piercing sinews and ripping ribs apart. I know what's going to happen."

He tried to move his arm, but could not do it.

"Take it slowly, brother," the man said. "The wound's still deep."

"Maybe I won't be able to write. I've never tried writing with my left hand."

"Maybe."

"But I hope I can still hold a sword and slaughter people. I need that."

All the way to Iraq, he thought of neither Ibn al-Mudabbir nor Ahmad ibn Tulun, but he did think about Judge Yahya. When and how had he betrayed him? How was it that the judge had been defeated? Every man has a passage of soft skin that can be penetrated by swords to reach the depths of surrender. With what had Ibn al-Mudabbir threatened him? What had he promised him? Did the judge think that if he separated Anas from his daughter, he would have defeated tyranny and helped the Egyptian people? What kind of naivete and despair had overcome the scholarly reader? No matter. Anas's father was still asking the waves for rescue, and his brother Ali was still stolidly facing down the whippers. Anas was still capable of revenge. The Tax Administrator must have been in despair, his mind destroyed by passion, to promise things he did not possess. It was a long war that had just begun. It would involve a certain amount of risk and a lot of careful planning.

Anas did not say anything to Al-Wasiti. All the way, he was stony-faced and his eyes meandered. After a while, Al-Wasiti said he knew what happened. He knew that Judge Yahya had retrieved or kidnapped his daughter before she could escape to Iraq with her husband. It was all done with Ibn al-Mudabbir's help.

"I'm going to get her back from the judge and Ibn al-Mudabbir," Anas told him forcefully. "That'll be when we've finished our business."

Al-Wasiti stared at him as though he were raving mad. He concluded that Anas's recent brush with death was forcing him to get a grip on himself and not shed tears over everything that he had lost.

Once they arrived in Baghdad, Anas and Al-Wasiti went to see the vizier, Hasan ibn Makhlad.

"My lord Vizier," Anas said, "how fortunate I am to have a meeting with you today!"

"You're unfortunate, fisherman's son!"

"On the contrary, I work with one of your commanders, someone who's always working on your behalf."

"Stop playing with words! I've heard that you translate and publish Greek ideas. I don't approve of them, nor do I appreciate a lot of argument. Now you've come, you'll be paying the price for all your actions. How can Ahmad ibn Tulun surround himself with killers? I've no idea."

For a moment, Anas looked down. "Will my lord permit me to speak?"

"Speak."

"There is a certain wisdom in the words and disputations of the Greeks. They state that the resources of men only emerge when they have in their hands both power and authority. You are a source of pure gold."

"Who said that?"

"Plato."

"Caliph Ma'mun was fascinated by it," the vizier said, "and Ahmad ibn Tulun as well. For my part, I want Muslims to stop arguing and fighting."

"My lord, disputation doesn't lead to conflicts; on the contrary, it brings people together. Has not God created us all different so that we can get to know each other? To know each other, there's no better way than discussion. But Plato also says that courage involves people knowing what needs to be feared and what does not. My lord caliph only fears God."

"I'm not following what you're saying, Egyptian. I don't know why Ahmad ibn Tulun appoints Egyptians. Don't speak the caliph's name."

"My lord, Ahmad ibn Tulun, the caliph's representative in Egypt, has a large army, bigger than many others. Does that make people afraid?"

The vizier stood up. "How dare you?!" he said. "Shall I kill you now?"

"My lord, let me first explain what I mean, then you can kill me. Forgive me; perhaps my Arabic doesn't enable me to express myself well."

"You can express yourself perfectly well when you want to do it. Say what you want, then you'll die. Try not to make too many mistakes; your accent's making me lose patience."

"My lord, the caliph's courage lies in realizing who his friends are. He has Ahmad ibn Tulun's army to serve him. He's the caliph; we pray for him from our minarets and aspire to earn his approval. Amir Ahmad is one of the caliph's men. Does the caliph disapprove of one of his own men being powerful? If Ahmad becomes weak and loses his momentum, doesn't that also weaken the caliphate? The caliph's courage also involves knowing which governors are causes for concern. Ahmad ibn Tulun has never been disloyal or treacherous. Long ago, he refused to kill the caliph, even though he was just a soldier with no authority. His morals are not those of other people, and his allegiance is to the caliph. If you keep him in Egypt, you will have support and power there. But I haven't come here to talk about that. I've brought you some gifts: pure Egyptian honey and dates that are different from the Iraqi ones."

"You've come all this way to give me dates in Iraq? Who gives Iraqis dates, man?"

"A slave-girl who can sing perfectly in every language in the world. Her voice comes straight from the heavens; it has a different flavor to it, with no parallel in any Muslim land."

"I'm going to kill you in any case. Ibn al-Mudabbir's anger at you ranges all the way from Persia to Byzantium."

"The Tax Administrator sends my lord the tax money loyally."

"I don't need you to know the caliph's men."

"But he's like a donkey carrying books."

"For insulting the Tax Administrator in front of the vizier, you'll get a hundred lashes before you die."

"What he sends the caliph," Anas went on hurriedly, "is not even half what lies hidden in Egypt's soil."

"Are you claiming that he's stealing the taxes?"

"I'm claiming that he doesn't know how to extract from the ground gold, garlic, and lentils. He makes do with less and leaves what is better. Forgive me; I can't say more. I've brought gifts for my lord amir and to surrender myself to the caliph. I've come here to petition the caliph to keep Ahmad ibn Tulun in Egypt. He himself is a support, and his army is a force at my lord's disposal. Beyond that, I wish to invoke the caliph's generosity by noting that I've come to request that I or someone else take back Ahmad ibn Tulun's family to Egypt—his wife and son. Year after year have gone by, and he has not seen them. How he longs to see his son! Once he sees and supports his own son once again, his loyalty to the caliph will be further enhanced, and he'll give him everything he has. My lord, I've brought you some gold."

"Do I need gold?"

"When you see it, you'll understand. There's gold and then there's *gold*, dinars and *dinars*. My lord Al-Muwaffaq is fighting the Zanj, and he needs money."

"Has he asked Ahmad for money without the caliph's permission?" the vizier asked without thinking.

Anas moved back. "Forgive me," he continued hastily, "I've gone beyond my own limits and spoken about something I neither own nor understand."

"You will remain in the palace prison until I have made up my mind about you."

"To be put in prison near the caliph is an honor."

"You keep playing with words. Are all Egyptians like you?"

"Yes, they are."

"What kind of country is it? They read the Greeks, argue, and speak Arabic with a foreign accent!"

"They keep trying, my lord."

"Do all Egyptians hate Ibn al-Mudabbir the way you do and love Amir ibn Tulun?"

For just a moment, silence prevailed.

"The things Egyptians love and hate should not concern my lord. Nobody bothers about such things. Let's just say that the Egyptian people admire the Abbasid caliph, the Commander of the Faithful, because he has chosen Amir Ahmad ibn Tulun as Governor of Egypt.

"But they don't admire him for appointing Ibn al-Mudabbir? Finish what you're saying."

"My lord, admiration for the caliph has nothing to do with one man or one choice."

"You're wriggling out of answering and dodging the question. You just said that their admiration is connected with Ahmad ibn Tulun. Never mind. Let's take a look at the singing slave-girl and Ahmad's gifts."

Anas spent a week in the caliph's palace prison. He was not sure when he was going to get out. There were no tears and no sorrow. Al-Wasiti was afraid that, under the weight of so much torture, Anas had lost his mind, or that his sorrow was even greater than tears or words. He was writing out some of Al-Khwarizmi's equations with his one hand, eating little, and not making any effort to take care of the wound where his other hand had been or complaining about the pain.

After a week, a guard arrived with orders from the vizier, who wanted to talk to him again. It seemed like his last chance. He did his best to organize his words as he had done the last time. The vizier was bound to inform him of a decision or some new event.

For just a moment he stood in front of the vizier.

"The new Governor of Egypt . . ." the vizier said slowly.

Silence fell, and Anas did not try to make out the rest of the sentence.

"Egyptian dates are excellent as well," the vizier added suddenly. "Ibn al-Mudabbir will stay in place. No governor will interfere with the caliph's decisions."

Anas said nothing.

"You were speaking to me a week ago," the vizier went on, "about the power of Ahmad ibn Tulun and his army. Answer me. Why did Ahmad form an army in Egypt? No other governor before him has done that."

"The caliph ordered him to do it," Anas replied, "when Ibn ash-Shaikh rose up in rebellion."

"Once we'd defeated Ibn ash-Shaikh," the vizier asked, "why did Ahmad keep his army? Why not just hand it over to the caliph?"

"My lord," Anas replied slowly, "you're well aware that keeping all the armies in Iraq appears to some people as a threat. It's not in the caliph's best interests. Even the most sympathetic people are afraid of armies."

"What are you talking about, Egyptian? Whom do you mean?"

"I mean that the caliph knows more."

"Perhaps you have someone specific in mind. Do you think I don't understand you? Are you daring to mention the caliph's own brother, for instance—my lord Al-Muwaffaq?"

"I didn't mention anything, my lord," Anas responded swiftly. "That's your guesswork and acumen talking. I have no idea what you're talking about."

"The caliph has appointed a new governor for Egypt."

Anas remained silent.

"Ibn Tulun's gifts are all acceptable," the vizier went on. "You're his envoy, but you're also a killer. You've called for a revolt against the caliph."

Anas still said nothing.

"There's a minor problem," the vizier continued. "The governor I've appointed for Egypt doesn't dare go there. That's what Ahmad ibn Tulun has managed to do with the caliph's men. He's turned them into cowards who are scared of his army and prestige."

Anas suppressed a smile.

"He's the caliph's soldier, my lord," Anas said.

"This has never happened before. Is Ahmad making Egypt independent? Is it over?"

"If you'll allow me, my lord. The caliph's own prestige is part of the Governor of Egypt's. If he was making Egypt independent, would he be sending gifts and asking for your favor?"

"He wants his son."

Anas did not respond. The vizier seemed somewhat baffled and even conciliatory.

"Ibn al-Mudabbir will stay in Egypt," he repeated, "and Ahmad ibn Tulun will stay for a while, but not forever. If he wants his son back, I'll send his wife and son with an emissary. But you're going to pay the price for your actions. You'll stay in prison for a year or even ten, till the caliph gives you a pardon."

Anas expected to stay in prison and was not surprised that the caliph had decided to send back Ahmad's wife and son. Ever since he had arrived in Iraq, he had sensed tension between Al-Mu'tamid and his brother, Al-Muwaffaq. Al-Muwaffaq seemed to be preoccupied with the war against the Zanj, and Al-Mu'tamid was not willing to share rule with his brother, as his father had wished. Indeed, he wanted to retain the rule for himself and to appoint his son to succeed him. At that point, Al-Mu'tamid did not have the power to engage in a fight with Ahmad ibn Tulun, and he had no desire to do so. Maybe Anas's words had had some effect. He did not know whether to feel happy or sad; happy that Ahmad was staying in power, or sad because Ibn al-Mudabbir was staying as well, while he, Anas, would be spending the rest of his life in prison. However, he could no longer feel either happy or sad; by now, he had learned how to endure and be patient.

The caravan took Al-Wasiti, Ahmad ibn Tulun's men, and his wife and son back to Egypt without Anas. When Al-Wasiti reached Ahmad ibn Tulun, he told him what had happened. Ahmad gave his wife and son a passionate welcome. He had no intention of forgetting about Anas, not merely because he was a friend, but also because he was one of his men. If the army got the feeling that Ibn Tulun would be willing to sacrifice one of his men for any reason, their trust would be broken, and collapse would follow. He went out to his army to speak to them and handed out all the gifts that had come from the caliph. He told them that Ahmad ibn Tulun's army was unlike any other. It was an army on Egyptian soil, a soil with all the magic of the ancients, astronomy, and the pen. Anyone who was honored to be linked to him, alive or dead, would be under the protection and patronage of Ahmad ibn Tulun. Wars were not for those who paid the most, but rather were intended to defend the truth and secure its triumph. This was a land with cities beneath it and above it. Between their folds, treasures would seep. Anyone fighting for the sake of gold would be ephemeral; those who would fight for building would remain. This was not an army to fight in revolt, then dissolve. It was an army to stay.

Ibn Tulun spoke about Al-Qata'i. He asked the soldiers if they knew why he had built his city. He told them that Al-Qata'i was a city without walls because it was the city of an unassailable army. Within its quarters, men could revive tales of the ancients, reading about the pharaoh and Moses and King Joseph. They would know about fallow years, wheat stalks, and the struggle between the powerful and the weak. Some people would oppress, then disappear; others would build and live. This city would survive because it had been built for an army that had chosen

Egypt as its homeland, even though its members came from every corner of the earth. People were simply words inscribed on an ancient document, some of them true, some false. Those who understood the words would not disappear; those who failed to read them would spend an eternity in meandering confusion. One ruler had followed another, leaving behind only those who trained men to fight, then built and instituted reforms. Those were countries that could not be tamed, just like wild beasts. Anyone wanting to use them had first to gain their trust and then respect their spontaneity and madness. Al-Qata'i would remain to provide witness of those who tyrannized, those who were just, those who built, and those who destroyed. Al-Qata'i would survive, like the statues of the ancients and their lofty temples, in order to tell of a glory that had returned, or nearly so, and paths that were partially above ground but mostly below. Those who walked through its quarters would need to consider what lay hidden in the depths and not just be content with what the eye could see.

Anas was one of Ahmad ibn Tulun's men, and Ahmad was not going to forget about him, as was the case with all the men in his army. Ahmad's army had no single skin color and no single language; they were all gathered together within a city on Egyptian soil. They were living in Al-Qata'i, adopting it as home and country. They were not just defending Al-Qata'i, but country and soil as well, a place where sons and daughters would grow up. When Ahmad departed this life, his army would remain like a single man's fist, with no distinction made by tribe, skin color, family, groups, or ruler. The army's strength lay in its unity and cohesion. It was an army brought together by a city; no one could tell apart the people who lived inside it.

Ahmad sent a letter to the caliph, asking him to pardon Anas. He had a wife, and was one of Ahmad's men. But the caliph regarded it as a simple lesson for Ahmad and an attempt to explain to him that the matter was not in his hands. In any case, the caliph had released Ahmad's wife and son. So why was he complaining?

Ahmad was increasingly frustrated, knowing full well that Ibn al-Mudabbir was in Egypt that day and the next.

The caliph's prison was wider than the space of the hammer's throw that Anas had hurled at Ibn al-Mudabbir's men. How many men had he put in prison? How many men had he killed in the last few months? They provided him with books and lamps, cleaned his prison cell every day, and fed him good meat and chicken. He smiled to himself. He had had a plan to teach prisoners in Egypt. With Ahmad ibn Tulun's approval, he had devised a new custom, bringing in teachers to teach the prisoners how to read and write. Those who learned quickly had their sentences reduced, and those who read poetry well had their sentences cut in half. He had been merciful and just, not seizing every opportunity, nor stealing money, nor giving the salt of the earth to his friends like Ibn al-Mudabbir. Now that same mercy was coming back, surrounding him with books in prison. But he could not find out anything about his wife, Ibn Tulun, or Ibn al-Mudabbir. Faced with his disappearance, had her mind dissolved again? Had the heart's demon taken control again and not left her any chance to escape? Was she, like him, a prisoner, trapped inside the darkness that had enveloped her before? If she was in prison, was he not the cause of all the misery she had suffered from the outset? He was the one who had married her, who had wanted her to stay with him, and who had left her for a whole year, exposing her to risks. He was the one who was preoccupied with the Tax Administrator and his father, preferring the overpowering waves to a life of humiliation. Why did his father have to plead with the servant? If he had intended to drown himself, then why did he submit to humiliation? Would it not have been better to surrender to the waves from the very beginning, before Ibn al-Mudabbir arrived? Did he wish his father had been more courageous? Did he blame his father for his humiliation? Had he wanted him to die first? If he had done that, then he, Anas, would have been the one who killed him. Had his father looked into his eyes? Had he heard his lips' silent whisper?

"I beg you," he had said bitterly, "don't do it. Don't humiliate yourself before the servant."

How he blamed himself for blaming his father! How feeble and self-centered he felt today! Who was he? A man seeking revenge on the person who humiliated his father and himself? Who was he? Someone who did not leave a single door Ibn al-Mudabbir passed through without it burning him. Who was he? Someone who could only think about his own trials, misfortunes, and struggles. And now, there was Maisoon. Was he the one who had made Maisoon lose her mind? He wanted to rip Ibn al-Mudabbir away from the country to which he was attached. Egypt was his country, his fish, and his salt. And Maisoon was his wife.

He could almost hear her screams and envision her twisting away from the shadow's flames and words. She might well accuse him of deserting her again. Did she realize that he had not deserted her? The whole thing was not in his hands. He yelled her name.

"You must realize, I was powerless this time. Stay strong, my wife. That's all I want of you. People in love stay strong, and those who persevere always win. A lover's heart cannot fold, nor can fire melt a lover's promise. If only you realized, it's a promise and solemn oath. And whatever you do, don't kill yourself, as my father did."

He banged his head against the wall, lightly and then harder. A bit of pain is always beneficial. People inured to suffering need to see its specter all the time.

Chapter 13

There is no escape or hope in slaughter. Maisoon disappeared from the earth's surface, like the remains of the cities of the ancients. People will say here that it was the Pharaonic capital; they built cities without walls just like Al-Qata'i, cities where people lived peaceful, stress-free lives. They built cities filled with palaces and weapons. People were constantly on the lookout for invaders and thieves. Swords were drawn, spears were raised, and women looked forlorn as they waited for the inevitable defeat to come. How had Maisoon disappeared? Her disappearance was certainly peculiar, but the change in her father was even stranger that the construction of the pyramid and its witch, whose origins were entirely unknown. How had Ibn al-Mudabbir managed to persuade Judge Yahya to retrieve his daughter from the bookseller? People said that Ibn al-Mudabbir had told the judge about the bookseller's past, but he must have known about that before. They said that Ibn al-Mudabbir had persuasive ways of talking, slippery as a crocodile, handsome as the new moon. He had sat with the judge for an hour, no more, during which he had told the judge that the bookseller had killed once, twice; he was not a suitable consort for her. He told the judge that God forgives all sins. He planned to change the way things had been: there would be no tax on fishing and no more pressure on Egyptians from then on. As an Egyptian woman, Maisoon could help him soften his heart and show mercy to the poor. Ibn al-Mudabbir went on to say that he might well have been cruel and harsh; he admitted as much. But times had changed, and love had softened his heart. The judge had a choice: between someone starting down the path of evil, or someone who was done with it. When the judge woke up in the middle of the night, his mind was made up. His daughter had come to say farewell; next day, she would be leaving for Iraq with her husband and not coming back as long as Ibn al-Mudabbir was in Egypt. The judge was no longer sure about Anas. Since he had become Deputy Police Chief, he had changed. Killing the tax workers was not the right thing to do, and his conflict with Ibn al-Mudabbir did not suggest any hint of decency or mercy. The Tax Administrator had promised in front of everyone to help the Egyptian people. Could he trust a man who had deserted his wife for a whole year, then punished her, and now wanted her to wander through many countries for no particular reason? Could he trust someone whose only goal was killing and torture?

At midnight, the judge left for Ibn al-Mudabbir's house and made a deal with him. He asked Ibn al-Mudabbir to prevent his daughter's departure. He was not to harm her in any way, but to return her to her father's house. Ibn al-Mudabbir agreed and repeated his promise. He seemed genuinely sorry; perhaps he really would change. The judge rubbed his hands together, beset by a feeling of impotence. He did not know if he was doing the right thing, but he was not going to leave his daughter with Anas. The country's interests were more important than the fisherman's son's revenge.

No sooner did Anas and his wife take to the streets of Al-Qata'i than Ibn al-Mudabbir set his men on them. On the city's outskirts, they kidnapped Maisoon and crushed her husband's hand. The judge knew nothing of that, but he was informed of his daughter's kidnapping. He waited for her to come home as Ibn al-Mudabbir had promised, but she did not arrive. Day came, and she still had not come home. He rushed to Ibn al-Mudabbir's house, regret gnawing at his heart. He yelled in Ibn al-Mudabbir's face that he had kidnapped his daughter. In his turn, Ibn al-Mudabbir acted concerned and confused. He told the judge that his men had indeed captured a woman walking with Anas. They had brought her to Ibn al-Mudabbir's house to take her back to her father. When they uncovered her face, it was not Maisoon. It was a slave-girl from one of the Al-Qata'i quarters. Ibn al-Mudabbir had seized her to get her to confess, but she replied that she did not know anything; she was walking with her master when the soldiers grabbed her. They tortured her, but she did not admit anything more. The judge lost his nerve and accused Ibn al-Mudabbir of kidnapping his daughter. He bitterly regretted trusting and aiding the Tax Administrator. How he had wronged Maisoon and made her burden intolerable! He was overcome by an unbearable sense of sin. He made up his mind to complain to the governor and the caliph. Ibn al-Mudabbir insisted that he was doubly sorry and doubly alarmed. Anas had played a dangerous game, but the judge responded that he, Ibn al-Mudabbir, was the one playing games, not Anas.

The judge did complain to the governor. Once again, it was Maisoon. Not a day went by without people talking about the judge's daughter. The judge rushed to see Ahmad ibn Tulun to complain, and so did Ibn al-Mudabbir. Anas sent the governor a message that they had kidnapped Anas's wife and amputated his hand. The caliph had put him in prison. Ahmad ibn Tulun sent spies to both Ibn al-Mudabbir's house and the judge's house to search for Maisoon. Whispers emerged from the Authority Town complex that the gorgeous Maisoon was crazy and had killed herself. She had drowned herself at night in the mighty river after running away from the soldiers. Screams could be heard from the judge's house. Lowering his eyelids, he let the tears fall.

Six months later, Ahmad ibn Tulun sent an important letter to the caliph Al-Mu'tamid. Ahmad did not feel safe sending it even by pigeon, so he dispatched Al-Wasiti to Iraq once again. In the caliph's presence, Al-Wasiti noted that the caliph's brother and fellow ruler, Al-Muwaffaq, was fighting the Zanj and trying to finish them off. That much was necessary and an object of admiration for Ahmad and all the Abbasid governors. But Al-Muwaffaq had also been demanding Egypt's taxes from Ahmad ibn Tulun. As Al-Mu'tamid was well aware, Egypt's taxes were not Ahmad's responsibility. Even if they were, he would never hand them over to the caliph's brother without the caliph's permission, first because he did not have possession of the taxes, and second the taxes rightly belonged to the caliph. If Ahmad were to be frank, the caliphate should not be shared like a common water glass. A shared water glass would only break, spilling all the water and disallowing anyone from drinking. Ahmad then informed the caliph that he was requesting him to set Anas free so that he, Ahmad, would not lose the respect of his soldiers. If not, then he would not be able to ask them to sacrifice themselves from then on.

On this occasion, the caliph was genuinely alarmed. He praised Ahmad ibn Tulun for telling him what had happened with Al-Muwaffaq. He then released Anas, ordering him to stay out of Ibn al-Mudabbir's way and not bother him.

Anas breathed in the fresh air and headed back to Egypt to see Ahmad ibn Tulun.

ᛘᛘ

Ahmad ibn Tulun thanked Anas.

"I'm aware of what you've done for me, my wife, and my son," he said. "I know."

"I'm a soldier in your army, my lord."

"Yes, and I will never abandon my soldiers, however much it costs. But you have the kind of knowledge that would change the situation if you could teach it to soldiers and other people. I want you to read and translate what you've read—in Greek and Coptic. I want you to translate and copy. Above all, I want you to teach my children and then the soldiers."

"My lord . . ."

"Anas, you were created to learn and teach. Teach my children Greek, Coptic, and algebra."

"My lord Ahmad ibn Tulun wants to dispense with my services in government and conflict," Anas said.

"I would prefer," Ahmad replied, "not to lose someone with your intelligence, if possible."

"I promised myself," Ahmad said forcefully, "on the day my father died, Ibn al-Mudabbir would leave this country."

"Do you think you're in charge?"

"I am, and he is not."

"Your Egypt is the Sultan's treasury. That's what the caliph says, as you recall."

"Any remaining dinars are the Sultan's. But the treasury is in my charge."

"Do you imagine that you can expel and arrest as you wish?

"It seems as though Ahmad ibn Tulun has surrendered to Ibn al-Mudabbir!"

For a moment, Ahmad said nothing.

"It's war and peace," he responded eventually. "Today you're at war. If you're defeated, you'll surrender."

"Ibn al-Mudabbir will either leave Egypt or die here," Anas said. "Until then, I am just another one of your soldiers. Appoint me Deputy Police Chief again. That is all I ask of you."

Ahmad smiled.

"You've already decided, Anas," he said. "It's as though I'm not the governor!"

"My lord, you are more powerful than the caliph."

"If the caliph heard you say that, he'd cut off your head and mine."

"The caliph knows it, and so do you. I made a promise a while ago, but I've been distracted and haven't kept it."

"What promise?"

"There's a skilled architect, an Egyptian named Saeed ibn al-Farghani. He worked with me and wants to meet you. I hope you'll allow it."

"Here you are interceding on behalf of Egyptians before army commanders!"

"Actually, I want you to hear what he has to say. You might well find him useful."

"You will forget about Ibn al-Mudabbir," Ahmad said forcefully.

"Forgive me, my lord. It's a matter of revenge. I have to."

"Then do it on your own. If he kills you, it's not my concern."

Anas remained silent. The tension held between the two men.

"There are times, Anas, fisherman's son," Ahmad continued, "when I think you're even tougher than Ibn al-Mudabbir. You never give up, never quit. You're as determined as an ant, as patient as a camel, and as vicious as a hippopotamus."

"These are times when careless people need to be taught lessons. If I wasn't determined, patient, and vicious, I'd simply disappear at the Sultan's court, submit to the Tax Administrator, or . . ."

"Or maybe follow my instructions, when I ask you to forget about Ibn al-Mudabbir . . ."

Anas smiled.

"I've spent much of my life waiting for him to fall. Don't deprive me of this. I've been working on it for years."

"The Tax Administrator will never fall."

"If you leave me in my post as Deputy Police Chief," Anas stated with resolution, "he'll fall."

"Anas . . ."

"You want him to fall even more than I want him to die. Let me have the chance. Give me a free hand with Ibn al-Mudabbir and his men."

"Anas . . ."

"Ahmad's dream has to be fulfilled. Today, Ahmad's army can defeat all the caliph's armies combined. This country will tell tales about you and your city, a city with no walls because everyone can live there in safety, more beautiful than all the cities of the Arabs and non-Arabs alike. It will remain a memorial of a king of the ancients, someone not born in Egypt, but who chose to make it his homeland. He followed in their footsteps, and learned their magic and knowledge. People will talk about an amir . . ."

For just a moment, Ahmad's eyes wandered.

"Anas," he said suddenly, "I've one thing to ask of you."

"My lord, your requests are my orders."

"Maisoon . . ."

"They kidnapped her, my lord. I'm going to find her. I have to find my wife. Judge Yahya betrayed me."

"That doesn't concern me. What does concern me is that I don't want to hear her name mentioned again. I've enough things to worry about without looking into matters involving women. Ever since I first came to Egypt, her name keeps entering the public domain. Can you put an end to the story so I can concentrate on more important matters?"

"When we've eradicated tyranny, my lord," Anas said, deeply affected, "and I've found my wife."

🏰

Ibn al-Mudabbir's visit to the Deputy Police Chief was expected. Ahmad ibn Tu-lun's continued presence in Egypt was disturbing his sleep. Ahmad was like an elephant, never forgetting or forgiving a slight. That day, what lay in the space between Anas and Ibn al-Mudabbir was blood, heart, and torn soul. Ibn al-Mu-dabbir came to see him, accompanied by his guards. But this time, his eyes looked crushed and watchful. Anas tracked his adversary's eyelids, following their movements and his heartbeats as they rose and fell along with the tension, despair, and disillusion visible in the Tax Administrator's gaze. Anas's gaze showed the same disillusion. In their last meeting, Maisoon had muttered to him some things about death and killing the heart. Would he ever see her again? He put his hand over his heart in the hope of stopping the ache, but it did not stop.

By the time Ibn al-Mudabbir left, Ahmad had already made his decision to tighten the siege and start hurling spears. He asked Mughith to arrest Abu Sha'ara, one of Ibn al-Mudabbir's closest confidants, aides, and supporters, guaranteed to laugh whenever Ibn al-Mudabbir did, and to feel sorrow the same way. When Mughith asked about the justification for arresting Abu Sha'ara, Anas told him that something had happened the day before in which Abu Sha'ara had been involved. While Amir Ahmad ibn Tulun had been inspecting Al-Qata'i, the women of the city had left their houses to watch the amir on his horse, escorted by his army and retainers. One of the women had leaned out on her windowsill and dropped a large jar on the ground very near the amir's horse, so close, in fact, that the horse had reared and almost thrown the amir to the ground. The woman who had dropped the jar was Abu Sha'ara's wife. Abu Sha'ara regularly scoffed at the amir and made fun of him. The Amir of Egypt had to be respected. Abu Sha'ara must be arrested, his wife would be pushed out into the street, and the house would be demolished, to be replaced by a garden with lofty trees and a lovely fountain. Mughith listened carefully to what Anas was saying.

"Do you plan to destroy a man's house, Anas," he asked, "and turn his children into vagrants?"

"Once he's received fifty lashes," Anas went on unconcernedly, "he can move his family's things out of Al-Qata'i. There's no room in Al-Qata'i for Ibn al-Mudabbir's men."

"Don't solve one problem, brother, by creating another."

Anas smiled. "Mughith," he said, "you're not my brother. My brother died at Ibn al-Mudabbir's hand. Abu Sha'ara's only the first to go. I want you to keep a close eye on all the men around Ibn al-Mudabbir. Anyone who makes fun of the amir or assaults the public I shall want to punish myself. Anyone who dares whip people for not paying taxes will be killed."

"Anas, you're launching an attack on Ibn al-Mudabbir's senior officials. That's not right. The police have never had any authority over tax officials."

"From now on," Anas made abundantly clear, "the police are going to be involved in everything. By the end of this year, I want Ibn al-Mudabbir to be the only one left, just like the fisherman's son was when his father drowned, he lost his money, and the servants acted brazenly against him. The police will search for Maisoon in Egypt, Iraq, Syria, and to the ends of the earth. I want my wife back, alive."

Anas dispatched spies to watch Ibn al-Mudabbir's men, and Ahmad ibn Tulun's as well. He kept track of everything that was said. Every night, he would perform the evening prayer, and then spend some time reading about what was going on inside the walls of the houses and palaces. Whenever he found out about someone saying bad things about Ahmad ibn Tulun, good things about Ibn al-Mudabbir, or praying for the caliph and not Ahmad ibn Tulun, that person would be arrested and put in prison. In less than three months, the prison was full. However, he was merciful with the prisoners. He decided to teach them how to read and write and to reeducate them. He established a special budget for teachers. Never for a moment did he think that he was doing something wrong. Every day he was closer to reaching his goal. Ibn al-Mudabbir sent a complaint to the caliph explaining what was happening with the amir and his aides, but the caliph ignored him. The caliph was worried about his own problems; he was fighting the Zanj and arguing with his brother. Ibn al-Mudabbir told his men to kill Anas at night, but Anas had hired some of Ibn al-Mudabbir's men as spies, and knew about the plan before it was supposed to happen. All the men involved were arrested, except for Ibn al-Mudabbir himself.

At night, his dreams were a mixture of Maisoon and Ibn al-Mudabbir. He dreamed that she was screaming, and he was running away with her. Ibn al-Mudabbir was grabbing at her hand and burying it in his, but Anas managed to pull her away from his authority zone. Her severed arm lay on the ground, blood pouring from the amputation. She was screaming, but he did not hear; she was calling for help, and he did not respond. He woke up with a start, missing her and fearing for her. Then love gnawed at his heart, and all he wanted to do was destroy the Tax Administrator. But the image of his wife, screaming and armless, haunted him. He closed his eyes tight to erase the terrible image. The following morning, he ordered a punishment for one, two, or three of Ibn al-Mudabbir's men.

Several months later, Anas requested another meeting with Ahmad ibn Tulun. The chamberlain refused to let him in, saying that these days, the governor was preoccupied with building projects and other matters. But Anas insisted. Two days later, Ahmad agreed to a meeting.

"What's the matter, Anas?" Ahmad asked impatiently.

"My lord," Anas replied, "I think our chance has finally come. I just wanted to give you the good news that there's a letter on the way from the caliph."

Now Ahmad looked at him. "It's a letter about the disagreement between Caliph Al-Mu'tamid and his brother, Al-Muwaffaq."

"Al-Muwaffaq is a partner in the caliphate," Anas replied, "but Al-Mu'tamid is the caliph. Discussions about forms of government and arguments between men have always worn me out. The caliph's going to ask you for help, my lord, and you're ready to give it."

"Anas," Ahmad said, "if you think you're giving sound advice, you're wrong. I know the letter's coming, and I know all about the dispute. Al-Mu'tamid needs money."

"My lord Ahmad, what Al-Mu'tamid wants is Egypt's taxes without his brother learning about it and without any consideration of brotherhood. He wants the taxes as caliph. However, my lord, Egypt's taxes are not at your disposal to give to the caliph Al-Mu'tamid. If they were, you could give them all to him."

Ahmad stared long and hard at Anas.

"I didn't realize that vengeance could produce such blatant iniquity," he said.

"If the governor had control of the taxes," Anas went on, "he could give it all to the caliph without Al-Muwaffaq knowing about it and without having to divulge the amount involved or what he proposed to do with it."

Ahmad smiled. "It's time to get rid of Ibn al-Mudabbir," he said.

"Yes, my lord, it's time. If my lord would be so kind as to ask the caliph to remove the Tax Administrator so that he would have control over Amir Ahmad's tax revenue and appoint someone else who was loyal and trustworthy, then Ahmad could make Egypt independent."

For a moment, there was silence. "What makes you think I wasn't already considering that?"

"My lord Ahmad thinks of everything. Getting rid of Ibn al-Mudabbir opens the path to making Egypt separate and fulfilling the dream."

"You don't know my dream."

"I can practically read it in your eyes."

"You've learned magic from the Pyramid Witch. Perhaps every Egyptian is good at magic."

"I'm just a soldier in your army."

"But when the amir dismisses the Tax Administrator, he'll be in greater danger. Wounded lions don't make any distinction between wolves and sheep."

"What do you intend?"

Ahmad brought out some papers. "The amir can read the letters that Ibn al-Mudabbir has been sending to the caliph over the past several years. I've kept them for this moment."

"I'm familiar with their contents."

"When the amir reads them," Anas went on as though he had not heard Ahmad's reply, "he'll impose a prison sentence on the disloyal Tax Administrator. If the caliph were to object, the proof exists. It's in the caliph's interests for the amir's army to be on his side."

"You're almost worse than Ibn al-Mudabbir."

"You can't equate murderers and those out for revenge. Swift action is needed."

Ibn al-Mudabbir anticipated the order and escaped before Anas could catch him. But deposing him was not enough; he needed to be in a dark prison. Anas knew prisons and was aware of the fact that bodily weakness and confinement do more to neutralize power than death itself. Someone used to walking merrily over the earth will never be happy to live in shackles, amid waste and the foul stench of dried human excrement. How would the Tax Administrator feel, he wondered, when he dressed his wounds with the salt of the earth that he claimed to be his?

How would he like the sea with all its fish rising up against him, the sea spume scorching him, and the black seaweed twisting itself around his neck? All he would have left would be a heart weakened, full of regret. With that regret he would ask for forgiveness. Anas dearly hoped that he would not make that request; he dearly wanted Ibn al-Mudabbir to roast forever in hell.

His days were totally preoccupied. How sorely he missed his wife. He let out yet another sigh. Had Maisoon really killed herself? He banished the thought, but that only brought back Ibn al-Mudabbir. How could hatred have so much power when his heart was sighing with the anguish of separation?

Ibn al-Mudabbir disappeared, perhaps to Syria or Iraq. He did not feel safe from Ahmad's ruthless actions. The people of Egypt cheered and felt able to breathe again. For the first time, they came out to the main square to congratulate Ahmad as their amir. Today he alone deserved that title. Women ululated and men chanted his name. They prayed for him and devoutly hoped that he would be able to change their predestined fates. They said that Amir Ibn Tulun was a powerful purveyor of good, generous in his charity; he had built his palace and created a square for all Egyptians to use. What use was a shaikh who prayed for them, but failed to raise his sword against the tyrant? The amir understood the language of the ancients, they said, and dreamed of kings and devout people. He was a Muslim, but a pharaoh as well—a commander, but one of them. Ahmad came out and spread largess with his own hands. They placed him in a position above the ground, just as a camel does with its rider. Men were frightened for him, but he did not care.

"The past is over," he said in his polished Arabic. "Egypt now is going to be a flourishing country."

He promised to build and populate what he had built; he would spend his entire life on defense and deterrence. He promised that treasures long buried would be used to construct imposing structures. Al-Qata'i, he said, was not like other cities; it was a place of justice and prosperity. Then he spoke the words that everyone had been waiting to hear with a dogged determination: all regulations enacted by Ibn al-Mudabbir were now canceled. There were no longer taxes on sea-fishing, natron, and sheep. He went on to say things that no one else had dared imagine. In a loud voice, he proclaimed that Egypt's taxes would be considerable, and he himself was in Egypt as a representative of the caliph. However, Egypt's dinars were for its own people. Once the land prospered and its people shared in its bounty, the tax revenues would be greater, not less. He would be spending the money for Egypt and would be remaining here in his country, the one of which he had long dreamed. He also promised to provide food for the public two days a week, eating with them on those two days, and listening to their complaints. From that very day, everything would change. He would build a hospital to treat both weak and strong, and he construct a school and a mosque.

But the Tax Administrator had not surfaced. As long as he remained in hiding, Ahmad would still be in danger and Anas in torment.

People say that the ancient Egyptians used to think of night-light as representing life in this world, while entering the next world was imagined as emerging into daylight. Was that why they appeared at night, Anas wondered, at the foot of the pyramid? Because they could enjoy their daytime in a better place? He walked slowly as he made his way to the Pyramid Witch. This time, he did not bother about who might be walking behind him or following his footsteps in this lower world. Ibn al-Mudabbir had been dismissed, and yet he was still fine, surrounded by his soldiers, decked in silk, and searching for Maisoon all over the place. The walls of his house were still protecting him, and Egypt's grapes still delighted his mouth. Anas stared at the Sphinx, as it awaited the arrival of the jinn from inside the pyramid. The silence was only broken by the whispering of statues. How strange that carved statue of the Sphinx was! It was by no means dumb; it spoke through every one of its senses. Its eyes screamed of the inevitable end to come; its nose foretold years of misery to come; its smashed hair spoke of a past like city walls and castle balustrades. The mouth never stopped talking: this one was a tyrannical king; that one was a greedy monarch; that one was a king who had defended and fought; still another had made sacrifices and been forgotten. This monarch had sought the day, while another had turned dark amid the folds of night. Here were days like passing cities, tinged with the scent of life and the conflicts of the weak—like cities that fade in the face of swords and stakes, but never vanish or desert the memory. They survive amid fragments of pottery and the smell of pen and ink. They survive in the vestiges of sweet water drunk by a child in search of justice, by a shaikh in search of contentment in the bowels of the earth, the pages of history, and the womb of hope. Those are cities built by the hands of the hopeful, the daring, and the courageous. Here the lover has mouthed his breaths of despair; here the man of passion has sniffed the scent of eternity.

He sat there, waiting for the witch or the ancestors. Eventually, he heard the sound of the palm branch that covered the door and moved slowly, understanding that she was allowing him to enter.

The witch did not look at him. Today, she was smiling, and her lovely face beamed with expectation.

"So, careless man," she said, "you're back!"

"I'm not careless."

She opened a secret door that only she knew.

"In the darkness of night," she said, "all humans are careless. When morning comes, they're even more careless. If only they realized, it would be better for them. You read, Egyptian, and think you know. Suppose I told you that the person who built this pyramid wasn't Surid and what you've read was neither truth nor knowledge? Suppose I told you that, would you believe me?"

He gave her a confused look. "I don't know," he replied. "You read more than I do. I might believe you or I might not. But tell me first: is she fine?"

"She's here," she replied.

"Is she fine?" he asked again, hesitant and fearful.

"You never ask about Bahnas," she replied. "I've told you for some time that you're responsible for me. But you're only worried about the beautiful woman."

"Bahnas," he asked again, his breaths quickening, "is she fine?"

"No, she's not."

He recalled the way the sword-blade had cut through the cuff of his hand. The mind can toy with us that way. How could such pain be stored away for years, like coffins of the ancients?

"Is she alive?"

"I've told you she's not well," she replied in despair. "If she were dead, she would be fine. She's alive, but not well."

Heart thumping, he moved forward. "My beloved," he said before even seeing her in the dark room, "it was all out of my hands. I was in prison, then observed by his men all the time. Don't be angry with me again. This time, I shall never leave you by choice. You realize that, don't you?"

He reached with his hand in the dark, searching for hers. She grabbed his hand.

"I knew you'd come," she said confidently.

He pulled her hand to his mouth and kissed it slowly. "My darling," he said, "every day I spent far away from you, I was lost and miserable."

He put his head in her lap, embracing her middle, but said nothing. She ran her hands through his hair.

"I'm fine!" she said firmly.

"I was afraid for you in the dark," he said, kissing her belly. "A whole year has passed, and last time I left you, you lost your mind."

She held his head, closed her eyes, and used her hand to search for his right hand.

"Delving into the heart demands effort and struggle," she said. "Trying to resist the shadow involves erasing part of the heart. What happened to you, Anas? Have I lost my mind?"

"Ibn al-Mudabbir cut it off," he replied clearly, "but he couldn't sever my heart. You know, this entire world involves tribulation. For some of us, that involves oppression from the outside; for others, it involves a heart that's never satisfied and never gives up. I don't know which is the more powerful."

She looked at his eyes in the darkness. For the first time, there was a glint of tears.

"Your tribulation," she whispered, "involves both oppression from the outside and a heart that's never satisfied."

"Maisoon . . ."

"There's no escape, Anas. You no longer have any choice. Maybe you never did from the outset. Are you crying?"

She wiped away a tear with her hand, and he kissed it.

"I've missed you," he told her. "I was afraid I'd lost you. If that had happened, I would have lost everything I have left."

"I'm so sorry for you, Anas," she said. "You can't fight your own shadow. You're like me. That's why you've loved me."

She leaned over and stretched out her arm to search for him in the darkness. She sniffed the air around him, and put his head on her breast.

"Your smell like light," she whispered.

When Anas had left her that year, he was sure he loved her, but he had been forced to leave her. But the shadow kept coming at night and whispering words of agony and rebuke, snuffing out all candles and smothering all hopes. The voice had said that Maisoon was always obstreperous; there was no hope for her. God had bestowed on her a face like the moon and a heart like a falling star that gleams and then disappears without trace. Another voice whispered that she was stubborn, bringing only destruction, and unfit to be either wife or daughter. Still another voice shouted that she was going to die, still longing for the contentment and security that do not exist in this universe. When the shadow obscured the light, she did not know who was around her. That had happened when he had left her for a year, but this time, it had not. Yet the shadow had still whispered to her, and the light had been obscured for some time. Every time he went away, clouds would appear, and confusion would prevail. She had no idea why she clung to him so hard, as though he were the only one who could fight the shadow and triumph over her recalcitrant heart.

She felt his eyes with her hands. He had not cried on the day his father died or when the two of them parted. Was he crying now for days long past, or for the torture of bones being severed? She did not know how to stop him crying or control her screaming heart. His tears were all drift and destruction.

She heard Bahnas's voice as she left the pyramid as usual at night to sleep outside. She wrapped her arms around his head as though to protect him from his own censorious self. She joined her body with his, and he plunged into her. Looking into her eyes, he tried to find out what she was giving him today. Her arms were wrapped around him, and he was almost fused with the darkness. Filling her body, he brought it to climax. His tears stopped and sheer passion took over and dominated all his senses. At that moment, he forgot about everything he had lost—hand, fingers, brother, and father.

"I've missed you," he whispered into her breasts, "oh, how I've missed you! When you give yourself so freely, you turn into moonlight as it draws near the traveler."

She ran her fingers over his face and sighed contentedly. When he had finished, he did not move away, but held her till she let out a contented sigh.

"Unlike you," she whispered, "I don't know how to talk like poets."

He heard Bahnas's voice as she came in again. He moved gently away from Maisoon.

"Very soon," he said, "you can come home to your house and to me. Be patient." She nodded.

He was frowning as he left his wife. His heart was wandering among the stones. He realized that he was being watched, still being watched.

"Maisoon realizes," Bahnas told him, as though she understood everything, "that men only speak body language. They know nothing of soul language. Are you now cured of your alarm, Anas, and reassured about your wife?"

"There's no cure for me, Bahnas," he replied. "I'm like you. I'll spend my entire life perplexed. You remind me of myself."

"Have you brought me what you promised?" she asked expectantly.

He emerged from the pyramid and returned with twenty or more books and a large number of cakes. He put them all down in front of her.

"Bahnas," he said impatiently, "you promised me to take care of her."

She looked eagerly at the books and picked up a piece of cake to eat.

"I've kept my promise," she replied.

He watched her eat the cake and waited for her to tell him something, but she remained silent.

"How did you prevent her from going mad?" he asked impatiently. "Her mind was half-lost and half-saved."

"People in books say that food helps the mad and hope puts an end to the heart's darkness. But what's certain, Anas, is that no devil can defeat it."

"But you only eat cake. Why don't you feed yourself the same way?"

"Whoever says that I want a sane mind in a world that is completely mad?"

"Please look after her," he pleaded, "until I come back."

"How wonderful is the lover's confusion and the absentee's doubts!" she said with a smile. "How I enjoy seeing your eyes plead and hope."

"I've kept my promise. You asked me for books and cake."

Anas had known Bahnas ever since he had arrived in Cairo after his father's death. The bookstore owner had told him that the Pyramid Witch needed books and food. At some point, she had helped him. Ever since, he would give her whatever she requested. On this occasion, he had set out with books and food. A strange friendship had developed between the two of them; they would talk for hours about the ancients and try to read the language of birds. Anas had become responsible for the Pyramid Witch.

He and Bahnas were the only ones who knew what had actually happened the year before. When he had made up his mind to take his wife with him to Iraq and told her father, he had felt uneasy and doubted her father's intentions. During his life journey, he had learned not to trust even the worthiest of men. Intentions could change and, like humans themselves, hearts had no firm roots or stable bases. He had also known he was being watched; Ibn al-Mudabbir was having him watched all the time. He had summoned a slave-girl and given her some money. Then he had set his plan in motion. There was not a lot of time to explain things to his wife. When he returned home, he told her that he was taking her to Iraq. Then he embraced her and whispered a few clipped phrases in her ear: as soon as they left the house and were walking in the dark streets, Gameela would take her to the Pyramid Witch and leave her there. He told her that he did not trust anyone else. Maisoon was to stay with her. The woman traveling to Iraq with him would be an unknown slave-girl, not Maisoon.

"Put your veil on," he told her, "and wait for me. It'll be a short time apart. I have no choice."

When she opened her mouth, he covered it with his hand.

"I love you," he said. "Nothing will keep us apart. This is just a temporary separation; I have no choice. Don't say anything, or you might be heard."

Remembering what had happened previously, he did not return to his house. He hung around the pyramid in the dark, waiting for Ibn al-Mudabbir to come. He was bound to come. Once he was told that Anas had gone to see the Pyramid Witch at night, he would come to search for Maisoon. For him, she was no longer just the woman he loved; she was life and purpose. She was a war zone involving two men.

Anas had waited for an hour, two, then three. He had watched as the moonlight came close and then moved away.

Was it possible for enemy souls to coalesce? Could he probe the inner depths of the tyrant and merge with him? How could he read the gaps in his mind and feel the torment of his angst? He had spent his recent years thinking about Ibn al-Mudabbir. The bond of those many hours that he had spent contemplating the moments of triumph and revenge all dissolved. He promised himself to forget the moment when tyranny would be erased, but he was still afraid of the moment when life would be at an end.

The witch had told her to eat, read, and go out for some fresh air, but only at night. In the darkness of night, goodly hearts emerge who are unafraid of shadows and specters, hearts of genuine folk who have no fear of the dark. Bahnas knew a great deal; from the tomes of the ancients, she had learned an herbal cure that calmed the mind without impairing it. She told Maisoon that when light disappears, the cause is the rustle of the heart's demon, it being the most powerful of all; it had made a home inside her soul and knew all its secrets. The shadow, she said, was not evil, but sometimes it would appear to help her transcend difficulties. Bahnas had a lot to say. Reading liberated the soul and lifted the heart to the daylight, as did both death and resurrection. Every time Maisoon read a book, she thought of Anas, and whenever she understood a symbol, she remembered who she was. The shadow would come when she was alone, and all she could do was to befriend it. To oppose it would be her end.

Anas had gone away against his will and promised to return. He had no idea when, but he had promised. He was away for a long time; he might be in prison or dead. If he were dead, then there was no hope for her. But he had said that the separation was only temporary. Bahnas had chided her for being so dependent; that was a human disease for which there was no cure. She told Maisoon that she could treat evil and greed, but there were two things on earth that she could not treat: dependency and weakness. Anyone afflicted with weakness is aware of the essence of being, and cannot return to earth with the enthusiasm of innocence and power of the heedless. Dependency is the bane of people on earth. Every single day, a man comes to earth, accompanied by a boy, money, influence, a woman, and occasionally his own self. There is no cure. The cure only comes along with weakness. Weakness brings a cure for dependency. Through knowledge, the feeble heart comes to realize that dependence on things we don't control is ignorance and illusion. Even so, Bahnas was unable to convince Maisoon not to depend on Anas. She could not find out what it was that Maisoon found in Anas to make him the pivotal point of existence and to distress her when he was away and comfort her when he was present. Perhaps Maisoon saw things that other people did not. She convinced herself to wait patiently till he came back. He had indeed come. He had made a promise, and this time he had kept it.

He would visit her every day, talking to her for hours, and reassuring her. But he was on the alert. The rapacious fish was bound to come; his father used to say that watching out patiently for rapacious fish was the essence of the fishing profession.

Every night, she waited outside the pyramid for him. He would come. He wondered if Ibn al-Mudabbir really loved Maisoon, or if she had simply become a cure for everyone, the baffled and the lost, whether weak or capable. Would Ibn al-Mudabbir come to the pyramid in search of Maisoon, or to listen to the Pyramid Witch? She could just as easily banish confusion as provoke pain.

Finally, Anas heard his footsteps and smelled his scent, like a wolf who recognizes the smell of sheep. Why did this familiarity with Ibn al-Mudabbir worry him? Why was victory more troubling than defeat? He was approaching the pyramid alone on horseback. Either he wanted to see the witch, or he was looking for Maisoon. He was coming because he was after Anas the way Anas was after him.

Anas did not try to hide behind a rock. How could he hide in that vast desert? Even without any moonlight, he could hear his shadow and feel his footsteps. Ibn al-Mudabbir dismounted, looked around him, and unsheathed his sword.

"Come on, Anas," he yelled, "I'm here. It would be a dastardly act to sneak up on me."

"Such acts have their own proponents," Anas replied, "people who flay the country's gentry in order to grab the produce of land and sea. I'm not out to kill you."

Anas looked at the shadow of the man in the distance. He appeared close, though he was a way off. He penetrated Anas's guts, the man's breaths foul and hateful—Ibn al-Mudabbir, the former Tax Administrator, the evader of prison.

"I knew you were coming. I know you better than you know yourself. Even though your coming would lead to your destruction, you were bound to come. The judge's daughter has rejected you. She's reminded you of how incapable you are when it comes to extracting good from the heart."

Ibn al-Mudabbir gave a rigid smile. "The bookseller," he said. "Who would have thought that he knew and understood? The evil's inside you, not me. You know me better than I do, that's certain. If you'd been in my place, you would have done what I did, and more."

"I'm not in your place," Anas replied, drawing his sword from its scabbard, "and I'm not you."

"How can you know, when you're not in charge?" Ibn al-Mudabbir replied. "To know whether you would give, you have to be in charge. To know if you'd oppress, you need to have power. To know if you'd be merciful, you need to be on top. What do you want?"

Anas raised his sword and slowly walked over to Ibn al-Mudabbir. Ibn al-Mudabbir did not move, and Anas placed the tip of his sword on Ibn al-Mudabbir's neck.

"It's you I want," Anas said.

"Maybe because I remind you of yourself. At least I was in love with her. You only saw her as a means for revenge. You exploited her affection to destroy her, no more. Year after year, you've kept her a prisoner like a plant with no water. Put me in prison, Egyptian, and I'll emerge in a year or two. You'll never escape me."

"I swear," Anas yelled suddenly, "that I know no one more evil than you."

The witch slunk out of the pyramid, followed by Maisoon. Ibn al-Mudabbir's eyes looked first at Maisoon, then at the witch.

"Tell them both," he said forcefully, "who it was loved you, and who wrapped you up like so much ancient parchment. Tell them both who sacrificed himself for you, and who sacrificed you for his own sake."

The witch smiled. "Are you talking to me or Maisoon?" she asked quietly.

"Do you know me?" Ibn al-Mudabbir asked, aghast.

"Yes, I know you, and you know me."

He gave Maisoon a pleading look. "Maisoon . . . ," he said.

She lowered her head and retreated back inside the pyramid.

Ibn al-Mudabbir looked at the witch. "It's your fault," he said. "Your witchcraft has affected her mind."

He was about to plunge his sword into Anas's belly, but Anas grabbed him and squeezed his wrists until he groaned. He took a rope out of his pocket to bind Ibn al-Mudabbir's wrists. Ibn al-Mudabbir kept struggling and resisting; he was trying to punch Anas, while Anas kept trying to hit Ibn al-Mudabbir so that he would give up. This went on for an hour or more, till they were both exhausted and Ibn al-Mudabbir gave up. Anas tied his wrists and put him on his horse. He headed for the main square and told his soldiers to put Ibn al-Mudabbir in prison.

He rushed back to his wife, lifted her in his arms, and ran with her, his heart almost floating in the clouds from sheer joy. What is strange is that joy is not like sorrow. It sneaks in from the edges of life like air, whereas sorrow lingers and burrows deep like soil and mountain rocks. Had he lost his hand, he wondered, for the sake of a fleeting moment in life, without even noticing and without nourishing a soul or quenching a heart's thirst? How deceitful is a world that errs and has no stability; that pierces, but does not stay; that digs in with its fingernails, but then pretends to disappear; that strikes with its sword, but then expires before you have time to breathe!

He took Maisoon back to their house in Al-Qata'i, full of hope. But Ibn al-Mudabbir was still alive. Once he died, the heart would no longer have to suffer. Why should he not die? As long as he was still alive, he might escape from Ahmad's prison. Who knows?

When Judge Yahya found out what had happened, he asked his daughter to return to his house and leave her husband. He claimed that Anas had deceived her father and made him yearn for his daughter. Maisoon declined diffidently. Ever since Maisoon's disappearance, her father had been struck by a peculiar illness. For years, he had been eager to be rid of her, regarding her as an affliction and disaster. But when his heart had turned into a void, assuming that she was dead, he had realized that maybe he did not really know what he had thought he had known; he had the feeling that he did not understand. His heart had softened and weakened; now, being close to even a small part of her was his every wish. As for Gameela, Anas had now taken charge of Ali's slave-girl. After freeing her, he had asked her to live with them in their house in Al-Qata'i and to look after his wife. He paid her a daily wage for her work.

After Anas took his wife home, she remained a bit confused, not knowing what had changed in a year or more. Her husband did not talk to her a lot. He seemed distracted, worried, anxious. He kept envisioning Ibn al-Mudabbir escaping from prison, or else getting his brother Ibrahim to petition the caliph and have him released, as though nothing had ever happened. He imagined Ibn al-Mudabbir living in peace, as though he had never killed or tyrannized anyone, and had not deprived Anas of the ability to copy books and, before that, even the ability to feel joy. No sooner had they returned to their house than Anas started treating his wife as though she had just returned from a savage war. He asked the servant-girls to help her with everything. He would hold her in his arms for hours without saying a word, and then he would start inundating her with affection and promises. He would never leave her again, whatever happened. He promised not to annoy her. Once in a while, he would stare into her eyes, worried that he might see a touch of madness, after which there could be no return to normal. Every time, he convinced himself that she knew who he was and had forgiven him. It had not been his decision; he seemed less confident and more fearful.

Every day, he woke up at dawn and dispatched one of his men to check on Ibn al-Mudabbir and confirm that he was still in prison. That done, he could relax for an hour or two.

One night, she told him that she missed her family and wanted to see her mother, her sister, and her father. For a moment he was silent, then he told her calmly that he would arrange for her mother and sister to pay a visit.

"What about my father, Anas?" she asked in all innocence.

He ignored the question. A few days later, her mother and sister arrived and sat with her. The atmosphere was tense. When Maisoon asked them about her father, her mother initially replied that he was busy but, when the meeting was over, she told Maisoon that Anas had sworn that she would never set eyes on her father as long as he was alive. Her mother had a lot to say. She said that her heart had been broken for Maisoon once again; she had told her father everything that had happened in the past, about Maisoon's illness that she had kept from him, and about going to see the Pyramid Witch. Then her mother told her about Anas's accusation, namely that her father was the one who had organized Maisoon's kidnapping. Her mother neither denied nor confirmed it. She spoke as though she had no idea what the actual truth was.

With that, she and Ruqayya departed. Maisoon was left alone to await her husband's return. That day, the shadow started toying with her again; it appeared in the morning, then vanished. She screamed suddenly, and then woke up from her stupor. When he returned and looked into her eyes, he knew. He sat down in front of her and held her hands.

"You do a lot of fighting, Anas," she said slowly. "If you'd told Ibn al-Mudabbir the truth about me from the start, he would have rejected and shunned me. Just tell him that Maisoon's mad. Her beauty is fading amid the dark regions of the heart."

He looked at her hand as though to read it.

"Even if I did that," he said calmly, "he would still desire you. You're not mad. All of us have a shadow that emerges in the dark, but we don't see it because we don't have your purity and knowledge."

"You're preventing my father from seeing me," she said bitterly.

He kissed her hand. "That's a permanent pledge," he replied forcefully.

She opened her mouth.

"Don't make me suffer the unbearable," he went on. "Didn't I tell you, Maisoon, that my own shadow never forgives or forgets?"

👥

However, Judge Yahya insisted on seeing his daughter. A month later, he waited until Anas went out, and then went to his daughter's house in Al-Qata'i. He banged on the door, and the slave-girl opened it. He asked to see Maisoon and sat there waiting with a longing, the origins of which were unknown to him. Maisoon came in, her eyes glued to the floor. She opened her arms, then dropped them.

"Father," she whispered, "I've missed you."

She was still staring at the floor.

"Forgive me," she said fearfully, "it was not in my hands. I swear that I've tried and I still am. I'll keep trying. I won't be happy . . ."

He grabbed her hand and gave her a hug for the first time since she was born. For just a moment, she gasped, then put her arms around his shoulders without saying a word.

"There's no cruelty," he interrupted her, tears in his eyes, "like children's cruelty. You obey your husband and crush your own father . . ."

"I swear to you that it wasn't me," she replied hurriedly. "I . . ."

"Perhaps you were just a bit cruel," he stammered. "Perhaps . . . , but then I always wanted something better for you. Perhaps it was your stubbornness that made me weak, Maisoon."

He wanted to tell her that he loved her, to ask her to forgive him, and to tell her how scared and feeble he had felt when she disappeared, but he could not do it. He let her go slowly and sat down in front of her. She looked into his eyes and could not believe what she saw there.

"Forgive me," she said forcefully, "if I desert your again. This time . . ."

But before she could complete the sentence, her husband entered. He stood there, staring at his wife and her father. Her father stood up.

"Anas," Maisoon said loudly, "I want you to welcome my father to our house. If you don't, I'm leaving with him now."

Her father smiled and, perhaps for the first time, looked at her with pride. Anas remained silent. Maisoon went over to him.

"For your sake," she told him, "I've put up with a lot. You know that. Year after year."

He remained silent, fighting his own shadow.

"Please don't make me choose between my father and husband," she pleaded. "If you do, you realize that I'll be lost. You know me and are aware of my condition."

"Welcome, Judge, to our house," he said angrily.

She gave a sigh of relief. "I'll get some juice and food ready, Father," she said eagerly.

She left the room, eager and happy. The atmosphere was tense and oppressive. The judge stayed silent.

"What's changed, Shaikh?" Anas asked.

"The country's interests are more important than me and my daughter," the judge replied forcefully.

"Did Ibn al-Mudabbir offer you a governor's post, I wonder," Anas continued, "or the caliph's own judgeship?"

"God alone knows what's in my heart, and no one else," the judge replied sternly. "Do you realize why I've changed, Anas? In your eyes, I see Ibn al-Mudabbir; we all do. You kill and oppress without the slightest hesitation. How many victims have you tyrannized? How much prey has the fisherman slaughtered? When I realized that you were even more evil than Ibn al-Mudabbir, I wanted my daughter to stay with me and not go back to either you or Ibn al-Mudabbir. Then came Ibn al-Mudabbir's promise to the Egyptian people. As you know, the public good is always more important than the individual. Then came that order in the past, and now it's over. Perhaps I did you wrong; maybe I behaved badly, maybe not. Let me see her, and forgive me. I did not anticipate what he'd do to you and your hands. I'm not happy about what happened."

Anas looked at him.

"You're always right," he said sarcastically. "Judge Yahya makes mistakes, even if he causes pain. He's misunderstood. What kind of delusions do you have, man?"

The judge looked nervous. He had not intended to acknowledge any mistakes. For a while, there was silence.

"Ahmad ibn Tulun likes to build things," Anas went on. "He's here to stay."

The judge responded. Conversation about the city and hospital that Ahmad ibn Tulun intended to build was without accusations or blame. Time passed, with the judge watching his daughter as she moved around with eager spontaneity. She kept talking to him with a certain reserve, but also with love and a sense of what she had been missing. After a while, she left.

"She seems happy with you," the judge told Anas. "Her mother told me about something that happened a while ago. It won't happen again. Maisoon's intelligent . . . , she's . . ."

He did not know how to finish the sentence.

"Yes, she's intelligent," Anas said, "and she's fine. There's nothing to worry about."

"If I die," her father said, "I want you to take care of her. Don't leave her, even if her mind deteriorates. How can I be reassured about her?"

Anas smiled.

"How can you be reassured about her," he asked sarcastically, "if you aren't reassured about me? You're right. But she's fine."

Maisoon was like a precious book with subtly colored pictures. She needed him to hold her carefully, gently, and patiently; she needed him to treat the colors inside the book with fear and admiration. If he was ever late, she would complain and start an argument with him as though it were something essential and important, even if it was actually trivial and did not concern her. She needed his involvement all the time; he would either give it voluntarily, or she would take it by force. Either he loved her passionately, or she would make him loathe her. But she could not stand living with tedium and futile feelings. He admired that about her: her desire to live amid nonstop ardor and continuous passion. She needed him to celebrate her with words, deeds, and touch. But she was also genuinely in love with him, far more than he had ever expected; he had no idea why, or why she had chosen him. In giving herself to him and showing her admiration for him, she was totally loyal. She realized that he was giving her all the attention she wanted. Even if he was delayed or somewhat distracted, he would be back before she burned the house down; every time, he could save himself from a predestined end. It was as if, every day, he was living in the midst of fires that he had to avoid. And yet he knew how to operate in such conditions and to make the fires warm him but not burn him. When he returned, she expected him to sit with her for hours and tell her what he had been doing, so she could live with him and be part of his work. She loved talking about government and rulers, cities and mosques, and wars. She loved it that sometimes he treated her like a soldier, while at other times, it would be like a princess, and at still others, like Ibn al-Mudabbir. But she was clever. She could understand the look in his eyes and know if he was worried or desperate. If he looked sad, she would talk nonstop till he responded to her with a smile. She took care of him and readily availed herself of his care for her.

Maisoon had moments of despair too, as he well knew. She closed her heart to the world and sat in her room without eating, drinking, or talking. It had all started a few months after her marriage, but the moments of despair had lessened and, with time, her heart had become more assured. She started relying on him just as much as she loved him; because of him, she grew to like the words and philosophy of the Greeks. She carried on making copies of books with him. Those were their most serene moments. As he dictated to her, talked to her, and argued with her over a topic or problem, she could feel how important she was to him. He would often carry her to their room and spend hours kissing her, and then continue the philosophical discussion. Her attachment to him was like that of fish to life at moments of guaranteed death. She was aware of her hidden madness and the way it might explode, something that now only happened rarely. But he knew it too, and did not hate her for it. Anas was both friend and remedy, serene and intimate.

Chapter 14

Ibn al-Mudabbir languished in Ahmad's prison. He tried to ask his brother Ibrahim to petition the caliph, but it seemed that the caliph was preoccupied with other matters. He seemed to have dispensed with Ibn al-Mudabbir. Ahmad put a stop to all Ibn al-Mudabbir's attempts to get out of prison. He spent his time reading Ibn al-Mudabbir's correspondence and finding out who visited him in prison. After a while, Ahmad ibn Tulun forgot all about him, but Anas did not forget. He swore that Ibn al-Mudabbir was going to die in prison. It seemed close.

"He's dying in his dark prison cell," Mughith said thoughtfully. "He's losing his sight more every day; that's what the guards are saying. I thought you might want to see him and have your revenge for everything that he did to you. They say he's lost all strength; his hair and beard are both long, and he's lost the will to live."

"When you've two strong legs that want to run," Anas responded, "prison becomes even harsher. If you amputated them, the burden of weakness would be less. When you have all the power in your hands, weakness is even more dangerous than death itself. I don't need to see him; I know already and can feel it."

"What happened to the Deputy Police Chief?" Mughith asked spontaneously. "By God, ever since I started work, I've never witnessed such cruelty as yours. Your heart has no soft spot, as though you've never imprisoned anyone, whipped anyone, destroyed houses, and made children homeless."

Anas was shocked.

"Everyone I've punished has deserved it," he replied.

"Anas," Mughith told him sarcastically, "who are you kidding, me or yourself? Come with me to visit Ibn al-Mudabbir. The very sight of him so weak should heal the heart. You need this. Don't pretend to be so superior! Will you come to see how many of his followers you've put in prison? You're the one who gave the orders. Don't you remember?"

Anas's look was a mixture of confusion and shock. Never for a moment had he thought he was doing something wrong. They all could die, Ibn al-Mudabbir's own men, everyone who loved him and encouraged him. They all deserved to die. He did not need to bother himself with their fate, nor had he gone too far in his killing and imprisonments. Not a moment passed without him thinking about the ravaged body of his brother and his father's body disappearing beneath the waves. There had never been any regret in his heart, even though his inner self was still baffled and seeking a peace that it had never found.

Every night, Ibn al-Mudabbir prayed to God to release him from Ahmad's prison, and every night his eyes grew dimmer. At first, he assumed it was because the prison and cells were dark, and then he was afraid it might be madness. He was a victim of the fisherman's son and Ahmad, of treachery and abandonment. The caliph had deserted him and left him in Ahmad's hands, even though he had spent his entire life protecting the caliphate and filling its coffers with gold and silver. Ibn al-Mudabbir was never going to see Maisoon again; not because he was going to die in prison, not because she would refuse to see him, not because he had been struck by a touch of madness, but rather because he had lost his sight a year ago. Everyone around him had faded away, as though he were the Samaritan, even though he had never indulged in calf worship or distorted God's word. He had performed his role proficiently and conscientiously. Sometimes he had been assertive because he wanted to be in control of things, not because he liked being a tyrant. He was a victim; that is what he told himself every single day, a victim of the curse of the ancient Egyptians. Maisoon had bewitched him because of her love for Anas; maybe Anas had bewitched him as well. The dungeon had doubled, and so had the bars of the cell. His entire self contracted, and his soul did not open itself up. He had been wronged; he was a victim. His very weakness was an indication of the power he had had in the past, and his lack of options now spoke to the truth of his words. He was Ibn al-Mudabbir, who used to wear silk and ride his way proudly through the markets with his fine horse and gold. Now he was living inside a prison, with darkness both inside and outside him. If the magic spell could be broken, he might be saved; if he died, he might be saved. The specter of Hamza al-Skandari drowning loomed before him. It seemed to be cackling happily.

"Come with me," it said, "let's play and have some fun! For an hour or less, this is a playground. You want things to end, you long for it. Welcome to the prison of despair and humiliation!"

He closed his eyes in pain and asked the guard to fetch the Pyramid Witch. He had heard of her astuteness. The guard told him that she only spoke Coptic and never left the pyramid. People said she only came out at night to keep company with the jinn and spirits of the ancients.

"Could you ask her a question or two," Ibn al-Mudabbir asked sadly, "and bring me the answers?"

The guard hesitated. "For your sake, my lord," he replied, "I'll do it."

"Ask her why I'm being subjected to such injustice when I performed my task perfectly. Ask her how I can be rid of a deceitful body and blurry eyes from which all light is fading. Ask her how Ahmad ibn Tulun has triumphed in spite of his disloyalty to the caliphate."

The guard promised to do it, but he forgot. Days went by without him doing it.

Ibn al-Mudabbir was overcome by a bout of depression, the impact of which was worse than any other disease. His limbs grew weak, and he stopped talking. At that point, the guard remembered and went to see the Pyramid Witch. She was expecting him and answered the questions without even hearing what they were. All the way back, the guard kept repeating the answers so he would not forget.

"The witch tells you, my lord," he whispered in Ibn al-Mudabbir's ear, "that weakness has not helped you learn, and the deceitful body is always destined for destruction. It's only for an hour or less that humans can control the world and be misled by it. She went on to say: 'For every human being there comes a moment when he realizes that weakness is an inevitable prospect; at that point, he has to realize the truth.' Then she said that she's not interested in the dispute between you and Ahmad ibn Tulun, but she does know that weakness does not discriminate between the tyrant and the tyrannized. It afflicts every human being, but the tyrannized person welcomes it, realizing that it is not the end, whereas the tyrant's heart lets out a snort like a whimper."

The witch's responses brought him no comfort. He continued cursing Ahmad ibn Tulun, Anas, and even Maisoon, who had preferred the fisherman's son to him. Overwhelming sorrow now took hold, and he died shortly afterward, still angry and frustrated.

With Ibn al-Mudabbir's death, Anas was able to pull the dagger out of the dark depths of his heart. But it left behind an empty spot to be seared by the breeze whenever it groaned and flared. Sometimes people can become so accustomed to grief that contentment turns into agony. When his father had died, humiliated and defeated, a soul full of contentment and an unruly and defiant heart died with him. The beating heart no longer brought with it the sound of singing birds; the tremulous soul no longer possessed the sound of waves in flood, blending fear with desire. There had been a time when he thought that Ibn al-Mudabbir's death would restore laughter to his heart and moisture to his ribs. He told himself that revenge would bring a cure and quench a thirst. However, what had been lost would never return; the departed would never be reborn in this world. Anas also had a shadow that trailed him throughout his life, a black shadow, pallid, fragmented, feeble, with complicated, crisscrossed lines like a spider's web. When he returned to his house, it was not to sacrifice animals or to celebrate joyfully. He returned in order to think and understand, but he did not understand and could not think. Temporary joy was an illusion. Any hope of returning to life as it had been before the onset of sorrow was as impossible as the resurrection of the dead and the ancient ancestors. He must accept the world with all its sorrow and dark hues. He should convince himself that the loss of ignorant innocence was both blessing and retribution. The vicissitudes of time leave gaps in the heart that can only be cured by death and resurrection. He wondered if the witch realized that. Did the ancients know that life was short, and time robs colors of their gleam?

He had thought that Ibn al-Mudabbir's death would bring back his father and brother, and imbue life with comfort after suffering. Ibn al-Mudabbir was dead now, just like his father and brother, and the same way as he and others would die. How futile, how delusional! This was life in this world, unfamiliar to us. If we reconciled ourselves to it, it would deceive us. If we fought it, it would win. Patient endurance of time was our only course; it was bound to come to an end; that was life's only certainty.

When he looked at his wife, he saw in her eyes a fear he did not understand.

"You know . . . ," he said assuredly.

She swallowed hard. "Ibn al-Mudabbir has died in Ahmad ibn Tulun's prison," she said.

He nodded, but said nothing.

"I wonder," she said without meaning to, "do you still love me?"

He held her hand. "There are moments," he replied, "when light radiates from the burning vault, and I see the gleam of life. That only happens when I'm with you. No, Maisoon, I wasn't married to you to take revenge. Now that Ibn al-Mudabbir is dead, I'll never leave you. You're the spark of life and waves of the living sea."

"I realize that, of course," she replied immediately. "I didn't doubt you. I was just . . . I don't understand why you're so sad."

"I don't know what's causing it either."

He would have to visit the Pyramid Witch. Whatever was worrying him was buried deep inside him, and he could not understand it or live with it. He decided to walk on foot from Al-Qata'i to the Great Pyramid in Giza.

The city of Al-Qata'i had both the magic and curse of ancestors. It had to be loved. The alleys were filled with the smell of baking bread and sweets to remind us of all the good things of life and the savor of passion. No one there could have enough bread and sugar; from hand to hand, from mouth to mouth, the wheat would gradually melt its way into the depths and then stimulate obscure memories. There was a tailor in the city who was making a pure silk garment; no one knew who it was for. Perhaps it was for a bride, full of love and hope, or else for the Tax Administrator, who was always happy to strut arrogantly through the land. Were the strands from which it was made entwined in hardship and suffering, or with patience and resolve? Here was hidden an incomplete joy and a weak body, even if pride had endowed it with sin.

There was also a smith making swords and wondering whom they were going to kill. He wanted them to put an end to all tyrants and greedy people. He realized that the swords would sever heads of the innocent, heads of some people wandering along entirely dark paths, and many heads belonging to fighters on behalf of memory that always slips between our hands. One store copied books about history past and another about the future to come, doing its best to gather the memory and record the wisdom of the ancients, but being thwarted in the face of fire and destruction. Once all trace of the city is erased and power overcomes memory, writing becomes essential. The preservation of documents is a kind of victory. Here died a shaikh who never veered from the truth; here departed a man, a victim of his own dream; here weakness was manifest to every strongman, frailty to every tyrant; here humanity discovered that it loses part of itself every single day that passes and that the end will inevitably come, duly accompanied by a degree of despair and a good deal of affection.

Anas crossed the Nile like someone in a daze or bewitched. All the way, he kept seeing Ibn al-Mudabbir, weak and alone inside his prison, captive of an unruly, fugitive soul, and a fickle heart. Without any thought, Anas put his hand over his heart, as though to check that it was still there. He opened his eyes, then closed them again in case the image disappeared. Instead, it was even clearer. He looked down and saw it on the walls of houses and all around the stones on the street. When he looked up, he could see it amid the clouds and stars. Ibn al-Mudabbir, it was Ibn al-Mudabbir. Crossing the Nile, he stared at the river water. He had not crossed. That image was fixed deep inside him, in the folds of his soul. He shook his head, as though he wanted to get rid of it, but could not do so. Tomorrow the Deputy Police Chief would go back to work. He would search every nook and cranny for a traitor, any who had defended Ibn al-Mudabbir; traitors would be punished without further thought. Tomorrow the Deputy Police Chief would go back to work. He would knock down houses and, in their place, put up fountains to wash the heart, but not cleanse it. He would destroy stores to fill his empty heart, but would never fill it with the demolished material. He had not made mistakes; he had only punished those who deserved it. Those who killed would be killed; that was certain. People kept saying that tax workers were under orders; they had no discretion. The Deputy Police Chief had killed some of them and imprisoned others, but they had had no choice. He had had no choice. This was a world that called for amputation and promoted sedition. He had spent years amid his books, but then the world had sneakily snatched him away from his manuscripts and not left him alone until he had become vicious. With that, he had triumphed, or nearly so.

He hurried to visit the Pyramid Witch, not knowing whether his heart palpitations were from joy or confusion. He went in without asking permission.

"Ibn al-Mudabbir's dead," he said.

"Did you see him, Anas, when he was weak?" she asked him, staring at his face.

"No, I didn't," he replied. "I decided that was impossible. It was revenge I wanted, not satisfaction."

"How merciful you are, man! So now the heart is relaxed, the sword's back in its scabbard, the world's adjusted, and heartbeats are regular."

"Yes, that's right. It's the happiest day of my life."

"And the saddest."

"Don't make me even more baffled."

"That's why you've come to see me."

"Which jinn touches you every day, Witch?"

"Your heart was filled with hatred of Ibn al-Mudabbir. Now he's dead, you're feeling a sense of loss without him, a big gap. Who's going to fill up your heart now, Anas?"

"My wife already does, she . . ."

"Ibn al-Mudabbir."

"What crazy nonsense are you talking?"

"He's dead, and you'll die, and so will Ahmad. Today you come here triumphant, but tomorrow you're going to feel sad. Today Ahmad stands victorious, but tomorrow he'll come here weak. If you realized that things spin incessantly, you wouldn't despair, grumble, and blame people. There's no victory on earth."

"It's the right of the oppressed."

"Why didn't you believe from the outset that it would happen?"

"I did my best."

"But God wills. Your efforts without His will don't mean a great deal. So leave here and seek refuge with Maisoon. She is still yours. You've a void inside you."

"It's as though I can see him in front of me, or actually inside me," Anas replied immediately. "Once he was dead, I assumed that my heart would experience some happiness, but Ibn al-Mudabbir . . ."

"That's because he'll never leave you. He's fixed and resident in your heart. He's destroyed past and present because he's fixed and resident. If you'd let him leave you, you wouldn't have come here today."

"What do you mean?"

"You know I don't like explaining things. Go your own way, and don't forget the books."

He left the witch with an anxious feeling, although he had no idea why. It was as though life had come to an end before it even began. As he entered his room, he wondered about life's purpose and time's end. The moment of victory was certainly not worth so many years of torment. Death would not come solely to the oppressor, but to the oppressed as well. Ever since Ibn al-Mudabbir had died, he had been constantly sad. He was afraid that he had spent his entire life breathlessly looking for a river, when it was actually flowing under his feet. He had been looking for a shining star in the heavens, but it had fallen all around in its search for him. Maybe he was feeling a pain in his chest. He looked at his wife who was asleep beside him. He woke her up.

"Maisoon . . ." he said.

She opened her eyes and looked at him. "What's the matter?" she asked.

"You know I love you."

"Yes, I do."

"I've always been happy with you. Maybe I could be even happier if you gave me the chance. Do you understand?"

She looked into his eyes, but did not reply.

"You've put up with me," he said with a smile.

"No," she replied, "you're the one who's put up with my madness. You've never tested me."

"Your madness is nothing compared with mine. I'm a bit confused; the earth's been quaking."

Next morning, he still felt a pain in his chest.

"I've no business working in the Police," he told his wife firmly. "I'm going to devote myself to books again."

She looked spontaneously at the spot where his hand had been severed.

"I may not be able to transcribe anymore," he went on with determination, "but I can still sell manuscripts."

She held his arm gently. "I can help you," she said. "I can make copies."

She stayed with her husband as he read books slowly and carefully. Ever since Ibn al-Mudabbir's death a month before, Anas had been sick, pale, and sad, immersing himself in documents. She put her hand on his shoulder. Even when she told him that she was pregnant, his mood did not change. With every passing day, he managed to fold away some of his despair and open a tiny crack through which a quest for the flavor of light and taste of understanding could seep out. When Ahmad ibn Tulun's procession passed by, Maisoon would go out to watch it, but Anas was not able to do so; he said that he was too tired.

The herald would shout out in a loud raucous voice: "Amir Ahmad ibn Tulun, Amir of Egypt, Syria, Hejaz, and Yemen." The soldiers would be arrayed in ranks: the cavalry wore colorful, embroidered uniforms, and the infantry were dressed in trousers, with shields and helmets. The procession went on its way as though it were endless, stretching all the way to Yemen on one side and Byzantium on the other. How could an army parade be as tall as mountains and penetrate the very heavens? Egyptian mouths gaped wide open as they watched it with drums beating. The inhabitants of Al-Qata'i crowded around to catch a glimpse of the amir, if only from a distance. He rode his horse, proceeding with a steady confidence amid his soldiery. He looked at the city all around him. The buildings all blended with the crowds of people, so that it seemed like a magic city where rocks could talk, rains splashed all around, and grape and fig plants sprouted on its edges. Clouds twisted, mists dwindled, and the star that had fallen ten years earlier shone bright, illuminating everything that remained. Here was a lofty mosque, here the Palace of the Square, here the hospital, factory, bridges, canals, fields, ornamentation, and lamps. Now at last, light could shine between the angles of the streets, interconnected as though they had been constructed a thousand years or more ago. Who was that smiling from on high? Was it not the person who had built the Great Pyramid, Surid ibn Salhouq, as the Arabs call him? Or maybe the Pyramid Witch, who knew the ancestors and spoke to them? People were smiling in pride today, gaping in surprise and realizing that time belonged to Amir Ahmad ibn Tulun; he filled the palms of his hands with it and drank its victories to the full. He wanted to build here, to make it his home and country, and perpetuate his own name alongside that of Surid, who had built the pyramid. He knew it and dreamed it. How many nights did he stay awake with it! He knew no other dream. Today every enemy would be afraid. Ahmad ibn Tulun would open his arms and reach out to enfold the whole of Egypt. The procession was awesome, warm, and intimate. Those walking and riding in the uniforms of infantry and cavalry included many Egyptians. A mother raised her hand in pride, and a wife bashfully suppressed a smile. People say that if you dig up the soil, you will find mud and gold; if you dig up the soil as a loyal citizen, you will find glory that never fades.

He could understand how she twitched nervously when she could not understand something, and how, once in a while, her mind would swing between illusion and madness. He did his best, as far as possible, not to bother her, but she could tell that he was not well. She brought in a doctor who said that Anas was physically fine. He might feel sad or downhearted; who knows? That often happened to policemen once they had left their jobs. Perhaps he needed to go back and work for Ahmad.

They spent a lot of time together, unbothered by feelings of oppression. Was it about a month after Ibn al-Mudabbir's death or a number of months while he was still in prison? He rued the number of days he had wasted without appreciating how beautiful she was as she lay in his arms. But he had been set on a course known only to the Creator, ever since he had watched as his father was whipped and humiliated.

"What's the matter with you?" she asked in frustration. "The doctor says there's nothing physically wrong with you."

"It must be in the heart then."

She looked at him, baffled, and then moved closer and put her head on his shoulder.

"How can I cure this condition?" she asked.

There was silence.

"Saeed, son of Katib al-Farghani, wanted to be my friend," he said, as he ran his hand through her hair. "At the time, I said no, but he knows me, perhaps better than I do. He's searching for his beloved, Maisoon."

"I don't understand."

"We're all of us pursuing the impossible. People who get tangled up with the impossible lose their minds. I want to see him. I'll send him a letter tomorrow."

"If that'll make you happy," she replied in despair, "then by all means send him a letter."

"Do you remember when I took you down to the river?" he asked, putting her head on his chest. "I carried you in my arms. The water dragged you down, but you managed to float. You yelled that you would never manage to see the river bottom. You're afraid of what you can't see."

"I floated because you were carrying me!" she replied with a smile. "I felt happy."

He rubbed his cheek against hers and mustered all his forces.

"Close your eyes," he said, "and think about our future together, days without end. Had we realized that separation was inevitable, we would not have wanted it to stay forever."

"What separation are you talking about, Anas?" she asked abruptly.

"The one in the past, Maisoon," he replied, "It's over."

👯

Two days later, Anas woke and looked around him as though he had been dreaming. He had recovered his strength and initiative. He had no idea why he had been sick for two whole days. Perhaps his conscience had pricked him about the past. All Ibn al-Mudabbir's men had deserved to die. He had been Deputy Police Chief, defending justice; there was no need to feel sorry for the death of traitors and tyrants. He needed to go back to Alexandria and be a fisherman, just like his father. He should take the boat out from the long-abandoned hills and use his arms to pull in the nets filled with good things. He suggested the idea to his wife, and she immediately agreed. He started making preparations. Ahmad ibn Tulun heard about his plan, gave him back the things that Ibn al-Mudabbir had taken, and appointed him head fisherman in succession to his father. He decided to sell his house in Al-Qata'i to Saeed, Katib al-Farghani's son, who had originally built it and now needed it. He sent Saeed a letter and eagerly awaited his arrival. Tomorrow Saeed would arrive, and Anas would return to Alexandria. Today he adored his wife with all the force of the pyramids and the obstinacy of the Sphinx.

"Anas," she said, opening her eyes in amazement, "you're feeling better. Maybe you needed to be thinking of the sea."

He held her in his arms.

"Maybe I needed the sea," he replied with a smile, "and you too."

As the light drew near, she could smell its scent. She slept peacefully in his arms. She turned over and opened her eyes. He pulled her toward him and hugged her hard around the waist. Staring out the window, she reached for the place where his severed hand would have been and squeezed it.

"I can't feel it, Maisoon," he whispered. "Put your hand over my heart; that would be better."

She placed her hand over his heart. "You've overwhelmed me with your passion," she muttered, "the way you did when you came crashing into my room at the Authority Town place. Do you remember? You were so intent on passion, fisherman's son, that I lost consciousness."

"There's nothing like passion," he replied with a smile, eyes closed, "to make you lose consciousness."

She fell fast asleep.

Next morning, Gameela carried their possessions out to a cart. Maisoon got dressed, and Saeed came rushing over after he received Anas's letter.

Maisoon went to wake up her husband, but he did not wake up. He seemed to prefer sleeping. He looked happy and peaceful, the kind of peace she had never seen in his eyes before. She stood still, not knowing what to do. She closed her eyes and hugged herself, as though expecting a wave of ice. The shadow emerged, then disappeared. She heard her own voice outside her body, chiding her for delaying and not understanding why. She recited some Quranic verses and then repeated some of Anas's own words. She did not know when he had said them: it would be a temporary journey. He had said: Won't you let the shadow take its place. He had said . . .

She screamed and called for Gameela.

"Help me," she cried, "I can't wake him."

Gameela went over to him, then recited some Quranic verses.

"My lady" she said, holding Maisoon's shoulder, "he's never going to wake up again."

▥

For the first time since she was born, her father held her hand gently.

"My daughter," he said.

She stared at him in confusion.

"Where's Anas?" she asked.

"Come with me," her father said.

She looked all around her, repeating the same words. Every time the shadow tried to penetrate her heart, she stopped it. She looked at the house wall and put her hand on it, as though to get some strength from it, then collapsed on the floor.

Her father stayed by her side for days. He was not aware of her fight with sorrow, with the shadow and darkness. Such wars were brutal. He could sense the depth of suffering in her eyes, but did not realize exactly what was going on inside her.

She kept looking all around the room in despair.

"Anas asked me to remind you," her father said, "that if darkness and the shadow prevailed, he would never meet you. I don't know what he meant. He said that you would understand. He asked me to tell you that every day."

"If only he realized how difficult it is," she said painfully.

"What's difficult, daughter?" her father asked.

"The shadow and darkness will never prevail," she replied without thinking.

Part Four

You wish to remain in an abode with no permanence;
Have you heard of an unmovable shadow?
—*Al-Tughra'i, 11th century poet*

Chapter 15

O ne year after Anas's death, it was clear that Maisoon had not lost her mind as everyone had expected. Her heart did not shun the pain; she realized the stealthy way it would whisper. She suffered in silence and enveloped her son in her love, having promised to take him back to Alexandria as his father had wanted before he died. She planned to do everything Anas had wanted: she would be selling the house to Saeed, Katib al-Farghani's son, and Ali, her son, would become head fisherman.

She started concerning herself with her mother's and sister's lives, listening to stories about Egypt and Al-Qata'i. She made the acquaintance of the women in the quarter and talked to them about their situations. She got to know the oven owner and sweet seller. She learned how to cook from some of the women and how to bake bread from others.

She was in the house when her father invited Saeed, Katib al-Farghani's son, to come.

No sooner did her father open the door than Maisoon was there with fruit juices, her face veiled.

"Welcome!" she said as she sat down. "Anas talks about you a lot. Forgive me; he wouldn't want me to show my face in front of other men."

Saeed was astonished at the way she was talking about her husband, as though he were still alive. Her voice may have been a bit weak, but her eyes were gleaming bright like stars on a moonlit night with no clouds and no shadows.

"I keep telling my father that if it weren't for Maisoon, the judge's daughter, Ahmad ibn Tulun's regime wouldn't have lasted."

Her father was nervous.

"There's no need for that now, my daughter," he said.

"I explain to my son," she went on regardless, "that, for my sake, the Tax Administrator was willing to forego the entire tax revenue of Egypt. But I chose Anas instead."

Saeed swallowed hard and had no idea what to say.

"Maisoon," her father told her gently, "come back to us. That was all in the past."

"What else is left to us to live in and for apart from the past? It's no longer past; it's us—me, you, and Anas. Anas always says that . . ."

Her father stopped her.

"Maisoon," he said, "your husband . . ."

"He says that there can be no separation between lovers," she went on as though she had not heard him. "There can be just a short journey-time, after which there's no travel and no distance. Anyone who thinks that it's separation doesn't believe in God; anyone who's afraid of evanescence has not let love into his heart. That's what Anas says. He loves playing with words. No matter! We want to carry out his legacy. He built this house for me, but I've only lived in it for a few months. There are lots of months in life—a complete era in itself, countless years not worth a single caliph's dirham or an Ahmadi dinar. Ahmadi dinars are heavy, made of pure gold. Anas says, Saeed, that you deserve this house most of all; you designed it and are familiar with its decorations and walls. Those who build the walls, my brother, most deserve the house. That's what Anas says.

"But tell me, brother," she went on eagerly, "how did Ahmad ibn Tulun build Al-Qata'i? How did you build this house? It was all for Maisoon, with whom Ibn al-Mudabbir was infatuated, while Anas wanted her for himself. It's a story, but if it weren't for her, Saeed wouldn't have built this house. Ahmad wouldn't have known Saeed nor would Anas, and Ahmad wouldn't have known Anas. Do you understand me, brother?"

Her father's patience was wearing thin, as though he had heard this tale thousands of times.

"There's no call for this kind of talk, Umm Ali," he told his daughter.

She gave him a chiding look.

"You have to know, Father," she said. "Didn't I determine the destiny of this country?"

To Saeed, it looked as though Maisoon was spending too much of her time alone, and wanted to tell her story at least twice every day. Perhaps she was not spending it on her own; having now lost her husband, she felt she had to talk about him. Saeed smiled to himself. Vanity was incurable! But actually, she was right: what she had done and what had happened because of her had, in fact, changed the destiny of humanity.

She stood up and put her hand on the wall of the house.

"Al-Qata'i, this magic city," she said, "is a little piece of paradise, the entire world on a single plot of land—white and black, Arab and non-Arab. You can hear every language here and eat varieties of food. If you're looking for gardens, you'll find them here; if it's plums and quince you want, they're here too. Even green apples and colored grapes are here. This city is here because of me.

"Brother Saeed," she went on eagerly, "but for Anas, Ahmad ibn Tulun would never have won, and, if he hadn't, Al-Qata'i would never have been built and would not be here. You'll see Al-Qata'i the way it was and will be. No matter! Let's talk about the purchase of the house. Anas hasn't specified a price. He told us that we should let you determine the price you want. But remember, brother, that you're not buying a house in Al-Qata'i with a fountain and windows that soak up sunlight; you're buying a house that within its walls has imbibed days of mercy and cordiality."

"I'm aware of that, my lady. I'll pay what you ask."

"When Ali grows up, we'll be living in Alexandria, and he'll be a fisherman like his grandfather. Ahmad ibn Tulun had already given Anas back some of his money and boats before Ibn al-Mudabbir died."

By now, the judge seemed to be feeling more patient with his daughter.

"Anas told us to look for Saeed, son of Katib al-Farghani, everywhere in Al-Qata'i. On the day he died, you disappeared, brother; I searched for you all over the place. You don't have a fixed abode, man. You're like birds, paying seasonal visits."

"I search for nectar in trees," Saeed replied, "and it's volatile and unstable. You need to keep moving. I'll pay whatever you decide."

Then he turned to look at Maisoon.

"My lady," he said gently, "your husband wanted you to have the most beautiful house in the whole of Al-Qata'i. His eyes shone as he looked at the plaster filigree, the fountain, and the hall. He was and was not a soldier. Do you realize that? I'll buy the house from you. My lady, Al-Qata'i is what remains of memories of my youth and creativity. It attests to the possibility of miracles; that, in the hands of ancestors, magic can build walls and offer protection from poverty and corruption. There are occasions when a man finds himself encircled by time on every side, delving into an obscure history loaded down with pictures and symbols and an ongoing quest for knowledge and victory. That victory involved those decorations and symbols, not so much in understanding them as in retaining them in the heart. This house is what I've longed for all my life."

She stared at him, then stood up suddenly and headed for her room. Saeed went over to the judge.

"Tell me, Judge," he asked, "how is your daughter?"

"Ever since her husband died," the judge replied, "she's refused to allow any-one to lament his passing or even to say that he's dead. She says that he's gone somewhere far away, and they'll be meeting soon. She keeps talking about him as though he's still with us."

"That's love, my lord," Saeed said.

"I've been learning from Anas," the judge replied. "He gave me advice and we talked about her."

"How can the judge learn anything from the fisherman's son?"

"There's no hope for a judge who can't learn anything."

"All of us here are a bit crazy," Saeed said suddenly. "It comes with the Nile waters and the pyramid nectar."

"Do pyramids have nectar?"

"Didn't I just tell you that we're all a bit crazy? Madness has its own magic and creativity. Be patient!"

Maisoon came into the room again.

"Saeed, son of Katib al-Farghani," she said eagerly, "now I remember. Anas left you a letter. I don't understand exactly what he means. He says you'll understand."

Saeed stared at her.

"Anas asks you to forgive him," she went on, eyes gleaming ardently, "because he was slow to learn. For a while, there was hatred in his heart, but for a while now, he's been trying to recover his real self. Anas says that he knows who the orphaned girl is that you've been searching for all over the world. She was around you and beside you all the time, but panic can always blind the sight and cloud the vision."

"Where is she? How did Anas find her?"

"He says he was watching out for her all the time, but only noticed her recently. She lives in the pyramid, the Pyramid Witch."

Her father was dismayed.

"Don't pay any attention to what she's saying," he whispered to Saeed. "Sometimes she starts raving."

"How did Anas know?" Saeed asked shivering.

"From the books she reads," Maisoon replied as she left the room. "You told him that she likes books and cake. Anas also says that you're his friend, even though he did not often try to see you. Friendship's a process, and meetings don't always have to involve the body. That's what Anas says."

The judge started talking and apologizing for the things his daughter was saying. Saeed kept shivering. Finally, Saeed left, tears pouring down his cheeks. After a while, her father chided her.

"There was no way of avoiding mention of the men who've admired you and wanted to be married to you," he said.

"That's all history," she replied forcefully. "It has to be remembered as it was."

She went into her room, mumbling to herself. Gameela brought her baby, Ali. By now, Gameela was used to Maisoon's moods.

"Talk to me, my lady," she said.

Maisoon took off her veil, walked over to the fountain, and stared at her reflection in the small pool.

"I promised him not to let the shadow take his place. I promised to put up with the heart's desolation and soul's loneliness until we meet again. He told me that, if I allowed the shadow to take his place, we would never meet. He threatened me; at times, he could be cruel. But he would also rock me and spoil me, just like a father, brother, son, and husband. He was more patient with me than my own father."

"Your father's a good father," Gameela said. "He loves you and is frightened for you."

"I know. Sometimes the shadow tries to lure me with its shining eyes. But then, I close my eyes and remember Anas."

"What do you remember, my lady?" Gameela asked eagerly.

"I used to look at my face in the water like this," she replied, speaking longingly of her husband. "He would come, or rather he'd sneak up on me from behind, almost out of his mind because I'm so beautiful. I won't hide it from you: I admired him too. Then there happened what happened and will happen. We built Al-Qata'i, gave Ahmad ibn Tulun executive authority, and put an end to Ibn al-Mudabbir. If I told you what we did, you'd think I was exaggerating."

"What did you do?"

"I tell my son and everyone. Whenever they spot a star falling from the skies or blazing on the green soil, they must remember, . . . whenever their eyes fail to see the beginning or end of the city, they must remember, . . . whenever the fire of love sears their hearts or the pain of distance severs their ties, they need to remember; to remember the judge's daughter, the most beautiful woman in Egypt, Maisoon."

Year after year, Saeed gathered his belongings and wandered the earth, staying in a house for a month or two, but no longer, and anticipating the day when he would find her. He would recall moments of fusion and coherence, others of joy from the depths of the soul to invigorate the heart and make limbs shudder. His orphaned beloved was everything he possessed, everything he desired. When he found her this time, he would never abandon her or be afraid. He had heard about the Pyramid Witch, who had ways of achieving things. She knew, understood, read, and memorized. People say she had an elephant's memory, could recite words like poets, and penetrate the earth like ancient temples.

He had thought he would ask for her help. Today Saeed, son of Katib al-Farghani, was different. He built out of longing; he created because he was deprived; he hoped as a lover and was vicious as an aspirant. He strode in to see the Pyramid Witch.

"I need to find her," he said without even looking at her. "Help me find her, and you can have whatever you wish."

The witch stared at him, but said nothing. He raised his eyes to look at her huge, black eyes. His heart quivered like wheat blowing in a storm.

"Save me, Pyramid Witch," he said in a despair accompanied by a degree of affection.

She approached him and stretched out her hand.

"Why should I save you, Copt?" she asked.

"I need you. Ever since I opened my eyes on the world, I've wanted you. You know that, Bahnas. Where have you been hiding from me all these years? You were close by, all around me, but I couldn't find you. How confused and deluded I've been."

"Even so, you've given up and surrendered."

"Wasted time. Forgive the one whose sole desire is self-sacrifice on behalf of his mother, father, city, and past."

"No, I won't forgive you. But no matter! What is it you want, Saeed?"

"I want you. I love you. Here no one will control us; no one will pelt us with stones. Al-Qata'i isn't like other cities; it values knowledge and difference."

She smiled, then held his hand.

"Here the city inhabitants won't see us," she said. "Relatives and neighbors will have no control over you. People will say you're in love with the witch who's kept company with the devil from childhood. She's weird and has no known family or ancestry. The Sphinx is actually her father, what do you think?"

He kissed her hand fervently.

"Forgive me," he said, "I'm just a mortal. My love for you is more than anyone can bear."

"It's love without courage. Love cannot exist among cowards. You'll be wandering for the rest of your days. You'll witness lovers, but not approach them. You'll see sacrifice and passion in men's eyes, but you'll envy them a courage you never possessed in your youth."

"You are a witch then; you strike me with your curse. You've never been in love. Lovers don't get angry and take revenge."

She smiled and kissed his hand slowly.

"The lover does not forgive, Saeed," she said. "How can you forgive someone who's robbed you of your soul? You were my soul."

He hugged her passionately to his chest.

"I'm still with you," he pleaded. "I've never loved anyone else, and I never shall."

She pushed him away.

"The Pyramid Witch gave herself to you one day," she said, "because she saw a truth. That day, her heart betrayed her. If she were to see such a truth today, she would not submit to it. When I gave myself to you, it was only you that I trusted, so much so that now I don't even know myself. Then your relatives managed to convince you that Bahnas consorts with the devil. I've never done that. I consorted with the ancestors because I was alone, even when I was with you. They were my friends and family. Stupidity and ignorance about them envelop you, so there's no escaping your own weakness."

"Are you condemning me to a life of wandering, like Moses's Jews, through mountain passes and in desert wastes in a fruitless search lasting forty years or more?"

"Forty years or more, Saeed. Only the creative ability inside you will be able to convince you. Cowardice has not won yet. Search all around you for motivation and passion. Observe the destinies of lovers. You'll encounter many of them."

"Who are they? I know of Anas and Ahmad ibn Tulun."

"Anyone who examines parchments will discover his goal between the lines. People who read with no understanding or passion have no hope of salvation. Make of your love a means of understanding. There can be no understanding without sorrow, and no love without weakness. This world does not provide us with the things we want, even if we kid ourselves that it is subject to our will. Achievement always involves error, and there's always hidden weakness in strength. If you're patient with your heart, you deserve to live a wanderer's life, never satisfied. Remember that you're not alone; we're all of us breathlessly pursuing eternity within a feeble and untrustworthy body that is defeated by the very first sword or plague. We're prisoners striving for freedom. Perhaps we shall meet again in God's heaven and recollect."

The world crumbled before him, and he could hardly breathe. Holding his breath, he embraced her again. She did not resist. He kissed her. As he put his arm around her, his entire life scattered. At that point, he wanted to throw his soul at her feet. He sighed, thinking about what he had lost and was about to lose again. She moved gently away.

"I feel really sorry for you," she told him emotionally. "How I have searched for you within my heart! Tomorrow perhaps or the day after, we'll meet again."

He did not understand what she was saying. At that moment, he could envision a mosque with a whole series of interconnected niches, confiding in God in heaven and praying for contentment and forgiveness, with no beginning and no end, their ribs created by the Lord. Then from her womb she produced the child—a communication between humans that is hard to explain, that from this, and this from that, a solid structure linking humanity. Even so, Bahnas wanted to crack open his chest.

"I can see them here and there in front of me," he said firmly, "all around you and me. How can you cleave what is linked with no beginning or end? You'll never manage to sever what is connected, one part with another."

She escaped from his arms. He was still roaming unconscious, as though inebriated by a powerful wine. She vanished, as though she had neither permitted nor yearned. She abandoned him in a wilderness like crocodile teeth, mercilessly piercing the flesh and with no known design.

On the Margins of the Story

ﬁﬁﬁﬁﬁﬁﬁﬁﬁﬁﬁﬁﬁﬁﬁﬁﬁﬁﬁﬁ

1918

After praying with Sultan Ahmad Fuad in the Ahmad ibn Tulun Mosque, people split up and went their own ways. Even the British scholar decided that he had done enough research and could now write his book about history. But Adil was not satisfied or happy. The image of Anas and Maisoon dominated his nights; he would see Maisoon even when doing his duty by his own wife. He would see her night and day. He obtained a photograph with Sultan Ahmad Fuad, and his wife was very proud of it. His heart was still sad. He realized that sorrow was all around him, and he had not been successful in either his job or his marriage; even his sons despised him. He was Saeed, son of Katib al-Farghani. Yes indeed, he was Saeed, with his cowardice and initial failure to engage, followed by his final regret and loss of direction. Pyramid Witch, when do you ever forgive?

"Bahnas," he muttered in his sleep, "what kind of heart do you have?"

He went back at night to the Tulunid house alongside the mosque and started digging in the rubble. A guard came over to throw him out. He gave the man some bread and meat.

"Let's talk, brother," he said. "What harm will it do you if I stay here?"

Adil brushed the sand off himself.

"Bahnas," he muttered, "Pyramid Witch, forgive me."

He pulled out a piece of decayed parchment and put it on his chest. He realized that it was one of Al-Khwarizmi's equations. Maybe Anas, son of Hamza al-Skandari, had transcribed it. He kept on digging and found an Ahmadi dinar that gleamed in the night like the steady eyes of the lower jinn. He turned and looked at the guard.

"Do you know Ahmad ibn Tulun?" he asked.

"No one knows him like I do," the guard replied. "I've spent my life guarding his mosque. Have you come to look for relics or treasure? Tell me the truth. What are you planning to do with that coin?"

"Do you realize," Adil responded enthusiastically, "that the spot where my foot is now used to be the city. This was the house of Anas, son of Hamza al-Skandari, that then became the house of Saeed, son of Katib al-Farghani. What do you see in the mosque, brother?"

"All I can see," the guard replied, confused, "is interlocking niches at the top of the balustrades. Look up, look at the balustrades decorating the mosque walls.

This mosque is unlike any other, but I've never understood the meaning of those balustrade shapes. I've never seen anything like them since I was born."

Adil sat down cross-legged, and the guard joined him cautiously, drinking tea and eating.

"People say," the guard said, "that Sultan, or King, Ahmad Fuad wants to be the Islamic caliph. The Ottoman caliphate has been defeated by the British, but where's the caliphate now? I've heard people saying that by praying the Friday prayers in this mosque, he's reminding people of ancient history or imitating Ahmad ibn Tulun by declaring the country independent."

Adil's eyes were glued to the Ahmadi dinar coin.

"People say," he replied with a smile, "that Ahmad ibn Tulun used to distribute bread and meat to the entire Egyptian people."

"Then let's pray to God," the guard responded, "that Sultan Fuad behaves the same way. But give me the dinar."

The Second Story: Ahmad's Dream
Part One

I weep for those who have given me a taste of their love,
So that, when they roused me in passion, they slumbered.
I shall depart from the world, their love
In my heart unfelt by anyone.
Twixt myself and sorrow have I extended an acquaintance,
Both of them never ending.
—*Bashshar ibn Burd, Abbasid-era poet*

His compassion for the people of Egypt surpassed all such sentiments,
so much so that it even went beyond that of father for son.
He would protect them, look after their circumstances and interests,
and fend off any adversity.
—*Abu Muhammad Abdallah ibn Muhammad al-Madini al-Balawi,*
writing about Ahmad ibn Tulun, 312 AH, 925 CE

Chapter 1

884 CE, 270 AH

Ja'far ibn Abd al-Ghaffar, Ahmad ibn Tulun's secretary, told me the following:
I used to accompany the amir of the Egyptian territories, Syria, Hejaz, and Yemen on his nighttime tours of Fustat and Al-Qata'i. He swore that never for a single day over sixteen years had he forgotten or neglected to investigate the circumstances of the Egyptian people. He used to dedicate two days a week to listen to their complaints and meet the people. The devotion of Ahmad ibn Tulun—God support him!—to the people of Egypt was abundantly evident, not just to me, an Egyptian, but also to his soldiers—Turks, Byzantines, Sudanese, and Nubians alike. Every Friday he would disguise himself as a merchant or craftsman and make his way through the alleys and streets, sometimes on his own, but with me most of the time.

I will not hide from you the fact that I used to quiver every time I accompanied him; I was afraid that he would be exposed by his servant Lu'lu' or one of his Turkish commanders. I was an Egyptian, and it was unusual for rulers of Egypt to have Egyptians as assistants. When he was made amir and I became his secretary, the entire world was turned upside down. People said, "Ja'far does not even know Arabic well. How can he manage the amir's affairs?" To which the amir—God protect him!—replied that even though Ja'far did not know Arabic all that well, he did know both Coptic and Greek, understood the country, and was steeped in the soil. As such, he could tell the amir some of its secrets and help him to distinguish the valuable from the cheap, to purchase what is precious, and to discard the dross. Then they said that Ja'far did not know anything about Baghdad and Samarra; he had never even visited them. To that Ahmad ibn Tulun responded that Ja'far knew Egypt, and his loyalty was to its amir. That made him preferable to many other people.

My worries about him did not stem from a lack of confidence in him, but rather a lack of confidence in his servant, Lu'lu'. I was aware that the amir could be brutal, but that was aimed at wrongdoers and people with evil intentions, not people like me. Yet monarchs have their own whims that cannot be understood. In a single day, they can make decisions resulting in the demolition of houses and the construction of palaces. I feared the amir—God protect him!—and my admiration for him increased as day followed day.

Today we walked on foot through the ice over four hours. He was forty years old, or almost. Yet it was I who was panting, and he made fun of me.

"If you can't keep up, Ja'far," he said, "I'll have to find someone else!"

"No, my lord," I replied quickly. "As long as I'm with you, I'm enjoying it."

He gave me a scornful look, and then turned his attention to a house on the mountainside, far away from Fustat and its suburbs.

"Come on," he said, "we're heading for that house."

"My lord," I replied gently, "caution can prevent risk. We've been walking for hours with no soldiers or guards. Who knows what awaits us at a house in the desert?"

He set out eagerly toward the house.

"It's always good to take risks," he said with a smile.

He banged confidently on the door, but the house owner did not open it.

"Nobody's home," I said. "My lord, with your permission, let's go back."

"No," he replied firmly, "I won't permit it."

He banged on the door again, until an old man approached and asked them to be patient. He opened the door.

"Welcome to the two strangers!" he said.

"We'd like a drink of water," the amir said, after returning the greeting. "We've come a long way and are not keen on going any farther."

The old man looked at the amir.

"Who are you?" he asked.

"A wayfarer," the amir replied.

The old man looked at me. "Who is he?" he asked.

"He works with me," I replied.

The old man looked at me, then at the amir. "You told the truth, my boy," he said. "If you'd told me he was your friend, I wouldn't have let you in the house. I detect fear in the eyes of your work companion. What's his name, and what's yours?"

"I'm Ahmad," the amir replied, "and he's Ja'far."

"Ahmad . . . like the amir's name," the old man said.

He gestured to us to come in.

"Come on in," he said, "while I get you some water."

"Why do you live so far away from Fustat?" the amir asked, as he looked around the house.

"Being close to people is of no use to me," the old man replied. "I prefer distance."

"Do you live alone, old man?" the amir asked him.

"I've four daughters. I never had a son."

He brought in some water in a jar.

"Don't drink all of it, my son," he said. "We don't get any water here. To get those few drops, I have to walk for days and pay silver and gold for it."

The amir took a sip or two.

"What's your trade, old man?" he asked.

"Tailor."

"What can you sew in this wasteland? For whom? Where are your daughters?"

The old man gave him a dubious look.

"Do your daughters live here with you?" the amir went on.

"That's why I moved to the mountains," he replied bitterly. "Two of them are married, and the other two live here with me."

The old man now stood up hesitantly, entered another room, and told one of his daughters to prepare some food.

"You've had a long walk, Ahmad," he said gently. "Stay and eat something."

At that point, the amir asked him another question.

"Is the amir interested in you?"

The old man said nothing. I was afraid of what he might say. If he said "no," then Ahmad might kill him on the spot for his honest response. On the other hand, if he said "yes," Ahmad might kill him for lying.

For a while, the old man said nothing.

"I've two daughters living with me," he went on. "One of them is beautiful enough to dazzle relative and stranger alike. All the men in Fustat and even the amir's soldiers have lusted after her."

"Pray for the amir, old man," I inserted hurriedly, "when you mention his name."

He ignored me.

"My other daughter, my eldest, has had nothing but bad luck. She's faded and lost all her beauty. She didn't have any children, boy or girl. Her husband threw her out the way ewes reject strange lambs. She returned to me, humiliated, but I have nothing. I decided to take my beautiful and rejected daughters far away. People had started saying nasty things about women rejected by their husbands and spectacularly beautiful girls."

"That's very clever of you!" the amir said with a smile. "But you didn't answer my question."

"Yes, I did, but you weren't listening."

I gaped in shock at the old man's defiance.

"You're right," Ahmad said. "Maybe I wasn't listening. You need to get your beautiful daughter married. Beauty like that is both temptation and war."

The old man was silent for a moment. "You could be married to her yourself, my son, or else your servant could."

"Are you offering your daughter to a complete stranger?" Ahmad asked in amazement.

"I don't trust relatives," he replied.

"How can I be married to her without even seeing her face? She might not be all that beautiful."

The old man hesitated.

"Do you want to see her face, just once perhaps?"

"No, I want to know why you're annoyed with the amir. Did you prefer Ibn al-Mudabbir, the Tax-Administrator, duly appointed by the caliph, who turned the Egyptian people against Ahmad ibn Tulun?"

"God forbid, my son," the old man replied. "Ibn al-Mudabbir was a catastrophe. Greed always leads to poverty. I've never seen anyone so evil since I was born."

"What about Ibn Tulun?"

"Do you work with him?"

"No, I do trade in Syria."

"Do you realize that he sends spies all over the place? No one dares speak the truth."

"Speak the truth now. Courage is always effective."

"I'll tell you something: Ahmad ibn Tulun's different."

"Different how?"

"He can see and understand what other people can't. People say that he sees the kings of the ancients in his sleep and managed to tame the caliph the way a man tames a lion, using tricks, negotiations, threats, and dialogue. Anyone who sees ancient kings in his sleep will always come out on top."

"Do you admire the amir?" Ahmad asked with a smile.

"I didn't say that. I don't like amirs."

I put my hand over my mouth, imagining the old man's head hanging from the gates to Al-Qata'i.

But the amir calmly asked him another question.

"You think the amir is after prestige and power," he said.

"No, I realize that he wants the best for Egyptians."

"So why don't you like him?"

"I don't understand amirs. I'm just a tailor. I haven't produced a son and I'm no good at fighting. Amirs, my son, are unreliable. They own the sun and the moon. People in power can be either aggressive or merciful. The heart is the site of both iniquity and piety, the former before the latter. For them, mercy becomes like precious water in the mountains."

"I don't like what you're saying. What do you want?"

"If I told you now everything I want," the old man scoffed, "what could you do about it?"

"Nighttime talk fades away in daytime. But night also brings out death agonies. How real they are!"

"At my age, my only wish is to shield my lovely daughter and have enough water around me."

Silence prevailed.

"You'll have what you want," Ahmad told him.

"Pardon? Do you have those death agonies, my son?"

"I'll give an order for water pipes to be extended to your house, and I'll see your daughter married to a soldier who'll take care of her."

"I thought that you were going to be the one to be married to her," the old man said suspiciously.

For a moment, the amir said nothing.

"Am I going to see her face?" he asked.

"I've told you I would allow it."

"How old is she?"

"She's my youngest daughter. But why are you raving like this? Did you drink wine before coming here? You must have, because now you're thirsty and incoherent. How can you give commands like this? Do you know one of the palace soldiers?"

"Old man," Ahmad said kindly, "don't say things you'll regret."

"I'm not scared of soldiers," the old man said firmly. "What can they do to an old man like me?"

"What can they do?" Ahmad replied without thinking. "Do you remember what the amir did to the caliph's secretary? He tied him to a wooden plank, then stretched his body till it came apart like a piece of lamb cooked slowly for a day or two over a warm fire."

"That was the caliph's secretary. I'm just an old man with no power and no son."

"Why don't you want your daughter to be married to one of the amir's soldiers?"

"You've come here asking for a drink of water. Any man who enters the house desiring sustenance makes a good husband."

The amir stretched out on the couch.

"Let me see her first," he said.

"I've told you, her beauty's peerless. She's a virgin, and every man in Fustat and Al-Qata'i is fighting over her."

"Let me see her first."

"Are you going to be married to her? I only want my daughter's face to be seen by the man to whom she's going to be married."

"How can I promise something I don't know? Let me see her."

He called his daughter. "Saneeya, come here!"

For a moment, the amir said nothing.

"Saneeya's your incredibly beautiful daughter," he said. "Isn't that right?"

"Yes."

"But she's not the one I want. I want to see your other daughter."

The old man opened his mouth. "I told you you're drunk!" he said.

"Yes, power has its own drunkenness," the amir replied. "Don't you like your other daughter?"

"She's over thirty, and has faded away after a profound sorrow. I told you, her husband threw her out like so many date pits. She's barren, and her features are very plain."

"What's her name?"

"Asma."

"Call her."

The old man brushed his hands together. "If you see her and don't like her . . . ," he said menacingly.

"Don't threaten me," the amir replied. "I'm not accustomed to such behavior. Call her. I've no need of beautiful women."

"How can a man not like beauty?"

"If beauty is readily available in life, the mind becomes more attractive and passion-rousing."

"I don't understand you, my son."

"Call her."

He called her. She came in with heavy steps, her face veiled. She was wearing a pair of old slippers.

"Yes, Father? she asked with little enthusiasm.

"Take your veil off," he commanded.

She stared at her father in amazement, then at the amir, and then at me. I could almost swear that she looked back at the amir, as though she could see no one else in the whole of Egypt. He was a young man, with black eyes and determined features. I always noticed the way slave-girls and wives would give him longing glances.

Their eyes met.

"Your father's asked you to uncover your face," he told her gently.

"I can't do that in the presence of strangers," she choked.

The amir looked at her father.

"Listen to what I'm saying, and no argument!" he told her firmly.

For a moment she hesitated, still staring at Amir Ahmad. Then she slowly took off her veil and lowered her head. The amir's eyes were focused on her face.

"Have you lost your sight, old man," he asked. "How can you not see such beauty? Cover your face again, girl."

She stared at him in amazement, then covered her face again.

"Do you still want her?"

"How could a husband leave such a woman?"

"He worked as a soap-maker. He must make a lot more money than you do. But even with all his wives and slave-girls, he didn't keep her. I've no idea why he was so angry with her. Perhaps because she had no children?"

Asma looked distressed and headed slowly back into the interior. The amir called her back.

"Why did your husband, the soap-maker, leave you, Asma?" he asked gently.

"I don't know."

"You don't know? Yes, you do."

"Has my father brought you water, sir?" she asked slowly.

"Your father says that water's scarce around here."

"Guests have rights."

"If I drank all the water, what would you do?"

"We'd look somewhere else, but you'd leave our house content."

"I'll be leaving content," he replied, looking at her, "that's for sure."

"When can I be married to your daughter?" he asked her father.

She opened her mouth, aghast, her heart pounding as never before.

"Promise me," her father said, "that you won't be sending her back to me in a month."

"Not after a month."

"Not after a year."

"Not after fifty years." The amir stood up and stroked the old man's shoulder.

"Look for a dowry suitable for an Egyptian woman," the amir told him. "She's entering the amir's household."

"Which amir, my son? She's not a slave-girl."

"Amir Ahmad," Ahmad replied. "She'll never enter the household as a slave-girl."

"Do you work in the amir's household, my son?"

"No, I am the amir."

"It's true, father," said Asma. "When he's married to me, he'll be more important to me than Amir Ahmad. For a wife, her husband is amir, king, and caliph."

"How dare you say such things?" her shocked father asked her.

The amir gave her an admiring look. "Yes indeed, Egyptian lady, amirs, kings, and caliphs are all husbands."

At this point, I intervened forcefully. "Bow down to the amir, my lady."

I turned to the old man and said the same thing. I had to assure him once, twice, thrice, that the person he was talking to was indeed Amir Ahmad himself.

I saw the old man shudder, then bend over and kiss the amir's foot. Asma fainted, falling to the floor like a bucket of water. Her sister came in and tried to bring her round. Opening her eyes, Asma bowed down to the amir.

"Forgive me, my lord," she said.

"Why are you asking for forgiveness?"

"I'm not worthy of you. The soap-maker deserted me."

"Egypt's amir is going to be married to you," he interrupted. "This life can take unexpected turns. You need to be always ready."

The amir—God assist him!—often surprised us with his decisions, and I never knew whether they emerged from deep in his heart or from his logical mind. From the time of my service to Ahmad ibn Tulun—may God prolong his life!—I never managed to anticipate his reactions or his next steps. He talked to me about his vision, his dream, and his charities. No one could ever disbelieve him. Power gives all actions a level of authenticity, while prestige always crushes the heart. When he was ten, he used to dream of a warm dinner served by his mother and longed for a morning when he would own the world or at least part of it. When his mother woke him up, he used to cry out, either enthusiastic or scared about something. He told me the dream, and no one else.

In the dream, he was a young man, not a ten-year-old boy. He would set out from sea to sea, and from river to river, with no boat and no sails. He would jump through the waves like experienced seabirds, or a lunatic. Then the sea would fade away, and the rivers would calm down. From the earth's mouth would emerge a king unlike any others, not wearing a crown like the Abbasid caliph or a gold-embossed cloak, and not brandishing a sword. He was stone, or something similar, with a crown extending from his head into the heavens and a black pearl set amid brilliant white. His face was human, but he had the body of a lion. The sheer power and vivacity of the eyes haunted Ahmad throughout his childhood and youth. He stood in front of the stone king, then moved back.

"Ahmad," the king said in a deep voice, "what is it you want?"

"I can see an awesome king," he whispered, his voice shaking.

"What do you want?" the king asked again.

"I want a dominion like yours."

"Do you dare ask? If I drown you now, you'll disappear. If I'm merciful, you'll live forever."

Ahmad started to cry and covered his face. He could feel cold water soaking his body.

"You're a liar, boy," the king said. "You don't want a dominion like mine. What you want is to live on earth forever like me. Why don't you stay here?"

"I've been searching for my home for years," Ahmad responded weakly.

"Where's your home? Isn't it where your father and mother are? That's Samarra, isn't it, in Iraq?"

"No, it's where sea and river come together—the meeting point of the two seas, where you are."

"Do you know me, Ahmad?"

He started regaining some of his courage.

"I'm looking for a house for which I was born," he whispered.

"You weren't born in it."

"No, I wasn't."

"You see yourself as the One with Two Horns [Quran 18 (The Cave), vv. 83 ff.], but you're just a puny boy. The only thing in your favor is your father's position and status with the Abbasid caliph. You're just a follower."

"No, I'm not a follower."

"Then who are you, boy?"

"I'm afraid to delve into my soul. I no longer recognize it."

"If you could master it, what would you do? How many kings have disappeared that way, leaving no trace!"

"No one will leave a trace like mine."

"You haven't asked me how kings come to disappear without a trace."

"Because it's a land that doesn't accept competition. You have to love it with your soul before your body. I realize that."

"How do you know that, when you're only ten years old?"

"When I'm searching for my home, I'll have to take care of it; it'll take over my entire life."

Ahmad swore that the king let a smile emerge from behind his stony lips.

"When it does that," the king went on, "then you'll own it. If you succumb to greed, you'll lose. If you get scared, you'll die. If you hesitate, you'll lose. But if it controls you . . ."

There was silence for a moment, and Ahmad's body quivered.

"Ahmad," the king went on slowly, "if it controls you, it will reveal its treasures to you. If it doesn't, it will hurl you into the abyss—you, just like everyone else."

"What treasure are you talking about, King?"

"Do you know me?"

"I swear that I don't know you. I've never seen anyone like you."

"Where's your country?"

"Where you come from."

"When do you want to go there?"

"Yesterday or a year ago."

"All triumphs involve risk. You're embarking on something that no Muslim has tried before."

"It's mine."

"It belongs to the Abbasid caliph."

"It's mine.

"As the Abbasid caliph's governor."

"No, it's mine, Ahmad ibn Tulun's. It's all mine, property and treasure."

"Are you planning to demolish it and toy with it?"

"No, I'll do whatever you want."

"Do whatever your soul extracts from the depths. Passion leads to salvation."

The king disappeared, and the boy started screaming. His mother comforted him. She did not understand why he was shivering and bathed in sweat.

"Ahmad," she asked him in curiosity, "was it a nice dream or a scary one?"

"It was scary, really scary. He almost got control of me and destroyed my mind."

"My son," she told him affectionately, "you're the most precious thing I have."

His eyes met his mother's. At that point, he could not know all she would do for him or how love could cover all paths and turns.

Qasim, Ahmad ibn Tulun's mother, lived with him and for him. She had no family and no man who deserved any self-sacrifice or trust. She was a slave-girl who had been kidnapped from Bukhara by slave-traders. Tulun, Ahmad's father, had acquired her. She had borne him a son, and he had freed her. Tulun, Ahmad's father, had also been taken from Bukhara by soldiers who had sold him to the Abbasid

caliph, Al-Ma'mun, son of Harun ar-Rashid. Tulun had been given a senior position and had risen through the ranks until he was commander of the caliph's
personal guard. When Al-Ma'mun died, his brother, Al-Mu'tasim, relied on Tulun, appointing him to various positions and giving him gifts. As time went by, he
moved from being a soldier for the caliph to becoming a general with possessions
and authority. When he purchased Qasim, he loved her like no other woman before, and her son acquired a status different from that of all his other sons. His
mother was afraid for him, anticipating threats, whether from a jealous wife of
his father or a brother trying to take over his father's affection. She would spend
hours with him as a boy, warning him about the dangers of relatives, even more
than strangers. She told the boy to trust only his mother, followed by his father.
Slave-girls had no status, the general was not one for words, and the caliph was
unreliable. Her entire life, she told him, was for him; keeping him content was her
goal, and achieving it was her success.

Ahmad's father died when he was eighteen years old. He emerged from the Samarra gardens, crying, on his own. He expected some kind of plot, as his mother
had taught him. His brothers were sure to put him in prison, or the caliph would
get angry with him and slaughter him either that day or the next. He was miserable
in Samarra. He had done military training and practiced the arts of combat, but
he was also fully aware of treason and lived with the insanity of Turkish militias.
He stayed far away from them, neither joining the caliph's coterie nor keeping
company with the Turks.

He watched from afar, absorbing and saying nothing. He preferred studying
jurisprudence to drinking wine, memorizing the Quran to debauchery. His prestige rose with the caliph and all the Abbasids.

Ever since the Abbasids had come to power, the status of Arabs had declined,
day after day. The Abbasid caliphs did not trust them. Arabs had families and
tribes, and their primary loyalty was to them. They were proud and arrogant, and
that stood in the way of any obedience to instructions. The caliphs had turned
to buying and training Turkish boy-soldiers. Once they had abolished the Army
Commission, Arabs no longer received gifts in Muslim lands, or had any kind of
status, involvement, or control in wars as they had in the past. Turkish and Persian
soldiers gained a wide reputation, and there was a noticeable increase in conspiracies and intrigues. Slave-girls gained influence inside palaces. Now brother killed
brother, and the caliphate turned into a position in which the occupant might die
between night and morning.

No one had as much courage as Ahmad. He quashed intrigues and emerged victorious whenever he commanded an army, whether inside or outside the realms.
The caliph Al-Musta'in liked him and made him his personal guard. However,
the loyal soldier is not always the person who arrives at a time when treason is
on the rise. The rivalry between Al-Musta'in and his brother, Al-Mu'tazz, intensified. Al-Mu'tazz's mother launched a conspiracy to get rid of Al-Musta'in and put

her own son in his place. She asked Ahmad, Al-Musta'in's personal guard, to kill him. She threatened him, made promises, and tempted him with money and gold. Then she offered him something that no man could resist: she would give him the governorship of Wasit in Iraq, even though he was so young. After his father's death, he had no means of support and no intercession from either soldiers or the caliph. Al-Musta'in was going to die, whether that day or the next, either at his hand or someone else's. He thought about it and made up his mind not to do what she had instructed. He went home to his mother, feeling distressed, and told her what had happened.

"I know you won't be disloyal," she told him gently.

"No, I won't," he replied, "but what's coming is even worse."

"Are you worried about the consequences of your refusal?"

"No, I'm worried about the consequences of killing the caliph. He's going to be killed. The slave-girl will do it."

"Watch what you're saying. Your mother was a slave-girl too."

"My mother was free. Time mistreated her, but then it dealt with her fairly. She possesses all the sincerity of free people and the strength of men."

She smiled and caressed his shoulder. "It's all in God's hands," she said. "If the governorship of Wasit doesn't tempt you, Ahmad, then what will?"

He remained silent.

"You only think about Egypt," she went on thoughtfully. "You dream about it at night, just like Qais dreaming of his beloved Laila. What you need is a wife to secure your position here."

"My position isn't here," he replied forcefully.

"That's either a dream or a nightmare that's stuck with you for ten years now. Listen to what your mother has to say. Secure your relationship with the caliph, and you'll succeed."

His eyes met his mother's. "Egypt . . . ," he said.

"Getting there is never straightforward," she said with a smile, "and leaving it isn't easy either. Anyone involved with Egypt can only leave it for wars involving seven armies or more. The caliph never lets anyone serve as governor there for more than a year. The Abbasids realize that; they read history. When Amr ibn al-As entered Egypt, he assumed that he had invaded and won. But it took hold of him, and his goal became staying there. He took a big gamble. If it's advice you need, then stay away from your heart's instincts."

"If I don't go back, I'll die."

"My son, you didn't visit it in order to go back."

"It's my place, ever since I had the dream."

"Ahmad . . ."

"Who do you want me to have as a wife?"

"Khatun, the daughter of the Turkish general, Yarjukh. You'll be protecting your back by being married to her."

"I accept, Mother."

"She's beau . . ."

"Engage me to her."

⚏

Al-Mu'tazz's mother swore to take revenge on Ahmad for refusing to kill the caliph. Soldiers kept harassing him, and various plots were hatched. His mother clenched her heart and suppressed her worries, which seemed to stretch as far as Yemen. Qasim, Ahmad's mother, resorted to another commander, also Turkish, who had been a friend of her master, namely her son's father, Bayakbak the Turk. With her heart quivering out of fear for her son, she spoke to him and asked him for protection. He had access to Al-Mu'tazz. It was one woman at war with another; one son's mother at war with another; a slave-girl soldier's mother at war with the caliph's own mother. She prayed, read the Quran, and waited for what she wanted. Then came the glad tidings: General Bayakbak asked to be married to her. She immediately agreed on the condition that he protect her son. When the time was right, he would give Ahmad an appropriate position. Ahmad had never been disloyal or made mistakes. He had fought and won, and he had defended the caliphate time and again.

General Bayakbak agreed, and for a while Qasim felt more reassured. He treated Ahmad as his own son out of respect for Tulun and love for Ahmad's mother. Qasim, however, reserved all her affection for her son. He was part of her; all other men were strangers.

⚏

I knew Amir Ahmad ibn Tulun—may God help him!—from close up. I learned about his history from him and his close associates. He was always serious, his gaze never straying from what he wanted. He was never tempted by slave-girls or influenced by entertainment clubs. The caliph gave him an indescribably gorgeous slave-girl named Mayyas, and he simply added her to his harem in Iraq. When the two of them first met, she gave him love just like other women, but she realized as well that, for Ahmad, love was self-torture; his wife was the daughter of the Turkish general Bayakbak, and she had a special place in his heart. She had borne him a son in whose features, from the very first day, Ahmad could see himself. He now started calling himself Abu al-Abbas Ahmad Ibn Tulun and tied his dream to his son, Al-Abbas. The first time he met Mayyas and lifted her head, he told her deliberately that he had never seen anyone so beautiful before.

"How can I reward my ability to capture hearts," she whispered, lowering her head again, "when it has made me free to love you? Such love, my lord, is freedom."

"Mayyas," he replied with a smile, "when the caliph gives one of his soldiers a stunningly beautiful virgin slave-girl, he either intends to kill the man or is scared to have him as an enemy. I wonder which of these fates awaits me?"

"I swear my only loyalty is to my master," she replied immediately. "You are my master."

"Caliphs have often made use of slave-girls to kill and betray people. With every beauty there is ugliness; with every eloquence, a degree of malice. Who are you?"

"Your slave-girl, at your command."

"You can sing, dance, recite poetry, and bombard me with words. But then what?"

"Do what you tell me to do."

"Khatun is my wife."

"And my lady."

"Al-Abbas is my son. He will inherit my property even if you give birth to a whole army of males."

She remained silent.

"Didn't you hear me?" he asked angrily.

"Yes, I did, my lord. But I don't know what property or inheritance you're talking about."

"When you look at me, what do you see?"

"I see one of the caliph's brave commanders."

"A client and follower."

"No, I see a loyal commander."

"You're bouncing words back and forth."

"I'm scared of the general's ambitions. I'll obey all your instructions."

"My son and wife . . ."

"Are my lady and my lord as well."

"I don't know you yet and don't trust you. I'm not tempted by beauty, Mayyas."

"Maybe beauty doesn't tempt you, my lord. But what's your reaction to someone who's tempted by your beauty?"

He embraced her, and she buried her breaths in his chest.

"If you're spying for the caliph," he told her, "I'll cut through your neck before my words even reach him. Listen to me carefully now. I own Egypt. One day I'm going to transfer the caliphate there."

She opened her mouth in sheer amazement.

"If there's loyalty and goodness behind all that beauty," he went on, "I'll free you and show you a world you've never dreamed of."

She leaned over and kissed his hand. "Give me the chance," she said, "and I'll prove my loyalty to you."

He grasped her hand.

"The one thing I'm not known for is patience," he said. "You're going to show me such loyalty now."

†π†

Al-Abbas ibn Ahmad was four years old or slightly more when he broke all the rules and embarked on an unprecedented adventure. All Amir Ahmad's closest associates heard about it. At midnight, Al-Abbas was sleeping in the children's room with his nurse; his mother was sleeping in the harem, and his father in his own room. Al-Abbas slunk out of the children's bedroom and wandered all around the huge house, looking for just one thing—not his mother's embrace, but his father's. Tears pouring, he knocked on doors and opened them. Eventually, he found his father's room, but did not knock on the door. Instead, he opened the door and stood there in front of his father. He looked like the ant standing gratefully in front of the mound, the lofty doors reflecting his tiny stature and need. Amir Ahmad opened his eyes and looked at the shadow of the little boy standing in the dark by the door. Lighting a candle, he went over to his son and asked him what he was doing there.

"I was looking for you," the boy answered spontaneously.

"Couldn't you wait till morning?" Ahmad asked.

"In the morning I won't see you, but my place is here with you."

Then the boy ran over, lay down on his father's bed, and pulled up the covers.

"Come on, Father," he said, "there's plenty of room."

Amir Ahmad smiled and stretched out on his bed.

"But this isn't right," he told his son. "You're a man, and should sleep in a room on your own . . ."

"I'm a man, and I sleep in my father's room, not with the other children."

He surprised his father with a big hug.

"Don't throw me out," he said.

"I'd never do that," his father told him with a hug.

"I'll be with you all my life. Rooms won't keep us apart."

Amir Ahmad smiled, knowing that love was buried deep in the heart, first for Al-Abbas, and then for any other person on earth. He also realized that love for his son would never leave his soul in peace. Of all his children, he was the most precious, a piece of his own soul or even more. Neither Khatun nor Mayyas would understand what he was saying, nor any other woman. Al-Abbas was himself. Ahmad looked at him, and saw his heart pacing the earth—his consolation in grief, his ornament on earth. He was companion and friend. No one else possessed Al-Abbas's spontaneity, affection, panache, and strength.

It seemed as if the kings of ancient Egypt were offering assistance to my lord—may God fortify him!—and supporting his successes. The Abbasid caliph had made Bayakbak, husband of Ahmad ibn Tulun's mother, Governor of Egypt, and the general had delegated the thirty-four-year-old Ahmad to go to Egypt. All I can think of doing is to compare him with the One with Two Horns. When it came to boldness and ambition, he had no equal. Was it the magic of the ancient Egyptians that motivated him, so that fate did not wish his mother's husband to be Governor of Egypt? Or was it that his mother made every effort on his behalf? God alone knows; I don't. Once he reached Egypt, he swore that it was his alone. How could a ruler inscribe his name on such a country? Gold prevailed in the South and the River Nile buried it in black mud. The only way for a ruler to gain control was with an army and a building program. He created an army and built a palace. But Egypt's wealth lay in other hands, those of Ibn al-Mudabbir, the Tax-Administrator. The caliph's secretary, Shuqair, spied on Amir Ahmad and sent the caliph details of every breath Ahmad took and every soldier he trained for his army.

When his mother's husband died, his father-in-law, Khatun's father, the Turk, General Yarjukh, took over as governor of Egypt. He sent his son-in-law a letter, telling him to continue to represent the governor, as before. So Ahmad continued governing Egypt on behalf of his father-in-law. He was in charge, or so he thought.

Never in my entire life have I encountered a father who loved his son the way the amir loved Al-Abbas. In fact, I do not know why this love was unique. God gave Ahmad many children, both male and female. Mayyas, his slave-girl, gave him Khumarawayh several years after Al-Abbas, and all his wives produced at least one son. I believe that the amir loved Al-Abbas so much because he was his first child and because he had had to leave him as a six-year-old when he went to Egypt. His wife, Khatun, and her children were only able to join him two years later. He used to write to Al-Abbas every day. The boy was so attached to his father that he refused to eat or sleep and cried continuously. That is what Khatun reported in her letters. When the opportunity arose, he brought his wife, sons, and entire harem to Egypt. On reaching out to his son, the boy dissolved in tears and blurted out that he was angry because his father had deserted him.

His mother slapped him. "Shake your father, the amir's, hand," she instructed him. "What's the matter with you?"

But Al-Abbas's instincts and passion made him retort. "But I'm angry with him," he said.

Ahmad knelt in front of his son. He explained to him why he had gone away. The boy listened, tears pouring.

"But you're going away again," he said.

"No, I won't," Ahmad said firmly.

The boy buried his head in Ahmad's chest and hugged him around the neck. "You've promised me not to go away again," he said. "You'll stay here with me."

His mother shook him angrily. "What are you doing, Abbas?" she yelled. "Have you lost your mind today?"

Ahmad hugged his son.

"Leave him with me today," he told her.

"Forgive me, my lord," she said. "I don't know what's happened. He was unhappy while you were away, but then, when he saw you . . ."

He lifted Al-Abbas in his arms.

"Will you stay with me all the time?" his son asked.

"Yes, all the time," Al-Abbas replied immediately.

Months later, Al-Abbas fell ill, and the fever worsened. It seemed as though someone had poisoned his food. The amir almost went out of his mind. One doctor after another was summoned and many were arrested. Ahmad prayed to God every which way; he gave alms and put on a disguise to go out to mosques and give people money and food. He asked people to pray for his son. In times of despair, a sense of attachment shows itself, and all finery vanishes. I swear that the amir told me that, at that point, he bowed down to God and told Him that he was not bothered about rule and prestige; he had no desire for wife or money. If God wished to take everything away from him and leave him just one thing, let it be his son, Al-Abbas. The sound of his son's voice echoed in his ears as the boy begged him for help and hugged him in his small arms as hard as he could. Those two feeble arms clung to him the way no woman's arms, no power, and no authority could match. Let him give up rule, let his entourage disappear, let him lose strength and youth, but keep Al-Abbas alive.

Shaikh Bakkar ibn Qutaiba stared at the amir for a whole hour without saying a word. Finally, the amir turned and looked at him.

"Let Him have everything," the amir said in despair, "if He keeps my son alive."

"God has no need of your possessions, Amir," Shaikh Bakkar told him gently.

"Let Him take everything I can give, but let me keep the part of me that I've no life without."

"My lord amir," Shaikh Bakkar continued, "God's decrees are not like caliphal pacts or general's agreements. We have to be willing to accept them, even when we can't control our sorrow."

"God has never taken away any part of me. He knows that I can't going on living without my son. God is compassionate, and must be merciful."

"You'll never be patient with Him, my lord. Don't ask about something you don't know."

"He's compassionate," the amir repeated insistently.

ﯨﯨ

Ahmad left Al-Abbas's bedside only to give out alms from time to time.

"Abbas," he said, shaking the boy, "can you hear me?"

The boy smiled, then closed his eyes again. Abbas shook him in despair.

"Do you know who I am?" he asked.

"My father," the boy replied weakly. "I know . . . Don't leave me here alone."

The amir grabbed the hand of his son. "I'll never leave you," he said.

Whenever his wife, Khatun, came in and suggested that he go to work while she looked after Al-Abbas, he would emphatically refuse, and the boy's expression would beg him to stay.

Then another doctor entered the room, fearing the amir's temper.

A week later, the fever subsided. The doctor said that the boy may not have been poisoned. Instead, he may have eaten some rotten food or strained himself while playing or training.

Ahmad praised God and donated a thousand dinars to the poor. All the time, his eyes enveloped the boy in an effort to protect him. He might be safe today, but tomorrow someone might manage to kill him. Who knows? He had to be cautious.

A dream kept recurring; he would see his son murdered in front of him or slaughtered, and he would not be able to do anything about it. Who would try to kill Al-Abbas, he wondered, whether the next day or the day after?

ﯨﯨ

I realize that Ahmad ibn Tulun's hands—may God come to his aid!—were tied when it came to the Tax-Administrator of Egypt, Ibn al-Mudabbir, who had given Egyptians a taste of real hardship and launched assaults on Muslims, Christians, and Jews alike. Ibn al-Mudabbir embarked on a policy of oppression against the Egyptians, revealing how avaricious and brutal he could be and how little he cared about Egypt. He even decided that the entire fishery of Egypt was his property; he would decide how much money to give to fishermen and boat owners. Natron was his personal monopoly; he would sell it and give only scraps to the Egyptian people.

When Amir Ahmad came to Egypt, Ibn al-Mudabbir, the Tax-Administrator, welcomed him with gifts worth more than ten thousand dinars. Ibn al-Mudabbir surrounded himself with powerful fighting soldiers. His closest colleague, Shuqair the Postmaster, was just as brutal and cruel as Ibn al-Mudabbir. Amir Abu al-Abbas Ahmad ibn Tulun turned down all the gifts and sent back the money. Instead of money, he asked Ibn al-Mudabbir to give him his soldier entourage. That event marked the beginning of the enmity between Ibn al-Mudabbir and Ibn Tulun. Ibn al-Mudabbir instructed Shuqair to send a letter to the caliph demanding that Ibn

Tulun be dismissed. It was Ibn al-Mudabbir's opinion that as long as Ibn Tulun would not accept gold, he was not to be trusted; there could be no safety with a man who surrounded himself with soldiers.

With my own eyes, I observed Ahmad ibn Tulun's frustration and the way he laid siege to Shuqair and his letters to the caliph. Every time Shuqair sent a letter, Ahmad anticipated him by sending one or two letters that offered clarifications and explanations. The amir appointed Anas, the head fisherman's son, as Deputy Police Chief, and Anas kept a close eye on the mail and on Ibn al-Mudabbir's men. If there was one man in the whole of Egypt who wanted Ibn al-Mudabbir to disappear, it was Anas. So widespread was the story of his hatred that poets composed poems about the two of them—a tale of suffering and tyranny enough to melt the heart, no less brutal than the famous story of Qais and Layla, except that Qais melted from love, whereas, with Anas, it was hatred. No matter; we were talking about Ahmad ibn Tulun.

Ahmad was much troubled by his inability to help the Egyptian people. Matters became even worse when he received a visit one day from the monk Anduna. There's a particular tale regarding this monk, the like of which I've never heard before. I will tell it now.

Ibn al-Mudabbir was inflicting more pain on monks and treating them badly, demanding unprecedented amounts of money from them. I realized that no monk would leave his monastery unless the circumstances demanded. People say that for monks, the monastery is like water for fish; if they leave it, they die. At the El-Qoseir Monastery,[2] there was a monk named Anduna who was renowned for his tolerance and serenity, but he had had more than enough of Ibn al-Mudabbir's ploys and tyranny. He had heard that an amir had come to Egypt to take over its administration, someone who was just, respected Christians, and made no distinctions between believers. The monk went to the amir's palace and asked for a meeting, but the chamberlain would not admit him. He waited for a whole day in front of the palace with no food or drink. Eventually he grew tired of waiting, and the chamberlain still refused to let him in. When it looked as though the monk was not going to leave, the chamberlain asked him why he had come to pay a visit, so the monk told him. The chamberlain threw a few dinars at him.

"Go back to the monastery," he told the monk. "What you're saying is dangerous. If news reached Ibn al-Mudabbir that you're complaining about him to the amir, he'd punish you and the amir. We've never had anyone like him. Take the money, and don't come back here again!"

The monk said nothing, but stayed a few more hours. Then he put the money deliberately on the ground beside the chamberlain and made his way back to the monastery without another word. When Amir Ahmad heard about what had

---

2. Translator's note: This Coptic monastery, at the time situated close to Fustat, no longer exists.

happened, he regretted the chamberlain's treachery. He ordered that he be given fifty lashes, and issued instructions that, from then on, a careful watch was to be kept on all chamberlains, spies, and freedmen, including me, Ja'far, his private secretary. That raises another point that I will mention shortly. When the amir heard about the monk, he sent some guards to chase after him and bring him back before the day was over. They brought him back, and he was received by the amir. Dismissing his assembly, the amir bid the monk sit, informing him that he was aware of what had happened with the chamberlain, who had now been punished.

"You are aware, my lord," the monk said calmly, "that our life is a struggle. We give up the short, defective life of this world for something larger and greater. It is not the money that Ibn al-Mudabbir is demanding that alarms me nor the brutal way he is treating monks. No, what's bothering me is a feeling inside me that I've been fighting off for days."

The amir looked at him with infinite admiration and surprise. "What feeling?" he asked.

"A hatred that I had overcome ever since my death and burial. It's come back and tested my faith. I've prayed for Ibn al-Mudabbir, but those who cannot be frank with their own heart are bound to lose it. My own heart almost loathes him, and that scares me. A dead person should not revert to feelings long since abandoned. It's like abandoning the world for the sake of a beloved, but then secretly betraying her. I'm still praying and asking God for strength. I can see no beauty within Ibn al-Mudabbir, even though he is part of God's creation. This is a fault in me."

"There's no beauty within him, brother," the amir replied with a smile. "That would be the case even if you prayed for him for a hundred years."

"I came to ask you to help me, my lord," the monk went on warily. "Leave the personal struggle to me, my lord. That's my fight."

"The personal struggle's yours, is it? What's your name?"

"Anduna."

"Can I call you that without a family name too?"

"What family name can a poor servant of God like me have?" he responded without thinking. "Of course you can, my lord."

"Ahmad."

"Pardon?"

"If you're a poor servant of God, then so am I. We're all in need of God's mercy. I want you to call me Ahmad; and sit here beside me."

The monk stared at him, hesitant and confused, then sat next to him, his eyes glued to the floor. At the time, I was almost fainting from shock. In all the time I had known him, I had never seen the amir ask anyone to call him by his own name.

"Anduna," the amir inquired, "your eyes don't even seem to register the beauty of the palace. Do you notice the gold on the fringes of the lamps?"

"I don't see the merely ephemeral," the monk replied shyly. "I've abandoned shiny gold for something more permanent."

"Have you really abandoned the world? Don't you love and hate? Don't you aspire and fear? Aren't you afraid?"

"Fear, my lord . . ."

"Ahmad."

"Fear, . . . er . . . Ahmad, . . . is a facet of this feeble world. With God, there's no fear. You worry about the money you've collected, which isn't yours. Like it or not, you're going to be rid of it. Then you're scared for a child, part of you, but you're going to leave him too, because you actually belong to him. You're afraid of a woman, when passion is ephemeral too. I do have an ambition, Ahmad, one that's maybe even bigger than yours; for a dominion that endures, a life that does not fade away, a heart with no fear, a life of love for the One who does not dissemble, but shows mercy and forgiveness. The body's a prison that becomes more brutal as time passes. I'm trying to transcend it in order to see the light. I'm no better than you, Ahmad. Maybe what I'm looking for is greater."

"You're looking for something greater," Ahmad repeated. "Do you realize that I've a heart that both loves and fears; and I struggle with it too? That's because I have a duty to help you and the people of this country. My heart is obsessed with Al-Abbas. I fear the likelihood of him dying, either by poison or murder. I have as many enemies as there are stars in the sky. I dream about it every single day. Do you have a cure for this fear of mine, monk?"

Anduna smiled and looked at Ahmad for the first time. "The amir is being very frank with me," he said, "and honoring me in a way I don't deserve. I'm just a poor servant of God."

"You have a magic, the like of which I've never seen. It's as if you're an old friend that I've been longing to see."

"Engage in the struggle, Ahmad. That fear is keeping you apart from God, fate, mercy, and God's kindness, even though it may seem otherwise. Your son, your palace, and your own self all belong to God."

"Unlike you, I can't leave the world behind. I've a role and a struggle to pursue."

"I've a role, and so have you. Yours may be the better . . ."

"By lowering your own importance, you raise it in my eyes."

"No, I lower it so as to raise it in God's eyes."

"Aren't you interested in the amir's opinion of you?"

"If I were, I wouldn't have died, and they wouldn't have chanted the prayer for the dead over me."

"Anduna, did you but know it, your strength scares me. But no matter! I can promise you that Ibn al-Mudabbir is going to leave Egypt. He'll either die or leave the country."

"I don't wish him evil. Indeed, I pray that he'll seek true guidance."

"You're simply demanding what is your right. Leave the affairs of this world to me, my brother. I continue to fear and aspire, to love and to hate. Don't criticize me if I neither forgive him nor pray for him to be rightly guided. Don't criticize me for having seen in human hearts obscenities that you have never witnessed. I have neither died nor deserted. I'd like you to stay with me for a while."

"I have no place in this lower world, or amid such wealth."

"Will you eat with me perhaps?"

"Yes, I'll sit with you, but I've imposed poverty on myself. I don't enjoy rich people's food."

"You even forbid yourself food!"

"Love of God sates my hunger. Anyone who witnesses His beauty will never taste life's bitterness."

The amir stretched out his hand. "I'd like to shake your hand," he said, "and visit you at the monastery from time to time. Will you allow me?"

The monk smiled and shook his hand. "You will be welcome, Amir," he replied, "now that you have so honored me and listened to what I have to say. Forgive me if I don't offer you any food appropriate to your station or wear clothes like yours. It won't be for any lack of honor and respect for you."

"When I come to see you, Anduna, I won't be expecting any food or luxury. When I come, it will be to contemplate and struggle with my own self. Even I need that from time to time. In the darkness of your monastery cell, there is a light that I need, one that I can't get from gold-embossed lamps. Go now in God's good care till we meet again, God willing. Pray for Ibn al-Mudabbir, but I'll be praying to put an end to him."

For a moment, Amir Ahmad stopped talking. "I really enjoy talking to you, brother," he said suddenly. "In our lower world, 'wealth and sons are the adornment of the lower world.' How can you expect me to dispense with both? Although it continues, 'The things that remain, righteous deeds, are better with God.' [Quran, S. 18 (Cave), v. 46] But mankind has differing provisions on earth."

"Your Holy Book says that 'wealth and sons are the adornment of the lower world,'" the monk replied calmly. "Isn't that right?"

"Yes."

"What's your opinion of 'adornment,' Amir?"

"Call me Ahmad, as we've agreed."

"What's your opinion of 'adornment,' Ahmad?"

"It provides us with moments of joy and splendor to delight the viewers."

"Without such adornment, would they not be delighted?"

"Without adornment, quarters, streets, and palaces look stark, sometimes gloomy, and often sad."

"That's what I wanted, Ahmad. You spoke the truth with no adornment."

"What do you mean?"

"Life without adornment may be stark, gloomy, and often sad. Adornment deceives the eyes. It gives humans some temporary pleasure that vanishes along with the adornment. That is bound to happen, because nothing remains in an ephemeral universe. That is why I've abandoned temporary pleasures for the continuous blessing that awaits us all."

"I can't be like you, monk."

"Bear in mind, my brother, that adornment only decorates the lusterless. Then it fades away by season and occasion. Do not become too attached to your son, your rule, your wife, your power, and your wealth. Otherwise, you will fail to see what exists beyond this world."

"What kind of logic is that? Everyone clings to their son, their daughter, their wife, their power, and their wealth."

The monk ignored his remark. "With a vision of the truth," he went on, "life becomes short, its end is known. Adornment will always fade in the light of eternity. We say: 'With You, I want nothing on earth.'"

"The monk is explaining the Quranic verse to me," Ahmad said with a smile. "If anyone heard us now, they might think that we were two lunatics wandering in the desert. I will come to visit you, Anduna. The company of those who are with God is all pleasure. Anyone who desires nothing on earth becomes the best friend for someone who wants to control it."

I will talk elsewhere about what happened to the Tax-Administrator and Shuqair. The amir made use of both cunning and determination to get rid of them both.

Once he gained control of the Egypt he had dreamed of, that same dream came back again. His mother had died, so he could not talk to her and ask for her help. One day, when he woke up, he called for me.

"Ja'far," he asked, "who's excavating the pyramids area?"

"My lord," I replied diffidently, "I don't know what you're talking about."

"For ages, people have been searching for 'claims' at the pyramids and all around the area."

"My lord," I replied gently, "Egyptians have been doing that for ages. They dig under their houses and discover treasure or 'claims.' They claim it's their property."

"They belong to the monarchs of Egypt."

"Whatever you command, my lord. But the ancient rulers of Egypt are long dead. We don't know much about them."

He moved closer and looked straight at me.

"Actually," he said, "we do know the most important thing about them."

"You mean 'the claims,' my lord?"

"No, I mean what we know about Egypt . . . what the king told me in a dream. He was the sole ruler, not subservient to caliph, Byzantine, or Persian."

"Egypt's been subservient to the caliph ever since I was born. My forebears told me about Egypt's subservience to the Greeks, and, before them, to the Ptolemies."

"And before the Ptolemies?"

"I don't know, my lord."

"The people who wrote in bird language were the ancient rulers of Egypt. Did they rule it as a province?"

"I know nothing about them."

"The king told me, and now I know. If you love Egypt alone, it lavishes riches on you. From today onward, no one is permitted to dig and look for buried treasure—for 'claims.' That belongs to the ruler, to be distributed fairly to all Egyptians."

"My lord, perhaps . . ."

"I want to go to the pyramid area myself and search for treasure there, beside the Sphinx."

You will be hearing a great deal about the treasure called "claims" that Ahmad ibn Tulun discovered at the pyramids. Some people assert that he did not find anything, while others suggest that he charged his men to look for gold in Aswan, as his Arab predecessors had done. But I will tell you what I know. The amir—may God assist him!—discovered treasure of such quality and quantity that I have never witnessed before—gold stretching so far as to fade from vision, decoration and statuary made of pure gold, so heavy that men almost perished while transporting it. When rulers discover such treasures, they usually keep them and give them to their children, but the amir did not do that. He regarded such treasure as a trust from an ancient monarch who would regularly visit him in his dreams. Ahmad decided to strip it down and ascertain its value. He built a mosque that could not be inundated by water or burned by fire. Then he built a hospital in Egypt to treat only sick from among the Egytian people, not soldiers or his own coterie. He constructed housing for the poor and filled the palace square with food for the "blameless" whom the rich regarded with disdain. He gave handouts to anyone who needed them. He built street fountains and schools. He started constructing a city to the northeast of the Abbasid capital in Egypt called Al-Askar. As for Al-Qata'i, he built it alongside Fustat. He increased the size of the army, and assigned designated soldier quarters for Byzantines, Sudanese, Nubians, Turks, and Egyptians.

Yes indeed, Ahmad did all of that, something that only ancient Egyptian rulers had been able to accomplish. He also added client Egyptians to his armed forces. His army had a unit of Egyptian soldiers, and he gave them an equal footing with other troops. He established a firm relationship with them and linked himself to them by marrying the Egyptian woman, Asma. That is a different matter.

When it came to Bedouin Arabs, Ahmad got them to pledge obedience and gave them gifts. He was extremely generous with them. He never marginalized them, and only fought them when it was necessary. Not only that, but he drafted some of them into the army and the police force. He said that the agreement with them would preserve Muslim blood. I accompanied him when he paid a visit to the Banu Salim tribe on the outskirts of Fustat. He brought them gifts, and their shaikh, Musa ibn Uthman, swore his allegiance in front of me.

The actions of the caliph and Abbasids, as they watched Ahmad ibn Tulun in sole charge of the Egyptian government, are a whole other topic.

I have now to acknowledge that I have never seen anyone who loved this country as much as Amir Abu al-Abbas Ahmad ibn Tulun. Nor have I ever witnessed Copts, Muslims, and Jews in Egypt united in their love for a ruler as they were in their love for Abu al-Abbas.

Ibn Tulun opposed and imprisoned some people, but he was always kind-hearted with the Egyptian people, devoting his gifts to them. He started making monthly donations to the poor and inviting them into his palace gardens every Friday. Every week, he would put on a disguise and go out into the quarters and streets in Egypt to listen to people and distribute gifts.

He had two different aspects. One was stubborn and short-tempered: he would cut up and crucify people, and imprison others, then forget about them, so they spent years in prison. But he was also sensitive, crying when he heard about the death of a shaikh, reading the Quran with great emotion, and deciding to pray in some unknown mosque behind a shaikh who would never know that the person praying behind him was the amir. Indeed, if the poor shaikh behind whom the amir was praying managed to jumble the verses, the amir realized that the shaikh must be going through some crisis or difficulty. The amir would then send me in disguise to find out about him. I would learn that the shaikh was in dire straits and needed money. The amir would instruct me to give him some generous gifts without telling him where they came from or who had brought them.

The people whom he treated harshly were those who preferred the caliphate and wanted to shake his regime and threaten him. I will not deny that he was particularly brutal with eighteen men who died in prison. He preferred security and stability to forgiveness, and Egyptian interests to fealty to the caliph. Whenever he had any suspicion regarding the loyalty of one of his subjects to him rather than the caliph, he would imprison that person without the slightest hesitation.

After a while and before he was forty years old, Ahmad was ruler of both Egypt and Syria. The world had come to him and surrendered, or that is how it seemed to him.

Chapter 2

Here is what I heard from Asma, daughter of Mahmud, the tailor, and wife of Ahmad ibn Tulun:

The Amir of Egypt, Syria, Yemen, and the Hejaz decided to marry the Egyptian tailor's daughter, a divorcée who had been rejected by her husband like a slab of meat that had lost its savor, without hesitation or mercy. My father almost died from the shock, and my brothers assumed that my father must be raving when he told them that the amir had paid him a visit in disguise and decided on the spot to marry me. To tell the truth, at the time I did not believe it either. With my minimal experience, I understood that he wanted to raise the profile of Egyptians and cement his relationship with them. That is the way it works with kings: family line, contract, and agreement. But I could not understand why his choice had fallen on the divorced elder sister rather than the spectacularly beautiful, virgin younger sister. For two whole weeks, I could not stop shivering as I prepared for the move to his palace in Al-Qata'i. My mind was a blur. I kept envisioning his wives scoffing contemptuously. I could see him disliking and rejecting me the way my previous husband had done. I imagined once again the way he looked: like a specter, neither fixed nor enduring. His black eyes kept enveloping me. My palpitating heart must have been audible when he came into our room. I sat there, enveloped in fear. He sat down beside me. My voice and my hopes emerged before his.

"My lord," I said submissively, "you have come to my aid and restored me. It is as if God has sent you to bring light into a darkness to which my eyes have been inured. But the amir does not need to be married to a woman like me. I've seen your wives and slave-girls, and I've none of their beauty and magnificence. You don't need to make sacrifices, my lord. You have been married to me and have raised my father's head. You don't need to make such a sacrifice or to live and consort with me."

He stared at me as though he did not understand.

"I'll stay here at your command for the rest of my days," I continued. "I'll obey all your instructions and make preparations for another wife for you, one who's more suitable, younger, and prettier."

"You're going to make preparations for another wife?" he asked with a smile. "How?"

"Someone who deserves you more, my lord. You'll soon be tired of me. Because I'm so fond of you, I'm afraid that this time I'll have a fatal breakdown."

She bent over and kissed his hand. "Your support is a great honor for me," she went on, her entire body shaking. "I'll live and die with it."

He stretched and held her shivering hand in his. "I thought you were a good person, Asma," he said, "but I didn't realize you could be this cunning."

"I beg forgiveness," she rushed to say, "if I've annoyed you."

"You don't want to have sex with me because you're afraid of your attachment to me? What kind of madness is that? Or are you even cleverer than other women?"

He was obviously trying to make me feel less anxious and afraid, but he did not succeed. My hand was shaking in his, and even my tongue started twitching and rebelling.

For a moment he just looked at me without saying anything.

"The amir now commands you, Asma," he said, "to get up and sit beside him."

I stood up and sat down beside him. "I was just saying, my lord," I said breathlessly, "that I . . ."

With a smile, he gripped my arms and laid my head on his chest. "Perhaps if you closed your eyes," he said, "you would forget who I am. When we're making love, you need to forget who I am. How can you be shivering like this when you're in your husband's arms? It's not right."

I closed my eyes and took some deep breaths, intending them to come out slowly, but instead they came out as short, rapid pants. He ran his hands over my hair and back.

"Why did your husband leave you?" he whispered. "There are only two reasons for a husband to leave his wife, no more."

"My lord, I gave him no children and I . . ."

"A husband doesn't leave his wife for that reason. He must have feared you. When a husband becomes scared of his wife, he has to crush her. I wonder, was he afraid of a mind that would demolish his own, or of a beauty that showed his own lack of initiative?"

I was fleeing my own worries inside his heart.

"I'm no beauty," I told him in a muted tone, eyes closed. "A woman like me has no mind of her own. My lord, I beg you to treat me kindly. If I learn to love you even more, I'll die inside the walls of your palace."

"I promise to treat you kindly," he assured her.

"Your very presence contents me," she said. "I ask no more. You can leave me, and my heart will be forever grateful."

He laughed, then pretended to be angry. "Are you rejecting me, Asma?" he asked, pushing her away and looking into her eyes. "Are you throwing Amir Ahmad out of your room, Egyptian lady?"

I let out a scream, then bent down and sat on the floor in front of him.

"Cut my tongue out, my lord," I said, head lowered, "if I intended any such thing. It's just that I'm confused. I realize that I'm never going to be able to please you. My body is no longer pristine; it's turned flabby . . ."

He put his arms round my waist. "I'm actually thinking of punishing you," he said firmly, "for all the instructions you've been giving me since I came in. I want you to give me a kiss and ask me to forgive you. Then I'll decide."

At that point, I did not even think. I kissed his mouth as hard as I could, hardly daring to breathe.

He started taking my clothes off. "That kiss was like no other," he whispered. "Are all Egyptian women like that, or is it that you're more scared and passionate?"

"You can discard me now," I muttered. "When you see . . ."

He put his hand up to silence me. "Maybe if you stopped talking," he said, "you'd give the amir a chance to forgive you."

He stayed with me for a day or two, or rather three or four, till he had taken control of my heart and inundated my vision. I could think only about him every day, as though I had never known or been wife to a man before. He completely erased memories of the past, and I understood why my previous husband had divorced me. I now realized what I had not been aware of before: my beauty had scared my previous husband and my love had made him lose confidence in himself. That is what the amir said. A woman like me, he told me, needs a complete man. He had a lot to say, and almost completely obliterated my memories.

When he finally stopped visiting me after two weeks, I waited for him night after night, but he did not come.

I started feeling more worried and cautious about the amir's palace. I had no idea how his children would receive me or how I would interact with his women. How vulnerable a woman in love feels whenever she must feel her way amid her husband's womenfolk, anxious as she is to glean a glance from his eyes or some expression of interest. He had made me "Amira" in seconds, but love's very ardor brings with it a different kind of bitterness. I understood that Khatun, Al-Abbas's mother and his first wife, had a status different from all the other women; she followed his instructions to the letter and treated me with a cordial politeness. I also knew that Mayyas, the mother of his second son, Khumarawayh, was a slave-girl given to him by the caliph. She was less confident than Khatun, shy and rarely saying anything. I met her son, Khumarawayh. A little boy without much to say, he showed little initiative. I learned that Mayyas did not socialize with his wives, preferring to spend most of her time alone. I saw his children, boys and girls, twenty or more; he would spend some time with them all every evening. He used to bring the entire family together for the evening meal, and then ask about each boy and girl, their education, training, well-being, and health. However, I noticed that every day his eyes would gleam especially bright for one of the children, Al-Abbas. He used to smile whenever the boy approached, but then deliberately suppressed his smile in order to maintain a more severe guise. But his eyes would betray his real love for the boy. I heard from the slave-girls that, when the boy was younger, he used to throw himself into his father's arms despite scoldings from his mother; he would cling to his father's neck and tell him how much he had missed him.

Today Ahmad and Al-Abbas had looked at each other, and a strange and anxious silence had fallen over all the children. Ahmad went over to Al-Abbas right in front of me and asked him how he was.

"I'm fine," Al-Abbas replied, "so long as the amir is fine—may God help and support him!"

Ahmad looked at all his children.

"The government of Egypt will remain with my family among all of you," he declared. "It's revealed its treasures to me, not because it does so for every inquirer, but because it makes the revelation to anyone whose desires lie beyond money and power, who realizes that ephemerality is fated, and that the human heart ordains evil. I take initiatives, making mistakes sometimes and getting things right at others. But Egypt must remain your primary focus. Do you hear me, Al-Abbas?"

"Yes, I always hear you, Father, . . . my lord amir."

He stroked the boy's shoulder. "When you become its ruler," the amir told him, "remember not to burden Egyptians with taxes. Do the things that King Joseph did in Egypt, not Pharaoh. Don't imagine that you can cut through the mountains; consider years of shortages before years of plenty. Never be wasteful."

Al-Abbas bent over and kissed his father's hand. "May God prolong your life, Father," he said.

The father grabbed his son's hand. "I don't know whether long life is a blessing or a curse," he said. "I want you to be a support for me to rely on. I want Egypt to remain in the hands of someone who'll work for the Egyptian people, not just for his own men and prestige."

Although I saw the amir every day at dinnertime when he brought his family together, he never looked at me or came to my quarters. I grew more and more anxious, to such an extent that, after a few days, I plucked up enough courage to whisper in his presence that, whenever he was absent, the darkness increased.

He turned and looked straight at me, then looked away without saying anything. My heart sagged and yielded. What kind of love was I expecting? If he had been my first husband, he would have thrown me out and sent me back to my father. So what did I expect from the Amir of Egypt? He had been married to me out of sympathy and as a gesture toward the Egyptian people. He had announced his marriage to Asma the Egyptian, and the populace had gathered all around him. He got married as though he were building a hospital or school. Even our passionate moments together were either an illusion fashioned by my thirsty imagination, or a charitable deed carried out by the amir in the same way as he invited the indigent to his palace square every Friday to feed them. Oh, for your ambition, Asma, and your lack of strategy!

But there is no cure for passion. Sometimes it can drive the person involved to take risks.

I took that risk and went to see Khatun, Al-Abbas's mother. I asked how the amir was and requested that she intercede on my behalf if he was annoyed with me.

She promised to talk to him, but he was absent for a month or more.

Then he came without appointment or warning.

I threw myself into his arms without saying a word.

"Did you resort to my wife," he asked slowly, "asking her to intercede with me on your behalf?"

"I'd resort to everyone on the face of the earth," I replied, hugging him around the neck, "in order to see you just once. I was worried when you stayed away, and afraid of clinging to the impossible. Why did you stay away?"

He did not reply. I realized that I might have gone too far.

"Forgive me, my lord," I said quickly. "I'll prepare some food for you."

"Asma," he said after quite a while, "when the husband is away, the wife has to know without asking . . ."

"Forgive me for being so forward, my lord. I realize how heavy your responsibilities are. I realize that I'm just one of your wives, and I'm not . . ."

"You keep asking and expecting a response," he interrupted. "That surprises me. When a husband stays away from a woman, it's either because she doesn't please him, or else she's penetrated deep and gained a stronger hold than is comfortable."

"My lord . . ."

"I wonder, Asma, is it that you don't please me anymore, or that you've penetrated too far?"

At that moment, I had no idea how to respond or even think. After a while, I nursed the hope in my heart of hearts that perhaps he really was fond of me. Whenever we met, the ardor was genuine and the affection firmly in place.

He let out a sigh as if he were dreaming, and I did not dare wake him up. When he did wake up, I asked him if, God willing, all was well.

"I've been having the same dream for two years," he replied sadly. "I'm afraid that Al-Abbas will be killed. They keep their eyes on him."

"Who would dare kill the amir's successor?"

"On the contrary, who wouldn't? Everyone wants him dead. From the Abbasid caliph to the palace slave-girls. We need to be careful. My dreams have often come to pass."

Next morning, the amir issued instructions that he would personally taste all the food offered to his son. His guards would keep a watch on all Al-Abbas's slave-girls and wives.

I must record here that the amir kept his promise. He sent water to all Egyptians and, immediately after his first visit to my father, he gave orders for wells to be dug. He also had water connected to the mountain where my father lived, to Fustat, to Al-Qata'i, and to the area between them.

Chapter 3

Muhammad ibn Sulaiman al-Katib, enemy of Ibn Tulun, told me the following: My story with Ahmad ibn Tulun is a long one, starting with premonitions of calamity and finishing—God willing—with his demise. I know of no tyrant or traitor to rival him. No caliph stood in his way; no one could intimidate him. People died in Ahmad ibn Tulun's prisons; he imprisoned seventeen thousand people or more. According to my commander, Lu'lu', Ahmad ibn Tulun's servant and one of his retainers, Ahmad spent a full year investigating each prisoner's case. If he did not release him within that year, the prisoner would remain in prison till he died, and Ahmad would forget about him. He dispatched his spies all over Egypt; husbands feared their wives and slave-girls worried about their master's wives. No one knew who would betray them in their absence or who would keep things secret. My lord Lu'lu' told me that Ibn Tulun summoned a group of Turks from Baghdad to Egypt and showered them with drink and gorgeous slave-girls. He then told one of his slave-girls to get the Turkish commander on his own, ply him with drink till he was drunk, and then ask him what he thought of Ahmad ibn Tulun. When the slave-girl did so, the commander cursed Ahmad ibn Tulun with every kind of oath and gestured with his sword that he would kill him this way and that. The next morning, Ahmad summoned the commander and told him what had occurred.

"My lord amir can hold me to account in the light of day," the commander answered fearfully, "but I beg him to forgive me. Things said when you're drunk and incapable are nightmares and drivel. I beseech the amir not to punish me for that."

"Actions are based on intentions, aren't they?" Ahmad commented at the time. "Such intentions only show clearly at dead of night."

Had Ahmad ibn Tulun been a normal kind of man, he might well have put the Turkish commander in prison, but he is a devil in human form. Instead of putting him in prison, he gave him gifts and slave-girls and told him to say nice things about him to the caliph. Otherwise, he would slaughter him, whether that day or the next. From then on, the commander spoke gratefully about Ahmad, his mercy, his very existence, and his loyalty to the caliph.

The truth of the matter is that Ahmad ibn Tulun intended to take over Egypt, and he did so. He had the determination of a whole colony of ants, building a house with King Solomon all around it. He was totally preoccupied with Egypt, as he was with no woman or gold. People said that as a child, he had had a vision: one of the kings of ancient Egypt had appeared and bewitched him. From then on, he had been crazy about Egypt, not seeing anything else. Egypt and its people dazzled his eyes. He no longer cared about the caliph or the Tax-Administrator. But the king who had so bewitched him—and how good those ancient kings were at magic!—gave him opportunities and had good fortune accompany him. His mother's husband appointed him the Egyptian governor in his stead, and his father-in-law made him governor without even leaving the country. By order of the caliph, the appointed governor would come to Egypt and live for a while in the city of Al-Askar. Within a year, or two at most, he would move, without taking up residence there or building palaces for himself. Then Ahmad arrived, stuck pegs in the ground like the ancient Egyptians, built himself a palace in the square, and constructed a city as large as Samarra and a mosque to accommodate travelers and fighters. Such is my resentment at the wrongs I have suffered that I have sworn to wipe off the face of the earth all traces of Ahmad ibn Tulun. Egyptians will forget that he was the independent ruler of Egypt who dedicated its taxes to building things for Egypt and its people. He ended his allegiance to the caliph and exploited the caliph Al-Mu'tamid's conflict with his brother, Al-Muwaffaq, to consolidate his rule and claim it for himself.

I will tell you what he did to me, but first I will describe the way he treated Ibn al-Mudabbir, the Tax-Administrator in Egypt and the person who controlled its wealth. The caliph had appointed him years before Ahmad's arrival. Ibn al-Mudabbir had welcomed Ahmad to Egypt with gifts, assuming that Ahmad was a man of his word, but Ahmad turned them all down and returned ten thousand dinars to him. Not only that, but he started taking Ibn al-Mudabbir's men away for his own army, demanding all of them, leaving the Tax-Administrator with no power. Ibn al-Mudabbir was collecting a lot of money for the caliph. He realized where loyalty lay and to whom. The Egyptians loathed him; yes, they regarded him as a greedy criminal stealing their money. Maybe so, but how long had the Copts controlled the position of the Tax-Administrator? In what era was this happening? The Egyptians were a difficult people to understand. They hated Ibn al-Mudabbir, but then submitted to Ahmad and adored him for no reason. They cannot be trusted; their feelings change as time goes by. In the era of the caliph Al-Ma'mun, they joined the Bedouin in rebelling against the Abbasid governor and wielded their weapons against the Abbasids in villages and cities until Al-Ma'mun managed to quell their revolt at the tip of the sword. At that point, the governor was dismissed, but they were still happy with Ahmad and celebrated him. Their avaricious eyes were only happy with someone who looked out for them and worked on their behalf. What loyalty, what ingratitude! Every single day, I expected Ahmad to announce Egypt's independence from the Abbasid caliphate. Once he had seized control of the tax system, the caliphate had no real presence in the country. Through cunning and trickery, he managed to persuade the caliph Al-Mu'tamid to dismiss Ibn al-Mudabbir as Egypt's Tax-Administrator after years of determined struggle. Egypt's taxes were then in Ahmad's hands, and he used the money to create an army for Egypt, not for the caliphate. However, Ahmad did not declare independence from the caliphate. Cunning oozing like blood out of every pore, he did something even nastier: when the conflict broke out between the caliph and his brother, Ahmad asked the caliph to make his way to Egypt, which would then become the caliphal capital. He was bold and cunning, aiming to control Baghdad from Egypt without cursing or opposing the caliph.

Ibn Tulun managed to get rid of Ibn al-Mudabbir after maligning him in every way possible in front of the caliph. Now that the caliph was only listening to Ahmad and trusting no one else, Ahmad made use of his control to punish Shuqair, who had previously been appointed by the caliph specifically to spy on the Governor of Egypt. Ahmad decided to kill him without delay, by splaying his body on a wooden plank and stretching him at both ends till his body snapped. But fate would not wait, and Shuqair died before he could be tortured. Ahmad intended to send a message to every spy so that the only ones left in Egypt would be his own. He was making clear that no caliph could intercede or offer protection from his brutal decisions. Ahmad's rancor was all-powerful.

As time went by, the only news that reached the caliph was whatever Ahmad dictated to his secretary. All links were severed, and Ahmad had exclusive control of Egypt, Syria, the Hejaz, and Yemen. He was a terrific fighter, undefeated, quelling revolts and gaining clients.

I came from nomads in Khurasan in search of a life in Egypt. I went to see Lu'lu', Ibn Tulun's servant and commander, who was his most loyal and beloved general. I was desperate; all I wanted was a job cleaning yards or tending horses. I worked hard, cleaning yards, without complaining. I did not say anything until Lu'lu's heart softened and he asked me to start military training. I joined his troops and met Ibn Tulun once or twice. He did not look at me, but it seems Amir Ahmad had seen some kind of vision or devil in his dreams, as though he had dreamed of me before he saw me. In his dream, I was not cleaning the yard, but was busy sweeping his palace, his mosque, and his city. Every time I pushed the broom, I was erasing some of its traces—first the palace, then the city, and finally the mosque. That day, he had woken up with a start, and it so happened that he was walking by while I was sweeping the yard. When his eyes fell on me, he gave orders that I was to be killed on the spot—no preliminaries and no trial. This amir, who was so celebrated and adored by the Egyptian people, ordered that a poor man with no resources should be killed, merely because the amir had seen a satanic vision in his dreams.

Lu'lu' intervened. "My lord amir," he said, "are we going to kill a man for no reason?"

"You'll kill him because I order you to do so."

"Your sense of justice will not allow a man who has come to Egypt seeking your protection to be killed."

"How many needy folk are basically wicked!"

"I beseech you, my lord, and ask you to show mercy. We can expel him, send him back to Baghdad, and tell him never to come back here again."

Lu'lu' kept begging him for two whole days. Ahmad ordered that I be returned to Baghdad, but only after I had sworn never to set foot in Egypt again till I died, and not till Ahmad died as well. He then ordered that I be given eighty lashes to remind me of my oath.

Ahmad did not realize, at the time, that oaths and swords placed on your neck have no value! When he ordered that I be killed, I loathed him. When he expelled and humiliated me, I loathed him. As each stroke seared my back, I swore to God that I would butcher him. Every time I begged the guard to treat me gently as he was whipping me, I swore to God that I would crush him and his entire offspring.

I am going to wipe his name off the face of the earth. He is as happy with his city as the infidels are with their victories. He calls it a city without walls because it is protected and inhabited by soldiers. I swore that one day I was going to erase that city, I myself and everyone who had suffered Ahmad's tyranny and realized the true value of the caliphate. I want Al-Qata'i to be a city with no trace; every stone to be broken up into tiny fragments, grains of sand too small to offer either cover or warmth, but simply floating in the air without purpose or goal. That city is destined for oblivion, for nothingness. If any part of it remains, we have lost. If even a tiny rock points to what once was, then there is no hope of eradicating insurrection and no way for predestined fate to empower the more powerful and learned. If only people would realize that Al-Qata'i has no origin; it never existed, it never was built. It was neither dream nor reality. Like legendary cities, it was merely words, scattered like vagrant grains of sand and then plunged into the wide-open sea without location or repose. It has neither origin nor source. The people who lived there and stayed will never tell their stories or write them down. If they were to tell you that, at one time, there was a city there called Al-Qata'i, then you would smile and say that it was like cities in folktales, disdaining time and failing to produce either goods or plants. Where are its remains? What is left? Is anything left? If anything is left, then it represents a defeat for me, Muhammad ibn Sulaiman al-Katib. If anything remains, then kill me at once and know that I have not won. Victory involves the erasure of arrogance, no more. Every trace that remains marks the spread of arrogance, like waterdrops on rocks. I promise you that it will be demolished and perish like animals. A city without spirit or purpose, it will be destroyed, and with it the dream of Ahmad and all who lived there.

Chapter 4

Ja'far ibn Abd al-Ghaffar, Ahmad ibn Tulun's secretary, spoke to me as follows:

You should know that Ahmad ibn Tulun was fascinated by the ancient kings, their buildings, their behavior, and their wealth. I know of no previous Muslim ruler who thought the way he did, made the country independent, and constructed buildings there in order to make it a homeland for himself and his sons. He built things as quick as a flash, as though fiery jinn were assisting him.

He kept building, as though he would last forever, or the country would. He employed the most skilled builders and chose expert architects. I was with him at the time when he had a close connection with Saeed, son of Katib al-Farghani, the young Coptic Christian whom Ahmad imprisoned, then immortalized. The story of Ahmad's relationship with him is a lengthy and incomplete one and may not be complete even today. He asked Saeed to build the spring and Nilometer for him so that water could reach the distant fringes of Egypt. Do you recall the visit we paid to the tailor, to whose daughter, Asma, the amir was married? Ever since then, the amir has been preoccupied with the matter of water and wanted it to be accessible to all Egyptians. Saeed built everything the amir wanted in the shortest possible time. He then asked the amir to come in person and inspect the spring and Nilometer. The amir arrived to inspect the spring, with me behind him with his horse. His horse's foot went into a ditch, and it fell. At the time, he assumed that Saeed had planned it. Rumors spread and spies intrigued, leading the amir to put Saeed in prison without compensating him for what he had built. Saeed remained in prison for a while, as the amir stumbled across some priceless ancient treasure by the pyramids. I swear to you that the amir—may God support him!—never took a single dinar from the treasure for himself, but used it to build the spring, the hospital, factories, and the city. He decided to make gifts to the poor and indigent for life, and then made up his mind to build a large mosque. He wanted it to be the largest mosque ever built in Egypt over the ages; it was to outlast the vicissitudes of fate and the ephemerality of rulers. People told him that building such a mosque would require three hundred church columns; he could make use of columns from ancient churches in the provinces and derelict villages. He thought about it, then lay down to sleep. While asleep, he had a dream that worried him for days. In the dream, he had built an enormous, lofty mosque, with his city, Al-Qata'i, extending from the mosque to Fustat and beyond, a never-ending city with radiant buildings and people living a life of ease and contentment. Then, suddenly, God had manifested Himself over the entire city, except for the mosque.

He left his bed, feeling shocked and pessimistic, and summoned shaikhs and sages to interpret his dream for him. They all failed, and some of them may have been afraid of saying something to annoy the amir, in which case he might take revenge on them. After a lot of thought, he told me one day that he wanted his mosque to be built without taking things away from ancient temples and churches; the dream he had had might be a message to him to stop doing such things any longer. People were confused by the amir's attitude and the question as to how to build the mosque without pillars. Then Saeed heard in prison what was bothering the amir. He told his guard to send the amir a message, saying that he would be able to build the mosque without any pillars, except for two for the *qibla*.

The guard sent the amir the message, and he ordered Saeed to be brought to him at once. He asked Saeed to draw him the plan for the mosque on a piece of paper. Saeed drew it enthusiastically. By that time, his hair and beard had grown long, and he looked tired and drawn from the time he had spent in prison. Saeed drew with a shaking hand, and the amir stared hard at the plans for an hour or more. He ordered Saeed to start work that day and to have it finished within two years. He told Saeed that he would give him as much money as he needed. The two of them had this conversation right in front of me.

"How many gates and windows will there be in a mosque like this?" the amir asked. "What kind of roof can withstand the intrigues of time and wars of the ages?"

"My lord, I'll be building it for you with buttresses rather than pillars. Their very height will reflect your justice and wisdom. We'll build the buttresses out of red brick. It'll have twenty-one gates to make it easy for the city's inhabitants to enter from any direction. The mosque walls will include four hundred and twenty-nine apertures. The mosque itself will have as its foundations mountain rock so that it will remain firmly in place even if cities are destroyed over time. I'll be using palm leaves for the roof."

"Palm leaves?"

"Will my lord grant me some freedom? Eventually he'll see whether I deserve to die or to be rewarded."

"We need to inscribe the whole of the Sura of the Cow [Sura 2] and Sura of the Family of Imran [Sura 3] on the walls as reminders. What's the significance of a mighty building without any words to encourage learning?"

"My lord, we have the very best calligraphers and laborers."

Saeed al-Farghani completed construction of the mosque, including the hanging of drapes and lamps. When the amir—may God sustain him!—entered, he was delighted by what he saw. He spent a while searching for Saeed in order to thank him. Saeed ran over and shinnied up the brass pillar.

"Your laborer desires reward and security," he shouted. "Don't put me in prison like last time."

The amir laughed.

"Climb down," he told Saeed, "or you'll die before you get your reward. You'll have all you want and more."

He handed him ten thousand dinars and, from then on, kept him close so that he became one of his important associates for the rest of his life.

For a moment the amir looked at the crenulations at the top of the mosque's wall.

"Saeed, son of Katib al-Farghani," he asked in a tone that was either annoyed or delighted, "what about those crenulations suggests love rather than worship?"

"Worship is an expression of love for God," Saeed replied firmly.

"They're not like anything I've ever seen, like embracing bridal couples, interlinked and connected to both body and soul. They're not like the ones in other mosques in Samarra, Egypt, or Damascus."

Saeed bowed to the embracing bridal couples raising their heads toward the heavens.

"My lord Ahmad," he replied definitively, "is not like other rulers."

"Explain to me what you meant by them. Make it short, so I don't throw you in prison again. Otherwise, I'll tell my men to destroy them."

"Kill me, put me in prison, and torture me, but don't destroy them."

Ahmad looked at him, waiting for his explanation. Saeed's response was self-assured, as he looked up at the crenulations.

"Separate crenulations," he said, "whether pointed or leaf-shaped, suggest a spirit that protects the location and dispels all evil and hatred. I could have made them in a pointed pyramid shape or like tree leaves. But protection involves a close union with spirits and their aspiration for their Creator. Those crenulations are united in their worship of God, work with each other for the better good, and continually longing for an encounter with Him."

Their eyes met.

"What about the Pyramid Witch," Ahmad asked, "who made you lose your mind? The whole of Egypt knows her story. Do you want me to order her to stop practicing magic and come back to you as a wife?"

Saeed gave a despairing smile.

"Bahnas will never come back to me," he said. "But she knows, or maybe she will know."

"Tell me, man, have you built my mosque with the heart of someone in love with a witch?"

"I've built it with the heart of one craving His forgiveness, someone who knows His mercy, and seeks His generosity. Anyone who has savored love is aware of the splendor of both the Creator and those whom He has created. How many bodies fight and destroy one another! People entering your mosque will remember that close union is the goal and complete harmony brings a waft of paradise. Make worshippers aware that Ahmad's crenulations are not like any others. When souls embrace, there is protection from weakness of heart."

"You can have all you want, Saeed, and even more. Just ask me, and I'll give it to you."

"What my lord can give me is enough. What I really want is not at your disposal."

Amir Ahmad invited all Egyptians to the Friday prayer in the mosque. However, some people spread the rumor that the amir had used the treasure of the ancients to pay for it, money that was tainted and, therefore, forbidden. The mosque's shape was different from other mosques. It had no pillars like the mosque of Amr ibn al-As. The amir heard about this before the Friday prayer, so he went to the mosque, gathered the populace, addressed them, and told them about his dream. He told them that he had not wanted to steal from any church or temple. The treasure belonged to the king who had visited him in his dreams from the first time, when he was still a child. So the treasure was legitimate. He had donated his mosque to Muslims and his hospital to Egyptians. The people gathered all around him and hailed him. This was the first Friday prayer in the mosque. On that day, the preacher, Abu Yaqoub al-Balkhi, gave the sermon and prayed for the caliph, but forgot to pray for Amir Ahmad. The amir turned to me.

"Ja'far," he said, "that preacher is to be whipped five hundred times for not praying for me."

I felt sorry for the preacher; maybe he had just made a mistake or felt a bit nervous. When the preacher came down the very first step, he remembered on his own. He went back to the top of the pulpit and said:

"All praise be to God, and His prayers upon our lord, the Prophet Muhammad. '*We made a commitment to Adam, but he forgot and We found no resolve in him.*' [Quran, Sura Taha (20), v. 115] O God, grant Your favor to Abu al-Abbas Ahmad ibn Tulun as deputy of the Commander of the Faithful!"

I heaved a sigh of relief.

"Instead of five hundred lashes," the amir said, "give him five hundred dinars."

Part Two

My complaint is to God: my tears have dried up.
Love for you has destroyed me with grief.
They said: Tomorrow separation. No doubt I said:
My soul will die before separation tomorrow.
—*Ibn al-Mu'tazz, Abbasid poet*

Chapter 5

Ja'far ibn Abd al-Ghaffar, Ahmad ibn Tulun's secretary, spoke to me as follows:
The conflict between the caliph Al-Mu'tamid and his brother, Al-Muwaffaq, intensified. The amir—God sustain him!—sided with the legitimate caliph, Al-Mu'tamid, who, in his weak position, resorted to him in search of Egypt's support. Indeed, the caliph encouraged the amir to add Syria to his Egyptian domains so that his brother, Al-Muwaffaq, would not gain control of it. The conflict between Al-Muwaffaq and Amir Ahmad intensified; it was as though the power of the Islamic world lay in the hands of two men, one in Egypt, the other in Iraq—Al-Muwaffaq and Ahmad. The caliph was increasingly weak, and his lack of options led Ahmad to invite him to make Egypt his caliphal headquarters. When it came to self-confidence and discipline, no other commander ever achieved the same level as Ahmad. He maintained his control of Egypt and kept his personal desires in check without being dominated by any slave-girls or controlled by desires. He had been trained as a fighter, and protection was his primary focus. Some people would suggest that he was impatient and dealt harshly with his foes; others that he was swift to show his brutality and domination of people; and still others that he had a predilection for controlling what people thought and spying on private whisperings. But I have never encountered or known an amir who loved Egypt as much as Ahmad did, who expended so much money and breath, and who melded with the Egyptian people the way he did. I will discuss the love that Egyptians felt for him elsewhere. When the conflict between brothers intensified and reached a crisis point, Al-Mu'tamid asked Ahmad to get involved and bring his armed forces to Syria in order to take over Syria before Al-Muwaffaq could do so.

On that occasion, Ahmad was full of confidence as he left for Syria. His boys were now men. Al-Abbas had been trained as a fighter, and now he was the pride of the country. Ahmad called his sons together and summoned Al-Abbas.

"You're my deputy in Egypt," he told his son. "You'll govern in my place until I return. You'll take care of the people and protect your brothers. You'll confirm your loyalty and courage."

Al-Abbas bent down and kissed his father's hand.

"May I be your ransom, my lord," he said.

"No," the amir told him firmly, "I want you alive when I return."

He then summoned one of his Egyptian men, named Ahmad ibn Muhammad al-Wasiti, and told him to assist Al-Abbas and serve as Egypt's prime minister till he returned. He was also to assume control of taxes. He was to provide support to

Al-Abbas in his decision-making. He also instructed him to consult Al-Wasiti before implementing any decision. He was increasingly worried about that poisoned dart that might strike Al-Abbas in the chest and asked Al-Wasiti to surround Al-Abbas with guards. He was to taste the food himself before letting Al-Abbas eat it and spy on all the palace's slave-girls.

The men all swore allegiance to Al-Abbas. As the amir headed for the city gates, his son stopped him.

"Father," he said, "I pray God that you will return safe and successful. Do not delay in sending letters so that my heart may be reassured and my eye soothed."

The amir rubbed his son's shoulder. "May your heart always be reassured, my son," he said.

Never in my entire life have I seen an amir so affectionate. I'll freely admit that I was very concerned about Al-Abbas while the amir was away. I had no idea from which direction the danger might come. Would Al-Muwaffaq send men to get rid of him and guarantee an end to the Tulunid regime, burning the father's heart in the finery of his own sons? Or would he be killed by one of the more ambitious men around him? Or even a slave-girl with similar ambitions? I was as worried about Al-Abbas as his father was, not out of love for Al-Abbas, but for the amir and a realization of the love that Al-Abbas had for his father. But departure was inevitable.

There were very few letters from Al-Wasiti to the amir. We all started to worry that something bad had happened to Al-Abbas or another member of the amir's family. The amir decided to send someone in disguise to Egypt to find out what was happening there. He was either to come back at the speed of lightning or else send a letter by carrier pigeon that would arrive days before he did.

A letter duly arrived, and the look on the carrier's face was fearful and gloomy. I noticed the expression in the amir's eyes as he stared at the letter carrier.

"If you tell me that Al-Abbas has been killed," he said in a despairing tone I have never witnessed before, "I'll cut off your head."

The man hesitated, then bowed in front of the amir.

"I beg your mercy," he said fearfully. "I'm just the messenger."

"If he's dead," the amir said in a quivering tone, "then get out of here now. I'll give you a few moments to get away from here, so I don't kill you."

The amir looked down and closed his eyes. I saw his fingers drumming on his chair as though he were entering a prison with no way out. The messenger was still standing in front of him, and the amir was still strumming his fingers as though engaging with destiny and fighting it.

"My lord amir," I eventually pleaded, "the messenger's afraid to speak. Please let him."

He did not seem to hear me.

"If Amir Al-Abbas has died," I told the messenger gently, "then leave now. Save yourself."

"He's not dead," the messenger whispered in my ear.

I heaved a sigh of relief.

"Amir," I said, "Al-Abbas's Egypt is doing fine."

The amir looked at the messenger. He was still waiting for the letter, not yet reassured.

The messenger said that Al-Wasiti was in prison and was thus unable to contact the amir. It seemed as though—God knows best!—Al-Abbas had taken two hundred thousand dinars from the state treasury and forced Egyptian merchants to pay an additional three hundred thousand dinars. When the amir heard this information, he did not believe it. He dispatched someone to confirm it and talk to Al-Wasiti in his prison cell. The real facts now emerged.

"My lord," the man said shyly, "it appears—and God knows best!—that a group of maligners have been stirring up intrigue between Al-Abbas and Al-Wasiti. They've maligned Al-Wasiti to Al-Abbas as an Egyptian who doesn't know Arabic well, mispronounces words, spies on your behalf, and gives you false information. They're all traitors, my lord, but Amir Al-Abbas is still certainly loyal to you."

The amir read between the lines, or did not. However, Al-Abbas left Al-Qata'i and fled to Alexandria for fear of his father's wrath or further intrigue. His father sent judges and shaikhs to him, encouraging him to return to Al-Qata'i and guaranteeing his safe conduct.

"Obeying your parents is an obligation," he said in his letter, "and rebelling against your own father is outright disobedience."

He said that he would forgive his son. Perhaps he had asked too much of his son in such a time of intrigue. He asked him to give back the money and return to Al-Qata'i.

Al-Abbas had left his brother, Rabi'a, in charge of Egypt before he went to Alexandria. It seems—but God knows best!—that the maligners had their doubts about the amir's letter and his real intentions. They told Al-Abbas that his father was always brutal with anyone who doubted him and showed no mercy. What would he do to Al-Abbas?

They went on to say that the amir's promise was a lie, that he really wanted to bring him back to Egypt so that he could deal harshly with him. At a certain point, there would be no mercy; Al-Abbas's only options were to win or to die. Al-Abbas sent his father a threatening letter. He surrounded himself with his army and men and headed for Barqa, and from there on to Tunis to invade, conquer, and then return to Egypt victorious after deposing and defeating his father. The traitors around him all told Al-Abbas that he was just as powerful as his father, and that time always honors those who secure rapid victory. We heard that in Africa, Al-Abbas ran riot, stole, and destroyed castles and houses until the governor swore that he would attack Egypt and Ibn Tulun. Fighting broke out, and it was reported that Al-Abbas had been killed. When the news reached Ibn Tulun, I have never seen him looking so distressed. He closed his eyes for a moment, then opened them again. For hours, there was silence, but then more news arrived: Al-Abbas was still alive.

Al-Abbas fled to Barqa once again. His father sent him letters telling him to return to Egypt. The son sent back a letter that I did not dare read. I thought the amir might strike its carrier on the neck.

I was there as the amir read it. What it said was that he, Al-Abbas, had no more loyalty to his father than did Abraham to his father in his unbelief. He was right, and the amir was in error.

A horrendous silence ensued.

"Dispatch an army to confront Al-Abbas," the amir said. "I want him alive. He must return to Egypt."

ᛉᛉ

The two armies, those of father and son, fought each other. Al-Abbas's army did not last long; people surrendered, and others were killed. Al-Abbas was captured and brought back to Egypt as Ahmad ibn Tulun had commanded. I do not know how to describe what Amir Ahmad was feeling because I did not encounter him. I know that he summoned the esteemed judge, Bakkar ibn Qutaiba.

"I've summoned you," he told the judge gloomily, "because I need to ask your opinion regarding disrespect for one's parents."

"It can destroy and crush the heart even more than the loss of children, my lord," Judge Bakkar replied definitively.

"It feels as though I've become weak," the amir said spontaneously. "I've no power and no purpose in the world."

"It's an unstable world, my lord, with no permanence for anyone."

"Has my own son been deceiving me for all those years past? I've been keeping watch on everyone close to me except for him. How could I feel his love all around me, only to have him betray me? Was he going to throw me in prison, I wonder, or kill me? My own son . . ."

For a moment, the judge said nothing, but then he looked at the amir.

"Being Amir Ahmad's son is the hardest thing in the world," he said, "if you want my opinion. '*God does not charge the self with more than it can bear*'. [Sura 2 (The Cow), v. 286] Be forgiving if you are able."

"How can I forgive someone who's ripped my heart to shreds in his hands? If it were a wife, I could forgive. But he's my own blood, my companion, my friend, my successor."

"He's not equipped to serve as your successor," the judge declared.

"What do you mean?"

"He has borne more than he can handle. He's not Amir Ahmad, but Amir Ahmad's all around him, looking down from every headland."

"I've never chided him. I've always wanted him to be better than me and more powerful."

"You haven't chided him, but he's chided himself for not being you. Whenever the world has drawn close to you and fallen into your grasp, the boy has felt how little discretion he has and how weak people regard him as being. Being the amir's son is perpetual torture. You're not Ahmad, and you can't be. Even so, Ahmad gives you responsibilities you can't take on."

"It's my fault then for wanting him to be my successor."

"That's the way of the world, my lord. It's not your fault. But it's a world that heaves with tribulations."

"I could survive all those tribulations except for this one."

"Be charitable and ask for forgiveness. That will help you endure. With that endurance, blessings from God will descend upon you."

"Ah me, what sorrow I feel, unlike any before! For my own son to kill me, disavow me, and forget . . ."

"Were this a haven of permanence, then it would be a sorrow. But, if you remember that it is purely transitory, then it is a tribulation with an end."

"It's as though I'm crying out in my life and death, like Noah beseeching God to save his son from the flood and fire that followed it. I want God to forgive his disobedience, but I don't want to forgive him. Even so, I yearn for him and sympathize. What kind of tribulation is that?"

Chapter 6

Here is what Asma, daughter of Mahmud the tailor, Ahmad ibn Tulun's wife, told me:

He did not write to me after I became a mother, but I was well aware of the love that a mother feels for her child. I could see Khatun's eyes quivering and felt sorry for her. But I felt even more sorrow and even worse pain for the amir. I have never seen a man so grief-stricken. When he returned, he came into the women's quarters, and I could see the lines around his eyes as though he were a hundred years old. He said a few terse words, then went into his room and did not call for any of us.

That day, something totally unexpected happened. Khatun came to my room, her voice and eyes flooded with tears.

"You have a major place in the amir's heart," she said.

"Nothing can possibly rival your place, my lady," I replied modestly.

Then I felt sorry for her, knowing what she was going to ask.

"I'll intercede for your son," I told her. "We all will."

"Ahmad was always afraid that Al-Abbas might be killed or might die," she said pensively. "He dreamed about it, tasted his food for him, spied on his slave-girls and retainers, all so that no one could harm him. You know that, don't you?"

"Yes, I do, my lady."

"Call me Khatun. He was afraid that someone would hurt his son, but now his son is doing it to him. What can I say to him?"

"He's his own son. He'll never hurt him."

"If a son turns against his own father, squanders money, and steals men, then declares war, what do you expect? If Al-Abbas had managed to take over Egypt, I wonder what he would have done to his father."

"It would have been fine."

"There's nothing fine about a son betraying his own father. How can I possibly ask that he be forgiven? No, Asma, I haven't come here to ask you to intercede for my son. Traitors should be killed. I want you to intercede about something else."

"My lady," I replied affectionately, "show a little kindness. Maybe he'll have mercy on his son . . ."

She interrupted me.

"I want you to intervene and ask the amir to kill him quickly, with no humiliation or torture."

"Let's ask the amir to pardon him," I replied.

"That kind of naivete only comes from someone who's only lived in palaces for a day or so. Will you come with me and have a meeting with the amir?"

We went in to see the amir with heavy steps. I was more afraid of his sorrow than his anger. I had no idea what to expect or what he would do once we started talking.

He looked at Khatun first.

"Have you come to intercede for him?" he asked her.

"I'll not intercede for someone who's betrayed you," she replied forcefully, "even if he is my own son. I want you to be as merciful as you have been loving."

"No, I have to be as sad as I've been loving. I must punish to the same degree, just as much as I have lavished my love on him."

"By all means, be sad, Ahmad," Khatun said, "but don't let your sorrow turn into bitterness and anger. How long have we been together? I know you and understand you. If you're planning to kill him, then be merciful. Don't sever his limbs and torture him deliberately."

He did not reply, but looked at the floor.

"What are you doing here, Asma?" he asked, looking straight at me.

"I've come to fill my eyes with your presence, my lord," I replied softly. "My lady allowed me to accompany her, and that's a great honor. I've come to ask you to apply your mercy rather than bitterness, your forgiveness rather than your anger, and your forbearance rather than your heart's inclinations."

He shook his head, as though he had not heard what I said.

"I hereby permit you to leave," he said.

Khatun looked at me, then opened her mouth.

"No more talk," he interrupted.

I moved backward along with Khatun, my hand over my heart. I had no idea what anguish would be filling the days to come.

Men took Al-Abbas, hands tied, all around Egypt and Al-Qata'i. He looked angry, but his heart was full of fear.

People clustered together behind windows, watching the meeting in the city square. The soldiers were assembled around Ahmad, while Al-Abbas and his men were in chains behind him, heads lowered in shame. Their eyes met, and, for just a moment or less, there was an affectionate look on the father's face.

"What's the penalty for treason?" he asked.

"Death, my lord," his men answered.

"What's the penalty for treason, Abbas?" he asked his son.

Al-Abbas swallowed hard and looked around him. "Sometimes, my lord," he replied, "realities are scrambled."

"Sometimes," the amir said, "treason shines bright. People talk about it inside their homes. The son betrays his father; the commander squanders his father's treasury that he's been saving up for the country's people. Who were the people who gave you advice? Abu Ma'shar? Who breathed hatred into your heart? Who exploited the obscenity inside your heart to make you liken your father to Abraham's? Do you see me as an infidel, Abbas? Or do you see me tossing you into hell as your reward for submitting to the Lord of the Worlds?

"No, I see you having given me peace, and then deceiving me."

"Yes, I gave you peace," Ahmad replied, "but you're the one who deceived me."

"My father . . ."

"I'm not your father. Today I'm your amir, and I disown you."

I watched with a quaking heart as the amir lifted his sword and put it on his son's shoulder. Al-Abbas was shivering, and his heartbeats could be heard all the way to the palace.

"Take the sword," the amir told his son. "I want you to sever the hands of Abu Ma'shar, who wrote the letters for you. Then cut off his feet in front of me and throw him down at the base of the mountain."

I closed my eyes so I would not see the blood flowing from the man's limbs. Then I had to block my ears as well so as not to hear the unbelievable screams. But I did hear Khatun whispering.

"You're going to torture him, Ahmad," she said. "I've asked you to be kind enough to kill him quickly, and you've refused. Are you going to use your own hands, Amir, to sever my son's limbs?"

"He won't do that," I responded immediately.

"Yes, he will."

"I know him. He won't."

"Well, I know him too," Khatun said. "He will."

The screaming stopped. I opened my eyes.

"Now cut off the limbs of every single one of your men, one by one," Ahmad told his son. "Then, right here in front of me, throw them away at the base of the mountain."

I closed my eyes again, and the screams reverberated all the way into my heart. Then I opened them again.

Al-Abbas's clothes were splattered with human blood as he put down the sword, panting. I could not tell whether that was because of all the energy he had expended or because he was terrified of what was to come. He looked at his father to see what he was going to do.

"You've sold your men," his father said, "and got rid of them without even trying to redeem yourself. I expected you to plead on their behalf. After all, they all fought for you, if you remember."

Al-Abbas did not respond; he looked distraught, convinced of what his fate was to be.

His father went up to him and gave him a vicious slap on the face, the echo of which could be heard where we were. Al-Abbas fell to the ground, his eyes bathed in tears. Ahmad grabbed his hand and pulled him up.

"Stop blubbering like a woman!" he told him.

There was complete silence. I could have almost sworn that the tears were not only in Al-Abbas's eyes, but it must have been just my imagination and naivete.

Ahmad looked at his guards.

"Take Al-Abbas away," he told them.

I said nothing, but heard Khatun let out a gasp. He went up to his son and slapped him on the face again.

"If I kill you," Ahmad said, "I'll be killing myself. If I let you live, you'll keep reminding me of my weakness and sorrow. Even so, those feelings are better than death."

"Take Al-Abbas to his house," he told his guards. "He's not to leave his house without my personal permission. Leave his women and children with him. No one else is to visit him without my permission."

At that moment, I heard the men praising him and thanking him for his mercy and justice.

Khatun gaped in sheer amazement. "He didn't kill him," she said. "Why not?"

"Because he couldn't," I replied in triumph. "I told you I know him better than you do. Do you remember?"

"But . . ."

"I'm afraid now for the amir," I responded without thinking, my eyes on the amir. "This is the ultimate agony, and he has a dagger stuck in his heart."

Chapter 7

Ja'far ibn Abd al-Ghaffar, Ahmad ibn Tulun's secretary, spoke to me as follows:
    No one dared mention to the amir his own son's revolt against him or his decision to remove him as his successor. In his place, he promoted his son, Khumarawayh, his second son, born to his slave-girl, Mayyas, several years after the birth of Khatun's son, Al-Abbas. He sat with Khumarawayh for an hour or more, then came out and told us that his son would assume the reins of power after him. That day, there was a crescendo of whisperings, not in opposition to Khumarawayh, who was regarded as being honest and merciful, but rather for fear of an Abbasid caliph who might not be happy with a Tulun descendant ruling Egypt, as though they were independent rulers like the ancient kings. Egypt had been subject to the caliphate ever since the time of Amr ibn al-As, but then Ahmad ibn Tulun had arrived, and everything had changed. One of the people present expressed his worries about the caliph, and also about his brother who had clashed with Ahmad ibn Tulun.

"Leave the caliphate matter to me," Ahmad said decisively. "I can handle that. It won't be long till, God willing, the caliphate's in Egypt."

When everyone had left, I was still feeling sorry for Ahmad, not as the amir dealing with dangers and betrayals, but as a father shattered by the treachery of his dearest son.

"My lord hasn't visited the harem for a long time," I suggested gently. "Women's company always provides some relaxation."

"Wait for me here, Ja'far," he said. "I'll change my clothes, then we'll go."

Later, as we mounted our horses, I was concerned.

"Where are we going at midnight, my lord?"

"To the monastery," he replied. "I haven't checked on the people there for some time."

"But in the middle of the night?" I pleaded.

"Do people devoted to worship feel any difference between night and day?"

"I'm afraid people there will be scared."

He did not respond. He took off on his horse, and I did my best to keep up with him. He was riding as though his life was at an end. When we reached the gates of the El-Qoseir Monastery at Al-Mis'ara, he banged on the door once, and it was opened by a monk whom I had known before.

"Welcome to the friend," the monk said, head lowered. "It's been a long time."

Ahmad dismounted, went into the monastery, and sat on the stone bench. Anduna the monk kept looking at him.

"I want to spend some time in retreat," Ahmad said.

Anduna nodded his head, then signaled to Ahmad, with me behind him. We went along a dark corridor, through a circular hall, and then yet another corridor, until we reached a room with only a stone bench, some water, and a single candle. Anduna opened the black wooden door.

"At your command, my lord," he said.

Ahmad went into the room and closed the door. He did not invite me to join him. Anduna and I remained outside.

"Is the cell secure from the inside?" I asked in alarm. "I'm worried about my lord."

"There's nothing to worry about here," Anduna replied with a smile.

"He's carrying some heavy burdens," Anduna said in Coptic. "I've never seen him so miserable."

I was afraid to say anything in case the amir cut off my neck. I wanted to ask the monk if he had heard about the business with Al-Abbas, but I did not.

"Only go in when he gives you permission," Anduna said after a pause. "Don't disturb him. Ever since he first came to Egypt, he's enjoyed the isolation here. If you need to check on him, just peer through the crack in the door. You can see the bench and him sitting on it. Whether he moves around or not, he'll be fine."

The monk moved slowly away, leaving me feeling confused. I tried to see the amir in the dark, but he did not light the candle or say a single word.

Placing my hand on my beard, I fell into a deep sleep till morning. I was already aware of the relationship between the amir—God help him and sustain him!—and Anduna the monk. It had begun when Ibn al-Mudabbir oversaw Egypt's taxes, going after the money of churches and monasteries, and imposing heavy taxes on Muslims and Christians alike. Anduna had come to see the Governor of Egypt to ask for his help. The amir had promised Anduna that Ibn al-Mudabbir would not have any authority over Egyptians for long. Anduna had invited him to visit the monastery, and the amir had done so. He felt affection for the Copts of Egypt, and admired and respected them. He would always say that houses where people prayed in quest of God's love and forgiveness deserved respect. Ever since, Anduna had been a close friend.

One night went by, then a second. I worried about the amir. He was not leaving the bench much. I called Anduna, and he knocked gently on the door, opened it, and went inside. The amir was spread out on the bench, his head against the wall. The room was completely dark. I moved back and stood by the door so I could listen and catch a glimpse.

It was the first and last time I ever saw Ahmad crying. I saw the monk sitting silently on the floor out of respect for tears that had never fallen before. Then I saw Ahmad use his hand to wipe away his tears.

"The pain's much worse," Ahmad said, "and it's spreading."

"The pain when a son rebels is the very worst," Anduna said calmly. "But show some tolerance. Forgiveness will bring you some peace before it does him."

"Was he planning to kill me, I wonder, or put me in prison? I was afraid to sleep at night for fear that someone might harm him, and I'd fail to protect him. I'd feel the pain of his death even though he was alive. His death might have brought me some relief from all this pain, but I couldn't kill a part my own self."

"Pain holds a lofty status with the Lord God," Anduna said. "Only those who have chosen it achieve such status. Perhaps it was God's will to open for you a light source, one that you can only see when you have grown accustomed to the darkness of this cell. Light never appears when anger is present. Show tolerance so that you can see; calm down so that you can hear God's voice."

"If only I could understand. Why did he do what he did? When he was just a boy, I used to see love in his eyes. Did my eyes deceive me or did he? Did his companions win him over, or can greed change the shade of feelings just like jasmine oil?"

"Close your eyes to see, and your ears to hear."

"Woe is me for what I can see and hear!" Ahmad retorted in exasperation. "If only I could neither see nor hear!"

"Ahmad," the monk said, "it is God's will. You need to accept that so He can make things clear to you. Show tolerance and forgive. Your anger is just as powerful as your love, your suffering matches your sympathy, and your penalty conforms with your sense of sorrow. Just remember that."

I was astonished to listen to this conversation between the monk and the amir. It was as though they were brothers and childhood friends. No titles were involved and no formalities.

For a while, there was silence.

"It's His will," Ahmad repeated, "but it's my torment alone and my defeat."

"Ahmad," Anduna told him thoughtfully, "this kind of grief brings with it a certain degree of death, and, in death, there's always life. You must die in order to live. You need to grieve in order to die, and then you can live a more profound and learned life with no pain before it. There can be no life with death before it, and no understanding without preceding grief."

"Do you realize, Anduna," Ahmad said at this point, "how much I envy you for abandoning this haven where there is no security? How I wish I could be at liberty to do the same!"

Anduna smiled, then said some words that I shall never forget as long as I live.

"In such abandonment there is both wisdom and a secret. You have to renounce the world when you are still eager and ambitious, not once you've despaired and withdrawn; you need to do it when the world has its arms open to you, not when you've savored the bitter taste of its sincerity and the reality of its brutal ways."

The monk stood, and returned with some bread and water. Ahmad ate the bread. We stayed at the monastery for another day; then we returned to the palace without a word.

🏛

Al-Wasiti and I interceded with the amir to have a meeting with his son, Al-Abbas, listen to his explanation, and forgive him before setting out for Tartus. For the first time, I noticed that the amir's gaze was unsteady as he stared first at the sky, then at the ground. Those days, I was very worried about him. I even felt sorry for him, something no one had ever felt regarding Ahmad ibn Tulun. After all, he was all sincerity, power, politics, and worldly wisdom—cavalier, brave scholar, just. We all wanted to be like Ahmad; but on that day, we pitied him coming to terms with treacherous fate.

Al-Abbas came in, head lowered, and hands tied and dangling on his chest. "I am hoping," he said in a soft voice, "that the amir will forgive me."

Ahmad raised his head. I knew what he was planning. He dismissed the assembly, but I stayed by the door so I could see Ahmad and intervene if necessary.

Ahmad went over to him, and Al-Abbas closed his eyes, as though he was expecting another violent slap on the face. However, the amir pulled on the hand-ropes, untied them, and threw them on the floor.

"I don't like to see my own son being humiliated," Ahmad said. "Lift your head up. You're Ahmad's son."

Al-Abbas raised his head slowly, and their eyes met.

"When you were young," Ahmad said, "you'd sit with me at the dinner table during Ramadan. You were always impatient. You'd fill your belly with tiny birds and be full before the sheep and chicken arrived. You'd stuff yourself with quail and jay; then you couldn't enjoy the yogurt with foie gras and baby kid. Why couldn't you wait till I was dead to inherit my position? Death's not that far away, Al-Abbas. Or did you want me to pray to God to hasten my death so that you could take over? Or was it that you wanted to confirm that you're better than Ahmad?"

"No one's better than you, Father," Al-Abbas replied without even thinking.

Ahmad grasped him by the shoulders and looked into his eyes. I was not sure whether he was going to hug him or slap him.

"I wonder," he said quietly, "when I go out to fight, shall I leave you in my place?"

Al-Abbas responded immediately.

"No," he said sorrowfully, "leave your favorite son, Khuramawayh, in charge. I'm not fit to govern. That's what people have been telling you."

"You were my favorite son, you idiot!" Ahmad yelled at him. "You were. I wonder, if I turned around, would you stab me in the back? People say that when a son takes over the rule from his father, he plucks out his eyes, so he won't be able to see forever. Were you planning to kill me or pluck out my eyes? If I left you here in Egypt, what would happen?"

"I beg you to forgive me," Al-Abbas replied listlessly. "Even Joseph's brothers listened to the devil, but then asked to be forgiven."

Ahmad nodded in acknowledgment.

"Are you asking to be forgiven so I won't punish you?" Ahmad asked, "Or so I won't be angry with you?"

"For me, my lord, your anger is more important than punishment."

"What you're saying sounds more like the Sphinx than my own son. How is it that I don't believe your words? I wonder, what did you expect from your father's love? Was it a women's conspiracy that changed your heart, or men's greed?"

Al-Abbas did not respond. He pursed his lips to suppress a deep-seated fury. The amir shook his shoulders.

"If I split your chest open, would I find my son's heart stolen or simply a void? There's no truth in your words, and no love in your eyes. It's an entire life wasted. But death is not far . . . Death is not far."

I went over to the amir.

"My lord amir," I said gently.

He looked at me. "When we leave," he said, "we'll take Al-Abbas with us. I'm not confident about leaving him here. There's loathing in his eyes. Nobody knows a son's eyes like his own father."

I opened my mouth to say something, but he gave me a look, so I remained silent. As long as I live, I can never forget the look in his eyes or the way he let his arms drop. He sat down as though he were carrying the entire world in his hands. He put his hand over his heart, as though he were searching for a knife that his son had thrust into him, or an arrow stuck in his back. That day, I saw death in his eyes and knew for certain, even though I did not acknowledge it to myself, that he was not going to live for long—Amir Abu al-Abbas Ahmad ibn Tulun.

Chapter 8

Muhammad ibn Sulaiman al-Katib told me the following:

Let me tell you about that devil in human form, Ahmad ibn Tulun. The Egyptians wept for him the way people weep for a master who has made them suffer. He had no creed or conscience to impede his evil. He exploited the struggle between the two brothers and the caliph's weakness to get the upper hand and take over Egypt and then Syria. Never in my life have I seen anyone spending as much money on his army as Ahmad ibn Tulun did, or increasing the size of the army the way he did. Ever since Amr ibn al-As conquered Egypt, I have never known a governor of Egypt who used common men as soldiers and built them houses in his new city, which one day I plan to raze to the ground over his head and those of his family and troops. He built that mosque which stretches endlessly between cities, as though a degree of piety had entered his heart whose primary characteristic was tyranny. People kept claiming that he never drank wine or bothered about slave-girls and had no cravings. They kept saying that ever since he was a boy, he had been a soldier, fighting sincerely and intelligently. For my part, I will say that he had wanted Egypt ever since puberty, when he had heard about it and seen it in a dream. Like a demon, he would alternate lenience and savagery, now affectionate, then brutal, whispering, then shouting, until he had put an end to his victim. Let me tell you what he did to Shuqair, the postmaster whom the caliph himself had charged with sending him information about Egypt.

From the outset, he loathed Shuqair and regarded him as a spy. He was obsessed about spies and madmen. As soon as the opportunity arose, he arrested Shuqair, tied him to a wooden plank, and then pulled his limbs till they tore apart a few days before he died. Needless to say, he died. He wanted to kill Ibn al-Mudabbir, the Tax-Administrator, as well. Because of Ibn al-Mudabbir's status with the caliph, he did not kill him, but he did manage to get rid of him in any case.

Talking about his espionage against Baghdad and all the caliph's retinue, this page is not big enough to recount everything he did. I will make do with what I was told by Al-Haitham ibn Abd ash-Shakur, a man of high status and repute. Someone came knocking on his door at midnight, and he found one of the amir's men telling him to come with him at once. The shaikh realized that this was the end. He bid his family farewell and hurried to the square. When he stood in front of the amir, he begged for forgiveness although he had no idea what he was supposed to have done.

"I've learned," the amir said, "that tomorrow you're going to be meeting some senior officials at a gathering to which you've been invited."

"Yes, my lord," the man replied, shivering all over.

"I want you to record in detail everything you hear," Ahmad told him.

Al-Haitham was upset by the idea of betraying his friends, realizing that intrigue was even worse than murder. He was aware, also, that if he did not carry out the amir's instructions, he would be killed immediately. He returned to his house in a quandary, not knowing whether to flee or carry out the amir's orders in order to save himself and his family. He reluctantly carried out the amir's orders, hating himself and despising his own cowardice. He wrote down everything he heard, with the men saying all kinds of bad things about Ahmad ibn Tulun. Next morning, he was summoned by the amir. He brought the paper on which he had recorded everything. Ahmad read it, then looked at Al-Haitham.

"Is this everything?" Ahmad asked.

"I swear to you, my lord," he replied with a shudder, "that's everything I heard."

With that, Ahmad pulled out another piece of paper and told Al-Haitham to read it. He did so and discovered the same things that he himself had written. It seems that the amir had appointed one spy to spy on the other; he did not trust either Al-Haitham or the other spy, and wanted to check on both. Al-Haitham left after receiving some money.

Al-Haitham was perplexed and saddened when he went home. He had no idea what had happened to his friends. He hoped that the amir would be merciful, or the caliph would intervene to save them. Two days later, he went to visit his friends and find out how they were. He could not find their houses. He thought he had lost his way, and spent an hour or more without finding any trace of their houses. In the place where the houses had been, there was now a park. He almost lost his mind. When he asked the neighbors what had happened, they told him that the amir's soldiers had drowned the house owners in the Nile, then demolished the houses and put a park in their place.

So that is Ahmad, if you wanted to know about his conduct. That is Ahmad, who used to spy on the prisoners in the notorious prison known the "the dungeon." He used to whip a recruit every two days till he bled, and then put him in the prison. In fact, he was one of Ahmad's own men over whom he had control. The prisoners all assumed that he was being tortured by the amir and was one of them, whereas he was actually working for the amir in secret. That was Ahmad, who used to spy on his wives and his secretary, Ja'far; Ahmad, whose own son rebelled against him, demolished his arrogance, and crushed his delusion. When Ahmad's servant, Lu'lu', who saved me one day, took refuge with Al-Muwaffaq, he sold Lu'lu's family in the slave market. Yes, indeed, he sold the women and daughters of his servant and general, Lu'lu', when he took refuge with Al-Muwaffaq! What kind of devil thinks that way?!

I have sworn to wipe all traces of Ahmad ibn Tulun off the face of the earth. No mosque or palace will be left standing, no son or daughter will be left alive. His wives and daughters will be sold by my own hand. He threw me out and humiliated me because of a dream he had had. He was going to kill me out of fear and self-delusion, as though he were a king who imagines that he can keep people alive or kill them. I shall make clear to him that the sun rises in the east, and he will never be able to make it rise in the west. However large his army, he is still weak.

No matter how many businesses he has built for Egyptians, how many poor people he has fed, and how hard Egyptians have prayed for his life to be long, he is still a tyrant.

Chapter 9

Ja'far ibn Abd al-Ghaffar, Ahmad ibn Tulun's secretary, told me the following:
Intrigue is more powerful than murder. Ibn Sulaiman has loathed the amir for some time, and so he lies and makes up information and stories about what transpired between the amir and the Coptic patriarch, Pope Mikhail, and between the amir and Judge Bakkar ibn Qutaiba. Ibn Sulaiman claims that the amir was jealous of men of religion and the way that people loved them; he was always out to crush them and make them aware of their limits. He only felt any affection for a few unknown religious figures, like Anduna, the monk, Shaikh Ali, the shaikh of a small mosque outside the city, and a few others. That is a completely false statement without any truth to it. I will tell you what really happened with the Coptic patriarch, a story that one of the corrupt bishops, Bishop Sakha, fabricated. He actually assaulted the Pope when he visited his church. When the bishop was late, the Pope himself prepared the communion elements. When the bishop finally arrived, he interrupted the Mass, grabbed the Communion elements, and threw them on the floor. The Pope then ordered that the bishop be deposed and someone else be appointed bishop. What then happened with this evil bishop was that he exploited Amir Ibn Tulun's need for money to fight his wars. He paid the amir a visit and betrayed the Pope. He concocted a story and told the amir lies. He claimed that the Pope was hoarding silver and gold when the country needed money, and that churches were full of gold and silver goblets and vessels. The amir summoned the Pope and laid out the accusations. He asked the Pope to give him some silver to be converted into money. The Pope tried to explain to the amir that the church vessels and the like were not his property, and he could not make decisions about them. The amir put him in prison for a few months until two Christian secretaries, Yuhanna and Musa, who were working for the amir, interceded. The amir then released the Pope. I can swear that the amir—may God come to his aid!—was the first ever Governor of Egypt who did not make use of church pillars or even pillars from ancient temples in the construction of his mosque. Throughout his reign, he never laid his hands on any church property. He had a fixed point of view, and was loved by Christians, Muslims, and Jews alike. They all prayed for him every Friday, Saturday, and Sunday.

His story with Judge Bakkar ibn Qutaiba is harsher and more complicated. I will relate it now.

I witnessed the encounter between the amir and the eminent judge and shaikh, Bakkar ibn Qutaiba. I have always wanted to forget it, and yet it has stayed with me through the years. When the conflict between the amir and the caliph's brother, Al-Muwaffaq started, Al-Muwaffaq started cursing the amir in the mosques of Baghdad. The amir decided to start praying for Al-Muwaffaq's deposition as caliph-elect, demanding that all shaikhs and judges do so. They all agreed, except for one judge, Bakkar ibn Qutaiba.

That judge refused to pray in mosques for Al-Muwaffaq's deposition. There was a deep-seated disagreement between the amir and Al-Muwaffaq. Above all, they went after each other over Ibn Tulun's presence in Egypt and his declaration of independence. When the conflict between Al-Muwaffaq and his brother, the caliph Al-Mu'tamid, worsened, the amir made a pact with Al-Mu'tamid, who never refused any of Ahmad's requests. He allowed Ahmad to govern Egypt as he wished and relinquished the country's products for its own people. The amir sang the caliph's praises and boosted his status, and that was even though—God alone knows—I was hearing a lot of rumors maligning the caliph Al-Mu'tamid and extolling the power of his brother, Al-Muwaffaq. People were saying—and God knows best!—that Al-Mu'tamid was giving himself over to pleasures and was not interested in matters of state. I am not sure whether the amir saw the caliph's weakness as an opportunity to declare Egypt and the border provinces independent. Or was he supporting him because he was the legitimate caliph? Actions are based on intentions. Everyone has such intentions, and it was difficult to know the amir's. However, I do know about his ongoing concern for Egypt and its people. When Shaikh Bakkar ibn Qutaiba declined to call for the deposition of Al-Muwaffaq, the caliph Al-Mu'tamid's brother, he was summoned by the amir, who greeted him coldly. They had the following conversation, which I have never forgotten.

The amir asked the shaikh why he was refusing to call for the deposition of Al-Muwaffaq. The shaikh, who was over seventy years old, was silent for a while.

"You're ordering me to be involved in worldly matters, Amir," he said. "I cannot obey an instruction that contravenes God's word."

"No, Shaikh, praying for Al-Muwaffaq is a worldly matter too."

"I have not seen anything objectionable in Al-Muwaffaq that requires me to call for his deposition."

"Your words are having a negative effect on the people. You're aware of that."

"I have not seen anything objectionable in Al-Muwaffaq that requires me to call for his deposition," the shaikh repeated.

"Are you pleased that he's cursing me from the pulpits of Baghdad mosques? Is spreading hatred an aspect of faith, Shaikh?"

"It has no place in religious belief."

"If that's what you admit, then call for his deposition."

"I have no role to play in struggles over power and rulership. Don't burden me with more than I can bear."

"No, you preach loyalty to Al-Muwaffaq since he was the one who appointed you judge here at the outset. I'm aware of that."

The judge did not respond.

"This is a war I did not want," the amir went on. "Al-Muwaffaq was the one who started it. Now it's not some stranger who's being a traitor against me; it's my own senior general, Lu'lu'. When that happens, you can't expect there to be any mercy."

A tense silence ensued.

"Amir," the shaikh said resignedly, "in my life, there are two kinds of men. One sees in the world things that delight and sadden. So he grasps what's left of his short life, and everything turns out the way he wants. The other also sees in the world things that delight and sadden. But he realizes that the world is ephemeral. What remains is very short, so he has to leave it in peace with himself and his Lord."

"There's another type that witnesses veneration and is then afflicted with arrogance. He has decided to stand in front of the amir, defiant and refusing."

"If you killed me, I wouldn't be the first to be killed; if you put me in prison, I wouldn't be the first either. If you tortured me, people would say that you tortured the Chief Judge. If you accused me of unbelief, I would be just like the pious people of old. Do what you will. I'm mortal, and so are you."

"I'm mortal and so are you. Fine! The darkness of prison has a magical effect even on those people who are followed and revered by people."

With that, the amir ordered that the judge be thrown into prison until he adjusted his tone.

The amir's final visit to the monk, Anduna, at the El-Qoseir monastery is also something that has stayed with me. Following his son's betrayal, Ahmad changed. His worries intensified to such a degree that it affected his heart and soul. When he next visited the monastery, he told Anduna that he would only eat bread.

"I want to eat what you eat," he said.

"Deprivation and voluntary poverty don't suit you," Anduna responded.

"On the contrary," Ahmad said, "deprivation and voluntary poverty are a test and guarantee for the soul and a reminder."

"I agree with you, Ahmad. They're a test for the soul."

"I used to think about God's blessings on me and thank Him for them. What can I dispense with in this world of ours? If I gave up power, for example, I'd be finished the same day. Without my army, enemies would hunt me down; without my resolve regarding people close and distant, ambitious folk would move. Without my power and army, I'm destroyed. It's impossible to simply withdraw."

"That's why I've abandoned power and brought my own weakness to God. He is neither greedy nor destructive, but rather generous and consoling. But I'm not bearing the responsibility for Egypt, Ahmad. I've abandoned that type of responsibility so I can draw close to Him and await the day of my encounter with Him."

"If I rid myself of all my money," Ahmad said, "how could I pay my soldiers? How could I make donations to the poor and indigent? Who would manufacture medicines for the hospital? I'm working for them, not just for myself."

"If you rid yourself of self-love, Ahmad," Anduna said with a smile, "you'd save yourself. That doesn't require you to hurt the Egyptian people. Too bad for anyone who injures the amir's pride! Get rid of that pride, Ahmad."

"I can do that with weak people, but I can't with the powerful, or else they'll pounce on me."

"You're viewing the world as though you're either someone who kills or is killed, defeated or triumphant. You see it as an ongoing war and conflict. For you, it's a continuous struggle, but the gains are fleeting. Abandon the part for the whole, the perishable for the eternal. I'm not asking you to do this all the time, but just for some time so that you can relieve your overburdened soul. The world's issues preoccupy the eye, and you need to calm your soul so that your eye can recover its gleam. When the world hurts you, don't give up. It's hurtful by nature and doesn't mean to hurt you personally. It's a faulty, imperfect world, with no fulfillment for the soul."

"It's as though you've reached a place where you're not really one of us. Don't you think like a human being? Don't you make mistakes, hate, and have ambitions?"

"Oh yes," Anduna responded with a smile, "I do all those things. I do my best to discard them and not cling to such things. Perhaps your soul is stronger. I've chosen to get rid of them, while you've chosen to get to your goal by clinging to them."

"Maybe you're humbler. You've defeated the arrogance in your own self."

"What's bothering you so much, Ahmad," Anduna asked suddenly, "about the judge's admission of what you want him to say?"

"Is Anduna defending the Muslim Judge Bakkar? Meddling in things that don't concern him? Daring to defy the amir?"

"Anduna's the friend who's challenging Ahmad and blowing away the dust of falsehood. Anduna the monk has nothing to gain from the amir's approval."

"The judge is defying me as though he's in charge of the country. He's the one who's being arrogant, not me. Every shaikh except him has obeyed my instructions. Al-Muwaffaq is cursing and damning me in mosques and trying to depose me. I'm not doing the same thing. I've just asked the shaikhs to obey the caliph."

"No, you're asking them to say what makes you happy."

"They have no say about government."

"When any one of them challenges you, you can't stand it."

"It's his self-delusion, not mine, that's stopping him declaring the truth."

"Set him free. There's no point in keeping a shaikh who's a weak old man in prison. Look on it as deprivation of self and crushing its arrogance."

"Ask anything of me, but not that. If I were to negotiate with him or anyone else, I'd be dead that day or the next. If I die, the Egyptians will die after me. I'm protecting them against unprecedented difficulties. Ahmad never negotiates or forgives arrogant rebels. Anything that threatens my rule is a threat to all Egyptians."

"Think about it. If you've come here to rid yourself of problems, then consider this the first step in the process of crushing your own arrogance. It's easy to deprive yourself of food and clothing for a day or two. But crushing one's own arrogance takes a lot of time, you army commander, enemy destroyer, and country uniter. Ahmad has a gentle streak that only I can see."

"Where's your slice of bread, monk? Let's stop talking about governance so you don't bring out the very worst in me. I've come here to get a burden off my shoulders inside the cell. I'm going to read verses from the Quran on my own, with no guards or wives."

When disloyalty involves people closest to you, it feels like an arrow stuck in the neck, preventing you from breathing and leaving you groaning in pain. Following the betrayal of his own son, Al-Abbas, there came the defection of Ahmad's general, Lu'lu', who not only went over to Al-Muwaffaq, but encouraged him to kill Ahmad ibn Tulun. However, Al-Muwaffaq was aware of the risks and consequences of doing so. Despite Al-Muwaffaq's enmity toward Ahmad, he still retained respect for a fighter, and admired Ahmad's strength and courage. He looked down on Lu'lu' and refused to work with him. Thus, Lu'lu' was left dangling between Egypt and Baghdad with no one to support him. When the amir—may God aid and protect him!—found out about the defection of Lu'lu', whom he had raised as a boy, he went berserk. He sold Lu'lu's entire family in the slave market as a punishment and a clear warning to others.

Worries continued to tug at his heartstrings, but he neither calmed down or relaxed. His servant in Tarsus, Yazaman, rebelled against him, so he mustered his army and left for Syria to fight him. Sorrow had taken the glint out of his eyes, and life had become like a lake with not enough water to quench its owner's thirst. The end seemed to be drawing ever closer. In Tarsus, I gave him some water buffalo's milk to drink that seemed to affect his stomach. He spat it out and refused to eat anything. The illness worsened. His Coptic Christian doctor believed his stomach illness had been caused by the milk, but I think that his stomach problem was something in his heart; sorrow is much more dangerous than any swords. We took him back to Egypt in the hope that he would recover there. But the illness worsened even more, and the doctor advised him to stay in the women's quarters; he could get some rest there.

Amir Ahmad—may God prolong his life and honor and glorify him!—asked the Egyptian people to pray for his recovery. They came out to the mountain in tears and prayed nonstop. Muslims read from the Quran and prayed for him; Christians read from the Gospel and prayed for him; Jews read from the Torah and prayed for him. Never in my life have I seen the light of so many candles illuminating the mountain as on that night, nor the people of the three Holy Books gathered together in their love for a man. But the disease continued to worsen.

In order to maintain my authenticity and record everything I know, I must note that when Ahmad ibn Tulun's illness worsened, he decided to visit the Pyramid Witch, and he took me with him. But he took Saeed, son of Katib al-Farghani, with him as well. At first, he asked the Pyramid Witch to come and visit him; he felt the end was nigh. But she declined; she would never leave the pyramid, it being her home and retreat. I do not know why my lord the amir insisted on this visit. He was carried on a wooden bed decorated with the finest kind of wood. I tripped while I was carrying him with Saeed, and he would have fallen off but for God's own protection. As we went in to see the witch, I was shivering for fear of him and for him. No sooner did she set eyes on us than she started talking in Coptic. I was surprised by the way she looked at Saeed al-Farghani, as deep as the earth's belly itself, while he looked at her with all the longing of a child for his mother. I could see affection and mercy, but I had the impression that they were just muddled dreams, no more. Saeed translated what she was saying for my lord, his eyes never leaving hers.

"Offer greetings to the ancients," Bahnas, the Pyramid Witch, said, "and thank them for preserving earth and gold."

"Are you going to greet me today," Ahmad asked decisively, "and thank me for preserving earth and gold?"

Their eyes met.

"Yes, I'll do it," she replied softly, "but on one condition."

"What's that?"

"That your trace should endure, O King of Kings," she said. "The ancestors are interested in you. You have done what others have not. I've been waiting for you, Ahmad. The weakness is not in your body, but in your soul."

He gave her an exhausted look.

She continued, "Your tribulations are not like others. When the heart loses its desire for continuity, it hands the reins to the soul to draw breaths. Tell me now. Which is worse, your own weakness or Ibn al-Mudabbir's? Is your sorrow more profound than Saeed al-Farghani's, he who's searching for his beloved and not realizing that she'll never forgive him? What weakness, what sorrow, and what treachery! You can recall my words . . ."

"My weakness is such that you can't describe it."

"Amir, armies have never defeated you, and neither governor nor caliph has stood before you. Ahmad ibn Tulun has always been the winner in conflicts."

"That's my defeat."

"Make your passion pure," she said, repeating words she had used much earlier, "and your purpose unwavering."

"I've done so," Ahmad told her wearily.

"Do you remember," she told him, "that I told you years ago that love always vanquishes? Love of a son rips the heart in two and tears at the very veins. You can recall my words: sorrow is for the mighty, and only hard hearts can bear the heavy burdens of worry. When misery is weighing down your heart, you should realize that you've been raised up, as though you're one of the gods of the ancients."

She stroked his hand without asking permission. Saeed look shocked, and Ahmad ibn Tulun seemed confused.

"Amir," she said, "no one is as sensitive to you as I am. If an army defeated you or an enemy killed you, you could still transcend that defeat. But the spear has penetrated to your very depths because, in this case, part of the heart means the entire heart. The spear that merely clipped your heart has actually hit your whole heart. How unlucky you are! You remind me of myself, Amir."

I can swear that there were tears glistening in the witch's eyes as she looked at Saeed.

"It's a spear from your own self that strikes your heart."

Ahmad opened his eyes in sheer amazement. I was thunderstruck and had no idea what would happen next. I saw Saeed ibn Katib al-Farghani's tears falling and the amir looking at the two of them.

"If I ordered you now to be married to Saeed ibn Katib al-Farghani," he asked forcibly, "would you disobey the command of the Amir of Egypt?"

In her eyes, he saw a glint of light in the darkness.

"Those interlocking crenulations are entreating God," she said.

"You're talking about the crenulations in my mosque. Why are you changing the subject? I'm talking about Saeed."

"I want to be married to you," Saeed told her. "I would be deeply honored. You're the purest woman in the whole . . ."

She interrupted him. "Are you seeking protection with your amir, Saeed?" she asked him. "The Pyramid Witch is only used to consorting with the ancestors. You're not afraid of loneliness nor do you need a wife."

"Your heart's turned to stone just like the stones of this pyramid!" Ahmad retorted angrily.

"My lord amir," Saeed told him gently, "Don't get angry with her."

For just a moment, there was a tense silence.

"Who built this pyramid?" Ahmad asked with a sympathetic smile.

She moved closer to him. "People say that it was King Surid," she replied, "but I say it wasn't him. If I said that to anyone else but you, they'd accuse me of being the devil's companion. But you know . . ."

"You can understand the language of birds," Ahmad said in a soft voice.

"I've been studying it for years, Amir," she replied assertively. "The truth will always emerge for those who seek it, admit their own stupidity, and then be patient about their learning. Tomorrow or in a thousand years' time, they'll realize that they're stupid. In that same time, your own traces will emerge, Amir, just like those of the pyramid builders, even though they don't realize the truth of it now. Today, Amir, you've become one of the ancient monarchs."

Chapter 10

Here is what Asma, daughter of Mahmud the tailor, Ahmad ibn Tulun's wife, told me:

Every day I was sleeping beside his bed with my head resting on his arm. I did not know whether he loved me as much as I did him. Was it sympathy or love that made him so affectionate and generous? I did not care. I had been divorced and discarded, living in the mountains, far from friends and feared by relatives. He had raised me to be queen of kings, the most respected woman in Egypt. I have no idea what he saw in me and why he did not choose my beautiful sister instead. I had no idea how his mind worked or how he made his decisions, but I had complete confidence in him as in no one else before. His sorrow was enough to break your heart, and his feeble eyes rendered all feelings useless. I asked Khatun and Mayyas to let me stay with him, and they reluctantly agreed. One night, he moved to change his position.

"Asma," he said, looking at me.

"My beloved, my lord," I replied, holding his arm.

"Why do you stay with me every night?"

"You ask why? You took pity on me and saved me. You're my entire life."

"How did I take pity on you?" he asked with a smile.

"Don't talk a lot. Shall I bring you some water?"

He shook his head. "I didn't take pity on you," he said. "You don't know a lot about men. It's not pity that makes a man long for a woman. I want to see all my children."

"Certainly, my lord."

"Al-Abbas too."

Before I could move, he held my arm.

"Look at me," he said.

I looked at him, tears flowing freely.

"Who am I, Asma?" he asked with a smile.

"Amir of Egypt, Syria, the Hejaz, and Yemen," I said, not looking at him, "my lord, and . . ."

He interrupted me. "Your husband," he whispered. "For years you haven't mentioned my name."

"Ahmad," I said, kissing his hand, "my beloved and my amir . . ."

"Whether through me or without me," he told her confidently, "you're going to be safe. I want you to be reassured. If you were crying because you're afraid of being belittled after I'm dead, then don't. If it was because you realize how lonely separation can make you feel, then, Egyptian lady, you're not the only one who's scared of separation. We're all impotent in that context. Don't cry from weakness. It's part of all of us."

Al-Abbas sat on the edge of his father's bed, his eyes glued to the floor.

"Look at me," his father told him.

He looked at his father for a moment.

"There is no sign of regret or affection in your eyes," Ahmad said slowly. "What's happened to you, I wonder. Are you angry with me because I haven't died yet? Or is it because I haven't made you my successor?"

"It's your dominion, my lord," Al-Abbas replied softly. "You can do with it whatever you wish."

"It's a trust from God. I'm handing it to someone who'll take care of it, not follow his own desires."

"It makes me sad that you don't think I'm fit for it. But then, I have no say in things that I don't control.

"You're talking about control as though it's mine, yours, or your brother's. That disturbs me. The country is God's possession."

He called in his son, Khumarawayh, and seated them both beside each other.

"What's weakened the Abbasid caliphate," he told them, "is the struggle between brothers and the people. The way for the government of Egypt to remain in your hands is for the two of you to be united. Do you both understand?"

"We always obey your commands, my lord," Khumarawayh replied forcefully.

He looked at Al-Abbas.

"You've never asked me to forgive you, whether today or yesterday," he told his son. "Even if you'd asked with your tongue, your heart would not have been in it. There's no sign of regret. From me you've inherited determination and risk-taking, but not prudence. Come here."

Al-Abbas moved closer cautiously, and Ahmad clasped his shoulder.

"Give your father a hug," he said, "so he can be content with you before he dies."

"I wish you a long life, my lord," Al-Abbas replied immediately.

Al-Abbas moved close to his father and hugged him. For just a moment, his eyelids quivered in sympathy. His father stroked his cheek.

"When I die," his father said, "if God has mercy on me and grants me the blessing of paradise, I shall ask to see you after a long life. I will need you and picture you not yet seven years old, boldly and spontaneously clinging to my shoulder. Do you remember?"

"How can I forget?" Al-Abbas sobbed.

"But you don't remember," the amir said. "If only you could forget to remember. Beware of making war on your brother. Promise me now in front of me and the two of you: don't fight each other, or else you'll fail and lose your spirit."

He looked at Khumarawayh. "Al-Abbas will govern Syria, and you'll govern Egypt," he said. "The army is your weapon. Look after it and keep your eye on it. Your troops are client peoples, Arabs, Turks, and people from Sudan and Nubia. Don't rely on Turks alone, and don't be extravagant. Remember that you're soldiers like your father. Soldiers don't spend a lot of money on pleasures, or else they're finished. Populate the city, give Egyptians the riches of the land, and treat them justly."

The two sons gave him their promise, then left. He then summoned Ja'far, his secretary, and asked him to go to see Judge Bakkar. He was to ask the judge to obey the amir's orders and pray for Al-Muwaffaq's deposition.

"If you find him praying in prison," the amir continued, "then wait until he has finished and tell him that I'll pardon him if he obeys my instructions."

Secretary Ja'far went to Judge Bakkar, found him at prayer, and waited until he had finished. He then informed the judge of the amir's request.

"Tell the amir," the judge replied, "that I will not do what he wishes. Tell him also that I'm very old, and he's seriously ill. Maybe we'll be meeting before God Almighty very soon. He will adjudicate between the two of us."

With that, he started praying again.

Ja'far came back and told the amir what had transpired. The amir smiled.

"O Lord," he said audibly, "be merciful to one so ignorant and deluded!"

With that, he recited the twin statements of faith and died.

Chapter 11

Secretary Ja'far ibn Abd al-Ghaffar told me the following:
The amir had charged me with delivering three letters following his death: one to Judge Bakkar, a second to Shaikh Ali, shaikh of the impoverished mosque that the amir was funding, and a third to Anduna, the monk.

He left a thousand thousand dinars, and seven hundred thousand specifically for the army. In the armed forces, he left twenty-four thousand men, among client peoples seven thousand men, seven thousand head of horses, three thousand camels, and a thousand mules. He left the country and its tax revenues with more than four thousand thousand and three hundred thousand dinars. He had spent a hundred thousand dinars on his mosque, twenty thousand on the hospital, and a hundred and forty thousand on the water supply. He spent similar amounts on businesses, fortresses, and the palace. He left a thousand dinars each month for charities, apart from other charitable gifts for the unknown and indigent.

Here is his letter to Shaikh Bakkar:

"Shaikh, when you receive this letter, I will have died before you. God willing, I will now be at peace. Whether or not you call for the deposition of Al-Muwaffaq will not concern me anymore. Opponents will always meet in the presence of God, but I do not wish to meet you when you are still angry. I did not dare release you when I was still alive because people would say that the amir feared death, whereas Ahmad never feared death, but rather expected his Lord to be merciful. When we meet before God, I shall explain that what I wanted was the public good. You will explain that you did not wish to follow your inclinations or feel any weakness of heart, even when your body was weak and feeble. God will understand and know, and it is not for either my mind or yours to understand what lies beyond words. When you receive this letter of mine, you will learn that I have ordered Khumarawayh to release you. I hope that you will pray to God to be merciful to me. I cannot give you any orders today, Shaikh. As God Almighty says: 'You love the hasty world and leave aside the hereafter.' [Sura 75 (Resurrection), vv. 20-21] These are short days, and we will meet each other in peace. With Him there is no other."

The shaikh received the letter and returned to his house. He died two months later.

The letter to Shaikh Ali, shaikh of the mosque for which the amir felt some sympathy, was in the form of an ongoing contribution that the amir designated to the shaikh for as long as he lived. I went to see the shaikh.

"Do you know who's giving you these donations each month," I asked him, "the person who's designated a sum of money for you each month? It's Amir Ahmad."

The shaikh smiled in a way that I did not understand.

"I'm not surprised," he replied, "and I'm not grateful either."

"You know the amir, don't you?"

"Who doesn't know Abu al-Abbas Ahmad ibn Tulun? His reign is over now. But his memory still lights up the horizon."

"Did you know him?"

"Today Ahmad's with God; he's no longer amir. What's the difference whether I knew him or not? Go on your way, brother, and pray that God will be merciful, as I shall be doing today and tomorrow."

Khumarawayh charged me with the task of personally delivering the amir's letter to Anduna before his death. I only opened it in the monk's presence. Amir Abu al-Abbas Ahmad ibn Tulun wrote it in Coptic. It was said that he was helped in writing it by his Egyptian wife, who translated it from Arabic into Coptic. In the letter, the amir said:

I have written this letter in your language so that it can go straight to your heart. Reaching the heart of someone who has abandoned this world is difficult, if not impossible. I am now on my way to abandon the part for the whole, leaving behind the world's sorrows for everlasting serenity. I await God's judgment and am prepared for it. I have tried and I have strived, but I have not been able to do without as you have or to follow the beloved, leaving behind my money, child, and wife. I know that He is merciful and forgiving and that He admires struggle and effort. I have asked the Egyptian people to pray for me, but I realize that the time has drawn close, and the final hour has come. I read in God's book and regret some things that I have not been able to accomplish. In our book, it is written that there is no loose talk or crime in paradise and that all malice is pulled from the heart on the day of the encounter with God. I am almost missing the people whom I will be leaving behind. Love for my traitorous son does not diminish, nor does my love for ephemeral glory fade away. I am leaving things unfinished, things that may never be finished. Will this letter reach you? Will my son, Khumarawayh, keep his promise? Will brother kill brother? Will there be stability in Egypt? Will the army fulfill its pledge? All these questions keep buzzing inside my head, with no clear answers. If I could get a glimpse of the unseen, then perhaps I would be upset or happy. I don't know, do you? Our friendship has a special flavor to it. No human can befriend the dead. How can anyone who pursues the things of this world befriend someone else who is leaving it behind? How can somebody who slaughters with the sword and severs limbs listen to a person who prays for his enemies?

Perhaps you have no desire to befriend a human being, but, for my part, I wish to keep my pact with you and the Egyptian people. This monastery is a refuge for all those who seek tranquility and trust, who crave eternity in a fleeting world. I entrust to my son the care of it and all churches and monasteries in Egypt. Peace be with you, Anduna, in both lives!"

I was watching the monk's eyes as he read the letter, and I can swear that I saw tears glistening. Then a solitary drop fell, and he shyly wiped it away, obviously deeply affected. He put on a display of fortitude and forbearance.

"I need to pray today," he said. "Forgive me."

I did not understand why he was asking me to forgive him or why he needed to pray. I assumed that he had been fonder of the amir than necessary, whereas his love should have been reserved for God alone. But I did not dare ask him.

"Amir Khumarawayh will fulfill his father's pledge to the Egyptian people," I said forcefully.

"May God preserve him!" he said, looking distracted. "And may He purify Ahmad's soul!"

***

You desire to remain in an unstable haven
Have you heard of an immobile shadow?
—*Al-Tughra'i, Abbasid poet*

1918 Cairo

As usual, his wife scoffed at him.

"You've started reading as well, have you?" Zakiyya said in a gentle tone with no connection to her real essence. "What are you reading? And, if you read something, man, are you going to understand it?"

Adil was expecting what was coming. She would scoff at the way he loved her, saying that he was no good at love; he was not a man. She would accuse him of never performing all his duties.

Before she said anything else, he read out loud a passage from Al-Balwi's biography of Ahmad ibn Tulun, written a thousand years or more ago, in which he described the way Egyptians prayed for him when he was sick.

"Muslims brought out copies of the Quran to the mountainside and prayed to God for him, invoking special intentions because of their love for him and their gratitude for the wonderful things he had done, for his knowledge and charity. When Jews and Christians saw the Muslims doing that, the adherents of the two faiths brought out their holy books, the Gospel for the Christians and the Torah for the Jews. The entire assembly gathered by the mountainside, praying to Almighty God and beseeching Him to restore the amir to health. It was an amazing day. They raised a daunting hue and cry that the amir could hear inside his palace. That made him cry, and he joined them in prayer to Almighty God. The end was nigh."

He finished by reading the account of Ahmad ibn Tulun's funeral:

"I went and saw an enormous crowd of people and a huge number of travelers, impossible to describe. I do not think that there was a single man or woman left inside the city."

His wife rubbed her hands together carelessly and accused him of being crazy. He decided to move away from her; if he tried to get close, she would stop him and make fun of him. That mockery was even harder to bear than Al-Abbas's treason against his own father. Would his own son betray him, he wondered, the son whom he neither understood nor knew? What did he have to do with Ahmad ibn Tulun? He was Adil, whose only task was sweeping up refuse. As usual, he made his way to the Tulunid house or what was left of it. He was still searching, and the story was only just beginning. The city could not just disappear without a trace. He found an old piece of parchment, picked it up, and looked at it. He blew hard to get rid of the dust; colors started to emerge, and shapes were clearly visible.

"Help me, Bahnas," he muttered. "Are you still in love with Saeed, son of Katib al-Farghani? Has your heart softened, Coptic lady?"

The Third Story: The Pledge

905 CE

291 AH

Part One

Chapter 1

Were my heart with me, I would not have chosen other than you,
Nor been content instead with others in love.
But it desires one who will make it suffer,
Accepting neither rebuke nor justice.
How long must I flatter one bent on my humiliation,
Making efforts to please her, while she remains vexed?
—*Antara ibn Shaddad, pre-Islamic poet*

The city became even more awesome, its length reaching the highest heavens. The human eye could not take in all the quarter subdivisions and the different hues of the soldiers. Saeed, son of Katib al-Farghani, pointed with his quivering, wrinkled finger: "That section's for Sudanese, that one's for Byzantines, that's for Turks, that's for Nubians, and that's for Egyptians. Can you see, realize, and appreciate it all?"

She shuddered, and it shook her entire body.

"How can I appreciate it all," she asked, "when I've never even seen a city before."

He gestured to his servants, and they lowered the wooden plank on which he was sitting so that his face was level with her ears.

"Aisha," he told her, "this city's future's in your hands. Not only this city, in fact, but the entire Tulunid house. You realize that, don't you?"

"Why did you choose me, Uncle?" she asked bitterly. "Couldn't you find anybody weaker or less capable than me?"

"It's all fate, my daughter. We all have a role to play in life, an appointed time, a day to live and a day to die. Today it's your time to live, and I've no idea about your time to die."

She pulled the veil over her face to protect herself from the city's winds.

"I'm choosing the man," she said. "If I have to take the risk and accept pain, I don't want to suffer for evermore."

"You will certainly have suffering, my daughter. Although I realize that this kind of luxury was not available to you in your own home, orphan girl."

"I'm not in my own home, Uncle."

"You must choose in the next couple of days. There's not much time left, and the Abbasids are at the gates. Muhammad ibn Sulaiman al-Katib is out for revenge; he loathes anyone who builds and succeeds. Such hatred is a fire that burns with no compromise. Here's Al-Qata'i right in front of you. Choose a husband from here, but remember: you'll need to give him a son as quickly as possible, or else al-Katib will kill you with his bare hands.

"You're asking a lot, Uncle."

"No, I'm giving you a chance to pick a man from among all the Tulunid soldiery, the finest soldiers on earth, men who've subdued seas and deserts from Yemen to Tobruk. If Amir Ahmad were still alive today, he would have emerged victorious with his usual mastery. But he's been dead for twenty years, and now's the time to make a choice.

Her mentor, Saeed al-Farghani, told her that from that day her life would change; she would have to put up with the pain in Egypt, lying as though telling the truth. Every person, he told her, has a day when she has to confront her own shadow; first it's captivated, then it collapses. She, in particular, would have to win; otherwise her defeat would be the end for the land of Egypt. Her mentor told her many things, but he was always patient with her. She wandered through the ranks of Al-Qata'i soldiers, but none of them attracted her, whether Byzantine, Turk, Sudanese, or Nubian. Her mentor told her it would be better if she selected a vagrant or thief. Honorable soldiers would never be able to tolerate such times as these or the inevitable destruction to come. He often spoke in riddles and played with words like a child while she was playing with stones. An orphan girl who had never left the city center could not understand everything at once, like a child wanting to run before learning to crawl.

After three days of searching, Aisha's choice fell on an Arab man who lived on the outskirts of Fustat. She had no idea what attracted her to him. She watched as he trained horses and examined their teeth. She saw him negotiating with merchants, bartering, arguing, and even challenging. His beard was trim, and his white turban emphasized his thick eyebrows and black eyes. He was wearing trousers and a white kaftan that contrasted with the brown color of his stern visage; his facial features were sharp as a spear blade. She felt drawn to him with all the power of winds, whether before or after a day.

"Do you like that Arab man?" Saeed asked her with a smile.

"You asked me to choose, Uncle," she replied bashfully.

Saeed looked at the man in question.

"Well, Aisha," he told her, "you're going to be the first girl in Al-Qata'i, Fustat, and the whole of Egypt who's ever set eyes on her husband before getting married."

"I'd like your opinion first, Uncle," she said.

The Arab man came a bit closer, but did not see the two of them. They were hiding behind a wall. He ran his hand over a horse's head as he spoke to it softly. He looked up at the sky, searching for some gain. She caught a glimpse of his shadow, enveloped in a brilliant light and beating heart.

"Abd ar-Rahman's from the Banu Saalim," Saeed said, "the Qais tribe."

"Do you know him, Uncle?" she asked.

"He works with the police, but he's a thief with no values or morals. He'll wrangle and resist. But gold's better at melting rocks than passion or wine."

"I don't understand you, Uncle."

"He'll betray and commit sin without the slightest hesitation."

"Then let's look for someone else," she replied without thinking.

"But Aisha, you like him, don't you?"

"I don't like traitors."

"I've told you, my daughter, that this is the age of destruction. The only people who'll succeed are brigands, vagrants, thieves, and wranglers. They're what's needed."

"After everything you've just told me, you still want me to be married to him?"

"If you like him, then marry him."

"Uncle . . ."

"The Banu Saalim tribe are part of the Qais tribal confederacy. They arrived here with the Umayyad army a long time ago. Like all Arab tribes, they made their living on army gifts. In the past, they fought in the army and acquired a status higher than that of any Copt. Then the Abbasids arrived and lost confidence in the Arabs and their tribes. They recruited Turks instead. At that point lineage became meaningless; for Egyptians, tribal names no longer meant much. Abd ar-Rahman's brothers abandoned the tribe and settled in the Nile Delta and Upper Egypt. They worked as farmers and were married to Egyptian women. They've forgotten about the Egyptian military, but Abd ar-Rahman hasn't."

"Uncle . . ."

"You need to understand what you're getting into. Even though you're going to trade in gold, Abd ar-Rahman is the youngest son of Musa, the tribal leader. He despises farming and has boycotted his brothers. He sees them as being weak traitors. His father used to raid fields in Ahmad ibn Tulun's time; he would rob and kidnap people. Eventually Ahmad ibn Tulun made a truce with them; they reached an agreement that they would guard the highways and, in return, he would give them gifts. This was the pact between them and the Tulunids. Today or tomorrow, they're going to break that pact. Once Muhammad ibn Sulaiman al-Katib enters Egypt with the Abbasid army, they'll be the first ones to join his army. Abd ar-Rahman's been corresponding with the caliph for a year."

She put her hand over her heart.

"He's working as a spy, Uncle," she replied. "I swear, I hate him now."

"Don't swear anything," he said. "Listen to me. The boy's spoiled. Self-love's a disease for which there's no cure. Abd ar-Rahman thinks he's going to restore the glory of the past and use his army to conquer one country after another. Ambition, Aisha, is a weakness, and his ambition is a door for you to enter; with that entry, you can fall in love with him if you like. Such suffering cannot be avoided. But just remember that this square, city, hospital, water supply, and mosque are all in your hands, a trust from God."

"I'm weak. I've never left my house before. Why are you asking me to do the impossible?"

"Destinies are in God's hands. He assigns each of us a role and advantage. Whoever would have imagined that I would build the mosque and water supply? Rely on Him, and we can start planning."

Saeed went to visit Abd ar-Rahman in his tent. They had a trivial conversation that lasted an hour or more. Abd ar-Rahman looked impatient.

"Have you come to buy a horse from me, man," he asked angrily, "or are you asking me about every single horse in Egypt? Be brief; I've a lot of things to do."

"No," Saeed told him, "I've come to give you something, my son, not to buy anything."

Abd ar-Rahman gave him a dubious look. "Give me what?" he asked. "These are times of novelties and wonders. What are you proposing to give me, man, after wasting an hour or more of my time?"

"We haven't eaten anything yet. Aren't you going to invite me for a meal? I know about the Arabs' generous hospitality."

Abd ar-Rahman gave him an angry look, then told his men to bring in some food.

"After the meal, you're going to leave, Uncle," he said. "You don't have anything suitable for me."

Abd ar-Rahman stood up to leave the tent.

"Is there a single man," Saeed replied immediately, "who doesn't want and appreciate gold?"

Abd ar-Rahman came back and looked at him. "Are you playing games, man?" he asked. "What gold are you talking about?"

"The gold that Ahmad ibn Tulun discovered thirty years ago."

The servant brought in meat and bread, and Abd ar-Rahman signaled for him to leave.

"Tell me about it," he told Saeed, "and be quick."

"A so-called 'claim,' gold of the ancients. I know where it is, or, to be truthful, she does."

"Who's she?"

"An orphan girl who's been raised by the secretary Ja'far ibn al-Ghaffar. Have you heard of him? He was Ibn Tulun's secretary. Her parents both died when she was a child. He adopted her. She became a friend of Ahmad ibn Tulun's granddaughter, Qatr an-Nada, and learned a lot from her about gold and Tulunid treasures."

Abd ar-Rahman gave a sarcastic smile.

"So," he said, "you've come to propose that I protect the girl and search for the gold. Is that it?"

Saeed looked angry.

"That's not it exactly," he said, "but . . ."

"The people manipulating the girl can protect her. I don't protect girls, man. Do you realize whom you're talking to and what tribe I belong to? Do you know who my ancestors are and my father?"

"I thought that, in your religion, everyone was as equal as the teeth on a comb."

"Equal before God. But, on this earth, there's neither justice nor equality. Why is this Christian offering a Muslim girl in marriage? Where's this Ja'far who's raised her?"

"He's still around, my son. Listen to me, so you'll understand what I want to say. Have a little patience. These days, young people are very impatient."

"Go ahead, I'm listening."

"Aisha has no family, and the Abbasids are at the gates. Ja'far is scared about what Muhammad ibn Sulaiman al-Katib is going to do to him. It seems that he already knows him, and there's a dark history between the two of them. Ja'far had to escape. I'm telling you the truth. I'm hoping that you'll stick to the old pact that I know existed between your father and Ahmad ibn Tulun."

"Ahmad ibn Tulun's dead," Abd ar-Rahman replied forcefully, "and the pact's over. Egypt has belonged to the caliphate ever since Amr ibn al-As conquered it."

"That doesn't concern me, my son. I want you to protect the orphan girl. I'll give you this gold so you'll believe me."

He put an ancient necklace in front of him; Anas's fisherman father had discovered it at the bottom of the sea, and Anas had given it to the most beautiful woman in Egypt at the time, Maisoon. Now it was with Saeed, son of Katib al-Farghani, who had been given it by Maisoon to save the city. Abd al-Rahman's eyes kept chasing the gleaming rubies, shining bright in their challenge to the ages. It was moon-shaped and inlaid with rubies and emeralds, heavy enough to weigh down a warrior's arm. In its folds were one or two stars made of pearls.

Abd ar-Rahman's eyes gleamed as he looked at it.

"That necklace is Greek," he said. "You're giving it to me so I'll marry an orphan girl with no family, when I'm the son of a tribal chief?"

"There's nothing wrong with a man being married to an orphan girl," Saeed responded, "and then later marrying a woman in his tribe. I realize that you're in love with your cousin. Everyone knows that. I know too that she was married to someone else and has divorced. You're planning to marry her. All that I already know."

"Do you also know that I've promised her that I won't touch another woman as long as she's alive?"

"No, my son, I didn't know that. When did you promise her that?"

"Three days ago. For three days now, I've been faithful to her alone. I've gotten rid of all my slave-girls and stopped going to bars."

"Three days. That sounds like a binding oath."

"It's one that I don't intend to break. You'll never marry me off to someone else. My cousin and I have a clear agreement. There's no place for your orphan girl in my life. Take your gold and leave."

"I understand you, my son," Saeed replied. "Forgive me. I just want to make clear that the orphan girl is a virgin; in fact, she's never been outside her house. But if you've sworn an oath, then no matter. I wish you well with your cousin."

He put the necklace back in his pocket and stood up.

"I thank you for the lunch," he said, "and the hospitality."

"Wait!" Abd ar-Rahman said quickly. "This orphan girl just needs a roof and food. Is that right?"

"Exactly right."

"Take the necklace out again and put it in front of me. Let me think about it."

Saeed sat down with a smile.

"Ask me anything you like about her," he said.

"When Muhammad ibn Sulaiman enters Egypt, will her presence in my household do me harm?"

"No one knows her. She's a totally unknown orphan."

"Fine. Is she going to ask for anything more than a roof and food?"

"She doesn't need clothing or jewelry."

"It'll be a marriage in name only. My only desire is for the woman I love."

"All the better for her."

"But this isn't all the gold. You said that she knows where Ahmad ibn Tulun's treasure is."

"She was a friend of Qatr an-Nada. It seems that she told the girl a lot and may even have entrusted gold to her."

"Just 'may.' If you aren't certain, then I won't be married to her."

"I swear to you that this isn't all the gold."

"Those Tulunids were stupid. People say that Khumarawayh built his daughter, Qatr an-Nada, a palace in every city where she stopped on her way from Egypt to Baghdad to be married to the caliph, Al-Mu'tadid. He used to put down a gold bench for her to rest on while she was on the way. But five years later she died, and the gold disappeared."

"No, it still exists."

"If I'm married to her, but don't find the gold, what am I going to do?"

"You have that necklace for a start. That's enough for anyone's lifetime."

"If I'm married to her, but don't get the rest of the gold, I'll either send her back to you or sell her in the slave market. Do you hear me?"

"You'll find it, my son."

"I'm not your son."

"Your lack of patience makes you different from your father and the men of your tribe."

"Have you come here to deliver your verdict on my morals or to ask for my help?"

"So then, we have an agreement."

"Yes, we have an agreement. Bring the orphan girl. I will provide her a shelter."

Aisha's wedding was neither a comfort nor a disaster. What had been a major disaster was her mother's departure a month before. She had hugged her daughter.

"Now it's your turn, Aisha," she had told her daughter firmly. "We all have a role to play in life, otherwise why would God have created us?"

"I've never left the house, Mother," she pleaded. "Don't leave me alone."

"People say that intelligence is innate; it doesn't come through experience. How many a woman has fate brought low through experience and suffering, so she's fallen into the well of her own self once or twice? I'm aware of your intelligence and upbringing. I and the whole city want you to help me. We'll meet again in a year's time, here by this gate in front of Ahmad ibn Tulun's mosque before the sun is high in the sky. I promise you that I'll come if I'm alive. If I don't come, then I'll have met my fate, and you're not to grieve."

"Mother . . ."

Her mother had told her that she was going to Alexandria. She was going to stay in Maisoon's house, but would not give her the address. With that, she vanished like a cloud, leaving Aisha in the care of Saeed.

On that particular day, she wanted to walk through the city streets before she embarked on a vague and scary journey to the outskirts of Fustat. She strolled through the quarters of Al-Qata'i, staring admiringly around her. She asked Saeed to buy her some sugared bread from the baker, and then some meat from the butcher. Her eyes took in the crowds of people, the voices of the vendors, and the different shades of the people, so much so that she forgot to blink, and her eyes soon teared up.

"Aisha . . . ," Saeed told her gently.

"What a beautiful city!" she said, looking at him suddenly.

"And you're going to preserve it," he replied.

Her heart leapt.

That day, Saeed spoke to her for the last time.

"Listen to me, Aisha," he said. "Abd ar-Rahman isn't the best of men. He's worse than what you're expecting, my daughter. But we don't need a good man for our task. The age of chivalry is dead, my daughter. He says that he's sworn not to touch any woman other than his beloved. Do you realize what that means?"

"Why should I come between a man and his beloved?" she asked with a naivete that Saeed did not know how to handle.

"You're fighting for life, not for love. There can be no love in times of danger, my daughter. You must be pregnant by him within two months."

"But Uncle . . ."

"That's an order."

"I don't know how . . ."

"Make sure you don't tell him where the gold is. If you do, he may well get rid of you even if you're pregnant by him. I don't trust him. Keep his dreams suspended till the time is right. I've given you the chance. It's his father you're after, the tribal chieftain. Before a year has passed, I want all of Egypt to be talking about the woman who turned everything upside down and altered the course of this country's history."

"'God only charges the soul to its capacity,'" she said, tears in her eyes. [Quran, Sura 2 (The Cow), v. 233]

"Precisely. That's what I wanted to hear. Your soul is capable."

Chapter 2

For Abd ar-Rahman, the world was turned upside down. His father chided him, and his cousin rejected him. She decided that she would never be married to him, even if he brought her the stars from the heavens. She accused him of reverting to his old, frivolous behavior that she hated. She insisted he had not changed. He was still pursuing his urges, flirting with women, going out to attack commercial caravans, stealing, and terrorizing people. He was still the same man she had rejected three years before; in fact, he was even worse. He had been married to a girl with no lineage, while still claiming that she, Azza, was the one he really loved. He explained things quietly to his father, who listened to him and thought up excuses. Abd ar-Rahman was his youngest son, the only one of his male offspring still with him, now that his other sons had decamped to the Delta and Upper Egypt where they were working as farmers like Egyptians. The father agreed, albeit without any enthusiasm. Then it was Azza's turn to speak. His father spent an hour or more talking to her. He swore that what his son was doing was not a real marriage, but an act of human kindness. He told her of the gold, and fabricated a tale about someone looking for the girl to kill her. Abd ar-Rahman would be protecting her, and would prove his good intentions and change his behavior. He would not be living with her in the same house, and he would not touch her. Azza could confirm it all for herself by staying with the new girl constantly. Azza was not convinced, but said nothing.

Aisha gave the Arab dwellings a sweeping glance. They had laid out for themselves a location in the desert far removed from Ahmad ibn Tulun's city. They had erected some buildings in the sand, pitched their tents in the middle, and constructed their mosque. Their houses were all joined together, but their territory stretched far into the desert, where horses galloped and camels and goats were raised. The tribe consisted of five hundred men and lots of women and children. The tribal chieftain, Musa ibn Uthmaan, was over sixty years old and was married to five or more women.

As Aisha approached the entrance to the houses, her heart started beating faster. She followed Saeed with heavy steps and a bemused heart. The Arab was now committed to her, without even having set eyes on her.

"Give me your hand," he said after acknowledging her.

Aisha held out her hand hesitantly. Abd ar-Rahman grabbed it and signaled to Saeed to leave.

"She's safe," he told Saeed. "Don't worry."

"Can I check on her once in a while?" Saeed asked.

"Maybe," Abd ar-Rahman replied after a pause. "We'll see. May peace go with you, Uncle."

With that Saeed departed, his eyes still on Aisha, who tried to interpret his looks, but without success. She walked behind the Arab, who was still clutching her hand, with her head turned to Saeed. She was blushing in embarrassment and thanked God that he could not see her face. She had never touched a man before, and his powerful grip was making it difficult to concentrate. Could she really love him after everything Saeed had told her? Why was her heart pounding and her limbs flagging every time he looked at her and tightened his grip on her hand?

"You're going to stay with my cousin for a while," Abd ar-Rahman said without looking at her. "I've agreed with Saeed that you're going to tell me where the gold is. Did he tell you that?"

He looked at her, expecting an answer, but she did not respond. He looked at her veil.

"Take off your veil," he told her. "I want to see your face."

She looked all around her, then uncertainly, wavering, took off the veil. She looked at him, and for a moment their eyes met.

"Put it back on now," he told her. "I've seen your face, and that's enough."

She had no idea whether or not he liked her face. Her mother used to say that she was beautiful, but she had never given any man the chance to look at it. Perhaps her mother thought she was beautiful, but men did not. Who knows? She did not dare ask him.

"Did you hear what I said about the gold?" he repeated, still holding her hand.

She still did not reply.

He let go of her hand and stood up.

"I need to make clear to you from the outset," he told her impatiently, "that I don't like haggling. We had an agreement."

"Uncle Saeed told me he'd given you gold," she choked in reply.

He looked shocked, grabbed her hand again, and took her to a small tent.

"No," he told her, "you seem to be an even greater haggler than your Christian uncle. Come here, we need to talk."

He pulled her down to the ground.

"Take off your veil," he said, "so I can see your eyes."

"You've already seen them," she replied without thinking.

"Take off your veil," he told her forcefully, "and don't argue with me."

She took it off and gave him a steadier look.

"Aisha," he said. "Your name's Aisha, isn't it?"

"Yes, it is."

"You're going to tell me where the gold is. You know, don't you?"

She remained silent.

"If I throw you out into the streets now," he said without thinking, "what's going to happen?"

A tense silence ensued.

"I'll tell you," she said.

"That's much better. When?"

"After you protect me."

"I've done that. It's over."

"Some army men have joined Muhammad ibn Sulaiman against the Tulunids," she said.

"Of course they have. Is anyone who wants to work under the command of a baby like Khumarawayh's son going to spend his time drinking and having fun?"

"Muhammad ibn Sulaiman is planning to enter Al-Qata'i," she said, as though she had not heard what he had said.

"Fine. That has nothing to do with me."

"Once he enters Al-Qata'i and Fustat, I'm in danger."

"Why? Why should an army commander like Muhammad ibn Sulaiman be bothered about you?"

"In Ahmad ibn Tulun's time, he used to clean the stables. He's bound to be interested in anyone who helped the Tulunids."

"I don't understand you. You're being manipulative again."

"Didn't Saeed tell you that the person who raised me was Ja'far ibn Abd al-Ghaffar, Ahmad ibn Tulun's secretary? Ja'far was one of Muhammad ibn Sulaiman's enemies. That's why he had to flee before his enemy arrived."

"Don't worry. I can promise you that a commander and teacher like Muhammad ibn Sulaiman al-Katib is not going to be interested in an orphan girl like you. He won't even get to hear about her."

"I thank you. Once the war is over, I'll give you all the gold you want. That's a promise."

"No," he replied nervously, shaking his head, "You don't understand. You're going to give me all the gold, whether today or tomorrow."

"I only want you to be patient."

"I'm not going to be patient."

"You've enough gold for now. Give me a chance, I beg you. I want you to protect me the way only men like you can do."

"You can relax today," he replied angrily, "but tomorrow you'll either tell me where the gold is or you'll be leaving here. I personally will hand you over to Muhammad ibn Sulaiman's men so they can sell you in the markets."

Standing up, he gestured to her to follow him to the house of Azza and her family. He told her to bang on the door; Azza would be waiting for her.

"Azza's going to be my wife before the end of this month," he told her before leaving. "Did Saeed tell you?"

"Yes, he did," she replied.

"We'll meet again tomorrow, and you'll tell me where the gold is."

ﬨ

Azza examined her from head to toe.

"Don't you even start to get ideas about Abd ar-Rahman," she told Aisha force-fully. "No dreaming about having him as a husband."

Aisha did not respond. Frozen in place and scared, she covered her body on the floor. Would Azza try to kill or humiliate her? Would Abd ar-Rahman sell her the next day as he had threatened? What kind of fate was awaiting her? She was the one who, in all innocence, had chosen him. She had had no idea that he was so greedy and vicious. Now there was no choice; she had started the journey and had to succeed. She pretended to fall asleep and closed her eyes to avoid listening to Azza's insults. Azza had not offered her anything to eat. At that point, she felt a certain degree of pride since she had argued and haggled with the Arab just like men. Yes indeed, she had actually done that. But how beautiful his eyes were! She remembered the way he had held her hand and sighed. She had forgotten every-thing he said; all she could remember were those eyes. Another sigh perhaps . . .

Then she heard Saleema, Azza's sister, talking.

"She seems like a viper, sister," she said. "Of course, he's going to have sex with her. If he's done it with slave-girls and party girls, then why wouldn't he do it with his wife? She's young and beautiful, not yet twenty. Think about it logically."

"He promised me he wouldn't," Azza muttered.

"How many times has he promised before, sister? Don't ask a man to do the impossible. There's no man in the world who can stay faithful to a single woman. If only you'd realize that. If you were convinced of that, you'd stay with your husband when he decides to marry another woman."

"You know, I used to hate him."

"That little viper can seduce him. All she has to do is move close, hug him to her bosom, undress in front of him . . . Women have a whole lot of tricks."

There was silence.

"If I were in your place, dear sister," Saleema told her, "I'd be happy for him to be married to her, and I would marry him myself."

Azza adjusted her position and looked at Saleema.

"As you know," Azza said, "I've been learning a lot of things about men. They're less honest than women. But they're Adam's progeny. The heart can only be in love with one person, even though men try to deny it. When a man is married to three or four women, his heart still only loves one of them. The others are like bread to decorate the table; their only purpose is decoration and boasting. Women realize that, and only give their heart to one man. Men don't even understand themselves,

Saleema. Abd ar-Rahman has been in love with me ever since we were children, even though he's had sex with other women."

"If you realize that, then there's no harm in willingly accepting this orphan girl, so you don't have to do it against your will."

"That's not going to happen. She'll be leaving here in two or three days."

ⵜⵜⵜ

She seemed to fall asleep after a while, but the conversation between Azza and Saleema stayed in her mind. It looked as if help would be coming from an enemy rather than a friend. She had to learn quickly; there was no time to lose. Her time with him was short. A slave-girl put some food in front of her, which she did not touch in case it was poisoned. After breakfast, Azza dragged her away to work with the women. She pretended to work, but actually did nothing. Her eyes kept searching for him among the men. While with the working women, she ate some stale bread and drank some milk, waiting for him to come as he had promised.

He was late. The sun had already set.

"Abd ar-Rahman wants to see you in his tent," Azza told her aggressively, "so he can ask you about the gold. I know everything, and I'm going with you. You're only going to spend a few seconds with him. Come on!"

She walked slowly, trying to ready herself for the confrontation amid so much hatred. Saleema had said that women have tricks, and that she was beautiful. If she threw herself into his arms, he would not object. Yes, she would close her eyes and throw herself into his arms. Saeed wanted her to be pregnant by him within two months. They were asking a lot of her, while all she wanted was her mother's embrace. Azza wanted her out of his tent fast.

He was sitting down as she went inside. Azza stayed outside.

"I can't stay out here in front of his tent," Azza shouted at both Abd ar-Rahman and Aisha. "But I'm warning you. If you're too long, I'm going to kill you with my bare hands."

Aisha did not respond.

He looked at her and removed her face-veil. She sat down in front of him.

"I'm not going to stay in the same house as your beloved," she told him before he could say anything. "She's just said that she's going to kill me."

"Be polite," he told her firmly. "You're talking to your master. Who are you in relation to Azza? She's my cousin and is going to be my wife. Make sure you . . ."

"I've just said that I won't stay with her," she interrupted defiantly.

"Then I'll throw you into the street."

"Do what you want," she said, standing up, "but you won't get the gold. I want to stay in a place on my own and make my own food. I haven't eaten since yesterday."

He stared at her in amazement.

"You seem to be used to giving orders, orphan girl of Al-Qata'i and Fustat," he said. "Who in your family was rich, your father or mother?"

"My family is none of your business. I've promised to give you all the gold once the battles are over."

He stretched out on the ground and leaned his head on the tent-pole.

"So, Aisha," he said, "you're defying me . . ."

She looked around, then moved closer and sat beside him.

"I don't want to defy you," she pleaded. "You're my husband."

He sat up and stared at her as though he needed to understand what she was saying. Taking a deep breath, she muttered some Quranic verses to herself, as though she were planning to cross a river on her own. She moved even closer to him and put her head on his chest quickly and anxiously, but without any hint of flirtation. She rubbed her body against his without saying a word.

At first, he did not move, not expecting her to behave like this. Then he put his hand around her waist.

"You're more dangerous than I expected," he whispered, their breaths blending together. "Saeed told me that you'd never left your house."

Her entire body was shaking because of her brazen gesture and her anticipation of the unknown.

"No," she replied, "I've never left my house."

She closed her eyes as though expecting a wind storm in the desert. She gave his shoulder a passionate hug.

He rubbed his cheek against hers, then kissed her cheek.

"Do you think you can control me with your body?" he asked her softly. "Who's taught you that?"

She blushed and moved away a bit.

"Forgive me," she replied bashfully. "I was scared and hungry."

He pulled her close again so her head was resting on his chest.

"No, don't move," he said. "Stay where you were. So, you want a house for yourself?"

She did not reply. Her own actions and his unexpected response were unnerving her. He kissed her neck gently.

"Do you know," he told her as he kissed her, "that I've made myself a pledge not to touch a woman until I'm married to Azza? I've told you . . ."

She had no idea how to respond to his kisses.

"Yes, I know," she replied.

"Even so, you're still this close to me and . . ."

"It's just that I'm scared," she said in despair.

"Aisha," he said, "I wonder what danger you're bringing with you. Is it despair that's driving you, or an evil mind planning destruction?"

He put his hands on either side of her face.

"Has a man kissed you before?" he asked.

"I swear to you . . ."

"Don't swear. I've never seen a woman as beautiful as you. If no man has ever kissed you before, then you really must have never left your house."

Her lips met his. She gasped in surprise. He gave her a long kiss which seemed to penetrate to the very depths of her soul. She clutched her shoulder, not sure what to do next. She shuddered and tried to move away, even when she was so close. His bold moves had made her feel happy, her aroused passion eager for more. He had swept away the earth's dust from all around her. Now she loved him; she must love him. Her heart had never beaten this fast for any man in Al-Qata'i when she was walking with Saeed. When he finished with her, she was shaking all over and her eyes were not focused.

"You weren't lying," he told her gently. "That was a first kiss. As I've told you, I've taken a pledge, and I'll never break it."

He stood up suddenly.

"It's as though what's just happened never happened," he said. "I'm still keeping my pledge to Azza, but I'm going to move you to my father's house. But make sure . . ."

He fell silent and looked at her. She collected the remnants of her mind and stood up.

"Make sure of what?" she asked.

"Make sure you don't try to seduce me or come that close to me again. I'm not a man to follow his whims. When I make a pledge, I keep it.

"I thank you," she said.

"Thank me for what?"

"For moving me to your family's house and for everything."

He moved close to her and put the veil back over her face.

"For everything," he repeated.

෴

Abd ar-Rahman's house gave her the opportunity she had been waiting for to enter his world, infiltrate his days, and, most important of all, to find a way to the tribal chieftain, Musa ibn Uthmaan. It was a two-story house with a fountain in the middle that was waterless most of the time. No sooner had she entered than she was greeted angrily by the chief's wife and with a minimum of welcome. After a while, Aisha learned that Atika, the youngest of the shaikh's wives, was as young as she was or maybe a year or two older. She was a close friend of Azza and Saleema. For that reason, she was never going to love or welcome Aisha. Atika, the shaikh's young wife, had not produced any children, and there were many stories about why not. Some people said that the shaikh was over sixty and could not produce children any more or even have sex with women. Others suggested that Atika could not bear children. Apart from his son, the shaikh had had other children with seven of his wives. In his youth, he had been married to his cousin, Khalisa, and had had five children with her. Of them, three boys had lived with them until they moved to Upper Egypt and had forgotten all about their tribe and lineage. After being married to Khalisa for five years, the shaikh had married another woman, but it had only lasted for a year. She had given him a son, but he had gone to the Delta with his mother. He had then married Abd ar-Rahman's mother, who had borne him three sons before dying when she was not yet thirty years old and Abd ar-Rahman was only ten. Abd ar-Rahman's brothers left for Upper Egypt, and only he, the last of the shaikh's sons, stayed behind. After Abd ar-Rahman's mother, the shaikh had married a young girl, but left her two years later. Most recently, he had married Atika, a tribesman's daughter and one of the tribe's most beautiful women. The only people now left in the shaikh's house were his son, Abd ar-Rahman, his wife Atika, and his first wife and cousin, Khalisa. For thirty years or more, Khalisa had preferred to disappear from view and now occupied a separate wing of the house with two slave-girls to serve her. She only ever wanted to see her own sons, and only once a year. She avoided contact with anyone else, and particularly her husband, the shaikh. She had never chided or blamed him, but she avoided seeing him. She was not curious enough to want to see his young wife, nor did she leave her wing of the house for any reason. She set up a small kitchen and had an oven in the garden. She used to bake bread every day and yell at the two slave-girls to such an extent that rumor had it she was the most difficult person to deal with. Her words would sting like a viper's, and her temper was merciless.

Aisha learned all this from the slave-girls as they were organizing her room. She listened silently and with a degree of curiosity.

"I want to visit the lady of the house," she said without thinking.

"Madam Atika is the lady of the house," the slave-girl told her.

Aisha was confused.

"But I thought you told me that Madam Khalisa was the oldest and first of the shaikh's wives."

"Ah well," the slave-girl replied, "she's no longer lady of the house and doesn't receive anybody. She just sits in her wing. If anyone came to see her, who knows . . . she might hit them."

The other slave-girl let out a laugh as she looked at her companion; perhaps they were remembering something that had happened before.

"Is she that scary?" Aisha asked.

"Worse, my lady. Don't go near her wing. My lord Abd ar-Rahman doesn't, and even the shaikh himself hasn't seen her for years. Her tongue's as long at the River Nile itself. Forgive me . . . Don't repeat what I've just said to anyone, or else they'll cut my tongue out."

"Take me to her wing," Aisha demanded.

The slave-girl did her best to get Aisha to change her mind, but she failed. She took Aisha to the wing, looking eagerly at her companion as though they were about to witness a murder and lots of blood before their very eyes.

When Aisha knocked on the door, there was no answer. She knocked again.

Khalisa stood up and walked over slowly to open the door.

"Who's the wretch who's banging on my door without an appointment?" she asked angrily.

She opened the door and stared at Aisha in amazement. Aisha looked at her carefully. Khalisa's white hair framed her face, and her body seemed plump inside her billowing black cloak.

"My lady," Aisha said, "I've come to make your acquaintance. I hope to be able to please you. I'm Abd ar-Rahman's wife."

"Abd ar-Rahman who?" she asked angrily.

"Shaikh Musa's son," Aisha replied in amazement.

Khalisa muttered some curses, although Aisha could not tell whether they were aimed at the shaikh or Abd ar-Rahman."

"Go away!" she told Aisha.

The slave-girl smiled and looked at her companion.

"My lady," Aisha responded quickly, "I'm a stranger here. All I want is to greet you. Please let me come in. I won't stay long."

"What do you want from me?" Khalisa asked, staring at her.

Aisha pulled the door open further, entered, closed it, and sat down.

"I've no family here," she said softly. "You're the lady of the house. I'd be happy if you'd let me visit you every day."

"I'm miserable, strange girl. Why should I bother about making you happy, you little idiot? In any case, what happiness is there in this dark world? What's brought you to this house? Who's deceived you, the shaikh or his son?"

"My lady," Aisha replied with an innocent eagerness, "I'm Abd ar-Rahman's wife. Not the shaikh's. He's the shaikh's son."

"He's a man, so he must have deceived you."

Aisha felt happy to be meeting Khalisa; she did not understand why.

"I love my husband, my lady. He's a man . . ."

Khalisa let out a bitter laugh.

"Yes," she replied, "he's a man. Is it his body or his words that you like? Does he recite Arabic love poems to you and adoring words?"

"No, my lady," she replied unreservedly, "he doesn't. Can I talk to you, Aunt?"

Khalisa opened the door.

"On your way! I don't know you."

Aisha headed, shamefaced, for the door.

"I'm sorry for disturbing you, Aunt," she said.

She was about to leave, but Khalisa stopped her.

"Did I allow you to call me 'aunt'?" she asked. "I'm not your aunt. Isn't that husband of yours in love with another woman? That's the way it is with men—only just enough desert sand to fill their eyes. Don't stick with him."

"Will you let me visit you sometimes," Aisha pleaded, "or is it that you don't want to receive me because I'm not from this tribe?"

"I don't want to receive you," Khalisa replied forcefully, "because I don't like humankind as a whole. You can visit me once in a while, but not too often.

Azza rebelled, despairing of ever reforming Abd ar-Rahman. Their love for each other had started when they were children, but any confluence of ideas seemed impossible. She was serious, whereas he was a persistent playboy. She wanted stability, but he was always attacking caravans and flaunting swords, horses, and arrows. His escapades with women and robbers in the past had worn her out, and she had married someone else. That had not lasted long; her husband did not love her or make any effort to make her happy or win her over. Once she was divorced, Abd ar-Rahman had come back to her. He had promised her that he would change, and insisted that she was his even if she resisted and left him again. She asked him to be satisfied with her alone and to settle down with her. He told her that he could be satisfied to have just her, but in the desert, he did not know what being settled meant. He had to keep striving. He could not do what his brothers had done, leaving the tribe and his father. Now he had to maintain his prestige within his family. If he stayed, he would have to take risks all the time. She did not understand, but his promise to be satisfied with her alone had calmed her down. But now, he had married and moved his wife to his house. Could he have deceived her again? What was to be the destiny of someone who was in love with a man like Abd ar-Rahman? Self-esteem had weakened him, and he had been defeated by love of money, sword, and women.

When he came to see her, he greeted her as usual.

"Our relationships's over," she told him firmly.

"No," he replied firmly, "it hasn't even started yet. I told you that I wouldn't let you search for our destiny again."

"You've had sex with your wife, Abd ar-Rahman. You lied."

"I gave you a promise, and I've kept it. Do you think I can't stop myself falling in love? Do you believe that I can use my strength to control horses, but I let my body control me? No! I've told you that it won't happen. We'll be married within a month. I've wanted you all my life."

His words flew straight to her heart.

"You're lying to me," she said softly.

"If I were lying," he shouted, "you'd know it. If I'd had sex with her, you'd feel it.

I'm used to that keen eye of yours, more astute than the perception of cavaliers and soldiers in Al-Qata'i."

"I don't want the gold, Abd ar-Rahman."

"Whoever finds gold keeps it. If it's right at our door, how can we refuse it? It's bounty and treasure."

"You've enough already."

"No, I've just enough to create a desire for a banquet that will leave us drowning in bliss for a lifetime. Be patient."

"That greed's going to hurt me."

"One last time."

"One last time."

"You know my father won't agree to the marriage, don't you?" she said thoughtfully. "He'll only agree if you leave the chieftainship of the tribe to him after your own father. He deserves it more, my cousin. He's older than you."

"He's going to agree, like it or not," he replied firmly. "The tribe's the right of the chieftain's son, not his brother."

"Are you planning to fight my father, Abd ar-Rahman?" she asked in despair.

"That's not going to happen," he replied gently. "He'll agree, and we'll be married. The gold's going to change everything."

Saeed had told her that she had to get pregnant within two months. Deep in thought inside her room, she hugged herself. If only her father had told her something about how to seduce men or even talk to them. The household women had closed the doors on her and her mother, keeping glances away so as to protect the daughter. Perhaps her mother had also hoped that she would stay with her and not leave her—who knows? Orphanhood felt like spume on waves; it split apart on contact with Abd ar-Rahman, then collapsed and vanished. She was an orphan, and needed to seek protection from a man who might perhaps fall in love with her. But she needed to trust him; that is what Saeed had told her. Caution, that was the way out and her only escape route. Even so, Saeed wanted her to be Abd ar-Rahman's real wife, but she had no idea how to do it. Saleema had said that if she took off her clothes, he might well give in to her. But he had sworn only to have sex with his beloved. What disaster awaited her, what defeat? She sat on her bed, took hold of her dress, and closed her eyes. Then she tried to take it off slowly, but she was ashamed of herself and quickly put it back on. "Impossible," she said.

But Saleema seemed to be right. Had he not kissed her as Saleema had expected? Why would she not pluck up the courage and take off her clothes in front of him? Then the plan would not work. What if he left her in contempt, thinking that she was cheap and dishonorable? Why was she so bothered about the way he looked at her? Had an Arab man overwhelmed her? She was in love with him; that might help. But overpowering her was something else. She realized that she was clever, and no Arab man, indeed no man, was going to dominate her.

She gave a confident nod. "Yes, indeed," she told herself, "he's not going to dominate me." Once again, she tried taking her clothes off, but she could not do it. She let out an angry sigh, praying to God to give her the courage or else to make him more gentle with her.

A slave poured water over the shaikh's hands, allowing him to wash after the meal.

"The end of the Tulunids is coming today rather than tomorrow," Shaikh Musa told his son. "The caliph Al-Muktafi is not like his father. These days, power and influence are changing. In Ahmad's day, all power was in his hands; he managed to rid Syria of danger and annex it to his territory. The caliph realized that he could not defeat Ahmad's armies. Next came Khumarawayh. When the Abbasids tried to enter his territory, he defeated them. Even so, he still honored them and had their name proclaimed from pulpits. Khumarawayh sent his daughter, Qatr an-Nada, to Baghdad as a peace offering. While he was able to remain exclusively in power and not send any money to the caliph, he continued his father's legacy and still respected the Abbasids. However, grandson is not like grandfather. Khumarawayh's son, Abu l-Asakir Jaish, is only fourteen and has none of his father's wisdom or his grandfather's vision. Like so many rulers' sons, he has turned to drink and pleasure. He killed his uncle, Abu l-Asakir Nasr; blood and lineage played no role. He was still a child, and no child can govern Egypt. When the army deposed him, they put his brother, Harun, in his place, although he was a child as well. What did they expect, other than the Abbasid army's entering the country? What I do not understand is why the Abbasid forces enter by land and sea. If the Tulunid commander is just a boy, then getting rid of him does not require armies, boats, and cavalry."

Abd ar-Rahman listened in silence. His father breathed slowly.

"Life's at its end, Abd ar-Rahman," his father said in a weak voice. "We've five hundred men who expect their chieftain to offer wisdom and guidance. You're all I have left."

"I shall do everything to earn your approval."

For a few moments, he looked at the door and then back at his father.

"You've spoken to the caliph's men," he went on firmly, "and I've some friends in Iraq who have status and influence with Al-Muktafi bi-llah. From today, we must make clear our allegiance. I'm meeting Muhammad ibn Sulaiman al-Katib very soon."

"We had a pact with Ahmad ibn Tulun," his father said hesitantly. "I don't want . . ."

There was a noise. To their surprise, the door opened slowly.

"Permit me, Shaikh," she said with a calm assurance, "and forgive me for intruding, but I've an important matter to discuss with you."

The shaikh gaped in amazement, and Abd ar-Rahman remained silent, not sure whether to kill her then and there or whip her. He did not look happy. She removed her veil and sat on the floor.

"Shaikh Musa ibn Uthmaan is one of the Banu Saalim," she went on immediately. "They're people of honor. He's not going to go back on a pledge. If he did so, how could men be loyal to him? Men learn from you, your wisdom, and your sense of honor. How often have I heard about your munificence and power?"

The shaikh looked confused and then looked at Abd ar-Rahman.

"Is this the woman to whom you've been married?" he asked.

Abd ar-Rahman gave a coarse smile.

"She's the one with the gold," he replied, "the orphan from Al-Qata'i. She's been spying on us and assumed I wasn't aware of her behind the door. She's a bit naive."

"Our pact was with Ahmad," the shaikh said forcefully, "not with his sons."

"No," she replied firmly, "it was renewed with his son, Khumarawayh. Pacts don't end with the death of one of the parties involved. They're like religion, valid through life and death."

"My goodness, how eloquent you are! Who are you, my daughter?"

She took the shaikh's hand and kissed it.

"Your servant and at your command. I desire the best for my tribe and family."

"Your tribe and family?" the shaikh asked.

She looked at her husband; he said nothing.

"I brought the gold in order to find someone in your tribe who would love me. Shaikh Musa ibn Uthmaan, who keeps to his pledges and shelters orphans, can protect me."

The shaikh stared at her.

"A child can't rule Egypt," he said. "That's not right."

"It's soldiers who rule Egypt, not the child. The soldiers of Al-Qata'i are the very best; their power has scared the caliph before."

"If Muhammad ibn Sulaiman enters Egypt, my girl, he's going to massacre everyone who does not acknowledge him. That's the way wars are. The victors take revenge, and the defeated tolerate and forgive."

"Are you really listening to this girl, Father?" Abd ar-Rahman asked in amazement. "Are you actually talking to her?"

He looked at his wife. "Aisha," he told her, "go back to your room, or else I'll throw you into the street where you can experience Muhammad ibn Sulaiman's power today."

"I'll always obey your orders," she replied firmly. "You've saved and protected me."

"Go back, no more words," he told her again.

She looked at the shaikh. "But I won't leave without the shaikh's permission," she said. "He's my father and guardian now."

Abd ar-Rahman stood up, grabbed her by the hand, and pulled her outside. "No," he said, "you'll leave when your husband tells you to do so. I'm your guardian. Go back to your room."

She went back to her room. Meanwhile, Abd ar-Rahman's father gave him a censorious look. "You're not showing me any respect, Abd ar-Rahman," he said thoughtfully. "How can you behave as though I've handed over control of my life to you? What that orphan girl said was absolutely correct, and . . ."

"Are you going to let a strange girl stand between us?" Abd ar-Rahman interrupted.

"She said she would only leave the room with my permission. She also said that pacts don't end when one of the parties dies."

"If we don't acknowledge Ibn Sulaiman," Abd al-Rahman declared, "our tribe's dead and gone. I'm trying to save men."

"If I decided to uphold the pact, would you defy me?"

For a few seconds there was silence.

"Father," Abd ar-Rahman said, "I don't dare defy you. That's impossible. It won't happen. Think it over, then we can talk again. Let me deal with the orphan girl. Don't let her put a wedge between us the way your wife did before."

"Beware, Abd ar-Rahman, or else I'll throw you out with no mercy."

"Forgive me, Father!"

"Don't test my patience."

"Of course not."

As he said that, his tone was full of rancor for one person, or maybe two.

She expected him to be furious and was ready for him. She had spent hours thinking about it. What she was fighting for was not just her life, but something much, much bigger. He might order her to be whipped or given a slap or two. That was certainly possible, or indeed a usual consequence. She had neither family nor ancestry. The very fact that she had listened in, then intruded, spoken, and objected was no trivial matter. He would be coming, and this time he could not avoid her as he had done the day before. He would be coming to express his anger, and it would be her very last chance for life itself, not just for victory. She wished that she had talked to her mother. How could a mother get rid of her daughter that easily and make her endure such an intolerable burden? How could she try to drown her, then ask her to save herself when she could not swim and had never set eyes on the sea? Did she like Abd al-Rahman? Did he like her? Had she fallen in love with him? She realized that she had fallen in love as soon as she set eyes on him, before he had even seen her. Her eyes had rejected him while he was training horses, but those eyes of his dominated both East and West. She had fallen in love with him and could not sleep for a night or two. If she loved her husband, that was a gift from God. She realized that he did not have a lot to say, but for her husband to love her was an unrealizable dream. His heart lay with another woman, and his mind was at odds with hers. There was no connection between them, neither today nor tomorrow. When he had kissed her, she had encountered passion once again; the heart overpowered all memories. She prayed and asked God that he would deal fairly with her. Her intention was to make one final effort to save herself from certain death.

She shuddered as she put on the flowing white gown with nothing underneath it. She sat down on the bed, hoping that he would come today, although he had not the day before. She closed her eyes in despair.

But he did come.

She started egging herself on, taking deep breaths and muttering a host of verbiage that only she could hear. She would take off her gown and, no sooner had he looked at her, he would dissolve in passion. Today he would tell her how beautiful she was and how much he loved her. Once he set eyes on her, he would lose his mind and all sense of purpose. Who knows, maybe he could be satisfied with her. Her fingers were quivering as she clutched the hem of her gown, but she used the fingers of her other hand to steady them. All the while, her mind was doing the rounds in the earth's belly.

He closed the door hard and sat down on the bed in front of her.

"I've given you two days to think," he told her. "Today, you're either going to tell me where the gold is, or you'll have no further life here."

She expected him to chide her for intruding or for speaking to his father. But now he was talking about the gold. Why was he haggling? Did she know everything about him? Maybe he was much cleverer than she was. Perhaps . . .

Her fingers were quivering even more as she clutched the hem of her gown. Even doing just that was proving impossible.

"Why don't you like me?" she asked off the cuff. "Am I really so ugly that you avoided me yesterday and the day before?"

He looked into her eyes. "Aisha," he replied with a smile, "what you want will never happen."

"I know," she said in despair, shaking her head. "You don't like me even though I'm in love with you. I swear that I've loved you ever since I set eyes on you."

He stood up with a laugh. "You're no good at seducing men either," he said. "The lie is visible in your eyes. You've come here with destruction as a goal. I've been married to you, and I'm after the gold. One of us is going to win. I can force you to admit where it is; you know that. But I'm being patient with you because you're delicate and unlikely to withstand torture.

"If I tell you not to spy, you'll still do it," he said, standing up again. "If I tell you to stay away from my father, you won't do what I ask. You've come for a specific purpose just like a soldier. Never mind! I want you to realize that I know and am being patient. No more than that."

He turned away and headed for the door.

"Abd ar-Rahman," she pleaded, "please stay."

He turned around. She clutched the hem of her gown with both her shaking hands and was about to take it off, but she panicked and the hem caught on the edge of the bed. She pulled at it nervously, took it off, and closed her eyes.

"You're my husband," she said.

He must not have left the room yet. If he had, she would have heard his voice. Was he staring at her body now, she wondered? Could he see every limb on her body shaking; even her legs would not support her. She could not open her eyes, but she could feel love's fiery passion all over her body. She realized that he had not left the room, and her entire body was visible to him, just as she had wanted. Her eyes were still closed as she involuntarily covered her breasts with her arms.

If Saleema was wrong, then Aisha's life was over now. That had been Saleema's suggestion, but she herself did not think that way. If he left her and went away, how would she dare face her own self? But then, even if he did not leave, how would she face herself? She did not see his eyes. He stared at her in total shock combined with a fire as though he was about to kill her at that very moment. However, his gaze roamed over her entire body. He could see her body shaking and her eyes closed, and that made him even angrier. Completely furious, he left the room as fast as possible, and, heart throbbing audibly, left the house. He was picturing her being torn limb from limb in front of him, chopped up into tiny pieces. Her image overpowered his imagination, blending with his own image as he tortured her. At times, he imagined himself torturing her and raping her, but also making love to her repeatedly. Closing his eyes, he mounted a horse and dug his heels in to make it gallop as fast as possible. But the fires refused to go out. She had wanted something and had almost achieved it. Almost, but then, it was not going to happen. Ever since Saeed the Christian had come to see him, he had been carrying out her instructions and their joint plan to the letter, just like a pliant horse. He dug his heels into the horse hard, till it neighed in pain. As he rode, the wind blasted his face, but the fires were not extinguished.

She put her gown back on, tears glistening in her eyes. Now she was just a slave-girl in the market, and everyone had rejected her. Why was she so depressed? She should have stood up to her own mother and Saeed. When he had told her that she had a role and duty and needed to become the Arab's real wife, she should have rejected the idea. She had to stop loving him; the marriage had been broken from the very start. She covered herself and bit her lips. The pain started at once. From now on, she could not face him any longer; he had rejected and discarded her like moldy date pits.

Hugging herself, she called out for her mother in pain, but there was no response. She curled up on the bed like an embryo searching for the warm embrace of the womb. An hour later, she shrieked when Abd ar-Rahman opened both panels of the door, and then closed them again.

She stared at him in confusion and noticed the fire in his eyes. She froze in place, not knowing whether he intended to kill her or make love to her. When he took a knife out of his pocket, she realized what he was planning to do. She closed her eyes and looked down, her heart thumping. He hurled the knife defiantly, and it stuck in the wall alongside the bed, right next to her ears. It stayed in place. She shrieked and hugged her body even harder.

"Please don't kill me," she begged.

He took off his cloak and sat down beside her. Pulling her toward him, he put his arm around her waist so roughly that it hurt.

"Do you want me as a husband?" he asked. "I'll be your husband, Aisha, and I'll do what you want."

"Please be patient and good with me," she replied, her head on his chest. "I don't want you to get angry with me and . . ."

"Today," he replied, taking off her gown, "I don't want to hear your voice."

She mustered all her courage so as not to scream or talk. When she felt him inside her, she groaned in pain.

"When you're fighting a lion," he told her firmly, "don't start groaning if it attacks you."

Amid all her confusion and fear, she could still feel some passion. There were moments when he even seemed generous with his own affection, but then he would pull back and remember who she was.

"I love you," she whispered sincerely as he kissed her body.

He hugged her so hard that she almost dissolved into him.

"I don't ever want to hear that word from you again," he told her.

Once he was finished, he pulled away, adjusted his position, and lifted her up to sit in front of him.

"Aisha," he told her, "put your gown back on. We need to talk."

She bashfully put her gown on, stared at the floor, and waited for him to say something. He pulled the knife out of the wall and clutched it.

"Who are you?" he asked, pointing the knife at her heart.

"Your wife," she replied, hesitant and scared. "Are you going to kill me now?"

She looked down at the blood of her lost innocence, hoping to use it in her cause. She swallowed hard as he ran the knife over her gown, almost tearing it.

"You're brave," he said. "Are you afraid of death?"

"Yes," she replied with a nod, "especially when the killer is my husband. You're my husband."

He threw the knife away and lifted her chin with his fingers. "I realize that," he said. "I also know that you can fight like a man. Those soft hands have never done any work, and you're used to giving orders. You've never left your father's house; he died before you were born. Poor Aisha! You've had to bear the angst of your entire family, Ahmad's daughter, while the men have played around and drunk themselves into a stupor."

She was utterly stunned. "Ahmad who?" she asked, her eyes wide open.

"Ahmad ibn Tulun," he replied gently, rubbing his hand over her cheek. "You know him, don't you? He ruled this country, but then he died, and his era and regime came to an end. I'm going to make sure it's over so that his daughters learn not to fool around with lions."

She swallowed hard again, but did not say anything.

"Did you really think," he went on, "that I would be married to you without knowing anything? Did you imagine that I would be deceived by your stupid, naive scheme with Saeed al-Farghani? How much sense do you have? I've spent my entire youth as a brigand and in bars. I can recognize lies and smell them. You'll listen to me, then talk. Ahmad ibn Tulun was married to Asma, the Egyptian tailor's daughter, so he could feel closer to the people. Egyptians heard about it and rejoiced. They forgot all about the thousands rotting away inside his prisons and the way he was defying the caliphate, insulting the caliph himself, and declaring Egypt independent. Instead, they talked about his marriage to the Egyptian widow who had been divorced by her soap-seller husband and had married the amir—a story straight out of legend. Asma had no children, or at least that is what she thought until, after eight years, she gave birth. When she told her husband, he was sick and totally preoccupied with the rebellion of his son, Al-Abbas. Ahmad ibn Tulun had thirty-three sons and daughters by his wives. Aisha, the last of them, was born after his death. By now, she would be about twenty years old. As Ahmad's sons squabbled with each other, Asma grew frightened for her daughter, and so she decided to live on her own in some of the palace rooms. She would raise Aisha herself and not ask for anything. Do you know Aisha? Her name's the same as yours. What I admire is that you didn't change your name. That's clever; you don't have to think whenever I use the name. The amir's own daughter here in my bed. Highly favored or unlucky? Which is it? What do you think?"

She stayed silent.

"You really didn't expect me to know?" he went on. "I was aware of it before we were married. I'm not one to be scared of adventure or to stay away from a bit of fun and games. You want some fun? Fine, let's play together. Saeed al-Farghani wants to protect what he's built: mosque, spring, palace. Now that he's constructed an entire culture, he wants to make sure that his own name endures. But what about you, Aisha? What do you want?"

She felt the whole world spinning around her, the passage of years breaking into pieces and scattering.

"I want you to be decent and honorable," she whispered.

"I'm neither of those things," he replied firmly. "I'll tell you what it is you want. You're aware that when monarchs invade a village, they destroy it. You realize that when Muhammad ibn Sulaiman al-Katib enters Egyptian territory, he'll have one goal, actually two. The first will be to erase all traces of Ahmad ibn Tulun on earth; the second will be to eliminate his heirs, men and women. Erasing every trace of Ahmad is the goal. So what's the orphan girl going to do, she who knows and appreciates what other people don't? She'll be looking for a man to protect her; then she can disappear into a tribe. It'll be better if she can have a child, so he won't tell Ibn Sulaiman who she actually is. Needless to say, Ibn Sulaiman will inundate with gifts anyone who tells him exactly where Ahmad's daughter is. Her husband cannot be trusted. But then, if she bears him a child, is he going to hesitate before handing her over to Ibn Sulaiman? What will Ibn Sulaiman decide to do about the Tulunid family, I wonder? Will he hand them over to the caliph, or kill them all himself? Nobody knows yet. Do you want to know more, or is that enough?"

"How . . . ?"

"Maybe one day I'll tell you how I found out, but not now. Once your husband feels loyal to you and your family, he may well fight and save the male children as well. Should he keep some Tulunid heirs alive, so one of them can seek power again in a year or two, along with the soldiers around him? Who do you want to save? Your little nephew, isn't that right—Khumarawayh's youngest son? He should be left alive, Ibrahim, the big hope?"

She put her hand over her heart.

"It's justice I want," she said.

"There can be no justice after deceit," he told her firmly, "no sincerity after lies and trickery. You're bringing destruction to this tribe."

"If you hate me that much," she replied angrily, "then let me leave."

He held her hand.

"No," he replied firmly again, "you've kept saying that the pledge is required. I've promised to protect you, and I'll do it. You gave me the necklace to protect you. That's what I'm obliged to do. But if you interfere or talk to my father, if you tell a single person about your lineage, I'll be released from my pledge and I'll take dire revenge."

"Well, if you despise me that much, then leave me."

He pulled her toward him, and she gasped. She tried to push him away, but he moved her hand and put his arm around her waist.

"No. As you said, you're my wife. A wife must obey her husband in everything.

Whenever I want you, you'll give yourself eagerly and willingly. Do you hear me?"

She fell into a deep well, something she had never encountered before. Trying to float on the surface did not work.

"I hear you," she replied.

He put his hands on both sides of her face.

"I want you now," he said. "No one's to know what's happening between us."

"Do you want me to deny being your wife?" she asked angrily.

"I want you never to speak about it to anyone."

"No," she replied without thinking. "If your cousin so desired, you would marry her, even though she knows that I'm your wife. In that case, you'd never touch me again. What if I get pregnant? How will you keep that from her?"

"I won't keep that from her, Aisha," he replied with a smile. "But no one has to know about who you really are. They all know that you're my wife."

"You promised her you would not touch another woman."

"You knew that, and still seduced me."

"You were married to me, not to her . . ."

"I've told you that you're used to giving orders. She's my beloved, not you, even though it's you I want now. Do you understand?"

"Yes, I understand," she replied superciliously. "Our agreement is for you to protect me, not love me."

"That's right."

When she gave herself to him this time, a bitter feeling enveloped her, and tears filled the well without actually falling.

He did not talk to her afterward. He turned his back on her and closed his eyes. She stayed awake, thinking about what had happened, what would be her destiny, and about a love that was bound to kill him before it could grow. How had he found out?

She had a memory of a past about which her mother had spoken to her day after day. On the day when her father had died, she had sat by his side, weeping as she held his hand.

"Don't leave me, my lord," Asma had said. "What will I do after you? I was so happy to be pregnant, but today I regret it. I didn't expect it or anticipate it."

"Asma," he managed to say, "it's happened to remind you of me."

"Can I possibly forget you, my entire soul?"

The mother related this to her daughter; her father had said the new baby would always remind her of him. She also told Aisha that she was a part of Ahmad, just as strong and beautiful. She was a princess and bore a heavy load. When her father had died, her mother had been five months pregnant. She had asked to see Amir Khumarawayh, who had succeeded her husband as Egypt's ruler, and he had agreed. At the time, he was just twenty years old. He had given her a warm welcome and told her that his father had entrusted both her and her child to his charge. She had asked him to let her have a separate wing in the palace where she could live with her child and not ask for much. She knew nothing about government; she just wanted to raise her child in peace. He agreed without hesitation and showered her with gifts. When she gave birth to Aisha, the power struggle between Khumarawayh and Al-Abbas had burst into the open, and neither the advice nor the words of their father had had any effect. All Al-Abbas would agree to and accept was to be ruler of Egypt as his father's successor. He refused to accept the governorship of Syria; in fact, he wanted to be ruler of both Egypt and Syria. When Khumarawayh asked him to swear his loyalty before the judges, Al-Abbas hesitated and haggled. Khumarawayh's confidants advised him to get rid of Al-Abbas. If Al-Abbas had been intent on ousting his own father without thinking of either fatherhood or blood, then he would not hesitate to fight or assassinate his own brother. Khumarawayh was forced to agree, and Al-Abbas was quietly killed. Asma gave birth to Aisha, the last of Ahmad's children. She shuddered when she heard the news of Al-Abbas's killing. She heard about Khatun's keening and the silence of Mayyas, Khumarawayh's mother, who was saddened by Al-Abbas's fate. Asma went to visit Khatun.

"It's easier to bear than other fates," Khatun told her resignedly. "Ahmad was my true love. If he had killed everyone my son loved, I'd have been split in two. But he didn't."

Asma made up her mind to hide her daughter far away and never take her outside the precinct. The daughter was twelve years old when she started to hear about the conflict between Khumarawayh and the Abbasid caliph in Syria. She heard how Khumarawayh had been victorious because he bore in mind the advice of his father, who had always told him that in order to solidify his rule, he should pay attention first to the army. Pay the soldiers and, before anything else, provide them with weapons and men. Her brother, Khumarawayh, was living in a section where her father had not lived, but he was still a genuine fighter concerned about Egypt and its people. He had so won the hearts of the Syrian people that they had closed the gates of Damascus to the caliph's troops when they had asked for lodging and food. He continued his conflict with the Abbasid caliphate and with those leaders who, year after year, tried to proclaim their cities or countries independent. Once he had defeated the Abbasid caliph, he decided to unite the families so that Tulunid rule of Egypt and Syria would be guaranteed for his children and grandchildren. He married the caliph to his daughter, Qatr an-Nada, who at the time was three years older than Aisha. She had been scared of the long journey and of her uncertain future, but her father had reassured her and sent everything she would need with her. He sent her uncle to guard her till she reached Baghdad. He seemed to have spent all of Egypt's treasures on her journey. No one knew why; perhaps he wanted to show the caliph how much power he had, or else was offering the caliph an oblation to confirm his allegiance.

When Khumarawayh reached Damascus, he died of poisoning, not yet thirty-two years old. He was succeeded by his son, Abu l-Asakir Jaish, who was hare-brained and irascible, and knew little about governing. Asma was worried about what Khumarawayh's son might do about her daughter. What scared her above all was that he was going to use her as an offering to one of the generals, so that she would be suffering the same fate as Qatr an-Nada, who had died after four or five years of residence in Baghdad. No one knew whether she had been poisoned or had died of an incurable illness. Aisha had vanished till everyone in the palace forgot about her, and she was never married.

When Abu l-Asakir Jaish was killed, Harun took over, and the caliph took control of Syria. It looked as though the Abbasid invasion of Egypt was imminent or worse. News spread that the commander of the invading army was Muhammad ibn Sulaiman al-Katib. Asma was well acquainted with him; he had often visited Ahmad ibn Tulun in his dreams. She decided to escape before she was killed or sent to Baghdad as a prisoner along with her daughter. But her escape to Alexandria on her own with her daughter had aroused suspicions, and she was easily located. For the first time ever, she left her daughter by herself; she had left her with one of her teachers, Saeed al-Farghani, who was in good standing with both Ahmad and Khumarawayh. Saeed knew it all and anticipated what would happen. He made the plan with Aisha, but he did not tell her what to do if the Arab found out who she was. No one had told her what to do now.

The next morning, Abd ar-Rahman got up and left without saying a word. Aisha sighed deeply, thinking hard as to how she could save herself and the city without treating her husband as an enemy. She thought all day, and recalled, in her conversation with his father, a certain inclination on his part to uphold the terms of the pact. But if she were to win over his father and create a rift between father and son, then the son would take revenge on her. She might seek refuge with the father, but, if she did so, the war between her and her husband would be made public. In that case, he would be able to tell everyone who she really was; she could be handed over to Muhammad ibn Sulaiman by her husband, Azza, or any man or woman in the tribe. There was no way out of this particular danger, not least because there was a man's heart involved, someone who hated her and loved another. If only they could live together in peace and try together to save her father's regime! What would the men of the tribe do when faced with the caliph's army? What kind of naivete and stupidity had hit her? She did not want Ibn Sulaiman to be defeated. All she wanted was to save the city and the Tulunid family; or, actually, to save the city, and Ibrahim, her brother Khumarawayh's son. A single son of the Tulunid line would be enough to restore prestige when the time was right. If she too could stay alive, then there would be two of Ibn Tulun's descendants in Egypt. It was possible to think of such a future. It was always feasible to win over soldiers, especially assuming that Muhammad ibn Sulaiman would leave. She would think about it all day and pray to God.

ııı

In the past, her mother had talked to her about the way things were; she was friend, sister, father, and support. She told her about her father, Al-Abbas, Khumarawayh, Mayyas, and Khatun. At times, her mother would talk to her with tears flowing, and the little girl would cry too. At other times, she would talk proudly about Ahmad, and the little girl would run among the gold-embossed palms and declare that she would run all the way to Baghdad. She would control the world and fight the Byzantines, and he would be even prouder of her than his own men. Her mother would laugh and try to catch up with her. Her mother also talked about the fear, intrigue, and sorrow that beset the palace when Ahmad, her beloved husband, had died—the amir with the dream, friend of the ancient Egyptian monarchs. She told her daughter about the treasure, the mosque, and Al-Qata'i.

Although she described Al-Qata'i in glowing terms, Asma refused to let her daughter leave the palace for even an hour. One day when Aisha was ten, she cried and told her mother that she was the only princess who had not seen Al-Qata'i. Another day she rebelled and accused her mother of keeping her a prisoner inside the palace. Her mother did not respond, but gave her a gloomy look and went away, leaving her on her own. Eventually she regretted what she had said and went to make peace and ask to be forgiven. Her mother handed her a piece of paper.

"Sometimes," she told her daughter, "people who see things have restricted vision and halting tongues. Those who use the eye to see fetter the heart and hamper its accuracy. Draw on this piece of paper. Make a drawing of Al-Qata'i, of your father, and whatever you want."

She drew her father tall, looking resolute and powerful, opening a door onto existence so that everything was manifest to him. He clasped the sun and hurled the moon at the city so as to wake up sleepers. She drew him carrying her on his back in the palace garden, as he petted one of Khumarawayh's lions and stared longingly at the horizon. Then she pictured him walking with her amid a never-ending paradise. She had never yet reached the end of the palace gardens. Did they have an ending? Her mother said that, one day, she tried to reach the end of the gardens only to return unsuccessful and out of breath that night. In her drawings, palms were blended with gold. Khumarawayh had covered the palm branches with gold and brass inlaid with silver. He had constructed ponds filled with jasmine to deceive the eye, called magic ponds. In every corner of the garden, Khumarawayh had placed a coverlet of pure silk decorated with stones. One day, Aisha had fallen asleep on one without intending to do so; it was meant for Amir Khumarawayh, parent of the armies. When Khumarawayh spotted her, he smiled. She stood up, terrified.

"Well, well, my adventurous little sister," he told her gently, "what brings you here with your pencil and paper?"

She put her hand over her heart.

"Do you remember me?" she asked.

"You silly girl," he replied, "how can I forget my own sister? Even though your mother's hidden you away because she's afraid for you, I can still remember you. You always have pencil and paper with you when you walk. What are you drawing today?"

She handed him the piece of paper and told him enthusiastically that she was drawing her father with his lion.

He looked carefully at the drawing.

"Would you like to shake the lion's hand today?" he asked.

She let out a scream, both fearful and eager. He took hold of her tiny hand and walked her to the place where the lion was. She shuddered, so he picked her up.

"Don't be scared," he told her. "Your brother's with you. The lion's my friend."

She closed her eyes, then, arms around his neck, she opened them again. She looked cautiously at the lion as it growled meekly in front of the amir.

"You're strong like my father," she said eagerly, "and brave as well."

He pointed at the trees. "Look at those quince trees," he told her. "I brought them specially to Egypt from Syria because my father loved them."

He looked a little sad. She was ten at the time and did not understand why. "Preserving Egypt is more important than anything else," he said as though talking to himself. "That's what my father said."

She was still scared of the lion.

"That's right, my lord," she said.

He took her away from the lion and put her down.

"You're a friend of Qatr an-Nada, aren't you?" he said.

"Of course."

"She's going to be married to the caliph."

She gaped in surprise. "Here in Egypt?" she asked.

"Aisha," he told her, "the caliph's not in Egypt. She's the apple of my eye, but I've given her to him while I'm still powerful after defeating him. That's so that the rule of Egypt will stay with the Tulunids. For Ahmad's sons to remain as rulers of Egypt, sacrifices have to be made. The time will come when you have to do the same, and myself as well . . . don't imagine that our life is all luxury and paradise. No, it's resignation and suffering. As I've just said, she's the apple of my eye, so I have to protect her and spend as much as I can to make her journey to Baghdad as relaxing as possible, even if that means building a palace in every city where she stops on the way."

"Will we be able to visit her there?" she asked sadly.

"Maybe. I'm going to send my brother and sister with her. Don't worry about her. But when your own time comes, Aisha, you'll have to realize that you're a member of the Tulunid family. Like me, your father, your mother, and everyone around us, you were born with a purpose and initiative in mind. This country stretches all the way from Barqa to the Euphrates River, from Asia Minor to Nubia."

She nodded enthusiastically in agreement and returned to her house, her mind full of concerns.

Years later, Asma had shuddered as she anticipated the request of Abu l-Asakir Jaish, who had succeeded as ruler of Egypt. She did not know whether she was worried about his request because she did not know this new commander who wanted to be married to Aisha, or because she did not want to have Aisha taken away from her. Was she being selfish, or was she worried that her own daughter might suffer the same fate as Qatr an-Nada who, while pregnant, had been poisoned in her own house five years after being married? She preferred her daughter to remain unmarried.

She listened to the request of Abu l-Asakir Jaish, who was not yet seventeen years old, just a few years older than her daughter, no more. She bent down and kissed his hand.

"The amir's request is a command for us," she said. "But allow me to say just one thing about Aisha that you may not be aware of, even though you are gifted with insight into the inner aspects of things."

He gave her an angry look.

"She's a little bit crazy," she said, looking all around her. "My lord, Amir Khumarawayh, knew about it. Her mind's tired and slow, and so I don't take her out of the palace in case people see her and say nasty things about her."

He looked at her in amazement, not believing what she was saying. She produced some of Aisha's drawings.

"Take a look, my lord," she said. "These are some of the things she's drawn on paper. Here's one of Ahmad, clasping the sun and hurling the moon onto the city."

Abu l-Asakir Jaish sighed and had Aisha brought in. Her mother had already talked to her and told her what to say.

"Why did you draw the amir that way?" he asked her.

Without lying, she told him that she had seen him do it. Now he was convinced that she was weak in the head. He was worried about what the commander would have to say if he was married to her. He decided to carry out her mother's wishes and keep her out of sight.

Her mother sighed in relief. It had all been Maisoon's idea. She had made Maisoon's acquaintance when Saeed had started teaching Aisha Coptic, as Ahmad ibn

Tulun had ordered. Saeed had told her Maisoon's story: how she had been married to Anas, the head fisherman's son, and about Anas's fight with Ibn al-Mudabbir. Asma had said that she would like to meet Maisoon, and so Maisoon had started visiting her in the palace every year. One day, Maisoon told her about her occasional bouts of madness and the shadow that dogged her every day and still frightened her. She counseled her that madness can sometimes provide an escape from a fate worse than being killed. Maisoon still talked about her beauty and complained about her son's wife and the way times had changed. But her friendship with Asma had provided the means of escape: when Maisoon had given Saeed the necklace, she was doing it because she knew that Anas loved Al-Qata'i and had watched every stone and street there being laid. She didn't want it to be destroyed.

***

Today Aisha was beset by memories that laid out an entire house for her. She was overwhelmed by a feeling of loneliness. She found her feet taking her to Khalisa's wing. Khalisa refused to open the door, but she persevered and insisted on going in. She kept pleading with her, as though she had known her for some time and Khalisa was of her own flesh and blood. Finally Khalisa opened the door in confusion, and Aisha went in and sat down. She complained about her husband's indifference, the lethal loneliness, confusion, innocence, and love. Khalisa was shocked and confused as she listened. She had no idea how this strange woman had managed to penetrate the barriers that she had erected for thirty years; she had done it so smoothly and without permission.

Isolation had nothing to do with place; it was all about passion and regret. At moments of confusion and weakness, loneliness can always slink its way into the folds of the breast.

***

Azza heard what had happened from Atika, wife of Abd ar-Rahman's father, Azza's friend, and Abd ar-Rahman's number one enemy in the shaikh's household. Atika told her that he had spent the night with his wife, providing a great deal of detail. Azza's gaze was fuzzy, and the words were all fabricated.

"I told you it was hopeless," Atika told her.

"You're right," Azza admitted.

Azza hurried back to her house, had a cry, and told her sister, who listened carefully.

"What are you planning to do?" the sister asked. "Are you going to marry him?"

"I'm going to confront him, of course," Azza replied. "He's a liar and deceiver."

"You idiot!" her sister said. "If you confront him, he's not going to deny it. He'll go back to her embrace for the rest of his life. As long as he does not tell you, forget about what happened. Hurry up and marry him. You're the one he loves, not her. Once you're married to him, he'll forget her. If you challenge him, you'll lose him. Haven't I told you that women have their own ruses, tricks, and wiles that you don't know? She's a stranger; we've no idea where she's come from or what she was doing before she arrived here."

For a while, Azza objected, but then she was convinced by what her sister was saying. She did not say a word of it to him. When she met him that day, she looked sad. He asked her what was the matter, but she did not say anything. All she asked was when they would be married. He told her that he was arranging the date with her father for that day or the next.

She vowed to expel Aisha herself on the day she married Abd ar-Rahman, but only after humiliating her and dragging her by the heels in front of the entire tribe.

Abd ar-Rahman spoke cautiously to his uncle, realizing full well his uncle's greed and the long-standing, latent hatred between the two of them. His father had announced that Abd ar-Rahman would become the chief of the tribe, and that had infuriated his uncle, Rabi'a, who considered objecting, but did not dare. When Abd ar-Rahman was betrothed to his daughter, he thought the family connection might make his own position stronger or weaker; as yet, he was not sure which. After Abd ar-Rahman's wedding to Aisha, everything had become clear. The uncle had stated that he did not expect Abd ar-Rahman to marry another after he had been betrothed to his daughter, and that he would not marry his daughter to any-one who had married some other woman before spending the wedding night with his daughter. He made it a condition that Abd ar-Rahman would have to divorce his wife first before he could be married to Azza. The uncle seemed to be mount-ing a clear challenge and declaring war on Abd ar-Rahman, who reminded his uncle that he himself was married to four women, and nobody had blamed him. The uncle declared that the brazen way in which the younger man had chosen to compare himself to his elders was the beginning of the end. Their eyes met, their swords sheathed, but poised and awaiting orders. Abd ar-Rahman walked without saying farewell.

Abd ar-Rahman spent the day convincing his men of what he planned to do and training them to use swords and lances. He spoke to them in terms of history and prestige, the past and what had been lost. He told them that the Banu Saalim tribe would need to revert to its old covenant; their rightful place was in the army. Turks were responsible for the Abbasid army's weakness, but once the caliph re-alized how strong and powerful they were, he would understand that Arabs were the most important soldiers. He reminded them of a time when the Umayyad caliph had bestowed lavish gifts on every Arab in Egypt and every army division, establishing a monopoly on the support of the Arab tribes. Their allegiance, he reminded them, had been to Ahmad ibn Tulun and his successor, Khumarawayh. With Khumarawayh's death, that allegiance had died. Victory always belonged to the strongest. He spoke about spoils and gold.

"This is a beginning," he told them all, buoyed by hope. "More than that, it's the beginning of our triumph and glory."

He reminded them all of Tulunid history.

"Ahmad honored the pledge," he said powerfully, "and understood how important the Arabs were. His son, Khumarawayh, did the same, and the army consisted of Egyptians and Arabs. But with the passage of time, things have changed. Ever since the arrival of Abu l-Asakir Jaish, Khumarawayh's son, everything's gone downhill into an era of darkness. Jaish was just fourteen when his cronies and generals took over; their loyalty wasn't to country or tribe, but to treasure and power. Whenever rulers are only faithful to themselves and their hold on power, regimes collapse. When Syria declared itself independent from Egypt, we realized that was the end. In Abu l-Asakir Jaish's reign, the governor of Syria, Tughj ibn Juff, declared independence. What did Abu l-Asakir Jaish do? He couldn't do anything. What a difference between grandfather and grandson! Whenever a governor rebelled, Ahmad ibn Tulun would go out to fight him in person. He was a real soldier, whereas Abu l-Asakir Jaish was just a playboy. When he was killed, we thought things would improve. One of Ahmad's sons would take over. But instead, the crooked clique preferred Abu l-Asakir Jaish's younger brother, the second child, Harun ibn Khumarawayh. He was even worse than his brother, wallowing in pleasures. Administrative affairs in Egypt were handed over to Abu Ja'far ibn Ali, who dealt appallingly badly with the Arabs, Egyptians, and even army units. Ibn Ali was frightened of Ahmad ibn Tulun's soldiers, who had been trained to be loyal to Egypt and not to any ruler or minister. For that very reason, he treated them badly, as did Badr al-Hammami when he took over the government in Syria. Once again, Egypt and Syria became sources of treasure for army commanders, no more. No attention was paid to the people, and there was no interest in matters of religion. Tulunid control of Syria had become purely superficial, and Badr al-Hammami was able to toy with the Syrian people and mistreat them, all of which led them to resort to the Abbasid caliph by themselves.

"No! We owe no allegiance to the Tulunids. People who don't guard their own house have no value. When the Qarmatians appeared in Syria and subdued it, the Tulunids failed to protect it. It was the caliph who did so, or to be precise, Ibn Sulaiman, the powerful commander who pledged his loyalty to the caliph rather than to a young boy who was toying with the country. So, who are we standing with? The one who liberated Syria from the Qarmatians or the one who's failed to protect himself and his country? Who are we fighting with? Someone who's maltreated

courageous soldiers and kept around him traitors and people with special interests, who are ruining our country, or someone who prefers the caliph's interests
and the Muslim people's unity?"

"My brother," Salih said in a lowered voice, "when the Egyptians and Arabs
rebelled in the time of Al-Ma'mun, he treated them severely, using vicious force to
suppress their revolt. Who can guarantee that the same thing won't happen in this
caliphate? The Abbasids regard Egypt as a province that the Tulunids have adopted
as a home and country."

"You're right," Abd ar-Rahman replied. "Al-Ma'mun took revenge on the Egyptians and Arabs when they rebelled against him. That happened, but he also
removed the tyrannical Abbasid governor, and eventually listened to Egyptian demands. If Syria falls, Egypt will as well. Today, Syria's in the hands of Muhammad
ibn Sulaiman al-Katib, Caliph Al-Muktafi's general. He took it over after the Tulunids failed to defeat the Qarmatians in Syria. Now Muhammad ibn Sulaiman is
on his way to Egypt, and, even before his arrival, the caliph's fleet has entered ports
and anchorages. Tulunid defeat seems imminent."

"It's only under Ahmad," Salih said, "that Egypt has known prosperity, almost
as though he knew Egypt, the way rivers recognize brides and pour forth in abundance. From Egypt he extracted such treasure as Egyptians never knew. Who built
factories and mosques? Who built the hospital? Who distributed rare medicines to
the populace that had previously been the exclusive reserve of the wealthy? Who
took care of Muslims, Christians, and Jews? Who sympathized with the people?"

Abd ar-Rahman interrupted him. "As I've told you," he said, "Ahmad died
twenty years ago. In the meanwhile, the light from his lamp has gone out; it no
longer exists."

"But Al-Qata'i is Ahmad," Salih replied. "He's there in his city, he's there with all
his prosperity, joy, factories, mosques, stores, palaces, and houses."

"When the son of the tribal chief is talking," Abd ar-Rahman told him impatiently, "everyone listens and no one interrupts. Ibn Sulaiman is on his way here
via Palestine with ten thousand fighters. He entered Damascus with no opposition.
The caliph's soldiers have prepared the way for him to reach Fustat and Al-Qata'i.
They've cut off reinforcements, burning the eastern bridge that connects Al-Qata'i
with Al-Roda Island and the western bridge linking it with Giza. When he enters
the city, it'll surrender. If we don't proclaim our allegiance to him, we've no place
in Egypt. The Tulunid army's split in two: some of them are faithful to power and
money; others to Egypt. When an army is split like that, territories come to an
end."

The men remained silent.

"When Ibn Sulaiman arrives," he declared loudly, "we'll to go to meet him and
negotiate in the tribe's interest above all else."

The men all cheered for Abd ar-Rahman. For the first time, he was seen as the
chieftain, the one in the know.

All the men declared their allegiance, save three: his uncle, all of whose children had already left the tribe and settled in the Nile Delta and Upper Egypt; his own father, who was still hesitant; and Salih, a young man from a poor and weak branch of the family. He continued to insist that the old pledge was still valid and that breaking it was wrong. Abd ar-Rahman turned and looked at him.

"Salih," he said, "I admire your courage. However, decisions about peace and war are made by the tribal chieftain and his son. You obey orders without arguing. Do you hear me?"

For a moment, Salih said nothing.

"Yes, I hear you," he finally replied.

Aisha spent much of the day thinking. She felt even more confused, and the ditch was narrowing around her. What was frustrating her was that inside she felt a genuine love for her husband. Every time he was close, flowers bloomed and the day shone bright. She was waiting for him today. When she set eyes on him, her eyes would glisten and her visage would blossom. Her heart would pound as though it had discovered its goal. How could she deny such love? What was she expecting if her husband continued to stand against her father? Her father . . . her first and last love. She had never seen him, but had only drawn him at the age of ten. She had kept her drawings to warm her heart and give her soul a sense of security. Her mother had told her that her father was exactly like the drawings she had made, with powerful black eyes, a round face, and a prominent nose. He had never worn a crown in his life or called himself a king, but she had given him a crown and called him a king. How often had her mother talked about the poor Egyptian girl to whom the king had been married so that she had become a queen, about her father's sympathy for the indigent, his love for the Egyptian people, and the hospital that he had made only for Egyptians. How often did she tell Aisha about Al-Qata'i, that city of legendary beauty where Muslims, Christians, and Jews lived alongside Zoroastrians, and people of every color—black, olive, white, and red—could mingle freely and peacefully. Nothing like it had ever been built in the world, and nothing ever would be in the future. Al-Qata'i was her father.

"Is it possible for someone to become a city?" she had asked her mother in surprise.

"Aisha," her mother had responded eagerly, "your father was his own city. He has died, but the city remains to remind people of who he was. Ahmad it was who brought men from all over the world to serve in his army. They lived in peace, black and white respecting each other, monk and shaikh as friends. Ahmad was Al-Qata'i, and if the city disappears, then so does Ahmad. Do you understand? My daughter, what's left for us apart from good works? What is there that's better than populating the earth? Ahmad's mosque, his channel that brought water to thirsty people, his hospital, his factories, his house—they all bear witness to his greatness till the end of time. You, Aisha, are a gift that he gave me after he had returned to God. If any one of your father's buildings is destroyed, then all trace of him and you will disappear."

Aisha frowned and mustered all her courage. She decided to find an opportunity to speak to her father-in-law on her own. She cooked him a sauce that her mother had taught her how to make, and then, with an innocent smile, asked his wife to let her see him. His wife was hesitant at first, but eventually she allowed Aisha to see him. She kissed his hand and sang his praises first, then handed him the dish she had prepared. She sat beside him, audibly thanking fate that was allowing her to meet him and to be acquainted with such a noble person. She expressed her gratitude for her husband's kindness and generosity.

"Uncle," she told him, "how I wept yesterday!"

"Why did you weep, my daughter?"

"For your sense of pride and honor. I recalled your pact with Ahmad ibn Tulun and your intention to adhere to it even twenty years after Ahmad's death. That's why I was weeping. Is there any man of such honor in this age?"

"But Abd ar-Rahman's right," he replied thoughtfully. "If we don't join Ibn Sulaiman, he'll finish us off. He spoke to the men today and tried to convince them."

Her heart almost stopped. "Convince them to do what?"

"To come to terms with Ibn Sulaiman." He looked at her in surprise. "How come you're interested in political matters?" he asked.

She almost exploded in anger in front of him, but managed to stay silent. "I just wanted to express my admiration for my uncle," she replied, controlling her temper. "I'd like your permission to return to my room."

Once back in her room, she banged her hand on the table; the purpose was now becoming crystal clear. There was no place for love in struggles for survival. If she had to make a choice between her husband and father, then the blood coursing in her veins would be witness to the one she would choose.

Her husband returned after a long day. He went into her room and took off his coat. She gave him an angry look, but said nothing. He sat right in front of her, and their eyes met.

"Aisha," he said, moving closer.

"Yes?"

He stroked her cheek.

"I like you, he said. "You're beautiful and clever, and infinitely crafty as well; a princess too. Today I want to make love to you and forget all about conflicts and wars. What do you say?"

She remained silent, doing her best to control her anger. She did not know whether to confront him today about his nasty behavior the day before or to wait. She was not sure what his intentions had been then, or what he was planning now.

He moved even closer and put her head on his shoulder.

"You realize, don't you," he told her, "that life's short? We need to enjoy it while it lasts. You're angry with me, and I'm angry with you. High walls are separating us. But I want you and like you. Who knows, maybe you like me too. Do you like me, Aisha?"

She remained silent, pursing her lips so she would not explode.

"Perhaps if our bodies coalesced," he said abruptly, "our souls might come closer. Who knows? Maybe one day you can convince me of what you want."

She moved away and gave him an incredulous look.

"I promise you," he said firmly, "that I'll listen to you, whether today or tomorrow. What do you say?"

He did not give her the chance to respond.

"Are you still angry with me?" he asked gently. "I realize that I wasn't kind with you yesterday. I didn't bear in mind that, for you, it was the first time."

She looked at him in amazement. She had no idea how he was able to read her thoughts. She did not say anything.

"Don't be scared of passion," he went on, kissing her and enveloping her entire being. "Yesterday I may well have been angry at myself because I couldn't resist your magic. I blamed you for having seduced me."

"I don't have any magic," she replied shyly, "and I'm no good at seduction."

"On the contrary," he told her with a smile, his mouth moving closer to hers, "you're both princess and charmer."

She looked scared and hesitant.

"Yesterday I scolded you," he told her firmly. "I realize that . . . there had to be some pain. But today, I'm promising you that it won't happen again. Do you trust me?"

"No, I don't," she replied without thinking.

"Wives must always trust their husbands," he told her gently as he stroked her hair. "I realize what's going through your mind, but I promise you that I won't blame you today. If you ask me to stop, I will. Do you want me to stop?"

He continued kissing her ears as he spoke. She shut her eyes and said nothing.

"Am I hurting you now?" he asked, rubbing his chin against her neck.

"No," she choked.

"Talk to me today," he asked as he kissed her. "Why did Saeed choose me? Or were you the one who chose me, Princess?"

She hesitated, but did not say anything.

He was kissing her all over.

"We shouldn't be shy," he told her with a smile. "Didn't I just tell you? Today, you're going to feel as if you're delving into your brother Khumarawayh's gardens with all their trees and rare flowers . . ."

She buried her head in his chest.

"Can we spend the whole day like this?" she whispered.

"Like what?"

"I mean, just in your arms, doing nothing else, and . . ."

"Do you mean that you just want me to keep kissing you?"

She nodded eagerly.

"There's no pain in kissing," she said.

He smiled. All the palace walls dissolved, and images of palms and quinces flooded his vision.

"Princess," he told her, "if only you'd trust me, we could float in the heavens like stars and leave the garden and trees behind . . ."

"I do trust you, but . . ."

"Don't answer yet. Did you see me before we were married? I'd like, I'd really like to know if the princess actually chose me out of all the other men."

Today was different. It was as if, when he took off his coat, he had rid himself of all his rancor. He was gentle and affectionate, using love's vocabulary, cooing at her and spoiling her. He kept kissing her with such perfect care that she almost lost her mind. The love that she felt for him rose to the surface to smother all fear and caution. When he had finished and she tried to move away, he pulled her toward him again till her head was resting on his chest again.

"You're beautiful," he whispered, kissing her hair. "Do you realize? Gentle as a princess, and yet as passionate as a desert adventurer."

She hugged his chest. "I want to spend my whole life with you," she blurted.

He smiled and started toying with her curls without saying a word. It was the most wonderful night she had ever spent in her entire life. Today she was a princess; no, a queen. She wanted to draw her own portrait, wearing a crown encrusted with gold, silver, rubies, and pearls. She closed her eyes, not wanting to sleep so morning would never come. Words would then fade away, and he would forget what he had said and done. She was suddenly afraid that everything that had happened had been a dream or jest. But she listened to his breathing and confirmed that he was indeed lying there in her arms. She kissed his chest with a smile.

"My husband," she whispered.

"Princess," he replied without opening his eyes.

She started drawing in her imagination again. The next day, she would put her ideas on paper. She would draw his handsome face, his thick, black eyebrows, and his sharp eyes and lips. How wonderful were his lips on hers! She would draw a horseman with a queen on his horse, taking her far away from wars and plots. She alone was his princess. He was all around her, giving her sweet water to drink from a small stream, then putting her on his horse and riding with her into the gleaming white desert untouched by evil. How wonderful passionate love was, with nothing to rival it. If only her mother were here so she could tell her about her love and the moment he had held her and given her more than she deserved.

She started tossing and turning in the bed as she imagined the picture. He grabbed her and put her on top of him. She squealed in surprise.

"I've no hope of getting any sleep," he told her, "unless I keep you locked up here."

She smiled and kissed him on the forehead. He moved her away a little, but she still felt like she was nearly sleeping inside him.

"Don't move," he told her firmly.

"Can I breathe?"

"Just a few breaths, yes."

Next morning, she felt him moving slowly. He put on his clothes, kissed her forehead, and left. After that, she did not dare open her eyes for hours; she was still drawing detailed pictures of the horseman who would be saving her and protecting her from all evil.

At midday, he came in suddenly and asked her to put on her cloak and face-veil. Then he grasped her hand and took her out to the desert. He told her eagerly that he wanted to introduce her to all his horses; each one had its own name and characteristics. She was so thrilled, she could not believe it. Every so often, she looked at him as he enthusiastically explained to her the horse's origins, its speed, and its particular features.

He told her how he had learned to use swords and spears and fire arrows. Ever since he was young, he had been learning from his grandfather, then his uncle who had gone to Bahnasa. His uncle had often talked to him about ancient glory. For years, he had worked in Ahmad ibn Tulun's police force, then he had decided to move to Bahnasa with his wives and children and work as a farmer. Ever since he was a boy, Abd ar-Rahman had dreamed of becoming the best archer in Egypt and had spent long hours practicing. One day, he knew he would join the army like his ancestors; when the time came, he would have to be ready. He took out his bow and arrow and fired off an arrow that hit the space between two horses close together without hurting them. Archers, he told her, were the key to every battle. Even though he had done sword training, shooting arrows gave him a feeling of strength like no other. Shooting arrows into the air, he could focus his eyes on the target; then he became monarch of the desert, wind, rain, and stars all combined. She listened to him lovingly, his every word entering straight into her heart. She could not tell whether her heart was especially open to him, or if he was just a good storyteller.

"If you trusted me," he said, stretching out his hand, "you could fly in the sky with me till you'd think you were a floating dove. But you need to close your eyes and trust me even though you feel you're tumbling from the mountaintop and start screaming as you encounter an unfamiliar gale. Can you do that, Princess? Do you have that kind of courage?"

"Yes, I do," she replied without thinking, holding on to his hand.

He took off with her on his horse, with her screaming in fear. Sometimes she would plead with him, at others she would let out an enthusiastic yell, and, at still others, she would lean into him.

"Are you ready for the biggest adventure in your life?" he asked her, his arms wrapped around her.

Without waiting for her answer, he pushed her off the horse with him, and she fell into a mountain of white sand. The horse kept going. She almost stopped breathing, and she may have screamed. Opening her eyes, she felt as though she had traveled into the heavens.

"Are you still alive?" he asked, with her still on top of him.

"Why did you do that?" she asked, still shaking.

"You're still alive!" he replied with a laugh.

She pushed him away, her anger mingled with a new kind of recklessness.

"That was not the kind of adventure I was expecting," she said.

"That's what adventure really is, Princess," he told her, kissing her hand. "Today you can boast that you fell off a horse, but weren't hurt. What's important is when and where you fall. Do you understand?"

He laughed again. How she loved his laughter!

"Do you know how to get home by yourself?" he asked.

She was not sure that she could stand up. "No, I don't know," she replied.

He lifted her up, held her hand, and walked beside her. He looked at her.

"Do you realize?" he asked her. "When you trust me, you can achieve all your dreams. Did I desert you today?"

"You never desert me," she said, her eyes enveloping his face, "but you certainly brought me down."

"Nothing evil will ever touch you."

She smiled to herself as she drew his face. She had no idea how it was that the goal had sunk to the very depths. For a while, she had forgotten about the gold and the city. All she could remember was his overwhelming affection, powerful embrace, and magic words. Her life had started anew.

If only Qatr an-Nada were still alive! She would talk to her and send her a long letter. She would say that the shaikh's house was smaller than the huts surrounding the palace where the slaves who swept the palace gardens lived. Egyptians did not seem to live in palaces like hers. No palace could compare with the one that her father had built. Her father was the finest man in the entire world. She would tell

Qatr an-Nada that she was not going to be living in the caliph's palace that Qatr an-Nada had described as being very modest, with no gold or ornamentation. No, she would be living in a house in the desert. Along with her husband, she could see the high wall made of gypsum with beautiful lettering, but could not see the low roofs that were almost stifling in comparison with her palace roof. That was all she could see. When she looked into his eyes, the house grew wider and the roofs extended further. When he was with her, all doors were open, waters flowed from every fountain, lions cavorted in the garden, and couches were decked in magical waters like lilies changing color—from gold to silver, silver to flaming red, and red to blue and green. When he hugged her, she would run around the garden amid the rare flowers and lofty palm trees, neither aching nor tiring. She would tell Qatr an-Nada a great deal; she missed her and maybe also felt sorry for her.

When she had finished her drawing, she wanted to share her joy with someone. Like sorrow, joy needs to be shared. She ran to search for Khalisa; as usual, she was sitting cross-legged, knitting slowly. She bent down and sat beside her.

"Aunt," she said, "do you see what I've just drawn?"

Khalisa looked closely at the drawing, as though she were trying to remember who Aisha was.

"That's Abd ar-Rahman," she said.

"That's right," Aisha replied eagerly, "my husband."

"What's he done," she scoffed, "to deserve you getting this piece of paper for his sake?"

"Forgive me," Aisha replied. "I'm the one who brought the paper and pencil. I can't live without drawing."

"You can't solve every problem with gold, my daughter," Khalisa said.

Aisha looked at her in astonishment.

"Khalisa knows everything," Khalisa said. "Who are you? Your appearance, your gait, your demeanor, and your words all suggest you're from a good family. Do you like Abd ar-Rahman?"

"He's my husband," she replied bashfully.

"Are you the only wife?"

"At this point, yes," Aisha replied, almost choking.

"Till he's married to Azza. Then he'll be her husband too, just her—who knows? What's he done: showed you some affection, told you how much he wants you?"

Aisha did not respond.

"When a man wants something," Khalisa continued, "he becomes as gentle as doves and sparrows. Once he gets it, he'll devour you like a lion. But it won't be like a lion, Aisha. Lions kill their prey first, then devour them. Men cut you up into small pieces while you're still alive. They're just like hyenas, gobbling down their prey without worrying about the screams of pain."

Aisha started feeling a bit scared.

"But I'm sure," she said, "that he's not lying. I can recognize when a man's speaking sincerely. I know . . ."

Khalisa gave a derisive smile.

"How do you know?" she asked. "You've never left your house all your life. I can swear that if he told you he was lying, you wouldn't believe him. Love is dangerous, my daughter, more dangerous than every single war and more harmful as well. Men aren't to be trusted."

"You've known Abd ar-Rahman ever since he was a boy. He's affectionate and good . . ."

"He's a man," Khalisa interrupted. "I love him because he's like my own son, but he's still a man. He was a good and affectionate boy, but now he's a man. Men are like fire; if you rush at it, you get burned, but if you stay far away, you die of cold. You need to approach cautiously and be aware of the risks."

"What do you yourself think?" Aisha asked her spontaneously. "Do you think he doesn't love me?"

"How can I see into people's hearts? I think he wants you."

"There's no difference, Aunt."

"Yes, my daughter, there's a huge difference. You're going to find out. Hasn't his heart been for his cousin for ages? Has his heart changed that quickly? Can we trust someone who changes his heart's desire that way? Use your mind, and don't draw imaginary pictures on paper."

Aisha stood up slowly and headed back to her room. The morning's joy was gone, but the passion was still burning.

She spent the rest of the day figuring out what to say and waited for him to come. When he arrived, he gave her a big hug that made her forget everything she was going to say. As she closed her eyes, the entire world was glowing with a powerful light that reached straight to the heart.

"Abd ar-Rahman," she told him at midnight, lying wrapped in his arms, "I've been wanting to talk to you . . ."

"Now?" he asked, eyes closed.

She sat up.

"I've been wanting to talk to you ever since the morning," she said. "Forgive me."

He pulled her toward him and put his arms around her waist.

"Fine," he said, "go ahead. I'm listening."

She took his hand to pull it away.

"I can't talk to you like this," she said. "If you'd sit with me for a while . . ."

He sat up and leaned his head against the wall. Then he lifted her and pulled her toward him.

"What's the problem?" he asked, arms around her shoulders.

For just a moment, she said nothing, unsure whether to move away from him or stay in his arms.

"You said you'd listen to me," she whispered. "Perhaps I can convince you . . ."

He rubbed his lips over her neck.

"Perhaps . . ." he whispered back. He kissed her neck, and she moved away, desire drowning all his words.

"I want to rescue Ibrahim, my brother's son," she told him in all seriousness. "I want to save the city, and I don't care who wins the war and who loses."

He looked straight at her.

"Who's managed to convince you that you can save the city or anyone?" he asked. "Who's persuaded you that you're more powerful than the caliph's army, more stubborn than all the palace intrigues? Don't take on more than you can bear, Princess."

"Why don't you want me to tell you how much I love you?" she asked suddenly.

"Let's leave love to poets," he replied. "They're the only ones who talk about it."

"You . . ."

"I what?"

She was afraid to ask him if he loved her and to hear today's soul-destroying opinion.

"I drew you on your horse today," she said. "You're the one who can save the city."

That made him laugh.

"With five hundred men," he said, "I'm going to save the city? Aisha, I realize that you're a princess and have never left your palace, but you must have learned and studied. You have to know and understand. Use your mind; that's a much better idea!"

"You're not asking me for the gold any longer. Why?"

He stayed silent.

"What I mean," she went on, "is that God instructs us to people the earth and that destruction is a major sin."

"God has a large number of instructions, and humanity is weak."

"Everyone has to strive and make an effort."

"God also instructs us not to expose ourselves to destruction. Are you aware that today your uncle, Sha'ban, killed his nephew, Harun ibn Khumarawayh, and took over as ruler?"

She swallowed hard from the sheer shock.

"When it comes to government, Princess of all princesses," he told her, "there are no ethics, justice, or benefit. If I were to subject all my men to destruction, God would certainly punish me."

"But if you stand aside while they destroy the hospital for the poor, how many people are going to die? If they demolish the mosque that my father built without stealing or robbing from churches or ancient kings' temples, how will you face your Lord? If they expel people from their houses, how can we live safe and sound inside ours? Whoever sees something reprehensible must change it. Maybe we need to come up with a plan, maybe . . ."

"Maybe what we need is gold."

She looked at him as though she did not understand. He stood up, took out the necklace that Saeed had given her for him, and placed it on her legs.

"Anyone who is married to a princess as beautiful as you," he whispered gently, "has to give her gold, not take it from her. Take your gold; I don't need it."

She gave him a fixed stare.

"Abd ar-Rahman," she said shyly, "it's your right. We had an agreement . . ."

He kissed her forehead.

"Did you but know," he whispered, "you're the most beautiful woman I've ever seen. Your innocence goes straight to the heart. Come into my arms."

Her heart almost cracked from sheer devotion.

"You're the only one for me," she whispered. "I'm a stranger here, alone, a feeling that only dissipates when I'm with you."

He inundated her with his kisses.

"I'm with you, Princess," he said softly.

✠

The echo of those words of his stayed with her all day. She felt a sense of wrongdoing as she stared at the necklace that he had given back to her. He was chivalrous; that much was clear. How she had wronged him and thought badly of him! He was heaven's gift to her, the answer to her mother's prayers to God. She sighed as she waited for him. When he came back, he took her affectionately into his arms, and she talked to him nonstop. She told him about her family, her childhood, the palace gardens, the lions, the flowers and trees, her mother, and the sketches that had saved her from the marriage plans that Abu l-Asakir Jaish had arranged for her. All the while, he was listening carefully and occasionally asking her a question.

"How could you sleep in your mother's room?" he asked.

"I used to go to sleep in her arms till she departed," she said, overwhelmed by nostalgia. "I'm scared of the dark and being alone. How welcoming her arms were! I used to sneak into her room at night and sleep in her bed."

"Maybe she was the one scared of the dark," he said with a smile. "She didn't like being on her own."

"She protected me against all intrigues."

"But why didn't she give you the chance to get married? Who knows? Maybe the husband whom Abu l-Asakir had chosen for you was suitable?"

"If I'd been married to him," she replied eagerly, "I wouldn't have been married to you. I can't imagine my life without you."

She talked about her father and Khumarawayh, who had been assassinated by traitors after he had defeated the Abbasid caliph and taken control of border provinces and ports. When he was murdered by his servant, he was not yet twenty-two and fighting revolts in Syria. They brought his body back to Egypt because he had said he wanted to be buried there by the mountainside. Khumarawayh was a bit extravagant and did not keep a close eye on money the way Ahmad had done. Even so, he took care of the army and was lenient and kind with all Egyptians. She told Abd ar-Rahman about Ja'far ibn Abd al-Ghaffar and Saeed al-Farghani, and their loyalty to her father even after his death. Both of them had looked after her and her mother. Saeed had become her teacher; instead of teaching her poetry, he had shown her how to draw. Aisha told him how she and her mother shared a secret language, Coptic, which only Egyptians could understand. Her mother had insisted that she learn the language so it could serve as a means of communication between the two of them when the whole family was assembled. She told Abd ar-Rahman how her mother had held her hand as she assigned her daughter to Saeed's care, informing her that the destiny of all Egypt was in her hands. For some time, the Tulunid family had been struck by a curse, and she, Aisha, Ahmad's daughter, was the only one who could save them from the curse. Aisha also told him the story of Anas and Maisoon, and the necklace that had been witness to love, disappointment, and loss.

She spent the whole day telling him fresh stories about the Tulunid house; sometimes about her mother and Ahmad, at others about Ahmad and the Egyptian monk, Anduna, and still others about Al-Abbas and the way he had betrayed his father and crushed his heart even before he had died. Aisha said that she knew all her father's wives, and respected Mayyas, Khumarawayh's mother, who never had much to say, and never interfered in anything or tried to dominate, even when her son succeeded his father. She sympathized with Khatun, Al-Abbas's mother, who spent the rest of her life sad and wounded. Her sorrow had started as soon as her son rebelled because she realized that her own son was as good as dead, whether at the hands of his father or brother, because he had so mishandled everything.

When Abd ar-Rahman asked her about Ahmad's prisoners, especially Judge Bakkar ibn Qutaiba, and Ahmad's impatience and stubbornness, she told him instead about his generosity, sympathy, and justice in dealing with the Egyptian people.

"Abd ar-Rahman," she told him eagerly, "if Ahmad had been a tyrant, why would Egyptians have gone out to the mountain to pray to God and ask that he be cured? Why would Muslims, Christians, and Jews gather and beseech God to preserve Ahmad's soul?"

"Aisha," Abd ar-Rahman responded, "if the ruler tells people to pray, then they're bound to go out and do that. Even when a ruler is close to death, he still knows how many people there are and what their names are. He can still take revenge on people who disobey his commands."

"If you're correct, my husband," she said gently, "then why did all Egypt come out for his funeral? When a ruler's dead, no one knows names any longer to take revenge. Isn't that so? Did a single Egyptian stay at home on the day of my father's funeral?"

He thought for a moment.

"I agree with you," he said, "that people who want to attend a funeral will do so, but cannot be forced to do so."

"At my father's funeral, Abd ar-Rahman, not a single child or woman stayed away."

"I don't know," he replied with a smile, "whether to be jealous of your mother who wrapped you in a love that leaves no place in your heart for anyone else, or of your father whom you never met but who is in complete control of your mind."

"You don't need to be jealous," she told him gently. "You're my treasure, my gold, my everything."

🏯

Abd ar-Rahman told her how he had found out that she was Ahmad's daughter. When Saeed had spoken to him for the first time, he sent some men to Saeed's house as though they were intent on housebreaking and burglary. They did steal a few things, but their real interest was to find out information about Saeed, maybe a letter he had written to someone who knew who the orphan girl was. The men came back with the entire contents of Saeed's house. He soon found a letter—from Qatr an-Nada to Ahmad's daughter, Aisha. Abd ar-Rahman handed Aisha the letter.

Here is the letter:

In the Name of God, the Compassionate, the Merciful.

May God prolong your peace, my dear; may He fulfill His blessings upon you; may He increase his goodness toward you and His preference with respect to you!

I am writing you this letter from the caliph's palace in Baghdad. How I miss our palace, Aisha, and how I miss you and taking walks through the quince trees. The caliph's palace is wide, but ours goes on forever. The caliph has lofty gardens, but ours reach up to the very heavens. The caliph's mosques are beautiful, but the alcoves of my grandfather's mosque are incomparable in their beauty and size. Can you imagine, Aisha, that the caliph's palace has no golden patterns and no delicate lamps like the ones in our palace? It is not comparable to our palace. I miss Egypt, Aisha, and realize that I will never return there. The caliph—may

God support him!—treats me well, but I am afraid of the intrigues all around me. I have heard it said that the caliph's favorite wife is bound to be poisoned by his slave-girls and die; any woman who bears him a child has to be killed. Every single day, I am afraid to eat and drink. I sit by myself in the harem, fully aware that death is my destiny. Ever since my father died, Aisha, I have been scared. May God help you, my one and only friend! Are you married now, dear sister? Forgive me. My letters have never arrived, and perhaps this one will not reach you either—who knows? How old are you now? You are about fifteen or so, and I am twenty, but I feel well over a hundred!

I wrote to you about the argument I had with the caliph. I was stupid at first; at the time I was still fifteen years old. On our wedding night, the caliph came in and greeted me.

"Khumarawayh's daughter," he said, "you need to thank me for keeping your father as Governor of Egypt, to be followed by his descendants for thirty years."

"My lord," I replied without even thinking, "you need to thank me because our marriage gives you a guarantee of safety from my father's armies that defeated the caliph earlier. Through your marriage to me you're acknowledging my father's rule."

With that, he left me for a month as punishment for speaking my mind. I felt a little sorry, but mostly happy. Do you remember, Aisha, when we talked about love? Do you remember your drawings of a cavalier who would rescue us and take us far away? Aisha, people say that that kind of drawing is forbidden. I think they're right, not because it angers God, but because it's a lie. Anyone associated with cavaliers tumbles into Joseph's well, but without finding any men to save and rescue them. Dear sister, we have no cavaliers or love for us.

If this letter reaches you, know that I'm still well, even though I'm pregnant. I'm scared in case something I drink will contain a poison that will slowly kill me. Never mind! All my prayers to God are for you! God bless you!

Your brother's daughter and sister! Asma, daughter of Khumarawayh, son of Ahmad ibn Tulun,

Qatr an-Nada.

Aisha clutched the letter affectionately and told Abd ar-Rahman about Qatr an-Nada's unhappiness and her marriage to the caliph.

Sometimes he would come by at midday and take her with him into the desert. He would talk to her, and they would exchange stories. She told him about her mother's strategy that had saved her from being married to a general. He listened carefully.

"Why do you keep drawing these weird things, Aisha?" he asked her. "Why do you draw things you don't see?"

"I draw what I do see," she insisted.

"But you drew your father holding the sun."

"That's the way I saw him."

"So, do you see things that we don't, or is it that you only see what you want to see?"

"Why do you live in the desert," she suddenly asked, looking all around her, "when the blessed River Nile provides its bounty and is generous to those near to it?"

For a while he said nothing.

"My brothers moved to the Delta and Upper Egypt and settled there," he replied. "They chose to be farmers, forgetting their ancestors' prestige. They're behaving like Egyptians, even though they're Bedouin Arabs."

"What's so bad about Egyptians, Abd ar-Rahman?"

"Egyptians are farmers, but Arabs are fighters. Ever since the time of Amr ibn al-As, Arabs fought in his army. Then in the Umayyad era, Arabs were army soldiers. We can't forget who we are. What my brothers did is a betrayal of our ancestors. Who conquered Egypt, Aisha? Arabs. Who conquered Syria, Iraq, and other countries? Bedouin Arab soldiers."

"But Ahmad ibn Tulun was in the Egyptian army too."

"He was an Egyptian of foreign birth, and always will be."

"But you're living on Egyptian soil."

"It's my country, and each of us has a role to play. I've a tribe and house in the desert. Desert-dwellers are not tempted by rivers. I'm going to wait for the day when our ancient prestige is restored. I shall keep training diligently every day. The day will come when the Abbasids will recognize the value of Arab soldiers."

"It's almost as if you think you're better than me," she teased him. "I'm Egyptian."

"I live on its soil; it's my country and homeland. You're Egyptian and I'm Arab. As I've told you, we both have roles. What my brothers did is a betrayal of our tribe. I'll never forgive them."

"I don't know what's so fascinating about the desert."

He held her hand and walked with her for an hour or more. He carried her to the very top of a hill, then pushed her so that she rolled all the way down to the bottom. He followed behind her as she screamed and tried to grab him. She kept laughing and asking him for help. She finally reached the bottom, panting and with him on top of her.

"What do you think of the desert now?" he asked her.

She looked into his eyes.

"I love it," she replied.

Aisha spent a whole month in paradise, with love growing every day. There was much talk and laughter. Everything was on an even keel. Every day, she would go to visit Khalisa, even if she refused to see her. She would talk to her eagerly, while Khalisa chewed her lips and said nothing. One morning, when Aisha awoke, an inner voice penetrated her mind, and she had a feeling of serenity. She went out to the desert and breathed in the air, then bent down and picked up some sand. She wanted just one thing, and that was to tell her husband where the gold was. He was faithful to her, affectionate, and loving, and always listened to her tales with a patient understanding. Indeed, she could almost swear that he now admired and revered her father and was convinced by her arguments. It could no longer be a barrier between the two of them. Who knows, he might use the gold to help her, save the city perhaps, and even . . .

She put her hand over her heart that was crying out with hot pain and joy as she contemplated these thoughts. Maybe he would never marry Azza and would be content with her alone, but then maybe not. She was not going to think about that now. At this point, she did not want there to be any barrier between them. She wanted to make clear how much she trusted and loved him. Who would not be in love with a man like her husband? She waited for him with all the eagerness of a young child who is going to confess to his father what has happened that day. As usual, she started talking to him nonstop.

When she finished, he kissed her so earnestly that she forgot what she was going to say and what was going to happen.

"Abd ar-Rahman," she said after a while, nestling in his arms, "if you promise to help me, I'll tell you today where the gold is. Tonight, I mean. I trust you. You've given me back the necklace . . . and I understand why you're annoyed. I promise that I'll never lie to you again. Just promise to help me."

"Why are you trusting me?" he asked, whistling in amazement. "What would you do if I did promise and then broke the promise?"

"You won't. You never break your promises."

"That's something different," he replied disconcerted. "I'm your husband, and . . ."

She opened her hand, and he kissed it.

"No man can possibly resist your magic," he told her.

"That's not what I meant."

"I promised Azza that I would marry her," he said without thinking.

She put her hand over her heart.

"If you promise me," she stuttered, "I'll tell you where the gold is."

He held her hand and rubbed it.

"What will you do when I'm married to Azza?" he asked.

"You'll save the city first."

"Why are you avoiding the question?" he asked, still holding her hand.

"Because there's nothing I can do about it."

"I promise to help you," he replied with a smile. "However, Princess, it's not for you to tell me where the gold is."

"On the contrary, you'll need it to help me," she replied assuredly. "I want to tell you."

"Only tell me when you're absolutely sure about me," he told her firmly.

"I've been sure for a while," she declared.

"How can you trust me when you've only known me for less than a month?"

"Abd ar-Rahman," she said, "I've given myself to you, body and soul. What's so important about gold? It's nothing when compared with the soul."

He remained silent.

"The adventurer is someone who's going to save the city," she went on slowly. "He's the cavalier, and you're the one."

He put his finger on her lips.

"I've promised to help you," he said. "Help's more important to you than my being married to Azza. Isn't that right? Do you trust me?"

"I love you," she said spontaneously.

"I didn't ask you about love. I asked whether you trust me."

"If I love you, I have to trust you. I've told you that before."

"You're tying love to trust and promises to gold. You keep drawing a cavalier on a white horse. Are all Tulunid princesses like you?"

"You're my husband and my beloved . . ."

He looked into her eyes. "Tell me," he asked with a joyful, triumphant smile, "why did Saeed choose me?"

"He gave me the choice of all my father's soldiers and men," she replied bashfully, stroking his beard. "I chose you. Ever since first seeing you, I've seen you with my heart."

"You chose me yourself," he said softly, "without knowing a thing about me. You've got insight, Princess of princesses. Where's the gold?"

Slowly she described the place at the bottom of the mountain where her mother had hidden it before she died.

"Abd ar-Rahman," she told him after she had finished her description, "I've entrusted my soul, my money, my entire life to you. I've given you everything. Don't betray me."

"We've been married for thirty days and nights," he replied as he held her tight. "You've known me for a month perhaps, and now you've told me where the gold is. You've had sex with me for even less time than that. Do you have a mind to think with?"

"I think with my heart that tells the truth."

"Your mother never told you not to think with your heart?"

"You'll never betray me, will you?" she pleaded.

"You're the one answering that question, not me."

She hugged him hard.

"I know the answer," she said.

"So do I," he replied, pulling her close to his heart. "I thought you were different when you came to me here in disguise and tried to seduce me, even though your innocence would make the very cradle blush. But you're not a baby in a cradle. Go to sleep, Princess. Who knows what tomorrow will bring?"

👥

The next morning, Aisha felt a bit sorry and anxious. She was somewhat doubtful, wondering if she had made a mistake in telling him where the gold was. She was worried that his attitude toward her would change and that everything that had happened between the two of them would disappear like foam in the sea. But when he came home as usual at night, he gave her the same loving greeting with the same passion. She chided herself for having doubts and thinking the worst. Every single day, he greeted her with the same passion, and she blamed herself more and more, feeling guilty about the Arab cavalier who never betrayed her or broke his pledge, a man who loved with all the subtlety of pre-Islamic poets and fought with the same level of savagery. As week followed week, the affection remained a constant. Then a visitor arrived, Saeed al-Farghani.

Saeed was feeling somewhat anxious as he stood there waiting for Abd ar-Rahman to come back. When he saw him, he asked earnestly about Aisha and requested to see her. Abd ar-Rahman invited him into the house and asked his wife to come and see Saeed.

She was delighted to see him and asked eagerly how he was. The delight in her expression made Saeed even more worried and pessimistic.

"May I have a word with Aisha alone?" he asked Abd ar-Rahman gently.

"No," he replied without thinking.

"She's like my own daughter, my son," Saeed said. "She's under my protection. I just need to make sure about her."

"That's my job. Her husband's her protector now."

Saeed looked at her.

"How are you?" Saeed asked in Coptic. "I don't know if he understands our language, but I doubt it. Arabs don't learn Coptic. Is he treating you badly?"

She looked at her husband who was resting his chin on his hand and staring at her without saying a word.

"He's a wonderful husband, Uncle," she replied in Coptic, "a genuine man who's promised to help me."

"So, you have your own secret language then!" Abd ar-Rahman commented with a smile.

"Uncle Saeed just wants to check on me, that's all," she pleaded with her husband. "Forgive me for talking to him in a language you don't understand."

Saeed gave her a chiding glance for asking Abd ar-Rahman to forgive her, as though she was being too submissive.

Abd ar-Rahman looked at Saeed as though he wanted to provoke him.

"Use any language you like, Aisha," he said. "I trust you."

Saeed looked at her in astonishment.

"How has he promised to help you?" he asked. "What's happened between the two of you?"

"He's a wonderful husband, Uncle," she said. "He treats me well; in fact, he spoils me. I don't do any housework; all I do is sit with him and wait for him to come home. He's kept his pledge."

"Does he know who you really are, Aisha?"

She looked at her husband who had turned away.

"Yes, he does."

"I knew he'd find out. He broke into my house one night and stole a letter from Qatr an-Nada. How can you trust someone who intrudes and steals things?"

"My heart believes him, Uncle," she replied firmly. "We lied to him, so what he's done was fully expected."

Saeed sighed in despair.

"Love always manages to scramble feelings," he went on angrily. "There's no point. Listen to me carefully. Love him all you want, but make sure you don't tell him where the gold is. Do you hear me?"

Abd ar-Rahman looked at Aisha.

"What's he saying? Is he threatening you?"

"Don't worry," she replied edgily. "He's talking about the past."

For some reason, she felt somewhat guilty.

"I've told him where the gold is, Uncle," she said. "Please don't be angry with me. I trust him."

"Have you gone mad?" he yelled at her.

Abd ar-Rahman looked at him, not knowing what Aisha had told him in Coptic to provoke such an outburst. But he did not say anything.

"Uncle," she said, "he's given me back the necklace without my even asking for it. He's promised to help me."

Saeed looked all around him, confused and in despair.

"How has he promised to help you?" he asked. "Has he said he'll attack Ibn Sulaiman?"

"No, he's said he'll help me."

"From his point of view, he's helping you now by protecting you against Ibn Sulaiman. Don't you understand? He hasn't promised anything. After a single month of marriage, love's blinded your heart. Did you but know, I feel sorry for you, your mother, and your father whom you've abandoned today. How many times have I told you not to tell anyone where the gold is, whatever happens?"

"I swear to you, Uncle, that I trust Abd ar-Rahman more than my own self."

"That same self was destroyed the day you trusted him. Passion has no place in the life of someone selected by destiny to save the city."

"Uncle, do not overburden me."

"You're no different from slave-girls. Love him all you want until he is married to someone else and throws you into some unknown room."

"You've never been this cruel with me."

"I didn't expect you to behave this way."

She blushed.

"I promise you, I swear to you that he's going to help us."

"You're swearing on behalf of a man about whom you know absolutely nothing."

"I believe him."

"That's because you're as naive as a ram before it's slaughtered. He must have hidden the gold by now. I can't even go and take it. If I did, he might well hurt you—who knows? I'm worried about you, my daughter," he said with a shrug. "Don't let him destroy you. He'll turn traitor. When he does, stand tall like a princess. You're Ahmad's daughter."

"Don't be angry with me, Uncle," she replied sadly.

Saeed left slowly, his shoulders sagging.

Abd ar-Rahman looked at her.

"What did he say to upset you so?" he asked her.

She stared at him.

"He reminded me of my father and mother," she replied. "Don't worry about what he said. He's a good man and looks on me as his own daughter."

After Saeed's visit, Aisha started concerning herself with the matter of Azza. She felt depressed and gloomy. Would he welcome her, she wondered? Would he marry her? Indeed, he had said that he would marry her. Had his father not been married to five women? What did she expect him to do? She closed her mind to doubts and decided to enjoy her time with him and relish the affection and tenderness toward her that came from deep inside him.

There was pleasure to be had in simply being around him, following his movements, feeling his veins pulsing inside his heart even when he was far away. She hurried over to him, carrying the food, and stood for a few seconds to feast her eyes on his face as he concentrated on training the horses. He noticed that she was there, but ignored her and went on working.

"I've brought you lunch myself," she said eagerly. "Do you realize, this is the first time I've brought lunch for anyone?"

"Thank you, Aisha," he replied without looking at her. "You can leave it here and go back to the house."

She was rooted to the spot.

"Are you meeting Azza?" she asked innocently.

He gave her an angry look.

"What business is that of yours? What kind of question is that?"

That response led her to ask the same question.

"Are you going to be married to her soon?"

"When I've fixed the time," he replied coldly, "I'll let you know. I don't like these questions."

For a moment, she said nothing.

"Go on, Aisha," he said, still looking at the horse, "go back to the house."

"I love you," she said spontaneously.

She had no idea why she had blurted that out. Maybe it was to reassure herself that they both shared the same feelings, or that he was behaving differently and coldly, as though erecting a wall between them.

He stayed where he was, as though she had stuck a sword in his back. He turned toward her slowly.

"Sit down, Aisha," he said.

She sat down and started arranging the food in front of him, not noticing his expression or his cold demeanor.

"Look at me," he told her.

She looked at him.

"I've told you before," he said softly, "that I don't like to hear that word. Do you know why?"

She felt annoyed and confused.

"That was before," she said, "but now . . ."

"Nothing's changed," he interrupted. "Tear up your paper, Princess. It's all imaginary; it was from your imagination in the past, and it still is."

She did her best to avoid understanding what he meant, since that would be the end.

"Why are you talking like this? Our relationship . . . everything . . ." She stopped talking, feeling utterly confused.

"You came to me asking for help," he said. "I promised to protect you. You weren't in love with me, nor I with you."

She still said nothing, his words tearing mercilessly at her heart.

"I've been in love with my cousin for ages," he went on, "before I ever saw you or knew you. My marriage to her has been delayed a while, but it's going to happen."

She kept trying to control her quivering hand and tongue.

"You've lied to me," she muttered bitterly.

"No, I haven't. You're beautiful, spectacularly beautiful. I like you, I want you, and you're my wife. That's all there is to it."

All she could think about was the drawing and how she could burn it.

"You've lied to me," she repeated blandly.

"You don't really love me, Aisha," he said in a cold tone she had not encountered before. "These days, you're confused about things because you're scared and bewildered. Princesses never feel real love in their hearts; their relationships are all governed by coalitions and treaties."

"You've taken my gold," she said angrily.

"It's not yours; it belongs to the monarchs of old. Your father found it, and I've taken it in return for giving you protection. From the very start, that was our agreement, and that's what Saeed promised."

"You've schemed against me."

"As you have with me. Do you remember? When we were married, you promised to tell me where the gold was, but you didn't."

She hugged herself, unable to speak. He stroked her hand.

"I'll never desert you," he said gently. "I've sworn and promised to help you."

"Are you going to make an agreement with Ibn Sulaiman?" she asked, holding back her tears.

"Yes, for my tribe's sake. Sooner or later, all Ibn Tulun's soldiers will do the same. 'For every appointed time there is a book.' For the Tulunids that time has come; it's the end."

"No," she muttered to herself, "it's your appointed time I'm hoping for, and at my hands. I'd like to see you bathed in blood before my very eyes."

He did not hear what she had said, but he still anticipated what she would say. He stood up.

"Don't leave the house," he told her. "I don't want the tribespeople wondering about your family and origins. People here are inclined to be nosy."

Once again, she did her best to prevent her mind coming up with words that would shatter whatever was left.

"You told me you longed for me and wanted me," she said. "You had a lot to say. Do you remember everything?"

The look he gave her was a blend of sympathy and frigidity.

"Yes," he replied, "I did long for you and want you. Separate body from heart, Princess, and then you'll understand what I'm saying. I get the impression that you don't want to understand."

She swallowed hard. His words were cutting into her body, and she wanted to find a fire that would burn her heart first and then him.

"You were . . ."

"I was . . ." he interrupted forcefully.

For a while she said nothing. She could not tell whether the prickling sensation in her body was a sign that she was losing consciousness or that the sheer shock was more than she could handle. She felt her legs to make sure that she could still walk.

"You make no distinction between a princess and a slave-girl," she said weakly.

He looked at her for a moment.

"You know nothing about men," he responded with the same frigidity. "When love is concerned, how many an amir has chosen a slave-girl rather than a princess? When a man and woman are in love, there's no difference between a princess and slave-girl."

"I'm nothing to you," she said without thinking, "just a soulless body."

He did not respond, but looked away.

"Arab man," she said insistently.

"You know the answer, Princess," he replied angrily.

"You lied to me," she said without thinking. "You told me that I had to sleep next to your heart every day . . . every single day.

"I'm sorry for you, Princess," she went on to herself, "for the place next to your own heart!"

Her tears dried up and refused to fall. He looked away carelessly.

"Why did you ask that of me?" she said suddenly. "You told me you wanted me beside you in your arms. That's what you told me. How come you lied?"

He raised his eyebrows, pretending to be shocked.

"If I said that," he told her, "it must have been under the influence of those lips of yours. The effect of passion doesn't last. Loving words are like a drunkard's ravings, totally unreliable. I forget what I said; what's happened between us is simply an agreement.

She grabbed the water jug that she had brought with her and started pouring water slowly onto the sand, looking down at the arid desert as it absorbed water, then dried up without any lasting effect. She started walking back to the house, feeling totally drained.

"Don't forget," he told her firmly, "that you're my wife. That's not going to change."

"God willing," she muttered, "you and Ibn Sulaiman will roast in hellfire!"

"What did you say?"

She did not respond. Hurrying back to the house, she went into her room and locked the door.

She stayed there for hours, taking in what he had said and what she had done, with Saeed's shouts still ringing in her ears. She blamed her mother for putting out the light so she had not glimpsed the world and for not letting her be married to any commander or other man, even though she might loathe him. What was the point of love in times of trickery and deceit? What could be the purpose of love in palaces and squares if the end result was bound to be betrayal? Had her own father not died of grief after being betrayed by the people most beloved to his heart? Had her own brother not been murdered by his most loyal servant? Had her brother not murdered Shaiban, his nephew? Not only that, but had that same nephew not killed one of his uncles and was at the point of killing the others as well? What did she expect? That the cavalier would be faithful to her because she loved him? Love never fosters feelings of gratitude in other people. It's a sense of loneliness, just like sorrow and loss. How hard that is for the pure soul, and how brutal are the hearts of men!

It was her own spontaneity that was making her suffer. Today she needed to talk to someone, and in that house her only friend was Khalisa. She went to see Khalisa and started talking to her in both anger and sorrow without going into her own lineage. Once in a while, Khalisa would laugh, but otherwise she was silent.

"Don't you feel sorry for me, Aunt?" she asked pleadingly.

"Why should I, you silly girl?" Khalisa replied. "I've told you before what he'd do with you. I did warn you. Do you want to burn the drawing now?"

Aisha said nothing.

"You love him like an animal longing for green grass," Khalisa went on with her habitual sarcasm. "You keep eating nonstop. The man told you, girl, that he was in love with another woman."

"Perhaps he's lying," Aisha replied in despair. "Maybe he doesn't realize the depth of his feelings for me. His affection gushed all around me, Aunt. I've never encountered anything like it."

"You stupid girl, I've told you that when a man wants something, his affection is like the devil's own plants, with no roots. Why don't you understand? Feel sad now, and rip up that drawing."

"I can't."

"Never mind," Khalisa went on. "You'll burn it, whether today or tomorrow. I'll give you a week before you start cursing the day you ever met him. What do you say?"

"Don't you have any hope of his loving me?"

"I don't have any hope of him loving in principle, Aisha," she said. "Men can only see themselves. They can only love themselves. You still long for him, and you're going to keep your drawings. Isn't that right? Fine! Come back in a week's time, you stupid girl, and you can burn them then."

"My mother told me," Aisha said in despair, "that my father always used to say that 'when a man leaves a woman, it's either because he doesn't like her anymore, or else because she's penetrated his heart and gained more control than need be.'"

Khalisa scoffed.

"What exactly did your father do, girl?" she asked. "He must have been a tailor. Didn't you tell me that your grandfather was a tailor? How can a tailor understand all men? Your father was a tailor, wasn't he?"

"Yes, he was," Aisha replied.

Her husband did not come at night as usual, and no one knocked on her door. After only a month of marriage, was he really bored with her and staying away? What kind of woman was she? Even if he was playing around, how could he shun her like this? Despising the part of her that was so in love, she tried to recall the goal in her marriage and the gold. It was actually his father who was the target, with no passion to tempt her and no headstrong heart like hers. Now the gold was lost, and so was her heart. With the heart's loss, she deserved what was happening. With the loss of the gold, it was terminal death, with no resurrection to follow. She waited for him to come eagerly to her room, take her in his arms, and tell her that what he had said was not true. He had discovered that he loved only her. But he did not do any of that. A whole day went by without him coming, and then a second.

After a week, she went to his room at night and knocked on the door. He allowed her to come in. He was stretched out motionless on his bed.

"I don't know what I've done to make you angry with me," she said.

"I'm not angry with you," he replied languidly.

"Perhaps you're bored with me. You haven't come to my room . . ."

She chided herself for saying those words without thinking. She blushed.

He looked at her for a moment.

"Why have you come here, Princess?" he asked coldly.

"I've come to ask you to keep a promise that you made to help me."

"Oh," he replied sarcastically, "and I was thinking that you'd come because you're missing me . . ."

She stared at the floor.

"You said you don't love me," she said, "and now I know you don't want me either."

He looked furious, and she could see his veins pulsating. She did not know whether he was angry at her or at the bold way she was talking.

"You promised to help me," she added quickly.

"I'm helping you," he responded coldly. "I'm still helping you."

"It's my father I'm really concerned about," she insisted. "You're right. Marriage is all negotiations and alliances. I made an agreement with you and gave you the gold so you could protect my people and save my city and family."

"I told you before that you're asking for the impossible. Ibn Sulaiman's arrived with an army of ten thousand soldiers. Do you really expect a tribe of five hundred men to confront him?"

"I don't know. Maybe you could save the city from destruction. I really want to save what my father built for Egypt."

"No, he built it to immortalize his name like the Egyptian monarchs of old. Didn't one of them come to him in his dream?"

"My dear husband, they may have been immortalizing Egypt, not themselves. You were born here, like me. Your brothers have scattered over its soil in search of its bounty. Now save what can benefit people so that God will be pleased with you."

"Do you and your family own God's pleasure? Enough of your tyranny! Don't you see? What truth don't you realize? Your nephew has now lost Syria, Tarsus, and the border provinces. The Qarmatians defeated him in a single night and day. Didn't he keep Syria through gifts rather than force? Do you know how he spent his time? Debauchery and drunkenness. Don't you remember that Khumarawayh's sons assumed the throne even though their elder uncles were much more qualified? It was the evil entourage that craved power while the uncles were left as weak as women. Didn't your mother teach you anything? When you were in the palace, didn't you detect any plots?"

"Everything you're saying is right," she replied eagerly, "but what's so bad about the hospital and palace, the city and its people?"

"Wars have their own rules, Princess."

"How do you want to help me? I've given you myself, then I've given you all the gold. What more do you want, chieftain's son?"

"I've taken everything I need. There's nothing you can give me now, daughter of Amir Abu al-Abbas Ahmad ibn Tulun. No one's taught you that you can't give before you've taken. I've given. But, because I'm generous with you, I'm going to continue protecting you, as I promised. Now, go back to your room."

She pursed her lips in anger.

"Sons of honorable folk keep their pledges," she said. "I thank you for the protection."

She left his room, but he stayed where he was. She went back to her room and closed the door. Perhaps he would still come; she still hoped that he would. There was Princess Aisha with her goal, and then there was a woman who had been unforgivably insulted. In days past, he had come to her after an hour; he was bound to come today. When she had gone to his room, he had yearned for her, had he not? She remembered their joint passion and the way he longed for her. Had he forgotten so fast? How much could men remember? If only she could forget! She felt certain that not an hour would pass before he was opening her door and taking her in his arms. He was pretending to be cold and cruel, but he has not like that. If she admitted that she had bungled matters of gold, heart, and body, then maybe she would have to die. She certainly deserved it. Was there a penalty for sheer stupidity? An hour passed, and then she heard the sound of footsteps near the door. She stood up, her heart pounding. It had to be him . . . he was longing for her and hesitating; maybe ashamed of what he had said and done. She opened the door slowly and saw Atika fetching herself a glass of water. Atika noticed her and gave a sarcastic smile of triumph.

"Are you expecting someone, stranger?" she asked.

"No," Aisha replied, holding back her tears.

Atika gave her a knowing look.

"What you're waiting for isn't going to happen," she said.

With that, she went away.

Aisha closed the door again and threw herself down on the bed. No, he was not going to come, not today or the next.

                        ﲒ

Breaking a pledge was despicable. Stealing her gold was despicable too. But shunning her and staying away, as though she were some scabby animal, that was a crime for which a price had to be paid. The chieftain's son was bored with the princess, longed for his cousin, and did not want anyone else. Aisha was absolutely furious and did not leave her room for two more days.

In her imagination, she composed another letter to Qatr an-Nada. In it she said that she was unhappy; the shaikh's house was narrow and smothered the heart. She told Qatr an-Nada that she was sleeping on her own every night; as the lonely feeling intensified, the doors would twist their wooden panels over her breast. She had gone to see him in person. He had not received her in his room or even noticed that she was there. What kind of torture was this? It was something she had never encountered before. Once the Arab had taken the gold, he had deserted her; it was as if he had only had sex with her to get the gold. Could Qatr an-Nada believe it? Could she even imagine that he had found nothing in Aisha to attract him? He kept pretending to be passionately in love with her while he was planning her defeat. It was as though all his kisses were simply phony, all those love phrases were false. Poisoned food was preferable to desertion. Staying in his house was like exile inside your own homeland.

In despair, she went to see Khalisa again.

"Aunt," she pleaded, "why is he shunning me? Is a single month enough for a man with a woman?"

"Sometimes, girl," she replied with a laugh, "a single day is enough."

Khalisa then gave her a different kind of look, as though she knew and understood.

"Your very soul's being squeezed between your ribs," she told Aisha. "You're longing for him and you hate him. You want him to die, and yet all you really want is to be in his arms. First fury's in charge, then longing. Sorrow stays hidden, never disappearing as days and years go by. When a man deserts a woman, my daughter, he tears her apart. Were Quranic verses not revealed, especially intended to urge men not to desert their wives?"

"What's hurting me," Aisha said bashfully, "is that he wants someone else, as though I'm not beautiful and maybe . . . I'm not as fully a woman. Has he lied to me? He pretended to be passionately in love while still shunning me."

"Perhaps he wasn't lying then," she said. "He certainly found you beautiful. You are beautiful, Aisha."

It was the first time that Khalisa had said something nice.

"I was beautiful too," Khalisa went on, "when my husband deserted me. That's the way men behave. Do you know what hurts me?"

"What's that, Aunt? Is it love for him?"

"No. What hurts me is that he's never realized that he tore me apart, cut me in pieces, and flayed me while my spirit was still pulsing. One day I want him to feel the same agony. If there's any justice in this world, then suffering needs to touch their hearts. But justice is in the hands of the Lord of all, so their ribs can roast in hellfire."

"Yes," Aisha responded eagerly, "I want to see him in hellfire, supervise the roasting myself, and add some saffron and clove spices."

"Who on earth adds saffron as spice for ribs, you silly girl?" Khalisa scoffed. "Do you even know how to cook? You need to use cinnamon, salt, and pepper. Then you cook them well till they are tender and dissolve in the mouth. I'd like us to eat ribs with them watching. We could enjoy eating while they're looking on."

"What a wonderful picture! I'm going to draw it, Aunt."

"Not until you've torn up the picture of him that you drew earlier."

"I want to die, Aunt," she said, shamefaced. "I miss him."

"Take care, do you hear me? Don't you dare submit to him. I'll tear you apart with my own hands."

"I won't do that; of course I won't. Even my Uncle Saeed told me that."

Today she cried, silently at first, but then with loud sobs. Tears pouring down, she buried her head in the pillow. If only her mother had taught her anything. Instead, she had stuck with her day and night, sleeping in the same bed and hugging her in order to protect her. She had stayed with her daughter and enveloped her, then abandoned her to this room amid the ice. Aisha felt scared of being on her own and wanted him to be with her. Not only that, but the dark room and the noise made by blowing grains of sand bothered her as well. If she went to see him now and told him that she was scared, he would think she was lying. He might think she was scheming against him or wanted him. She stood up and headed for his room. She bore in mind what Saeed and Khalisa had both told her: she should not humiliate herself. She should certainly not do that. But what if he saw her crying? She wiped her eyes nervously. She opened his door. He was asleep, his head buried in the pillow. She clutched her chest, as though to prevent her heart from trembling.

"Abd ar-Rahman," she whispered.

He did not open his eyes.

"Can you hear me?" she asked.

"Yes," he replied.

Once again, she wiped away her tears nervously.

"I wanted to speak to you," she said.

He turned his head away, eyes still closed.

"Go back to your room, Princess," he said.

She opened her mouth in anger, her heart racing.

"I haven't come here," she said, "to throw myself into your arms and then have you send me away. I have a right to speak to you. This is wrong. Give me back my gold."

He stretched.

"Tomorrow," he told her, eyes still closed. "Now back to your room!"

She banged the door angrily and went back to her room. She berated herself, blaming her heart for letting her be so insulted. He had realized, he must have realized that she really wanted to sleep in his arms and for him to reassure her. He knew that she was a princess with a weak soul, easily humiliated a thousand times over as time went by.

Abd ar-Rahman started training his men to fight. The battle was coming; that was certain. Nothing made him happier than training to fight. It did not matter who was friend or foe. The adventure of war brought with it a special elation, a sense of relaxation that would cause no exhaustion. In war's embrace are treasures for man, unparalleled by any others; and nothing can rival the satisfaction of victory. When a soldier is victorious, he is in control; with that, he is content. He longs for such contentment. All the earth's beauties will bow down before him, and he will be able to choose whichever one of them he desires. He will feel content, relaxed, and satisfied.

One of his men told him that someone had been waiting to talk to him for some time. He stopped his training. Taking his sword and spear with him, he went to meet the man. It was Saeed al-Farghani. Abd ar-Rahman gave him a frigid smile, then started cleaning his sword.

"Welcome!" he said. "Have you come to check on the princess or to talk to me?"

Saeed sat down and fixed his gaze on Abd ar-Rahman.

"I want to talk to you," he said.

Abd ar-Rahman sat down too and continued cleaning his sword.

"I was angry with you, Saeed," he said, "when you spoke to her in Coptic, knowing that I don't understand it. It was as though you were talking to my wife about me. That's not right."

He was using a mocking tone, blended with a sense of power and superiority.

"Listen, Arab," Saeed said. "There's no call for arrogant boasting. You're only winning against an innocent orphan."

Abd ar-Rahman pretended to be angry.

"Who says that I've won? She's my wife. Everything she owns is mine. There are no secrets between husband and wife. She obeys my orders, not those of a man like you who has no connection with her."

"Will you be happy when you get hold of the treasure? Will you control the whole world? My son, I'm older than you. The world only gives to those who are willing to withdraw. You go after everything; you're eager to achieve, but all you'll find is a mirage. On your path, Arab, there's neither water nor palm trees, just desiccation and drought. People who drink mirages are never satisfied; they need water, but find none. You'll keep trying, but you won't get there."

"I don't like such complicated words. Say what you want, then leave. I don't have the time."

"I'm worried about Aisha."

Abd ar-Rahman gave him a furious look.

"Why?" he asked. "You aren't her father or uncle. You've nothing to do with her."

"Have you deserted her, or not yet? Have you discovered the damage you've inflicted on her? She loved you and chose you out of all the men in Al-Qata'i. Do you realize that?"

Abd ar-Rahman looked at his sword, which reflected the image of his face.

"Yes, I do," he replied.

Saeed looked at the sword.

"And now you plan to help her father's enemy," he said, "and witness the destruction of Fustat and Al-Qata'i. When Ibn Sulaiman decides to knock down the mosque, what do you plan to do? Such a person is an enemy of humankind. Those who build are saved from oblivion. Reformers are not like corrupters, nor are builders like destroyers."

Abd ar-Rahman tossed his sword aside.

"Saeed," he said, "rulers can build, construct, tyrannize, and oppress. Building only means that they want to memorialize their own names. Ahmad means nothing to me; I wasn't around during his era. All I know is that eighteen men died in his prison. So how is he different from Al-Hajjaj ibn Yusuf ath-Thaqafi?"

"Ahmad had a dream," Saeed responded forcefully. "He treated Egyptians fairly, gave them victories, and dispensed justice among them. He built things for them and gave them preference. Ahmad . . . But you'll never understand. Demanding times always blind the vision. If Muhammad ibn Sulaiman destroys the mosque, you'll be just as culpable."

"I'm really surprised," Abd ar-Rahman scoffed, "that a Christian is so upset about a mosque founded by a man with stolen treasure."

"And I'm surprised that a Muslim is so unconcerned about the fate of a house of God. Yesterday you and your men went out to attack peasants. You never tire of such assaults, I realize; brigandry is the only thing you know. You attacked peasants, stole their money, wheat, and cattle, and distributed it all to your men. You did that so that tomorrow you could order them to join Ibn Sulaiman's army and thus break your pledge to the Tulunids. You're bribing them with stolen property. That's just the way you are, man."

"Leave here now," Abd ar-Rahman responded in fury, "or else I'll put an arrow through your head. You're an old man. You won't survive."

"I'm leaving, Abd ar-Rahman, but we'll be meeting again. I'll be able to tell you that you've lost a princess who's given you everything with nothing in return, that no treasure can ever quench the thirst of greedy people, and the earth's very structure is the foundation of your faith. I'll meet you again in a year or less to inform you that you've lost and found neither happiness nor rest. For you, there's neither peace nor farewell."

"Don't come here again," Abd ar-Rahman told him angrily. "From today onward, I'm going to stop her meeting you."

"Even though she's soft-hearted," Saeed said, "she's still powerful. She obviously knows what you're really like. She's grown to loathe you. Now she's full of regret, and that's the first phase in maturity. The princess doesn't need me. But don't you dare treat her badly or betray her. I'll kill you with my own two hands. Don't force her or humiliate her. Do you hear me?"

"Get going, man," Abd ar-Rahman said with a chuckle. "The princess is totally infatuated with me. You're well aware that such love is always humiliating."

"You like your own youthful vigor and strength, and you're seduced by gold and glory. You'll carry on living in your own erroneous ways because people like you don't possess the vision needed to regret. You'll look for slave-girls in palaces and have sons. Maybe you'll be married to your cousin, but you still won't be satisfied. You'll never be satisfied."

Abd ar-Rahman gave him a smiling look of triumph.

"I'm satisfied already, man" he said, "and that's the end."

The news was confirmed: Muhammad ibn Sulaiman had left Palestine and was now in Egypt. He had pitched an enormous tent on the outskirts of Al-Qata'i and was waiting for the opportunity to attack it with his soldiers. War would flare up all over Egypt, and no one would escape the consequences. Once Shaiban had replaced his nephew, Harun son of Khumarawayh, he put together a huge army with the intention of holding firm and defeating Ibn Sulaiman's forces. The Tulunid army could still frighten people near and far, being renowned for its victories and courage. No other army had its capabilities or its power to stand firm and resist. Ibn Sulaiman was well aware of all that, so he stayed inside his tent, planning a different kind of strike that would be totally unexpected. That day, bridges were burned, and no supplies reached Al-Qata'i. Faced with the caliph's army, only the city would remain. Ibn Sulaiman's goal was to erase Al-Qata'i altogether and, if he could manage it, maybe its inhabitants as well. He now summoned to his tent the tribal chieftains and the soldiers who had deserted the Tulunid ranks. Sometimes he wanted to win by strategy, and, at others, by betrayal. He threatened any tribal chieftains who refused to accept his cause that their homes and families would not be safe.

Abd ar-Rahman sat down that night to ask for his father's advice and make a careful selection of the men who would go with him to Ibn Sulaiman. Aisha listened to them from behind the door, her heart being torn to shreds. Abd ar-Rahman selected three men, one of them named Salih. His father said that he did not trust that man and wanted to keep him close where he could keep an eye on him. Abd ar-Rahman's father grasped his son's shoulder and thanked him for taking charge of the tribe's affairs in such difficult times. He told him that he was still feeling badly because he was breaking his oath and annulling the pledge they had made to the Tulunid house. Abd ar-Rahman reassured his father, pointing out that no pledge could be secure when faced with swords and no oath would work in times of slaughter. Abd ar-Rahman prepared himself to go to Ibn Sulaiman, and Aisha returned to her room and pulled the coverlet over her head, almost exploding with anger. It felt as though every mountain rock was pounding her head and crushing her chest. At dawn, he came into her room. She got out of bed and gave him a hateful look, but said nothing.

"As usual, you were spying," he said. "I know. Don't dare do that, do you hear me? Don't leave the house till I return. Don't talk to anyone outside the walls of this house. Even with the people inside the house, speak carefully and be succinct."

"If you took me to Ibn Sulaiman," she said dryly, "he would give you double the amount of gold you took from me. What do you think?"

She wanted to annoy him, and maybe she had.

"You're right," he said thoughtfully. "I'll think about it. Till I've made up my mind, don't say anything to other people."

"I don't love you anymore, Abd ar-Rahman," she said as he was leaving the room. "I want you to know. I don't love you or want you."

"That's much better," he replied, as though the words had not reached him. "Now we can treat each other honestly, without hypocrisy."

"You're always honest, my husband."

"I'm honest," he replied dryly, "when you tell the truth, and a liar when you don't."

"Are you going to give Ibn Sulaiman my gold?"

"You don't have any gold, Princess. It's mine."

With that, he closed the door behind him and left.

After her husband had been away for two days, news spread about Ibn Sulaiman's tent, where he had received the tribesmen, and about her husband. The women celebrated the news even before the tribesmen came back, and that day, they—and especially Azza, Saleema, and Atika—repeated the information in Aisha's hearing. Atika called to Aisha and asked her to sit with them. Aisha stared at the floor in silence.

"Do you know what happened to Abd ar-Rahman?" she told Azza. "Ibn Sulaiman gave him two stunningly beautiful slave-girls; he chose one for himself and gave the other girl to one of his men. They say he's spent some fabulous nights with her. She's not like other women: she's Byzantine, trained to sing and draw, with eyes as blue as the sea."

Azza gave Aisha a long, hard stare that said everything. "He's betrayed you and me. You're no different from any slave-girl. He's spent hours with this girl and hours with you, but his heart's with me. That's the way it will always be."

Atika looked at Aisha's crushed, quavering expression.

"I wonder if he'll bring the slave-girl here," she said. "Will you keep her, Azza, once you're married?"

"If it makes him happy," Azza replied with a smile, "then I'll keep her. But I'm sure he won't need anyone else once we're married."

"He's just like his father," Atika said. "Do you realize that he was married to five women, but now it's just me? He doesn't need anyone else."

She whispered something in Azza's ear, and it made her smile.

Aisha stood up slowly. Saleema stuck out her foot so it bumped into Aisha's and she tripped. She fell flat on her face and felt her bloody chin. She managed not to cry, stood up to the sound of Atika's laughter, and went back to her room.

Azza chided Saleema.

"Why did you do that?" she asked.

"I don't like her," Saleema replied "That one's a man-stealer.

"Did you see her look when she heard about the slave-girl?" she went on. "There were tears in her eyes as she fell to the ground like a camel. Did you see the blood on her chin?"

Azza did not laugh with her.

When Aisha went into her room, she did not cry. Wiping the blood off her chin with the back of her hand, she looked for the drawing she had done, picked it up, and took it to Khalisa without saying a word. Lighting the fire, she burned the paper slowly as the smoke mingled with her burning breath.

"I told you that you'd be destroying the drawing," Khalisa scoffed, "and here you are doing it in my room. A little intelligence is always helpful, Aisha. Why are you crying?"

The edge of the drawing was still in her fingers as the flames finally reached them. She paid no attention.

"When you burn your fingers," Khalisa asked, "will that put out the fire inside your heart?"

She covered her head with her hands, but did not cry. On one side was Saleema with her insults, sarcasm, and hurtful behavior, and, on the other, there was his sarcasm and hurtful behavior. His cruelty and hatred far surpassed Saleema's.

"Stop thinking!" Khalisa told her. "No man's worth your suffering this way. I've told you before, men are like fires, but you're getting too close and being burned. So the drawing's gone. What do you expect from him now? For him to be satisfied with just you and stay away from other women? Do you believe poets, you silly girl?"

"If the desert would just swallow me," Aisha whispered, "and I turned into pieces of sand wafting through the air, I'd be content."

"You stupid girl, you're going to die for the sake of a man? They've no loyalty. They're like wild cats. You can feed them for your entire life, and they'll pretend to be happy in your arms, but then they'll desert you, rebel, and even maul you. Come over here . . ."

She hugged Aisha.

"Why aren't you crying?" she asked. "Doesn't your chin hurt?"

"I regret what I've given."

"Don't! Generous people always give to meanies. You gave because you're generous, but he can't because he's mean. It's not your fault. You gave because you have a proud, decent heart."

"I hate him."

"No, you don't. You adore him. The only cure for that is death. That type of love never changes, my daughter, like craving for food when giving birth. I know."

"So I'm going to die."

"No, you're going to crush some seeds with me. Like them, your heart is splintering into pieces. You can calm down and get some sleep."

"I'll kill him with my bare hands."

"You're going to lose twice if he spots any weakness in your eyes. Take care . . ."

She moved away a little.

"I don't understand you, Aunt," she said.

"Listen to me and understand what I'm saying. Make sure you don't seem weak in front of him; no hatred or sorrow. Make sure too that he doesn't see any signs of love in your eyes, or else you'll be like a dog panting behind its master even when he's far away."

"You're asking a lot. I've no love left inside me; it's only hate and disgust."

"Didn't I tell you? Inside hate and disgust is love and passion. With time you'll understand. When he comes back, you'll treat him as the wife he wants, with no love or rebuke."

"As though I've no life."

"As though you've no life, so he won't be able to put an end to what's left of your heart. Listen to me just once. As I've told you, the man's like a wild cat. So, he comes and goes as he wants. He's not reliable and has no need of stability. Don't hang your heart on him again. Forget whatever happens during lovemaking. Like this ephemeral world, like a mirage, that all vanishes.

Part Two

Has it deceived you about me that your love is killing me,
And that my heart does whatever you command?
Your eyes only flow with tears in order to strike me
With twin arrows in the fragments of a ruined heart.
—*Imru' al-Qais, pre-Islamic poet*

Chapter 3

How did Muhammad ibn Sulaiman manage to achieve the rank of general in the caliph's armies? No one knows exactly, but men relay the story of a self-made man. Ahmad ibn Tulun almost killed him when he was young for no apparent reason. The only person who interceded on his behalf was Lu'lu', one of Ahmad ibn Tulun's generals. Ahmad ibn Tulun then told him to leave Egypt, and he went to Baghdad and worked at any job he could find until Lu'lu' rebelled against Ahmad ibn Tulun and left Egypt for Baghdad. Muhammad ibn Sulaiman made every effort to meet him, and Lu'lu' welcomed him and trained him to use a sword. Lu'lu' came to rely on him and trust his fidelity. He presented him to Al-Muwaffaq, the caliph's brother, and thereafter Muhammad ibn Sulaiman never left the caliphal palaces in Baghdad. He learned quickly and showed a good deal of enthusiasm and courage. For all the intervening years, he had just one single goal: revenge—putting an end to Ahmad ibn Tulun. However, fate did not give him the chance; Ahmad died before he could kill him with his bare hands. Even so, the things that Ahmad had built and his reputation were still powerful structures in their own right. He had sworn to eradicate every trace of the Tulunid dynasty and what Ahmad had built.

Abd ar-Rahman brought Muhammad ibn Sulaiman gifts and booty. He instructed his men not to talk in his presence or tell anyone else what transpired between the two of them.

He went into Muhammad ibn Sulaiman al-Katib's tent and was welcomed like a friend. Muhammad was sturdy and powerfully built; he looked like a veteran warrior. He sat Abd ar-Rahman down beside him.

"You're the son of my good friend, Shaikh Musa ibn Uthmaan," he said. "Your visit is reassuring and shows both foresight and understanding."

"What are your intentions in coming to Egypt?" Abd ar-Rahman asked him after an initial greeting. "Today you're at the gates of Fustat and Al-Qata'i."

"My brother," Muhammad ibn Sulaiman replied, "Ibn Tulun's regime was a distortion of reality and a gross error in the history of the caliphate and this country. For the first time in Islamic history, one man took a country like Egypt for himself, commandeering its finances and forming an army. It was Ahmad ibn Tulun's army, not the caliph's. That has never happened before, and it won't ever happen again. People have short memories, and their lives are even shorter. The passage of time always crushes the vestiges of memory with pain. I don't want Egyptians to remember him; all traces of him must be erased so they'll forget."

"I don't understand you, Sir."

"Never mind, Abd ar-Rahman. You'll soon understand. Only one army has any legitimacy, and that's the army of the caliph in Baghdad. The Egyptian army has no legitimacy. Even so, its numbers were larger than the caliph's army. Did Amr ibn al-As declare himself independent ruler of Egypt, even though he loved the country? No, he didn't. He conquered it and saved it from the Byzantines. But he never ruled it independently, nor did he dare form a separate Egyptian army. Ahmad ibn Tulun is the only person who's done that, dragooning Egyptians and Arabs and not being satisfied with Turks and Byzantines. He was ambitious and tyrannical. In the entire history of Islam and earlier of the Romans, I've never heard of anyone using Egyptians as soldiers. Did the Romans use them? No. Did the Umayyads or Abbasids? No. But then in comes this soldier from Bukhara and uses Egyptians as soldiers. What danger awaits the caliph, and what kind of example does Ahmad set of resistance and falsehood?"

"But he gave Arabs their rights," Abd ar-Rahman replied, "something the caliphs had ignored. Forgive me for being so frank. What are you intending to do when you have authority over Egypt?"

"Arabs always have their rights," Muhammad Ibn Sulaiman replied without even thinking.

"My father's often chided me for my blunt talk," Abd ar-Rahman replied, "but I need to be honest with you. You're a brother and commander. Ahmad ibn Tulun and later Khumarawayh enlisted Arabs in the army and showered them with gifts."

"Today or tomorrow, they're all going to die in the fighting," Muhammad ibn Sulaiman responded impatiently. "If they don't give me their pledge, I'll slaughter them."

"I'm hoping that the commander will pause; he is not yet in control of Egypt. Tulunid armies conquered Syria and reached the borders of Africa, Yemen, and the Hejaz. I'm asking you, General, to keep a promise and not make threats until we can find a point of agreement."

"All that was in the past. The Tulunids have now lost Syria and the frontier regions. It's no longer a real army, brother. Al-Qata'i is fractured and dominated by greed. The rulers are children."

"Some people will still fight," Abd ar-Rahman insisted, "even though the Tulunids themselves may surrender."

"Who'll dare fight me now that Syria's gone over to me, and I've saved it from the Qarmatians? Have you come here to challenge me, Arab?"

"No, I've come here to open your eyes, so you can win. Egyptians who are serving in the army today will not accept the fall of the Tulunids, even if their amir is a silly child. Once you realize that, you won't be so indifferent anymore. When you're in charge, it's difficult to lose. I'm warning you about the troops from Egypt, Sudan, and Nubia. Their fealty isn't to Harun or Shaiban; it's to Ahmad, and the people who show that they're still with Ahmad's regime."

"Ahmad died twenty years ago. He's dead and gone."

"No, he's only getting started. If you want to win, then don't kill too many people. If you want to stay, then don't erase history. Even if you demolish Al-Qata'i, its story will remain in the heart and its destruction will be stored in the soul till the demise of humanity. Just as pain stays with us and we forget our joys, General, so will Ahmad's mosque remain. You must leave the city standing, and deal gently with its people."

At this point, one of Muhammad ibn Sulaiman's deputies, named Qasim al-Khurasani, came in.

"No," he said, "the mosque will be destroyed before the city's burnt."

For just a moment, there was silence.

"Do you intend to destroy a mosque," Abd ar-Rahman asked, "a building based on pious devotion to God?"

"No," Qasim replied, "it was based on stolen money. Ahmad had two mosques: the mosque of Enlightenment and his big mosque. I'm going to erase all trace of both."

"Brother," Muhammad ibn Sulaiman told him gently, "we don't have Fustat or Al-Qata'i as yet. I plan to deal mercifully with the Egyptians and come to terms with the Arabs. Today, I have a brother and friend here, Abd ar-Rahman. You're going to fight with us, aren't you?"

"My men aren't ready to fight," Abd ar-Rahman replied.

"So what's the point of your visit? Have you just brought gifts and a slaughtered animal?"

"Our soldiers will be standing guard. If the fighting intensifies, they'll join in. We're not fighting with Tulun, but I don't want what's left of my men to be destroyed. If the fighting's fierce, my men will enter on your side."

"Who's to decide if the fighting's intense? Your men are under my command."

"Forgive me. You're asking me to give up everything I possess. Our men will only obey the tribal chieftain. There was a pact between us and Ahmad, Sir. Today I've broken it for your sake. Don't force my men to rebel against me and those I choose to support. For Arabs, a pact is a debt that does not die when its originator does. Even so, I prefer to form an alliance with you."

"So I won't be asking the Arabs for help, and the caliph won't do so unless it's absolutely necessary."

"But you need them today."

"You'll keep the roads safe for me, offer protection, and not attack."

"Agreed."

"I'll give you the gold and weapons you need."

"No, let's come to an agreement about how things will be in the future."

"Ask away . . ."

"Donations to my men for thirty years," Abd ar-Rahman said, "supervision of police matters, as was the case in Ahmad's time and also that of his son, Khumarawayh, a stipend for the shaikh and his son for the same period, and for every tribesman. We'll put it all down on paper and have it witnessed by your men and the judges."

"You're asking a lot for having just five hundred men not attack."

"No, I'm only asking for it because of security and the roads, if you want to be in command."

"That's all I want. You'll get all you want and stay here with your men till the entire situation is clearer."

Abd ar-Rahman agreed along with his men.

"As long as you're with me," Ibn Sulaiman went on, "I'm going to give you two slave-girls as a gift, and one for each of your men."

"Your generosity has been well known for some time, Sir."

He moved closer to Abd ar-Rahman.

"I'm giving you a stunningly beautiful slave-girl," he said. "She can sing, dance, and recite poetry. She'll transform your future days."

"How can I turn down such gifts when I've come to ask for them?"

"I like you, brother."

Tulunid forces encircled Fustat and Al-Qata'i. Even though the two cities had no walls, it was impossible to get in. Horsemen were there with spears and swords, and infantry patrolled night and day. Once Shaiban had killed his nephew, Harun, he started protecting himself with Sudanese soldiers and used other soldiers to secure the borders.

Ibn Sulaiman's forces engaged in a brutal battle with the Tulunid armies. They expected to enter Al-Qata'i by sunset, but that did not happen. He was impatient and in despair, recalling how things had been. It was like reliving the past, one he could not decide whether to forget or remember, in order to encourage himself to continue. How could ten thousand soldiers not defeat the Tulunid army? How could a fragmented force put up such fierce resistance?

He summoned Abd ar-Rahman.

"We need your men today," he told him forcefully.

"If you take my men today, Sir," Abd ar-Rahman replied, "they'll be slaughtered before sunrise. Keep them in reserve in case you need them later on."

"I don't understand why their army's resisting," Muhammad ibn Sulaiman said. "What perfidy for an army to resist the caliph's forces!"

"They regard Ahmad as a dream and symbol."

"Ahmad . . . he's responsible for all the disasters. He's dead and gone. His memory keeps ruining my life. I'm going to erase his very existence; I swear it."

He summoned one of his men and asked him to take a letter to Shaiban, Ahmad ibn Tulun's son, the current ruler of Egypt. In the letter, he said that, sooner or later, the Tulunid army would surrender and the caliph would emerge victorious, whether that day or the next. No reinforcements would arrive, and no eastern border regions would be coming to his aid. Syria was now in the caliph's hands, and the people of Fustat and Al-Qata'i would be suffering the cruelties and impact of war. If Ahmad were still alive, he would much prefer people to be safe and for Egyptians, Al-Qata'i, and the armies to be at peace. By acknowledging the caliph and surrendering, he would be saving both himself and his army so that he would not have to witness the disappearance of the city. Who knows, maybe the caliph would appoint him Governor of Egypt. Ibn Sulaiman promised him that if he surrendered that day, he would ask the caliph to appoint him governor. He finished by saying that he was granting safety to himself and the entire Tulunid family.

He then shouted the same thing in front of Abd ar-Rahman and all his men.

"Let it be witnessed that I hereby grant safety to the Tulunids. I prefer people's well-being and survival to the horrors of war. Before these men, I swear that Shaiban's surrender will save the city and everyone in it. They will not be harmed. Egypt will be restored to the caliphate, and the matter will be closed. The Tulunids will remain in Egypt as lords and amirs. Tell Shaiban that I have sworn this oath in front of all these men; the pledge is firm till the Day of Resurrection. Tell him that, if he wishes to surrender, he and the entire Tulunid family should head unarmed toward my tent. I trust that he will not play any tricks; he and his father before him are persons of honor."

"Sir," one of the soldiers commented, "he might be planning a trap for us with his soldiers."

Ibn Sulaiman thought for a moment.

"He and the Tulunids should come first," he said, "and then the army can follow. Monarchs' words never scare as much as an unbending sword."

The vicious fighting continued, and Ibn Sulaiman began to feel even more desperate about victory. He expected the caliph to kill him when he returned to Iraq. At dawn, the good news arrived. Shaiban had agreed to Ibn Sulaiman's terms. He heaved a sigh of relief as he awaited the arrival at his tent of Shaiban and his troops.

Abd ar-Rahman and his men stayed in the tent, looking on in silence. Salih came over to Abd ar-Rahman.

"I don't trust Ibn Sulaiman's promises," he said.

"That's none of our business," Abd ar-Rahman replied. "Don't say anything now. In desperate times, cruelty prevails. If he hears you, he'll kill you on the spot."

Shaiban arrived with the entire Tulunid family. Ibn Sulaiman gave them a warm welcome in his tent. He then sat down in front of Shaiban and asked to be introduced to every member of the family, both men and women. He was recalling a day when he had been at Ahmad's mercy, but he had honored him and let him live. Shaiban started saying the names of all the members of the Tulunid family.

"Ibn Sulaiman," he said, "you've sworn before all the men to guarantee our safety."

"Yes," Ibn Sulaiman replied, "I have sworn and I never break an oath. You and the entire Tulunid family are objects of my beneficence. Ibn Tulun had thirty-three sons and daughters. Some of them are dead, but I'm asking about his Egyptian wife, Asma. Where is she?"

"How do you know the name of my father's wife?" Shaiban asked in dismay.

"I know the entire family. We had an agreement that the entire Tulunid family would surrender. You know what I mean. There's been intrigue inside the Tulunid household. If one of them gets away, then the surrender is useless. He'll muster an army, and the entire game will be repeated. If Ahmad's wife were to be married to a general, then your own surrender would be totally insignificant, Amir. So where's Asma?"

"She ran away months ago. No one knows anything about her whereabouts."

"Where's Ahmad's daughter by her?"

"You mean, Aisha?"

"Yes, where is she?"

"How am I supposed to know? She ran away with her mother months ago."

"You haven't looked for them?"

"I was in my nephew's prison, man," Shaiban replied. "Also her mother kept her daughter apart from the rest of us. She only left the women's quarters on rare occasions. She was a fox, shy of humans and hiding inside her den."

"Foxes are a danger to the caliphate. I want Aisha, Ahmad ibn Tulun's daughter."

Shaiban shrugged his shoulders.

"I know absolutely nothing about her," he said. "I just told you that. Since when is the caliph concerned about women?"

"I've heard she's beautiful," Ibn Sulaiman said. "I've always wanted to be married to the daughter of a benefactor."

"If I ever found her, I'd marry you to her."

"Well then, we must find her. I won't leave Egyptian territory till I find her. Now, where's Ibrahim, Khumarawayh's son?"

"Ibn Sulaiman, you're treating me as though I'm your prisoner. I'm still amir of this country and Ahmad's son."

"Ibrahim, Khumarawayh's son, is still a boy, not yet ten years old," Ibn Sulaiman insisted. "Where have you hidden him?"

"I swear to you that I haven't hidden him. He was kidnapped two nights ago. At the time, I thought that you were the ones who'd done it to use his life as a bargaining chip. You now have all the male and female members of Ibn Tulun's family. You keep asking about a girl who's run away and a little boy with no power."

"Egypt's rulers for the last ten years have been boys, Amir. Where's your army and entourage? Order them to surrender."

"I've already done that."

But the army did not surrender.

Ibn Sulaiman ranted and raged. In desperate, fearful times, the truth will shine clear, and all veils will be lifted. Shaiban's cavalry surrendered, but his infantry did not. When he asked Shaiban why, Shaiban replied that the news of his surrender may not have reached them. Ibn Sulaiman was baffled about the infantry and vowed to teach the Egyptians a lesson that very day. He summoned Abd ar-Rahman and asked for his opinion. He informed Abd ar-Rahman that the Tulunid infantry had not surrendered. They were still fighting even though they knew that he had won. Why were they exposing themselves to certain destruction? They were still fighting for Shaiban, while the amir had already surrendered. What were they doing and what did they know?

"They know more than Shaiban," Abd ar-Rahman replied. "They've lived in the country and inherited Ahmad's dream."

"What dream? Ahmad's dead."

"People have said that Ahmad used to dream of the monarchs of old," Abd ar-Rahman told him, "when Egypt was the center of their civilization—silly, deluded dreams, Sir, with no value."

"I want your men to get involved."

"Today the war's on your side; you don't need men. They're just foot soldiers, nothing for you to worry about, Sir. They're fighting for an illusion, for stars in the sky that shine at night, then disappear. Let them be till they surrender."

"Ahmad's more dangerous than we imagined, whether dead or alive."

Ibn Sulaiman then ordered the slaughter of the entire Sudanese contingent and started the burning and demolition of Al-Qata'i and Fustat. The caliph sent reinforcements, fierce and powerful soldiers from Khurasan. He ordered them to slaughter the Egyptian soldiers who had refused to surrender and those who had done so. He slaughtered all the men who had not joined the caliph's army before Shaiban's surrender. Those who fight for a dream have no guarantee of safety. We can parley with others who fight for a general or amir, but, with dreams, there's no way in and no heart to pierce with a sword. Within a week, the fires started. The Khurasani Bedouin entered Fustat and Al-Qata'i and started raping women, killing men, and destroying homes, bakeries, and factories. But Al-Qata'i had a thousand houses or more, so one week was not enough time to demolish them all; Ibn Sulaiman would need months.

Qasim al-Khurasani approached Ibn Sulaiman in Abd ar-Rahman's presence.

"We're destroying it house by house, including the hospital and the main square," he said, "but that won't erase all trace of Ahmad. If you destroyed his mosque in Al-Qata'i, then all trace of him would disappear. Before long, there won't be a single mosque in the camp or in Fustat. But his mosque in Al-Qata'i was built by an Egyptian who's a genius at magic. It will never be destroyed, even in a thousand years' time. If we managed to destroy Ahmad's mosque, his city would no longer exist. If we burn down the city but the mosque stays in place, it'll remind people of times past and the dream of an ambitious man like Ahmad."

"People will say that Ibn Sulaiman is destroying God's own mosques," Ibn Sulaiman said.

"In Al-Qata'i we've burned and destroyed mosques already," Qasim replied forcefully. "I demolished the Enlightenment Mosque with my own hands, then burned it. No one objected; nobody dared say a word. If we spread the rumor that Ahmad's mosque was built by a Coptic magician, and the treasure that Ahmad stole and used to build the mosque was forbidden money, then people are not going to care. That's not a fake story, it's the truth."

Ibn Sulaiman looked at Abd ar-Rahman who seemed to prefer silence.

"What do you think?" he asked.

"I'm duly honored to be in your presence, Sir, and to have your trust."

"You haven't said what you think."

"I think that destroying a mosque is a very bad omen," he replied, "and sets a dangerous precedent."

"No, mosques have been destroyed before in the Umayyad period. Wasn't the Kaaba itself attacked and demolished by catapults, then rebuilt by Abdallah ibn Zubair? Even the Kaaba is not safe from attacks."

Abd ar-Rahman remained silent, and Ibn Sulaiman seemed hesitant.

"Just let me destroy it," Qasim said eventually, "and it need not involve you at all, Sir. Don't involve yourself in small details. We need you for bigger things."

"I want all Ahmad's treasure," Ibn Sulaiman said. "Everything in his palace is mine. Have soldiers entered the palace yet?"

"Not before you give orders, Sir."

"My soldiers should enter and bring me everything, cheap and dear, from inside the palace. I want to double the search for Aisha and Ibrahim. I want the two of them caught before the month's out."

At night, the argument between Ibn Sulaiman and Qasim al-Khurasani over the importance of demolishing the mosque started again.

Abd ar-Rahman soon understood and realized what Ibn Sulaiman's intentions were, he being a close aide: it was the two of them, the general and his servant, Qasim from Khurasaan, who had brought the Bedouin from there because they were fierce fighters to their dying breath, never complaining or bothering about wounds, whether deep or on the surface.

Qasim al-Khurasani would carry out orders before he even heard them. He was not just loyal to Ibn Sulaiman, but to his ideas and dreams as well. Ibn Sulaiman had told him what Ahmad had done to him, going into great detail as they sipped wine and enjoyed the services of slave-girls.

"If you intend to erase all traces of Ahmad," Qasim said firmly, "then you have to eradicate his city, but first destroy his mosque and sever his line of descendants. The mosque and the descendants are all Ahmad."

"People say," Ibn Sulaiman said thoughtfully, "that when he built the mosque, he said that water wouldn't drown it and fire wouldn't burn it."

"That can work for us, Sir. Only catapults can demolish the mosque."

"People will say that Ibn Sulaiman demolished a mosque where people pray."

"When the Umayyads hit the Kaaba, people did not blame them. The people who speak have the power; the weak just listen. Now that you've won, you have to clear the space of Ahmad. You can be married to his daughter or kill her. Do whatever you like with her, but the mosque has to be demolished."

"You're the one to do it," Ibn Sulaiman said.

"I'd carry out your orders even if you were in Baghdad."

"What if we fail to demolish it, Qasim?"

"Then we've also failed to defeat Ahmad. He knows, and so do you."

"You're right. When are you going to start?"

"When the city's defeated and its buildings are reduced to desert rubble."

Qasim al-Khurasani's eyes met Abd ar-Rahman's.

"My Arab brother, Abd ar-Rahman ibn Musa," Qasim said, "don't you like what I'm saying?"

Abd ar-Rahman stared back at him.

"What does my opinion matter compared with yours, Commander?" he said.

Qasim moved closer and sat beside him.

"What do you think of the slave-girl?" he asked. "I selected her for you myself."

"That's alarming, brother," Abd ar-Rahman replied. "I've no idea what I told her during lovemaking."

Qasim laughed.

"I don't know a thing about Egyptian women," he said. "I've never tried any. But you, Abd ar-Rahman, do you have any experience with Coptic Egyptian women?"

"I don't know anything about Egyptian women," Abd ar-Rahman replied. "We prefer to be married to tribal women."

"Ahmad ibn Tulun was a wicked man. If he had decided to be married to an Egyptian woman, he'd have found something different."

"Are you planning to be married to an Egyptian woman, brother?" Abd ar-Rahman asked Qasim.

Qasim laughed.

"Why should I be married to an Egyptian woman, Ibn Musa?" he asked. "Every woman in Egypt's my prisoner."

For a moment, there was silence.

"Do you intend to put women in prison?" Abd ar-Rahman asked. "Egyptian women aren't slave-girls. If Arabs put Egyptian women in prison, no Egyptian will ever be loyal to us. Egyptians will never forget that; sooner or later, they'll get their revenge."

"Egyptians aren't Arabs, Abd ar-Rahman," Qasim said.

"For them," Abd ar-Rahman said, "honor is more precious than life itself. I was born in this country and know it well."

"Are you going to come with me tomorrow," Qasim asked defiantly, "and watch me subdue and overpower the women right in front of their husbands and children?"

"Don't do that!" Abd ar-Rahman replied. "If you do, there'll be consequences."

"From you or Egyptians?" Qasim scoffed. "Here's this person talking about piety when he raids the peasants whenever he's short of food or money! Everyone knows that Abd ar-Rahman steals grain and animals, and then spends the money on fun and games . . . Now he's advising me to stay away from Egyptian girls!"

"Stealing animals, brother, is not the same as stealing honor," Abd ar-Rahman replied. "But I'm also afraid for the caliph's prestige."

"Prestige only comes through cruelty and victory. Once they're defeated, people forget things that happen during wartime. Periods of weakness are inevitably forgotten. Don't bother yourself about what I'm going to do. Just enjoy your slave-girl."

A tense silence ensued.

Women's screams expanded to envelop the whole of Egypt. The evil reputation of Ibn Sulaiman and the Bedouin of Khurasan spread far and wide till people accused them of unbelief, of being merciless and unforgiving. They were intent on taking revenge on the inhabitants of Al-Qata'i and Fustat. Soldiers went into Al-Qata'i with fire, catapults, and weapons. They demolished houses on top of the people inside, and set fire to grocery stands, bakeries, factories, perfume shops, slaughterhouses, grills, baths, ovens, and mills. Then they set alight the small mosques, went inside houses, raped girls in front of their families, and stole things from the people living there. Then they made their way into Ahmad's palace. Ibn Sulaiman went inside, surrounded by his men, his face wreathed in smiles. He told his men to take all the gold and jewelry and anything else of value to his tent. He then proceeded to destroy every wing one at a time, deliberately and delightedly. He set fire to valuable wood and rare trees, slaughtered wild animals, transferred various types of food to his tent, and distributed them to his soldiers. Every single day, he personally supervised the demolition of Ahmad's palace and central square.

"Do you see me today, Ahmad?" he yelled, looking up to the sky. "Do you feel regret or any grief for your mercy and cruelty toward me? Did you flay me for a dream, you tyrant? That dream became a reality, and now you no longer exist. The remaining men and women of your household are under my arrest. I can be merciful or punitive, as I wish. I have your entire treasure. Even though all Egypt loved you, you were a tyrant. I know how you really were, Ahmad, and I'm the only one who does. I've seen your cruel eyes and known your ruthless hands. You'll become a symbol, just like Pharaoh. People will recall you as a ruler who left no trace and built nothing. Today, Ahmad, you're forgotten, as though you never were."

He then ordered the entire Tulunid family to be imprisoned until the caliph decided what to do with them. He also ordered his soldiers to find Aisha alive or dead that same day, and Ibrahim as well.

"You've broken the pledge, Ibn Sulaiman," Shaiban pleaded. "You've broken the pledge. I surrendered to you on the basis of your promise of safety and a peaceful existence in Egypt. Now you've put us in prison."

"No, Shaiban," Ibn Sulaiman replied forcefully. "You don't exist anymore. If I'm made governor of this country, you're going to die before the year's out. I don't make pledges with thieves. You're a thief, as was your father and the entire Tulunid family."

Ibn Sulaiman laughed. For a moment, Abd ar-Rahman stared silently at him.

"You seem happy, Sir, about your victory," he said.

"My victory hasn't even started yet."

"Will you permit me to leave? I need to protect my tribe and reassure them. Or am I a prisoner too?"

"You're a brother and ally," Ibn Sulaiman replied, looking at the ground, "but you haven't helped me. Your men did not participate in the fighting, nor did they keep the roads safe."

"They didn't fight against you, Sir. You don't need my men when you have the Arabs from Khurasan."

"What about when I do need them?" Ibn Sulaiman asked forcefully.

"They're yours whenever you need them."

"Do you swear loyalty to me?"

"I swear loyalty to the caliph."

"You can leave . . . but if I need you, you'll bring your men."

"Immediately."

Abd ar-Rahman thought for a moment.

"I've a question that I'd like you to answer, Sir," he said.

"Go ahead."

"Why are you being so cruel with the Egyptians? If your fight was with the Tulunids, why are you taking vengeance on the Egyptian people?"

Their eyes met.

"Egyptian soldiers kept fighting," Ibn Sulaiman responded, "even after Shaiban had surrendered. Do you remember?"

"Those were soldiers, not the general public."

"Actually the general public is even stronger and more dangerous. They closed their doors to our soldiers and treated us like infidels. Christians who bowed down to Ahmad and his dream. When you're fighting a dream, you have to be cruel. Do you know what kills dreams, Abd ar-Rahman?"

"What?"

"Humiliation. It's even more crushing than death or weakness. When a mother watches her son being slaughtered, or a husband sees his wife underneath a Khurasani soldier, he realizes that there's nothing he can do. Ahmad's declaration of independence was a crime that deserved to be punished. Do you understand?"

"I'm trying."

"Does the slaughter of Egyptians grieve you?"

"Raping women does. Destroying honor is not a trait of either Muslims or Arabs."

"So you're passing judgment on soldiers then. When soldiers get a taste of blood, they inevitably place the burden of killing on women's shoulders. That's just the way wars are."

"I wish you well!" Abd ar-Rahman said after a pause.

He then left, along with three men, Salih and two others. He did not head for the tribe, but ordered Salih to go back ahead of him. The two other men stayed with him. He decided to go through Al-Qata'i and see the destruction. He heard women screaming and saw fires consuming people, faces, and limbs.

"If I see a Khurasani soldier," he whispered to his companion, "I'm going to kill him."

His companion looked at him in alarm. Abd ar-Rahman raised his bow ready to shoot, and aimed it at a soldier who was grabbing a girl not yet thirteen years old and ripping her clothes off. He fired and hit the soldier square in the back. He fell to the ground screaming, and the girl ran away. He hid his bow inside his kaftan amid the crowd of people, and shouts arose. He took off calmly as though nothing had happened.

"Why did you do that?" his companion asked.

"They've made us suffer," he said nonchalantly. "Along with suffering comes risk."

"I don't understand you, Abd ar-Rahman."

"I don't understand myself. Let's go home."

Chapter 4

These days, she hugged herself constantly, needing the warmth of his embrace amid the ice that surrounded her. He had had sex with the slave-girl and would do so with his cousin and other women too. He might even leave her alone in her room. She sometimes detested and often rued what she had given him with no return. What stunned her soul was not the gold he had stolen from her, but what she had given during lovemaking. She had entrusted herself to him and poured out all her feelings without restraint. Then came regrets. She regretted every single kiss she had lavishly bestowed on him and every endearment she had spoken without the slightest caution. She would write to Qatr an-Nada again and tell her everything. Even if Qatr an-Nada died, she would still hear her. She would tell her that he had deserted her and had sex with the slave-girl; he had deserted the Princess, Ahmad's own daughter. She would tell her that sometimes she despised herself because he had not found anything to like in her. Sometimes she did not even know her own heart or why it seemed to be intent on killing her. She would tell Qatr an-Nada that princesses should not pin their hearts on men; they had different duties and traditions. She would tell her that she had chosen the Bedouin Arab from among all the soldiers, and he had chosen the slave-girl.

Her husband came back. She could hear the men's voices talking, but stayed in her room. He looked gloomy and worried, and that froze her heart somewhat. She gave him a frigid welcome, and their eyes did not meet.

She was amazed that he had come into her room, as though he had never been away and betrayed her.

"I need to wash," he said, taking off his coat. "It's been a long day, full of dust. Prepare some water for me."

She nodded. No sooner had she left the room than she let out a long sigh and closed her eyes to stop the tears from falling. She felt an unspeakable loathing for him, and his sorrowful eyes pained her. She would have to take it all out on him that day. She hoped he would die the way he had killed her, that he would burn the way he had plucked out her heart and thrown it on the fire. Had he hugged the slave-girl and slept in her arms after making love? Had he shivered as he whispered how beautiful she was? Had he run his fingers affectionately through her hair?

"Aisha," she heard him say, "where's the water?"

Was he happy about the pact with Ibn Sulaiman, the man who used to clean the yard at her father's house? Was he content that the vile had defeated the great? She took the bowl of water back in, put it on the floor, and looked at him without saying a word.

"Help me wash," he told her, taking off the rest of his clothes.

"Didn't you bring your slave-girl to help you?" she asked without thinking. "Princesses don't have to help anyone; that's the way we were brought up. If you have a slave-girl, I'd like you to ask her to do those things."

"Even a princess has to obey her husband," he said after looking at her.

"Where's your slave-girl?"

He picked up the flannel, grabbed her hand, and put the flannel in it.

"Come on," he told her, "help me wash."

She took the flannel, turned around, and started scrubbing his shoulder so he could not see her face, fire emerging from her cheeks. She needed to recall Khalisa's words.

She concentrated on the waterdrops on his shoulders and slowly wiped them away, although she was not sure whether it was to erase all trace of the other woman or the vestige of the love inside her.

"What's making you so angry?" he asked her all of a sudden. "Are you unhappy because Ibn Sulaiman's won? Did you ever doubt that he would win?"

She did not respond, but kept slowly wiping the water off his shoulders.

He turned to look at her.

"Is the fire that's burning your heart because the Tulunids have been defeated, or because I've acquired a slave-girl?"

"It's your right," she replied, avoiding his eyes, "your absolute right to acquire slave-girls and be married to whomever you wish. I'm grieving for a beloved people who've been humiliated in an era when all truths have become confused. Forgive me, husband. I've not seemed all that enthusiastic about your return from being with people who've usurped my father's rights."

"Your father died a while ago; just remember that. One ruler was a child who just played games, and he was followed by an uncle who killed his nephew along with a cluster of corrupt associates."

He moved closer and put his hands around her face.

"But that's not the only reason," he said.

She moved his hands away.

"Are you going to rebuff me today?" he asked.

She hurled the flannel into the water, which splashed both their faces. She stood up.

"What's changed?" she asked. "Didn't you desert me for two weeks even before you went away? Now you've had sex with that slave-girl in the tent of the man who used to clean my father's yard. Why do you need me?"

He wiped the water off his face.

"What kind of question is that?" he asked. "I can want my wife at any time without question."

She started breathing faster. She imagined herself picking up the bowl of water and throwing it in his face. She would have liked it to be boiling hot, enough to scorch his face. Maybe she could take the bowl, heat it to boiling point, and bring it back. That would be better.

"Aisha," he said, "your clothes are wet. Come on, take them off."

"Do you realize, husband," she said in a quavering voice, "that when you mistreat and flay an animal, you can't milk it the same day. People say that animals never forget."

He smiled as though he had not understood.

"But you're a princess," he said. "Princesses do forget. Come here."

She grabbed her hands so as not to dig her nails into his face.

"You've told me before," she replied in fury, "that there's no difference between a princess and a slave-girl. Do you remember? You're not in love with me any longer."

He stared at her in amazement.

"I never said that," he replied. "Where did you hear it? The difference is that a princess knows her duties and avoids women's usual inanities. Don't fuss about slave-girls."

She gave a wan smile.

"I'm not going to rebuff you," she said. "You're my husband, and, as you said, I have to obey you."

"That's much better!"

He stopped washing and put his hands around her face again. Then he kissed her passionately, and she accepted it stalwartly. Her heart was closed to him. Whenever her body melted to his touch, she saw him in her imagination in someone else's arms. Her body froze and was subject to her will. She let him do whatever he wanted. He hugged her hard and kissed her. His passion seemed to be sincere, and it was always that sincere passion that led to degradation. She suppressed the tears that refused to fall until he had finished. She moved away, but he pulled her toward him. She moved his hand away.

"A husband should not force his wife," she told him firmly. "I've done my duty. Now let me go to sleep."

He did not speak.

She moved as far away as possible, her tears now cascading down her face.

"Why are you crying?" he asked, sitting up.

"I'm not crying," she said. "Actually, I am crying—for what's been lost."

"What's that, Aisha? What's been lost wasn't yours to begin with."

"I thought it was. That's my mistake and delusion."

"Come here," he said, holding her by the arm. "You used to sleep on top of my heart. Do you remember?"

"No, I don't," she replied, removing his hand.

A tense silence ensued. She wanted him to leave the room now, or for dawn to arrive unawares. He pulled her toward him, but she moved away again. He asked her to move closer, but she refused outright. She did not get any sleep, but next morning she felt him get up. He fetched a piece of paper and pencil and sat down. He called to her, and she opened her eyes and looked at him.

"Come here, Aisha," he told her firmly.

She sat down beside him, and he handed her the pencil.

"Make a list of all the contents of your palace," he told her, "everything: gold, animals, ornaments, embroidery, silver, bronze, all the lamps, curtains, and furniture."

She stared at him in amazement.

"Come on," he told her, "what are you waiting for?"

"I don't understand," she replied.

"There's nothing to understand. Maybe if you start writing and remembering things, it'll help you move on beyond what's happened. Come on, start writing."

"Give me some time."

"There's no time. Start writing now."

She started writing things down slowly. Every time she remembered something, it made her more miserable.

He was staring at her hard.

"I don't want to write anything," she told him uneasily.

"I didn't ask you what you wanted," he told her angrily. "Just do what I tell you without saying anything. Make sure you don't forget anything."

"I can't remember all the details."

"Didn't you spend twenty years inside the palace? You must remember."

He rubbed his hand over her back.

"How many slave-girls did your father own, I wonder," he asked, "and how many wives?"

She understood his point and did not respond.

She moved away from him.

"I can't write with you so close," she said.

He moved even closer till his breaths scorched her cheek.

"You didn't answer me," he told her. "Was your mother angry about your father's slave-girls or his other wives? Did she receive him with a frown on her face?"

She pursed her lips, feeling an overwhelming desire to pierce his eye with the pencil she was holding.

"No, she didn't," she replied. "You'll have to forgive me because I'm not as good or as generous as she was."

She moved away.

"I've just told you that I can't write this way."

"Stop objecting and write. Come on . . ."

"Why are you taking revenge on me like this?" he asked after a while. "I've not done anything. All that frigidity toward me yesterday. Do you think I don't know?"

For the first time, she felt proud.

"Once or twice," she said without thinking, "I've stood by your door."

She regretted what she had just said.

He rubbed her back again.

"It didn't happen," he said.

She put her feet on the floor.

"I'm not a piece of rag in your hand," she told him firmly, "nor am I a panting dog eager to do your will. I came to you . . . I was alone and afraid. I was . . . Oh, you'll never understand."

He did not respond.

She started writing quickly, filled a whole page, then stopped.

"That's all I can remember," she said.

He grabbed the piece of paper and read what she had written carefully.

"That's enough," he said.

She held out her hand to take the paper back.

"Leave it with me for a while," he said.

"I thought you wanted me to keep it," she said.

"Yes," he replied, "I did want you to keep it, but then I changed my mind. I'll see you this evening."

As he left, her mouth was gaping in surprise.

That day, she decided to take a walk in the desert; she was almost suffocating inside the house. She sat by herself on a rock and started throwing stones, angry and desperate. Just then, she heard a voice and put up her veil.

"Never in my entire life," Salih said, "have I seen a sweeter and lovelier face. Forgive me, my lady."

She stood up.

"Who are you?" he asked.

She hurried back to the house with him following behind.

"Forgive me," he said. "Don't blame me. I've come to complain to the desert about the betrayal."

She stopped for a moment.

"I have to obey the chieftain's son," he said, "but my conscience wants the Tulunids to win. I realize that what I'm saying may lead to my death, but such a lovely lady will never be a betrayer. Who are you?"

"You want the Tulunids to win, but how?" she asked without thinking.

"With my heart. I can't do anything else. Maybe in the future . . ."

"They don't have a future."

"People are saying that Ibrahim's run away, or else one of his men has helped him."

"Do you know where he is?" she asked without thinking.

"Who are you, my lady? The tribe's chieftain will kill me if you say anything."

She ran back to the house feeling scared, regretting that she had spoken to a man she did not even know. His words stayed with her.

"You think the war's over," he had said. "It hasn't even started yet. You're beautiful, and yet you seem very sad. Who are you?

"I'm Salih," he had continued, walking behind her. "Should you need anything, you'll find that I'm ready to obey you and carry out your instructions. Every day, I'll be waiting for you."

♟

Khalisa sat Aisha down beside her.

"Come here and listen," she told her. "Don't say anything."

Khalisa looked at the slave-girl sitting there modestly, stunned by how beautiful she was.

"Who is she, Aunt?" Aisha asked.

"You know," Khalisa replied, pursing her lips.

Aisha clutched her heart.

"Where have you brought her from? Why?"

Khalisa hit her on the hand.

"Khalisa knows everything," she replied. "She'll tell us the truth about everything."

"I don't want to know, Aunt," Aisha pleaded. "Please be merciful with me."

"There's mercy in knowledge."

Khalisa looked at the slave-girl.

"You promised me to tell the truth," she told her.

"My lord, Abd ar-Rahman!" she replied admiringly. "My God, I've never seen such a handsome and strong man before, and . . ."

Aisha interrupted her.

"What happened between the two of you?" she asked.

"I swear that I wanted to stay with him for the rest of my life. He didn't look at me or even notice me. He had sex with me, of course. Faced with my beauty, there's no man who doesn't lose his mind. We had sex, but his mind wasn't with me. When he'd finished, I moved closer, wanting to make him happy. But he pushed me away roughly and told me he didn't want me to sleep with him in his bed. He asked me to sleep in another room. Three days later, he gave me to my lord Salih, but he never even came close to me. He told me that his heart was filled with an impossible love or something like that. I don't understand, my lady."

"How did you know his heart wasn't with you?" Khalisa asked thoughtfully.

"I know, my lady. I can sense men's feelings and understand them."

"How can you understand?" Khalisa insisted.

The girl thought for a while before going on. Meanwhile, Aisha dug her nails into her hands till they bled as she looked at the girl's breasts and svelte figure.

"His touches had no warmth to them," she said coquettishly, "and no quivering passion. His eyes were looking at me, but when I told him how much I longed for him, he didn't respond, as though he hadn't heard or didn't believe me. In moments of sheer rapture, I told him that he was the best of men and I wanted to spend the rest of my life with him, but again he seemed not to hear, even though words like that can melt men's hearts. Then . . ."

Khalisa looked at Aisha, whose lips had turned white in fury.

"Then what?" Khalisa asked.

"When he finished, he did not kiss me or turn toward me, even though no woman can rival me when it comes to love. My generosity with men is well known and my sheer perfection makes even Ibn Sulaiman forget who he is. Abd ar-Rahman asked me to get dressed, and I slept in another room. I won't hide from you, my lady, that I still desire him. Such a strong, determined man impresses me . . .

"But he's given me to Salih," she went on with a sigh. "He doesn't even touch me . . .

"But I made Abd ar-Rahman happy," she went on maliciously. "He admires beauty and openness. I saw pleasure in his eyes. Love's an art that has to be perfected."

Aisha felt a pain in her heart as never before and closed her eyes.

"That's enough, Aunt," she told Khalisa.

Khalisa gave the slave-girl some money, then allowed her to leave.

"I don't understand what you're saying, Aisha," she said, "but you must understand."

"I can see him slaughtered in front of me and moaning. His blood is soaking the house. Then I go over, rip out his heart, and tear it into little pieces while he watches impotently. Could I do that, I wonder? Why did you bring her here?"

"Because there's salvation in knowledge, even if it's marred by pain. What can you see as well?"

"Maybe I'll burn his heart, Aunt, and mix it with your wheat."

"He's aware and awake, right?"

"Yes."

"Then tear your own heart out."

Aisha nodded. Khalisa was still confused.

"The slave-girl said that she couldn't reach his heart," Khalisa said. "He was distracted."

"His heart can burn. Let him die a thousand times over."

She leaned her head against the door, listening to the conversation between the guest and the chieftain. When she looked at him through the narrow crack, she recognized who he was: the young man who had seen her a few days ago and spoken to her. He sat down beside the chieftain.

"All praise to the One who teaches and humbles!" he said. "Shaikh, I have seen Al-Qata'i with my very own eyes, like a pile of discarded furniture. Ibn Sulaiman has a long-standing vow of vengeance against the Tulunids. He doesn't want any of them left in Egypt; who knows, he may kill them all. I don't trust him; I don't trust his word or his promises. Has your son told you what's happened?"

She clutched her heart and choked as never before.

"You know Ahmad ibn Tulun's palace and the main square, don't you?" Salih asked. "It was a palace that no one could view from outside. People said it had all kinds of plants and animals. They said that Khumarawayh kept white and black lions in the palace garden. We used to weave entire stories and fables about the palace and its beautifully designed gardens about which we knew nothing. We used to stop in the main square as children and eat halva; we would then imagine what was behind the gate and huge wall. Now Ibn Sulaiman's burned it all in front of my very own eyes. I watched the lions roaring in the flames and stood by as Ibn Sulaiman's men systematically knocked down the walls and trampled the flowers. It was just like the Day of Resurrection, Shaikh. I wept for a palace whose walls we used to look at as though they would never be destroyed. But now they've been demolished in a day or less. Ibn Sulaiman is not to be trusted, but Abd ar-Rahman is parlaying and making deals with him."

"Abd ar-Rahman's my successor," the shaikh said slowly, "and I've handed things over to him. He knows best what the tribe's best plan is. Make sure you don't defy him!"

"I'll never do that," Salih replied immediately. "You know me, Shaikh. I just wanted to tell you what's happened and to ask you about . . ."

Suddenly he fell silent.

"Ask me about what?" the shaikh demanded.

"I thought I saw a strange girl in our midst."

"You saw her face?" he asked angrily.

"No, I didn't. But I've been hearing about a strange girl here . . ."

"What business is that of yours?"

For a moment, he said nothing.

"I was inquiring as to whether she had a husband or needed protection. I came to see you to . . ."

Aisha put her hand over her mouth as she heard the shaikh yell.

"If Abd ar-Rahman heard your question now, he'd cut your head off. Forget what you've just said. She's your master's wife!"

"Forgive me, Shaikh," he replied immediately, in a total panic. "These are bewildering times."

"Never mention that again. Regarding Al-Qata'i, the entire Tulunid family has surrendered."

"Except for two. Two of them haven't surrendered yet."

"Who are they?"

"There's Ibrahim, Khumarawayh's son. He's a young boy, and it looks as though someone's kidnapped him, maybe in order to bargain with Ibn Sulaiman. Who knows? Then there's Ahmad's own daughter whom we didn't find in the palace. Of his thirty-three children, we know who's been killed, who's surrendered, and whom Ibn Sulaiman's arrested. But Ahmad's daughter is still a fugitive."

"Why's Ibn Sulaiman so interested in one of Ahmad's daughters?"

"Because she's of his progeny. Anyone married to her, Shaikh, could demand to be ruler of Egypt. Ibn Sulaiman wants to take her to Iraq."

"Do you think he'll hand over Shaiban and his coterie to the caliph?"

"No," Salih replied confidently, "I think he'll get rid of them before that. His whole purpose in coming was to erase all trace of Ahmad on the earth's surface. He plans to stay in Egypt so he can even destroy the mosque. He has a servant named Qasim, a really evil man."

"That's enough talk about Ibn Sulaiman," the shaikh said "You should be talking to Abd ar-Rahman about him, not me. He's your commander. Don't forget!"

Salih stood up and headed for the door. He kept looking around, as though searching for her. He did not find anyone.

"How I pity that strange girl," he said in a low but audible voice, "whose husband fools around with slave-girls and doesn't appreciate the jewel he has—a tribe that's not to be trusted."

Her tears poured down as his words rang in her ears. Al-Qata'i, a city that had lived in her imagination, although she had only seen it once. She wanted to try the pastry baker's cake, but she had not had the chance, nor had she purchased any silk or watched the soldiers' parade.

Later that night, Abd ar-Rahman came into her room. Taking a deep breath, she clasped her husband's shoulder.

"I'll help you take your cloak off," she said.

He gave her the kind of look that she had never understood and let her take off his cloak.

"Abd ar-Rahman," she pleaded, "all I want is for you not to cooperate with Ibn Sulaiman. I don't want you erecting barriers between us. I realize that you don't want to fight a losing battle, but if you remained neutral, it would be better for us. You have the gold and don't need Ibn Sulaiman . . ."

He sat on his bed.

"Don't poke your nose into things that don't concern you," he replied sternly.

She did her best to control her sorrow. "I've heard about the destruction of Al-Qata'i," she said. "Are you happy about that?"

He did not respond.

"Are you going to give my gold to your new lover?" she asked, avoiding his eyes.

He gave her an angry look. "You don't have any gold, Aisha. As I've told you before, you don't own it, nor did your father before you."

"Nor do you either."

"You keep tossing words back and forth. I don't like it."

She remained silent. She was not sure whether she could stay with him in the same place for a single day longer. Turning away, she made up her mind. Whether the next day or the day after, she would go to her palace before long, even if it was in ruins. She needed to see her city. It had been entrusted to her, but she had not been able to save it. Why had Saeed asked her to do something that she could not manage? She was just a girl, with no power or authority; a girl deceived by the fox that had pounced on her, leaving her no power even to scream out loud.

Had he held the slave-girl all night, she wondered? Maybe he had . . . the slave-girl was lying. Had he whispered in her ear how beautiful she was? Why could she not rid herself of the image of him with the slave-girl? It was overpowering every other image, even that of the city.

He left the room at dawn.

That day as well, she left the house to look for a way of getting to Al-Qata'i. She went to the place where he used to train his horses, not knowing whether her inquisitive instinct was making her chase after him or she was actually looking for a way to get to Al-Qata'i. If she asked him, he would not take her there; that much was impossible. That day, he was not training his horses. Looking all around her, she used her hand to block the burning rays of the sun. Then she found him. He was holding a pigeon; then he released it, letting it fly far away. He was sitting on his own by the pigeon towers. Was he sending messages? What was he doing with the pigeon and what was he planning? People said that Abd ar-Rahman was an adventurer and risk-taker who had played for his entire life. He had never grown up or had the world's realities made clear to him. But he was even more dangerous than she had expected and people had said. Azza may not have understood him, and she herself certainly had not. There was no limit to his cunning and deviousness. He had his own personal goals and did not care about the feelings and goals of anyone else. She hurried back to the house before he spotted her.

All day, she tried to put his image out of her mind as she tried to come up with a way of getting to her city. She remembered a childhood long ago and her own image as she ran for hours amid the flowers, trees, and park with their heavenly scent. In those days, she had owned the whole world, even though it loomed like a huge giant far from the horizon. She had opened her tiny arms to embrace the dewdrops and breezes, then folded them again so as to trap them in the folds of her bosom.

With a smile, she had told her mother that she could understand the language of birds and knew what the breeze whispered to the trees. Her mother believed her; she always did. She picked her up and spun her around till her tears started falling from the wind brushing against her cheek. She laughed as never before and never after, her laughter blending with the sound of the palm trees and stretching away to the outskirts of the city.

"If I shouted and yelled," she asked her mother with innocent enthusiasm, "would he hear me?"

"Your father hears you and adores you," her mother replied. "He told me that yesterday."

"How did he say it yesterday?"

"In the dream. He said you're the best of his children, the one closest to his heart. He realizes how brave and capable you are."

"Does he know that I understand birds and trees? Have you told him, Mother?"

"I'll tell him today."

"Does he know that I'm the fastest runner in this park, and can reach the edge before it turns around?"

"He knows."

"What does he think of my speed?"

"He thinks you're remarkable. Your strength transcends the boundaries of Al-Qata'i."

"But Al-Qata'i's wide, and the park is lofty. I don't know where the city ends. I've never seen its streets."

"One day you'll walk along the streets, Princess, your head raised high because you're Ahmad's daughter."

Aisha closed her eyes, feeling the pain as the words echoed . . . "Head raised high because you're Ahmad's daughter." How could she leave this place now to look at her city? How could her heart that was betraying her at every moment crumble away?

That day he came back late, looking glum as he sat to eat his dinner. She sat down in front of him.

"In my imagination," she said angrily, "I'm seeing destruction, fire, and a city groaning from catapult strikes and women's screams. Are you happy about such devastation, I wonder?"

He looked at her without saying anything. She could not understand what it meant.

"Who's been talking to you?" he asked.

She gulped in surprise. "No one has," she replied anxiously.

"Yesterday and today, you talk about the city and the devastation. Who's been talking to you? Speak!"

"Have I been so wrong," she replied nervously, "to be worried about my city, my palace, and my entire life? Have I done something wrong by hating devastation and wanting to preserve what my father built? Where is the wrongdoing, son of the tribal chieftain?"

He grabbed her wrist all of a sudden and pulled her close.

"Who's spoken to you, Princess?" he asked. "I'll know if you don't tell me. If I know, I'll slaughter him, then flay you till you ask to die. Who told you that the palace was destroyed and robbed?"

"I knew without anyone having to tell me. I expected that to happen . . ."

"Don't lie," he interrupted, pulling her wrist toward him. "You're no good at lying."

"Let go of my wrist," she pleaded. "You're hurting me."

He let go.

"You're going to tell me everything now," he said. "Be careful, do you hear me? Make sure you don't even think of going to the city. If you do, I'll kill you and knock down all the remaining buildings."

She stood up, ready to head for the door.

"If you hate me this much," she whispered, "then leave me."

"Leave you how?"

"The way your father left Khalisa. Leave me here and be married to the woman you love. Enjoy all the slave-girls you want. Just leave me to myself. Don't make me suffer for no reason or benefit."

She did not listen to his reply. She opened the door to leave.

"Come back in," he told her in a scary tone. "Close the door, and come over here."

She came over with heavy steps and sat on the floor. He grabbed her arm, and before she could object, pulled her to his chest.

"Did you talk to Salih?" he asked in a sneaky tone.

She tried moving away, but he kept his hold on her.

"Leave me alone, Abd ar-Rahman," she begged.

"Stop resisting. Just answer my question."

She pushed against his chest.

"I don't know that name," she said. "I've heard some men talking about what's happened to the city when I was outside. That's all. Are you going to stop me going outside from now on? Will that accomplish your plan to humiliate and crush me?"

For a moment, he remained silent.

"I don't want you leaving the house till Ibn Sulaiman has gone," he said. "He's searching for you in person."

This was the first time he had explained anything to her.

"Is he bothered about my fate?" she asked bitterly. "Wouldn't my death make you happy?"

He moved her away a little. She could see an inexplicable suffering in his eyes.

"I want you to love me the way you used to do," he told her softly. "Do you remember?"

"The same way she did?"

"Forget her. She's nothing to me."

"Did you want her because she's more beautiful than me?"

"Kiss me," he said with a merciless affection. "I'm your husband. You want me just as much as I want you."

"And if I don't, will you flay me or slaughter me?"

"Forget about such talk. I long for you."

She moved away, shaking her head.

"Don't do this to me," she said. "I no longer know who I am."

He kissed her cheek, then her neck.

"I know who you are," he said. "I'll remind you."

"Do you want me to betray my father?"

"Don't think about your father when you're in my arms."

"My father . . ."

"Not now."

"He'll stay with me."

He kissed her on the mouth.

"Kiss me back," he said, "the way you used to do, eagerly, innocently, with your whole heart and soul. Come on . . ."

Her heart was pounding. The bitter passage of time suddenly exploded, and jealousy went on forever.

"Did she kiss you back innocently as well?" she asked.

"She's nothing."

"But you wanted her. You'll be married to Azza and other women, and get one or two slave-girls as well . . ."

He ran his hand over her back.

"If I did," he replied, "that's my right."

"Don't ask of me something I can't give."

"You're in love with me. Someone who's in love hands over the reins to love, without stinting or being cruel."

She sat up, breathing hard with a suppressed anger.

"I gave you my love," she said, "and you tossed it into the garbage. You crushed it first, then . . ."

He held her hand and kissed her arm.

"Love is not given," he interrupted. "It can't be controlled. It lurks in the very depths, waiting for its owner to appear. It has no end or beginning. Do not deceive yourself."

His caresses were making it difficult to concentrate.

"But passion for the body does come to an end," she said.

"If it springs from a passion for the soul," he replied, "it doesn't come to an end. Come here. If I love you now, it won't be a defeat for you. I realize that you're angry. Put that aside for a few hours. It won't go away."

She looked into his eyes as he drew close. When he held her hand, she could not stop him.

"Kiss me today," he said again, "and you can be angry tomorrow . . ."

"Do what you want, Abd ar-Rahman," she replied bitterly. "Then finish and leave me alone."

He ran his hand through her hair.

"If you give me a kiss," he asked her gently, "will the world come to an end?"

"No, but my heart will. I'll burn it and loathe it."

She let him rub his hand gently over her arms and shoulder. As she closed her eyes, passion began to melt her anger. Confusion can always sear and humiliate.

He kissed her neck, then her ears.

"The Princess must obey her husband," he told her gently, "and stay loyal to him. She has to kiss him and give herself to him. That's required, even if she's annoyed."

Eyes closed, she tried to push him away.

"What do you gain by humiliating me?" she asked bitterly. "You've taken the gold and . . ."

He kissed her hand, and his arm was still wrapped around her body.

"I promise you I'll forget," he interrupted.

"Forget what?"

"I'll forget that you kissed me, that you still love me and long for me as I do you. We won't talk about it again . . ."

"Why?" she asked in despair. "Why can't you be kind?"

As he kept kissing her, his caresses were making her lose her mind.

"I'll be kind tomorrow," he said. "I promise. But today, I'm being cruel and giving you orders. You're going to kiss me and tell me how much you long for me."

He put his hands around her head and put it on his chest.

"I've longed for you," he said.

She put her lips on his chest, smelled his scent, and felt him overwhelming all her senses.

"Didn't you stay away from me before your journey?" she asked. "Didn't you desert me?"

"That never happened," he insisted.

"Don't make me lose my mind," she said, getting up. "You did it. I came to you, and you told me to leave. I waited day after day, but you never came. The princess got bored very quickly."

He pulled her head down onto his chest again.

"Haven't I told you," he replied, "that night erases the memory? Why are you talking about a past that I don't remember?"

He kissed her face, shoulder, and arm.

"If your husband wants you," he asked gently, "why are you so angry? Would you prefer me to leave?"

"Yes," she replied without thinking.

"You're lying," he whispered. "Don't lie, Princess. You're no good at it."

"Only you are."

"Tell me you want me to stay."

"Kill me, then I'll never say it."

"Kiss me, Aisha," he commanded. "That's an order."

She did not move. He moved closer. Grabbing hold of the shreds of her anger, he tore them apart with his hands like pieces of paper and old wrappings. His caresses kept tearing at her mind.

"You were waiting for me day after day," he whispered, "longing for me and remembering . . ."

She pushed him away.

"You're the one who forgot," she said.

"Pour out all the desire in your heart," he said. "I'll forget that too, Princess."

She was feeling passionate; he was not lying. She was suffering from his brutish behavior. All she wanted was for the room to expand with his breaths. She had never had to cope with this kind of humiliation! But those breaths of his were filling her heart and liberating her imprisoned body. If she kissed him, would he promise her not to go away?

Times and crises blended.

"Don't desert me again," she found herself saying unconsciously. "Don't leave me in your house as a stranger with no friend."

He put his hand over his heart.

"That's a promise on my part," he replied seriously. "If you kiss me today, I won't leave you again."

She hesitated for just a moment, then put her arms around his chest and kissed it with a mixture of pain, longing, and sorrow. It was an order; that is what he had said, and it had to be carried out. She kept her lips on his chest as she rubbed her hand over his arm.

"This tyranny has to be paid for," she whispered. "What you're doing to me is unforgivable. Do you realize that I'm afraid of being left alone? Did you think of me? My misgivings and worries? I'd only left my own mother's protection a month before. Then you started making me suffer."

"If you'd told me you were scared," he replied softly, "I'd have come back. Aisha, I'm taking you in my arms."

She kissed his neck slowly, then put her arms around it. As she closed her eyes, her kisses were more intense and profound.

"Princess of unparalleled beauty," he told her affectionately, "your kisses are just amazing. Do you realize? They penetrate to the very depths."

She wanted to yell in his face how much she loathed him and how furious she was with him. She wanted to tell him what he had done to her and about the fire that was burning her heart. She felt that she was in hell, but she could not do it. As before, she had given herself to him with an innocent longing and desperate love.

She realized that she would regret it all, and the crime would gnaw at her insides, for not safeguarding her father's memory and her own self-respect. Giving herself to him was humiliating, but revealing her own weakness and begging him not to leave her again was a betrayal of her entire being.

Once he had finished, her head was still resting on his chest and her lips over his heart. She could not move them. Then she turned away and hugged herself. The image of her father chiding her would not leave her imagination. He pulled her toward him again, put his arms around her waist, and lifted her on top of his body as he had done before. This time, she did not sigh, but simply closed her eyes.

"What do you want from me?" she asked. "You want love and realize that you've gained my heart. Does that please you? Do you feel more successful when you confirm your total control or when you know that you've crushed me the same way the city's been destroyed?"

"I didn't destroy the city," he whispered gently in her ear.

"We're all too weak to resist, sometimes willingly, sometimes unwillingly. How many times does my father scold me? I sacrificed his treasure, and then . . ."

"Why's your father still with us today?" he interrupted her. "Leave him outside the room. I'm your husband. I demanded obedience. I now command you to stay sleeping on top of me."

"You'll choke if I stay there too long."

"Don't worry about me now."

She shifted her position so that she was half on top of him and half in the bed. She then fell sound asleep, knowing that it would not last. Whenever his affection gushed, he covered the soil, and it turned into gold. Whenever she tried to move, he pulled her toward him and wrapped his arms round her shoulders even though he was asleep. What would he do when he was married to Azza, she wondered. His affection would smother her too. Aisha would stay in the room next door, realizing that he was now with the love of his life. Azza might get annoyed with her and give her details of his lovemaking—who knows? The slave-girl had said that he did not sleep with her in the same room or take her in his arms. He still wanted her; that was certain. But why did that feeling not make her happy? Why was she bothered about him? Why was she still longing for him, even though he had told her long since that he loved someone else?

She woke up in the middle of the night and banged on his chest.

"You said you don't love me," she told him. "Do you remember? You love Azza. That's what you said."

He sighed sleepily and did not respond. She shook him angrily. He ran his hand over her body.

"Can you still be that angry?" he asked. "Come here."

She grumbled and resisted.

"Promise me you won't sleep in her arms," she whispered. "Let me have just one thing."

She had no idea how or why she said that. He kissed her body.

"Today I'll promise you anything," he said. "That's enough talk!"

"You're promising me now, and then you'll break it tomorrow morning."

"It's not morning yet."

"You wriggle and slither away like a snake."

He made love to her again till the passion exhausted her. Now she slept without moving. At dawn, he put out the lamp and ran his hand over her chin.

"What's that wound on your chin?" he asked, eyes closed. "Did you fall down?"

She swallowed hard, remembering her weakness with Saleema. Weakness was a fault, but, for princesses, it was death.

"Yes," she replied, "I fell down. The wound's healed."

He wrapped his arms around her till the morning. When she woke, he had already left. She tried to remember his whisperings from the day before. What had he said while overpowering her body?

"There's no one like you, Princess," he had said. "You're the most beautiful of all, the most wonderful. You're a magical lady!"

"But you deserted me," she might have replied.

"I've promised you double love. Doesn't that satisfy you?"

"No, it doesn't. You've come back from seeing the traitor."

"No politics during lovemaking. Enough talk! Today, I'm not going to leave till your tongue can't talk about anything but love. I'm going to erase your memory and drown your sorrows."

"You won't be able to do that."

"Don't defy me, Princess!"

He did it. For hours, she was lost in a drunken stupor of love.

The next morning, she looked at the sky through her window.

"Forgive me, Father," she said. "I'm not the best of your children; I'm the worst. Please don't be angry with me. I'm a girl with no power or discretion. I used to think that I was the commander's daughter, the monarch with whom no one could compare since the Prophet Joseph. But I'm not fit to be your daughter. My weakness blinds me, so I can't see. Degradation keeps me in its clutches like a drowning beloved. I could not save your city or even hate the traitor. If you were still alive, you would be angry with me and even sadder than you were over Al-Abbas's betrayal. But then, at least Al-Abbas was strong, but I'm . . .

Along with her feeling of wrongdoing, there was also a sense of pleasure as a woman. She did her best not to think about it, but she could not stop feeling happy that he still wanted her. He had been close, then far away; he had deserted her, then come back.

She put on her clothes and made up her mind to go to the city that day, even if she died or was killed, or her husband decided to kill or flay her.

She looked all around her as she left the house and headed for Al-Qata'i, concealing a knife under her clothes. As she was walking nonstop, she ran into a donkeyman. After paying him some money, she asked him to take her to the palace. He told her that the road was dangerous; the Khurasani Bedouin were killing women, and he was afraid for her. But she still insisted on going there.

She heard screams and smelled fresh blood. The donkeyman stopped by the city gates and told her that he could not go any farther. She begged him to wait for her and gave him a large amount of money, telling him that all she wanted was to cast a last look on the city.

There was the palace. That day, the soldiers were burning the trees, leaving only the roots and unknown bits of wood. No one would remember how splendid they looked or the leaves that used to extend far and wide, changing color throughout Egypt. There was a day when she thought that, with its towering roof, the palace could not be overpowered by anyone. Her gaze could not even extend as far as the end of the roof or the boundaries of the walls. Now the only things to be seen were scattered bits of smashed stone where her mother's and her own rooms had been. Her father's room was now a black pit filled with vestiges of the fire. Soldiers were still busy, carrying out withered rosebushes and scattered pieces of bronze that they were secreting in their pockets as fast as possible. It was a new sensation for her to look at her roots completely burned, leaving her only the vestiges of a past life. It was as if they had left the wood without roots, and everything that had been was now unrecognizable relics and remains. Every time a sword chopped down an orange, apricot, or lofty palm tree, her heart burned.

She screamed as she had never screamed before.

"Mother," she shouted at the top of her voice, "where are you? Don't leave me alone . . ."

She collapsed on the debris and covered her face with her quivering hand.

"Father," she said, slapping her cheeks, "forgive us, forgive us all."

A hand touched her cheek, and she leapt to her feet, terrified. She knew that face and voice; it was Salih.

He moved away.

"Forgive me," he said gently. "I saw you crying. Please don't cry, my lady . . ."

Her eyes were still glued to the debris and burning fires.

"Leave me to my own devices," she said without thinking.

"Princess," he told her gently, "be reassured. Ibrahim is safe."

She stared at him in amazement. Looking all around her, she saw that the soldiers were busy knocking things down, burning, and stealing whatever they could. No one even noticed she was there.

"What's that you're saying?" she asked.

"That I know you, Princess of Princesses. I'm protecting Ibrahim and the entire

Tulunid family if I can. I'm not breaking the pledge; it stays in place till the Day of Judgment, and . . ."

He fell silent.

"Well then, don't betray your pledge to the tribe," she said firmly. "You realize that I'm the wife . . ."

"He doesn't deserve you," he interrupted, "or appreciate you, as I've told you. But he . . ."

She headed toward the donkeyman, nervously wiping the tears from her eyes.

"Don't say another word about my husband," she interrupted him, "or I'll tell him."

***

She heard Salih groan as the arrow hit him in the chest. He fell to the ground, and she sat down beside him in total shock, looking around to see where the shot had come from. One of the soldiers must have killed him. How cruel Ibn Sulaiman's soldiers were, how . . . Her mouth gaped and her shock only worsened as she looked at her husband, the source of the shot. Her husband had just killed Salih. She had no idea how or when . . .

"Why, why, why?" she asked hysterically.

He pulled her up.

"You go out without my permission," he told her angrily, "you talk and flirt with a man who's not your husband, and then you ask why?"

She resisted him as she went over to Salih.

"He may be still alive," she said. "Let's try to help him. Why did you kill him? How can you possibly kill a man like that so simply? What kind of devil got into you, or rather, what kind of devil are you?"

He grabbed her arm roughly.

"He's dead," he said. "It's over. Come on, let's hurry."

She brought the knife out from under her dress.

"I swear I'm going to kill myself now," she said, semi-conscious. "I'm not going back with you, never."

She moaned and cried. "Ah, Father!" she called out, slapping her face, "Ah, Father, everything you built is gone. Forgive me. Father, forgive me. Ahmad! I don't deserve to bear your name . . ."

Before he could grab the knife from her, she aimed it at her heart.

"Death's easier than going back with you," she said.

She did not know exactly what happened. He was about to grab the knife, but she resisted him. The knife cut her arm. She heard him curse her and utter oaths. Putting the knife in his pocket, he dragged her over to his horse against her will, put her on it, and left.

The wind brushed her cheeks as she recalled the killing, the fire, her mother running with her in the palace gardens, and making love with her husband not too many days ago. The scenes all melded together, just as her breaths mingled with the hurtful wind. She lost consciousness.

Maybe she had to kill herself. Did she prefer to be a prisoner of Ibn Sulaiman or return to her husband? Perhaps, as a princess, she needed to kill herself and not subject her father to any more humiliation. She could not stop crying and shivering.

"I don't want to set eyes on him," she insisted, as she asked Khalisa to help her. "I'd rather die. If he even comes close, I'm going to die."

Khalisa gave Abd ar-Rahman a scolding look.

"What on earth did you do to her today?" she asked.

"She wounded her arm," he replied, ignoring her question. "We need to clean the wound."

He threw her down on Khalisa's bed.

"I don't want . . . ," she muttered.

"Stop talking," he interrupted.

Aisha started sobbing, the image of the slain Salih still with her. Truth was now completely jumbled. The city had been burned—the main square and palace park. What had happened to the animals, she wondered. Had all the lakes dried up? Could water not triumph over fire? Even the walls had been knocked down, and the gold-encrusted palms had been pulled out by the roots. How foul gold was, making men lose their minds and provoking all kinds of cruelty and deceit. She could see her mother chiding her for what she had done, talking to her about her wonderful father, and then seeing the palace in ruins, burned to cinders like heretics on Judgment Day.

And then, there was him. He had now burned her childhood and youth. She could not see him clearly, but he was hurting her, body and soul. She groaned.

"I told you not to go out," he chided her, "but you did. They're out to destroy everywhere, not just Al-Qata'i. Does your arm hurt?"

She groaned again and pulled her hand away. He grabbed it again.

"You deserve it and more. If I killed you today, I could relax."

"Do it then, and we can both relax."

He put some herbs on the wound. She suppressed another groan, while he bound it up.

"Women who disobey their husbands deserve to be flogged and locked up," he said. "When you're feeling better, we have to talk, talk a whole lot."

"Do you ever show any mercy?"

"Do you see any mercy around you, Princess, so I can be merciful too? If I did, I'd die. If I died, then Ibn Sulaiman would get you. He might not kill you, Princess. He might want to be married to you so that he could humiliate your father every single day. Does that fate appeal to you?"

"How's that fate any different from my fate today?" she muttered. "He's a killer, and so are you. He . . ."

"Be careful!" he interrupted. "Don't say anything, or else I may flog you today, even if you are wounded."

He told her to sleep on her right side.

"Why haven't you killed me?" she muttered. "If you did, all these problems would be over. You've taken everything you want: gold, body, and heart. What is it you want now?"

"What you need is rest and food," he insisted. "You must eat something."

She sat up and looked at him.

"I'm going to die now and won't set eyes on you ever again. That's all I want."

He ignored her and called out to Khalisa, who had left the room.

"Look after her, Aunt," he said, "and make sure she eats something. I'll tell the servants to prepare some food. The wound's small, but deep. We don't want it to get infected."

She shuddered.

"I swear, I'm going to kill myself," she mumbled. "I'm not going to stay with you. I'm going to kill myself today."

He went over to her and pulled her head roughly toward his face.

"If I hear you say that one more time," he told her, "I'm going to tie you up here for the rest of your life. Is that what you want?"

"No, I don't," she whispered.

"You're going to eat and do everything I tell you."

She said nothing.

"Do you hear me?!" he yelled at her.

"Yes, I do," she choked.

With that, he left her.

"I don't want any knives in this room," he told Khalisa. "This child is stupid. She hasn't learned anything all her life."

The next day she seemed to have a fever; she could not see or sense anything around her. Sometimes Khalisa came over and put some water on her forehead. He, he was always there in her imagination. He put his hand on her head and ran his fingers through her hair.

"Aisha," he said.

She did not respond. Clenching her eyes shut, she dearly wanted to rip his heart out. He was still being loving and affectionate. He ran his hand over her wound.

"You'll be fine," he said.

He lay down behind her and put his arms around her waist.

"You said you hate me," he whispered. "I know."

She grabbed her hand and dug her nails in, all the while chiding her body for pulsating with love after everything that had happened. Maybe if she pretended to be asleep, he might stay with her for a while. If she woke up and pushed him away, she would be able to preserve whatever was left of her mind. She could feel his breath on her neck and his arms hugging her waist so it almost meshed with his chest. She could not push him away.

"Who knows?" he told her. "Maybe you'll get your wish and not see me again. Is that what you want?"

Whenever he yielded, he won. She needed to remember that. It had happened before. He did it a lot.

He grasped her shoulder to turn her toward him.

"Look at me," he said.

She shook her head, so he sat up and turned her around. He hugged her to his chest.

"Do you really loathe me?" he asked.

She nodded her head eagerly. He embraced her hard as though to take revenge for what she had just said. She almost stopped breathing. In fact, she closed her eyes, dearly wishing she could stop breathing.

"Woe is me for such hatred!" he said again. "It's even harder than your love, did you but realize it."

He moved away, stood up, and grabbed her arm. He opened the bandage he had put on the wound. She closed her eyes, expecting it to hurt. He put his finger on the wound to check it.

"Were you out to hurt yourself?" he asked. "That's stupid. It's not worthy of you. I'm sure your father would despise you for what you did yesterday. Don't try that again. You say he was courageous. How can a courageous man produce such a cowardly daughter?! Don't ever say those words again."

She turned away.

"Why did you kill him?" she asked. "Because he wanted to help me? For you, amputation's so simple. You wipe out everything in your way."

"You need to ask?" he said rudely. "You dared speak to him?"

"He didn't do a thing," she replied immediately, "nor did I. I was going over to the donkeyman to bring me back here. You know that."

"Why don't you wake up?" he yelled at her, grabbing her wrist. "Why don't you think? Sometimes you make me feel sorry for you, but then I despise your naivete. Why did our paths cross? Why did you come here? You've brought nothing but ruin. I told you from the start."

She remained silent, feeling afraid because she had never seen him this brutal before.

"Look at me!" he said, putting his hands around her face.

She looked at him.

"How I wish I'd never met you or set eyes on you," he said. "I curse the day when I first saw you. I detest everything that reminds me of you, even my own house and tribe . . ."

She opened her mouth.

"I don't want to hear your voice," he yelled. "Don't you dare, do you hear me? Don't disobey me again, or else I'll make you regret not dying with Salih yesterday. You're going to stay here in Khalisa's room and not go out without my permission. Do you hear me?"

"Yes," she choked.

He looked straight at her.

"What happened yesterday," he told her, "never happened."

She nodded her agreement. He put his hands roughly around her head.

"If I hear you talking about the city or palace or raising any objections from today on, I'm going to cut off your limbs. You saw me yesterday . . ."

"You saw the blood oozing out of Salih's body," he whispered in her ear. "Now you realize that I can kill. Your existence in my life is a tribulation that I must endure . . ."

"If you left me, I'd die," she said.

He cut her off.

"If you do something stupid again," he yelled at her, "if you try to kill yourself, I'll save you, then torture you for the rest of your life. Listen to me and don't utter a word! From now on, I don't want to see you or hear your voice."

He went over to Khalisa, who was watching them both.

"She needs you," he said. "Stay with her. I've told her she can't leave the room without my permission."

"You amaze me, Abd ar-Rahman," she scoffed. "Your father's cruelty is nothing compared with yours. You come close, then go far away; you're vicious, then affectionate. You must want to do away with her altogether!"

He did not respond, but left without a word.

Khalisa shrugged.

"That boy's lost his mind," she said. "What did you say to make him so furious?"

"I don't know," Aisha replied in despair.

The next day, he did not come by. The fever went down, and she ate gloomily. She did not talk to Khalisa. She needed some time to take in what was happening and what had happened. Ever since she had known him, tears had sometimes gushed in silence; at others, they were accompanied by a scream at what had been lost. She tried to go to sleep, but could not do it.

The next morning, she stayed in bed, not wanting to see or talk to anyone. Khalisa came in and sat beside her. She had a lot to say, but Aisha did not hear her. He had not come that day or the day before. Maybe he was now married to Azza. Who knows? Or perhaps he had purchased a new slave-girl. On the third day, Khalisa woke her at dawn.

Khalisa shook her. "Are you awake?" she asked.

"I didn't get any sleep, Aunt," she replied sadly.

"Come with me," Khalisa said with a frown, "and hear what's happened."

"But he told me not to leave this room," she replied hesitantly.

"I know, Aisha," Khalisa replied, "but he's not here now. We might not ever see him again. Come on . . ."

Aisha followed Khalisa, her worries about him overpowering any anger. She looked everywhere but could not find him. She picked up some gossip from the women, but did not understand. She waited for his father to come back. At dinnertime, she left the room and headed for his father's chamber. After asking for permission, she went in to see him. Looking into his eyes, her heart plunged into the abyss.

"Is Abd ar-Rahman all right?" she stammered.

She assumed that he had learned about Salih's death and had punished his son. She stayed silent, waiting to hear more.

"Yesterday at dawn," the father told her, "Ibn Sulaiman's men came and arrested Abd ar-Rahman."

She shrieked from shock, but said nothing.

"I don't understand anything," he went on. "These are dark times. Soldiers have surrounded the tribe. Abd ar-Rahman and his men could have resisted, but he preferred not to do that so tribesmen would not have to die. He went away with Ibn Sulaiman's soldiers."

"Why did he do that?" she asked sadly. "Hadn't he made a pact with Ibn Sulaiman?"

"These are days of trickery and betrayal," the father said, rubbing his hands together in despair. "I used to tell Abd ar-Rahman that we needed to keep our pledge to Ibn Tulun, but he disagreed with me. He himself went to see Ibn Sulaiman and reached an agreement with him. Now the soldiers are accusing him of betrayal. How can that be?"

"What did the soldiers say, Uncle?" she asked.

"They said that he killed Salih. Why did he kill Salih? Why's he accusing Ibn Sulaiman of killing Salih? They said that Salih was one of Ibn Sulaiman's men. Can you believe such madness? Salih, who used to oppose Ibn Sulaiman and curse him and his army? Abd ar-Rahman, who . . ."

He fell silent.

"He'll kill Abd ar-Rahman, whether today or tomorrow," he went on. "They're saying that Salih knew where Ibn Tulun's daughter is hiding. What kind of madness is that? Abd ar-Rahman's my son. I have no other . . ."

She slapped her cheek and opened her eyes in shock and total dismay, now faced with something that she did not want to understand, but inevitably had to realize. She left the shaikh's quarters and went back to her room.

"You were right, Abd ar-Rahman," she whispered, clutching her head. "All I've brought is ruin. You were right!"

She closed her eyes as reality loomed clear and burned the entire universe. Her husband had not betrayed her. He had promised to keep her safe, and he had done so. The traitor was the one who had seemed to be a friend. The enemy was the one who had kept the pledge. If only realities would follow regular laws, like the rising and setting sun. We anticipate their arrival and departure. If only existence and reality swam in a single firmament, as though reality were what we reach in the end, but not before. We follow behind it, desiring it, and yet it only manifests itself to those who abstain and withdraw. Her husband, the love of her heart and craving of her very soul—today she had killed him. He would die without her giving him a final kiss or kneeling before him to beg for forgiveness. For the rest of her life, she would be wishing for his forgiveness. But life would not be long enough for her to ask him.

She let out a loud grown. Her inner heart was disclosing the secret . . .

Abd ar-Rahman was deliberately cautious because he realized that Ibn Sulaiman was treacherous. He did not expose his men to destruction or listen to what she wanted because he knew a lot more and understood authority and the way that relatives and allies could betray you. He wanted to steer his tribe to a safe haven and keep her safe as well. Then what had happened? Had he become one of Ibn Sulaiman's enemies? When had Ibn Sulaiman recruited Salih? Perhaps he had had his eyes on the tribe from the very beginning. Maybe Salih's words about Ibn Tulun were intended to attack those people who took over from the Tulunids and rebelled against them. But then, what had happened? How had Abd ar-Rahman come to anticipate Salih's betrayal? When Salih had told him that he had heard some men talking? Or before? Perhaps Abd ar-Rahman had had someone spying on Salih. Who knows? Maybe he had doubted Salih's intentions when he had been so excessively enthusiastic about the Tulunids. So, he had used spies . . . spies . . . and the slave-girl . . .

Shocked, she shrieked and slapped her face again. That slave-girl who was so jealous of her had been given as a gift to Salih. She said that Salih did not touch her. Maybe she was lying. She had spied on Salih, and Abd ar-Rahman had thus confirmed that he was a traitor. Then, when she—Aisha—had left the house, he realized where she was going and rushed after her because he knew . . . he knew that Salih was a spy; maybe Salih doubted that she even existed, or else had discovered who she actually was. How had he found out? Maybe he had asked someone or heard what she looked like . . . or . . . or . . . But he had made sure when he set the trap for Aisha. He had told her what had happened to her city and palace so that she would go there to confirm things for herself. If she really was a member of the Tulunid household, she would certainly want to confirm things and see the destruction of her former abode. He would follow her too, but his intention was to take her to Ibn Sulaiman. He had confronted her with her real identity, presumably planning either gradually to win her over to Ibn Sulaiman's side or to kidnap her if she resisted. Had he said he knew where Ibrahim was? Ibrahim, who knew where he was? Where was he? Then her husband had arrived and killed him on the spot. He had rescued her again. She chided him and said she wanted him dead. If she died now, that would be much better.

She let out a scream. She wanted to see him once, to ask him to forgive her, and tell him how stupid she was. She longed to hug him just once and tell him how much she loved him even though he did not love her. She wanted to tell him how incredibly brave and generous he was, that she was the one responsible for keeping Azza apart from him. She would be the one to make sure that he was married to Azza; she would not be angry and would stay tied to him for the rest of her days. She would tell him that she was naive, neither aware nor knowing. Her only concern was his safety and her own loyalty to him.

𝍐

Every day, she passed by the chieftain's quarters, asking him to go to Ibn Sulaiman and intercede on Abd ar-Rahman's behalf, but he would refuse, claiming that it was not the right time yet. After a week, she lost patience.

"He's going to have him killed, Shaikh," she said impatiently, "before it's time."

Then she apologized and kissed his hand. Once again, she begged him to intercede for Abd ar-Rahman. He seemed of two minds. He sent men to meet Ibn Sulaiman, who refused to consider any intercession or even meet the men. He was determined to kill the traitor so he would be an example and lesson for all the Arab Bedouin in Egypt, even if he was the shaikh's own son. The shaikh asked for a delay in the killing of Abd ar-Rahman so he could negotiate with Ibn Sulaiman. He asked for some time, no more.

Atika whispered in the shaikh's ear that Abd ar-Rahman had brought shame on the tribe. Anyone who killed a fellow tribesman could not be trusted. He could never be a suitable tribal leader; men would not obey him, nor would women feel safe with him. As she had expected, his son had turned out to be a traitor and adventurer. He had been reckless and fickle all his life, only ever thinking about himself. She moved closer and whispered that she had never trusted him. Abd ar-Rahman was an act of retribution on the tribe, and Musa's brother, Rabi'a, would be a much better successor to the tribal leadership and would be shaikh after a long life. The shaikh chided and rebuffed her, banning her from his room for two days. She asked him to forgive her, and he let her come back to his room, but she started talking all over again.

The tribesmen were divided. Some of them still trusted Abd ar-Rahman, and many of them hated Rabi'a. He was stingy and gruff, and neither friend nor foe was safe when it came to his brutality. Men started coming up with excuses for Abd ar-Rahman and talking to the shaikh every day. Some of them even offered him money and cattle to pay for Abd ar-Rahman's ransom. In spite of his young age, he was gentler and more understanding than Rabi'a. During the Tulunid war with the caliph, he had honed his intelligence and his ability to dispel dangers. He had not exposed his men to destruction, nor had he parlayed with the Tulunids. He asked his men to be cautious and take the general atmosphere into consideration. He seemed more intelligent than Rabi'a. The men could not understand why he had killed Salih. That would only happen with the chieftain's son if Salih had committed some major crime; if he had, then he should have been tried before a tribal assembly. Rabi'a now started cursing and attacking Abd ar-Rahman. He refused to allow anyone to pay compensation to Salih's family before Ibn Sulaiman had adjudicated the matter of Abd ar-Rahman. In fact, it seemed that Rabi'a was visiting Ibn Sulaiman in secret and demanding that Abd ar-Rahman be killed as soon as possible. The women heard what had happened in the tribal assembly. Azza went bashfully to see her father and sat beside him.

"Father," she asked, "is Ibn Sulaiman going to kill Abd ar-Rahman?"

"Let him do it!" he said decisively. "It's none of your business. Don't mention his name again. He's a killer and traitor. He can't be trusted. I've known that for some time. From today, your engagement's off."

She opened her mouth to speak, but was scared by her father's brutal response. That night, she did not sleep and cried for hours.

"All our problems stem from that strange girl," Saleema told her dryly. "If she died, we could all live in peace."

Chapter 5

"Y ou're going to be killed too," said a voice in the dark prison. "Ibn Sulaiman wants to kill the entire army if he can."

He did not respond.

"I heard them talking about you," the voice went on. "You're an Arab Bedouin from the Banu Saalim tribe. They're going to kill you tomorrow. Are you afraid of death? What do you miss? Whom do you want to see? Whom do you want to kill before you die?"

"All these questions for a dead man," Abd ar-Rahman replied softly. "Be nice, brother. Who are you?"

"Khafif from Nubia."

"Your name's Khafif?"

"No, man, it's a nickname. In the whole Tulunid army, there's no one as fast and competent as me."

"I wonder when you're going to be killed."

"Today or tomorrow. Death doesn't scare me, brother. We've been trained for it and already confronted it. But what about you?"

"About me . . . ?" Abd ar-Rahman replied.

At that point, he opened his eyes and moved in the direction of the voice. All he could see were the outlines of a Nubian face. He did not know why Ibn Sulaiman had insisted on making his prison windowless—an underground pit that would make prisoners think they had died and gone to hell. Darkness did not scare him; indeed, it lifted the cover from his eyes. He closed his eyes, then opened them several times. He eventually decided to close them. When he did so, he could see a lot more, and the darkness dissipated. In its place, the light of the past and moments of a genuine love glistened in the darkness; more than that, the gleaming light almost dazzled his vision. But, just as soon as it appeared, it quickly disappeared. He remembered the day twenty years earlier when his mother had died. He was ten years old. She had gradually stopped breathing. Three days later, his father had married a fourth wife. His mother had a particular tune that she used to hum when cuddling him. He could still hear it, sad and desperate, but flowing with an unrestrained love. His mother . . . and then Aisha had come, flowing with an unrestrained love as well. She was not his mother, but she was just as sad. He envisioned her, singing the same tunes.

How wonderful to walk in a circular world with no end and without achieving a goal or even knowing what that goal and purpose was! He toured the circles of life, snatching moments of incredible happiness, sometimes raiding a caravan or pouncing on a traveler—but for sheer adventure, not for money. Yes, he had stolen and plunged into life's delights. He had consorted with slave-girls, but on waking, he had not been able to recall their faces or their role in his drunken stupor. It had all happened. He had fallen in love with Azza and longed for her, as though she were a dream with no compass. Perhaps, but the adventurer has different rules that most people do not understand. His father used to scold him and say that he was his only hope, but he did not care. Azza would blame him too and marry someone else. He would raid a caravan, squander all the money, ride his horse through the sands for a day or two, then forget. All the money was his, and so were all the women, sand, and horses. He had given life a free hand, and it had let him overpower it and plunder. Then it had seized his soul and crushed his heart. Oh, the perfidy of days and convulsion of time! If only life could come to a stop today and start again. This was a life that played games and deceived, reminding us that, however powerful we may be, we were still weak. The end was coming, even though people walked in endless circles.

Then the orphan girl had arrived with the gold. With her, he did not need to dominate or pilfer. She handed him body, heart, and gold, without him threatening or brandishing a sword. Simplicity can have the impact of a whip, and innocence can be as cruel as any sword and as brutal as any raid. The princess had arrived, looking first blaming, then suffering, baffled, and passionate; then suffering all over again from despair, defeat, and surrender. She had done it all. She had slaughtered the soul that no one could reach. She had dug her way inside and shattered its foundations. Abd ar-Rahman had no conscience, but love can always deliver a shock, arousing all feelings and everything good and evil.

When she had started digging, he had decided to stay away, mistreat her, and constantly remind himself of who he was so that he would not drown in her arms. He vowed to stay away and arouse her before himself. The princess had to realize that her drawing was the product of a naive imagination, with no firm basis. Her pained expression brought him relief and reminded him of who he was. At the time, he had told himself that he would be marrying Azza the next day and would forget the princess. He started spending the gold, foregoing his escapades. He would keep her and rub her out, but she would never get into his soul and splinter it. She had come to his room, and he could see the love and pain in her eyes. He had been insistently cruel with her. When she had left, he had grabbed his own hand, dearly wanting to pound his chest because it was throbbing with love for her. She was just a woman, even though love came cascading from her bosom and pierced the heart with life. She was just a woman; if he had sex with another woman, he would forget her. If she found out, she would stop loving him. If he killed her, she would stop butchering his soul. This was not him; he no longer knew who he was. She wanted him to be a swashbuckling hero, saving the city and fighting like legendary cavaliers. She wanted him to come from the world of red-horned jinn, unbeatable by human beings. She wanted a hero who knew the secret password, could dissolve barriers and rebuild what had been destroyed; who could protect the princess with one hand and fight the enemy with the other. She wanted him to be superhuman. When her eyes had fallen on him, she had decided that he was her hero and support. She was just a silly girl who had never left her palace and had been protected from conspiracies by her mother. She had not realized that inevitable destruction was on the way. Ever since Adam's time on earth, treachery had been the predominant feature in life: brother against brother, men with their love, and swords with their owners. The princess wanted him to die; that was certain. There was nothing that he could do about her love and ignorance. After a while, he had understood. He had been cautious in going to see Ibn Sulaiman. Abd ar-Rahman's loyalty was only to himself. He did not trust anyone or concern himself with anyone else's business. No pledge mattered to him and no oath could divert him from his own decisions.

His story with Ibn Sulaiman was no different from the one with his uncle or any caravan he might attack. What he wanted was success and security for his family. Then he had changed his mind and wanted to kill Ibn Sulaiman and his entire army.

Yes, on the day she had come to his room, he had chided his body for its passion and threatened to get rid of it if it did not obey him. He was strong, and no desire or passion was going to dominate him. His challenge had been successful, and he had won. He felt proud and happy. He had managed to resist.

The slave-girl was more beautiful than the princess. She had perfected the art of loving and knew how to please her man and make him happy. So why had she not made him happy? There was a world of difference between the innocent princess, with her hesitant kisses, seeking a safe haven amid the forests, and the slave-girl's perfect performance and professionalism. She could melt stone with her love arts. But the pain never left him as he was having sex with her. She was his, his property, and the princess had no right to object or protest. In any case, he would soon be married to Azza, whom he had dreamed about from his childhood and youth, not the princess who would object. So what to do about his heart, longing for the princess's hesitance, confusion, and tentative touch, all pouring forth and cleaving to the soul; a heart that longed for the moment of climax when it could only see the princess's face as she frowned shyly and tensely at the crucial moment? She would be bashful, let out a sigh, kiss his chest, and bury her head inside his heart. How could his heart be so distracted at such moments, and not recall what the slave-girl had done and how much pleasure she had given him? Yes, he had had sex with her, but his heart would only consort with the princess. Perhaps the body could deceive, while the heart remained loyal. But what betrayal? The slave-girl was his, so why was he thinking about the princess? Had his father not been married to five women? He had divorced whomever he wished, and kept whomever he wished. None of them had objected, so where was the betrayal?

Perhaps he did not enjoy any other woman because she was different, nothing else. Yes, she could not have imprisoned his heart in this darkness forever. Where was the man who could be satisfied with one woman and not desire another? Even if such a person existed, he was not Abd ar-Rahman!

He had gone back to her, even more in love and desiring her alone. He had brought a heavy load with him; hatred was already a load, but conscience was even heavier. Ibn Sulaiman had mentioned her name, eyes shining. He wanted her. Why had he been so troubled to hear her name mentioned? Why was fear whispering malicious thoughts to a courageous heart?

He had come back with a frown, because love was tearing at his guts. He had come back worried, because he had no idea who he was, what he was after, and where his spoils were. She had given him her body, but not her heart. He had lost his temper and been furious. He had made up his mind to punish her. Why not punish her, then forget her? Why could he not do it? Why had she managed to master and control every pulse of his heart, so he could not see or desire any other woman? He felt ashamed of his loyal and simple heart. He had wanted her to love him the way she had in the past; just once more, maybe, and holding nothing back even as he could see the pain in her eyes. As usual, she had given of herself, asking nothing in return. He realized then that he was hers alone and belonged to no one else, whether that day or the next. He hated his own heart which refused to forget her and only remembered her lips, her laughter, and her eyes. The behavior of his unknown soul troubled him, and he was angered by the way in which his mind submitted to a conscience that he did not control and never had.

Salih. Every time he remembered him, he wanted to kill him all over again. He had doubted Salih's intentions from the outset. His voice was high-pitched and his enthusiasm was phony. Abd ar-Rahman knew the men well. He had stolen with them and gone into a drunken stupor with them. He knew their strong and weak points. Abd ar-Rahman had asked his slave-girl to spy for him. Promising her gold, he learned of Salih's intentions. He understood that Salih had his doubts about Aisha. But then, her naivete had led her to go to Al-Qata'i. He had wanted to whip her five hundred times. She had fallen so easily into Salih's trap. When he could not find her, he knew where she would be and who would be trying to get to her. He had understood all of it, and had rushed there as fast as possible, his heart thumping like the beat of horses' hooves. He feared for her like an overwrought teenager and hoped she would see him as the fearless cavalier that she had drawn. Perhaps it was his own naivete and the fact that he had become like a flag blowing in the wind that was making him so furious. How had she managed to penetrate his very depths and seize control of its circles? Why was he thinking today about the way she would look on his perfidy and killing? How would she remember him after his death, like one of the pre-Islamic poets? He would be dying in a few hours and the darkness all around him would dissipate, but Ibn Sulaiman would still be combing the whole of Egypt looking for her.

When he went to see Ibn Sulaiman, he was not out for war. He wanted to save the tribe with minimum losses. Seeing what the Khurasaan Bedouin were doing to the people of Egypt, the eventual goal made its way slowly into his inner psyche. The goal was not destruction, nor was the demolition of mosques the method. The assault launched against the women of Egypt made it impossible not to declare war on Ibn Sulaiman. At first, Abd ar-Rahman had been cautious and suspicious, but then caution had turned into hatred and suspicion into a desire for revenge. He no longer knew himself. He no longer wished or was able to control his rebellious heart. He no longer resented the prison she had imposed on his soul, with no way out.

"Where have you gone, brother? Have you died and risen again?"

He looked toward the voice.

"Khafif from Nubia," he said, "I'll remember your name. Who knows, maybe we'll meet in the world to come."

"It's Ahmad I want to meet."

"Ahmad's the one responsible for all our problems," Abd al-Rahman said. "Ahmad and his dream, his mosque, his city and palace, Ahmad and Egypt, Ahmad and the caliph. I don't want to meet him."

"I want to meet him," Khafif replied eagerly, "so I can find out the secret of the monarchs of old and why they chose him in particular. What were they looking for, I wonder, in the leader and monarch? Was it endurance, total love of Egypt, or reverence for the blessed Nile? What were they looking for when they helped one ruler rather than another?"

"Do you believe in the magic of the ancients?"

"Who among us doesn't believe in it? Of course I believe in it, but they offer support to only a precious few. I want to find out why they supported Ahmad, but not others. Egypt has had one ruler and governor after another, but only a few of them have managed to take control of it. Do you understand what I'm looking for? Amr ibn al-As conquered the country, served as its governor, wanted to stay here, and built his mosque. But then he died without really establishing himself as ruler or settling down and delving into its people's lives. Ahmad, on the other hand, built his mosque and city just like Amr, but he became its exclusive ruler. He enlisted its people and created an army like the caliph's. Ahmad wanted Egypt to be a home for himself and his family, and chose it as his residence and headquarters. That never happened before, and may never happen again."

"Who knows, maybe it will."

"Brother, Ibn Sulaiman is out to erase all traces, and then memories as well. There can be no memory without traces left behind. The only things we know about ancient monarchs is what remains to be narrated and told. If Ibn Sulaiman erases everything, we'll forget. If we forget, then we'll be left to trail behind the caliph all over the earth because we know nothing about our former monarchs. We no longer know the language of birds well, but we understand what Ahmad has left us very well. Do you know what Ibn Sulaiman is planning to do with the remains of Ahmad's army? He's going to kill some of them and send others as prisoners to Baghdad. He doesn't want to leave any of them in Egypt until he's finished his erasure game. If I have any luck, maybe it'll be to go to Baghdad tomorrow and not be killed. I'll be living on other soil, far removed from my family and children. Abd ar-Rahman . . ."

"How do you know my name?"

"I know you. Who knows, maybe we'll meet again. If you don't die tomorrow, then we'll meet as prisoners in Baghdad. If you die tomorrow, I'll know that it'll be as a hero and cavalier."

"Why are you so sure?"

"Anyone killed by Ibn Sulaiman is a hero for sure."

👪

He slept in his cell, his mind focused on the next day. Then he sensed the guards bringing in a new prisoner and whispering to each other that he was going to be killed next morning. They said he was Ja'far ibn Abd al-Ghaffar, Ahmad ibn Tulun's secretary. They finally located him in his hideout. Ibn Sulaiman had ordered that he be killed the next day in front of the Egyptian people.

Once the guards left, Ja'far whispered something to Abd ar-Rahman without even asking who he was.

"My son, there's no way out of Ibn Sulaiman's prison. For months he's been searching for me in the various quarters, and now they've found me. Why does he want to get rid of me, I wonder. It's because of what I know. For Ibn Sulaiman, knowledge is his most dangerous foe."

"What is it you know?"

"I know all about his origins and his hatred. Hatred's an incurable disease. But what delights my heart is that hatred does more harm to the hater than anyone else. There's no peace or rest for the heart. We all spend time with people, but everything we encounter is like a single hour or less. Just look at me. If you ask me how old you are, I'll answer: less than a year. Do you know why? Because what I can remember is just a few jumbled moments switching between suffering and bliss. Just a few hours; that's all there is. In his final days, Amir Ahmad said that our temporal world leads people astray more than the next. Do you know why? Because the temporal world rushes people toward an inevitable end with no mercy. We hurry along with it, desperately hoping to snatch a few moments of pleasure, along with all the defeats. But too bad for people who chase after the temporal world as though chasing their own shadow, never reaching or touching it! Mirage and water mingle with memory, my son. Life seems swift and empty, like motes in the air."

"Swift and empty. You're right."

Ja'far was talking quickly, as though to conceal his fear or even hide it from himself.

"Long ago," he went on, "the amir met a monk, and a friendship developed between them, the like of which I've never seen before. It was spirits coming together, my son. Sometimes contrasting spirits will come together, and each of the two will find respite with the other, realizing that in serenity trust is to be found. Now, as my hair turns gray, I realize the deception in victory and the dust of defeat."

"Aren't you interested in anything at your age?"

"How do I know? I'm still scared of death like a child confronting a lion. Every time I feel older and death approaches, I'm more afraid. Ibn Sulaiman knows that; that's why I'm still here, so he can see me humiliated. I knew he would destroy the city and demolish the mosque with catapults. He has a servant named Qasim from Khurasaan who's set his eyes on erasing every trace of the amir."

"How many traces of an amir have been erased before, Shaikh? That's nothing new in this country."

"I wonder if anything of Ahmad will be left. If so, what will it tell us?"

"Can stones speak?"

"Yes indeed, only stones can speak. Words come out of our mouths, then vanish like motes in the air and screams of war. But stones remain to remind us of what was. If it weren't for the stones of ancient monarchs, Ahmad would never have built his city and mosque."

"But, Shaikh, he didn't use the stones of the ancients to build his mosque, did he?"

"No, but if he didn't have the stones of the ancients right in front of him, he would never have built the mosque."

"I don't understand you."

"Just look at the mosque's balustrades. They're crenulations embracing each other as they bow down to God. Heaven is their focus, with no eyes or nose. From the distance, they look like human beings. Do you want me to tell you his whole story?"

"But all we know about the ancients are stories in the Quran."

"That's enough. Listen and read."

"Tell me the story, then."

"Storytelling always overcomes fear."

"In times of danger, storytelling is comforting."

"Storytelling," Ja'far said, "is knowledge, love, desire, and escape. We, all of us, long for happiness, and that is not of this world, but the next; it is one of the features of paradise. Storytelling reminds us all that what we see and what we do is not sufficient. We wage war and win, but what we don't do is much more than what we do. Listen to me. Genuine storytelling brings a lot of comfort and a little sadness.

"Do you realize," he went on, "that I understand the monk now. In discarding the world, he became stronger. He died while still alive. He was no longer afraid of being killed. His renunciation gave him power and strength. Now I'd like to renounce it. It no longer pleases me."

"Then renounce it."

"Renouncing the world when it's defeated you, Abd ar-Rahman, is different from doing it when you own it with no rivals. They're both renunciations, but the force comes when you are in charge and not when you've lost. Anduna renounced the world as a fit young man. He knew and understood. If I do it now as an old man, it's from weakness. One day, the monk told the amir that there was wisdom and joy in renunciation. You need to do it when you still have wishes and ambitions, not in moments of despair and deprivation. You have to deny the world when its arms are wide open with hopes and not when you've tasted the bitter fruits of its brutality. I'll tell you everything."

Ja'far kept telling his story till morning. As dawn approached, his voice started to quaver, and the words caught in his throat. That morning, the soldiers took him away to slaughter him in front of the people.

Chapter 6

Two weeks later, Aisha rushed to see Khalisa. Looking at her wan face and swollen eyes, she made a strange request. She said that she wanted to check on Saeed al-Farghani. She needed to see him, if it were possible for Khalisa to send someone to look for him in his house alongside the mosque. His house was actually attached to the mosque. He would never leave it, even if Ibn Sulaiman burned it down. If he was still alive, he would be inside. Khalisa could not understand why Aisha wanted to see him now, but she was upset by Aisha's despair and nonstop crying. In Aisha's love for her husband, she found a kind of sanctity and loyalty that she thought had disappeared from the human heart, the kind that would light up the dark spaces in the soul and command respect. Khalisa managed to locate Saeed and arranged for them to meet secretly in her wing of the house, with her present.

Saeed looked pale as well; his health had deteriorated badly. He came in to see Aisha.

"The city's lost," he told her in despair, "and soon they're going to knock down the mosque."

"Ibn Sulaiman's arrested my husband," Aisha rushed to tell him. "He's planning to kill him."

Saeed looked shocked but said nothing.

"Uncle," she said, "the gold's my only hope."

"Your husband's taken it, of course," he replied.

"No, I'm sure he hasn't taken it yet. He was for Ibn Sulaiman. The gold's still in place; no one's taken it yet, and no one realizes where it is. I need it, Uncle. I can't go to the mountain now, but I really need it. Please help me."

"It's your father's gold. Why are you so determined to give it to your husband?"

Over time, she had learned to control her tongue and not tell people what she knew, even those closest to her.

"It's my gold, Uncle," she insisted. "I want to give it to him, and I'm hoping you'll help me, just as you pledged to my mother."

He shook his head. "You've lost your mind, Aisha."

"What use is the gold now the city's been destroyed?"

"Who knows? Maybe you need it to save yourself. Ibn Sulaiman's looking for you in person."

"I need it today."

Saeed reluctantly agreed. He found the gold in its hiding place and brought it to her two days later.

Past midnight, Aisha rushed out of her room. She headed for the chieftain's room and pounded on the door. Atika opened it.

"Have you gone crazy?" she told Aisha angrily. "How dare you come here?!"

"I need to talk to the shaikh at once," she replied breathlessly. "Wake him up."

"You crazy girl!"

"Come in, Aisha," the shaikh said.

Aisha went in.

"Send your wife away," she said. "Forgive me, but what I have to tell you is dangerous."

He sent Atika away.

"What is it you want?" he asked her, sitting up.

"I have something we can use to ransom my husband. It's enough to make Ibn Sulaiman let him go."

"What treasure or gold is going to be enough to make Ibn Sulaiman release him? Even Ibn Tulun's gold won't be enough."

"It's not just any treasure, Uncle," she told him hesitantly. "It's the ancient 'claims.'"

"The treasures of the ancient monarchs, you mean?" he asked.

"Exactly. They'll save Abd ar-Rahman. We must go to see Ibn Sulaiman today. Otherwise, he'll have killed Abd ar-Rahman."

"We must go, you say. What have women to do with this?"

"I have to see him. If Ibn Sulaiman was intending to kill him, then I must see him. Take me and Azza with you. I want to see him, and he wants to see Azza."

"Impossible," the shaikh replied.

"The gold in exchange for seeing him. I must talk to him."

Aisha knocked on Azza's door in despair. She opened it and stared at her angrily.

"What do you want?" Saleema asked derisively. "Isn't it enough that you've destroyed this tribe and ended its men's lives, you utter disaster?!"

Aisha ignored her.

"Azza," she said breathlessly.

"Don't use my name, when I'm your mistress," Azza said.

"Listen to me."

"We've nothing to say to each other."

"Abd ar-Rahman loves you; he still does. He told me."

Azza gave a proud smile but said nothing.

"You need to go with the shaikh to Ibn Sulaiman," Aisha pleaded. "If Abd ar-Rahman sees you, he might have the drive to save himself. He wants to see you; he's hoping to see you."

Azza gave her a defiant look.

"If you realized that he loved me," she asked Aisha, "why did you come between us?"

"Forgive me," Aisha begged. "I made a mistake. I beg you to come with us."

"With us?"

"Me, the shaikh, and some tribesmen."

"Did you go to him? How can the shaikh allow women to go to Ibn Sulaiman? He'll take the women as hostages."

"Never mind," Aisha responded at once. "This may be the last time we see Abd ar-Rahman. Ibn Sulaiman has said that he plans to kill him. I want to see him, but he wants to see you. Do you understand?"

"No, I don't. I'm willing to go, but only on one condition. That you don't go."

"That won't work," she replied without thinking. "I need to see him."

"Your selfishness knows no bounds. Go to prison, then. I'm not going."

"If he dies, you'll be sorry. Don't you love him?"

"Yes, I do," she replied proudly. "But I don't want to risk my own freedom and annoy my father."

Aisha turned and left her, running as fast as she could to catch up with the shaikh.

Ibn Sulaiman left them standing by the door of his abode for a whole day. He was now living in the house of Badr al-Hammami in Fustat. He had readied the house and sent a message to the caliph, saying that he wanted to stay in Egypt so he could serve as its governor. He had gone to war and recovered Syria and Egypt. All he wanted was to stay in Egypt. He had not yet received a definite reply from the caliph, but he was certain that the caliph would let him remain. News of his victories and loyalty had reached Baghdad. Now all that remained was to demolish the mosque. In fact, Qasim al-Khurasani had decided to finish that project before the week was out. He did not need to demolish all of it; the minaret and alcoves would be enough, and maybe the pulpit as well—why not? He would destroy what could be demolished, the parts of the mosque that no future ruler in Egyptian history would be able to reconstruct.

At day's end, Ibn Sulaiman sent his secretary to listen to what it was that the shaikh wanted. He duly listened and sent a message to Ibn Sulaiman. The next day, he allowed them an audience. Ibn Sulaiman gave them a cool reception. The shaikh offered his apologies and told Ibn Sulaiman that he had brought some treasure of unparalleled value; he wished to use it as ransom for his son. Aisha stayed silent, her disgusted gaze fixed on Ibn Sulaiman from behind her veil. Here she was now, standing in the presence of her father's killer. He was killing her father today, and not on the day he died. Here was the stable cleaner who had stolen and destroyed what the soldier had built. She had to clutch her hands as her limitless hatred boiled over. Ibn Sulaiman listened and then said that he wanted to see the treasure. The shaikh produced a piece of gold.

"I'm asking you to be generous, Sir," he said. "The enmity of the Banu Saalim is not something to be taken lightly by any commander, but we hold you in affection and loyal respect."

Ibn Sulaiman looked at the piece of gold. "That looks like the gold Ahmad found," he said. "Where did you get it?"

"Men found it years ago. We've kept it for a trying time like this."

"I can take the treasure today," Ibn Sulaiman said, "and throw you and your men out."

Suddenly he turned and looked at Aisha. "You've brought women with you as well," he went on. "Why such despair, Shaikh?"

"I want to save my son, Sir. He'll be shaikh of the tribe after me. I'm sure that, once you've taken the treasure, you won't break your word. You're a commander and model for us all. Will you allow me to see him?"

Ibn Sulaiman looked at Aisha's veil.

"I'll allow you to see him, but only you."

Aisha clasped the shaikh's hand.

"I and everyone with me, Sir. What can two men and a woman possibly do in Ibn Sulaiman's prison?

"Fine. Then you and the others come back so we can talk."

Her heart was thumping and shuddering as she looked for him in the dark prison. She called his name, but there was no reply. She became even more desperate.

"Here he is," the shaikh said finally.

Iron bars separated them. She put her hand out, trying to find his, but he did not give it to her.

"Abd ar-Rahman," she said in despair, "can you hear me?"

"Yes, I can," he replied with a reassuring steadiness.

"I want to tell you that . . ."

He reached for her hand as though to stop her saying anything.

"And so can all Ibn Sulaiman's guards," he said.

"I can't see you in the dark, but I want to tell you that Azza is waiting for you. She was going to come today, but my own selfishness knows no bounds and willed that I see you myself. I can't see you. Are you well?"

"If you kept quiet and didn't come, that would be better. If you don't talk, my wife, I'll be well. Don't say anything and don't remove your veil."

"Yes, I promise."

"We're giving Ibn Sulaiman the gold," the father said sadly, "so he won't kill you. Then we'll negotiate your freedom. He was going to kill you today."

"What gold?"

"That doesn't matter."

"Why did you bring her here? Since when do women come to prisons?"

"She insisted on seeing you."

"If we're going to talk to Ibn Sulaiman, my wife has to go. Otherwise, there's no point in talking."

"I won't go," she insisted.

He clasped her hand, desperate and angry.

"I've told you before that you have to obey your husband's orders. I don't want to see you here, and I don't want to hear your voice."

"I realize you're angry with me," she said sadly.

"I said I don't want to hear your voice," he replied firmly.

He moved closer.

"Just tell me," she stammered, "that you're not angry with me."

His patience finally snapped.

"Take her away from here," he told his father.

"I won't talk, I promise you," she said, clutching his hand.

"Make sure you don't, do you hear me?" he said. "Whatever happens, don't say a single word. Do you want me to live?"

"That's all I want," she replied forcefully, "even if I have to die."

"Those words don't help me. All you need to say is 'yes.' If you talk like that, I'm bound to die. You must remain silent in front of Ibn Sulaiman."

"I will."

Ibn Sulaiman's guards told them to leave the prison. Once they left, they waited for another chance to meet Ibn Sulaiman. He granted them another meeting and had Abd ar-Rahman brought in as well. Qasim al-Khurasani sat beside him, his eyes glued on Abd ar-Rahman.

"He has to be killed," he whispered in Ibn Sulaiman's ear. "He's dangerous for us."

His gaze met Abd ar-Rahman's, and they exchanged hate-filled looks.

The tension increased, and everyone sat in front of Ibn Sulaiman, who was surrounded by soldiers.

"General . . ." the shaikh began.

"No," Ibn Sulaiman told him, "call me 'Teacher.' That's all they call me now.

I've taught armies how to fight and surpassed Ahmad. He pirated the rule of the country and stole the treasure in order to use it to build his mosque. I'm going to demolish it, whether today or tomorrow. Before I leave Egypt, there won't be a single vestige of Ahmad."

Aisha swallowed hard and clutched her hand so she would not say anything. Her eyes met her husband's, and he shook his head as though ordering her to stay silent.

Ibn Sulaiman looked in her direction.

"Who's she?" he asked. "I didn't realize that Abd ar-Rahman had a wife. Is she from your tribe?"

"Yes, she is," Abd ar-Rahman responded immediately, "from a poor branch. She's an orphan I took in."

"She must be beautiful," Ibn Sulaiman responded with a sarcastic grin. "I've not known you to be that generous. Do you know what Ahmad did to his general, Lu'lu', when he rebelled against him and sought refuge with Al-Muwaffaq, the caliph Al-Mu'tamid's brother? Do you know?"

He did know, but he remained silent.

"He sold his family in the slave market," Ibn Sulaiman said. "Can you imagine? He sold the children and wives of his general in the market like slaves. He deprived them of any honor. What wretch would do such a thing?"

She pursed her lips and closed her eyes as the words relentlessly penetrated her eyelids. She muttered something.

"What did you say?" Ibn Sulaiman asked, looking straight at her.

She did not respond.

"Ahmad's a moron, as corrupt as the Quraish infidels. I'm going to exhume his body and empty the remains all over his city so that Egyptians will realize that he was a tyrant and now he's been defeated."

"God have mercy on the dead," she muttered audibly.

Ibn Sulaiman whistled in surprise.

"Your wife's talking," he said, "and showing mercy for the dead!"

Her husband closed his eyes, feeling desperate. Then he opened them, went over, and slapped her hard on the face.

"When men are talking," he told her, "I don't want to hear your voice. Learn your manners when you're addressing the Teacher."

He looked at Ibn Sulaiman.

"If that whip were mine," he said, "I'd whip her fifty times. I want her to leave, Sir. She doesn't belong here. In fact, I don't want her as a wife anymore. I'm going to leave her in the house today and make her an example for her brazen talk.

"Take her away, Father, and leave," he went on, looking at his father. "Come back on your own."

"No, she stays," Ibn Sulaiman replied firmly.

Ibn Sulaiman gave her a long, hard stare.

"Your husband's a traitor," he said. "For Ahmad, death commanded no respect. He used corpses as examples and severed limbs. Ahmad was the most despicable and vile of men. Take your veil off."

"No," Abd ar-Rahman insisted at once. "If the face of the wife of the tribal chieftain's son is uncovered, even if it's in front of you, Sir, then the Arab Bedouin command no respect."

"People who are loyal to me command that respect. Her accent's not Bedouin; she's Egyptian. Have you been lying to me again?"

"Her mother's Egyptian, Sir," the shaikh intervened quickly, "but her father's from our tribe. He's come here today and is at your command."

"She deserves to die for her conduct here," Ibn Sulaiman said.

"She does deserve to die," Abd ar-Rahman said immediately. "If you like, I'll whip her now right in front of you. Give me a whip, and I'll punish her. She spoke without permission."

Abd ar-Rahman did his best to change the subject.

"I killed one of my men who betrayed me," he went on. "How does that do you any harm, Sir?"

"He was my man."

"If I'd known that, I wouldn't have killed him. I thought he was one of the Tulunids' men. He used every occasion to defend them."

"Stop playing games, Abd ar-Rahman."

"I killed him because he kept defending the Tulunids, as everyone in the tribe can vouch. How was I supposed to know that he was one of your men?"

"Who's hiding Ibrahim?"

"Do you really think, Sir, that I'm hiding Khumarawayh's son? How could I do that? When he was kidnapped or escaped, I was spending the night with your slave-girl. You know that. I've no idea. The person who did it must have been an army commander. Maybe the boy died of fright, or else his uncles killed him. Who knows?"

"Where's Ahmad's daughter? I'm not bothered about his wife. But where's Aisha, his daughter?"

"Are you asking me about the whereabouts of the Tulunid princess?" Abd ar-Rahman said. "I live on the outskirts of Fustat, and the palace is in Al-Qata'i. Maybe she's dead, or they escaped to Upper Egypt. How am I supposed to know, and what do I have to do with the Tulunids? I've never set eyes on any of them."

"If you found Ibrahim and Aisha, I'd set you free."

She clutched her heart. Abd ar-Rahman gave her a horrifying look, as though he would cut off her head if she spoke.

An abrupt silence followed.

"Salih told me he had important information," Ibn Sulaiman said, "and that he would be bringing me Aisha. Then you killed him. What does that mean?"

"He was a greedy liar, as I expected and told you before."

"Or you killed him because he knew . . ."

Ibn Sulaiman looked over at Aisha.

"Do you understand, Shaikh," he said, "what happens to people who betray me? Ahmad whipped me thirty times simply because he had had a dream. He severed the limbs of men who had worked with his son and then tossed them from the mountaintop. In my case, I'm going to sever your son's limbs slowly and then leave him to die in a day, a couple of days, or a week, and right in front of you and his wife."

Aisha throttled the tears in her throat.

"We're paying blood money in gold," the shaikh said. "That's an issue between ordinary men, Sir, not rulers."

"How can I be sure?"

"It's a lot of gold," the shaikh continued. "Making a truce with the Bedouin Arabs is much better than declaring war on them. Killing Abd ar-Rahman will kindle a fire in the tribes, and not just in Egypt but in every country—Syria, Yemen, the Hejaz, and Iraq."

Ibn Sulaiman looked at Aisha again, as though noticing her again.

"Qasim al-Khurasani is determined to demolish the mosque," he said. "He tells me it'll only take a month. As you know, all the mosques in Al-Qata'i have already been demolished, and Ahmad's is no better than the others."

"What do you think . . . What's your name?"

"Women have nothing to say on matters involving men," Abd ar-Rahman insisted. "I'm hoping that you, Sir, will respect the sanctity of the harem."

She remained silent, her cheek still smarting from the slap he had given her, and fire burning in her eyes. She realized that he had saved her from a dire fate, but Ibn Sulaiman's statements about her father were humiliating and crushing her.

"I'll bring you the gold today," the shaikh said, "and then you can release him."

"I'm not going to release him because I don't trust him. If you give me the gold, I'll take him with me to the caliph who'll decide his fate. I won't kill him today. That's all I can promise you."

"Let him go with me," the shaikh said.

Once again, there was silence.

"You can give me the gold today," Ibn Sulaiman said eventually, "and he'll go back to you tomorrow."

The father heaved a sigh of relief.

"But just for one night," Ibn Sulaiman continued, "before I take him with me to Baghdad. There the caliph will decide his fate."

"I'm giving you all the gold, Sir," the shaikh said.

"And I'm saving him from death."

"He'll be killed on the way to Baghdad," Shaikh Musa said. "I know that and so do you."

"That's a risk you'll have to take. He'll return to you tomorrow for a night till daybreak. If he even thinks of escaping, the soldiers will kill him on the spot and set fire to the tribe and all its buildings."

The shaikh remained silent. He stood up, supported by Aisha.

"You can wait," Ibn Sulaiman said, addressing her. "Today I've been more merciful and virtuous than Ahmad. I want to hear what you think . . ."

"Forgive me, Sir," Abd ar-Rahman interrupted. "Women's voices are defective; that's why I slapped her. Don't make her get another slap or even divorce."

"Fine," he responded with a laugh. "Tomorrow your husband will come back for just one night, and then he'll leave. That may be the last time you set eyes on his face. Who knows?"

Ibn Sulaiman left and gestured to his men to leave as well.

"I'll leave you with your son for a few minutes," he said, "so you can appreciate my mercy and then leave."

Abd ar-Rahman looked at his wife.

"What you've done today is unforgivable," he told her. "You're going back to your family, woman. You're no good as a wife. Father, take her back to her family even though the tribe will be annoyed. I don't want her."

Aisha remained silent. She was well aware that all Ibn Sulaiman's men were listening, that Ibn Sulaiman himself wanted to confirm her origins for one last time and still had his doubts about both her and her husband, and that she had spoken out of turn, contrary to her husband's instructions.

Ibn Sulaiman's decision not to kill him but instead to send him to Baghdad, along with all the other prisoners and soldiers, astonished Abd ar-Rahman. However, he was able to predict the reason before it was actually confirmed. The caliph had received a letter, accusing Ibn Sulaiman of stealing money, the contents of Ahmad ibn Tulun's palace, and the entire Egyptian treasury. The letter apparently provided details of everything that Ibn Sulaiman had stolen, suggesting at the same time that, when Ibn Sulaiman had sent the caliph the contents of Ahmad's palace and treasury, he had not told the truth. Instead, he had kept for himself a lot of money and all the jewelry and gold. The caliph told him to hand over the governorship of Egypt and tax revenues to a new governor, named Isa an-Nushari, and not to take any action regarding his prisoners. Instead he was to send them to Baghdad for the caliph to determine their fate. Ibn Sulaiman was forced to give in. He arranged to take all his prisoners with him to Baghdad. Before he left, he handed over all the country's business to the new governor of Egypt, Isa an-Nushari. Ibn Sulaiman swore that he knew who had betrayed him and blackened his name with the caliph. He stayed in Egypt for four more months and left with more treasure than a thousand or more men could carry. The caliph ordered him to hand over all the money that he had not declared to Isa an-Nushari.

When Abd ar-Rahman emerged from prison and was heading for his tribe, he found Qasim al-Khurasani standing in front of him. Their eyes met for an instant.

"I want to talk to you before you go to Baghdad," Qasim said. "Maybe I won't see you again."

Abd ar-Rahman gave him a cold stare. "That's an honor I don't deserve, General," he said, turning away.

"I wonder, Sir," Qasim said, "who sent that detailed letter with information about Ibn Sulaiman to the caliph? Who wanted to finish him off? Who knew about everything inside Ahmad ibn Tulun's palace? It's really baffling, brother."

"Are you implying that I wrote the letter," Abd ar-Rahman replied, "when I've been in prison here for a month or more? Ask your men. They're the culprits. Thieves always count their spoils and know them very well."

"Do you dare accuse me of stealing, man?"

"In wartime, theft is legitimate. Those are your own words. Women's honor is a legitimate target, and slaughter is permitted. I always have your words in mind, General; I learn from them."

"I'm sorry for you, Abd ar-Rahman. You'll never be coming back to Egypt."

"Are you feeling sorry for someone who's going to be in the caliph's coterie in Baghdad?"

"You'll be leaving your family and spouse."

"I'll be married to someone else in Baghdad."

"Do you think you're going to stay alive? Do you really think so?"

"Our lives are in God's hands, General," Abd ar-Rahman responded with a smile. "But all I wish for you is a long life and that you'll stay here for a long time."

Qasim moved closer.

"It's as though you're putting a glass barrier between yourself and everything that's happening. I don't see you, I don't understand you, but you're a traitor."

"That word 'traitor' is being bandied around by everybody these days."

"No, it describes people who aren't loyal to the caliph."

"It's as though people loyal to the caliph only want to please him."

"What do you mean?"

"I'm talking to you frankly, General, because I know you'll never kill me. I know that I'm going to be killed near Syria. I learn fast."

"Maybe I can help you."

"Maybe you need to break the glass to find out what's inside it. It's the love of exploration, which is what expelled Adam from Eden. I know you, so how is it you don't know me?"

"Yes, I do know you, Abd ar-Rahman."

"You're an Arab, and so am I."

"I'm here, and I'll stay till Ibn Sulaiman goes. I'll confirm that you're dead—today, in a year, or in ten years. Before you die, I hope to see you covered in ignominy."

Abd ar-Rahman looked down. "I've never encountered such a temptation," he said.

"What do you mean?"

"As long as you're alive, I'm going to die. What do you expect me to do to save myself?"

"Are you threatening to kill me?"

"No, I'm trying to make you happy, General, you and the caliph who appointed you and whose orders you consistently obey. Maybe we'll meet on the Syrian border and maybe not. But I can almost swear that I've never met anyone like you."

"My courage and loyalty, you mean?"

"Your loyalty, your determination, your . . ."

Abd ar-Rahman fell silent.

"Go on," Qasim said defiantly.

"Your hatred of this country."

"No, my loyalty to the caliph."

"Love never leads to hatred, General. But let's just say that your loyalty is stronger than your sense of mercy, and your determination overwhelms your good instincts."

"You . . . ," Qasim said.

"What did I do?" Abd ar-Rahman asked.

"You're the one who betrayed Ibn Sulaiman. You don't want the mosque to be demolished. I don't know why. Is it love for the Tulunid house or something else? Today I swear to you that I'm going to tear it down and kill you. Do you want me to make a pledge?"

"We've had enough of those, General. Your oath convinces me and confirms how powerful you are."

iii

While the shaikh and a few of his men waited for Abd ar-Rahman by the doors of the houses, Aisha rushed to Azza's house. She pleaded with her to be married to Abd ar-Rahman that day; he would be leaving the next day. She begged her to receive him. He had said multiple times that he wanted no one else. Azza was hesitant; she did not trust Aisha. She then declared that it was not appropriate for her to receive him when he was not her husband yet. If he really wanted her, he should ask her father again. Aisha left her and went back to the house. She went inside, sat down, and wrapped her hands around her head, feeling weak. A soldier came in, bringing Abd ar-Rahman. The soldier was carrying a sword and had a contingent of some two thousand soldiers at his back. They scattered all around the Bedouin tents, and especially his. As soon as his father saw him, he clasped his hand with a mixture of affection and pity. His uncle's look was one of threat and rebuke. They all went inside together.

Aisha was waiting impatiently inside the house. As soon as she set eyes on him, she whispered his name. She really wanted to throw herself into his arms in front of all the men, but she did not dare. She stared at him, and he stared back. Neither of them spoke. He turned away and looked at his uncle.

"I'm planning to come back," he said calmly as he sat down, "even if that's not Ibn Sulaiman's plan."

"Since when do we kill our own tribesmen?" his uncle asked angrily.

"Since they became spies," he replied.

"In that case, you tell your father. You don't do it yourself."

"Abd ar-Rahman's my successor," the shaikh said assertively. "He'll take over the tribe after me."

"And who's going to do that till he comes back?" his uncle asked angrily. "If he comes back, that is."

"I'm still alive," his father said.

"You'll have to pay compensation to Salih's family," his uncle said. "You'll have to explain to the tribesmen why the shaikh's son came to play a dirty trick and killed one of their own blood."

"They already realize," Abd ar-Rahman said, "that betrayers are killed, even if they're my own brother."

"Or your uncle? We've become just like the Tulunids. The man can kill his own uncle in cold blood, and the uncle can kill his nephew without a second thought."

"Excuse me, Uncle. Don't misunderstand me. We're all family."

"If you've any respect for the family, then ask your father to leave me in charge."

"No," he replied firmly as he stood up. "Excuse me, I want to get some rest for a while. I'll come back, Uncle. Don't worry."

He opened the door, and Aisha was standing right behind it.

"Well," he said, "at least you haven't changed your habits."

She looked around her.

"Can I have a word with you?" she asked.

"Lots of words," he replied angrily. "I warned you not to disobey my instructions. Do you remember?"

She nodded.

"I don't dare ask you to forgive me," she stuttered. "You've a perfect right to kill me. Do what you will."

"You came to his house!" he yelled at her.

He grabbed her shoulders and shook her.

"You spoke to him and objected. Were you even thinking? Understanding? Then you give him the gold!"

"I was scared for you," she mumbled.

"You're making me lose my mind with your utter naivete. What am I to do with you? How should I punish you?"

His father came out of the room.

"Abd ar-Rahman," he pleaded, "treat her gently."

He ignored his father.

"Come in here," he told her.

His father grabbed his arm.

"She seems to be from a rich family, my son," he said. "She's not used to such cruelty."

He shoved her inside the room, followed her inside, and shut the door. She said nothing, but stared at the floor. Affection could not get the better of her that day. Love had to involve progress and giving. She decided that he belonged to his beloved and not to her. She would never touch him. If she even meshed with his chest, she would inevitably be selfish. She closed her eyes in pain and moved away from him.

She looked at the whip she had concealed in her clothing, grabbed hold of it, and reached out to hand it to him.

"Princesses have to learn that punishment is in accordance with the crime involved," she said firmly. "They need to endure the punishment."

He opened his eyes wide in utter amazement.

"What do you want me to do?" he asked.

She opened his hand and put the whip in it.

"I disobeyed your instructions," she said, "and caused everything that happened to you."

He relaxed his hand, and the whip fell to the floor. He raised his hand again, put it on her head, and ran it through her hair, as though to make sure that she was fine. He moved closer and kissed her head. She gave a slight shudder, suppressing the tears in her throat. He snorted angrily.

"Lift your head," he told her, "and look at me. Come closer."

With heavy steps she moved closer and lifted her head slowly. He passed his hands over her eyebrows, eyes, and lips.

"Do you want me to whip you," he asked, pulling her toward him, "and have an end to it?"

"Do whatever you want," she told him, her head lowered, "but stay alive. I can't stand being apart from you."

He swallowed hard and clasped his hand to stop himself from hugging her.

"Didn't I tell you not to speak in front of Ibn Sulaiman?" he asked. "You were asking to be forgiven . . . What happened? Come here!"

He pulled her toward him, and she rested her head on his chest.

"I'm going to punish you," he said, "but later. For now, I want you here, close to my heart."

She held his hand.

"Today you're going to your beloved," she said. "She deserves it."

He did not understand what she meant. He did not know his own self.

"You have to be punished," he told her gently, as he clasped her hand in his. "This time, your tricks, words, and touches won't work."

He smelled her scent. Leaning over, he kissed her cheek, as the sheer agony of worrying about her transfixed and overcame any kind of risk.

"Aisha," he asked, "do you regret going to see Ibn Sulaiman, and . . . ?"

"I ask you to forgive me," she replied without thinking, "because I didn't understand. But you would also need to forgive me if I told you that I don't regret going to see Ibn Sulaiman, what I said, and handing over the gold. Having one second to spend with you would be worth all that and more."

He could not say anything. Once again, she had managed to defy him and demolish all his powers. He tried to sound serious.

"What did you just say?" he asked.

She moved away.

"I said that having one second to spend with you would be worth all that and more," she repeated.

He pulled her closer.

"You're still saying those stupid things," he said angrily, "and behaving like an idiot. You don't regret a single thing. You're still defying me, Princess."

She bowed in front of him and lowered her head.

"I swear," she said, putting her hand on his leg, "that I'm not defying you. Regret is consuming my liver. Forgive me!"

His breaths emerged confused.

"Get up, Princess," he told her, doing his utmost to control his distracted heart, "and come over here!"

She opened his hand and kissed it.

"There isn't a lot of time," she said. "I want you to spend the night with the one you love."

He stared at her, not understanding.

"I don't know if your uncle will agree," she went on, "but he must. You're going to be married to Azza and spend the night with her. I've spoken to your father. He says he's opened the subject with your uncle. Forgive me for coming between the two of you for so many months."

He opened his mouth to speak, but she put her finger over it.

"Don't say anything," she said. "Just forgive me. I didn't know or understand. I was stupid. I only saw what I wanted to see."

"You only ever see what you want to see," he repeated. "Come here!"

He pulled her toward him and hugged her so hard that she almost melted into his chest.

"You've been nearly killing yourself," he said, "and each time you head straight for danger with all the enthusiasm of a child who can't discriminate."

"Your death would slay my entire soul, not just me," she whispered in his ear.

"Don't say such silly things," he told her, doing his best to seem serious. "Listen to me!"

She moved away.

"Not till you go to her," she insisted.

He stared at her in amazement but said nothing.

She moved still farther away.

"Today I'm not going to let you sacrifice yourself for my sake," she said. "Today you're going to go to Azza—now. When you come back, I promise you that I'll be waiting with the same love and longing, even though I realize that she's your wife and she loves you as you love her. You'll be able to find me any day you want me."

"Is that because I'm going to die afterwards?"

"Don't say that," she said, looking straight at him. "How I regret every day I've wasted when you were close by and I was angry with you, every moment when I haven't slept in your arms. I deserve to have you leave me today and go to your beloved."

He pulled her to him again.

"Ever since I've known you," he told her, giving her quick kisses, "you've been weaving tales, drawing people, telling stories, burning and destroying. Didn't you realize? Maybe if you stopped drawing, you'd see things better."

"At first, I was seeing things with my heart," she said distractedly. "But then it left me after causing me so much pain."

"Go back to it and ask for forgiveness. Your heart had the eyes of a falcon, but your eyes neither see nor understand. Does your heart tell you that I see no one but you?"

She looked all around her, not knowing how to react at this point and who her husband was. Was he the horseman whom she had burned before? Was that not an illusion? Maybe she saw things that he did not. Maybe she had opened up his heart before he had hers. Perhaps the end had come as quick as a flash.

She put her hands around his face.

"Intense passion leads to a more profound selfishness," she whispered. "The world turns into a flood, with rescue to be found in your eyes. Life becomes starless, and the bright star refuses to appear. Affection is a disaster, just like self-love. Today I am learning that a life of darkness, with the star fixed in place, is much preferable to asking that same star to draw near, only for me to end up burning it. Forget about me and everything I've asked of you."

He did not respond. He stared at her, as though he were trying to respond to what she was saying, but not daring to do it. He moved closer to her, wanting to kiss her, but she moved away.

"Your father's waiting for you," she said, "and your uncle's outside."

He moved closer again and kissed her on the lips before she could move away. She tried pushing him away.

"Do what I tell you!" he whispered.

She kissed him with all the power of her love.

"Don't move away again," he said, fighting for breath in his longing for her. "Do you hear me?"

She wrapped her arms around his neck and kissed his shoulder.

"Don't do this to me," she said. "Go to Azza. I've kept you two apart for so long."

"Here you are, ordering me around again. You must have stayed in the dark. You haven't realized yet where the star is fixed or how it preserves its light."

"Abd ar-Rahman . . ."

"I came here to punish you, but now you've removed all cruelty from my heart. I've no hope with you, Princess."

She hugged him, as though she wanted to be crushed inside him. He squeezed her as though he wanted her to be crushed inside him.

He pushed her down on their bed and enveloped her with his body. That day, she loved him, knowing full well that it might be the last time she would see him. She gave in profusion as though she had all the generosity of the intrepid and the enthusiasm of the voyager. For his part, he poured out all his love, as though doing his best to avoid his responsibilities. Then she moved away, her expression a tissue of sadness.

"So, here's my selfishness winning yet again," she said. "Tonight was going to be her night, but all I can do is stay in your arms. Do you really want Azza? Please don't lie to me."

"What do you think?"

"I no longer understand anything. I don't deserve your love. I've brought disaster to you and your family. If I died now, it would be better. You have to live, but I and my very existence are without value."

"Ibn Sulaiman wouldn't agree with you about that, Aisha. Your existence is tremendously valuable. You're the princess."

She leapt up, her thoughts in pieces like scattered soldiers. "Your uncle doesn't want you to come back," she told him, "and Ibn Sulaiman is bound to do his best to kill you. What are we going to do? The soldiers? Do you know any of them?"

He held her arm. "Come here into my arms," he said. "I love you."

"One day you told me not to say that word," she said. "Today I'm asking you not to use it."

"Are you taking revenge on me today?"

"No, I'm just trying to preserve what's left of my sanity. I don't deserve you."

"What is the connection between love and gratitude? Love has nothing to do with what I want and don't want. I wanted not to fall in love with you. I went against my own heart and abandoned it. Even when I was making love to another woman, I was always thinking of you. I could see your image in front of me, picture the passion in your eyes, and taste the truth of your lips. I used to think about my longing for you, waging war on my own self and killing it so that it would not surrender to you. But it did anyway, without my permission. Do you realize what has removed all the resentment and anger from inside me? Your love digs deep, without giving any warning, sneakily and perfectly, just like water in mountain crevices. I hated you while hating myself. I was angry with you because I was angry with my own soul. I could not stop my longing and desire. I may have been unkind because I was swamped by affection. I can't breathe any more. I was cruel so that I could float on the waves, but instead I sank to the very bottom with no hope of rescue. Do you understand?"

She put her head on his leg and kissed his hand.

"I'm trying," she stuttered. "I despise my selfishness."

"Princess," he said with a smile, "affection's selfish, love is selfish. Intense passion is like excessive killing. You don't get fat, you don't profit from hunger. No, it just makes you weaker and more desperate."

He stroked her face, neck, and hair.

"The problem is," he went on, "that you've pictured everything with an honest spontaneity. You gave me everything. At the time, I thought I was betraying you and winning; that your treasure was my due, as were you. I didn't realize that you were giving me the key but putting my own hand in chains so that I could neither strive nor betray."

She kept his hand over her mouth without uttering a word.

"I did it all because of you, even though I managed to convince myself that I was doing it because I loathed the destruction wrought by Ibn Sulaiman. You were always standing there in front of me."

She was still kissing his hand over and over again.

"Please," she begged him, "stop saying those things."

"It may be the last time. I want you to know . . ."

She jumped up and hugged his stomach. "I beg you not to say that," she said fearfully.

He kissed her head.

"No, Aisha," he told her, "I don't love Azza and don't want to be married to her. I may have been infatuated, but I was never as angry with her as I was with you. I didn't hate her as much as I did you, nor did I envy her as much as I did you, for not realizing the agony and failure I felt when faced with your sincerity and belief in me. Princess, you're merciless in inflicting wounds."

"No," she interrupted, kissing his lips, "you're my amir, my husband, my entire life."

She made love to him again, twice, till she felt sated, but still giving.

"Abd ar-Rahman," she whispered, still enfolded in his arms.

"Yes?" he replied, eyes closed.

"You must come back. I need you, and so does your child."

"I want you to stay with Khalisa," he replied with a big smile. "Don't ever leave the house. Will you do what I tell you?"

"Yes, I will," she replied definitely.

As he stood up and put on his clothes, her eyes followed him, desperate but confident.

"I love you," he said, giving her a powerful kiss.

"And I adore you more than anything else in life," she said.

He went out and closed the door. She suppressed a scream but did not dare leave the room or listen to his conversation with his father.

Before dawn, he waited in the usual place where he would go to meet her as a young man. She saw him coming and went over to him.

"You haven't asked to see me for some time," she said as soon as she saw him. "I assumed you'd forgotten my name and our meeting place."

She looked at him and could see the suffering in his eyes, but it was not because they were about to part.

"You're not the man I used to know," she said forcefully. "That strange girl's bewitched you and finished you off. You won't be coming back to this tribe. What do you want of me?"

He opened his mouth, but she went on immediately:

"Your eyes don't even see me, cousin, and you've little to say. It's not your fault. That girl's dominated you from the very start; you're finished, cousin. She made you kill a fellow tribesman. Don't you have any loyalty at all?"

He did not respond. She looked straight at him.

"I've waited for you for years," she said. "Your marriage has been full of suffering from the start. Through that suffering you could have learned and grown. You got married, leaving me on my own, but you didn't care. You didn't learn or grow. Instead, you indulged in games, wine, and women. Then that strange girl appeared and aroused all the grief and despair pent up inside you. Did you want to make me suffer so that you could relax, or did you need her magic in order to understand? It was your destiny to suffer from love of her, while mine was to suffer for love of you. I hope you don't come back. Indeed, I hope you're slain or crucified, cousin, and the birds can chew on your skull."

She left him without any further word. He just stayed where he was, as though ingesting her words, then proceeded with a soldier outside the bounds of his property. Azza was right. The strange young girl had extracted his grief; indeed, she had grabbed the strings of the impossible within him. He had become as desperate as the love poet, Majnun Layla, or even worse.

But Aisha had never moved away; always at his beck and call, available and present all around him. Even when she was furious with him, he had managed effortlessly to extract all the love and passion from her heart. All his life, he had never witnessed the like of her spontaneity and sincerity. Even at painful moments, she had always told him that she loved him. So why the sorrow? Maybe because her love imposed on him an unprecedented burden. He was not capable of defeating the caliph's armies or restoring the former glory. Perhaps it was her love for him that had led her to ask that he become like the monarchs of old, like a pharaoh of the pillars, and construct a palace to reach the very heavens; maybe it was her spontaneity that enabled him to suppress his own weakness above all else. Her passion reminded him that his own prestige was ephemeral and, at that point, his history was of no value. The noble son no longer conquered countries or protected ports. Perhaps through her feelings about his courage she was actually blaming him for not being Ahmad. He could never be Ahmad. How he loathed Ahmad! No soldiers all around him, no gold, no prison to house the enemy, no monastery, and no mosque.

So who was he? Someone who lived with the dream of heroism, conquests, gifts to soldiers, and distinguished status. Then the strange girl arrived to probe his dream. With her, he had discovered that it was a dream, nothing more—no props and no palaces either. He was not an Egyptian from the times of ancient kings, nor was he an Arab general with Amr ibn al-As. Let the strange girl ask questions about his brothers and his uncles, all of them wandering aimlessly amid fields of wheat and vegetables, having completely forgotten their lineage and history. Or had they understood their real powers and bulk, in which case why did she not realize it as well? Even saying farewell today, she had given him a charge that he could not fulfill. How could he defy death? How could he come back to her? Sometimes he would be angry with her, while at others, he wanted only to see her happy. If she was really his, in his arms, and obeying his instructions, then why the yearning, suffering, and dreaming of the impossible? If only Qais and Antara would come today to hear him tell of his trials and tribulations! If only everyone who has lost his way because of an impossible love would come so that he could tell them that, even enfolded in his arms, she would be angry and suffering. And yet, he longed to see a look of happiness in her eyes, like a young child longing to see his mother smile. He was ashamed of his weakness and hated her for it. In the past, he had tried to punish her, but had only managed to punish himself. No consolation, and no forgetting. He had been struck by a curse.

Chapter 7

A few hours later, she headed with heavy tread for Khalisa's rooms. Khalisa looked at her in dismay.

"Aunt," Aisha said, "today I need you. I love him, oh how much I love him! Please help me!"

Khalisa pounded the ground twice with her stick, then sat down.

"Come here!" she said.

She opened her arms, and Aisha threw herself into them and burst into tears.

"The man was telling the truth," Khalisa said thoughtfully. "He can kill just like the sword. His truth is harsher than either his lies or his fidelity. Sometimes it can burn even worse than his betrayal. Didn't I tell you that men are fires that burn anyone who comes too close? That boy's in love with you; he's different from his father. But in wartime, there's no point in being in love."

"I'm praying for him, Aunt."

"And I'm praying for you, hoping that, unlike me, you don't have to live a life of fatal loneliness for the sake of a man who abandoned you in order to die or betray you. If he betrayed you, you might hate him; but if he dies, you've no hope of being rid of him."

Her visit to Azza that day had saddened her and aroused mixed emotions. At times, she felt sorry for Azza; at others, she was scared of her, and, at still others, she felt a sense of wrong. It was the sorrow that prevailed, a sorrow felt by all lovers at the pain of separation.

Azza was talking nonstop to Atika and Saleema, and her sister stroked her shoulder as she cursed Aisha. Aisha paused for a while, then left her room slowly and went in to see them. The flames had been kindled and not died down.

"I want to ask you to forgive me," Aisha said.

For a moment, Azza looked at her, then she clenched her fist and punched her in the face. Aisha fell to the floor.

"So now the slave-girl slut is asking me to forgive her," she said. "You've wrought destruction, killed men, and panicked the tribe. If you died now, everyone would be better off."

The world all around her was whistling from the impact of the blow on her ear and cheek. She stood up slowly but said nothing. Saleema gave her a contemptuous look.

"You belong on the floor," she said in a fury. "You've no right to sit with us."

As Aisha attempted to stand up, Saleema kicked her leg, and she fell down again with a groan. Saleema pounced on her, kicking her nonstop in the shoulder, face, and stomach. Aisha screamed, unable to resist. Atika enjoyed watching the scene, while Azza kept telling Saleema to stop, but without success.

A powerful voice emerged behind them, a stick pounding on the floor.

"Get up, Aisha!" the powerful voice said.

She tried to stand up, clutching her stomach and worried about the fetus within her.

Khalisa pounded the floor seven times. Silence ensued.

"Come here, Aisha," she ordered. "Sit here in front of them."

"I want to go to my room," Aisha said in pain.

"No, you're going to stay here. Sit here as I ordered."

Then she looked at her younger rival-wife.

"This house has one woman in charge," she said, "me!"

"Aunt," Atika grumbled, "you shouldn't get involved in women's quarrels."

"I'm not your aunt, you stupid woman. From now, you're going to do everything I say."

"We need to talk to the shaikh before . . . ," Atika interrupted angrily.

Khalisa hit her on the shoulder with her stick.

"No," she said, "from this day you'll only talk to me. I gave you free rein and thought you had some value. The shaikh carries out my instructions, young lady. From today onward, you'll answer only to me. Don't you dare defy me, or I'll finish you off and you'll be back the way you were, nothing. You realize that I can do that. Aisha is the lady of this house, the wife of the shaikh's son and successor. She deserves respect and due service from you, Azza, Saleema, and all the tribeswomen."

"The strange girl deserves no respect, Aunt," Azza said. "She's only brought us devastation."

"This is her house," Khalisa stated forcefully. "You and your sister need to apologize to her for what you just did."

"That'll never happen," Azza replied defiantly. "My father will be tribal chieftain, not Abd ar-Rahman. Abd ar-Rahman's made it clear before that he's not fit for the task, and he's not fit now. That's if he stays alive, but I hope he dies."

Aisha stood up unsteadily and stood behind Khalisa to protect herself.

"Do you realize," she told Azza, "that your kind of love, a blend of selfishness and arrogance, puts men off?"

Azza gaped in amazement.

"First you love him," Aisha went on, "then you take revenge on him by marrying someone else so as to teach him a lesson, then you abandon your husband and come back asking him to love you. And when he doesn't, you want him to die.

I just wanted him to be alive and happy, even if it was with you. Do you see the difference? Do you know anything about love? I asked you to come with me to see him in prison, but you refused. It's your selfishness that's in charge, Azza, not your love. He realizes that, and that's why he loves me."

"I'm supposed to learn from you, you slut! Tell me how you made him love you. Did you take your clothes off and give him your body even though he didn't want you, or . . ."

Khalisa interrupted her.

"Shut your mouth!" she yelled. "Apologize to Aisha for what's happened. As you well know, Azza, your father's not fit to be chieftain. He has no conscience or loyalty."

"My father's more noble than Abd ar-Rahman. He doesn't consort with strangers and prefer them to his own family."

"Either apologize to Aisha," Khalisa insisted, "or else get out of this house and don't come back."

"It's my uncle's house."

"And Aisha's under my protection. Whoever hurts her hurts me."

Azza stood up and headed for the door.

"You're tearing the tribe apart, Aunt," she said defiantly, "and challenging my father."

"Aunt," Aisha pleaded, "I can understand why Azza is annoyed . . ."

"I despise you," Azza interrupted, "and the man who made you a wife of his."

With that, she pulled her sister up and left the room.

Khalisa grabbed Aisha's hand.

"Tell the servants to move all my things to the main room," she said. "Your room will be next to mine."

Khalisa's return to the main part of the house roiled the servants and the chieftain himself. Atika felt frustrated and confused. When the shaikh returned, Atika started wailing, informing him of what had happened with his wife. He listened gloomily, then went to Khalisa's room for the first time in thirty years. She did not look at him. Aisha was in the room and was about to leave, but Khalisa stopped her.

"Shaikh," she said without looking at him, "I'm returning to my place as head of this household, and your son's wife holds the place immediately after my own."

The shaikh said nothing, but Aisha noticed how intimidated he was by Khalisa, like a child who's just lied to his mother. He looked like a boy who has eaten all the sugar, with bits of sugar all around his mouth and nose revealing his crime. He stood like a repentant child in front of his mother. Then Khalisa looked at him.

"You're the mistress of this house," he said, "but Atika's young, so be nice . . ."

"Yes, she's young," she interrupted, "and needs guidance and instruction. There's only one woman in this house to control things and make decisions. If that young girl is rude to me, nothing will stop me using my stick on her."

"Khalisa . . ." he said.

"You haven't uttered my name for years, Shaikh," she interrupted. "I assumed you'd forgotten it. Leave the house management to me and attend to tribal matters so that your son can come back."

With that, he left the room. Khalisa remained silent, but Aisha could see sorrow in her eyes.

"You're so determined and strong, Aunt," she said affectionately. "One day, I hope to be like you."

"Don't hope for that. You deserve better."

⛪

"We have to preserve Abd ar-Rahman's status as tribal chieftain after his father," Aisha told Khalisa enthusiastically a few days later. "I want to visit the women, Aunt, and get to know them, but I'm a stranger. Nobody knows me."

"That'll never happen," Khalisa responded firmly. "What are you thinking?"

"You're my only family, Aunt," Aisha pleaded. "Please do this for me. You've left your own room and gone back to the main room to protect me. God has sent you to me as friend and protector. I want you to help me. I know you want to."

"Even my own children didn't dare ask me for that," Khalisa said. "Khalisa hasn't left her room for thirty years."

"I'm like your daughter too."

"Why are you so worried about a woman you've only known for a few months?"

"You're everything I have here, my family, my people."

Khalisa was determined to refuse, and Aisha was equally determined to go with her. Two days later, Khalisa reluctantly agreed. Khalisa left the house leaning on her stick, accompanied by two slave-girls carrying sugared bread for the tribes-women. Aisha walked beside her, holding her steady. She started doing the rounds of the tribe's houses. Every day, they would visit two houses, and the women would be astonished; it was a while since some of them had set eyes on Khalisa, which had led them to believe that she was either crippled or had a fatal disease. Many of them had never seen Abd ar-Rahman's wife. Khalisa told them that Aisha was a relative of her mother's and under the protection of the Banu Saalim tribe. Aisha took her paper and pencil; when she was along with the girls of the tribe, she drew pictures of men on horseback. The girls all groaned and said that drawing was forbidden, especially drawings of faces. Aisha told them that the drawings were only for them, and there was nothing either forbidden or wrong about them. The men were not real. The girls asked to keep the pieces of paper, and she agreed even though she did not own much paper. Then she sewed and stitched a few pieces of colored wool for the tribeswomen. She spent her time either on preparing the sugared bread or stitching wool. Then she sent gifts to the tribal elders and did her best to earn the women's love.

After several visits, she explained to the men that Abd ar-Rahman had done what he had out of fear for the tribe. She spoke at length and with great sincerity, and they listened to her in silence. She then went to visit Salih's family; Abd ar-Rahman's father had already paid them blood money. She took Khalisa with her on that visit, offered them sugared bread, and asked them for immunity and friendship. Their welcome was unenthusiastic, but they did welcome her and accepted her gifts. She never went to sleep before midnight, and busied herself day and night, with Khalisa looking on with a sarcastic grin.

"This love is going to be the death of you!" she said mockingly. "Haven't you learned anything over the past month?"

"I've learned a whole lot," she replied, pretending to be strong.

Khalisa pursed her lips.

"A lover's mind is like a sparrow's," she said. "All it can see is its nest. It doesn't understand bird language. Let's see what's to be the end of this love, Aisha. Let us learn from you."

"No, I've learned everything from you, Aunt. May God keep you alive for my sake!"

"Keep me alive just for you? What kind of selfishness is that?"

Aisha smiled.

"Yes, keep you alive just for me."

"Don't put your sail up," Khalisa said seriously, "and then discover that the water's stagnant. Abd ar-Rahman may well be killed. Indeed, it's highly likely. Perhaps he'll come back and be married to Azza, and maybe . . ."

"He'll come back," Aisha insisted.

"What if he's married to Azza?"

"He'll never do that," she said sadly. "But I swear to you that I owe him a lot. Even if he married her, I wouldn't be angry. I'll only work to make him happy."

Khalisa smiled.

"Your mother didn't teach you anything," she said. "Didn't your tailor father tell you that men can't be trusted? Never mind."

Part Three

They said: Did you so wish, you could forget about her.
I told them that I did not so wish.
A love for her grows in my heart,
Even restrained, it has no end.
—*Qais ibn Lulawwah (Majnun), romantic poet*

Chapter 8

iiiiiiiiiiiiiiiiiiiiiiii

Abd ar-Rahman traveled, along with a group of Egyptian soldiers imprisoned by Ibn Sulaiman, ordered by the caliph to be brought to Baghdad. Some of them had been commanders in Ibn Tulun's army, while others were youngsters overwhelmed by Ahmad's dream.

All the way, he kept thinking about Ibn Sulaiman. His letter had managed to reach the caliph in time, before the mosque was to be demolished and he himself killed. No sooner had Ibn Sulaiman arrived in Baghdad than he was arrested and had his entire property sequestered. He had stolen from Egypt a thousand thousand dinars that the caliph had been expecting and the Baghdad treasury was missing. He had stolen gold as well; it had to be taken away from him. How had the gold been stolen from Ibn Sulaiman's caravan? Abd ar-Rahman had planned for this day, realizing that Ibn Sulaiman could not be believed or trusted.

After Aisha had made him a list of the palace's contents, he had sent it to the caliph. He had visited the caliph's palace before, and had some friends among the caliph's scribes. When he sent the list of contents to the caliph, he accused Ibn Sulaiman of theft and lying. In his letter to the caliph, he pointed out that Ibn Sulaiman had not mentioned the things he had stolen. When the caliph asked him about Ahmad ibn Tulun's treasures, he described them to the caliph without saying where they were. Ibn Sulaiman was not to be trusted, even though he had defeated the Qarmatians in Syria and the Tulunids in Egypt.

Ever since Abd ar-Rahman had visited Ibn Sulaiman in his tent, things had become clearer to him, as well as himself. Maybe he had been prepared to fool around in the past, not bothering about the fate of caravans as he proceeded to rob them. But now a city, and then a mosque, had been demolished, women had been raped, and men had been slaughtered. That was more than he could bear, just as breaking pledges was something that only despicable people would do. But he was not concerned about his father's pledge to Ahmad. No, the pledge that changed his mind was the one that Ibn Sulaiman had given Shaiban, safety for him and his family. Ibn Sulaiman had broken that pledge, putting Shaiban in prison and then having him killed two days after he and his family had left Egyptian territory. Shaiban had been killed before they even reached Aleppo.

When are heroes born? He smiled as he thought about it. They are born in the medial space between the hubbub of the ambitious and the brutality of the killer. No hero is ever born inside his own home, with a nice warm fire and comfortable woolen wrap. He envisaged himself as one of the pre-Islamic brigands. It was only when he had made a pact with Ibn Sulaiman that he realized how much he loathed him. Yet his hatred of Ibn Sulaiman was nothing when compared with the way he hated Qasim al-Khurasani. If only he could stop him from demolishing the mosque! He was much more dangerous than Ibn Sulaiman himself.

The entire caravan was made up of defeated soldiers. Their fate was death. However, the caliph had summoned Ibn Sulaiman and would be putting him in prison. That was a victory of sorts.

Ibn Sulaiman rode at the head of the caravan, along with Shaiban and all the Tulunid family. Ibn Sulaiman was expecting the caliph to reward him, then send him back to Egypt and appoint him governor. He did not yet know the fate that awaited him in Baghdad. He may have had his doubts, but Abd ar-Rahman knew, and that was a kind of victory too.

Qasim al-Khurasani was still in Egypt. That was a sign of a major defeat. He kept whispering to Isa an-Nushari that the mosque needed to be destroyed. He was still carrying out Ibn Sulaiman's plan to erase all traces of Ahmad. Isa an-Nushari walked through the streets of Fustat, then Al-Qata'i, and observed the destruction and still-burning fires.

"In order to secure Egypt for the caliph," he declared forcefully, "and for me to trust Egyptians, all trace of Ahmad has to be erased. Just a few houses are all that's left of the city."

He walked to the mosque and noticed a house beside it still standing. He asked his friend about it.

"It belongs to Saeed al-Farghani," Qasim told him, "one of Ahmad's men. He's old and senile, nothing to worry about. If I wanted, I could kill him today and destroy the house on top of him."

"That small house doesn't bother me," Isa said.

"As long as Ahmad's mosque is left standing," Qasim said, understanding his point, "we've no hope. It's the largest mosque I've ever seen. I'd gladly demolish it if you gave the order. Do whatever you think is in the caliph's interest. You have absolute freedom."

Qasim al-Khurasani smiled, realizing what he needed to do.

This journey was going to define their destiny—his, the Tulunid family, and all the soldiers and commanders. Shaiban had been killed, and that was that. None of the other Tulunids knew what their fate was to be. Was it in the caliph's hands? Some quick thinking was needed.

There was no way out now. He had done his best to stay out of a conflict that did not concern him, but now he found himself deeply involved in war. If he could not grab a sword, he would be killed in seconds. It would be better if he could escape somehow. Ibn Sulaiman was at the front of the caravan, along with the Tulunid family. Abd ar-Rahman was surrounded by ten thousand soldiers; there was no hope of escape. Like it or not, he had become part of history. His ancestors had summoned him and asked for his help; he would be fighting for Ahmad's side.

On the road to Syria, he looked at the soldier riding beside him.

"What's your name?" he asked.

"Muhammad ibn Ali al-Khalanji," he replied despondently.

"Who was your commander?"

"Safi al-Rumi."

"You must have been one of the strongest soldiers. Your accent's Egyptian. What's the caliph going to do with you, I wonder? Maybe he'll pardon you and put you in his army in Baghdad."

"I've no interest in Baghdad at this point," Muhammad replied forcefully. "My wife and son are in Egypt. I don't like a lot of talk; I don't trust anyone."

Abd ar-Rahman offered Muhammad ibn al-Khalanji some food, but he declined. They had now left Egyptian territory and were heading for Syria, then Iraq. Every time Abd ar-Rahman tried to talk to him, Muhammad cut him off and refused to listen.

"You have to listen to me," Abd ar-Rahman said to Muhammad after it was dark. "We've left Egypt now and reached Aleppo. In less than a day, the order will be given to kill me. Killing prisoners is against Islamic practice."

"Why should I be bothered about you being killed?" Muhammad asked angrily.

"Ibn Sulaiman's going to kill me before we get to Iraq. Do you know why? Because of what he's stolen and the fact that his primary goal was wiping out all trace of Ahmad and not simply returning Egypt to the caliph's fold."

"Shut up! If you're one of Ibn Sulaiman's spies, I've nothing to say to you."

"When you see the mosque being demolished before your eyes," Abd ar-Rahman said, "then you'll remember that you're an Egyptian. You were in the Tulunid army, then you were defeated by Ibn Sulaiman."

Muhammad drew his sword and put it on Abd ar-Rahman's neck.

"If I kill you now," he said, "it might be better for both you and me."

"Because you don't want to listen. Where did you get that sword? Have soldiers been hiding their weapons?"

Muhammad dug the sword into part of Abd ar-Rahman's neck, and blood flowed.

"Shut up," he said, "or I'll kill you."

"If I'm going to die, then at least give me a chance to challenge you."

"No one can beat me at sword-fighting."

"So Ahmad taught you himself."

"Don't you dare talk!"

"Then fight me. If I win, just listen to me. If you win, then kill me, and Ibn Sulaiman will reward you generously."

Muhammad looked all around him, then brought out another sword from his cloak and gave it to Abd ar-Rahman.

"Now, defend yourself," he said.

A savage sword fight ensued, and neither man was victorious. They both collapsed, exhausted and breathing heavily.

"Since when is an Arab Bedouin bothered about Egypt?" Muhammad asked. "Isn't your tribe enough?"

"Now you want to talk," Abd ar-Rahman replied, "after your strength has exhausted me. I can't talk now. Wait till I catch my breath."

Muhammad sat on the ground beside him.

"I've waited," he said. "Now talk!"

"How can I not be concerned about the land where I'm living?" Abd ar-Rahman replied, panting.

"Now what?"

"I know what you're thinking. I used to think the same. Corruption was widespread all around the young amir. After a while, he was killed by his own uncle. Once his uncle had severed that family kinship, loyalty to him was out of the question. The corrupt generals and their control of the young boy robbed the Tulunid dynasty of all respect and put an end to their rule. How many dynasties have come to an end because of their corrupt members! How many have disappeared when their children opposed each other! If only the amirs had learned from the Umayyads and then the Abbasids, the struggle between Al-Amin and Al-Ma'mun, intrigue, and the evil ways of men! It's a world in which men live in ignorance. Even if they know, they forget; and if they think, they pretend to forget when greed takes over. In Ibn Tulun's time, General, all that was good in Egypt was for the Egyptian people. The authorities were from them and for them. Egypt had an army, and in Tulun's army every Egyptian was a commander. You're an Egyptian. If they let you live, you could become a soldier in the caliph's army. You'd be involved in conflicts far removed from our faith, and you might never see your country again. If only money could make up for what the human soul has lost from the earth! What can you say, General, about Ibn Sulaiman? What has happened to the Tulunid gold? It's in his pocket. What's happened to Al-Qata'i? He's destroyed every trace of it, and he's still knocking down stones one by one. In his place, he's left Qasim al-Khurasani, one of the nastiest people I've ever met. He won't leave the country until he's demolished the mosque. Are you going to stand there with a shrug while the mosque is knocked down? Ibn Sulaiman's word is completely untrustworthy. Now that the Tulunids are gone, this country will not see prosperity. Remember Ahmad and his dream; never forget it."

For a moment there was silence.

"From the very beginning, "Abd ar-Rahman went on, "I've noticed in your eyes a nostalgia for the past and the glory of old. Once the city is erased, the memory of victory will remain, but after a few years, it too will dissipate, and Egyptians will think that their only recourse is to submit. Do you understand me? How did you feel as Ibn Sulaiman's soldiers were raping women and slaughtering men on Egyptian land? Why did they have to take revenge on Egyptians and destroy Fustat along with Al-Qata'i? What did Ibn Sulaiman discover in the Egyptian heart? A dream or sense of honor that he had to crush? What fate could possibly be worse than having to watch your sister, wife, or daughter with a Khurasani Bedouin on top of them, sullying their honor? That can crush any soldier, my brother, and destroy the wildest of dreams."

"Even supposing you're right," Muhammad responded, "you're still a traitor. Even if we assume that you're right, what do you expect me to do today? Ibn Sulaiman's killed Shaiban and no one knows what's going to happen to the rest of the Tulunid family. I expect they've either been killed on the way, or else they're going to be put in prison when they get there."

A tense silence followed.

"If you plan to reveal my identity," Abd ar-Rahman said, "then at least promise me that they'll kill me without torture."

"What do you mean?"

"Promise me first."

"You can't be trusted. Why should I make a commitment?"

"Not true! I was committed to Ibn Tulun, brother, and not to anyone else. Bedouin Arabs never betray."

"No, there was betrayal!"

"Promise me that my slaying will not involve torture."

"I promise."

Abd ar-Rahman looked all around him. "Ibrahim ibn Khumarawayh is still alive," he said. "He's in Egypt."

Muhammad gaped in amazement.

"I've ways of knowing how I'm going to die before I reveal his whereabouts," Abd ar-Rahman went on. "There'll be no point in torturing me. I have some poison inside my mouth that I can swallow now . . ."

There was silence. Muhammad began to have his doubts, or was it certainty? Who knows?

Confirmation came two days later, a letter from one of the soldiers informing them that Ibn Sulaiman had been arrested in Aleppo on orders from the caliph. They said that someone had betrayed him to the caliph, telling him that Ibn Sulaiman had stolen close to a thousand thousand dinars from Egypt. The caliph ordered him to return to Baghdad. In Aleppo, the caliph's deputy had ordered him to give back the gold, money, brass, and silver he had with him. Then he arrested Ibn Sulaiman.

Now Muhammad was even more confused and uncertain. At nighttime, Muhammad approached Abd ar-Rahman.

"What you're demanding is risky," he told Abd ar-Rahman. "Death would not be sufficient punishment for us."

"Punishment for us, you say. That's great news! Are you going to let Qasim al-Khurasani go on corrupting life in Egypt? Can you forget that Egypt had its own army separate from the caliph's, and that the caliph himself asked for its help? But for Ahmad's death, the caliphate itself would have been transferred to Egypt. Can you forget how kindly Ahmad treated Egyptians and how justly he dealt with them? Can you forget that Qasim al-Khurasani is still hell-bent on demolishing the mosque?"

"Where's Ibrahim?"

"That young boy needs a commanding authority figure, an Egyptian general trained under Tulunid rule."

"You're whispering like the devil himself."

"I'm with you, along with my men. If you ask the soldiers today, you'll find that they're all with you."

"The caliph's army will defeat us."

"You've soldiers with you who've refused to surrender as prisoners. Make use of them. Use your soldiers, my men, all those who yearn for Tulunid times, everyone who regards Egypt as their homeland and doesn't want to leave it, their spouse, and their family."

"We'll be defeated and die."

"If you save the mosque, brother, it will stay there to remind people of you and what you did. Death is not punishment; it is a genuine certainty. It'll come, whether today or tomorrow. Put your trust in God!"

"What do you want in return?"

"All of us who live on Egyptian soil watch and survive. When crises erupt and hard times come, we all starve, thirst, and die. No distinctions and no advantages. I'm with you."

"I don't have any money."

"I've spent my entire life wanting money. I've felt so ashamed for not being able to come to the aid of a young girl who was asking someone to rescue her from her rapist. What I want today is power."

"It sounds as though you're boring into your heart . . ."

"No, that's been your desire from the outset," Abd ar-Rahman said. "I'm the one who's brought out what you've been hiding, the inner voice of your heart. The resources of this country are endless. We're bound to acquire money and gold in profusion."

Abd ar-Rahman turned around to look for Khafif the Nubian, who was walking, desperate and with heavy tread, behind the prisoners, his hands and feet fettered in irons.

"Release the prisoners with the weapons you've concealed," Abd ar-Rahman told Muhammad, "and let them join you. Go back the way you came. There's still a Tulunid descendant in Egypt."

Abd ar-Rahman himself released Khafif the Nubian, who stared at him in amazement. He then released the rest of the prisoners.

"We want to go back to the Egypt we know," he shouted. "Who wants to go back with us?"

The soldiers all shouted enthusiastically.

The Egyptian soldiers agreed that as long as Ibrahim was still in Egypt, the Tulunids should stay in power. The Tulunid era had been both just and abundant. The soldiers had no inclination to leave their homeland. They numbered just a thousand, no more. They swore allegiance to Muhammad ibn Ali al-Khalanji. With their horses, swords, and tremendous enthusiasm, they turned back toward Egypt. As soon as they reached Ramle in Palestine, fighting started between Ibn Wasif, the governor, with five thousand soldiers, and Muhammad ibn Ali al-Khalanji with just one thousand. Ibn Wasif had never seen the kind of fervor that Muhammad al-Khalanji's troops were displaying, even though they had fewer weapons and equipment. It was as if they all came from the same tiny village, or had been locked up in a dark prison, and their only chance of escape was by fighting Ibn Wasif. He had never encountered such violence and brute force. When despair is combined with love of homeland and children, things get out of hand. Ibn Wasif retreated, and his army was defeated before he could send a message to the caliph and governor of Egypt telling them what had happened and warning them about the extraordinary danger coming from an army of soldiers, most of whom were Egyptians. Muhammad pitched his tent in Ramle, surrounded by his soldiers. He asked the local people for food and water, and they were pleased and delighted to provide them, whispering to themselves that Ibrahim ibn Khumarawayh was alive in Egypt and this had to be his army. The men held a meeting to discuss the next step, which would be more dangerous and difficult. They had no food, money, or equipment. They were horsemen with swords; horsemen would not win a war with the caliph.

"Once we get to Egypt," Muhammad said, "we'll be able to find the tax revenues so we can get the necessary equipment and pay the soldiers' salaries. But what do we do until we reach Egypt? How can we get there with no food or drink?"

"Till we reach Egypt," Abd ar-Rahman said confidently, "the local people will give us food out of the goodness of their hearts. We don't need money that we're not fighting for. In the Friday prayer, we'll pray from the minarets, firstly for the caliph, then for Ibrahim son of Khumarawayh, then for you as his deputy.

Muhammad stared at him in amazement.

"Me, and not you?"

"You're in the army. I can't give orders to soldiers. We're all with you. When the preacher gives his sermon, he'll explain who we are. They'll welcome us."

Two days later, Muhammad gave instructions to the preacher, and he duly prayed for the caliph, then for Ibrahim ibn Khumarawayh, son of Ahmad ibn Tulun, and then for his deputy, Muhammad al-Khalanji. The congregation prayed for support and assistance for Ibrahim ibn Khumarawayh and his army and brought food and weapons from every region. They were joined by men from everywhere, without money or salary, just out of fidelity to Ahmad ibn Tulun's legacy and the benefits he had brought to the country. The soldiers were delighted and continued their journey back to Egypt.

News reached Isa an-Nushari, whom the caliph Al-Muktafi had appointed Governor of Egypt, about what the Egyptian general and his supporters had done. He downplayed their importance, they being the same soldiers who had fled from Ibn Sulaiman. Of course, they had stolen horses and weapons, but they had no supplies. In a couple of days or less, hunger and thirst would wear them down. Even so, he had a nagging suspicion about Egyptians. They had adored Ahmad ibn Tulun, and some of them still remembered his reign, his generosity, his gifts, his justice, his buildings . . . He worried that, if this soldier Muhammad al-Khalanji entered Fustat, Egyptians might join his ranks and celebrate his arrival. If that were to happen, the caliph would command no respect. From Isa's point of view, all these problems were caused by Ibn Sulaiman's soldiers. They had spread corruption all over the country, plundered houses, and treated Egyptians as badly as the Byzantines or even worse. What did he have to do with Ibn Sulaiman's actions? Ibn Sulaiman would be punished for his greed; that much was certain, but now he was the one reaping the crop of Ibn Sulaiman's stupidity and arrogance. But a cluster of rebellious men was not a threat to the caliph's armies. Isa decided to show the Egyptians how courageous and resolute he was. He himself set out for Gaza to confront the soldiers fleeing from Ibn Sulaiman and defeat them. He could then go back to the Egyptian people and control the country's affairs with no rival. Isa readied his army and set out to confront Muhammad al-Khalanji's soldiers in Gaza.

The new men were trained in horseback riding and sword-fighting for a week; Abd ar-Rahman trained them in horseback riding, and Khafif from Nubia handled the sword and spear training. Putting their trust in God, they set out to confront Isa an-Nushari's armed forces. They knew the desert roads very well and spread out. The initial contact with Isa's army only involved a quarter of the fighting force, while the rest hid in the desert. Isa's men thought nothing of the men they saw and launched a full-scale attack. Once the battle had started, the other men emerged from their hiding places and surrounded Isa's army on all sides.

Isa was more shocked than he had ever been; he had never seen soldiers so fired up, well trained, and maneuverable. He ordered his troops to retreat to El-Arish, and the fighting resumed there. Isa's army was defeated, and the news flew back to the whole of Egypt by pigeon. Some troops from the Tulunid army had defeated the caliph's armed forces, and the governor had fled from El-Farma to El-Abbasa. The road to Fustat and Al-Qata'i was now short, and Muhammad's troops were eagerly and confidently pursuing Isa and his soldiers. Muhammad reached the city of Jarjeer. Isa fled to Fustat, and Muhammad's army approached its outskirts.

†††

As Muhammad's army approached Egypt, Isa an-Nushari recalled what Ibn Sulaiman and General Damian of Tarsus had done a little over four months earlier when they had entered Egypt. They had burned the bridges to East and West so that no supplies could arrive. Soldiers and the Egyptian people in general would have no food; they would have no choice but to surrender. Every bridge in each direction consisted of boats tied together. Isa set fire to the boats, and the bridges collapsed. He then began to feel worried about the enthusiasm of Muhammad's soldiers and the reactions of the Egyptian people. He therefore decided to leave Fustat and cross the river to Giza, deliberately leaving the country with no governor, no police, and no army. Thieves and murderers emerged from their lairs, and there was general chaos and destruction throughout the land. Isa was out to take revenge on Egyptians and show them what he could still do, even if he had fled beyond the capital's boundaries.

†††

Aisha knocked on Shaikh Musa's door as usual. Much to the annoyance of Atika, who was jealous of the way Abd ar-Rahman's wife was able to influence his thinking, the shaikh allowed her to enter. She spoke to him enthusiastically about what was happening. Like everyone else in Egypt, she had heard the news. The Abbasid Governor of Egypt had fled across the river to Giza, leaving Fustat and the remains of Al-Qata'i with no army and no police.

"That's right," the shaikh responded ruefully, "and now thieves will come in, and there'll be general destruction."

"No, Uncle, that's exactly what Isa wants to happen. You must talk to the tribesmen."

"What's that got to do with you?"

She responded calmly that she anticipated that some of the men would revert to their old ways, attacking farmers and stealing crops and cattle. Some of them would feel confused and feeble. They would start cursing the Tulunids and the Egyptian general who had managed to expel the Abbasids with just a few men. She spent a whole hour talking to him and explaining that he needed to talk to the tribesmen. They needed to protect their homes and wait for Abd ar-Rahman to return. He was on his way; that much was certain. God willing, he was closely involved with this army. Ever since he had left, she had been hoping that he would return safe and sound. She herself had acknowledged the defeat and never expected the Tulunids to return in her own lifetime. Every day, she said two prayers to God: that her husband would come back safely, and that God would preserve Ahmad's mosque. But ever since Isa an-Nushari had taken over, she had been afraid of his accomplices. He had kept on demolishing and erasing all traces of the city. She assumed that he too was intending to demolish the mosque or part of it. She had never even dreamed that an Egyptian soldier would be in command of a Tulunid army. That dream was exactly like Ahmad's dream involving the Egyptian monarchs of old, something remote and inconceivable, but still possible and permissible, indeed necessary for salvation.

Musa listened as she told him eagerly what to say to the tribesmen and what needed to be done. She told him that resolve was crucial; he had to stop the men stealing from Egyptians. The Banu Saalim tribe would fight with the Egyptian general, Muhammad al-Khalanji, because they had taken a pledge to support the Tulunids. The Banu Saalim tribe would have a key role to play, and its men would become generals and ministers in the future. The men had to behave responsibly, protect women, and not assault anyone.

Next morning, she left the house with her face-veil on. She listened to what the shaikh was saying, a smile on her face, and she repeated the words along with him. They were her words. She put her hand over her heart and said a prayer for her husband, the mosque, and the baby inside her.

Women complained about the lack of food, the dangerous road to Fustat, and the general chaos that the Egyptian general had wrought after Isa an-Nushari had run away. The men complained about spending night and day guarding houses and tents.

Then came the news. That day, Muhammad al-Khalanji and his soldiers had entered Fustat.

Egyptians had gathered to wait for Muhammad al-Khalanji's arrival and entry into Egyptian territory and Fustat. Men, women, and children all gathered and bought costly saffron to decorate the horses of the brave cavalrymen, Ahmad ibn Tulun's and Egypt's cavalry. Hearts fluttered, and women and children laughed. Young men looked on admiringly. No sooner had Muhammad entered on his horse than Egyptians tossed saffron over his horse's face. They sang paeans of praise, and then tossed more saffron on his companions' horses, those of Abd ar-Rahman, Khafif an-Nubi, and others. Abd ar-Rahman still had his face-veil on, and he looked all around him with a sense of pride that he had never experienced since he was a boy. He was eager to tell her about what had happened. He might even admit to her that she had been right about some things, but not everything.

Aisha went out; she could not stay inside or welcome the people who had defeated her own family. She convinced the shaikh to go out with her in case they encountered Abd ar-Rahman. There was a huge crowd, and she could not get near the procession. She threw roses and saffron, and then spotted a veiled horseman she knew. Her heart leapt for sheer joy as she cried out Abd ar-Rahman's name as loudly as she could.

He did not hear her; she did not expect him to hear. He was still alive. Would he remember her, she wondered? Would he visit her? When would she throw herself into his arms? She gestured to the shaikh, and he tried to see his son but could not.

Muhammad made his way around the city, shaking people's hands and listening to their congratulations, joyful shouts, and exclamations of victory. Then he prayed in Ahmad ibn Tulun's mosque. The preacher gave the Friday sermon. Then, leading the people in prayer, he prayed first for the caliph; then for Ibrahim ibn Khumarawayh, son of Ahmad ibn Tulun; and finally for Muhammad al-Khalanji.

As soon as Muhammad al-Khalanji entered Egyptian territory, fifty thousand men or more joined his forces, the defeated Tulunid army and young men who believed in Ahmad's dream. Muhammad had not been expecting such a welcome or that number of soldiers. He assembled his soldiers and told them that when Isa had fled, he had taken the entire police force with him, leaving the city in chaos to punish Egyptians for their devotion to the Tulunids. Indeed, no sooner had Muhammad entered Fustat than he discovered that, before fleeing to Giza, Isa had made off with the tax revenues and all the papers and records of Egypt. So Muhammad had no evidence and no money. In talking to the soldiers, he said that he had no experience as a ruler and would not even be able to pay their salaries or give them gifts. In response, the soldiers told him that they did not need any gifts and could wait for their salaries until things in the country settled down. Muhammad asked some of his men to take over the running of the police and keep people safe so that they could fight Isa and expel him from Egypt. Abd ar-Rahman decided to remain concealed and to keep his face covered all the time, even when he was riding alongside Muhammad. That was for Muhammad's benefit, since he could then ride freely among the people without being recognized by friend or foe. Abd ar-Rahman then sent some soldiers to his tribe with orders from Abd ar-Rahman that invited them to join Muhammad's army. The men set off eagerly. Abd ar-Rahman, Muhammad, and Khafif an-Nubi adopted as their headquarters and residence the house of Badr al-Hammami, where Isa had been living and Ibn Sulaiman before him.

She saw men preparing to go to see Abd ar-Rahman and went back to her room, feeling annoyed. She had expected him to come and see her if he was in Fustat. She wanted him to make an effort to see her. Had he forgotten her again? How many slave-girls did he own now that he was settled in Badr al-Hammami's house?

Two days later, he sent some veiled men to collect the commander's wife. She ran as fast as she could, joy bursting from her eyes. She entered Badr al-Hammami's house, anticipating an encounter and passion with no end. She waited patiently in the room till she felt the touch of a man with his face covered.

"The Princess!" he said.

She turned and opened her eyes, her heart pounding. Looking all around her, she stood up slowly and bowed to him.

"My lord General," she said, "the people of Egypt all thank you today."

"All of them?" he repeated as he raised her to her feet.

She threw herself into his arms and clung to him as hard as she could. He put one hand around her waist and the other on her head.

"Yes, all of them," she replied. "They've charged me with sending you a message of greetings and peace."

She buried her head in his chest.

"And a lot of love as well," she went on. "They all adore you and long to see your face. They're with you for the rest of your life."

"I never realized," he said as he stroked her hair, "that Egyptians could be so affectionate and gentle."

She moved away a little and removed the covering from his face.

"I knew you'd come back," she said as she kissed him multiple times. "My mind and tongue are totally incapable of describing how much I admire you. When I fell in love with you, I did not realize the full extent of your soul, the power in your heart, and your understanding. Forgive me for submitting to my limited mind. I had no idea that my husband was the bravest and most intelligent of men."

"I used to think," he whispered in her ear as he kissed her, "that the bravest of men was your father, Princess."

"My father was the bravest of men because he built and made reforms. You're the bravest of men because you want to preserve what he built. His courage would not be complete without yours. What's the point of building something if it's inevitably going to be destroyed? What's the point of reform if corruption is bound to follow? When he built things, he may have been sure that someone like you would arrive one day to fight for the preservation of what was left. Every man who preserves what Ahmad built is maintaining good in the face of evil and granting victory in the midst of greed and hatred. What you're doing, General, will linger in the land."

"Not so fast with your encomium! I'm not the general. That's Muhammad al-Khalanji."

She kissed his chest and put her hands around his arms.

"Yes, you're the commander," she said, "and the cavalier!"

"You're drawing castles in your imagination again."

"You told me that my heart could see things. My heart's telling me that you're going to save the mosque from the barbarous instincts of Qasim al-Khurasani. I need to reassure you and let you know that the tribe's waiting for you. Your position is secure."

"How's my position secure?"

"I'll tell you everything."

"Let's postpone stories and chatter for a while."

She moved away from him gently and looked into his eyes. "I shouted to you," she told him. "Did you hear me?"

"When?"

"You were astride your horse and trotting alongside your general. Egypt's women were all around you, tossing flowers and saffron. You didn't hear me, of course. I wonder, how many women did you admire on the way, General? How many slave-girls fell in love with you?"

"If you were half human," he replied with a smile, "and half jinn, you'd have bewitched me. It's hopeless; I only ever think of one woman."

She stroked his body. "Maybe you're thinking of two or three . . ."

"Just one."

"You've been away for a month."

"I've been longing for that bewitching woman."

She spent hours in his arms, her heart bonded with his. She took a chance.

"How does Muhammad al-Khalanji's army stand against the caliph's armed forces?" she whispered.

"The same way Ahmad and Khumarawayh's army did against the caliph's forces." Silence ensued.

"There's something I want you to know," she said, kissing him on the cheek.

"What's that?"

"I need you to be safe," she said, and then went on, "If you're fighting for my sake . . ."

"Fighting for your sake?" he responded with a smile. "What kind of woman are you that war should be declared for your sake? Are you really half human and half jinn like the legends of old? Yes, yes, I just said that you're half jinn. Didn't I just say that?"

"What I mean, Abd ar-Rahman, is . . ."

"Of course, I'm fighting for your sake," he went on immediately.

"Please don't equivocate. I don't deserve anything."

"You're the one who's equivocating! You start by extolling me and encouraging me to be resolute. Then you ask me to stay safe and sound. Then you tell me that the caliph's army is powerful. You're more dangerous than you think. Where did you learn such methods? If I'm going to lose my life for the sake of the amir's daughter, then you'll need to give me something in return."

"I've been entirely yours from the start," she told him, hugging his shoulders. "I want to stay with you. Don't make them take me away."

"It's best for you to stay with the tribe, Aisha. The caliph's army's on its way, and I'm scared for you."

"I'll stay with you for a day or two, then leave."

He seemed hesitant. She kissed his hand, then put it on her cheek.

"It may be two days or a week, then we'll know before any army gets here."

She kissed his hand again and clasped it with her other hand.

"I'll stay in the room," she went on, "and no one will see me. I won't bother you. When you find some time, you can come to see me."

He thought for a while.

"No," he replied, "not when you're pregnant. You'll go back today, and when things are over . . ."

"No," she interrupted, clutching his hand, "not today . . ."

She drowned him in kisses.

"I'll stay for two or three days, no more," she said. "What difference does a day or two make? Please let me stay. I haven't asked you for anything before . . ."

"It's risky," he replied with a frown, "you realize that."

"I won't leave my room."

"I don't like this idea," he replied angrily. "Two or three days," he grumbled, "no more."

Maybe for the first time she laughed.

"Yes, indeed," she said, "no more. Now go to work or else you'll be late."

Abd ar-Rahman sat down alongside Muhammad, listening to him addressing the soldiers. He was asking them to fight the corruption that Isa an-Nushari had deliberately left behind him and to punish thieves. Muhammad was joined by Egypt's Christians and Jews, in addition to the Muslims. From his army ranks, he selected two Christian brothers to take charge of his ministry and taxes. Ibrahim ibn Musa the Christian was appointed Tax Administrator, and his brother as minister. He handed over the police to Ibrahim ibn Fairuz. For a while, things settled down in

Egypt. Khafif an-Nubi managed to use his troops to force Isa an-Nushari out of Giza. He fled to Alexandria, with Khafif chasing after him. Isa was expecting to defeat him as he waited for supplies coming from Baghdad.

Ibrahim ibn Musa explained to Muhammad al-Khalanji that the coffers were empty and the records had been stolen. He had no idea who had been paid and who had not. No army in any country could hope to win with no money or gold, however loyal the men might be and however willing to sacrifice their lives. They needed food and weapons.

This then was the major challenge, a crisis that neither Muhammad nor Abd ar-Rahman had anticipated. Ibrahim suggested that they take money from merchants and landowners and give them a written pledge to give them back what they had taken when the fighting was over.

"Are you planning to take the money by force?" Abd ar-Rahman asked.

"We've no choice," Ibrahim replied. "In a month's time, soldiers will be starving, and we'll be closing offices. Without any food, there'll be general chaos again, even though we've controlled the corruption and arrested the thieves. If the system collapses, then the caliph's governor will be back even more vicious and violent, and the Egyptian people won't be able to stop him. They're used to long years of stability. They're fighting on our side today, but what they want is the prosperity, stability, and justice of Ahmad's time."

"If you take the money by force," Abd ar-Rahman said, "merchants, farmers, and local leaders in Egypt won't trust you."

"We'll give them a document," Muhammad said, "stating what we've taken from them. I'll sign it myself."

Abd ar-Rahman remained silent, panic-stricken. He could not think of an alternative solution. There was none.

Every day, he would wait till work was over before returning to her. She was too insistent and domineering, but he no longer cared. One day she would have to go back to the tribe. But every day, he postponed that return, and every day he asked her listlessly to go back. Today he realized that a whole month had passed, not just a few days. Aisha had to leave; her staying with him was a risk with unknown consequences. When he went into the room and before he even greeted her, he avoided her gaze and told her that she would be leaving the next day. He would be arranging everything.

She held her stomach and said that she was tired. She was worried what the effect of the journey would be on her pregnancy. He gave her a dubious look, well aware that she was lying. She grabbed his hand, sat down, and sat him down beside her.

"I can't leave you," she said softly.

"You're going tomorrow," he told her, pretending to be cruel. "When the danger that Isa an-Nushari poses is over, we can live together for the rest of our lives. Having you here in the middle of Fustat is an unnecessary risk. The Abbasids are still searching for Ahmad's daughter and Ibrahim, Khumarawayh's son."

"I wanted to ask you," she asked in all innocence.

"Ask me what?"

"Where Ibrahim is."

"Don't change the subject," he replied with a smile.

"Where have you hidden him and why? You trusted Ibn Sulaiman at first, didn't you?"

"I don't trust anyone, Princess."

"Not even me?"

He put his hands around her face.

"I might trust you if you went back to the tribe."

"Have I disobeyed your instructions? Have I left this room? Has anyone set eyes on my face?"

"No."

"Let me stay here and wait for you. When I look around me, the world seems in balance from here. Do you realize that I wait for you to come back every single day?"

He swallowed hard and put his mouth close to hers.

"How's that?" he asked.

She gently touched her lips to his, then carefully ran her fingernails over his neck, shoulders, and chest. She moved away.

"I used to live in paradise gardens," she said, "waiting for a day when my loneliness would disappear and my vagrant heart would settle down. I realized that, even though the rooms were huge, I was still a prisoner. My destiny would be the same as Qatr an-Nada and other women in my family. Then you came along . . ."

She kissed him quickly on the lips and could feel his ribs trembling.

"You liberated me," she went on, "if you but knew. You made the garden boundless and the rooms open up to endless seas and rivers of sweet water. I set out with you, even though I had been imprisoned by walls. Now you want to leave me . . ."

He tried to kiss her, but she moved away.

"I'm staying with you," she said.

"Where did you learn those words?" he asked.

"From you. Aren't you a poet and an expert heartbreaker? Shall I stay with you?"

"For a while," he responded hesitantly.

Muhammad al-Khalanji's great challenge was a lack of funds. There was no shortage of either men or enthusiasm, but the merchants' complaints about sequestration were important, while farmers complained that they had already paid their taxes to Ibn Sulaiman. Ahmad's dream was still the roaring gale that could overwhelm trees and force twisted leaves into compliance. The whistling wind could make its way through windows and fill the ears of young and old alike. Abd ar-Rahman wanted to slow it down so that it would not fizzle out all of a sudden. He was afraid that it would pass through, then die down, or else strip the trees of leaves on its way. Here they were, trying to feel their way to the very core of Egypt's records without either a thousand years of experience or the ancestral gold.

"When is Ibrahim, Khumarawayh's son, going to show up?" Muhammad asked Abd ar-Rahman. "The people need to see him."

"If he appears now," Abd ar-Rahman insisted, "Isa an-Nushari's men will kill him and defeat us on the very same day. We have to keep him safe."

"If we're fighting the same fight," Muhammad said impatiently, "we have to trust each other somewhat. At least tell me where he is."

"No," Abd ar-Rahman replied, "it's better if we don't tell each other what we know. If either of us is arrested, we don't want that to be the end."

"That's madness."

"Has someone asked about Ibrahim? I can tell you that he's fine. He'll appear when the danger that Isa an-Nushari presents is finally over."

"What if he shows up and decides to rule on his own?"

"He's only a ten-year-old boy, brother!"

"What if he appears and surrounds himself with corrupt people, as they did before with Khumarawayh's sons?"

"Our presence will keep that from happening. I'm more concerned about the caliph. If we can manage to secure the country and re-establish its independence, then everything will be easy after that."

ⅲ

On the day when Aisha had her baby, she was afraid that her husband would be annoyed because she had not given him a male successor. She was worried that he would ask her to go back to the tribe, or even take another wife. But he did not do any of those things. She did not know why she was feeling so desperate and frustrated.

"I haven't given you a son, Abd ar-Rahman," she told him despondently, as he sat down beside her.

"It's God's will," he insisted.

"What'll happen to the tribe?"

"Why are you worrying about the tribe?" he asked, stroking her hand. "Take care of your own health and our daughter."

"Tell me now," she asked impatiently. "Are you planning to marry someone else?"

He was totally nonplussed.

"No," he replied. "What's the matter with you? If you don't produce a son and so some other tribesman takes over from me, it could be my daughter's husband or some other man. Who knows, I might die first in any case."

"Don't say that," she said, tears pouring down her cheeks.

"You're tired," he said gently, giving her a hug. "Your daughter's as beautiful as you. What are you going to name her?"

"Khalisa."

"I thought you'd choose your mother's name."

"My mother won't be upset. Khalisa has saved me over and over again. If my mother were here, she'd choose Khalisa too."

She calmed down after a month. Her husband did not change his attitude or ask her to leave. At night he stayed with her to reassure her and gave her the kind of affection that she could not imagine doing without.

There were times when he seemed distressed. He had not opened his heart to her yet. Did he not trust her, she wondered, or was he worried about her naivete and usual enthusiasm? Her impetuosity alarmed him. Even now, she had not convinced him that she could tolerate heavy burdens, even though she alone was carrying her own father's burden, had assumed the burden of the entire tribe around him, and his own father listened to what she said and acted on it. But Abd ar-Rahman, no. She swore that today was going to be different; he had to talk. She started figuring out what she was going to do and say, and then reorganized her thoughts. The burden he was carrying on his shoulders was a major one; he could not carry it on his own. Why could a man not put some of the load on his wife's shoulders and confide in her? He must not trust her; no love could be perfect without trust, and no heart could find peace without fidelity. When he came into the room, his expression a tissue of sorrow, she helped him take off his clothes and asked him to lie on his stomach so she could massage his back and press down on all the painful spots.

"Where did you learn to fight?" she asked softly as she massaged his back. "You're an expert swordsman and spearman. It's as though you were born to be a fighter."

He was enjoying the feel of her hands on his back.

"Indeed, I was born a fighter," he replied with a smile, eyes closed. "My father told me about the glories of the ancients. He said that his tribe was with Amr ibn al-As when he fought and defeated the Byzantines. We conquered Egypt ages ago and awaited a day when those same glories would return and be renewed. But they didn't. Now the Abbasids bring in Turkish soldiers and put them in charge. But I haven't given up. I've dreamed ever since I was a child . . ."

She clutched his shoulder. "So you had dreams too," she said, "just like my father . . ."

"It was a different dream, Princess," he said. "I dream that I'm fighting and doing sword training. My father trained me first, then one of my uncles before he left the tribe. I've told you before."

"At the time I thought you were lying."

"I never lie to you."

She felt more optimistic. He had been talking freely and nonstop. "What's troubling you?" she asked.

"Let's stop talking while I'm enjoying having your hands on my back," he said, closing his eyes again. "I don't want to think about what's troubling me."

She drew closer and kissed his back. "You're worried," she insisted. "Don't you trust Muhammad? Are you worried about the caliph's army or the lack of money and gold?"

He did not respond.

"You're going to tell me," she said as she sat beside him.

"Don't stop," he told her, his eyes still closed.

"I won't stop if you tell me . . ."

She kissed his shoulder.

"Trust me," she whispered. "You're all I have. As you know, I've no family or status now. In fact, men are looking for me. I trusted you without even knowing you, but you don't want to trust me, even with so many soldiers around. How fair is that?"

She kept pressing on his back, waiting for him to say something, but he did not.

"Is Muhammad al-Khalanji jealous of you?" she asked forcefully.

"Of course not!" he replied at once.

"Is it because you always have your face covered so no one can recognize you, or because you're not after a position or tax money?"

"Because we both have the same goal in mind."

She allowed herself a smile of triumph. He had spoken at last.

"Is that goal difficult, or impossible?"

"We've taken over the government of Egypt, Princess. That was the goal. But money's the problem. Isa an-Nushari isn't Ibn Sulaiman. He's more cautious and knows more about the tricks of government. He's planning to come back; that's for sure. How are we supposed to govern Egypt with no money, no records, and no plans? It feels as though we've entered a dark room with a huge pit in it. We're feeling our way, avoiding the pit, and promising people light without knowing where it's to come from."

"Things have settled down in the country now. Don't be alarmed. The Egyptians are with you."

"The caliph's not going to leave us alone. When the fighting gets worse, we're not going to be able to sequester the wealth of every single Egyptian. Needless to say, they'll end up hating us.

"If they hadn't stolen all my father's money," Aisha said angrily, "we could locate a lot of it, but they stole it . . ."

"That's what happens in wars. When people invade a country, Princess, they steal."

She remained silent.

"Now you're depressed as well," he said. "You wanted to know what was making me unhappy."

"We'll find a solution," she replied enthusiastically. "The Egyptians will never get rid of you."

"Egyptian soldiers have been fighting for us without pay for months. Egyptians are all patiently bearing the brunt of war and the scarcity of necessities. But you can't overburden people. The Nile hasn't flooded, and the war that's been going on for years keeps destroying things and not making any headway."

She rested her cheek on his back.

"We'll find a way out," she said lovingly. "Why are you staying incognito with people, when you're as much of a hero as Muhammad al-Khalanji and Khafif an-Nubi?"

"So I won't expose you to any danger. If people find out who I am, they'll start asking themselves about where my wife came from and they'll investigate."

She sighed, then hugged his back, her breasts resting on him.

"Where's Ibrahim, Khumarawayh's son, Abd ar-Rahman?" she asked.

He turned around to hug her, but she moved away coyly.

"I haven't finished my questions yet . . ." she said.

He pulled her by the wrist and brought her face close to his.

"This crafty attitude doesn't suit you, Princess," he said, his lips almost touching hers. "If I haven't told Muhammad al-Khalanji himself, do you suppose that I'm going to tell you? Once the war's over, he'll reappear and take over the government."

Almost a year had gone by, changing her entire life—partings and meetings, passion and suffering. Her mother had gone away almost a year ago, and it was just a short time before they would see each other again. They had agreed to meet by the Mountain Gate at Ahmad's mosque. She had a lot to tell her mother: about her husband, love, gold, her baby girl, Khalisa, the tribe, the Egyptian general, the city that she had seen burning right in front of her, and Ahmad's mosque that was still standing, thanks to her husband and Muhammad al-Khalanji. She would tell her mother that her own fate was much better than Qatr an-Nada's; her husband had managed to erase any moments of pain through his generosity and decency.

It was as though he had waged his wars for her sake, changing the scenario and defying the caliph. She would tell her mother about the cavalier who made her shudder whenever he approached, penetrated her very heart when he appeared, and pinched it hard whenever he was far away.

She could remember the day a year ago when her mother had clasped her hand. "Aisha," she had said, "you'll be fine. We'll meet in a year's time."

At the time, she had begged her mother not to leave her, but she had refused. Within seconds, she was gone, leaving her a helpless stray, like an orphan child. She had left her daughter in a totally unfamiliar world after being her entire world for years. She had not slept for a week. Now she was thinking about the meeting, her mother, and the year gone by. Tomorrow she would be hugging her mother, never to leave her again.

Muhammad looked worried. Khafif an-Nubi was still pursuing Isa an-Nushari, but Isa had laid a trap for him in Alexandria. There was a fierce battle, after which Isa fled to Upper Egypt. He managed to lay the bait for Khafif and his exhausted army. Khafif was defeated after a good deal of bloodshed.

The caliph dispatched spies to search for Ibn Tulun's daughter, she having in her hands the end to the wars. He was no longer concerned about Ibrahim and his fate. He was just a child who had not even appeared yet; Egypt was being governed by an Egyptian general, and that would not last. If Al-Muktafi could track down Aisha, Ahmad's daughter, the wars would come to an end and rule of Egypt would revert to him. The caliph Al-Muktafi had decided to marry her immediately. If she was already married, he would have her divorced or widowed. That did not matter. He needed to nail down his own authority over Egypt. The Egyptian people had never forgotten Ahmad's rule and his dream. By allying himself with Ahmad's daughter, he would be able to pitch his tent peacefully in Egypt.

Muhammad conveyed the information to Abd ad-Rahman who listened in silence. His wife Aisha had given birth two months earlier, no more. She was still staying with him in Badr al-Hammami's house, only rarely leaving her room for a short time and not knowing anyone.

"So the caliph wants to marry Ahmad ibn Tulun's daughter, Aisha," Abd ar-Rahman said, as though to confirm what he had just heard.

"Khafif an-Nubi's been defeated by Isa an-Nushari, Abd ar-Rahman."

"How does he expect to find her?" Abd ar-Rahman asked, going back to the previous topic.

"He's the caliph, brother. He'll find her. He's not Ibn Sulaiman, he's the caliph of the entire country. He'll send men to spy and give rewards to people who show him where she is. He'll find a way to marry her. That needn't bother us. Maybe if he's married to her, his heart will soften, and we'll be able to negotiate with him over Egypt's independence . . ."

"Impossible."

"Abd ar-Rahman . . ."

He left and went to his wife's room.

In just a few hours, she would be seeing her mother after a whole year. The very first thing she would do would be to hand her mother the baby girl to hold in her arms. Then she herself would hug her mother as she had done as a child. She would wander with her through the various parts of the mosque. Her mother might be sad, who knows? The destruction of the palace and the entire city might well make her sad. They had agreed to meet by the Mountain Gate, which was still standing. She would be there at sunrise.

Abd ar-Rahman looked upset and impatient as he entered his wife's room.

"You're going to leave for Upper Egypt now, along with all the other women," he told her without even looking at her. "Don't argue. Don't even open your mouth."

"That's impossible," she replied without even thinking. "You know that I'm going to meet my mother tomorrow in front of the mosque. I told you earlier."

"I didn't ask for your opinion," he replied firmly. "You're leaving now. By tomorrow morning, you'll be well on your way to Upper Egypt. Come on, put your face-veil on. It's a long way, and you'll reach Esna after several days. My nephew lives there, and he's been told that you and the whole tribe are coming."

"Why are you doing this?" she asked, not understanding anything. "You know that I've been waiting for this day for a year. Who knows, maybe I won't see her for the rest of my life."

"Keep talking while you're getting dressed," he said, handing her the veil. "There's not a lot of time."

"I don't understand. I thought you were going to look after me."

"I'm looking after your very life and something even more important for me . . ."

"Abd ar-Rahman . . ."

"The caliph's after you, Aisha," he went on impatiently. "He wants you for a wife. He's searching for you, and he's going to find you unless you leave here. If he finds you . . ."

She screamed, then opened her mouth in total shock and slapped her cheek. "How has he found out?" she asked.

"He has found out, and that's the end of it. There's no time for talk. You're leaving for Upper Egypt now, along with the tribe."

She grabbed his hand. "Are you coming with us?" she asked.

He pulled his hand away. "Of course not!" he replied angrily.

"I may never see you again."

"Maybe not," he replied angrily, recalling that the caliph himself wanted his wife. "That doesn't matter. What matters is that you and my baby daughter are safe."

She avoided looking straight at him so he would not see her tears. "I'll get ready," she said, "but my mother . . . can you find her? Do you know her? She'll be waiting for me tomorrow . . ."

"I'll do it if I can."

"Maybe you won't be able to do it. Death may envelop me, and you and my mother as well. Maybe I won't see you again."

"Maybe the caliph will find you and add you to his harem in Baghdad. Does that destiny meet your approval? Of course it does! Caliph's wife or wife of an ordinary man . . . ?"

"I have a husband," she interrupted, "and I don't want anyone else."

She dressed herself as she was talking and wrapped her daughter in a woolen blanket. Without saying a word, he took her hand and left for the place where the tribe was gathered. He took her there on his horse, then lowered her in front of the caravan, his gaze as hard as stone. She reached out to touch his hand.

"Come on," he told her angrily, "get on the camel."

He grabbed hold of her, lifted her up, and put her on the camel.

"Whatever happens," he instructed her, "make sure you don't say anything. You're Abd ar-Rahman's wife, and that's all. My father will take care of things for you till I return. If I don't return, you'll still be where you are, raising my daughter along with the tribe."

"If I die," he went on forcefully, "don't get married again. That's a pledge between us."

"I'll do as you ask," she replied without thinking.

He then ordered the veiled men to start moving.

"Whatever happens," he told her again, "make sure you don't say anything. Do you understand?"

She nodded.

"You'll come to us, won't you?" she asked.

He ignored her question.

"Don't interfere in tribal matters," he went on. "Stay with Khalisa. I've entrusted you to my father and the tribesmen. They know how to protect you. No one can reach you in the desert."

"You will come, won't you?" she asked again.

He stared at her for a moment.

"It's a long trip," he said. "Look after my daughter, Khalisa."

He looked away and ordered the men to start off. She could not even cry. She looked back at him, standing there watching as the caravan gradually disappeared over the horizon. He looked far away, then turned into a drop of water in a parched desert, hard to see and disappearing into the sand. Closing her eyes, she remembered his laughter, and at times his enthusiasm and expressions so full of life. Why had he not said farewell, held her in his arms, and told her he loved her? He had not done any of that. She had no need of words or touches. In her memory, she could see him hugging her hard, her body floating with his, heartbeats racing as she listened to his sighs and hers, recalling how she would shudder with passion when she spotted him or saw him approaching. She remembered how she had watched him for the first time, training his horses. Perhaps she had fallen in love with him at that point. Her heart could still remember his scent and his breath. Even so, she had wanted to say farewell and to tell him how much she loved him. Why had he not given her the chance to tell him? Now he had vanished. She screamed involuntarily.

"I want to go back to Cairo," she told the tribesman.

"That's not possible," the veiled man replied, leading the camel.

"I love you," she muttered. "Why didn't you let me tell you? Do you know? I wonder, do you need to hear it? How many times do you need to hear it? How many times will you come back safe and sound?"

She hugged her baby even closer and rested her head. Once again, her heart was breaking into pieces. Ever since she had known him, her heart would break into pieces, burn, and melt.

✴✴✴

His eyes searched for Asma, Ahmad's Egyptian wife. Even if she was wearing a face-veil, he was bound to recognize her. He would know her from the way she was looking for her only daughter, breathing and sighing for someone she had missed. But she had not come, or else he had not recognized her. His patience was wearing thin, and he was beginning to despair. Eventually he encountered a woman who tapped hard on his shoulder with her fingers.

"Are you the Arab?"

He looked at her eyes. They gleamed like the moon, and the kohl only served to enhance her attractive eyes. Her forehead and eyebrows were lined, and she seemed about the same age as Aisha's mother. Abd ar-Rahman stared at her, his face still veiled.

"Do you need something, Aunt?" he asked.

"You're the one who needs something," she responded arrogantly, "not me. You've come here to wait for the mother of . . ."

"I've come to wait for . . ."

"She won't be coming."

He looked at her. She removed her face-veil slightly.

"Forgive me," she said. "I can't remove my veil any more than that. My husband's jealous of everyone, young or old."

"Your husband?" Abd ar-Rahman asked, baffled.

"Don't you recognize me? People always recognize me from my eyes. That necklace she took was mine. There's no other like it in all of Egypt. I'm the reason this city exists, and now I see it in ruins. Today Anas will be furious and full of sadness. Do you recognize Maisoon, Arab?"

He looked at her without knowing how to respond. He did not understand what she was talking about.

"Have you ever heard of Ibn al-Mudabbir, the Tax Administrator? The one who humiliated the whole populace? Perhaps you haven't. I'm the one who made him disappear. No matter! These are days of darkness and ignorance. The young don't know the old. Tell the girl that her mother's now with the One who neither harms, nor deserts, nor forgets. The mother has no need to stay hidden today."

"She's dead!" he said forcefully.

"I tell you that she's with the One who does no harm, and you ask me if she's dead! She died about a year ago, Arab, when she came to me with the disease still rampant. She made me promise to tell her daughter that she had never abandoned her. Even from a distance, she had enveloped her in prayers."

She rubbed his shoulder without the slightest compunction.

"Don't abandon the one you love," she told him. "The lover must always make sacrifices and never think about himself. Send my greetings to Saeed. I'm going back to Alexandria now. My son's waiting for me. How come you don't know Maisoon? Everyone in Egypt knows Maisoon. Wait a while, and I'll tell you about her."

She talked for two hours or more.

War rattled the Egyptian people, and deprivation prevailed. Funds ran out, and Muhammad could not return the money he had taken from the rich, acquire more, or pay his men's wages. Even so, they continued to fight without surrendering. A fearsome army sent by the caliph entered El-Arish on its way to Fustat. Muhammad faced it with his own forces in El-Arish, while Abd ar-Rahman remained behind to protect Fustat. People suffered from food scarcity, extortionate prices, and ongoing destruction that had not stopped from the time Ibn Sulaiman arrived a year ago to the present day. Their hearts were with Muhammad al-Khalanji, but their stomachs were groaning from hunger and longed for rescue as soon as possible. News arrived that Khafif an-Nubi had been killed by Isa an-Nushari's troops in Upper Egypt, but Muhammad refused to surrender. He took his army out to confront the caliph's forces, but was defeated and retreated. The caliph's army reached Fustat, entered Badr al-Hammami's house, and found it empty. No one knew exactly who the Arab commander was who had fought alongside Muhammad al-Khalanji, or where he had fled with his soldiers. Some people said he belonged to Bedouin tribes from Syria, others that the tribes were from Yemen, and still others that they were from the Arabian Peninsula. Isa decided to look for him once Egyptian affairs were firmly under his control; he would look first for Muhammad al-Khalanji.

The reign of Ibrahim ibn Khumarawayh, no trace of whom was discovered by the Egyptian general, Muhammad al-Khalanji, lasted for about seven months. Shaikhs prayed for him in mosques and the Egyptian people were happy. Between their bafflement at having an Egyptian general running their affairs and the possibility of a return to the glory days of the country's ancient monarchs, the primary need was for food. The dream floated away like clouds, and there was no way of holding on to it.

Qasim al-Khurasani stayed in Egypt, giving Isa an-Nushari support and advice. Qasim told him that he knew the identity of the Arab commander who had fought against them. He needed to be captured and killed immediately so that the situation in the country could be stabilized.

Following Muhammad al-Khalanji's defeat, he went into hiding and Qasim al-Khurasani spent days searching for him. He searched his wife's family dwelling, the places where his soldiers lived, the banks and shores of rivers and seas. Eventually he found Muhammad, arrested him, and was on the point of killing him. However, Isa an-Nushari wanted to hand him over to the caliph. What this soldier had done was something no one else had ever dared do, and it was also crucial that no one dared do it again. Muhammad had to be used as an example for anyone else who might contemplate opposing the caliph. Isa sent Muhammad to Baghdad, where the caliph's men paraded him in chains and humiliated him. Then they killed him in full public view so that he would serve as a lesson for any soldier who rebelled against the caliph.

Abd ar-Rahman took his men, fled from Fustat to Giza, and camped in the desert, far away from soldiers' eyes. He had heard about Muhammad al-Khalanji's death, Isa an-Nushari's fixture as governor, and Qasim al-Khurasani's ongoing search for Abd ar-Rahman. He realized that, as a result, he was unable to either contact his own family or face the Egyptian people. What had happened? Some fifty thousand soldiers had joined Muhammad's forces without the promise of money or gold, but it had proved impossible to run the country without either records or money. Isa realized that, and so did the caliph. What could mere enthusiasm achieve when faced with hunger, and how could good intentions confront corrupt thieves and robbers? How long would merchants be willing to wait to recuperate their losses? When would the time come for the craftsmen to announce his surrender? What had he expected? For months, he had owned the world and seen in its eyes a craving felt by all the earth's people. His vanity had been complete and his heart satisfied. He had become the cavalier, the general, all the kings of yore. For a few hours, he had been Ahmad himself. Then came collapse. He had tripped and fallen into the very depths of all the seas combined. He had suffocated between the grains of salt and the sea's foam. Now there was no going back, no escape. The world had contracted and become like the cave where he was hiding. He was now ant-size, but unable to carry even that insect's loads.

The next day, Qasim would demolish the mosque or part of it. Perhaps he would aim his sword at the foundations, ensuring that, whether in one year or a hundred, the mosque would turn into a ruin. If he struck the buttresses and stones, that would be enough. If he aimed some blows directly at the roof, he would have won. How many buildings and shrines had disappeared before, and how many houses of God had been destroyed due to man's brutal vanity and overweening power! No matter. Perhaps he would die in his cave or be killed by Qasim. Maybe he would go back to the princess without any hands; she would give him a sympathetic glance and patiently put up with him. What a gloomy fate! It would be better never to go back. He had to stop thinking about the princess and what she would do. He had become obsessed with her eyes, the looks of admiration and affection that almost drove him crazy.

Then what? What came after the madness? He would either die or go back. The caliph would find her and marry her. She was a princess, and the right place for princesses was the caliph's mansion. Once there, she would forget about the Bedouin Arab, their love for each other, and the moments of truth and tranquility. She would take his daughter there; he would not be able to see her ever again. She would never know anything about her father, the way he had become a hero after changing sides, and then had to flee. A nagging doubt started whispering in his ear: how long would she wait patiently? When would she surrender? If she did, how many daggers would she deserve? How many stars would sear his veins and gush through his limbs?

Chapter 9

A isha had no idea what was going on around her. She felt dominated by the sound of her husband's voice, ordering her to leave without any farewell. The journey was long and exhausting. She covered her daughter's face to protect her against the dust, wind, and sun. Before they reached Esna, she heard Atika let out a loud scream. The caravan halted, and the camels lay down on the ground. Aisha dismounted and rushed over to discover that Musa ibn Uthmaan, the tribal chieftain, had died just before they got to Esna. His brother, Rabi'a, decided that he would be buried in Esna and told the women to stop wailing. Aisha went looking for Khalisa and found her watching the scene in silence. She went over to her.

"What's going to happen to me now, Aunt?" she asked.

"I'll protect you, Aisha," Khalisa replied forcefully, "you and baby Khalisa."

Aisha looked at her frozen expression. "Aren't you sad, Aunt?" she asked.

"No, I'm not," Khalisa replied firmly. "My tears dried up as soon as he left me."

"Abd ar-Rahman's nephew, the one who's going to help us," Aisha asked anxiously, "do you know him, Aunt?"

"Yes, I do," Khalisa replied, her eyed fixed on Musa's body. "He's fine. He doesn't involve himself in problems. His father died when he was a boy, and he decided to settle down here. He has status and family here. Don't worry. If you want to stay alive, you have to stop worrying."

"I'm worried for my daughter."

"Put your trust in God. He'll protect her."

Aisha sat down submissively beside Khalisa as the sound of men's voices rose and fell. The women all around them were whispering and pointing at Aisha. Azza kept talking about what trouble the strange girl caused, bringing down destruction on the tribe and the entire country. Now she had finished off both father and son. Aisha shrank where she was, clutching her baby daughter. Khalisa grabbed her hand.

"Stay calm," she said.

Aisha started nursing the baby and covered its face with her veil.

"Who's going to be jealous of your baby?" Azza asked angrily. "You walking disaster! Why couldn't you have had a boy? If your daughter grows up like you, she'll bring shame to the whole country . . ."

"Be polite, Azza," Khalisa told her firmly.

"Don't give me orders, Aunt," Azza replied equally firmly. "My father's the tribal chieftain now."

"No," Khalisa replied, "Abd ar-Rahman is."

No sooner did Azza hear that name than a blend of anger and sympathy took over.

"Abd ar-Rahman doesn't exist anymore," Azza insisted. "He's going to die, and we'll all be relieved."

Before Khalisa could respond, Uncle Rabi'a knocked on the door. The women all donned their veils.

"The men will start building houses for us," he said, "and pitching tents. Today I'm tribal chieftain, and, after several months, I'll be married to Atika."

Atika smiled happily and removed her head-covering. Aisha opened her eyes, trying to make sure that what was happening was not a nightmare.

"From today," he said, looking at Khalisa, "Azza and Saleema are responsible for you, Khalisa, you and the strange girl."

He turned and looked at Azza.

"Tomorrow," he told her, "you'll be married to your nephew, Saalim."

"As you wish, Father," she replied gloomily.

"Our confederacy and family have honored us," he went on, "and given us houses and land here. But the country's still at war, and inflation is affecting all parts of Egypt. Drought is spreading, so women are going to have to work like men. The strange girl can stitch and sew."

He looked at Saleema.

"I'll take charge of her, Father," she said.

"That may be best. Your sister's going to be preoccupied with her marriage. We're going to need to be careful about distributing food and drink. We're right on the cusp of famine, drought, war, and devastation."

"Don't worry," Saleema replied. "I'll make sure to carry out your orders."

Rabi'a spoke to his nephew. He told him what had happened to Abd ar-Rahman; whether today or tomorrow, the war would be won by the caliph. Abd ar-Rahman was bound to be killed, along with all the other people who had defied the caliph. He convinced his nephew, Saalim, that he was the oldest and most experienced, and that the tribe could not stay without a chief. Today, he had a hundred men. That was after Abd ar-Rahman had cajoled four hundred men into joining his forces and defying the caliph. Rabi'a offered Saalim his daughter, Azza, in marriage. Saalim already had a wife, but he immediately agreed. He could still remember how beautiful Azza was, even as a child. It all worked out well for Rabi'a. However, even amid the fields, food was both little and scarce.

For several days, Aisha tried to make sense of what had happened afterward. She had enough time. Khalisa asked to stay in the same room as Aisha; Saleema refused. She was rude to Khalisa and threatened her. She then separated Khalisa and Aisha, assigning them to different rooms. Khalisa's room was tiny and shoddy; Aisha's was large, but had no bed or blanket. Instead, there was a loom, spindle, and a lot of wool. Saleema pushed her inside, and she crashed to the floor with her baby. She hugged the baby hard so she would not be injured, and stayed silent.

"You're going to work for your food, you slut," Saleema said. "Do you know your measurements and description? There are no men here who want you—your breasts and waist, you harlot! You've been living by opening your arms and legs, but now you're going to live by working, you source of all destruction and debauchery!"

Aisha's face turned red, and her eyes filled with tears. She was furious.

"Don't insult me!" she said.

Saleema let out a dry laugh, then looked around her.

"Are you angry, you little slut?" she asked. "Why weren't you angry when you were offering your body for trade? You're dirtier than a foul-smelling rag."

Realizing that this battle was lost, Aisha took some deep breaths.

"What do you want me to do?" she stuttered.

"Spin, then turn what you've spun into fabric for sale, as you've done before. We've heard that your father was a tailor. You'll work all day, and I'll bring you food and drink once a day. If I don't like what you've done, there'll be no food or drink. You'll die, and your daughter even before you. Then we'll be spared the shame of her."

"Why do you hate me so much?" Aisha asked assuredly. "Is it because you're hollow and have no feelings? You're no good as a wife or daughter. You're just jealous of me."

Saleema raised her hand to hit Aisha, but Aisha grabbed it. Saleema pushed her, and she fell down. Saleema now screamed to the women for help.

"The whore's hitting me," she said. "Save me, Aunt!"

The women came in and broke up the fight.

"She started it," Aisha said immediately. "She's trying to starve me and my daughter. I want any one of you to take charge of me, but not Saleema."

"Those are the chieftain's orders," Saleema responded loudly.

She moved closer to Aisha.

"If you don't behave properly," she said, "I'm going to strangle your daughter and toss her in the garbage. No one will care. If you don't apologize now in front of all these women, I'll kill her at night. You know I can do it."

Aisha shuddered, but said nothing.

"Ask for forgiveness, Stranger," she yelled. "You've dared to defy your masters. You hit me, you whore, and threw me to the ground. Now kiss my hand."

The women whispered to each other in confusion.

"Leave her alone!" one of them said.

"She hasn't learned any manners," Saleema said angrily. "I have to teach her, or else she'll be rude to me every day, and I won't be able to control her."

Saleema grabbed the baby.

"Perhaps, Aunt, she's not the right person to take care of the baby," she said. "It might be better for you or me to do it. Otherwise, the baby may turn out . . ."

"I'll apologize," Aisha interrupted her, holding the baby's hand. "I'll do what you want."

"Don't be insolent with me," Saleema replied with a smile.

Aisha tried to take her baby back. "I won't," she said.

Still holding the baby in one hand, Saleema held out her other hand, expecting Aisha to kiss it.

"Hand her back first," Aisha said.

"Not till you apologize . . ."

Aisha bent over and kissed her hand. "Forgive me," she said. "I did you wrong."

The women were still silently observing the scene.

"That's enough, Saleema," one of them said.

"Can't you see, Aunt," she complained, "how she struck and hurt me?"

"That's enough," the woman said again. "Give her back her daughter."

She gave Aisha back her baby.

"I hope you've learned a lesson today," she said.

"Yes, I have," Aisha choked.

Their eyes met, then Saleema left and shut the door.

No tears fell, reminding her of the way she had been humiliated and crushed. She hugged her daughter, all hopes of her husband's return vanishing into thin air.

After a week, her milk began to dry up, and her eyes roamed. At night, Saleema would come in with a piece of bread and some water, but that was not enough to satisfy either her hunger or her baby's. One day, when Saleema came in, she found Aisha's hand shaking; she was working very slowly. Saleema told her that as long as she was not working hard and doing it well, she would not be getting any food. Aisha pleaded with a stammer that she really needed some food and promised to produce double the next day.

Saleema refused and took the food and drink away. She was about to lock the door, but Aisha grabbed hold of her and pushed her outside where she collided with two fat women. They pushed Aisha back inside. Aisha cried out for help, but nobody answered.

"Haven't you learned anything from what happened before?" Saleema asked her angrily.

She went up to Aisha.

"Your fate's in my hands, Aisha," she said. "You're at my mercy. I can either kill you or save you. You must understand that."

"Why are you doing this?" she asked ruefully.

"I hate you. Just like love, hate happens for no reason. I don't like you. You destroyed my sister's heart."

"She doesn't hate the way you do."

She slapped Aisha on the face.

"You're being cheeky again," she said, out of patience. "I've told you, you're at my mercy. If you die, for example, who'll care? Khalisa? She's a senile old woman who never leaves her room. Nowadays, everyone's concerned about their own food."

Aisha rubbed her cheek.

"God sees you," she said, "and knows."

Saleema grabbed her dress and pulled her close.

"Do you curse me?" she asked.

"I beg you to give me some bread," she said, "for the baby's sake. She has no power or strength of her own."

"If you stop objecting," Saleema replied, "I'll think about it. If you begged maybe . . ."

She held out her hand, and Aisha planted a kiss on it without speaking.

"Aren't you going to beg?" Saleema asked. "I'd give you some bread. Won't you ask for forgiveness?"

Aisha remained silent.

"If you kissed my feet," Saleema continued, "I might give you some water too. What do you think?"

Aisha did not reply.

"Never mind!" Saleema said as she stood up. "Tomorrow you're going to kiss my feet. You can cry for hours, but regret won't work."

Saleema locked the door, cursing and swearing as she went. She left Aisha sighing and moaning, while her starving daughter kept crying.

She hugged her daughter, fully expecting that she or her daughter would die either that day or the next.

She had some regrets about not humiliating herself even more with Saleema, but at the same time, she felt proud that she had not done so. She was Ahmad's daughter; she should not forget that. Her memories of her time with her husband were now far distant, and the sound of his voice had faded away like the clouds in the sky. Her father's voice came through loud and clear: "You can die, Aisha, but never humiliate yourself; your daughter can die, but never kiss anyone's feet." She smiled, but then her daughter started wailing. She went over and started desperately banging on the door.

"Saleema," she yelled. "Come back. I'll do whatever you want. Don't let her die."

She did not come. She started pounding the wall.

"Why did you leave me, Abd ar-Rahman?" she shouted. "Why did you leave me? I'll never forgive you. Where are you now, Mother? My father? Don't ask me to take on more than I can bear. You always do that. I'm just a weak girl, no more."

She heard the door opening that night, but paid no attention. Azza shook her hard and put some food and water in front of her.

"Here," Azza said, "eat this quickly before Saleema comes."

She ate quickly and drank the water. She almost stopped breathing because she was swallowing the food and drink so fast.

"You look like a hungry dog," Azza told her contemptuously. "Where's your fabled power and control over men?"

She did not reply, but started desperately nursing her baby till she felt the milk coming out of her breast.

She looked up at Azza. "I don't know how to thank you," she said pleadingly.

Azza looked at her. "Do you realize how much I hate you?" she asked.

"Yes, I do."

"You know that you put an end to my life. Do you realize that as well? Do you realize that, because of you, I'm now married for the second time to a man I don't love?"

"All I want," she replied desperately, "is for my daughter to live."

"I hope you both die. But I'll feed you this once."

Aisha had an overwhelming feeling of humiliation. "I beg you," she pleaded, "just bring me some bread at night. What your sister's giving me isn't enough. I don't want my baby to die," she went on. "I beg you. I'll do anything. I'll sew night and day. I'll make you a beautiful dress. I'll do everything to make you happy."

Azza thought for a few seconds. "Abd ar-Rahman," she said.

"If he comes back," Aisha said firmly, "I don't want him. I'll tell him that. You were right: I shouldn't have been married to him. He loves you, and I stood in the way."

"You're a devil."

She stayed silent, not knowing how she could make Azza happy.

"But he'll never come back," Azza said decisively. "You realize that, don't you?"

Aisha shuddered. "Perhaps," she replied.

Azza looked at her.

"If he came back and fought my father," Azza said, "one of them would have to kill the other."

"Ask me for anything," Aisha replied in despair. "Give me orders, and I'll do it at once. But let my daughter live."

"I'm afraid one of them will kill the other," Azza said. "I'm afraid that Abd ar-Rahman will either die or come back. Do you still love him, you bringer of disaster?"

"I want my daughter to stay alive," Aisha replied in despair.

"If he returns and fights my father, I'm going to kill her right in front of you. I'm going to help you and bring you bread at night, but if Abd ar-Rahman does come back, you'll have to stop him fighting my father."

"I'll do it," Aisha replied forcefully. "I swear that I will, even if I have to kill myself in front of him."

"And if you don't . . ."

"Do what you like with me."

"That's a pledge between the two of us."

"You're better than me," Aisha declared, "and better than him too. It's a pledge."

"Make sure you don't tell Saleema about it," Azza said, "or anyone else."

"I won't."

"I want you to realize," Azza told her, "that there's not much food in the house. None of us has a lot to eat. Prices have gone up, and there's a drought. Don't think my sister is making you suffer unnecessarily."

Aisha nodded. "I understand," she said.

Azza left. Aisha cried for an hour or more, then fell asleep with her baby in her arms.

"I love you," she said, shouting her husband's name. "Oh how much I love you! This time, I'll never forgive you for leaving me."

Next morning, she started working in earnest. When Saleema came into her room at sunset with a small piece of bread, she took a look at Aisha's work.

"That's a lot better," she said.

As usual, Aisha wolfed down the bread and drank the water in one gulp.

Aisha was carefully sewing in different shapes, colors, and decorative patterns.

"I want this piece as a present for Azza's wedding," she said.

"Why Azza?" Saleema asked, suspicious. "And who are you to decide how we use the embroidery?"

"I was just thinking," Aisha replied immediately. "You're the one to decide, of course."

Saleema thought for a moment.

"Maybe I will give it to Azza," she said, "as a present for her wedding."

At midnight, Azza arrived with some bread and water and a cup of goat's milk.

"I've embroidered a piece of cloth for you," Aisha said immediately. "I want you to get it. Your sister has it."

"Maybe some other time," Aisha went on, "we might have shared friendship and affection. You're generous, and I want that piece to be yours."

Azza was suspicious and narrowed her eyes.

"I don't trust you, strange girl," she said.

"I know and understand. I can feel your sorrow and bitterness."

Their eyes met.

"A man may be married to a lot of women," Azza said, "but he only really loves one. He doesn't have two hearts inside him."

"But he loves you," Aisha replied immediately. "He told me so."

"Maybe in the past," Azza said, "but not the way he loves you."

"Even though you're better and more generous than me," Aisha declared. "I don't know, if I were in your place . . ."

"I've felt like killing you many times," Azza said with a smile. "But he's never coming back, so there's no point in our being enemies. I'll let you know what I think of the piece of cloth, tomorrow or the next day."

Saleema had innumerable peculiar ways of crushing her. Sometimes she would come in smiling, put some food in front of her, and ask her to start work. But no sooner had Aisha started her sewing than Saleema would slap her on the back. Aisha would shut her eyes in pain, but not say a word.

"Oh," Saleema would say, "did I hurt you unintentionally?"

Aisha would not respond. On other occasions, Saleema would slap her hard or push her so she fell flat on her face. Aisha still refused to let her win by groaning or complaining. She bore it all in silence, and then had a little cry on her own.

Two days later, Azza brought her some bread and milk.

"I like your embroidery," she said. "You were right; it's different."

Aisha gave a weary smile.

"Keep it, sister," she said.

"We're not sisters," Azza replied.

"You're a lot better than your sister."

"Don't be rude about my sister."

"I hope your husband realizes how valuable and generous you are."

For just a moment, Azza looked at her.

"He's better than my first husband, that's for sure," she replied, as though she had forgotten who Aisha was.

"I hope you'll be happy," Aisha replied cautiously. "You deserve it."

Aisha asked Azza for permission to see Khalisa, even if it involved Azza being there, but she refused. Such a meeting might make Saleema suspicious. Aisha wondered how it was that Saleema had the kind of power that her sister did not possess. Saleema was the elder sister and seemed to have a way with her father. She was married to one of the tribesmen and had children. So why so much hatred? Did she hate her husband? Was she angry at the entire world? Had she herself been born with the heart of an incorrigible whore? Was it her ability to do whatever she liked with Aisha that made her so vicious and defiant? Aisha had plenty of time to think.

Her daughter filled her life and turned her prison into a fascinating garden. That day, the little girl had started smiling, and she had spent hours talking to her. She told her daughter about Abd ar-Rahman; she said that she had her father's eyes, and her father was a warrior who had been defeated. He might be dead perhaps, or even still alive. No one knew for sure.

Within a month or two, Aisha had learned endurance; she could make do with just a little food. Work was the first thing she did every day. She overcame her hatred for Saleema, and no longer felt humiliated or sad in her presence. She learned to control her spontaneity and adjust her feelings. She prayed every day, asking God to bring him back, then prayed some more, asking Him to preserve her father's mosque, it being all that was left. Then she asked God to look after her daughter. She spoke to God a lot. She only ever heard snippets about what was happening outside her room. When two months had passed, Azza came to her room one night and told her that Saleema was not at home that day, and she could take her for a walk outside the house. Aisha donned her veil, wrapped up her baby, and went outside to sniff the air for the first time. She asked Azza why Saleema was keeping her a prisoner, but Azza did not reply.

Soldiers entered the tribal borders without permission, and the women screamed. The men gathered, and Aisha hid behind Azza, worried in case Saleema appeared. But Saleema did not seem to notice her.

The Abbasid Commander addressed them all.

"The caliph is searching throughout Egypt," he said, "for Ahmad ibn Tulun's daughter. Anyone caught hiding her will pay for it with his life."

"We all pray for the caliph, brother," Rabi'a said. "Our tribe doesn't have any strangers."

The Commander looked at the women. "The caliph's told us," he said, "to go into every household and question every man and woman. If we don't find her, Egypt as a whole is going to suffer."

He then brought out his record.

"Give me the name of every woman in the tribe," he said, "along with the names of her father and husband."

She put her hand over her heart. "Can I go back to my room?" she whispered to Azza.

One of the soldiers seemed to hear her.

"Tell all the women to come outside," he ordered. "Today soldiers are going to search every house."

"That's not right, brother," Rabi'a protested. "The harem is inviolable."

"Those are the caliph's orders. It's not just your tribe, but the whole of Egypt. We started two months ago. If we don't find her, the caliph's going to punish us."

As the soldiers started asking the women their names and writing them in their records, Aisha was shivering in fright. When her turn came, the soldier asked for her name, and she told him in a quivering voice. He then asked her for her father's name.

"He's a relative of my aunt, Khalisa," she stuttered. "She's here. I can ask her."

"What's his name?"

She looked at Khalisa.

"He's my niece's husband," Khalisa replied at once. "Her mother's an Egyptian woman."

It seemed as though the soldiers did not believe Khalisa.

"Did she leave the room without permission?" Saleema asked immediately. "My lord, she's a stranger with no family and no background. Khalisa's lying."

Aisha's heart almost stopped, and she stayed glued to her spot.

"Take off your veil," the Commander ordered.

She did not respond, and the Commander yelled at her again. She removed her veil. He looked at her.

"What's your name?"

"Aisha."

Silence now fell, so that the sound of flying cockroaches overwhelmed her senses.

The Commander looked at his colleague and whispered something in his ear.

"Aisha's the name of Ahmad ibn Tulun's daughter," he said.

He looked at Rabi'a. "How long has this strange girl been with you?" he asked.

"Ever since Abd ar-Rahman was married to her over a year ago," he replied. "This orphan girl can't possibly be an amir's daughter."

"My lord," Aisha stuttered, "Aisha's the name of about half the girls in Egypt."

He looked at her carefully again and noticed her hands with scars from so much sewing and her eyes surrounded by deep wrinkles.

"Take the veil off your hair as well," he told her.

"That's not right, my lord," she replied.

"Do what I tell you! Where's your husband?"

"Dead," Rabi'a replied.

He did not dare say that Abd ar-Rahman had been fighting against the caliph. The entire tribe would be punished, not just a few of its men. If the Banu Saalim were to become one of the tribes that had angered the caliph, they would have no hope. The drought and hunger they were already suffering was enough. She slowly removed her veil.

"Why are you shaking?" the Commander asked.

"My husband's the only person who's seen my hair before now," she replied.

The Commander looked at her long, black hair and her gentle features. But her hands suggested hard labor. No princess would be able to do that kind of work.

"Open your hands," he told her.

She opened them, swallowing hard, and he looked at them.

"Where did you learn to sew and embroider?" he asked.

"In my father's house," she replied. "We all worked, then he died and . . ."

"What?"

"I kept on working till I was married."

Suddenly he looked at Azza. "What do you think?" he asked her. "Is she Ahmad's daughter?"

She gave Aisha a baffled look. "I don't believe she is, my lord," she replied.

"Has she told you anything? Who are you?"

"I'm her friend," she replied firmly, "her husband's cousin. She's a poor orphan. I know her family; they're relatives of my aunt, Khalisa, as she just told you. But we haven't seen them for ages."

Her father gave her a dubious look, and Saleema stared at her in reproof. The soldiers whispered to each other.

"If you hear about Aisha anywhere," the Commander said, "you must let me know. Whoever finds her will received a thousand dinars from the caliph in person."

With that, the soldiers left, and Aisha rushed back to her room, with Azza following her. Azza closed the door and looked straight at Aisha.

"Who are you?" she asked.

"As you said, a poor orphan," Aisha replied panting.

"Liar!"

Azza left, and Aisha listened as Saleema chided her sister for what she had just said. How could she say that she was this strange girl's friend? Saleema locked the door, and Aisha threw herself on the bed, hugging her baby and trying to calm her fears.

As the months passed, Aisha learned to ignore Saleema's taunts and assaults. Sometimes it involved curses, but at others, the assault was physical. Every time, she simply ignored her and did not cry, plead, or lose her temper. She learned to present Saleema with a lifeless visage, as though she was asking to die. After a while, Saleema was bored with the game. She started bringing her food and taking the fabric away without a word. Aisha learned how to control her willful self. A cautious friendship developed between her and Azza, perhaps out of curiosity on Azza's part; Aisha could not tell. Every week, Azza would come at night, take her for a stroll outside, and bring her back without anyone knowing. Aisha asked her for a comb and some water to give herself a wash. Azza brought them for her in secret. Aisha's sole purpose in life involved waiting for the chunks of bread to arrive and talking to her daughter for hours, lamenting and telling stories.

"If your father comes back today," she told her daughter one day, "he won't like me. I'm skinny and pale. Saleema wants me to look ugly by way of revenge. Do you think I've changed a lot?"

Azza never had a lot to say, but one day, she brought the fabric that Aisha had made. She sat down by Aisha.

"These patterns are different," she said thoughtfully. "They're completely unfamiliar to us, like stars in the heavens and colorful flowers. These five-lobed leaves are strange. How did you come up with them as designs?"

"They come from Al-Qata'i, where I was living."

"They're royal designs, strange girl."

Aisha looked at her. "I don't know what you're talking about," she replied.

"Let's suppose," Azza said thoughtfully. "Let's just suppose that you're the daughter of Ahmad ibn Tulun, the mighty amir. You escaped when Ibn Sulaiman attacked. You promised Abd ar-Rahman the gold, so he married you. I wonder, does he know as well?"

"That's nonsense. I'm an orphan with no family."

"As I told you, Aisha, we're just suggesting. Don't be scared. I'm thinking along with you. Abd ar-Rahman may well be dead. In fact, he must be dead because the war's over, and he hasn't come back. Isa an-Nushari is securely in place as governor, and Abd ar-Rahman hasn't returned. The caliph's still looking for Ahmad's daughter. I don't think he wants to kill her. Have you heard anything about the caliph Al-Muktafi?"

"I don't know him," Aisha replied exasperated.

"I've heard a lot about him. He's a handsome young man, gentle, and a poetry lover. Not like his father, who was married to Qatr an-Nada. I think Al-Muktafi wants to be married to the amir's daughter. What woman could refuse to be married to the caliph, Aisha? For example, let's just suppose that you're the amir's daughter, would you refuse to be married to the Caliph of all Muslims?"

"I have a husband," she replied without thinking.

"What if he's died?"

"I'd refuse."

"Why? Because you love Abd ar-Rahman? Or is it that you prefer to still be humiliated like this? Can you imagine how your daughter would grow up in the caliph's house in Baghdad? Do you dream about that? If you were accustomed to palace life, what's to keep you here as a poor orphan?"

"I promised Abd ar-Rahman not to be married to anyone else, even if he died."

"Abd ar-Rahman is unbelievably egocentric! He's in charge, both living and dead. Think of your own daughter's future."

Aisha held the fabric in her hand. "Keep this, Azza," she said, "and pass it on to your children. Forgive me!"

Azza stared at her long and hard.

"I will keep it and pass it on to my children," she said. "But I'll never forgive you."

Three months later, she received a strange letter. She expected it to be from Abd ar-Rahman, but he had not tried to contact her. Had he been killed, she wondered, or was he afraid the letter might fall into the soldiers' hands? She dearly wished that he would write anything to take away her sorrow and despair over what had happened to her, her worries about the unknown future, and her despair at not seeing him. She had dearly wished to have a single chance to say goodbye and tell him what had happened. But as time passed, any such meeting became impossible and all hope vanished. Azza brought her this letter. She had read it; a little boy had handed it to her. Azza told her that it was lucky the letter had not fallen into either Saleema's or Rabi'a's hands. It was a short letter in Coptic. Here is what it said:

> We have been searching for Amir Ahmad's daughter. If she were married to the caliph, he would not destroy Ahmad's mosque. Only Ahmad's daughter can save it. In just a few days, it will be demolished. The wife's intercession will save the father. People say that amirs' houses are regulated by affiliation and loyalty, not love. The entire population of Egypt is hoping and waiting.

Aisha burst into tears as Azza watched her attentively. Aisha understood Saeed's letter. He had found her, knowing everything and realizing that the tribe had moved to Esna and that, this time, love was preventing her from self-sacrifice.

She grabbed the letter and tore it up.

"You were always unkind, Uncle," she declared audibly. "You're asking a lot of me."

"Has he asked you to be married to the caliph?" Azza asked. "Who sent the letter?"

She did not respond.

"Think of your daughter," Azza said. "Abd ar-Rahman's egocentric, but a mother should think of her child. Do you want her to spend the rest of her life under Saleema's tutelage? Do you want that or the caliph's residence? You want to sacrifice yourself. Fair enough, but why make a powerless little girl suffer? If a mother's a real mother, then she's prepared to make sacrifices. I'm not saying that because I want Abd ar-Rahman. I've married someone else, and he'll never be coming back anyway. I'm saying it because I know what awaits you here. Who can give you a guarantee that my father won't forcibly marry you off to one of the tribesmen after a while? What fate awaits you, Princess?"

"I'm not a princess."

"Yes, you are," Azza replied firmly. "I know that, but you're a mother too. A mother always makes sacrifices for her daughter. It's the mother who has to do it. Your daughter's not safe here. In a year or less, my father's going to marry you off to a tribesman. Time's passing, and hope's vanishing. Make your mind up now before tomorrow."

Chapter 10

I sa was now securely installed in Egypt. He produced the records that he had hid-den, concerning Egypt's taxes, as well as the money he had taken with him from the treasury. As he spoke to people, he made promises and threats. If they wanted stability, they needed to forget everything that had happened. He would forgive Egyptians for their support of Muhammad al-Khalanji. He would forget what had happened on condition that they forgot that Ahmad ibn Tulun had governed the country. Fustat would again be the capital city. Isa would provide people with food and chop off the hands of robbers. He would put things in order and encourage merchants and landowners. The only people he would punish would be soldiers who had fought against the caliph, fifty thousand of them. They had scattered throughout Egypt, and it would be difficult to arrest them all. But many of them had fled south. He started encircling Bedouin tribes that had helped Muhammad in order to make arrangements for them to be punished. Some of them he already knew, others he did not. Tribes started moving from their locations, and it became impossible to find them. In Qasim, Isa found a stalwart support and strength.

Qasim al-Khurasani was still planning to demolish the mosque; he would be starting either that day or the next. The caliph's soldiers were pursuing anyone who had helped Muhammad al-Khalanji, the Egyptian commander, and everyone who wanted a return to Ahmad ibn Tulun's regime in Egypt and its independence from the caliph. Qasim al-Khurasani started taking the caliph's armed forces through the streets of Fustat and Giza, searching for particular names among Egyptians, Arabs, Turks, Nubians, and Sudanese. They would either be killed in Egypt or sent to the caliph in Baghdad to be killed there.

The ongoing search for Aisha, Ahmad's daughter, and Ibrahim ibn Khumara-wayh was continuing; indeed, it was a goal involving the potential collapse of the caliphate itself. The caliph Al-Muktafi's mercy and intelligence had both made him eager to marry Aisha. That marriage would be a gesture of truce with the Egyp-tian people and would also mark a triumph and an end to the Tulunid regime. If Aisha was not dead, then she was still somewhere in Egypt; and as long as she was there, Qasim al-Khurasani had to find her. It was more important for the caliph to find her than to locate Ibrahim, who was just a child. Muhammad al-Khalanji's army had not defeated the caliph, but the caliph still needed to consolidate his rule over Egypt. Marrying into the Tulunid household would enable him to realize the dream and soak up all memories of the past. The police started searching in every village, city, house, and quarter.

Qasim was aware that some Arab Bedouin tribes had supported Muhammad al-Khalanji, as had all the Copts, Christians, and Muslims. But then the curse had struck them, so there was no point in exacting punishment. Prices were soaring, and there was general drought. They all realized that people who angered the caliph had no hope of a decent life. Qasim al-Khurasani again spread the rumor in the quarters of Fustat that the mosque was about to be demolished, and it was the duty of every Egyptian to tear down a mosque that Ahmad had built using stolen money. News also spread that, once things in Egypt had settled down, Isa an-Nushari was planning to build a new mosque even bigger and more splendid. The previous era was over and gone, and Egyptian territory would be restored to the caliphate. Egyptians locked their doors and blocked their ears. No one listened to Qasim, and no one trusted him. After what had happened, nobody dared come out in opposition to Isa an-Nushari. Instead, every household was concerned with finding bread and water. Everyone else mourned the glory days of the past, times of plenty when meat was available to Egyptians, decorations filled the streets, crafts and agriculture flourished, and happiness pervaded every segment of society. That is the way things were—and all praise to the One who exists forever! Everyone suppressed their bitter feelings and carried on in silence, the visible involving submission, but the invisible anger. Memories were still fresh and alive, and the mosque was still there, disturbing the sleep of the caliph, the governor of Egypt, and Qasim al-Khurasani, not to mention that of Ibn Sulaiman inside his prison.

Soldiers started searching for the Banu Saalim tribesmen; Abd ar-Rahman had to have been one of those who helped Muhammad al-Khalanji. He had either to be killed or handed over to the caliph to be paraded around Baghdad, then killed, humiliated and regretful. But Abd ar-Rahman seemed to have vanished, as had the Banu Saalim men with him. The Banu Saalim tribesmen in Esna had not supported Muhammad al-Khalanji; that much was clear. It was just a question of a hundred men or fewer. Isa doubted that Abd ar-Rahman, whom Qasim accused of helping Muhammad and supporting the revolt, existed. Nobody had seen his face, but everyone knew that a veiled Bedouin Arab had been assisting Muhammad. No one knew his name or what had happened to him. Qasim spread his men out all around the Banu Saalim in Esna and the outskirts of Fustat. The search for a veiled man was almost impossible. Even so, the demolition of the mosque or part of it would be finished within what remained of that day's waking hours.

Saeed al-Farghani had lived through all the recent conflicts—Muhammad al-Khalanji's victory, then his defeat. Doubts beset him, hope intoxicated him, and defeat aroused him. He realized that the inevitable end was nigh; he was still living in the small house he had built for himself alongside the mosque. It had not been demolished yet, and he was living amid all the destruction and vestiges of past glory. Every day, he spent hours looking at the mosque, then went into his house and stayed there. He cried a lot, and these days his tears would arrive without permission—weak bones perhaps, failing strength, old age mercilessly weighing him down. Ah, woe for an age that takes and gives nothing, crushing the heart and leaving wounds untended! The beloved is far removed, and what is past and gone turns into a heavy-laden cloud. All he had left was what he had built. Now time wanted him to stay alive in order to live with oblivion and to remember; to witness the demolition and be humble; to be crushed and grow strong.

A stranger knocked on his door. When he opened it, he was looking into the eyes of a veiled man.

"The Arab," he said, as he let him and his men inside.

The veiled man closed the door and then removed his scarf. Their eyes met. Abd ar-Rahman looked defeated and maybe even sad. Saeed looked submissive and desperate. The men spread all over the tiny house.

"I thought badly of you," Saeed said. "Forgive me. You're better than I expected."

Abd ar-Rahman gave a bitter smile. "What I've done my best to preserve," he said, "is about to be demolished. You've no hope, Saeed."

"I know. How is she?"

Abd ar-Rahman dismissed his men.

"I haven't seen her for three months," he said. "I was fighting with Muhammad in Fustat, then El-Arish. After we were defeated, I've been hiding with my men."

"Have you come to chide me for what I told you a year ago?"

"No, I've come to find out how you are."

"You're not an easy man, Abd ar-Rahman. Do you think I don't know that? You act at random and take risks. Have you had your fill of adventure yet? You needed her in your empty life."

"A man has to take risks at least once in his life. Otherwise, he'll die without ever knowing the craving for satiation."

"You're due honor for having tried."

"Isa an-Nushari is much more dangerous than Ibn Sulaiman," Abd ar-Rahman said. "He's clever and unambitious. He carries out the caliph's instructions without having any money put in his pocket. We've no hope. Qasim is still helping him."

"Qasim still wants Aisha."

For a moment, there was silence.

"That'll never happen," Abd ar-Rahman said.

Saeed smiled. "You realize, don't you," he said, "that if the caliph were married to Aisha, he might save the mosque. Aisha could persuade him to keep it. No one else could do it."

Abd ar-Rahman kept his anger under control. "I may die," he said, "and she may die, but she won't be married to him. She already has a husband. If I die, she won't marry anyone else."

"Men's egotism has no parallel, no different from their greed! Today she's defying the caliph and standing in front of him. Do you realize that?"

"I'm confident that she's not going to betray me, even from a distance. She'll keep our pledge."

"There's no cure for love," Saeed said with a sigh. "It kills without mercy. I didn't expect you to fall in love with her. There she was, in your hands. Why did you fall in love with someone who gives for nothing in return? I thought Arabs composed poetry for the absent beloved, not for someone who submits and obeys. She was yours, and I assumed that you would be looking for a woman who was independent. Men always look for someone who'll make them suffer . . ."

"No, they'll be looking for someone as a companion . . ."

Saeed moved closer. "Her mother never taught her," he said, "that princesses don't fall in love. They sacrifice themselves for their country and fathers. If only Asma had taught her anything! I'm not concerned about love, Abd ar-Rahman. What I'm concerned about is the mosque. There is glamour and life to be found in sorrowful love stories. Have you ever heard a happy love story lasting till today? Take me, for example. My own suffering has engendered the most wonderful aspects of love. Do not be frightened of heartbreak at the moment of parting. I've been separated from my own beloved for years, and yet here I am standing before you, still fighting and striving . . ."

"I realized that that's the way you'd be thinking," Abd ar-Rahman responded. "I've come to see you. If you're planning to help Isa find out where she is, I'm going to kill you today and put an end to you. You're never going to find her, even if you spend the rest of your life trying."

"I'll find her," Saeed replied with a smile. "In fact, I know where she is."

Abd ar-Rahman drew his sword and placed it on Saeed's neck.

"Don't you dare," he said.

"Let her choose, either to save what her father built or to stay with you. Maybe she already realizes what her duty is and what she needs to do."

"I'll kill her before she even gets to the caliph and before you could get to her."

"There's unparalleled violence in lovers' despair. I can still remember when I came to visit you a year ago. You had a triumphant smile on your face after you'd completely dominated her. You had learned all her secrets, controlled the world at the time, and assumed that you were powerful. How did she manage to take control of you afterwards? If only I knew! But then, lovers' lives are full of incomprehensible surprises. Love's just like life itself; you can never predict. You're never going to see her again, Abd ar-Rahman. Do you realize that?"

"Qasim has to die," he replied, ignoring the question.

"Do you want to save what Ahmad built for her sake or for your own ego?"

"No, for the dream."

"So what am I supposed to do? I'm just a feeble old man with no power."

"If Qasim dies, we'll save the mosque."

"And you'll die too."

"My dying is predestined fate. I'm not afraid of death."

"Haven't you had enough adventure?" Saeed asked.

"I long to live with her, but there's no escape from death."

"Ibrahim, Khumarawayh's son."

They stared at each other.

"I'm not sure," Abd ar-Rahman replied with a smile. "Was my meeting with you a year ago the worst thing that ever happened to me, or the best? I'm not sure yet."

"Well, I realize that your malice is unrivaled. How does the princess deal with you?"

"Saeed, I'm not going to kill you today because we've a common goal, but that's all. But forget about Aisha, forget that you ever knew her. And don't let useless ideas get hold of you."

Abd ar-Rahman and his men hid in one of the demolished houses in Fustat. It was becoming difficult, if not impossible, to persuade the men to say with him. There was no money or food. The goal was still clear. Four hundred men. But if they rose up against Abd ar-Rahman and killed him, no one would blame them. They had fought without success or spoils, and then become powerless fugitives, living like stray dogs amid demolished buildings and smashed walls.

That day he spoke to the men and asked them to go back to the tribe if they wished. No one would recognize them; the war was over. They asked him why he would remain a fugitive. Why would he not try to go back too? He did not respond, then told them that his task was not finished.

Most of the men decided to go back to the tribe, except for ten who decided to stay with him till he returned safe and sound and took his place as tribal chieftain. He knew that his father had died and his uncle had taken over as chieftain. He also knew that his wife was well, but that was all he knew or could find out. The men left at night, and he stayed with the ten men, wondering how to tell them what his intentions were. Nights were now shorter than days; days were endless. After the defeat, weakness had reared its ugly head. With that realization, life became difficult. Leaning his head against the wall, a sense of weakness squeezed his heart and removed all evil thoughts from his soul. Today he was standing against the caliph, hostile and defiant. Today he expected her to forget who she was for his sake. Today he was going to die, with no hope of resurrection.

His mother had spoiled him when he was a child. He could not remember her ever scolding him. Till she died, she would give without recompense. All he could recall was her smiling face. When she died, he lost his way. All his friends were horses; he used to talk to them, scold them, and tell them about the glory days of old. He felt overwhelmed by an oppressive loneliness that he could never dispel. He had wasted his life on pleasures, but never achieved anything. He had fallen in love with Azza, but that did not satisfy him. He had vied for power, but never found it.

Then Aisha had appeared, wiped the dust off his heart, and given assurance to his confused soul. She had arrived like a passing cloud, unattainable and not lingering. What was he expecting? For her to stay with him while he was a fugitive, when he was as good as dead? Now that he was defeated, could she still save what her father had built and be restored to her former prestige? What kind of vanity had hold of him? He pounded the wall with his fist. Who was he, when faced with the caliph? A young man? Powerful? The caliph was a powerful young man too, and he also held every single Muslim country in his hands. Too bad for Aisha if she betrayed Abd ar-Rahman! He would never forgive her. In fact, he would kill her before she left. He would have to do it. He would want to see her blood flowing all around him, just as she herself would be mangling the innards of her own heart if she even thought of going to the caliph in Baghdad. His own love was a mixture of dire affection and cruelty whose destiny was unknown to him. Why had he fought, and why had he been defeated? He had enjoyed the adventure and spent years waiting for her, hoping that the old prestige would come back. But she had always been the focus of his attention, and he had wanted her to know what he had done and achieved. Why had he fought and taken risks? He had wanted her to know that he was a fighter, no less than her own father. She was there, standing in front of him all the time, flooding the whole of life and enveloping the passing days in her grasp. Ah! Pure suffering, incurable, unforgiving. Ah, the sweet agonies, much desired, ungiving. Could he break free? If only he could! Hold fast and hope. But with hope there was temptation and betrayal. It is hope that erases the day and turns nighttime into perception. It is hope that cancels the desire to live and survive; with it, there is neither compensation nor surrender.

He had heard about the monk, Anduna. Ja'far had told him in prison about the monk's story with Ahmad. He envied the monk for having departed this world and realized that he could not announce his death today. The monk had died by his own choice, whereas he was going to die by hers. She would be prioritizing her father's interests and the dream. She had made sacrifices for the dream before, and now she would do so again. Whenever he thought about it, the fires inside him started raging.

"Don't you dare, Aisha!" he said audibly, as his very weakness oozed out of his pores. "I swear that, if you're married to him, I'll go to Baghdad and kill you myself."

The next day, he met Saeed and told him about his plan to kill Qasim al-Khurasani. Saeed listened carefully. He asked Saeed to sit in the mosque courtyard when Qasim al-Kharasani and Isa an-Nushari arrived to demolish it. The guards would try to take him outside, and it was his job to defend the mosque as though it was the very last time he would be seeing it. He had to attract both Qasim's and Isa's attention. Abd ar-Rahman would fire an arrow at Qasim and then flee. It might not be possible to escape because there would be guards all around the mosque. They needed to think of a way out. Only Saeed, who had built the mosque, knew how to do it. Saeed asked him if he could fire the arrow from a distance and then climb the minaret. Abd ar-Rahman produced a sheet of paper and asked Saeed to do a drawing of the mosque and its gates. He told Saeed that he intended to stay alive. If he could escape to the mountains, the soldiers would have a hard time finding him. They were full of dark caves that could not be blockaded. After a few days, his men would be waiting for him with the horses, and he would return to his tribe. No one knew him, and no one had seen his face. Even if Isa had his doubts about Abd ar-Rahman, it would be difficult to track him all the way to Upper Egypt. Saeed drew the mosque and then gave Abd ar-Rahman a thoughtful look.

"You'll have to choose between scrambling up the minaret or running fast," he said. "For me, at least, escape looks impossible."

"Perhaps if my men could spar with the soldiers," Abd ar-Rahman said, "it might be possible to escape. But that's asking a lot of my men. They won't realize what this escapade is about."

Saeed went into a room and came out with some gold.

"Give them this," he said. "I know that the country's current state matters to them."

Abd ar-Rahman looked at him. "Why are you helping me?" he asked. "Is it just because you want to save the mosque?"

"Arab," Saeed replied, "I sent Aisha a letter asking her to make the sacrifice for her father's sake."

Abd ar-Rahman grabbed him by the collar. "If you weren't an old man," he said, "I'd beat you to death rather than shoot an arrow that kills you."

"I'm surprised to see you feeling so weak, Abd ar-Rahman," Saeed replied. "It's what you need. I can still recall the triumphant smile with which you greeted me just a year ago. You need to learn a little humility. Nothing softens the heart as much as the passion of weaklings."

"I'm not weak," Abd ar-Rahman replied forcefully. "I'll die before that ever happens."

"You don't own the land as well."

"Nor does the caliph. And, even if he did, he'll never own my wife."

"Why are you angry with me? I haven't forced her to do anything. Or is it that you're not sure she'll choose to stay with you? She'll just stay in the deep South, with no family and no prestige. For your sake, she'll erase everything that her father built with her own hands, even though she does not know whether or not you are coming back. Your self-confidence is without peer. Or is it perhaps that you don't have the power to defy the caliph? Do you want to save the mosque for her sake? So you know that you can indeed defy the caliph? Or do you want to save it because of Ahmad's dream?"

Abd ar-Rahman grabbed one of the smashed rocks inside Saeed's house and hurled it against the wall as hard as he could.

"Shut up," he yelled, "so I don't kill you!"

"Don't destroy what's left of the house," Saeed replied with a smile.

"There's not much left, man," he replied.

"If you're successful," Saeed said, "you'll leave, and I won't see you again. Maybe I won't see her either. In fact, it's certain that I won't. If she decides to go to Baghdad, I won't see her; if she decides to stay with you in Esna, I won't see her. I don't have much life left. Do you realize, Abd ar-Rahman, that I'm indescribably happy when I look into your eyes and see how miserable you are? Do you know why? Not because I hate you, but because for some time you've impressed me. You used to roam the world, seizing moments of pleasure without even thinking about the consequences or the people around you. But then your camel stumbled, and you were stuck in a deep hole with no way out. While you were there, you were liberated from pleasure, and the world expanded before your eyes. Whether or not you find her waiting for you, you'll still be the person you've been for a year now. If you don't find her, you'll have to forgive her. She's only human."

"You're deliberately prodding fresh wounds," Abd ar-Rahman responded angrily. "No matter. We were talking about the men who'll help me escape."

Saeed stared at him.

"We'll save the mosque together," he told Abd ar-Rahman calmly. "We'll try. Then you'll go back and find that she has gone. You'll wander in the desert, collecting memories, and imploring the stars at night to give you a glimpse of her face in your dreams. You'll live a long life, befriending every stone and every raindrop, begging God to let her visit you in your imagination, holding out your arms to embrace her shadow in the noonday light. The sun will shine into your eyes, and agony will cleave your heart. Whenever she is absent, the entire world will seem more brutal. Everywhere will be calm until you scream in the desert, to be heard only by the echo of your own voice. Then, Arab, you will realize, you will learn that you are not the world's pivot and that children of the nobility have no special place in destiny. Weak, sorrowful, and defeated, they live in perpetual longing for what was and what will never be again. Tomorrow, you're going to be looking at the mosque's balconies, crenulations suspended in the skies and aspiring for something loftier and more sublime. Tomorrow, you'll realize that loss can lighten heavy burdens and make spirits soar like the crenulations in the mosque's balconies. Ephemeral beloveds and an everchanging world are no cause for fear. Tomorrow, you'll come to know and appreciate my own sorrow."

Abd ar-Rahman stared at the floor.

"Your hatred of me is without parallel," he said after a pause. "You read Arabic poetry. Who taught you that, Copt?"

"The man who's been chasing you everywhere," Saeed responded with a smile. "Ahmad ibn Tulun."

"Amir Ahmad, you mean. He told me that, before I built the mosque, I needed to visit Samarra and read about love. Only desert dwellers had perfected the art."

He looked at Abd ar-Rahman. "Do you know," he asked, "why desert dwellers have so mastered the art of love? It's because they all realize that departure is inevitable. Their kind of passion is always impossible. Clinging to impossibilities is madness. Madness always leads the mind astray before the heart. The princess needs to be married to the Commander of the Faithful, to wear silk, to be swamped in jewelry, to run through the palace rooms, and live in the luxury of which you've deprived her. You must learn not to think only of yourself. A year ago, I came to see you and told you that you'd be sorry. You would be sitting in front of me, enveloped in sorrow. I'm always right, Arab. How happy I am to see you so miserable today. I won't hide it from you. When I met you after you'd betrayed her, I wanted to kill you, but I didn't."

"We've met since then, Copt."

"Yes, but I've never seen you this miserable. That sorrow will intensify and deepen."

"I'm the only one who knows the princess," Abd ar-Rahman responded forcefully. "She'll never leave me."

"No," Saeed replied with a smile, "I'm the only one who knows her. She's going to leave. When she does, and you're feeling even more desperate, go and find the Pyramid Witch. Tell her that the love of Saeed, son of Katib al-Farghani, is more profound than yours. He's stayed loyal even though there have been moments when cowardice has taken charge. But you've hated and punished an entire lifetime. Tell her: 'Saeed has his dignity. He won't beg you, and he'll never visit you.'"

"What witch are you talking about?"

"You'll go to her. I know you will. When you do, as we all do, tell her that she may have read, but knows nothing about love.

Saeed, son of Katib al-Farghani, now took out a piece of paper and started writing on it:

In erasing the city is the scent of fear and the taste of danger.
In erasing the city is war on the memory with swords and spears.
In erasing the city is vengeance and blessing. Cities that are gone linger in the
    memory.

Cities that are gone linger forever in bright sunshine with lofty buildings.

In searching for the city, the heart draws its final breath.

The city is remote; the traveler wakes up.

The city is nigh; its inhabitants are heedless.

This is the tale of a city unlike others; in its structures an encounter between foe and beloved.

In its alleys, an approach to a chasm full of treasure, merciless with the hesitant, devoted only to those who lose themselves therein.

People said it was neither here nor there. Rather, it was beside a mountain warding off death.

People say that its inhabitants scattered all over the earth with neither memory nor knowledge.

They say that ancestors collected its stones in a pit, its bottom even deeper than the seafloor.

They then demolished its features so as to protect the papers from destruction.

They said that time destroys hearts, weakens the body, and demolishes all cities.

However, on this earth, traces do not vanish nor is history lost.

Here people are expert preservers of documents, even if they do not read them.

Come now, let me tell you about the city, lovers, the dream, achievement, wandering for forty years or more.

Abd ar-Rahman stared at him, more frightened than he had ever felt before.

ᛉᛉᛉ

Abd ar-Rahman started hearing voices, whispering in his ear and sometimes chiding him. Beautiful Maisoon warned him not to chase his own shadow, but that shadow of his would not leave him, even for a few seconds. Now here he was inside the mosque—Abd ar-Rahman in Ahmad ibn Tulun's mosque. He had protected it.

The vision became clear in the dawn light. It was strange for the call to prayer to sound while the mosque was empty. He did not know exactly where the sound of the calls came from, but it was not from Ahmad's mosque. Ah, Ahmad, your grief today over your end! Ahmad stood in the mosque courtyard.

"Abu al-Abbas Ahmad ibn Tulun," Abd ar-Rahman yelled, "you're chasing me with your dreams, and in my dreams too! Ah, how full of sorrow you are today over your disappearance and your obliterated vestiges! People say that the monarchs of old did not take their revenge with torture or death, but instead by erasing all traces. How cruel and mighty they were!"

He looked up at the stars.

"What do you want of me, Ahmad?" he yelled. "Stop whispering inside my heart!"

In his vision, the courtyard widened to encompass the whole of Fustat, then to the borders with Syria and Iraq, and then to India. He could see the world as both broad and narrow. In the mosque courtyard, he could picture the void of painful times and the power of moments filled with love. He had come here to save the mosque, but all he could see was his own shadow in the alcoves, by the mihrabs, around the pillars, and the tips of the balustrades. Ah yes, Saeed al-Farghani's balustrades and the trouble he had with them!

He sank to the mosque floor and closed his eyes. In his heart, he could see all the details of the place traced on a plaster wall. In the mosque courtyard he could not appreciate its scale or prestige: square-shaped, elaborate, uniform in its sections, maybe just like Al-Khwarizmi's equations that he had heard about from his wife. In the middle was a huge courtyard with nothing in the way to block out the stars in the heavens. In his imagination, he could see the sun taking over the space, its fingers almost shaping the edges of the four arcades. The largest of them was right in front of him, the qibla arcade, containing five colonnades. If a man emerged from each one, Isa an-Nushari's soldiers would be blindsided, and their swords would be useless.

With his eyes shut, Abd ar-Rahman could see five plaster mihrabs in which a veiled Arab Bedouin might be able to hide, then escape over the big wall surrounding them. If there were forty-two gates, then escape was possible. His closed eyes focused on the leafy filigree on the gates' wooden passageways. If two expert runners hid themselves in the mosque's alcoves, then there would be no hope of catching them. In this mosque, the alcoves rested on a hundred and sixty buttresses rather than marble pillars.

The buttresses were made of red clay, their four angles shaped like blended pillars, each one topped with bell-shaped crowns, coated with gypsum and decorated with fivefold leaf designs that wrapped around the buttress in twin rows. Each buttress also had pointed arches in a horseshoe shape. The entire extended building that Qasim al-Khurasani was planning to demolish that day rested on those buttresses. Ahmad had built his dream on them, and a Copt from Farghan had carried them out. Ah me, Saeed, how did you manage to make those columns so perfect?! Who suggested those designs to you?

The pillars were topped with ornamental crowns that served as the pivot-points for the mosque's roof. Then the mihrab . . . One wonders, what was it about the main mihrab that could inspire such sorrow? Why was he seeing in front of him a tablet on which was inscribed the name of the mosque's builder in clear characters, almost piercing his closed eyes? The mosque was built by Abu al-Abbas Ahmad Ibn Tulun . . . Abu al-Abbas. Betrayal can amputate like the edge of a poisoned sword; it can infect the body with fever and only finish it off after much suffering. He knew about the suffering Ahmad had endured at the hands of his son, Al-Abbas. When the sword tip penetrates and lodges in the heart, it does not kill, but just throttles the breathing. Beware, Aisha! Make sure you don't behave like your brother! But then, maybe she thinks that if she keeps her pledge to her husband, she'll be betraying her father. Being married to the caliph will save what is left of her father. If she is thinking that way . . .

When he opened his eyes, he could no longer see the details of the mosque. All he could see was bright sunlight scorching relentlessly. He looked at the mosque walls and the battlements on top, looking like interlocking crenulations looking upward in prayer. What made them look so sad, one wonders, and why look up to the heavens? How sad you must be, Saeed, and how amazing! As though you were possessed by the spirit of the ancient magicians and built this mosque just as they built the still-standing pyramid. Your sorrow, Saeed, extends all the way up to the heavens. I can almost feel it in my own emotions and the pulses of my soul.

He closed his eyes again with a sigh. He recited the whole of Surat al-Baqara [The Cow] and Surat Al-Imran, both chapters of the Quran inscribed inside the mosque in clear script. The hour drew close, and he had to think fast.

The winding minaret had an external spiral staircase topped by a dome. In that spiral lay his escape, but falling off it would mean certain death. He could hide inside the dome, but if Isa's and Qasim's soldiers started clambering up the winding stairs, then what?

The moment for which Qasim al-Khurasani had been waiting for a year or more had finally arrived. Isa an-Nushari hesitated and told Qasim that destroying the mosque would bring down disaster on the caliph. In reply, Qasim told him that all the mosques in Al-Qata'i had been demolished, even though they had not been built with illegal money like this mosque. Isa had continued destroying what was left of Al-Qata'i, burning down houses and stores.

Qasim prepared the catapult, then took his men into the mosque courtyard, along with Isa an-Nushari and the caliph's soldiers. Egyptians did not leave their houses; every man closed the house up out of fear for his children and worries about the problems of hunger and thirst. However, one man did come out and sat in the mosque courtyard, barely able to speak or walk. No one knew who he was. Isa an-Nushari supposed that he was a madman. Killing him would cause all sorts of problems; all they needed to do was to move him away.

The soldiers did that, with him grumbling, yelling, resisting, and demanding to meet either the caliph or the governor of Egypt. Where was the governor? Isa gave him a confused look. Some soldiers looked on from afar, while others carried him out of the mosque, with tears streaming down his face.

"Look up at the crenulations first," Saeed al-Farghani yelled as loud as he could while they were carrying him out. "Just see who's praying to God today . . ."

Qasim raised his hand to signal to the soldiers to begin the demolition. Voices rose, and there was widespread chaos—shouts, yells, and the sounds of swords and arrows. No one knew what was happening, so the soldiers quickly covered Isa an-Nushari and hurried him out of the mosque. The old man was still there, watching everything that was happening.

Some veiled men seemed to have taken the mosque as a place to conceal themselves for an hour or less; they may have slunk in while the caliph's soldiers were making preparations for the demolition. One of the veiled men, who was a superb shot with bows and arrows, had climbed onto an alcove roof and fired straight at Qasim's head. The other veiled men rained arrows on the caliph's soldiers, then ran out of the mosque as fast as possible, passed through the gates, and vanished in seconds. Some of them took off their garments and face-coverings and mingled with the Egyptians who had clustered in the middle of the mosque courtyard amazingly quickly as soon as they had heard the shouting. Others ran to the mountain and hid in the caves. Isa gave orders to chase the veiled men and either kill them or capture at least one of them.

The soldiers' swords and arrows now started hitting some of the men who had not run as fast as they could. Two of them were killed immediately. When the caliph's soldiers removed their clothing to look at their faces, they were wearing Egyptian dress. No one knew who they were. The soldiers surrounded Qasim al-Khurasani, who had died with an arrow through his head.

The Egyptians now started yelling, cheering the brave heroes who had just saved the mosque. They said that God had protected His house and Ahmad's spirit was still haunting the location. The crenulations on the buttresses would protect the mosque for evermore. It would only be destroyed on the Day of Resurrection. Women wept for Ahmad, as though he had only just died. Memories were still fresh and a sense of caution was still enough to keep Egyptians scared. They had not expected to recall all the details, and that same caution had also troubled Isa and the caliph. More men and women clustered in the mosque courtyard. Voices rose, some of them mourning Ahmad, others praying for him. Some people started blaming the caliph and the governor. Isa did his best to listen. He clearly understood the message and told his soldiers to take him back to his residence.

He wrote to tell the caliph what had happened. That day, Qasim al-Khurasani had died, apparently killed by some Egyptians. Soldiers had managed to kill two of the killers, and the rest had fled—a hundred or more. He wrote somewhat diffidently that Egyptians were odd, still believing in magic, the power of ancient kings, and the curse that would strike down anyone who angered the statues of the ancients or even gave them disparaging looks. The Egyptians treasured this mosque, as though it were one of their own children. They had appeared like lightning when the fighting had started. They were so happy that Qasim al-Khurasani had been killed. Isa pointed out modestly that he could not punish the entire Egyptian populace; wars had already worn them out enough. He wrote too about the heaven-directed crenulations on the mosque buttresses. He did not know why the person who had built the mosque had designed them that way; he had never seen anything like them before in other mosques. Their existence must have something to do with the mosque's permanence. He wrote his letter carefully. Only the Abbasid soldiers attended Qasim's funeral. The caliph's letter came back, fast and explicit.

The caliph accepted the governor's suggestion not to demolish the mosque, but he forbade any prayers in it. Time, he said, would see to its destruction. All trace of Amir Ahmad ibn Tulun would vanish from the earth's surface, whether that day or the next, while the caliph's name would survive. If they simply ignored the mosque, it would be destroyed by an earthquake or perhaps another ruler in a hundred years' time. The caliph finished by saying that he had not seen the crenulations on the buttresses and would never believe in the magic of the ancients.

☗

Abd ar-Rahman hid inside the Great Pyramid. He had lost two of his men. The tribesmen would be asking about them both and why they had taken the risk. The gold that Saeed had given him would not be enough to quell the screams of women and children. But the admiring and joyful looks in the eyes of the Egyptian people certainly intoxicated his other men, who had not expected such a rapturous reception. Some of them hid in Egyptians' homes. They were given a warm welcome, as though they were family members. They were proposed with marriage to the family daughters. People said that the men who had saved the mosque were heaven-sent heroes—magicians, seers, not just humans. They possessed powers greater than sultans, like those of history, the pyramid stakes, and the sheer awe of the Sphinx. Abd ar-Rahman stayed inside the Pyramid for a week, while Isa's men searched all around it; he could almost hear their voices.

She was obviously waiting for him; his heart kept talking about her, telling him that she was still faithful to him. Was not she the one who had taught him about faithfulness, sincerity, and keeping promises, about giving without recompense or expectation? Had she not overwhelmed him with her spontaneity, drowning him in carefree kisses and talking from the very depths of her heart without shame or trickery? The princess. She could not be weak now. If she were married to the caliph, would she love him the same way, drowning him in kisses and passionately waiting for him? Would she now deprive him of his daughter for the rest of his life? That would not be the final journey. If she were to be married to the caliph, he, Abd ar-Rahman, would plan to go to Baghdad to find her. He swore he would do it. He was almost going out of his mind. Loneliness always brings out hidden fears and causes doubts. Sometimes he could imagine them back together again, but, at others, he pictured his own wife in the arms of the caliph Al-Muktafi. At times he would cry out; at others, he would have trouble breathing. This passion was a form of madness. He had saved the mosque, although he was not totally sure whether he had done it for her sake or his own; or because his soul did not approve of so much destruction. He had never for a moment expected to be thinking about building and destruction or to be bothered about something that did not concern him. Perhaps he did not actually know what did and did not concern him. This was Egypt, and every building in it was part of him and belonged to him. It was his country, the place where he was born, and it controlled his heartstrings. The heart was a strange phenomenon, moments of awareness arriving when least expected, while an error would stretch over a lifetime. In the past, he had stolen, robbed, and perhaps ill-treated people, but without caring. In moments of loss, he longed for her, not knowing what surprises his heart was hiding till those moments arrived, moments of awareness, regret, sorrow, and risk.

Every day, one of the Egyptians would bring him food; the men had agreed to do that. It was too risky for his men to come to his place now. He agreed with them that they would go back to the tribe before him, and he would come back once he was sure that the soldiers were no longer searching for him around the pyramid. The Egyptians brought him food and drink and informed him that, on orders from the caliph, Isa had decided not to demolish the mosque. He went on to say that news had arrived that the caliph was to be married with the Tulun family and the marriage would be celebrated for fifteen days in Baghdad. The caliph wanted to use this marriage as a way of endearing himself to the Egyptian people. The man went on to say that poor Qatr an-Nada's father had wanted her to be married to Ali Al-Muktafi bi-llah, who at the time was a handsome young amir. But the caliph Al-Mu'tadid had wanted her for himself. She had died of grief in the palace. Aisha, Ahmad's daughter—indeed she was Ahmad's daughter who was going to be married to the caliph. The woman who would marry the caliph had to be Aisha, Ahmad's daughter. His daughter would be living happy and content with a handsome young man who was also Caliph of all Muslims. People said that Al-Muktafi loved poetry. How many poems, one wondered, would he chant in love of Aisha? Ahmad's daughter was not like other women . . . speaking in Egyptian and having a lot to say. Abd ar-Rahman broke the bread up into pieces but did not comment. He could still remember what she had said.

"I was living in the gardens of paradise," she had said, "waiting for a day when the loneliness would disappear and my wandering heart would settle down. I realized that I was a prisoner in those massive rooms. My destiny was like that of Qatr an-Nada and others in my family. But then you came along."

Could a woman's heart change like the seasons, or was it that fate had no sympathy for lovers? Abd ar-Rahman threw the chunks/loaves of bread onto the fire. It flared up, but neither warmed him nor satisfied his hunger.

Part Four

A close friend, far-reaching in his demands,
For me, death is far easier than aggravating him.
If my heart suffers long,
It soars in longing to meet its tormentor.
An ardor that sacrifices the self; were there anything dearer, he would use it.
—*Al-Buhturi, Abbasid poet*

Chapter 11

He closed his eyes and wept. He had never wept before, not because it was only women who wept, but rather because he always ignored pain, buried it in a pit inside his heart, and refused to deal with it. Today he wept, silently. In the past, despair had been blended with a profound love for cruelty that would urge him to kill and dismember bodies. But now, weakness and sorrow were firmly in command, and that was the end—the end of all endeavor and resistance, total defeat. He did not blame her or hate her. He had simply allowed his heart to express what was lurking deep inside him. He liked the pyramid; it suited his sorrow. Only rarely did he feel any affection. These days, even breathing had become difficult. He liked sleeping on damp rocks and staring up at the bat colony's nest as they twitched and hovered in the air as though they were about to choke. He enjoyed living amid the corpses, surrounded by ice. Time would stop moving; maybe he would stay inside the pyramid for a hundred years, but without a dog to stretch its legs or a companion to share his indifference. It was time for delusion and a long sleep, a time without stability or support. How could he pitch his tent in a world moving as fast as clouds and suns, a world wrapping itself around his neck and leaving him suspended in the air like bats, a world with no goals and no trust? Ah, the sagacity of that monk and his own ignorance; a life where effort and courage were useless, days when he was ignored and not given a single glance! He had assumed that suns orbited his universe, whereas they neither knew he existed nor recognized him.

Had she thought about the oath and pledge, he wondered, before giving in to the caliph? Had she remembered him at all before traveling far away? Had his uncle made her suffer, so that she had decided to flee? Perhaps she hated him because he had not asked about her. Maybe she thought he was dead. Maybe the caliph had not married her. That hope approached diffidently, knocking on the door and asking to come in. He was not sure he wanted to let it in today. Hope can hurt even more than defeat, burning and destroying even more than soldiers' swords in Al-Qata'i. But hope did open the door, entering bashfully without waiting for permission. What if he went back to Esna and found that she had kept the pledge? If all the stories were merely rumors? If, if . . . Maybe the caliph had married someone else. But who would that be?

Madness also comes in without asking permission. What would he plan to do if he went back and found that his wife and daughter had left him? Would he roam the desert? Chase after them both? He vowed to go after her. Anger, that was hope.

Now anger was in command, and weakness disappeared along with the possibility of finding her in Esna.

All the time he had stayed inside the pyramid, he had expected to see the Pyramid Witch and listen to her. People said that she kept company with the jinn, she being half-demon perhaps. Saeed had spoken about her, the Copt who would summon her in his dreams. Her name was Bahnas. But he never saw her; that is, until his seventh day there, when she came in slowly.

Her voice sounded as sweet as the chirping of hoopoes.

"You've come to the Great Pyramid, Arab," she said, "but you're not scared. Didn't they tell you about the Pyramid Witch and the tombs of the ancients?"

He could see her eyes in the darkness; it was almost midnight. She had appeared with her impossible beauty and glistening despair, neither startling nor consoling his aching heart.

He did not respond, but closed his eyes and leaned his head against the wall.

"How many men come to see me," she said calmly, "after they've messed up their lives! Just like a snake toying with a frog in its fangs. Are you regretful or desperate?"

"Afraid. If she's gone, then my whole life's wasted . . ."

Silence ensued.

"Saeed al-Farghani built those crenulations praying to God on top of the mosque wall," she went on gently. "They embrace each other, their souls uniting and their features dissolving. He used to say that things joined cannot be separated, and things that cannot be divided will never be destroyed. At one point, he asked me to forgive him, but how can you forgive someone who kills the soul? Even if the body were ephemeral, the soul has to remain."

"Saeed al-Farghani," he muttered, "he wanted me to give up everything I owned. He wanted me to tell you that he is still keeping his pledge. He loves you . . ."

"When did the noble Abd ar-Rahman ever contemplate giving up anything?" she asked with a smile. "How can Saeed keep a pledge that he never agreed to and give up the pledge that we both accepted? When I was his, he never helped me. When I left him, he did. That's the way it is with human beings. It is only through conflict that they achieve their goals. But in life, insight is not there and never wins."

"Tell me," Abd ar-Rahman pleaded, "that she won't leave me. Everything I've done is for her."

"What you learned from her," she told him with a smile, "is priceless. You know that, and so do I."

"What do you know?" he asked, baffled.

"You've been talking to me about what you've given and fought for," she told him. "That's typical of men. But you're never going to tell me about those moments of regret and realization when souls coalesce and plunge into the very depths. Now the brigand has turned into a cavalier, when it's obvious that he's still a brigand. She's managed to penetrate your heart and seen the cavalier there, but all your heart can see is the brigand. She trusted your ability and conscience, while you kept on collecting your spoils and making preparations to get rid of her. She was teaching you, but you were bent on taking the gold for yourself. But then what? You left it where it was, and she took it, but not for herself. Instead, she gave it to her father's enemy to save you. So what exactly has the princess taught you, noble scion of the tribe?"

"Is Aisha keeping the pledge?"

"She was the one who taught you to stick to pledges," she replied with a smile. "She may also have been the one to teach you that there are pledges that can't be kept, even if you try."

"You're not giving me any comfort; you're fanning the flames. A pledge is a pledge; breaking it is a betrayal."

She used her fingers to draw the crenulations on the pyramid wall.

"How many pledges have been broken!" she said. "Give Saeed my greetings and tell him that the Pyramid Witch does not forget love or renunciation . . ."

"I'm not a messenger between the two of you. Tell me what it is you want."

"No, you're the one who's come here on a mission. You've come to see the Pyramid Witch because you're scared and desperate. I'll only be meeting Saeed when our twin souls are suspended in the heavens like the buttress crenulations in the mosque."

He gasped in surprise.

"You're lying, Witch!" he said all of a sudden. "You claimed not to know Arabic, but here you are talking with all the fluency of the Qahtan tribe! Is lying a characteristic of witches? Or are they able to comprehend all kinds of words? Or is it that you realize that now all Egypt will be speaking Arabic and forgetting Coptic?"

She rubbed her hand on the pyramid wall, her eyes gleaming with a heart-rending beauty.

"You don't understand my language," she whispered. "That's why I'm using a language that you do understand. But then, love doesn't involve language, but sacrifice—and that has its own special language, as thirsty as arrows piercing and lodging inside the heart."

"As thirsty as arrows," he repeated, feeling a kind of sorrow he had never felt before. "If only she realized . . . so that she wouldn't leave."

"Abd ar-Rahman," she said, turning toward him, "greet the ancients and thank them for preserving the land and gold."

"I'm the one who's preserved the land and gold," he replied forcefully. "You know that. Whatever's left of Ibn Tulun, I'm the one who's helped preserve it."

"So then, Arab," she replied with a smile, "you're one of the monarchs of old, even though you've lost Ahmad's daughter and your language isn't mine!"

With a smile, she disappeared.

Next day, he asked the Egyptian to bring him a horse and gave him some gold. He started the long journey to Esna, moving as quickly as possible. Isa's men had disappeared from the area around the pyramid a few days earlier. He could not stop, even though his exhausted horse's neighing was deafening him.

After seven hours of nonstop travel, he had to stop. Now his impatience was even tougher to handle than anger, stronger than whole armies. He was panting after hope and scared of the despair that might follow it. She had sworn to him that she would never be married to anyone else, even if he were to die. That pledge was an unbreakable pact, she had said. But then, perhaps she had lied; she had weakened, having lost all hope of his return. Perhaps her circumstances had changed after his father had died; for the past three months, he had not managed to get any information about her. All he knew was that his father had died, his uncle had become the tribe's chieftain, and she was fine. He knew she was alive, but no more than that.

In his memory, the day loomed when she had departed for Upper Egypt. He had not said goodbye or told her how much he loved her. He had not kissed her or given her any reassurance. Jealousy beset him and robbed him of all affection. Fear always begets cruelty, and jealousy's cruelty has no rivals. She had asked him to go to her mother the next day and tell her what had happened. He had kept the pledge, but she had not. Ah! Those words of Saeed . . . !

Saeed always knew everything, memorizing stories and poems, understanding passion and greed, and reading hearts and souls. He would draw just like the princess and keep his drawings and words inside the walls of his house. Drawing, he would say, purges the heart of its hatred. When he was a young man, he would remark, he would build mosques to secure his own prestige and make a lot of money. If Ahmad asked him to build the mosque now, he would do it, but in order for it to remain and be remembered, not for youthful ambition or heartfelt desires. With the passage of time, he had understood and learned. Now he was following Abd ar-Rahman's every step like unforgivable sin.

He allowed himself a bitter smile. Maybe Saeed had been right. How could patience be this bitter? It felt as though it would be easier to discover that she had left rather than to await his own arrival in Esna. He did not sleep and continued the journey at dawn.

It was still a long way to go, and with every passing hour, the meeting seemed even further away. He needed at least a week to get to Esna. He tried to think about things related to his own life, how his uncle had usurped his role in the tribe. How was he going to face him? Was he going to fight him or kill him? Would the tribe be split? What if his uncle had informed the soldiers that Abd ar-Rahman was working with Muhammad al-Khalanji? What if his uncle had betrayed his plans? Isa an-Nushari had no proof, nor did his uncle. He had not left any traces behind him; he had been veiled the whole time. What would the tribe be doing in Esna? Would they settle there, and the men work as farmers? There was no longer any hope of joining the armed forces or seeing the return of the Tulunids. They would have to settle in Esna. The blessed River Nile was always generous to its people, even if occasionally it was dry and cruel.

Thinking about those details helped keep him patient, forcing him to focus on life's details. But then it turned against him, as he thought about her and his daughter. As the second day passed, his longing intensified and his sense of loss drew closer. His remaining patience vanished. Drawing his sword at night, he started fighting his own shadow, slashing to left and right with a degree of hope he had never experienced before. It was as if hope were more vicious than all enemies at once, more unruly than wild horses.

He remembered what Maisoon had said. He had met her only once in the mosque. She had come to let him know that Asma, Aisha's mother, had died. Asma had had to go away and leave her daughter so as not to be a burden during wartime. Before Maisoon had left, she had looked into his eyes.

"Fear your own shadow, Arab," she had said. "There's no enemy like it. If it haunts you, make a truce. You can't fight it."

He did not understand Maisoon's words then, but perhaps he did now. Maybe she was right. All he could see around him was his own shadow, and now it was withdrawing and being disloyal.

Aisha would be dressed in silk. She would ride around the palace on her white horse. She would raise her daughter among the princesses of the caliph's household. Then she would have some of the caliph's own children. Her son would become caliph. Aisha.

It was still a long way, and arrival was far distant and not getting closer. He set out at dawn on his third day. His thoughts turned to quince trees, although he did not know what they looked like. How was it that he had not seen them before? They were inside the palace. Khumarawayh had brought them from Syria. Aisha had told Abd ar-Rahman about them, about their taste with sugar, and the sweetness of their leaves. She told him that when she was young, she had thought that quince trees were her private property which she would protect with her own hands. As time passed, she said, the trees had been knocked down, pulled out by the roots. He smiled as he recalled her eyes shining as she told him the story, just like a little girl. She had raised her eyebrows eagerly and demonstrated how tall and wide the trees were. At the time, he had assumed that he was the one betraying her, whereas he did not realize that she was betraying him. He kept listening eagerly to locate the gold, or so he imagined. He became accustomed to her stories without even realizing and looked forward to her embrace every night. Then he had gone away, assuming that his destiny was in his own hands, but what he did not realize was that she had managed to take control of him, root and branch. She was his big mistake. Why had he fallen in love with her? He had no idea how to respond.

He spurred the horse and rode for hours. He waited for the following dawn, heart quaking, and started his fourth day of travel. As Esna drew closer, hope was both near and far. At the end of the day, certainty arrived and gave him a jolt. She had not gone away. She could not leave him. Her love was sincere. She had welcomed love before he did and had suffered for it. She had drawn his picture as a cavalier, then burned the piece of paper. She had drawn it again. She could not possibly leave him. His heart was inspired and then saw clearly. The day passed well; every time doubt tried to make its way into his heart, he expelled it forcibly. As he slept, he was confident that the night would be short and the next day even shorter. They would soon be reunited, and he would spend months in her arms. He would lock all the doors and hide her from public view. No caliph would reach her, not any of the monarchs of old. On the fifth day, he set off with all the enthusiasm of a youngster and the indifference of the powerful. On his way he started thinking about the details of their reunion: would he hug her to his chest or drown her with kisses? Would she dissolve in tears or shout out his name, her heart aquiver? How would the princess welcome him?

He slept soundly, enveloped by hopes like quince leaves. He dreamed about his quince tree and Aisha feeding him from it. In the dream, she was telling him that she still loved him and he was more important to her than any prestige or warfare. When he woke up on day six, despair had managed to burrow its way inside yet again. After the delight of sharing food and kisses, he found her fading away and disappearing. He would never find her. Once he arrived, he would find a gigantic chasm inside his heart, growing larger and larger till it swallowed the remains of his soul. He no longer thought about anything and erased her image as soon as it appeared. Now his father appeared to tell him that his mother had died.

"You've all the household's women," he told his son. "Choose one of them as your mother."

He had given his father a look of dismay, concerned above all that his father did not seem to realize how weak he was; his words would not give him strength, but only make him feel even weaker. What woman would he choose? One of his father's wives? An aunt? In other words, no substitute for his dead mother. But his father did not understand. For him, all women were the same; anyone could take another's place, just like kaftans and turbans. He had not cried. Azza had chided him for fooling around, even when he was only ten. He could not remember a lot about her at this point, but she had always been better than him.

This journey was wearing him out, as though it would never end. If he abandoned the world, he could relax; if he abandoned her before taking his revenge, he would never relax. Once again, he vowed to follow her to Baghdad. If possible, he would kill the caliph himself; that would be best. She had no excuse. She had betrayed him; that was all. He spurred on his horse, burning with hatred and eager to arrive. Only one day remained now, and he would be arriving either the next day or the day after. He stopped to drink some water and get some rest. He said a few words to the water-seller to make sure that his mind was still functioning. He asked if the caliph had really been married into the Tulunid family. The man replied eagerly that the news had spread throughout Egypt and the caliph had announced it with the goal of ingratiating himself with them. Abd ar-Rahman blocked his ears. The man might be lying. Perhaps the caliph had located another Tulunid woman. Hope would never disappear, but then, maybe it had.

"Wake up, you idiot!" he yelled at his own heart. "People are telling you that the caliph is married to a member of the Tulunid family, and here you are thinking about the crenulations on the mosque wall! You're just like Saeed! You're swinging between madness and hope; your shadow's taken over and is in charge. Wake up, Abd ar-Rahman! The princess isn't yours. She only ever was in moments of despair and defeat. The princess is married to the caliph!"

He went into a small mosque, lay on his back, and closed his eyes. She seemed far away. He remembered the days when she had told him where the gold was, when she had asked him to go to Azza, and when she had risked her life by visiting him in Ibn Sulaiman's prison. For the dawn prayer, he prayed behind the shaikh. He spent a few moments summoning up his courage to continue the journey. What awaited him there might well put an end to whatever remained of his heart.

"You look worried," the shaikh said kindly. "Do you need my help?"

"I need God's help," Abd ar-Rahman replied.

"Are you going to a new house or returning to an old one?"

"I'm not sure yet, Shaikh. The world's turned on me. I've been to war and lost. Then I scored a minor victory, only to find myself in a fight with someone bigger and more powerful."

"What fight's that? To me, you look like a strong enough man, someone who could not be defeated."

"Just picture yourself, Shaikh," Abd ar-Rahman replied, "confronting the caliph's massed armed forces and power on your own. What would you do?"

"I leave such things to God. But why would I embark on a conflict where I've no discretion?"

"Maybe because the more powerful entity wants to seize everything that's yours when he already owns everything."

"Perhaps God will do something about it. Never despair of God's mercy. Do you know the story of Anas, the head fisherman's son? Egyptians tell it every single day. Anas the fisherman defied the Tax Administrator and was married to the beautiful Maisoon. But he wasn't satisfied with his victory. They say he died soon after Ibn al-Mudabbir. So, even though your beloved has left you, don't despair. For God, the way out is easy, but not for you and me."

"I believe in God's mercy, but I'm not sure whether she has kept the pledge or will simply submit to power and armies."

The shaikh stayed silent, perhaps not fully understanding what Abd ar-Rahman was talking about. Abd ar-Rahman changed the subject.

"People say that some time ago, Ahmad ibn Tulun had a dream," he said, "in which God revealed himself to his city and everything inside it, but not his mosque. But that dream has always baffled me. Do you have an interpretation of it, Shaikh?"

"We were talking about the caliph," the shaikh replied, "but now you're talking about Ahmad ibn Tulun. Who are you, my son?"

"Do you have an interpretation, Shaikh?"

"If God revealed himself to the mountain, it would bow low for fear of God. If He revealed himself to the city but not to the mosque, that means that the city will disappear, and the mosque will be the only thing left out of all the amir's buildings. It's a message. Are you interested in the mosque?"

"Not at first, but then I was, maybe because of her, and a pledge that I made with myself, one that no one else heard."

"Is she the one who's made you so desperate?"

"Perhaps."

"I don't know what you're talking about, but I do understand how sad you are. If she was yours, then there's no one who can take her away from you, even the caliph. But if she wasn't, then no war will work and no pain will help. In both cases, it's God's will. Leave your burden with Him and be on your way. If He wants something, he just says: 'Be,' and it is."

Abd ar-Rahman stood up to leave.

"Believe me, my son," the shaikh said, "some rich, powerful person in your village is after your wife, is that right?"

"Yes, Shaikh."

"Can you complain to the governor, for example?"

Abd ar-Rahman sighed. "Maybe," he replied.

For just a moment, the shaikh said nothing.

"If she submits to powerful people, don't blame her," he said. "Maybe she has no choice. Forgive her."

"The Pyramid Witch says that the body is ephemeral," Abd ar-Rahman responded in a low voice. "You can forgive someone who kills it, but how can you do that with someone who kills the very soul?"

The shaikh gave a bitter smile. "Youthful anger dominates the senses," he said, "and renders any understanding impossible. Maybe in ten years' time, you'll be able to forgive."

Abd ar-Rahman remained silent as the lines of his life loomed before him.

"Remember," the shaikh went on, "that God is merciful."

"God is merciful," Abd ar-Rahman replied, "but I'm not. Don't worry about me. As you said, it's all God's will."

Leaving the shaikh, he set off on his horse.

He was going to try to arrive the next day, even if it was nighttime. He knew where his cousin, Saalim's, house was; the tribe had to be nearby. On the seventh night, he got no sleep. Hope broke down every barrier; it pounced on his every sense and even the blood in his veins. There was no remedy. He would arrive and find her, and they would live together for the rest of their days. The princess was not like other women, just as his mother was not; she was irreplaceable. He instructed his mind to think only of her, as though he were not a strong man, and was either crazy or possessed. Men were not supposed to be distracted from the entire world by a woman. He was supposed to think about horses, swords, wars, and victory; to crave gold, collect dinars and silver, and have male children so that his line would continue forever in his offspring. Then he could enjoy all women, with his gold and silver, order men around, and lead. So what had happened to him? Why was he thinking about her all the time, as though she were all the suns and stars together? Why were his heartbeats thumping, and doubts taking over and destroying everything? What thief is it that can seize control of hope's certainties? Was he crazy already, or not yet? Why was he being chased by that evil shadow that was sucking away at his blood whenever the sun moved its position?

He was close to Esna and stopped to catch his breath and make sure his mind was working properly. It was midnight, and he could not wait for daylight. He reached Saalim's house, tied up his horse, and paused for a moment's thought. Should he go looking for the tribe nearby or wake up Saalim? He decided to look for the tribe; they could not be too far from the house. The houses were all silent, as though the town had no hearts and no conflicts. Even the trees were not moving. He followed the paths slowly and quietly; he may have died and been born again. He moved away from the trees and toward the desert. Maybe this was the end to all his suffering, doubt, love, despair, and hope. Ah, love that slays without mercy!

He found where the tribe was and recognized the tents and houses attached to them. He took his horse into the camp and stopped in the middle of the desert place where the tribe had erected its tents and the tribesmen had taken their houses. He called out to his household and banged hard on the doors. Azza came out. He recognized her, even though she was wearing her veil, and she recognized him in spite of the veil covering his face. Their eyes met, and she may have smiled.

"I thought you'd been killed ages ago," she said.

He dismounted and took off his veil.

"Where are my wife and daughter?" he asked.

For a moment, she said nothing. He repeated the question impatiently.

"You haven't even greeted me, cousin," she said.

"You haven't answered my question, cousin."

"So, you've come with destruction in mind."

He headed for the door.

"Is she inside?" he asked, with his heart listening.

Azza did not reply.

"Why don't you reply?" he asked angrily.

"Why should I, cousin? Am I your wife's guard? Look for her yourself."

"Azza," he said, looking at her, "it's been a long journey. I give you my greetings."

"There's never been any greetings from you, Abd ar-Rahman," she replied painfully. "For me, you're just suffering, loss, and pain."

"Where is she? Has she gone?"

He went into the house.

"There are women inside," she told him hurriedly. "Wait here till . . ."

Her father woke up, came outside, and looked at Abd ar-Rahman for a moment.

"You've no place here," he said.

"No, this is my place," Abd ar-Rahman replied furiously. "This is my tribe. Where's my wife?"

"She's asleep inside," Azza replied quickly.

His heart jumped, then settled down again. He was afraid that Azza may have noticed the slight twitching of his eyes and his bodily jerks. So, she was here; she had not betrayed him or left. Of course she was here. What would you expect from a princess? She had made him a promise and kept it.

"I want to go in to see her," he said gently.

"Tomorrow morning," his uncle said.

"Now," he replied firmly.

Azza held her father's hand. "Let him see her, Father," she told him gently. "You're the tribal chief. You've taken care of her even though he's been away."

His uncle moved to one side.

"He can go in to see her now," he said, "then leave as soon as possible tomorrow."

Abd ar-Rahman did not respond but looked toward her room. Azza unlocked it.

"Are you keeping her a prisoner?" Abd ar-Rahman asked in shock.

"My father keeps all women locked up," she replied. "You should be thanking God that she's well."

He paid no attention to what she had said but looked straight at the door. He went in, and Azza locked the door behind him. For a moment, Azza stood behind the door, swallowing tears that would not fall. Then she went back to her own room.

Aisha woke up as soon as the door was locked. She recognized his scent and his spirit. She could sense his presence in the dark.

"Abd ar-Rahman . . . ," she said, hugging herself.

He knelt on the floor where she was sleeping and picked her up in his arms without saying a word. The best thing about darkness is that it hides weakness and fragility. It can also conceal overpowering passion and tyrannical yearning. She clung to his shoulders as hard as she could, while he hugged her in his arms till she almost choked; but she did not care. She rubbed her cheek against his neck, and he kissed her cheeks. For an hour or more, he kept on hugging her.

Her tears kept falling for the entire hour; from time to time, he could hear her sobbing. Her tears kept falling on his neck and face, but he did not wipe them away or ask her why she was crying.

Now, after a life of wandering, here he was, settled in her arms. After so much suffering and humiliation, she had now found shelter. As long as he was with her, she was a princess; if he left her, she became a slave-girl, caught between vicious poverty and female domination. Now he had come back to take over all her burdens. Now he was back, she could weep over the past and be relieved of a heavy burden.

After so many days of madness, all he wanted was to hug her silently. If she wept, then no matter. She was weeping on his chest and inside his bosom as well. Could she feel the devil whispering in his ear, he wondered? Did she realize the madness gripping him? Had she expected him to be wandering around the desert, surviving the fiery wind and being plastered in dust till he almost suffocated to death? Was that what she expected? Did she picture him that way? Saeed had told him that she would leave. Why did he say that? He had felt like cleaving his chest open with his sword. How affectionate her arms were, and how delicate her heartbeats!

"Abd ar-Rahman," he heard a soft voice say, "My father doesn't want you here. You must leave and come back tomorrow."

He moved away, but Aisha clutched at him. "Don't leave me," she whispered.

He pulled her toward him again. "I swear to you, I'll never leave you."

"Leave us for now," he said to Azza. "We can talk tomorrow."

"Abd ar-Rahman," Azza said, "I don't want you causing a fuss today. Leave the house now. You're not welcome here."

He pushed Aisha away gently, picked up his sleeping daughter, and gave her a kiss.

"Come with me," he said to Aisha as she wiped her tears. "We'll leave here together."

She clasped his hand as hard as she could. Carrying his daughter and holding his wife's hand, he opened the door and walked past Azza without saying a word. His uncle stopped him by the door.

"Take your wife and daughter, and leave this town," he said.

Aisha clung to his hand, tears still falling.

"I'm going to set up my tent here," Abd ar-Rahman said. "If you plan to kill me, all the tribesmen will testify against you. I'll take my wife, my daughter, and all the men who wish to join me . . ."

He did not wait for a response, but left the house with his wife. He stopped there, right in the middle of the desert space where his tribe's tents were. Some men came out to welcome him and started helping him put up his tent. The men started whispering. Some of them had not expected him to come back; others were delighted that he had; others were tired of war; and still others did not want him there. He put up his tent, while she held on to her daughter and waited. Then one of them gave him the floor covering, and he went into the tent, with her behind him. She sank to the floor and put her daughter beside her. He closed the tent, lit a candle, and hugged her again even harder than before.

"Did you think I was never coming back?" he chided her. "Did you think I would leave you for the caliph to take?"

She did not reply.

"I almost lost my mind," he groaned. "If only you knew . . . and could feel it. I'll never forgive you for months of sheer torture, between hope and despair, with my life in your hands, either to slaughter me or keep me alive. I'll never forgive you."

"Did you think I'd break my pledge to you?" she asked in amazement.

He looked at her.

"When I gave you my pledge," she told him, "I did it to the extent that I could, not what I could not. I can't stand being apart from you. I pledged to myself that I was yours, whether you were dead or alive."

"Death is separation, Princess."

"No, death is a journey, with a promise of meeting later. That's what Anas the fisherman's son told his beautiful wife, Maisoon. My mother told me their story. If you'd died, I was going to wait to meet you again. No one else was going to touch me. Traces of you will remain on my body and soul."

"Did you but know it," he said as he kissed her shoulder, "you've saved my soul."

"But you've come back," she said forcefully. "You're not going to die because of the tribe. The tribe can go to hell. I want you with me alive."

Suddenly he could feel her shoulder bones. She moved away, and he tried to see her features in the darkness. She looked strained, pale, and skinny. Cursing and swearing, he stood up and left the tent. He asked one of the men to bring some food. He came back with bread, meat, and milk. Abd ar-Rahman put it all down in front of his wife. She wolfed it all down in seconds, while he took a good look at her for the first time since he had returned. He looked at her hands covered in scars, at her skinny arms, and her eyes that had sunk deep into her face. He stared at her in utter shock. When she had finished eating, he laid out the rug for her and pulled her to him. She hugged his neck and closed her eyes. She fell sound asleep as though she had not slept for ages. He stayed awake, now fully aware of what had happened and doing his best to understand what she had had to bear. She spoke in her sleep and kept groaning.

"Have you really come back, Abd ar-Rahman?" she asked, clutching his chest.

"Yes, I have," he replied, holding her hand.

She had two hours of undisturbed sleep during which she dreamed of her palace garden.

"How I've longed for you," she heard him whisper as he kissed her, "the way an eye longs for lamps on a dark night."

He plunged into her with no preliminaries.

"Now you've confirmed," she went on with him still inside her, "that it's not a dream."

She wanted to keep him as part of her, inside both body and soul for the rest of her life. He seemed to have the same idea.

"If I stayed inside you like this," he said, "I could guarantee that we'd never be apart. My heart could relax."

"It's as though you're killing me every day, every hour," he whispered when he had finished. "You're in charge and have grabbed hold of my soul. There's no escape."

She had never heard her husband using words like that before and had no idea how to respond. She decided to say nothing, but pulled him toward her, as though she were planning to swallow his heart.

He looked at her for a moment in the dawn light.

"Who did this to you?" he asked in a tone of voice that really scared her.

"Did what?" she stuttered. "I'm fine."

"No, you're not," he replied in fury, although she did not know if it was aimed at her or someone else.

Coming close, he opened her hand and took another look at the cuts all over it. He then took another look at her lusterless eyes, now sunk deep into her head, the dark lines on her face, and her thin, colorless body.

"I'm going to slaughter him now," he said in a voice that really terrified her, "him and all his men."

"Will you give me another hug?" she asked in a tired voice.

"Not till I've killed him."

"Please give me a hug," she said, holding out her hand. "I really need it now."

He paused for a moment. "He didn't even give you a blanket," he said.

She rested her head on his chest and hugged his shoulders. He remained frozen, unable either to calm down or to hold her. He had assumed that the caliph would take her away from him, but not that his own family would humiliate her, starve her, and leave her uncared for in their midst. She took his hand and put it on her shoulder.

"I'm fine," she told him, "and so is your daughter."

"Don't lie," he responded furiously, his anger aimed at himself, not at her or even them for now. "Tell me everything from when I left you to now."

"There's been a widespread drought," she told him, her arms around his neck. "I kept sewing, weaving, and selling things to help the tribe. Azza turned out to be a friend and support. I haven't seen Khalisa. I'd like to see her."

"Did they keep you locked up?"

"No, that didn't happen."

He did not seem to believe her or maybe he was not listening. "He's going to pay the price," he said, kissing her hair. "Anyone who does that will pay the price. Anyone who humiliates my wife will be slaughtered in front of the men. It's my fault. I didn't plan for this day. I left you with thieves and highway robbers, not family . . ."

"You're not going to fight your own family," she interrupted. "I'm not going to let you."

"Get some more sleep," he told her, standing up.

"I want you with me," she said.

"I will be in a little while."

"Don't fight your uncle!" she told him firmly.

He gave her a look that really scared her. "Go to sleep, Aisha," he said.

"I beg you to listen to what happened," she said, hugging her daughter. "Give me a chance to explain."

He pulled his hand away and disappeared.

She fell sound asleep. Then she woke up, ate, and drank till she was full, and went back to sleep. When she woke up again, her mind was confused; people were all jumbled up with each other. There was Azza and her pledge; her own mother whom she had not seen, who had not kept her pledge, and who had met her at the mosque gate; her husband who had vanished right in front of her while the desert was long, far, and filled with stones; Saleema with her nasty voice and bread, scattered chunks filling the tent, while she was drowning with milk, water, and bread all around her, and her daughter was screaming nonstop. Was it all a dream? Nonstop screams. Half-awake, she nursed her daughter, then fell sound asleep again, as though she had not slept for three months.

She awoke to the sound of Khalisa's voice that she had been missing.

"I've been missing you and your lovely daughter," she said to Aisha as she entered the tent.

She picked up the baby.

"What's this lovely face?" she asked with a smile.

"Where's Abd ar-Rahman?" Aisha asked dubiously.

"Men are just like children," Khalisa replied. "They squabble over trifles. Forget about him now and tell me how you are."

Aisha stood up, put on her veil, and left the tent to look for him. The tribe seemed ready for a fight. Abd ar-Rahman had gathered the men and spoken to them. He had told them that he was the one who had made the agreement with Saalim that they would settle in Esna. His father had entrusted responsibility for the tribe to him. His uncle had accused him of being irresponsible and exposing the tribe to peril. Ten men had died because of Abd ar-Rahman's involvement in the war, and they had received no money or booty from it. Abd ar-Rahman's decisions could not be trusted. Abd ar-Rahman responded that he had kept the pledge that his father, Musa, had made with Ahmad ibn Tulun; that was a necessity. He said that he had fought in order to save one of God's houses from destruction. Populating the earth was the essence of faith. Women gathered around the tent, listening in silence.

"Abd ar-Rahman's escaped from the caliph," his uncle insisted. "He may be arrested, whether today or tomorrow. Isa an-Nushari will be looking for him and will eventually find him. When he does, he'll either kill him or put him in prison. How can he assume the responsibility for the tribe?"

"If you're planning to betray your nephew," Abd ar-Rahman replied, "then the tribesmen have to be told. That'll set a sorry precedent for all the tribes, that a tribesman can betray one of his fellows to the governor."

Silence ensued.

"That's not going to happen," the uncle said by way of denial. "But you've no place here, Abd ar-Rahman."

"No, this is my place."

"Saalim, with whom you made the agreement, is now married to my daughter."

"That kind of kinship does not negate the pledge. This is my tribe, and they're my men."

"I'll kill you with my bare hands."

Abd ar-Rahman went up to him. "I'm going to slaughter you for what you've done to my wife," he said, voice lowered. "Just killing you isn't enough, Uncle."

Abd ar-Rahman came into his tent, getting ready for a sword fight with his uncle. Some tribesmen who had nursed a secret loathing for his uncle for years joined him, while others sided with the uncle because he was older. They tried to dissuade Abd ar-Rahman from fighting his uncle, but without success.

Aisha grabbed his arm. "Why are you doing this to me?" she asked. "I have you back after three months of torture. Now are you fighting again, to die and leave me to them again? What are you thinking? I wish you'd not come back and given me hope. Why don't you leave this place? Why are you so set on dying?"

He did not respond.

"I beg you," she pleaded, "don't do this to me again."

He looked at her, but his desire for revenge was flooding his heart.

"I'll be back," he said, not even seeing her. "Don't worry."

"I made a pledge," she said forcefully, "that you wouldn't kill you uncle."

"With whom?"

"The one who saved my life, Azza."

"That's nothing to do with me."

She stood in front of the tent door and opened her arms.

"If you kill your uncle," she said, "I won't live with you. I'll leave."

He was stunned as he looked at her and made her sit in front of him.

"Who hit you?" he asked.

"No one did," she replied, swallowing hard.

"You're lying. Was it Azza or Saleema? If you don't tell me, I'll find out anyway."

She remained silent.

"As I've told you," she went on, "if you kill your uncle, I won't live with you."

He headed for the door.

"Don't threaten me," he yelled in her face. "I'll fight my uncle and kill him, and you will live with me."

He left the tent before she could say anything.

Her husband arrived, followed by his men, and so did his uncle with his. Each of them drew his sword. She ran as fast as she could, fully expecting her husband to explode at her. She stood in front of him with his sword drawn.

"Don't kill your uncle," she told him forcefully. "I've made a pledge with the person who's saved me. Pledges are a matter of faith."

His voice was enough to terrify lions in the desert.

"I'm going to kill you first, woman, if you don't get out of the way," he yelled.

"Go ahead and kill me if you want," she replied. "But I've given my pledge to the person who saved my life."

He ignored her.

"Well, boy," the uncle scoffed, "have you agreed with your wife to have her interfere because your cowardice won't let you fight?"

Abd ar-Rahman pushed her away, and she fell to the ground. He raised his sword again, and the fight between the two men began, with her looking on in fear. Her eyes kept searching for Azza. When she found her, Azza gave her a chiding look and shrugged her shoulders as though to say, "It's out of my hands."

As the two men sparred with each other, the pulse reverberated in the women's ears. Sweat was pouring off them, and the killer instinct was even greater than any human's desire to slay his brother.

"Don't kill your uncle, Abd ar-Rahman," she yelled. "I made a pledge."

He did not seem to hear her. He managed to slash his uncle's arm, then pointed his sword at his heart.

"You don't respect women's sanctity or blood ties," he told his uncle. "You've treated my wife like an animal. I might have shown you some mercy if you'd done the same to a woman on her own with no support or husband . . ."

This time, he heard another voice. Azza went over to her father.

"Please don't kill my father," she begged Abd ar-Rahman.

For a moment, he paused, his sword still pointing at his uncle's heart.

"You've no business here," he said, not even looking at her.

"Don't kill my father, cousin," she whispered, "you who won my heart from the outset."

No one else heard her. He paused for a moment.

"There's no room for both of us here," he yelled, grabbing his uncle's sword. "Either Rabi'a stays or I do. I'm the one who made the agreement with our family here to come to this place. Those who want to leave with Rabi'a can go. Those who want to stay with me can stay."

His uncle opened his mouth to speak.

"If it's war you want," Abd ar-Rahman said, cutting him off, "then I'll fight, but I've no desire to shed the blood of kinsmen."

"We'll discuss the matter," his uncle said, getting to his feet.

"Don't try any tricks," Abd ar-Rahman told him. "If you do, then you and those who join you will have no security."

For just a moment, his eyes met Azza's; Aisha watched them without understanding anything. Then he grabbed Aisha by the hand and pushed her inside the tent.

"You leave the tent," he yelled at her in front of Khalisa, "and defy me in front of the men! You disobey my instructions. What's the matter with your mind?"

"I told you," she insisted, "that I'd given a pledge.

"I gave it to your very own beloved," she went on angrily. "You listened to her today, but not to me!"

"Women!" Khalisa commented with a sarcastic grin on his face.

Aisha looked straight at him.

"She loves you," she told him. "She still loves you, even after you've been married to someone else. It's truth that a lover speaks, my husband, not lies."

He stared at the floor.

"Saleema must be punished," he said.

"Don't do that, Abd ar-Rahman. It wasn't just her decision. There was drought, war, and inflation. We came here with nothing, looking for help from your family. If you punish your cousin now, you'll open up an endless cycle of hatred."

He did not seem to see her or hear what she had said.

"She'll be thrashed eighty times for what she did to you," he said.

"She didn't do anything," she insisted.

"Don't tell lies," he told her impatiently. "Do you think I don't know her? Hatred and malice dominate her entire behavior. She definitely made you suffer."

"Can you even see me?" she asked. "Are you concerned about me? It's you I need now, not your revenge. If you just looked at me, you'd understand. But all you can see is your own self and your sense of honor. If you're the tribe's chieftain, you have to think sensibly."

For a moment, he hesitated, but then he sat down in front of her. Khalisa took the baby and left the tent.

"I'll stay for a while, but then Saleema and Rabi'a have to pay the price. Whipping's a minor punishment. Killing and amputation would be better."

"If your uncle and his family leave," she said gently, "we'll be rid of them for good. We don't need to bring down revenge on our children. We were all poor and in sorry straits, but it was Azza who felt sorry for me and helped me."

He held her hand and noticed how swollen and scarred both hands were. Slowly she rested her head on his chest.

"I thought I'd never see you again," she choked. "When you win, Abd ar-Rahman, you can be merciful."

He stretched out on his bed and pulled her toward him.

"While I was being humiliated," she told him, wrapping her arms around his neck, "it was your arms that I wanted. I just wanted to tell you how much I love you."

She ran her hand over her face.

"I'm not beautiful the way I was," she said. "Isn't that right?"

He gave her an admiring look.

"You're even more beautiful," he replied with a smile. "Where's your food? I want you to keep eating to make up for months of starvation."

He looked around for the food tray, then picked it up and put it in front of her.

"Come on," he said, "don't be slow."

"My mother," she said all of a sudden. "Did you meet her?"

He sat up. "She never came, Aisha," he replied sadly.

"Perhaps you didn't go."

"Yes, I did. I went in person and waited. I met her friend, Maisoon. Your mother had died. I'll tell you everything."

She listened as he told her everything, but without tears.

"Where's Ibrahim?" she asked. "You're the only one who knows. Will I get to see him?"

"When the time's right," he replied, "but not now. The mosque's still there, Princess, unharmed. Qasim al-Khurasani's dead."

She put her hands around his face. "One day, I'll tell my daughter about you: the cavalier, the hero, someone who has no idea about the sheer bulk and depth of his own soul, a quality that I was the first to notice; someone who thought his goal in life was fun and games, without realizing that his heart aspired to something much greater. I'll tell her about the veiled warrior who never bothered about spreading his reputation and words of praise. He set off into the desert wastes to preserve what was built and would remain. I'll tell her how to discover the real essence of gold when it melts and how heroism is engendered in the midst of destruction, and all in a spontaneous moment when humans choose life and are not distracted by ruin."

He held her hand and kissed it. "Will you tell her that you're a princess?" he asked.

"I'll tell her that I'm the chieftain's wife," she replied proudly.

ᛘᛘ

Rabi'a and half the tribesmen decided to go north to Bahnasa where Rabi'a's brother lived and to settle there. Saalim wanted Azza to stay with him in Esna, but she refused, saying that she had to stay with her father, but still hoped that he would visit her at least once a year. Her husband objected, but she insisted, and he was forced to give way. Meanwhile, Saleema groaned and cursed Aisha, who had brought down destruction on them all. A deep-seated hatred, ineffective and untamable, left her moaning. She rushed to talk to her husband about it, and he slapped her hard several times right in front of her father and sister. It seems that her husband would hit her frequently, but she never complained or spoke about it. That day, the general atmosphere in Esna was one of gloom, and the camels bore the brunt of it. Aisha went out of her tent to watch silently, and her glance met Azza's. She was not sure that Azza would want to bid her farewell. She stayed where she was, no longer as impetuous as she had been. Azza came over to her.

"I never liked you, Aisha," she said.

Aisha was surprised.

"I know," she replied, "but you were still kind to me. Loving me and being kind is to be expected, but hating me and still being kind is a sign of your goodness and nobility. I also realize why you're so determined to leave. It's not because you don't want me to be jealous of my husband as long as you're still here . . ."

Azza smiled bitterly.

"No," Aisha continued, "it's because it would be even more painful for you to be close to him. You're the very best among women, and I wish you all happiness. I hope you'll keep the dress."

Azza moved still closer. "I know you, Princess," she said softly. "Do you know what made me certain that you're a princess?"

Aisha gaped.

"Saleema was out to crush you," Azza continued. "Yet, even as you pleaded, your eyes never lost their powerful and proud gaze."

"It was your proud glances that I admired from the very start, Azza."

Azza did not respond, but nodded in agreement. With that, she joined the caravan.

Once Rabi'a had departed, Abd ar-Rahman gathered the men together and explained to them that times had changed. Now they were settled in Esna, they would have to work. He now realized that farming was neither a crime nor a sin. What had annoyed him about his brothers in the past was their sense of superiority. Each of them had settled on his own in a different town. They had been married and had forgotten all about the tribe. Now the situation was different. The entire tribe would settle in Esna and look for some fertile land to farm. There were still lands with no owners. The tribe would put its foot on land, farm it, and not subdivide. The families would all stay together as one. This was virgin, fertile land that would provide them with its bounty. Here was the blessed River Nile, only rarely stinting them of its waters. The river would flood on the morrow, and there would be general prosperity.

Word had spread that the caliph had been married into the Tulunid family. Eventually, things became clearer: he had married Salma, Qatr an-Nada's sister. She had been Qatr an-Nada's companion for years. At the time, she had just been a little girl, and she had grown up with her elder sister in Baghdad. The caliph had wanted to marry Ahmad's daughter, but when he found out that would be impossible, as Aisha may have died or been killed, he decided to marry Ahmad's granddaughter, Khumarawayh's second daughter.

Chapter 12

Years went by after the tribe split into two. Azza had five children and Aisha had nine. Aisha told them about their father and their grandfather, Ahmad. She said that Ahmad's secret had to remain inside the family home and that his dream had been even greater than all the caliphs combined. She told them many things, and each year she asked her husband if she could visit the mosque. He refused; as long as Isa an-Nushari was still governor, her presence in Fustat would be too risky. When An-Nushari died, a new governor arrived. People had forgotten about the princess, but they had not forgotten about Ahmad. After ten years had passed, Abd ar-Rahman agreed that they could all go to Al-Qata'i and see the mosque. All that was left was the mosque itself, the remains of the home of Saeed, son of Katib al-Farghani, and a few other poor houses.

There was no information about Saeed; he would have been over seventy, and Abd ar-Rahman had assumed that he was dead. He had long wanted to see Saeed and Anduna, the monk about whom he had heard so much. But it turned out that Saeed was actually still alive. When they reached the mosque, the children scattered all over the empty courtyard and ran around as though it were wider than any palace gardens. Abd ar-Rahman looked at the small house attached to the mosque. It was still there, surrounded by rubble. Saeed had rebuilt part of his house and settled there. Abd ar-Rahman called out his name, expecting him to be dead. He wanted to say his name: "Saeed al-Farghani, where are you?"

Two hours later, Saeed appeared, carried by two servants. His hair was white, and he had a cover over his eyes, as he could barely see any more.

"I thought I'd never see you again," Abd ar-Rahman said as Saeed drew closer, "after our last meeting ten years ago. There you were, sitting in the mosque court-yard like the bravest man in the land."

"I built it all with my heart," Saeed replied with a throat-rattle. "It's all I have."

"By God, I've never met anyone like you. What kind of man are you?"

"While I was building it," Saeed went on as though he had not heard what Abd ar-Rahman had been saying, "I kept praying to God to keep me alive until I'd finished it. Once it was finished, I wanted God to keep me alive so I could see it every day. Then Ibn Sulaiman arrived, bent on finishing me off by demolishing the mosque. And then, a demon named Qasim al-Khurasani arrived. You killed him. How are you, Arab? Are you still arrogant and impulsive?"

Abd ar-Rahman smiled and looked at his wife.

"My hair's gone white," he replied.

"You're saying that? What about me?!"

"I've never felt entirely at ease, ever since I first met you," Saeed said, rubbing Abd ar-Rahman's back. "How did I ever cooperate with you, I wonder. Miracles can happen when you're desperate."

"I've never felt at ease with you either," Abd ar-Rahman replied.

"But you saved the mosque."

"As you've just said, miracles can happen when you're desperate."

Saeed went over to Aisha.

"That husband of yours," he told her, "is the craftiest man I've ever met. Do you realize that?"

She looked at her husband with a smile but did not respond. Saeed looked at Abd ar-Rahman.

"Aisha," he asked, "do you know where Ibrahim, Khumarawayh's son, is? He's the one that Muhammad al-Khalanji had people pray for in Egypt's mosques, and for whose sake Muhammad al-Khalanji went to war. He's the one in whose name Muhammad al-Khalanji, the Egyptian soldier, ruled for seven months. Do you know where he is?"

"My husband promised to tell me," Aisha replied, "once Ibrahim was no longer in danger. He told me that Ibrahim was safe."

Saeed gave a derisive smile, but then started a hacking cough. Eventually, he managed to continue:

"Yes, he's safe, Aisha!" he said.

Aisha looked at her husband, and he stared straight at Saeed.

"Stop laughing, Saeed," he said. "You'll die if you have another coughing fit."

"Abd ar-Rahman," Aisha asked, "is Ibrahim still safe?"

He did not reply.

"He's safe, Aisha," Saeed replied. "Don't ask. Your husband always lies. He's safe because he's dead."

She clutched her heart, and her husband remained silent.

"When your husband visited Ibn Sulaiman years ago," Saeed went on, "he already knew everything. The only people who knew were him and me."

She looked at her husband in total shock.

"When Ibn Sulaiman's soldiers launched their attack on Al-Qata'i," Saeed continued, "Abd ar-Rahman had the idea of kidnapping Ibrahim. He was thinking of his own and his tribe's interests, and maybe yours as well. I don't know about such matters of love. He made an agreement with one of his men that he would accompany the soldiers to Al-Qata'i and look for the boy. But the boy had already disappeared from the palace. Just when Shaiban was negotiating with his men on terms of surrender, the servant-girl who was looking after Ibrahim wandered away to eavesdrop on the men's discussion for fear of what her own fate might be. The boy left the palace and was hit by an arrow. Abd ar-Rahman's man recognized him from his clothes and shape. I had come to look for him as well, and also recognized him. He was my very last remaining hope. The man saw me carrying the boy and trying to revive him. He watched as I shed tears over the end of all hope. I hugged him and concealed his body inside my clothes, then buried him in a spot that no one knows. The man followed me and found out where the boy was buried. He told your husband, Aisha. Ever since war broke out, he's known that Ibrahim was dead. He also knew that I knew, and expected me not to say anything. What your husband wanted was for me to need him. Even though I don't like his vicious behavior, I still admire his intelligence and impetuousness. Muhammad al-Khalanji waged war against the caliph and had Ibrahim prayed for in mosques. Ibn Sulaiman and the caliph both searched for Ibrahim and raised heaven and hell in the process. As you said, Aisha, he's safe; he's in the place where all is safety."

Aisha did not respond.

"Well, Arab," Saeed went on with a derisive grin, "you've deceived armies and caliphs. How did you manage to motivate armies with just a few words about a Tulunid child?"

"Ibrahim was the dream," Abd ar-Rahman replied, "and the dream does not die. It wasn't Ibrahim, son of Khumarawayh, who motivated the armies, Copt. It was Ahmad's dream. I realized and understood. From the very beginning, I envisioned things that no one else did. I learned from her . . ."

He looked at his wife who had scarcely blinked since the story began.

"It was from her that I learned," he continued. "The dream was greater than any rulers. He was the leader, and rulers were merely soldiers following his orders."

"Do you realize, Arab," Saeed said as he signaled to his men to carry him out, "I believe that I don't actually hate you. I've come to admire you."

He looked at Aisha.

"Does he treat you badly, Aisha?" he asked her.

"No," she replied, her eyes still fixed on her husband's, "he never has."

"Ah, I think you're lying. He did treat you badly. Do you remember?"

"All I remember," she responded forcefully, "is that, for me, he's a gift from heaven."

Saeed sighed. "I don't think I'm going to see you ever again, Arab," he said.

"Maybe, maybe not, Saeed al-Farghani. All will be recorded . . ."

"Indeed it will," Saeed replied. "I shall be recording what the scribe, Ja'far ibn Abd al-Ghaffar, and Asma, the Egyptian tailor's daughter, told me, and what I heard Muhammad ibn Sulaiman say about Ahmad ibn Tulun. I'll write about the fisherman's son and Maisoon, and about you, in particular."

Abd ar-Rahman smiled and looked straight at Saeed.

"Every time you've lorded it over me, Copt," Abd ar-Rahman said, "I've felt like slapping you. But then I've said that he's the great man, and I have to respect him."

"I've often lorded it over myself when you've been with me," Saeed responded. "I've felt like killing you, but then I've told myself Aisha loves this man. She'll blame me if he dies."

"You deserve only the best," Abd ar-Rahman told him with a laugh.

"Remember that, but for me, you wouldn't have saved the mosque."

"I know."

"Remember too that your wife's a princess. Treat her well."

"Less talk and less advice, Copt," Abd ar-Rahman told him. "As you know, I don't have much patience. Make sure you take care of your health."

Saeed looked at Aisha again.

"Are you sure he treats you well?" he asked.

"For me, he's everything," she replied firmly.

Abd ar-Rahman gave him a look which was half-threat and half-joke.

"As I've told you, take care of your health."

Abd ar-Rahman held out his hand.

"I'm honored to be able to shake hands with this expert architect who's perfected the magic arts."

They shook hands.

"Friendship's like love," Saeed said. "It always comes when you least expect it—no principles, no planning. I had a friend who had no time for me, named Anas, son of Hamza the fisherman, but I'll never forget him. And now, I've a friend named Abd ar-Rahman, but I'm going to do my best to forget him. I can't stand his vanity . . ."

"No," Abd ar-Rahman responded with a laugh, "you won't forget me, nor will I you. You spoke about friendship with no principles or planning. This time, I think you're right.

"Saeed, son of Katib al-Farghani, farewell and peace to you!"

"Come on, Aisha," he said, holding out his hand.

She looked at her husband, held his hand, and kissed it slowly.

"I don't know how to thank you," she whispered.

"We won't be able to visit the mosque for a while," he told her, ignoring her remark. "Feast your eyes on it now, then we must go back to Esna."

"I know."

As she left the mosque with him, her eyes were still riveted on the courtyard as her tears fell. The mosque seemed to be floating in the clouds. A distant gleam was emerging from its mihrab, drawing near, then disappearing. Its courtyard had expanded to envelop sea and river, then float in the vault of the heavens, swimming in the cotton clouds. The courtyard now had no limits, growing wider as she moved farther away, accompanying her on her journey back and not concluding at journey's end.

Before her very eyes, the mosque's alcoves were transformed into gates that swallowed the world. The alcoves of the mihrab reverberated with cries of "God is great!" in a sweet, profound tone of joy. The end was in sight, but it was actually the beginning: one colonnade belonged to the past, the other to the future. That courtyard would still be there in a thousand years. How had a weakling constructed something so powerful? How had an ephemeral human being built a structure for eternity?

Her tears poured even harder, covering her entire face. She felt her husband's hand on her arm, urging her to leave. As she moved away, Ahmad did not seem far away, but rather inside her, even if she could not see him. His eyes were in hers, and his limbs were around hers. That mihrab was her, that alcove her heart, that city her memory. Her mother would never return. Perhaps she had known from the start that her mother was ill—who knows? Perhaps she had been certain from the very first moment that she would not be coming back. Humans hold to the promise of a constantly postponed rendezvous. She continued to weep, and the tears erased the rubble and ruins, allowing her to see the mosque courtyard stretching away to infinity.

The eye is just as weak as the heart and body; it can only see what lingers on the earth. But memory is like the mosque courtyard, limitless. The mosque gradually disappeared over the horizon.

"Don't worry," her husband said. "It'll always be there."

"I can't see it anymore," she replied. "I realize that I'll never see it again."

"We're leaving," he said, "but it'll be there. Here are the battlements with their crenulations suspended without barriers or gaps, like a building aligned with the same features and colors, and like human beings before hatred makes its way into their hearts. Those crenulations will remain in an eternal embrace, a memorial to what needs to be, but what we've failed to achieve, what we need to preserve, and what of piety and iniquity remain inside our hearts. It is a single soul, one that no color, clan, or distance can separate from the Creator; a soul from which the Creator fashioned the whole of humanity, just like those crenulations that are now disappearing over the horizon."

1918 Cairo

When Adil finished reading, the affectionate words on the pages lingered before him, coursing off the sheets of paper and painfully penetrating his heart. He could hear his wife's voice, chiding him, blaming him, and asking him to be better. She kept asking him to change himself; if he did, would she love him? That was a question he needed to ask her. Perhaps he should tell her about Aisha, who by now had become both companion and friend. Or about the Arab, the monk, or Ahmad himself. Maybe if he told her about Ahmad, he would know the answer. Even in their more intimate moments, his wife would snarl at him angrily and ask him to leave her alone. Had she been in love with someone else, he wondered, before they were married? Sometimes he pictured himself banging her head with a heavy hammer, but she would not die. She would raise her head to chide him because he had not accomplished the murder. He was no good at anything.

"If you keep reading those old documents," he could hear her chiding, "you're going to lose your job."

Perhaps she was right. His memory was deceiving him, leaving him to float on dreams and fancies. He looked at the papers as though he had found his goal and desire. He had dedicated his life to stones and pillars. What a wonderful fate!

"Adil," she said, "do you hear me?"

"If I stopped reading the documents," he asked, frantically folding up the papers, "would you love me?"

She opened her mouth in shock, as though he had just accused her of betrayal.

"Those documents have destroyed your mind," she replied.

"Do you know Ahmad, Zakiyya?"

"Ahmad who?"

"The one who built the mosque where Sultan Ahmad Fuad prayed."

"How on earth could I know him," she asked impatiently, "when he died thousands of years ago?"

"Just one thousand."

"Are you calling me stupid, man, or just ignorant?"

"I was asking you about our life after tomorrow. Once I've stopped reading, what's going to happen?"

She gave a shrug and called out to her children. As usual, she started complaining, and they listened to her sympathetically. It had all happened ten years earlier. He had been married to her without even setting eyes on her face. She was prettier than he had expected. Then, on their wedding night, she had rebuffed him and burst into tears. She had decided that she did not want him. She had had five children, still hated him, and had no need of him. He thought about leaving her; he could not divorce her, but he could forget that she was around. He could leave and not come back; that would be better than divorce. When he complained to his mother, she scolded him. His wife had done nothing wrong; she was a model of the ideal wife. Her house was always tidy, and her children were always dressed in the nicest and cleanest clothes. She was generous and talked sweetly. The fault clearly had to be his.

⛫

Adil looked at the words written by Saeed, son of Katib al-Farghani. He would miss those words, but they may have been the last thing that he wrote. He read:

My beloved Bahnas,

All trace of the city has been erased, Pyramid Witch; it is as though it never was. All that remains now is the mosque and the wall of my own house. It was our house. I could see you inside, illuminating its corners with the light of your knowledge and wisdom. Among the ignorant, those who know are purely ephemeral; among those gone astray, people of wisdom need to be punished. You saw what we did not; you realized what we did not. Forgive their narrowness of spirit. It is the curse of vision that afflicts everyone in moments of confusion.

Do you hear me? I am still living in the house, waiting for you in Al-Qata'i. Let us recall moments, laughter, breaths unlike any others, emerging with spontaneous purity. Human beings have vanished from my surroundings, but sorrow still lingers around the walls. As long as I am breathing, that sorrow lingers. Why have I not died? Why have I been fated to stay in love for these past forty years? When will you take pity on me? You told me that cities have a life just like humans. Inhabited cities provoke sedition and invite raiders to attack their walls. Al-Qata'i was a city with no walls. There I built what I built, my love for you never fading. Pity me, my beloved!

Today I searched for you inside the Great Pyramid, but did not find you. All I heard was my own voice echoing in the dark chamber. You have disappeared without trace, Bahnas. Have you left the world, or just the Pyramid? Your books still protect the wall, and the vestiges of your cake still invite the mice to a sumptuous feast. But you have left, perhaps along with or after the city itself. I have no idea. It is my personal vanity that has stopped me communicating with you for years. Do you remember? The destruction of the city partially erased my memory, but my heart led me to the right place. I discovered that the Pyramid Witch had gone. So I have collected my papers and written down the necessary words in the hope that, when everything else has disappeared, they may survive and serve as a reminder for people who can benefit from memoirs.

Adil packed his suitcase and made ready to leave in search of the Banu Saalim tribe. He wanted to reassure himself about the accuracy of the manuscript and the kind of people with whom he wanted to live. What if he abandoned this age and world, went back to Ahmad's era, and looked for a woman like Maisoon, Asma, and Aisha? Actually, the one he wanted was Azza. What had happened to her, he wondered.

Yes, he would go in search of the Banu Saalim tribe and take along the manuscript as evidence. The tribe had split up, or that is what the manuscript had said. He would go to Esna first, then Bahnasa. Once he had found out, perhaps he could learn the truth about his wife and decide what to do with her: kill her, divorce her, or learn to live submissively with her. He would leave without a word. Fate would be waiting for him when he came back.

His wife asked him where he was going, but he did not reply. She threatened and promised, but he still said nothing. He left by train. Closing his eyes, the characters in the manuscript stayed with him, breathing and chattering inside his heart.

When he reached Esna, he asked about the Banu Saalim tribe. Everyone in the city knew about them, the oldest and largest tribe of all. One of the men took him to the tribe's chieftain, who spent hours with him without saying a word. Adil told him that he was investigating the tribe's history, but the chief did not trust him. Adil told him that he needed to find out more about their ancestry, but the chief was not convinced. Adil left, feeling frustrated and anxious. He gave some money to the guard who had brought him to the chieftain.

"Do you want to hear the tales?" the guard asked him eagerly. "You need to talk to Shaikh Dimyati."

"What brought Dimyati to the south of Egypt?"

"He's from the south, but his name's Shaikh Dimyati. He knows everything. He sits in the local cafe from sunset prayer till evening prayer to smoke and drink tea. I'll introduce you to him."

Now hope seemed nigh. He sat down in front of the shaikh, who was smoking a nargileh and blew the smoke in Adil's face. Adil blew away the dust and, with a cackle, the shaikh blew in his face again. The routine was repeated.

"I've come here to talk to you," Adil said patiently, "and to hear your stories."

"I don't have any stories."

"But the guard . . ."

"If it's history you want to hear, that's different. But I don't tell stories like the dramas in Cairo."

"Its histories I want to hear, about the origins of the Banu Saalim tribe."

"Do you mean the Banu Saalim in Esna or in Bahnasa? The tribe split up a thousand years or more ago."

Adil was even more excited now.

"Tell me, Shaikh," he said.

"Shaikh Dimyati knows it all."

"Why did the tribe split up?"

"They say it was because a strange woman was married to one of the tribesmen, and the other men rejected her. They separated from the tribe."

"Who are the Banu Saalim?"

"Grandees of the town and significant figures."

"And who's the strange girl?"

"That's a story with a long explanation. People say that she was a relative of Qatr an-Nada—her sister or aunt, no one knows for sure. They say she was a Tulunid princess. She fell in love with an Arab Bedouin and was married to him. When the Tulunid era came to an end, they fled to the south. That was . . ."

"Who's Tulun?"

The shaikh shrugged his shoulders.

"There's a huge mosque in Cairo named after him," he said.

"Who is he, Hajj?"

"I can't even remember my own children's names. You expect me to remember someone who lived a thousand years ago?"

"What happened to the strange girl?"

The shaikh stood up.

"Come with me," he said.

He took Adil to a small house on the banks of the Nile and asked him to wait for a while. He came back with another shaikh who was even older and more feeble.

After exchanging greetings, the shaikh produced an old piece of paper with drawings and names on it.

"Our Banu Saalim tribe is the tribe of mighty men," the shaikh said. "It's one of the Qais tribes from the Arabian Peninsula. The name of its chieftain is recorded here on this page."

Adil read the name Abd ar-Rahman and Aisha, his wife, and his heart relaxed.

"Abd ar-Rahman was married to Aisha," the shaikh went on proudly, "and they had ten children, as far as I'm aware. Our tribe is the largest in this region and around this city."

He looked at the page again and pointed his finger at the name of Aisha's son.

"Her son, Uthmaan, was married to four women," he said, "but Abd ar-Rahman was only ever married to Aisha."

"Why?"

"She had blue blood, just like Sultan Fuad, maybe even better. People say that the Arab Bedouin adored her. She was able to dominate him to such a degree that, for her sake, he went to war against the entire armed forces of the caliph. That's the way it is with women; all they bring you is worry."

Adil could hear his own heart pounding.

"But you've evidence to support the fact that Aisha was a princess. She was a member of the Tulunid family."

"Aren't my words enough?" the shaikh asked. "There's nothing to confirm that here, but you'll find confirmation in Bahnasa."

"Let's go there together," Adil suggested.

"I'm an old man. I can't undertake such a long journey."

"You don't know how much you'll be helping by coming with me."

Shaikh Dimyati shook a man's hand warmly and introduced Adil as an old friend interested in the tribe's history. They all sat down together inside the tent of Shaikh Shauqi in Bahnasa. He too produced an old sheet of paper and pointed to the names of Rabi'a and his wife.

"Do you know about Qatr an-Nada?" the shaikh asked. "She was from our tribe."

"How could that be? Wasn't she Khumarawayh's daughter and Ahmad ibn Tulun's granddaughter?"

"I don't know who that Khumarawayh is. But she was from our tribe, our own flesh and blood. Hasn't Shaikh Dimyati told you the story about the princess who was married to Abd ar-Rahman?"

"But that may all be just tales and fables," Adil said, still feeling overjoyed. "Who can confirm that it's true?"

"Come with me."

The tribal chief in Bahnasa took Adil to his house. He brought out a large box from his storeroom and produced a sheaf of old papers which he opened slowly. It looked like a silk garment a thousand years old or more, almost melting away in the man's hands.

"Do you see these shapes?" Shaikh Shauqi asked him. "Five-pointed leaves— royal emblems. The princess gave them to her husband's cousin, who was a close friend of hers. Our ancestor preserved it a thousand years ago, and we've inherited it. This is the confirmation that the tribal history is true. Just look at the colors: bright red and vivid blue, as though defying time. Colors can defy the passage of time: colors, plants, and certain fabrics. We humans are the very first to perish, and yet we still strut around, ranting and raving in our arrogance."

Adil put his fingers close to the cloth. "I know this cloth," he said. "It's what Aisha gave to Azza. Can I touch it?"

"It'll fall apart in your hands, my son. No one touches it, even me. To preserve the shapes and colors, you have to handle it gently. But Bahnasa is known for its weaving. We've cloth just like this or even more beautiful."

"In a distant time," the shaikh continued, "long, long ago, there was war. The monarch died and so did most of his family. The only exception was his daughter. She managed to escape the aggressor's violence and war's savagery. Caliphs and governors searched for her all over Egypt, but they never found her. She hid inside a man's tent. He hid her from everyone and fought on her behalf. She fought on his."

"Who's this monarch?"

"It doesn't matter. He was Qatr an-Nada's father, one of the monarchs. Who cares about the names of ancient monarchs, man? I know that our king today is Ahmad Fuad. People say that some kind of revolt is stirring in Cairo. What's the king doing?"

Adil shrugged his shoulders.

"Have you found what you're looking for?" the shaikh asked him.

"What sort of question is that? That's the hardest question I've ever heard in my life. Of course I haven't, not yet."

Have you found what you're looking for? That is an impossible question for human beings to answer. He had not decided yet whether to return to Zakiyya or leave her. Between a man and woman more than love is needed for there to be fulfillment; sometimes it comes from discovering secrets, understanding riddles, and reading ancient documents. It may even come from living inside a tale involving giving and sacrifice. Was fulfillment awaiting him, he wondered. Was he living in this world? Why was he trying to find water deep in the desert, when the river was right in front of him with its sweet waters? But then, the search for water deep in the desert was more fulfilling than searching for it around rivers. The search itself was what he needed.

"You have to go into retreat when you're still longing and eager," the monk had told Ahmad, "not when you're already desperate and abstaining." But he was beyond mere retreat; despair had been a constant forever. Today he was Ahmad after he had uncovered his own son's betrayal. Today he was Abd ar-Rahman, his innards torn to shreds by whispered rumors, his vanity melted by sheer weakness. Today he was Saeed, his worries about what he had built intensifying. Today he was Shaikh Dimyati, eagerly opening the sheaf of papers to preserve the fabric with its colors and complex designs. Saeed, Ahmad, Abd ar-Rahman, Shaikh Dimyati, he was all of them, all those men possessed by the dream, having left everything else. But he still was not convinced about his own dream and its value. People were saying that revolt was stirring throughout Egypt. It had not proved feasible for Sultan Fuad to become Caliph of all Muslims, even after he had prayed the Friday prayer in Ahmad ibn Tulun's mosque. Who would be praying in the mosque the next day, he wondered. Who would remember the dream of the ancients?

The world is on fire and dying. His wife never stops blaming and criticizing him. People have died. Human beings have woken up to the color of blood. His wife is still blaming him and complaining. His first resort was to God to complain about his troubles, then to the priest in his church. He asked Adil to be patient.

"He who loves his wife," the priest told him gently, "loves himself. You love her even though your self tells you the opposite."

"No," Adil replied miserably, "I'm afraid I've hated myself solely in order to please her."

He went to the El-Qoseir Monastery. For months, he had been thinking about Anduna, the monk. He liked going on retreat, leaving behind more things than wars. He had decided to become a monk. The words that he had heard inside the monastery kept repeating themselves: "With You, I need nothing on earth." He had been visiting the monastery for months, but today the abbot told him that it would not be happening. Those who abandon the world must do so without constraints or difficulties. They must still be capable of showing courage. Retreating because you do not want to face struggles is a kind of cowardice entirely inappropriate for monks. Anyone who comes to the monastery to get away from his wife and children is different from someone else who comes in spite of having a wife and children. So there was no hope.

Zakiyya was all around him. He found himself heading for the pyramids. Where did the Pyramid Witch live, he wondered? What would she have to say today? He stopped in front of the Great Pyramid. In front of him, he saw the caliph Al-Ma'mun knocking down stones so that he could discover what lay hidden beneath the sands of time. He could hear the sound of the stones moving slowly and swore that he could hear the Pyramid Witch's voice whispering.

"It's here," she was saying, "not just in the mosque and the remains of the houses. It's here, and in Esna and Bahnasa as well. It's present in every single moment when the heart coheres and trembles, in every painful sigh of loss, in every footstep that proceeds without understanding or knowing where destiny will take it. It's here, in the heart's very core, never leaving, amid the twists of pulsating veins, the serenity of acceptance and pleasure . . . Al-Qata'i . . . a city. As with life, sometimes it plays tricks, while at others it appears in all its brilliance and then fades away to nothing, like the body."

"Bahnas, Pyramid Witch," he yelled, "why did you destroy Saeed's heart? Have you no mercy? Why couldn't you forgive? Are all women the same, with no forgiveness in their hearts? What about you and time, Pyramid Witch? You suffer, and we suffer with you. Are you even listening, I wonder?"

On the Margins of History

ꔛꔛꔛꔛꔛꔛꔛꔛꔛꔛꔛꔛꔛꔛꔛꔛꔛꔛꔛ

Completed in 879, Ahmad ibn Tulun's mosque is considered the oldest mosque still standing in Egypt and the largest in area. Even though Amr ibn al-As's mosque is actually older, it has gone through a number of alterations and suffered the effects of time, while Ibn Tulun's mosque remains intact in spite of the passage of time and a number of different rulers.

Specialists in Islamic architecture have been much impressed by the colonnades of the Ahmad ibn Tulun mosque and the interlacing crenulations atop the mosque walls, bowing to the heavens. Right up to the present day, no other mosque built before or after Ahmad ibn Tulun's has anything like them.

All that remains of Al-Qata'i is Ahmad ibn Tulun's mosque and the house, part of which has been discovered by archaeologists, as in the novel. There is also the aqueduct which Ahmad ibn Tulun constructed in the Al-Bustan quarter in Cairo, one of the oldest Islamic monuments.

In the Fatimid era, governors ordered a wall to be built around the ruins of Al-Qata'i so as not to offend the gaze of people passing by on their way to Cairo. The historian Al-Maqrizi notes: "Know that all trace of Al-Qata'i has disappeared, and no plan of it is known to exist."

Ahmad ibn Tulun was the first to establish an independent dynasty in Egypt during the Islamic era and the first to create an independent army since the Pharaonic period. The Tulunids were followed by other dynasties, like the Ikhshidids, and the Fatimids, to be crowned by the Mamluks, who adopted the Tulunids as a model for success and power. During the Mamluk period, the Abbasid caliphate was actually transferred to Egypt. The Mamluk Sultan, Husam Lajin, was one of the most important figures in the repair and reconstruction of Ahmad ibn Tulun's mosque. The Mamluk dynasty was much inspired by Ahmad ibn Tulun in creating a powerful army, assigning command of it to a powerful warrior, and honoring its soldiers.

Ahmad ibn Tulun allowed Egyptians to enroll in his army, gave them gifts, and housed them in his city. He is the first person to have created an army with Egyptian soldiers since the Pharaonic era and a thousand years before Muhammad Ali's army in the nineteenth century. Muhammad Ali al-Khalanji, the Tulunid Egyptian general, ruled Egypt for seven months.

Saeed, son of Katib al-Farghani, settled in the house of Anas, son of Hamza al-Skandari, in Al-Qata'i, which he himself had built. The British archaeologist discovered, alongside the mosque, the wall of a house constructed of gypsum with filigree decorations like those of Samaraa' in Iraq. Saeed hailed from Farghan, currently situated in Diyarb Nagm in Egypt's Sharqiyya Province.

In Al-Balawi's biography of Ahmad ibn Tulun, there is mention of the wife of Ahmad ibn Tulun who was from the client people, in other words a non-Arab, an Egyptian woman. His daughter's name is also mentioned: Aisha.

Bahnasa is still well known for its fabrics. Many Bedouin Arab tribes have settled in Upper Egypt.

Like all dream cities, Al-Qata'i managed to contain every race on earth in peace and cooperated with its folk for thirty years. Once all traces were erased, it left no memories for centuries, nor were there any memories of Qatr an-Nada, Maisoon, Aisha, and Asma, the Egyptian woman married to Ahmad ibn Tulun. The city's disappearance only serves to enhance its awe and radiance. Between the acts of building and erasure, there are many tales to tell. The fragrant light reminds us of what was, who knew, who tyrannized, who won, who roamed in passionate love, who forgot the neighborhood amid terrors, who set the stars before his eyes, how the star shone bright, how it fell, and how it gave light.

THE END—PRAISE BE TO GOD

Afterword

The name Ibn Tulun is primarily associated today with the mosque named after him, one of Cairo's most spectacular Islamic monuments. The mosque is situated toward the southern part of contemporary Cairo. To the north lies the Khedive Ismail's nineteenth century Cairo, modeled on Haussmann's Paris and linked via Ataba Square to the earlier "old city" whose quarters are celebrated in many of the earlier novels of Naguib Mahfouz, with its tenth-century Al-Azhar Mosque and fabled bazaar, Khan al-Khalili. On a ridge protruding from the Muqattam Hills is Saladin's citadel, now topped by the Ottoman-style Muhammad Ali Mosque. To the south is the oldest part of the larger urban region of Cairo, Fustat, so named after the Latin word for "trench," *fossata* (although other sources suggest that it originally meant "tent"). Fustat is the site of the earliest monuments in the history of Cairo, including famous places of worship for the three monotheisms originating in West Asia and North Africa: the Coptic Church dedicated to the Virgin Mary, the so-called "Hanging Church"; the Ben Ezra Synagogue with its important storehouse of "Geniza" documents; and the Mosque of Amr ibn al-As, named for the commander of the Muslim army that invaded Egypt in 636 CE.

While two of Reem Bassiouney's previous excursions into historical fiction, *Awlad an-nas* (2018; *Sons of the People*, 2021), and *Sabil al-ghariq* (2020; *Fountain of the Drowning*, 2021), have also been set in specific historical periods, in this novel, *Al-Qata'i*, the period involved is the Tulunid dynasty in the ninth and tenth centuries in Egypt and beyond, which is especially fraught with conflicts in both broader regional and local terms. The tensions between the Abbasid caliphate in Baghdad and the administration of Egypt and its people bring into play many significant historical figures—caliphs, governors, army commanders, Tax Administrators, judges, and religious scholars—all of whom are to play important roles in the novel's three "stories."

The Arabic title of this novel, *Al-Qata'i*, is a word—a place-name—that is derived from the verb meaning "to cut." While I have chosen to preserve the Arabic term as the title of this translation, it seems useful to point out that the word means something like "sections" or "subdivisions." It is thus a direct depiction of the way in which a completely new city was created to the north of Fustat by assigning building lots (*Qata'i*) to the soldiers who had joined the rapidly expanding Egyptian army and who were too numerous to be accommodated in the older Fustat barracks.

In this new and carefully planned urban landscape, a magnificent and unusual mosque is to be constructed. As the novel opens in 1918, the reader is immediately made aware of both the mosque's significance in Egyptian history and the eventual fate of the city of Al-Qata'i. Egypt's Sultan Fuad has indicated his intention to pray in the historic mosque located in what was once a complete city but is now only represented by the mosque and some adjacent ruins. A group of archaeologists has been conducting research at the site, and one particular house has turned out to be that of the mosque's Christian architect, Saeed, son of Katib al-Farghani. His detailed account of the tumultuous circumstances of his life and the enormous building project that he has organized is recorded in a set of papers that emerge from the ruins. In the novel's three "stories" that follow, the reader is taken back to those very same circumstances and the historical era in which they occurred.

Those "stories" describe the events of the Tulunid era in their historical sequence, with each narrative exploring the careers and motivations of many of the principal participants in the era's events. On the broadest scale, the Abbasid caliphate in Baghdad strives to maintain control of its Muslim territories during a particularly fractious period. Ahmad ibn Tulun, of Turkic extraction and born in Baghdad, has been sent to Egypt as an Abbasid administrator, but almost immediately finds himself confronting the powerful and corrupt Tax Administrator, Ibn al-Mudabbir. This confrontation occupies most of the first "story." However, the title of that first "story" is "Maisoon," a reference to the beautiful and strong-willed wife of Ahmad ibn Tulun's loyal helper, Anas the bookseller. Her tempestuous relationship with her husband and her unconcealed fury at his frequent and lengthy absences on Ahmad's business, all set against Ibn al-Mudabbir's lustful attentions to her, make full use of domestic turmoil to provide the reader with a vivid reflection of the broader conflicts and tensions of the period in question.

The second story consists of accounts of Ahmad ibn Tulun's period as Amir of Egypt. It is told from three very different viewpoints: those of Ja'far, his personal secretary; Asma, his Egyptian wife; and Muhammad ibn Sulaiman, a former retainer who has defected to the Abbasid cause and who, in the third story, will return to Egypt as the head of an Abbasid army determined to erase every trace of Ahmad ibn Tulun. The dream which gives the story its title is one in which Ahmad envisions a restoration of the glorious centuries of Egypt's past history. Indeed, following the devastating privations visited on Egyptians by Ibn al-Mudabbir's taxes and regulations, the Egyptian people do thrive during Ahmad's regime. The economy prospers, the city of Al-Qata'i provides all sorts of services, and the great mosque is completed. Ahmad seeks advice from Bahnas, the Pyramid Witch. Her brutally honest wisdom and respect for history is to be shared with many of the characters, both male and female, who populate the narrative, and Bassiouney's historical fiction generally. Ahmad also finds solace in the isolation offered him by Anduna, a monk at a nearby monastery. Of the three records of the era, it is Ja'far's that provides the account of Ahmad's final days. Following visits to both Bahnas and Anduna, he summons his sons and appoints one to govern Egypt and another, Syria. But, as the third story is about to illustrate, events are to turn out differently.

The lengthy final story, "The Pledge," recounts the complicated aftermath of Ahmad ibn Tulun's period as Amir of Egypt. A constant factor is the determination of the Abbasid caliphate in Baghdad to return Egypt to its former, pre-Tulunid status. The Abbasid army invades Egypt under the command of Muhammad ibn Sulaiman, who is hell-bent on destroying everything that Ahmad ibn Tulun has built. As the systematic destruction of the buildings in Al-Qata'i proceeds, the architect Saeed al-Farghani finds himself in need of a strategy to save the mosque that he has designed. His plan introduces into the narrative another of Reem Bassiouney's notable female characters, Aisha, a young girl initially presented as an orphan adopted by Ja'far, Ahmad's personal secretary. However, as later emerges, Aisha is actually Ahmad's daughter by his Egyptian wife, Asma. As with Maisoon and Anas in the first story, the tempestuous relationship between Aisha and Abd ar-Rahman, son of a tribal chieftain, comes to personify the complexities of the broader landscape, as their growing love for each other provokes all kinds of tribal dispute and rivalry, not least among the women. When the tribe decides to re-locate and join another of its branches in Upper Egypt, the narrative divides in two. While Abd ar-Rahman sends his now pregnant wife, Aisha, with the tribe to the south, he and a small select group of tribesmen go into hiding, determined to prevent the demolition of Al-Qata'i's great mosque. When a group of Ibn Sulai-man's soldiers arrives to commence the task, they are attacked by Abd ar-Rahman's men and the group's leader is killed. The project is abandoned, and the mosque is left standing. To escape capture, Abd al-Rahman spends several months in hiding. Eventually he is able to travel south, rejoin his tribe, and celebrate with his wife the birth of their daughter.

The third of the novel's stories also concludes on a happy note, and Ahmad ibn Tulun's mosque survives the demolition of Al-Qata'i. To conclude the novel, the author takes the reader back to its starting-point, the year 1918. An Egyptian, who has joined British archaeologists in their exploration of the ruins adjacent to the mosque and is now reading the recently discovered record of its architect, finds a letter addressed to Bahnas, the Pyramid Witch. Like so many of the characters in the novel, he too wants to question her and seek her counsel. In the novel's final sentence, he wonders if she is even listening. Had he had access to Reem Bassiouney's superb novel, he might have found some answers.

In conclusion, I would like to express my thanks to the staff at Georgetown University Press for the care they have taken in bringing the English translation of Reem Bassiouney's novel to publication. In particular, I express my gratitude to

Hope LeGro and Melanie Magidow for their meticulous attention to the English text. As a result, readers of English now have access to this superb example of the contemporary Arabic historical novel, fulfilling, one might suggest, one of the genre's traditional functions by making use of illustrations culled from history to offer its readers possible lessons for the present and future.

ROGER ALLEN

Timeline

750–1258	The Abbasid Caliphate (based in the newly built city of Baghdad, Iraq from 756), except for the Samarra' period (836–92)
833–42	Caliphate of Al-Mu'tasim
836–92	Beginning with Al-Mu'tasim, the Abbasid Caliphal capital is in Samarra', Iraq
855	Death of Tulun, Ahmad ibn Tulun's father, commander of the Caliph's personal guard
861–71	Ahmad ibn al-Mudabbir is Tax Administrator in Egypt and an opponent of Ahmad ibn Tulun
868	The Abbasid Caliph Al-Mu'tazz appoints Bayakbak, a Turkish military commander, Governor of Egypt, and he in turn sends Ahmad ibn Tulun to Egypt as his deputy
868	Ahmad ibn Tulun begins the process of wresting control of the country from Ibn al-Mudabbir and achieving his goal of an independent Egypt
869–93	The Zanj Revolt, beginning in the Iraqi city of Basra, a rebellion against the Abbasid Caliphate
869	Death of Abbasid Caliph Al-Mu'tazz
869	Ibn Tulun's stepfather, Bayakbak, is murdered; he is succeeded as caliphal supervisor of Egypt by Yarjukh, father of Ibn Tulun's wife, Khatun
870	Construction of the new city of Al-Qata'i begins
870–92	Caliphate in Samarra' of Al-Mu'tamid, largely a figurehead, in that his brother, Al-Muwaffaq, exercises a good deal of control, including the conflict with the Zanj rebels
871	Ibn al-Mudabbir is imprisoned, then released and sent to Syria
872–84	Ahmad ibn Tulun establishes himself as ruler (Amir) of an independent Egypt
875–76	A dispute erupts between Al-Muwaffaq, the caliph Al-Mu'tamid's powerful brother, and Ahmad ibn Tulun over tax payments; the army dispatched by Al-Muwaffaq fails to engage with Ibn Tulun's forces
877	Ahmad ibn Tulun captures Damascus and sends Ibn al-Mudabbir back to prison in Egypt
878–80	Construction of the mosque of Ibn Tulun in Al-Qata'i, designed by Saeed ibn Katib al-Farghani

879	Al-Abbas, Ibn Tulun's eldest son, rebels against his father, but his forces are defeated and Al-Abbas is paraded through the streets on a mule
882	Lu'lu', one of Ibn Tulun's army commanders, defects to the Abbasids
882	Yazaman al-Khadim (d. 891), servant of the governor of the Cilician borderlands; appointed leader of local forces, he rejects Ibn Tulun's rule and affiliates with the Abbasid Caliphate
882–3	Ibn Tulun takes his army to Tarsus in Syria; his camp is flooded by Yazaman al-Khadim, and he returns ill to Egypt
883	Ibn al-Mudabbir dies in prison
884	Ahmad ibn Tulun dies (in May), and his son, Khumarawayh, succeeds him; Al-Abbas, Ibn Tulun's eldest son, is assassinated
884	Ahmad ibn Muhammad al-Wasiti, former senior general of Ibn Tulun, encourages the Abbasid Caliph to attack Khumarawayh's forces in Syria
885	Battle of Tawahin in Syria; the Abbasid army of Al-Muwaffaq is defeated by the Egyptian forces of Khumarawayh
886	Khumarawayh is recognized by the Abbasids as Governor of Egypt and Syria
896	Khumarawayh is murdered by one of his servants; his fourteen-year-old son, Abu l-Askar Jaish, takes over
896	The short reign of Abu l-Askar Jaish ibn Khumarawayh; he is deposed and killed
896–904	The reign of Harun ibn Khumarawayh, Abu l-Askar's Jaish's younger brother; he is killed in an army mutiny
903	The Abbasid Caliph Al-Muktafi, sets out to defeat the Qarmatians in Syria; his generals, Muhammad ibn Sulaiman al-Katib and Badr al-Hammami, rout the Qarmatian forces near Hama
904–5	Shaiban, son of Ahmad ibn Tulun and uncle of Harun, succeeds his nephew; he surrenders unconditionally to the Abbasid general, Muhammad ibn Sulaiman al-Katib, ending the Tulunid dynasty
905	Egypt is reclaimed by the Abbasid Caliphate, and Al-Qata'i is razed, leaving only the Mosque of Ibn Tulun

About the Author

Reem Bassiouney is the author of nine novels and a scholar of Arabic linguistics. She was the first woman to be awarded the prestigious Naguib Mahfouz Award from Egypt's Supreme Council for Culture for the best Egyptian novel of 2020 for her bestselling novel, *Sons of the People*. Bassiouney's novel *The Pistachio Seller* was awarded the King Fahd Center for Middle East and Islamic Studies Translation of Arabic Literature Award in 2010. She also won the 2009 Sawiris Foundation Literary Prize for her novel *Professor Hanaa*. Five of her nine novels have been translated into English, Spanish, and Greek, including *Sons of the People, The Mamluk Trilogy* (forthcoming) and *Fountain of the Drowning* (forthcoming), both translated by Roger Allen; *Mortal Designs,* translated by Melanie Magidow; *Professor Hanaa*, translated by Laila Helmi; and *The Pistachio Seller*, translated by Osman Nusairi.

Bassiouney is a professor of sociolinguistics at The American University of Cairo. She has published eight academic books and is currently the editor of the Routledge Series of Language and Identity.

About the Translator

Roger Allen is retired from his position as the Sascha Jane Patterson Harvie Professor of Social Thought and Comparative Ethics in the School of Arts & Sciences at the University of Pennsylvania, where he also served as Professor of Arabic and Comparative Literature in the Department of Near Eastern Languages & Civilizations for forty-three years. Among his published studies on Arabic literature are: *The Arabic Novel: An Historical and Critical Introduction*, and *The Arabic Literary Heritage*.

He has translated many fictional works by modern Arab writers. He is the celebrated translator of the Egyptian Nobel Laureate, Naguib Mahfouz, including translations of a collection of his short stories, *God's World*, and his novels, *Autumn Quail*, *Mirrors*, *Karnak Café*, *Khan al-Khalili*, and *One Hour Left*. Other Arab authors he has translated include Jabra Ibrahim Jabra, Yusuf Idris, 'Abd ar-Rahman Munif, Mayy Telmissany, Bensalem Himmich, Ahmed al-Toufiq, and Hanan al-Shaykh.